Enemy Within
The Executive Office

Tal Bauer

A Tal Bauer Publication

www.talbauerwrites.com

This is a work of fiction. All characters, places, and events are from the author's imagination and should not be confused with fact. Any resemblance to persons, living or dead, events or places is purely coincidental.

All rights reserved. No part of this publication may be reproduced in any material form, whether by printing, photocopying, scanning or otherwise without the written permission of the publisher, Tal Bauer.

Warning
This book contains sexually explicit content which is only suitable for mature readers.

ISBN: 9781520907932
First Edition
10 9 8 7 6 5 4 3 2 1
Copyright © 2017 Tal Bauer
Cover Art by Natasha Snow © Copyright 2017
Interior Artwork by Tal Bauer © Copyright 2017
Edited by Rita Roberts
Published in 2017 by Tal Bauer in the United States of America

Dedication

To my husband, the love of my life.

To Christina and Rita, two friends who helped make this possible.

To all of my readers, for your unending awesomeness, and your love of these characters. You keep the stories alive.

The Executive Office Cast

White House

Jack Spiers: President of the United States
Ethan Reichenbach: First Gentleman & former head of Presidential Secret Service Detail
Scott Collard: Presidential Secret Service Detail Agent/Lead
Levi Daniels: Presidential Secret Service Detail Agent
Luke Welby: Presidential Secret Service Detail Agent.
Elizabeth Wall: Vice President
Pete Reyes: Press Secretary
General Bradford: Chairman of the Joint Chiefs
General Harris: Vice Chairman of the Joint Chiefs
General Bell: General, SOCOM
Olivia Mori: Deputy Director of the CIA
Senator Stephen Allen: Republican Senator, Chair of Senate Select Committee on Intelligence
Jason Brandt: First Gentleman Press Secretary
Barbara Whitley: White House Social Secretary
Jennifer Prince: White House Floral Designer

Russia

Sergey Puchkov: Russian President
Sasha Andreyev: Former Air Force officer
Ilya Ivchenko: Director FSB (Russian State Security Services)
Aleksey, Anton, & Vasily: Russian Federal Police aligned with Sergey Puchkov
General Moroshkin: Russian General; overthrew Sergey Puchkov

Marine Corps Special Operations Team

Lieutenant Adam Cooper
Staff Sergeant Wright
Staff Sergeant Coleman
Lance Corporal Park
Corporal Kobayashi
Lance Corporal Ruiz
Corporal "Doc" Camacho
Corporal Fitz - deceased

Madigan's Faction

Former General Porter Madigan: Traitor to the United States
Former Captain Ryan Cook: Former Army Captain convicted of war crimes

Saudi Arabia

Prince Faisal al-Saud: Royal head of the Saudi Intel. Dir.
Prince Abdul al-Saud: Governor of Riyadh

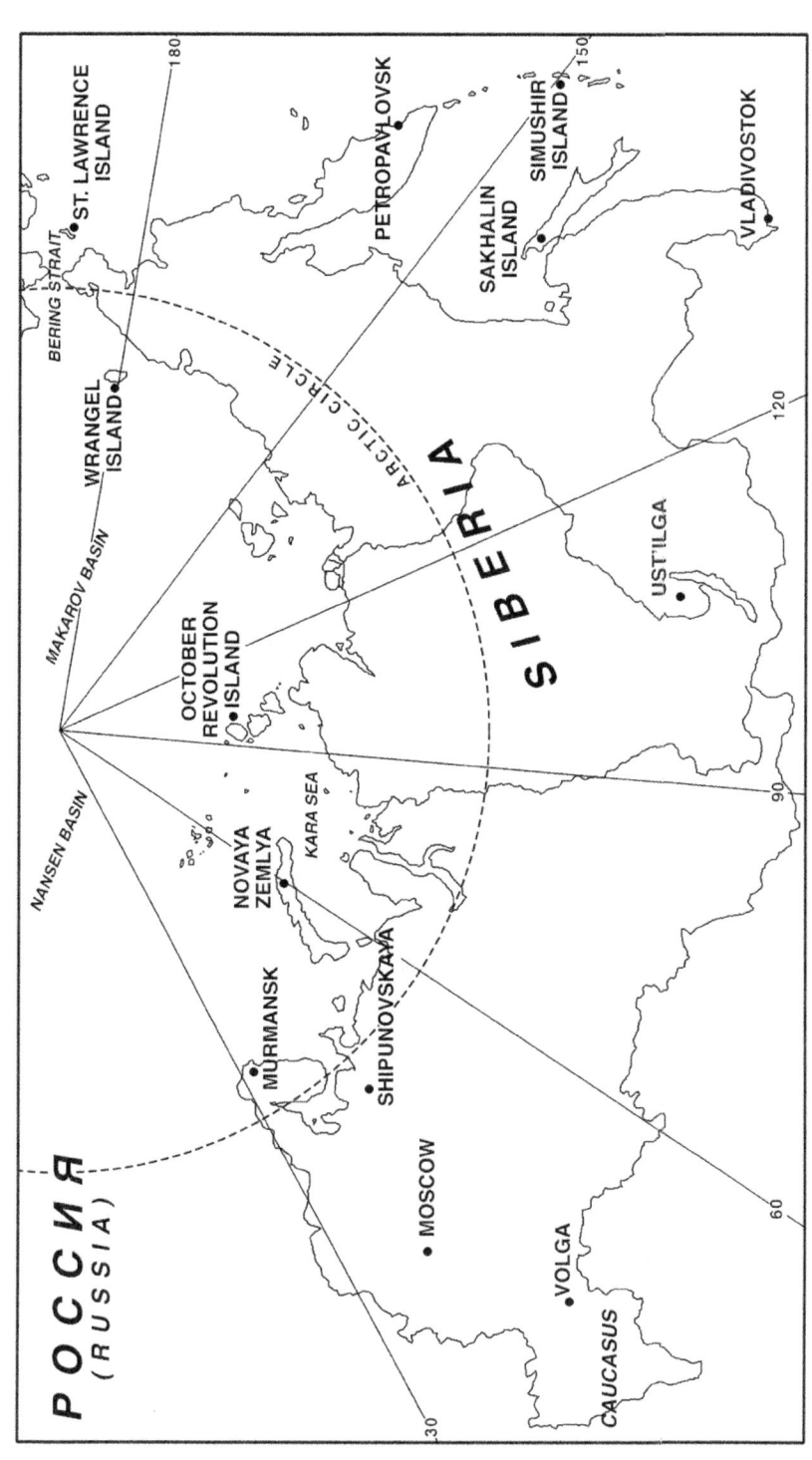

1

Kara Sea

IN THE FROZEN ARCTIC, one mile seemed as vast as a thousand.

Circling around former General Porter Madigan, as far as the eye could see, was a haunted, whitewashed wasteland. A howling storm had blitzed the RusFuel station they'd taken over, and after the storm, the ghostly sky seemed to fuse with the endless expanse of desolation and ice. Fog and a swirling snow haze hovered, wisping through the distance. The mist was so thick that the lights on the snow tractor, parked feet away from the station, were only faint flickers amidst the gloomy, endless miasma.

Somewhere out there, the midnight sun shone, spiraling in an endless circle over the horizon. The Arctic summer had arrived, just barely, just enough to keep a gloomy light hovering through the frozen fog.

Thousands of miles of ice surrounded him, and beneath him, under the ice pack, a frigid ocean quaked and roared.

Madigan smiled, his ruddy cheeks pulling against the bitter cold beneath his fur-lined hood. The Arctic suited him. The rawness, the violence, the brutality of the place. As peaceful and serene as people might imagine it to be, the Arctic was everything but. A truly harsh place, with vicious realities. Smooth ice and gentle snow hid the raging, turbulent ocean. Ice ridges thrown up by the crash of glaciers shared space with ragged fractures, bisecting the ice and opening up leads where waters carved and splintered into the ice cap. Scars marred the expanse, the wreckage and rubble of a thousand violent collisions throughout the centuries, spread across a wild emptiness.

"General."

Madigan turned and faced former Captain Ryan Cook. Cook's dark eyes fixed on his, deep set in his angular face. Like Madigan, he wore a thick snow parka with the hood pulled up to cover his head. Beneath the fur-trimmed rim, Cook's eyes glittered, like black diamonds lit by firelight.

"Status, Captain?"

"The storm didn't delay our progress. Our men were able to shelter on the ships. Some of the hired help suffered exposure. Frostbite on their hands, feet, and face. The main teams are back at work."

"Exposure? They were supposed to be sheltering away from the storm."

"Their failure, and their condition, is a personal problem, General. Not ours."

Madigan grinned and turned back to the unforgiving landscape. Their hired help was generally good, but not perfect. His criminal army, they were men who had been sprung from the worst prisons in the world and banded together under Madigan's banner with a promise for a better life—or at least, a life more suited to them than the present world offered. They worked for a debauched and bloody future that they could practically taste. They were brutal men, hardened by their captivity and hardened further by Madigan's mission and Cook's relentless training.

"Cut them loose. They can deal with their personal problems on their own."

Cook stepped to Madigan's side, and Madigan caught the curve of his smile from the corner of his eye. "Already done, sir. They were last seen walking away from our ships under the watchful gaze of my team."

He grinned again, his chapped lips catching beads of ice blown up by the polar winds. Naturally, Cook had already implemented his orders. Never had Madigan found a more ruthlessly efficient man than Cook. He was singular in his focus, exacting in his execution. Mission first. Mission always. All else was secondary. Any tactics were on the table. He was a force of nature.

Madigan was glad Cook was on his side.

And Cook's team. A group of men as close to Madigan as Cook was. True believers, in every sense of the word. They'd come to his side over the years, the most loyal officers and military men he'd encountered. Men who believed as Cook did, and as Madigan did. That the world had gone astray, and it was up to them to set it to rights. To put the strong back on top. To put the rightful, and the powerful—truly powerful—in charge again.

Millennia ago in ancient Sparta, a secret unit of warriors was kept buried amid the ranks of the legendary Spartans. The *Krypteia*, a unit hand-selected from the best, the most trustworthy, and most bloodthirsty, and charged with keeping order in the kingdom. A security arm of sorts, they terrorized and murdered their fellow citizens to keep order and control.

It was time for the *Krypteia* to rise again. For the strongest to dictate that order and control in a world gone awry. "All operations are proceeding on schedule. Ventilations of the methane hydrate are in the redline." Cook spoke again, and as he did, Madigan pictured the cannibalized chemical indicators they had ripped out of the destroyed oil derricks and RusFuel stations they'd taken over in the Kara Sea. A few adjustments, some carefully placed explosions in the ice, and the indicators redlined, signaling massive ventilations of the dangerous gas into the air. Once it ignited, waves of fire would roll across the skies, a cleansing burn that would raze the old world to cinder and ash.

"And our other team?" Turning, Madigan raised one eyebrow.

Cook nodded back to the base behind them, a bare-bones, prefabricated structure formerly used by RusFuel scientists on their polar oil explorations. "Sonar has pinpointed the location. The divers are surveying the site now. We've salvaged enough equipment from the RusFuel station, and after the dive teams complete their survey and draw up the plans, we'll begin placing pistons underwater and beneath the wreck."

"How long until we're able to raise it?"

"Days, General. We won't know for sure until the dive team returns. And after—"

Madigan held up his hand. "We must get our nuclear tech here before we speak of anything else. We've come this far by being practical. Measured. Let's not get ahead of ourselves, Captain. Stick to the plan. Have you heard from our man?"

Cook hesitated, for just a moment. "Not yet. He's on the move. He hasn't made contact since his team mobilized."

"One step at a time. We maneuver him here. His utility is best served with us now. His undercover mission is over. Have him cut loose. You know the drill."

"When he makes contact again, I'll give the order."

Madigan took a deep breath. Ice crystals melted in his throat, and frigid air filled his lungs. The cold reached deep inside him and curled around his fast-beating heart. So close. They were so close.

So close he could taste it.

"Excellent, Captain." Madigan clapped Cook on the shoulder. "And our last little problem?"

Days before, a rogue MiG had overflown their base camp in the Kara Sea and the Russian destroyer *Veduschiy*, which General Moroshkin had so graciously gifted them. Madigan's men had fired on the pilot, and *Veduschiy* got off two missiles. One burst apart in the pilot's flares, but the other had chased the MiG down, destroying the jet over the empty taiga, the seemingly endless boreal forest that stretched across northern Siberia. Somehow, the pilot had managed to eject just before the missile's impact. *Veduschiy* picked up his distress signal after his ejection.

Whoever the pilot was, and whoever he was working with, he had to be eliminated. While Madigan would have preferred the pilot to be killed in the shoot down of his MiG, his ejection wouldn't save him. Thousands of miles of snow-packed forest stretched around him, a prison of ice and snow and unforgiving wilderness.

Frowning, Cook glared into the snow haze and the flickering light that might have been the sun. "The *Spetsnaz* unit you dispatched after the downed pilot hasn't found him yet, just his landing site. His rig and parachute. He ditched the radio and made off on foot. They're tracking him."

"Give them time. Siberia is a large place."

"You trust these men, General?" Cook's eyes narrowed as he turned back to Madigan. "They're Russians. We're supposed to be using the Russians. Not trusting them."

"Trust? No. But *these* ones are useful. They're hunters. Predators. They'll find this pilot and they'll kill him. Of this, I have no doubt."

The unit loaned to him by General Moroshkin was a Siberian *Spetsnaz* unit, made up of men forged in the dark heart of the frozen taiga. Hardened warriors, already fierce due to the land of their making, and refined by their training into something even darker. Moroshkin had handpicked the men and gifted them to Madigan. A thank you present, of sorts, for his assistance in Moroshkin's coup against President Sergey Puchkov.

To a man, the Siberian *Spetsnaz* troops were cut from the same black depths as Cook. In place of a heart, they had been born instead with bottomless wells of emptiness and rage, wells from which brutality and viciousness could be honed and sharpened. They were weapons as much as men, and utterly lacking in compassion or the trifles of morality.

No surprise that Cook's hackles rose around them. Like recognized like, and fought back.

Cook's glower pierced Madigan.

He smiled at the younger man, squeezing both his shoulders as he faced him. "Focus on our mission, Captain. This pilot is already dead. He simply doesn't know it." Madigan hesitated, and his grin turned wry. "I promise, you will have plenty of opportunities to hunt on your own when we are through. You are not missing anything. And—" With another squeeze, he let go. "I need you here. At my side. You are my right hand."

Cook visibly relaxed, the tension snaking out of his spine and his shoulders. He nodded once.

"Excellent. Now, show me the updates from our dive team. I want to see their progress."

Together, Madigan and Cook headed into the base, leaving behind the Arctic wasteland and the frozen, howling wind.

Nation Rocked By Revelation of Langley Bomber's Identity

The nation continues to reel following revelations from the White House regarding the identity of the Langley Bomber being a clone of Captain Leslie Spiers. Captain Leslie Spiers, President Jack Spiers's deceased wife, was supposedly rescued in Russia in the midst of the coup against former Russian President Sergey Puchkov. She had reportedly been held captive for sixteen years by former General Porter Madigan.

However, the White House now says that the woman recovered in Russia was not Leslie Spiers, but was a clone of Mrs. Spiers, created by Madigan as a Trojan Horse against President Spiers and the United States government. The White House credits swift, decisive, "on the ground" intelligence collection for the discovery of the clone's true identity.

The night of the bombing, the clone had been arrested in the White House Residence and taken to Langley for interrogation. President Spiers was observing his cloned wife's interrogation when she detonated her bomb, concealed within her disfigured limb in an "extremely advanced manner", preventing security personnel from discovering its existence.

Senator Stephen Allen, famously hostile to the Spiers's administration, has called for an investigation into the bombing, and the events that led to the clone's arrest. "What transpired between Sochi and the Russian coup and the night of the blast?" he asked, speaking to reporters on Capitol Hill. "How did President Spiers allow such a dangerous lapse in security to occur?"

President Spiers remains on life support at Bethesda Naval Hospital and is not expected to recover.

Tributes, flowers, candles, and pride flags have blanketed Pennsylvania Avenue, and a crowd of mourners continues to grow, even days after the attack.

First Gentleman Ethan Reichenbach, who did not return to the White House following Mrs. Spiers's seeming return from Russia, has not been seen since the Langley blast.

2

Southern Siberia

A BRANCH SNAPPED NEARBY, in the gloomy, pre-dawn darkness.

Ethan's eyes flew open.

He sat in the back seat of his and Jack's jeep, leaning against the frost-crusted window while Jack slept between his legs. Jack's back rested on Ethan's chest, his legs stretched out on the bench seat. One of Ethan's legs was tucked around Jack's, and his other foot braced on the floorboards.

Two stuffed quilts covered them both, pulled up to Jack's chin. Russian-made, they were thick, filled with feathers and lined with fur. Ethan had grabbed both when they passed through yet another desolate Russian ghost town two days before. Like the other villages they'd passed, it was deserted and bore the hallmarks of recent savagery.

One of Ethan's arms rested under the blankets and wrapped around Jack's chest, holding him tight.

His other hand gripped his pistol.

He'd kept hold of his weapon all night long. At the slightest noise, he'd had it up in the darkness, ready to fire.

Another snap, and then crunching footsteps in the snow, coming up the side of the jeep.

Ethan's arm tightened around Jack, and his gloved finger hovered on the trigger. He held his pistol steady, pointed at the passenger window, and waited, not breathing.

"Good morning, sunshine." Ethan relaxed at the familiar voice as Scott appeared at the window. Scott opened the door and peered in. He was bundled from head to toe, a balaclava pulled back to expose his face. His hair, perpetually messy, stuck up at odd angles. A thick, bulky sweater made his camo jacket puff out around him. Like Ethan, he wore dark gloves and cargo pants tucked into his boots.

Exhaling, Ethan lowered his pistol and groaned. "Already?"

Scott nodded and took a long pull on a cigarette, then blew the smoke away from the jeep. "Does sleeping beauty need more beauty rest?"

Ignoring him, Ethan blinked hard, trying to force himself awake. Night after night of being on edge had worn him thin.

Scott jerked his chin toward Jack as he took another drag on his cigarette. He arched his eyebrows.

"He's good." Ethan dropped a light kiss to the top of Jack's blond hair. Jack shifted, burrowing against his chest, and ducked partially beneath the blankets. "What'd you guys find?"

Every morning, Scott and Sergey took a small team from their convoy out before dawn, scouting ahead on their route. They moved fast, reconnoitering the terrain, and then were back at camp by dawn. Speed was of the essence, but so was stealth.

So far on their drive from the Volga river valley to the east coast of Russia, Sergey had kept his insurgency, their convoy, off the main roads and away from the cities. They moved overland, on rough tracks and barely-stable game paths, slipping through dense-packed Russian forest. It slowed them down, but they made up for it with their grueling pace. There was no time to lose; they had to be at Simushir Island, in the Kuril Archipelago north of Japan and stretching toward the Arctic Circle, in just a few days.

But so much was stacked against them.

The convoy was moving farther into Siberia, and into the mountains, where snow built beneath their tires and the temperature kept dropping. It was late spring according to the calendar, but in Siberia, deep snow drifts and thick ice kept the ground frozen, and the temperature hovered in the thirties. It would only drop as they kept going.

Warm, according to the Russians they were moving with.

Every day, the air was thick with frost-laden clouds that tangled in the branches of the forest trees and alpine woodlands they'd plunged into. They followed tributaries when they could, sometimes named, sometimes not. For every named river in Russia, there were another ten that couldn't be found on any map. Surrounding the convoy, encircling them in every direction, mountain peaks faded in and out of the harsh gloom, a mess of smeared steel skies and threatening snow clouds. Loose black dirt skidded beneath their tires and their boots, the whine of their jeeps' engines and muttered curses in Russian and English the only noises in the vast wasteland.

Siberia was silent. Eerily so. Like the land had swallowed up all life deep within its frozen core. Behind every tree, ghosts seemed to linger, the foggy air heavy with a sense of harshness and cruelty that came from the land and its history. How many had died in Siberia, throughout her long, long history?

They were almost halfway to the Russian east coast, and, for Ethan, the faster they put Siberia behind them, the better. Ahead lay the winding, frozen mountains of central Asia, with frigid cold and late-season snow storms. To the south lay the tri-border region of Kazakhstan, Mongolia, and China. Another tense border region in an already too-tense world.

They had to keep going, keep moving. Had to make it all the way to the coast, and then beyond, to Simushir Island. It was an island so remote, it wasn't on most maps. Of course, it also held the remains of a secret Soviet submarine base. That helped keep it hidden.

President Elizabeth Wall, president of the United States since the attack on Jack and Langley at the hands of Madigan's most cruel agent, had promised to send aid and a submarine attack squadron to the base to meet up with them.

And from there, they were finally going on the offensive. Taking their fight—for no less than the safety of the world—straight to Madigan, and his ally, General Moroshkin, the self-appointed leader of Russia following his coup against President Sergey Puchkov, with Madigan's aid and assistance. The coup that had left Sergey in hiding, leading an insurgency, and Madigan in control of his clandestine Arctic mission with his brutal criminal army.

There was no time to waste. They drove all day and into the night until they had to stop for just a few hours when the forest closed in and the darkness was practically a knife, slashing at their jeeps. No one wanted to pitch sideways down the mountain or slide into a ravine. Even their stops for supplies were lightning fast, darting into burned farmhouses and bomb-cratered villages to hunt for tins of food, eggs left in chicken coops, and cans of fuel. Blackened skeletons of vehicles lay in heaps in the few roads they crossed, bearing the scars of General Moroshkin's war for the soul of Russia. Moroshkin may have taken Moscow, and a large part of the Russian military, but the populace fought him tooth and nail, especially in Siberia. And paid the price.

They were racing against time. Madigan hung on the top of the planet, intent on razing the world to the ground by igniting a thermobaric explosion that would incinerate the atmosphere. General Moroshkin led his Russian charge over the North Pole and into Canada, an invasion pointed at the heart of America. Elizabeth was locked in a heated standoff with Moroshkin and his forces, and the only intelligence anyone had on Madigan's actions in the Arctic came from Sasha's sacrificial flight in his MiG and a rickety, ancient Swedish weather satellite.

The world was falling apart around them.

Scott shook his head. "The route for this morning is clear. This deep inside Siberian territory, we should be safe from Moroshkin's troops."

From the Volga valley to Siberia's borders, the convoy had dodged Moroshkin's forces holed up in towns and cities, at roadblocks and checkpoints across highways and backroads, and in tanks and massive anti-aircraft weapons platforms deployed in fields and farms. Nothing flew overhead in Russia anymore, except for Moroshkin's forces.

Scott sucked down more of his cigarette. "We're getting off the mountain and back on the roads, too. No more navigating through the trees. We saw a couple farms around us. A destroyed village. We got some fuel out of the trucks they left behind. To the south, there were what looked like some Chinese units hanging out near the tri-border region. Guarding their border, or making a push into Russia, I couldn't tell."

Ethan frowned. "What did Sergey say?"

"Not much." Scott fixed Ethan with a hard glare.

It had been four days since Sasha had flown off for the Kara Sea, volunteering his life on a one-way intelligence mission to the Arctic.

Sergey Puchkov, deposed president of Russia, leader of the Russian insurgency and of their convoy, had always been an enigma to Ethan. He'd met Sergey a year before, when Sergey and Jack had been at odds, striking and parrying at each other in the international arena. They'd formed a tentative alliance in Prague, but when Jack had come clean to the world about him and Ethan and their relationship, Sergey had backpedaled hard and fast.

And then returned, when it became clear Jack wasn't going anywhere. After Ethan had stopped Madigan's attempted coup against Jack, and Madigan's plan to devastate the Middle East that would have murdered thousands of Russian soldiers. After all that, Jack kept being the president, a foiled coup under his belt and Ethan on his arm, and he stared the world down and waited for someone else to blink.

Somehow, Sergey had become Jack's closest political ally on the world stage. More than that, even: a good friend.

Along the way, Sergey had befriended Senior Lieutenant Sasha Andreyev.

Another riddle of a man. A former Russian Air Force officer, MiG pilot, and the survivor of a brutal anti-gay beating by his former Air Force comrades. Half-dead, he'd made his way to Moscow in a delirium, where Sergey's personal physician found him collapsed outside the Kremlin's walls. Sergey had kept him in the Kremlin as his physician nursed Sasha back to health, and then offered Sasha a position as his senior aide. He worked closely with the head of the Russian FSB, Sergey's friend, Ilya Ivchenko.

From strangers, they had become a nearly inseparable pair. Sergey had glossed over most of the details when he first told Jack of Sasha and how he'd come to be at Sergey's side. But it didn't take a psychic to see the way Sasha felt about Sergey. Ethan could read it in his eyes, and in the way every part of him was tuned to Sergey, at the State Dinner and after. Sasha had fallen and fallen hard.

But Sergey never saw Sasha's feelings. Whatever their relationship was to Sergey, he hadn't seen how Sasha had felt.

Until the very end.

Sergey had been bitterly opposed to Sasha's Arctic overflight, petulant in his anger. He'd confronted Sasha after snapping at him for hours. And then—

Whatever had happened between the two of them, out on the flight line by Sasha's MiG, was a mystery.

Something *had* happened, though. Sergey came away knowing how Sasha felt. His Russian temper had flared after Sasha's takeoff, and he'd lashed out at Jack, roaring, "Everything was *fine* until you! You changed the whole *world*, and *my* world!"

Devastation had slammed into Sergey. Ethan had watched it, watched Sergey's knuckles go white as his fists clenched, and he'd fought for something to say as his world rearranged itself, pieces to a broken puzzle that suddenly wouldn't align. "He said *nothing*!" Sergey had hissed. "Why did he not *say* anything?"

Sasha's last satellite call, and the screech of metal and the roar of flame, haunted the silent places in their convoy and hung like a cloying shroud around Sergey. Tragically faithful to the last moment, Sasha had given everything to Sergey and his mission. Even his life.

After that, it seemed like Sergey had been turned inside out. He moved in a daze, his eyes wide, gaze shattered, limbs listless. Normally full of life, his long arms brimming with energy, his hands always moving as he spoke, he'd lapsed into a dull, heavy melancholy. Scott said that the days crawled by, riding shotgun in Sergey's jeep as they drove at the head of the caravan, Sergey silent at his side and with all the energy of a sucking black hole.

Scott blew another puff of cigarette smoke away from the jeep. "Vasily ransacked a chicken coop at one of the farms. He's scrambling eggs if you want to get up and get some. We move out in ten."

Finally, Jack stirred in Ethan's arms and let out a soft groan as he came awake. His hand stroked over Jack's chest beneath the blankets, and Jack covered his hand with one of his own. "Is there coffee?"

Scott snorted. "Whatever it is they pretend is coffee is boiling." He held out his cigarette, offering it to Ethan.

Ethan shook his head. "You know Stacy is going to kick your ass for smoking again."

"I know. I love it when she gets all protective." Another long drag, and then he stamped out the cigarette. "Don't tell her I said that." He wagged a finger at Ethan before picking up the cigarette butt. "You and I smoked in Fallujah to keep ourselves awake." Scott shrugged. "It does its job."

Ethan dropped another kiss to the top of Jack's head, just before Jack opened his eyes. "Things are different now."

Scott rolled his eyes, but grinned and walked away from their jeep, back to the center of camp. It was less a camp and more an array of parked jeeps crowded together in a defensive ring. Clumps of snow covered the ground and clung to the evergreen branches overhead. Thick, fog-shrouded forest surrounded their convoy, stretching as far as Ethan could see, giving the landscape the feel of a cemetery. It made Ethan's bones pucker and his skin tighten. He wanted out.

Ethan had tucked his and Jack's jeep in the back of the camp, at the base of a thick pine. Opposite them, Sergey and Scott had parked theirs. The rest of the men were in between.

The sounds of the convoy coming alive in the frosty morning started clattering through their patch of snowy forest. Grumbled Russian, squeaky metal hinges and slamming doors, the crackle of logs in a fire, and the clang of pots and pans that Vasily had insisted on bringing from Volga.

Jack nuzzled at Ethan's neck, and the roughness of his beard, grown thick in the five days they'd been on the road, scratched over Ethan's skin just before Jack dropped a kiss beneath his jaw. "Morning, love."

Ethan smiled down at him, de-cocked his pistol, and slid it into his hip holster beneath their blankets. He wrapped both arms around Jack as Jack turned and faced him. "How are you? Are you warm enough?" As Ethan spoke, his breath clouded the air between them.

"I'm good." Jack peeled off his gloves beneath the blankets and snaked his warm hands up under Ethan's jacket and sweater. His gentle, searching fingers found the long line of ragged stitches in Ethan's side.

Ethan flinched.

"Sorry. You know we need to check them." Carefully, Jack felt around the stitches, testing the skin, and then rested his palm over the top of the mostly-healed wound. "No heat. No swelling. No pus. No infection." He smiled. "You had me worried after yesterday."

Ethan ducked his head, his cheeks warming. While rummaging through an abandoned barn, he'd walked right through a rotted-out baseboard and fallen into a cellar, into the rough, loose earth. Not his finest moment. They'd wrangled some supplies, but he'd come away filthy and bruised, his ego smarting. Jack's worried eyes and his gentle ministrations after they'd stopped for the night had helped soothe the ache.

Jack's gaze darted over Ethan's face, searching. He frowned. "Did you get any sleep?"

"Some."

"Liar." Arching an eyebrow, Jack sat back but kept his hands under Ethan's clothes and on his skin. "You should let me watch over you at night, too."

"I'd rather do it. I have you close to me." He patted his hip and his holstered weapon. "I have constant protection on you all night long. There's no way anyone can get to you. Not without going through me."

"Literally." Jack smiled, but it faded fast. "I'll drive during the day again. Rest, and let me watch over you." He squeezed Ethan's hip.

Ethan nodded, and the corners of his lips quirked up. This was new, this give-and-take of caretaking and watching out for each other. In DC, at the White House, there had been their jobs and their duties and the world to react to. They took care of slights and wounds inflicted by the press, their suits and ties a kind of armor against the world. Out in the wilderness, in the forest, they'd fallen into a different kind of caretaking. A sharing of two lives, each supporting the other's existence. It was primal, in a way, how they had fused together. Half of his life was in Jack's hands, and instead of feeling vulnerable, it was the most natural feeling in the world. "Deal." He pressed a kiss to Jack's lips.

A question hovered in the forefront of Ethan's mind, weighing on his thoughts. Every morning, he felt the weight of his secret resting over his heart: two rings, made before the world fell apart around them. Some moments, asking Jack was on the tip of his tongue, ready to tumble from his lips with his next breath. He forced himself to swallow the words. Not yet. It wasn't the right time. Not yet.

Jack leaned into Ethan, and his hands wound around Ethan's back beneath his sweater. "At some point, we won't be sleeping in this jeep anymore," he whispered into their kiss. "We'll have room to stretch out… share a sleeping bag…"

Smiling, Ethan pulled off his gloves and brought his hands up to Jack's face, his thumbs caressing Jack's cheeks. "We don't need a sleeping bag…" One hand snaked around Jack's neck, and the other dropped to his hip.

In a flash, he flipped Jack, laying him on his back across the bench seat. Jack wrapped his legs around Ethan's waist as Ethan slid his hands through Jack's blond strands.

Jack grabbed his shoulders and pulled Ethan closer, his legs holding Ethan in place. He captured Ethan's lips, kissing greedily as his hips rocked upward. Even through the layers they wore, Ethan felt Jack's hard cock pressing against his own.

"I want you," Jack breathed. "I want you to make love to me."

Ethan's blood burned, searing through his body from his head to his toes, and part of him wanted to tilt Jack's head back and ravage his throat, work his way down, unwrap him like a present until he found his cock. Suck him deep. Work him open with his tongue until Jack begged for more, and then sink his cock into Jack's warm, tight body. Jesus, he wanted Jack. So much.

The springs on the jeep's suspension squeaked with their rocking, and the tires groaned and crunched against the snow on the ground. In the distance, low chuckles sounded, and one catcall.

Deflating, Ethan dropped his forehead to Jack's chest. He rode Jack's heaving breaths and listened to his racing heartbeat. "I don't want an audience when I make love to you again."

Jack's legs dropped, one falling over the back of the front seat, and the other squishing against the window. His hands stroked over Ethan's back and tangled in his hair. "I don't want to have to be quiet."

"Jesus." Ethan gripped Jack and surged against him, thrusting against his hard cock. "That's not helping."

Smiling, Jack rocked his hips up once and then scooted backward, propping himself up on his elbows as Ethan sat back and tried to straighten out his clothes. A prominent bulge strained the front of his cargo pants. He ached, painfully hard for Jack.

From the center of the camp, Scott called, "Coffee's ready if you are!"

Rumbling laughter, deep and throaty, from nearly all the men.

Shaking his head, Jack started to pull himself together next to Ethan and fished out his balaclava from the pocket of his cargo pants. Outside of the jeep, he wore a full-face balaclava and, on their drive, he kept everything but his eyes covered. Ethan insisted, and Scott and Sergey both backed him up. The members of their convoy, of course, knew who Jack was, and just after Jack had shown up, Sergey had delivered a scathing speech in Russian to his people that had had even Ethan flinching, though he didn't understand a word that had been said. But they were traveling through a war zone, parts of Russia that were contested in the coup, under attack from Moroshkin's forces, and had been bombed by the United States and other nations, all trying to stop Moroshkin.

Who knew what was out there, or *who* was out there. Jack was, to the world, brain-dead in Bethesda Naval Hospital. A front-page picture of him alive in Russia would go over as well as a nuclear bomb.

"Scott came by?" Jack tucked his undershirt into his pants and took a moment to readjust. His cheeks were dusted crimson, a faint flush Ethan wanted to nibble.

"Yeah." He tore his eyes away from Jack and fanned the bottom of his sweater, trying to cool his body.

"How'd the scouting go?"

"The route is clear for the morning. More abandoned villages. They found fuel and some supplies. Vasily is cooking eggs." Ethan reached out and traced Jack's spine through his sweater and jacket. "And you should talk to Sergey."

Jack turned and stared at Ethan.

"I think Scott's worried about him." A tight, strained smile curved his lips. "And that's saying something." Scott's trust in Sergey, and in their Russian allies, stretched from meal to meal. Day to day, hour by hour. If everything came apart, Scott would be the first to say "I knew it".

"He hasn't wanted to talk to me." Swallowing, Jack leaned back with a sigh. His hands dropped to his lap, and he picked at the wool fibers of the balaclava. "He's kept his distance since Volga. I'm not sure I'm the person he wants to see right now."

Nodding slowly, Ethan frowned. Sergey's harsh accusations, thrown at Jack at Volga air base, had been the last direct contact the two had. "After all this time, you think he's pulling away because of…"

Because of their love? Because he and Jack were together? Because Sergey had been loved by a gay man? Was this some kind of reaction, a fear that falling in love with another man "was contagious", as he'd hurled at Jack?

"He's pulled back before." Jack sat forward, slipped the balaclava over his head. He tugged it down around his neck. "I want to do the right thing by him. I don't want to piss him off." He frowned, deep lines furrowing his brow. "But, no matter what else is going on, he's devastated about losing Sasha. I remember what it felt like when I thought you were dead. I can at least try to talk to him about that."

Ethan's chest constricted, and his heart almost seized. Was it only a week ago that he'd thought Jack was dead as well? Never, ever, again. He'd do everything in his power to keep Jack safe, keep him from ever coming to harm. And, he'd never lose faith like that again, either. The darkness that had swallowed him on his race from Saudi Arabia to Russia. The emptiness, the silent scream within his soul. The way he had wanted to die, had begged the world to kill him.

Together. They'd face everything together from now on. No matter what.

Adjusting the balaclava, Jack leaned over and pressed a chaste kiss to Ethan's lips. "Time to face the music, love."

Ethan pulled out his own balaclava, tugged it down around his neck, and gripped the door handle. They piled out of the back of the jeep, and Ethan caught the smothered grins and barks of laughter sent their way. Scott raised a dented metal mug toward them both. Jack headed for him, and for the small fire where Vasily was cooking.

One of the Russians who went out with Scott every morning, Aleksey, slid up to Ethan. Middle-aged, Aleksey had been a federal police officer in Sochi and had fought with Sergey against Moroshkin and Madigan's forces the night of the coup. Now, he was one of Sergey's officers in the insurgency. He had a small beer gut and a thick salt-and-pepper mustache beneath ruddy, pockmarked cheeks, a sharp smile, and perpetually messy hair.

His eyes glittered as he clapped Ethan on the back. "You are good Russian lover!" he crowed. "Quick!"

Others laughed, and Ethan spied Jack smothering his grin and rolling his eyes as he took the coffee Scott offered. Scott shrugged and hid his smile in his next sip.

Ethan clapped Aleksey on the upper arm, smiling along with the others. When he and Jack had first met the men in Sergey's insurgency, they'd worried about how they would be received. Two men in love in a country where only months before, Sasha had almost been killed for being gay. Another man, Evgeni Konnikov, *had* been murdered.

Sergey's men, however, had been nothing but accepting. They were believers in Sergey's government, after all, and Sergey had made equality a foundational platform of his politics and administration.

They just showed that acceptance through good Russian ribbing and teasing. The more ribald, the better.

"If we had actually got going," Ethan began, first winking at Jack and then sending Aleksey a grin, "we'd be here for *days*."

More laughter. Aleksey wagged his finger in Ethan's face and squeezed his elbow before handing him a cup of bitter, sludgy coffee. Vasily waved him and Jack over, and he scooped the last of the eggs into a scavenged plastic bowl they shared. "I save for you," Vasily said, pointing to them both.

Jack thanked him. As they ate, Ethan spotted Sergey standing in front of his jeep, his hands resting flat on a spread-out map of Russia draped over the hood with his head bowed low. He looked up, and his piercing gaze fell on Jack. There was a moment where his face flickered, something dark passing through his eyes, but it was gone before Ethan could catch it.

And then Sergey folded up his map and climbed into the driver's side of his jeep. He kept his eyes downcast, not once looking at Jack again.

3

Northern Siberian Permafrost

WHOMP WHOMP WHOMP.

The helicopter was still out there, tracking over the taiga.

Sasha ran through the dense alpine forest, the trunks only feet apart, and stumbled through knee-deep snow. He dragged a pine bough behind him, hoping it would obscure his footsteps. Anything to cover his tracks.

The forest cover above thickened, branches overhead tangling together, coated in massive clumps of snow and ice. He hesitated, crouching next to a fat pine trunk, and tried to catch his breath. Chest heaving, he closed his eyes, listening.

The helicopter's rotors slowly faded.

It was veering off.

Perfect.

He ditched his pine bough and dropped to his knees, digging frantically in the deep snow. The day before, the fragile, ice-crusted snow he'd been walking on had collapsed, plunging him into a snow drift over seven feet tall. He'd been a shivering mess when he finally managed to climb out, hours later.

The ice crust on this snow, however, was thicker and refused to break.

The rotors sounded again, grinding over the trees. The rumble grew, growling in the sky. The helicopter was coming back his way.

Grunting, Sasha kicked at the ice, slamming the heel of his boot into the crunchy snow, over and over.

Whomp whomp whomp

Closer... closer...

Finally, the ice cracked, and the snow beneath puffed up, exploding over Sasha's legs and his filthy, tattered flight suit. He cursed and went back to digging, quickly scooping out clumps of snow to make a deep, angled trench.

The ground trembled beneath him.

Time was up.

Rolling, he ducked into his trench, hiding under the overhang of snow that he'd left. He reached out, smearing one arm through the drift he'd left behind and knocking over the pile he'd dug out, and then dragged the pine bough over the opening. With luck, and obscured through the forest, his hiding spot would look like an animal den.

He curled tight, barely breathing as the black helicopter passed above the trees. Closing his eyes, Sasha imagined the *Spetsnaz* team leader's face.

Once, he'd let the team get too close, close enough to where he'd had to hide, pressed in the frozen dirt beneath the warped boards of a trapper's cabin in the empty forest. He'd peered out from under the floorboards, his face in the dirt, watching the men search for his tracks.

And he'd first laid eyes on the lieutenant. The *Spetsnaz* lieutenant was a hard man, a Siberian, with a weathered, sharp face and a cutting gaze. A long scar curved over the right side of his face, from his temple to his jaw. His eyes were sharp, with a predator's instinct. Sasha had stopped breathing when his gaze swept over the cabin.

The *Spetsnaz* lieutenant was a hunter in his own lands, and Sasha was his prey. How had he ever managed to last this long? He should have been killed days ago. Every moment he kept going was borrowed time.

Sasha held his breath and tried to blank out his mind.

Sergey's face, and the memory of his smile, his laugh, played in the darkness behind his eyelids. He almost groaned as yearning, painful, aching *want*, slammed into him.

Finally, the helicopter moved off, the heavy cut of rotors against the frigid sky fading into the distance, heading back the way it had come.

Sasha went limp, boneless, his head resting in the snow as he let out a shaky breath. His gloved hands gripped the strap on the emergency pack he'd pulled from his ejection seat, but they were trembling, both from the freezing cold and the strain of being on the run.

His emergency pack was nearly empty. Russian pilots were only supposed to have to survive seventy-two hours before being rescued. He was working up to one hundred hours on his own, stumbling through the vast wilderness of the Siberian taiga. He'd stretched the food, but his water was gone.

He scraped snow from the wall of his tiny cave and held it in the palm of his gloved hand. Blowing on it, he tried to melt the snow, bring it above freezing. He was already cold, his body temperature too low. Eating snow would only lower it further. How much more until he was dangerously hypothermic?

Finally, the flecks melted, and he licked the frigid water from the palm of his filthy glove. Not enough. Not nearly enough. And it was still too cold.

What he would give to be warm again…

Sasha's eyes slipped closed.

In his mind, he was back in the Kremlin, in Sergey's presidential apartments, laughing and sitting across from him at the gaudy state dining table, one end piled high with briefing papers and binders. There was a fire roaring in the fireplace along the wall, and he had a glass of whiskey in his hand. Sergey's smile, though, was warm enough to reach his bones, set him on fire from the inside, fill his whole world up with heat and light—

Jerking, he snapped awake, his forehead slamming into the snow overhead. He'd closed his eyes for a moment, but that was all it took to slip into an exhausted slumber. Damn it. He snagged what rest he could, digging out snow burrows and nesting with pine boughs and fallen branches, but it wasn't ever enough. He was almost delirious with exhaustion.

Outside, the sun had fallen, and only a dim glow blurred through the forest.

And he was shivering, his jaw clattering loud enough to wake the dead. His snow trench was too cold. He had to get out of there.

Sasha pulled his pistol out of his pack and checked the chamber. Evening meant bears, and the bears in Siberia thought nothing of swiping at a lone, wrecked human wandering through their range. He'd be a tasty meal for a bear working out its hibernation hunger. Not that a pistol would do much against an attacking bear, but he might be able to scare it off.

He shook his head, trying to shake the haze of exhaustion. *Keep heading southeast.* If he was where he thought he was on the map, then he was deep in the Sakha Republic. Indigenous Siberian territory. Tribal lands. And days away from Simushir Island.

He had to keep going.

Sasha slid out on his belly, wincing as snow poured down the front of his flight suit. Damn it, he couldn't stop shivering.

Gripping his pistol as tight as he could in his shaking hands, Sasha set off into the forest. He stumbled and nearly fell, and his body felt like it was trembling apart, but he kept moving. One foot in front of the other, into the deep snow.

Each step was one closer to Sergey.

4

Washington DC

"MADAM PRESIDENT." GENERAL BRADFORD nodded to Elizabeth as she strode into the White House Situation Room. He and all the others around the conference table stood when she entered.

Elizabeth's throat clenched. She used to stand with them, her former colleagues, and greet Jack when he entered. His arrival had always calmed the room, his eyes bright and sharp, and with a soft smile at the ready, no matter what. He'd embodied that balance of intensity and perspective, especially so after Ethan had joined him at the White House. The team—*Jack's team*—had truly felt connected, especially after Madigan's betrayal. It felt like they were united, serving a purpose bigger than themselves, bigger than politics, even.

That camaraderie had evaporated, vanished with a sucking pop. Hard stares followed Elizabeth to the head of the table, everyone still and silent as she pulled out the chair—*Jack's chair*—and sat down. She laced her fingers together, rested her elbows on the edge, and stared at General Bradford. "Let's hear it."

General Bradford didn't blink. "Madam President, after the initial strike, we successfully pushed the Russians' first invasion wave into Canada back from Yellowknife to what we're assuming is their rally point in northern Nunavut. We're currently engaged in a standoff with General Moroshkin's Russian forces in the Canadian Nunavut and Northwest Territories. We've mobilized the Second Infantry Division out of Fort Lewis, the Tenth Mountain out of Fort Drum, and the Fourth Infantry Division from Alaska, as well as Marines from Pendleton and Kaneohe Bay. The Air Force has fighters from Elmendorf and Eielson in the air. The skies over the polar cap are stuffed full of additional Russian transports, and more Russians are coming in via Baffin Bay and over the pole. At best estimate, they have at least three subs under the ice and four destroyers in the water. And the Russian aircraft carrier has been spotted."

"Moroshkin hauled that bucket of bolts out? I thought it was being mothballed." General Harris glanced at Admiral McDonald, Director of Naval Operations, who stayed silent. Harris was the vice-chairman of the Joint Chiefs, a position formerly held by General Madigan.

"Reports from fishermen off Greenland and Nova Scotia show it crossed through the GIUK Gap and headed up Baffin Bay. We believe she's offloaded her fighters to the Arctic Bay Airport, at the north end of the bay." Bradford called up a series of maps along the far wall of the Situation Room and overlaid the surveillance images they'd managed to grab from overflights and the few satellites they had left that could reach the polar orbits.

"The Russians have established a defensive line at Kugluktuk. It's a hamlet in Nunavut, on the shore of the Arctic Ocean. North of there, the Russians control the Arctic. The islands, the seas. Everything."

Shit. A dull pain pounded behind Elizabeth's eyeballs. Once, she had wanted to be president. What she wouldn't give for Jack to be back and sitting in the big chair. "How many people are up there, General?"

"Very few, Madam President. Mostly tribal settlements and research stations. We have American scientists at the research station at Resolute, and we had an Army unit at Alert Station. Both facilities have gone dark."

"Any word from them?"

"We haven't been able to establish radio contact."

"What the hell is Moroshkin doing, General?"

A momentary pause from General Bradford as he stared her down. "This is an invasion, Madam President. It's not how we expected a Russian invasion to happen, especially not in this century, but the Red Bear has come to our door. And Canada is stuck in the middle."

"What has Canada's response been so far?" Elizabeth turned to her former deputy Secretary of State, Paul Heng, now acting in her old secretary of state shoes, ostensibly until she and Jack put together a list of replacement candidates.

"They're outraged. Publicly, they've asked for our military aid, and they are sending their military units alongside ours against the Russians with the caveat that we *do not* strike first. Privately, they're deeply concerned about loss of life and loss of infrastructure. The number of casualties in the first wave of the invasion is estimated at just over a thousand. That's too many for them. They're willing to consider all options to avoid further casualties."

"Even surrender?" Her voice chilled, cold enough to cut diamonds.

"Yes, Madam President."

"That would give the Russians a clear path to the US," General Harris growled.

Elizabeth gave Harris a long look. "Paul, I want to know the moment that the Canadians and the Russians start talking. If anything happens between them, at any level. Backroom or a direct phone call. I want to know." She nodded to Acting CIA Director Olivia Mori as she spoke. The CIA would need to help with that.

Mori nodded back. Her arm was in a sling and half her face was black and blue after the explosion at Langley. Her eyes were clear, but pinched. If

Elizabeth had to guess, Mori wasn't taking her pain medication. Considering a building had fallen on her, that said something.

This was crunch time. The Russians were coming, and they were headed for their back door. There was no time for pain.

"Options." Elizabeth peered around the table.

"Our defensive line is holding firm for now." Bradford gestured to the map on the large display screen across the front wall. "The Russians are pushed back to Kugluktuk. They haven't advanced any farther south."

"But they will."

Bradford nodded, once. "Undoubtedly, Madam President."

"Madam President." Admiral McDonald, Director of Naval Operations, leaned forward. "The *Nimitz* Strike Group is already on their way north, heading up the Pacific coast of Canada. The rest of Carrier Strike Group Eleven is moving up from San Diego. Three subs from Bangor are sailing with the *Nimitz*. We can strike the Russians at their rally point north of Nunavut and send in fighters and sorties after."

General Harris spoke again. "The ground troops we've mobilized can sweep up the mess after they're done."

"The Canadians have *expressly* forbidden any air strikes in their territory, directed to either side." Heng flipped a pencil back and forth between his fingers, the eraser slamming into his notepad over and over, beating out a dull *thump thump thump*. "The prime minister issued an emergency address to the nation and the world, and explicitly ordered both the Russian forces *and* our forces to *not* conduct airstrikes. Their biggest concern is further civilian casualties."

Harris snorted. "Does the prime minister honestly think the Russians will abide by that? They bombed their way to Yellowknife and sent missiles toward Toronto and Vancouver—"

"Which mostly landed outside the cities," Heng interrupted Harris. He swallowed audibly, his eyes wide, but pressed on. "After the prime minister's statement, all Russian bombing stopped."

"Moroshkin is trying to appeal to the Canadians." Elizabeth let out a slow breath as she squeezed her hands together. "They know what's most important to them: their people. If we strike first and hurt anyone up there, we're opening the door for the Canadians to turn against us."

"They wouldn't *really* allow the Russians to invade their territory—" Julian Aviles, Secretary of Homeland Security, protested.

Elizabeth's mind ticked ahead, her years of backroom diplomatic deals and tit-for-tat negotiation providing the twisted roadmap. "If the Russians and the Canadians sign an agreement after the fact, then it's not an invasion. It's the Canadians inviting the Russians to use their land. In exchange for the protection of their population."

General Harris snorted.

Elizabeth's eyes flashed to him. "General, wake up. The United States has taken some pretty big hits in the past few years, if you haven't noticed. Several huge blows in the last week. We lost our president, and a rogue general—your predecessor—has played the bulk of our intelligence agencies and military like fools. We've been caught with our pants down, and we don't have many friends in our corner right now."

Silence.

"The Canadians and the world might very well pivot to the next big player that gives us a bloody nose. Moroshkin knows this. He'll push us until we bleed, and he'll force the world to take sides."

"NATO has condemned the invasion," Heng said in the silence that followed. "But none of our NATO allies are offering military aid to us or the Canadians at this time. This could be the final break."

Elizabeth exhaled and dropped her head forward, letting it hang between her shoulders for a moment.

"Madam President?" Admiral McDonald spoke while Harris kept quiet, looking like he was chewing nails. Bradford glared at the map on the far wall as if he could make the lines move with his concentration alone. As if he could banish Moroshkin's Russians from the map, and the world.

Elizabeth frowned.

"You personally ordered a deployment of four subs from our base at Pearl Harbor. I can't get answers about where they're headed or why. Everyone is buttoned up tight. Under *your* direct orders."

Heads all around the table whipped toward Elizabeth, unasked questions building into a near-crackling tension in the air.

She caught Bradford's eye. He stared right back, not blinking.

Harris scowled and looked around the table as if searching for someone to come forward with the answer. "Madam President—"

"Their mission is classified." She rested her hands on the tabletop. "I want to know the instant the Russians or the Canadians make a move. Any move. And I want to see options for addressing the Russians that the Canadians will be on board with. Insertion teams. Special Operators. A small footprint. And—" She sighed. "See if you can find anything about the Americans who were up there. Let's not leave them behind."

Hard gazes and narrowed eyes speared her from around the table, the rest of the Situation Room standing slowly after her. She hadn't won any points with that one. *Jack... You made it look easy.* "Thank you, everyone. You're all dismissed. General Bradford, Director Mori, stay behind."

Padfolios closed, papers shuffled, and feet thudded toward the door. Weighty silence clung to the paneling, to the sound-dampened wooden walls, almost as loud as a scream. Mori and Bradford stared at their notepads, not meeting anyone's gaze as their colleagues trudged out of the Situation Room. By the door, Secret Service Agent Levi Daniels gave Elizabeth a long look, a different heaviness etched into his gaze.

The last staffer slipped out of the Situation Room, leaving Elizabeth alone with Director Mori and General Bradford seated at the table, and Levi at the door. Bradford's eyes flicked to Levi.

"He stays." Elizabeth dared Bradford to protest, glaring down the table at him. "There are precious few people I *know* I can trust. He is one of them."

Bradford said nothing.

"Now," she said, sighing. "What's going on in the Russian Arctic?"

Bradford changed the screens, calling up a new series of grainy satellite images, the detail nearly obscured, the picture a wash of white snow and gray clouds. Unusable. "We're still having a hard time getting accurate intelligence."

A new series of images, data from a weather satellite with the raw scientific information in Swedish still displayed on the bottom of the picture, came up on screen. A wave of gas, colored in a haughty, vibrant fuchsia, leaped off the black-and-white image, stretching across the northern tip of the Russian nation, across the Sakha Republic, the Chukotka Autonomous Okrug, with wispy fingertips pointing toward Alaska.

"We can confirm the gas cloud is growing," Mori said. "And it's growing at a rate that doesn't suggest natural release from the seabed or the Arctic ice," she finished carefully.

"Madam President, why don't we launch a full strike against the location immediately? Obliterate this man once and for all?" Bradford's cheeks were dark, his mouth pursed like he'd sucked the bitterest lemon.

"For the first time in a year, we know exactly where he is." Elizabeth sighed. "And we can't launch a damn thing against him. The science advisors tell me that any significant explosion at that location, where the density is highest, would trigger the ignition of the entire gas cloud. A cascading fireball that would sweep through the entire damned thing. From Russia to Alaska."

Bradford didn't look convinced.

"Are you familiar with the Tunguska explosion in Siberia? In 1908? Two thousand kilometers of forest was flattened and burned to ash. Trees the size of buses were shattered like toothpicks. Every single thing was destroyed. One theory about how that destruction was caused is exactly this." She pointed to the screens. "A methane fireball erupted, burning its way through Siberia. Now, imagine that level of destruction rolling across the globe. We *cannot* let this happen."

"Madigan will detonate it when the cloud is larger. Detonate it like a missile strike." Mori shifted in her seat, the briefest flicker of pain scratching across her bruised face. "He must have some means of creating a large enough blast to ignite the gas cloud."

"That's what I'm afraid of." She rubbed her hands over her face, exhaling into her palms as she closed her eyes briefly. *Jack, how do we do this? Where are you?* It had been days since she'd heard from Jack. Russia was large, she reminded herself, near-constantly. Racing across a continent took time. Still, she held her breath every time she turned on the news or opened her email, fearing the pictures she saw in her nightmares would be splayed across the screen: Jack, bloodied and disfigured, captured or worse, in some far-flung corner of the globe.

Why had she agreed to his insane plan? What on earth had she been thinking?

"All right, we need options for addressing this threat that aren't liable to blow the planet off its axis. What can we deploy immediately?"

Bradford tapped at his tablet, and a flag popped up on the map onscreen. A blip in the middle of the ocean. "We have a SEAL unit operating onboard a sub patrolling the north Atlantic. They tracked the Russians across the GIUK gap and have been monitoring deep underwater for any additional Russian subs or ships coming south out of Murmansk and making a run for the gap. They can make way for the Arctic and deliver the SEALs."

Elizabeth nodded once. "Send them in, then send the sub back to monitoring Moroshkin's movements." The SEALs were the best. They could get this done. Put Madigan down once and for all, and then Jack could come home. The subs going out to meet him wouldn't be needed for anything other than humanitarian relief, and then to join the fight against Moroshkin in Canada. And if Madigan fell, his puppet Moroshkin didn't stand a chance either.

She could hope.

"Madam President?"

Mori's voice broke her wandering thoughts. They shattered to the table, her fears falling into her center, a thousand pins hitting her heart. "Director?"

"About the other intelligence you have. The pilot who managed the overflight. Who is he? Where did you get this intel? What's your source? How are you getting out information out of Russia—"

She stood, her chair pushing backward across the carpet too fast. "That information remains on a need-to-know basis. General, deploy the SEALs. Director, I want to know everything that comes out of the Arctic. Keep me updated on the gas and its growth. And keep your eyes and ears fixed on Canada and Russia. Canada's flashed their hand. If they cave to the Russians, we'll have an invasion at our back door faster than you can say *privet*."

Mori and Bradford stood and nodded, their expressions drawn, exhaustion in their gazes and tension in their shoulders.

"This is war," Elizabeth breathed. "Or the last gasp before it begins."

5

Somewhere over the Atlantic Ocean

THE AIRPLANE HUMMED AROUND Doc, the in-flight rattle of a jumbo jet hurtling at thirty thousand feet in the air and screaming halfway around the world. It was the second, no third, flight for the team, a mind-numbing series of trips that had spanned almost three days already. From Jeddah, they'd flown to Riyadh, and from Riyadh to London. Now, from London to Seattle. Back to America.

Scattered around the cabin, not sitting together, pretending to not even know or care about one another, were the rest of the team. Sergeants Coleman and Wright, each snoring in window seats. Park, Ruiz, and Kobayashi, the remaining junior members left after Fitz's murder, were sitting through the third round of in-flight movies and numbly chewing crackers and pretzels. And Lieutenant Adam Cooper sat ahead of him, hunched and glowering at his feet.

Doc rolled his head along the seatback, looking to his left. A fat, snoring Brit sat between him and the last member of their team: Faisal.

For the length of each flight, Faisal sat silently in his coach seat, staring out the window at a shifting landscape of desolation and empty skies. His face betrayed nothing. As fucked up as Adam appeared, Faisal seemed practically impervious to emotion.

Fuck, the argument over Faisal coming with the team had been epic. Doc hadn't thought Adam could get that pissed. Granted, he'd seen a brand-new side of him over the past few weeks, but the shit-fit Adam threw had been beyond anything he'd imagined.

And Faisal. Shit, did looks deceive. He stared hard at Faisal's profile, remembering the final climax of Adam and Faisal's argument. It had happened right in front of him, for fuck's sake.

He'd been working with Adam in Faisal's space-age kitchen, their truly astounding array of weaponry spread out in front of them. They'd already decided they were sneaking back into the States under the radar, which meant traveling commercial. Which meant no weapons. At least, none that could be found. Faisal had scrounged up secured, false-bottomed bags, and Doc had volunteered to help Adam disassemble their covert, untraceable assault rifles into their little hardened plastic pieces and load them up.

And then Faisal had walked in.

The argument was already days old, stale in the broken air of the Jeddah villa. The whole team tiptoed, as if walking on shattered glass, questions burning from their gazes. What was *up* with the L-T and Faisal?

Doc knew. But he kept his damn mouth shut.

"You're *not* coming," Adam had hissed. "Jesus, Faisal. How could you even ask? You're still recovering!"

Faisal's eyes had narrowed. "I am doing fine. How could *you* imagine that I would be all right with you leaving? *Yallah!* Without being by your side?"

"I *swore* to your uncle—" Adam's voice had shaken, his words quaking as his hands balled into dark fists.

"You said you never wanted to leave."

"I swore to keep you safe!"

"*Wallah*, Adam, the only times I've ever been hurt are when you are gone."

Fuck, that had been a low blow. Doc watched Faisal's words slam into Adam like bullets, each one driving the air from his body, making him step back, and drain the blood from his face.

"There's no place for you."

"You are down a man. I can fill in for Fitz. *Bismillah*, let me help, Adam—"

Adam's fists had hit the counter. A disassembled rifle part clattered to the floor. "Not *you*. You can't—"

And then, Faisal had moved. Hands darting out, he'd picked and grabbed from the pieces of ten different weapons spread across the marble counter, assembling, before their eyes, a perfect AR-15 in under a minute. He'd pressed the rifle stock to his shoulder, turned to the living room, and raised the bore. The patio door had been left open, the breeze from the Red Sea floating through the house. He sighted the rifle, exhaled, and squeezed the trigger.

A perfect hole had appeared in the center of the middle pylon on his pier. If a bull's eye target had been fixed to the wood, he would have landed his shot dead center.

Doc's mouth had dropped open. He'd stopped breathing.

Faisal had turned back, disassembling the rifle as he moved until it was nothing but pieces scattered on the counter again. "You forget where I came from, *habibi*," Faisal whispered. "And our history."

Silence. Doc's eyes had bounced from Adam to Faisal and back again like he was watching an invisible game of tennis.

Adam had shoved away from the kitchen counter with a snarl and walked out.

Later that afternoon, the rest of their supplies had arrived, and that evening, they were on their first flight to Riyadh, Faisal sitting squished next to Doc. Since the kitchen, not a word had been spoken between Adam and

Faisal. And once they left the villa, everyone had ignored each other. They were, to the outside world, strangers.

Or they would be, except, Doc thought, glaring at the back of Adam's head, *for Adam*. He was doing a shit job of acting like everything he wanted in the world, and who he wanted to turn to, wasn't sitting four rows behind him and to the left. As Doc stared, Adam leaned forward again, wrapping both hands around the back of his neck, and tried to surreptitiously glance beneath his bent arms to their row.

Doc met his dark, hooded eyes. Adam looked away, fisting one hand and holding it in front of his pursed lips.

"Excuse me."

The fat Brit snorted and then glared as Faisal squeezed his way through the seats and into the aisle of the jet. Doc tried to catch his gaze, but Faisal, far more so than Adam, was keeping to their ruse of not knowing each other at all.

He turned, watching Faisal head down the aisle toward the rear of the plane. Passengers watched, too, Brits and Europeans with narrowed eyes and suspicious glances turned Faisal's way, watching him with a predatory intensity. One man unbuckled his seat belt as Faisal drew near, as if readying himself to lunge.

Fuck it. Doc rose, heading down the aisle. He glared at the businessman ready to leap after Faisal, now relaxing back in his seat since the Arab had passed him by. Shit, out of anyone, Faisal was the least likely to ever start something. He was the tech nerd, the skinny guy with the computers and the awesome house. He called Adam *habibi*, and he'd put them all up over and over again, never asking for anything. And with the tiny bit that Doc *did* know about Adam and Faisal, well—

Faisal had put a roof over their head, food in their bellies, and intelligence in their hands, even though it meant having his ex, a man he still loved, in his face. Using his palace like a personal base. And ignoring him, and their history.

Faisal didn't deserve to be side-eyed like he was some kind of dangerous terrorist. Without him, would their team have accomplished even half of what they had? It was Faisal who'd put the pieces together with the Yemeni tanker and found Noah in Ma'an. Hell, they were all just Faisal's muscle, at this point.

A part of Doc twisted at the thought, his gut clenching against that mental sucker punch. His words, thrown at Adam days before, echoed in his ears. *Serious foreign influence violations*. They all trusted Faisal, Adam especially. But why? What did they have to go on, other than Faisal's endless consideration and politeness and his and Adam's mercurial connection?

What kind of world was it where Saudi princes became frontline allies against a rogue American general?

Doc followed Faisal to the back of the plane, catching every sidelong glance and lingering glare sent Faisal's way. Even the flight attendants disappeared when Faisal neared, their heels click-clacking against the corrugated cabin flooring as they fled.

Sighing, Faisal leaned against the plane's bulkhead next to the rear door and ran his hands over his face. His lips moved as if whispering, but Doc couldn't hear a thing over the drone and rattle.

"Hey." He leaned back, his shoulder blades digging into the knobs and toggles and levers along the rear compartment wall, the stowage area of bins and trays and carts the flight crew used.

Faisal's eyes popped open. He spotted Doc and snorted. "Of course. *Yallah,* you would ignore the rules about not interacting."

Doc shrugged, one corner of his lip curling up in a smirk. "I'm sure people just think I'm trying to get into the mile-high club."

Faisal shook his head.

Doc's smirk faded. "How you doing?"

Faisal stilled, and a shroud descended behind his gaze. "Fine."

Lolling his head toward Faisal, Doc's eyebrows shot high on his forehead. He said nothing.

Neither did Faisal.

Time for a different approach. "I didn't know you were such a badass. Thought you were just a computer nerd."

Faisal chuckled softly. His eyes sparkled. "There's quite a lot you don't know about me. I am an al-Saud. My family subdued the Arabian Peninsula. We wrested control from the tribes of old and stitched together a nation made from blood and conquest. We may look like fat, wealthy Arabs, but we carry the hearts of conquerors."

"Now I see why Adam took an interest in you."

Faisal's eyes darkened, and his expression went brittle, like holding his tiny smile in place was all that kept him from breaking apart. He shrugged. "I suppose that's one reason." He looked away, staring at the bulkhead and the jump seat for the flight attendant as if it were a priceless artifact.

"You guys okay?" Doc crossed his arms and frowned.

Silence.

Shifting made one of the drawer handles dig into the center of Doc's spine. He leaned back, pressing into it. "I don't really know the L-T all that well…"

What the hell was he trying to say? He barely knew Adam at all. Adam had been their team leader for a little over a year, and he'd gone from being a stick-in-the-ass perfectionist when they'd met him to a rough-edged brawler with the shadow of some huge weight dragging him down. Months ago, Adam had been thrown in the stockade by General Bell, and the team had gone out to drown their frustrations in liquor, anticipating their collective stand-down and reassignment to a new team lead.

Color them all shocked—and hungover—when instead they were on a black-ops White House mission to South America at midnight.

"I know he's a private guy..." Doc shrugged. What he knew about Adam could fit in a paragraph. The most important fact about Adam was what he and Faisal were to each other. Not just, as Adam had claimed in the highland sands of Ethiopia when they first ran to Faisal and his safety net, someone he'd worked with in the Middle East.

Adam had seemed to unbend with Faisal, just slightly, around him and Reichenbach. Had at least acknowledged that Faisal was someone to him, someone special.

That had all changed when the team arrived. Adam had locked up tighter than a missile defense shield. Even Doc had felt the reverberations of Adam's distance echoing painfully off Faisal's confused heart.

"Having the whole team here is probably hard for him," Doc finished lamely, shrugging.

"I appreciate what you are trying to do," he said, meeting Doc's gaze. "There are... larger problems, though."

Doc shifted again, the levers grinding against his back. "Like what?"

Faisal stayed quiet, his gaze seemingly turned inward, and Doc watched him pick and discard words as he licked his lips. "This is the third time he has walked away from us. Each has been difficult. The first..." Faisal's voice faded away, and his eyes slipped closed. "I've never felt anything like that. And I never want to again. After the second, I tried to put us back together. I thought if I reached out, if we could just connect again—" He shook his head.

Doc tried to add up what he knew. He frowned. "When was this?"

"After Ethiopia."

Doc thunked his head against the cold metal. So, when they'd first run to Faisal when they were presumed dead, killed by their own government, Adam had found comfort in Faisal's arms. And then left again. After Ethiopia, and after the White House, Adam had started his slow slide, his descent into gruff silence and barroom brawls, and a prickly hardness that had the whole team on edge. "And now?"

"This is the third time he has turned away from us. I thought, after the hospital, that things would be different. He *seemed* different. But it is all just the same. He is not ready to love."

"He was fucking crazy at the hospital. I mean, just fucking desperate to get to you. I thought he was going to get himself killed. He wasn't faking that."

Faisal glared at him when he cursed, a flat stare that broadcast his displeasure. He sighed. "Three times is significant in Islam. We do things that carry great meaning in threes. *Al-wudu*, the ablutions before prayers, done three times. In *Salat*, prayers are repeated three times. And—" He inhaled, holding his breath. "*Talaq*, to divorce someone, must be done three times before it is final."

Shit. Doc's eyes flicked up the aisle of the plane, as if he could spot Adam in the rows and rows of passengers. "You think he's trying to *divorce* you? You're not *married*, right? I mean, I thought that couldn't—"

"I think," Faisal said, interrupting him gently, "that three times is three times too many. This hurt I feel is not right. This is not the way it's supposed to be. Pursuing this again would be wrong."

"Then why did you insist on coming?"

Faisal's expression softened, though his eyes shone with a cutting pain. "How could I not? I still love him, even if he does not feel the same. I will do everything I can to help him. Always."

Halfway up the plane, a man stood, stretched like he was a bad actor in a soap opera, and turned around, leaning against the front of his seat as if he wanted to stand for a while. He stared toward the rear of the plane, his eyes laser-like in their intensity. He spotted Doc, and Doc stared right back.

He watched Adam look down at his seat cushion and pick at his fingernails.

"He doesn't deserve that from you."

"We have a long history." Faisal smiled, almost wistful. "That's how I choose to remember us. What we were. Not this. Not what we have become." Straightening he cleared his throat and rubbed his hands together. "*Alhamdulillah*, it is time for prayer."

"You're going to *pray* on an airplane?" Doc's eyebrows shot sky high again. "Do you want to get jumped? There are about twelve dudes out there right now who wouldn't think twice."

"Not my full prayers." Regret laced through Faisal's voice. "But the practice grounds me. I find peace in the ritual when I seek *al-nafs al-mutma'innah*. My tranquil self. My peaceful self."

"I think Adam could use some of that."

Faisal sighed, a harassed, harried look crossing over his features as he stared at Doc. A moment later, he smoothed his expression back to his practiced neutrality.

"Sorry." Doc raised both hands, and he shuffled sideways, trying to give Faisal space. "I'll, uh. I'll hang out here with you until you're done. If that's okay."

"More than okay." Finally, Faisal truly smiled. "I've always hated being alone."

6

Northern Siberian Permafrost

His BREATH CAME FAST, fogging the air in front of his face. Cold sank its teeth into his back, right between his shoulder blades. The freezing temperatures squeezed his skull, made his skin feel slapped, and peeled his lips back from his teeth. At least his teeth had stopped chattering, though.

In some corner of Sasha's mind, he realized that was a bad thing. He should still shiver. His teeth should still chatter. But he couldn't remember why.

On he trudged, stumbling through the snow. Tree trunks faded in and out of focus, switching places in front of him. He held out his hands, trying not to run face-first into a pine that seemed to jump ten feet to the right in a moment.

He couldn't feel his fingers anymore.

Dropping to his knees, Sasha buried his hands beneath his armpits, rocking in the snow. Slowly, agonizingly, circulation returned, lancing pain spreading fire through his fingers. Gritting his teeth, Sasha screamed, and a tear slipped from the corner of his eye.

It froze before it reached his chin.

Frigid cold penetrated his entire body, wrapping him like a shroud.

He was so tired.

Just lie down. It will be okay.

Sergey's face flashed in the darkness behind his eyelids.

No, I have to get to Sergey. I have to.

Sasha tried to stand, stumbled, and fell to his knees again.

But a warmth started to spread through him, starting in his thighs. Finally, he wasn't cold anymore.

Sasha rose, shaking, and took one step before collapsing face-first into the snow.

7

Southern Siberia

"*HOLD UP. THERE'S SOMETHING AHEAD.*"

Scott's voice broke over the scratchy radio as Sergey's brake lights flashed, their jeep ahead of Ethan and Jack slowing to a stop on the snow-dusted, two-lane Siberian track. Potholes the size of their jeep dotted the muddy roadway, and the convoy snaked around cracks and fissures. The road had been built sometime in the late Soviet period and never maintained, and it showed. Dense forest clustered close to the edges, and rugged mountainside stretched up one side and plunged into a dark ravine on the other.

Ethan and Jack shared a look before stopping their jeep. Behind them, the rest of the convoy ground to a halt, brakes squealing. Ethan grabbed the radio. "What do you see?"

Static, and then Scott's voice. "*Ethan, you'd better get up here.*"

Another long look passed between Jack and Ethan. Jack put the jeep in park and clambered out with Ethan, both of them jogging ahead. Their breath fogged the air, the cold slicing at bits of exposed skin around their balaclavas as snow fell, blanketing the air with silence.

They slid into the backseat behind Scott and Sergey, shaking off a dusting of snow from their gloves and jackets.

Scott and Sergey were peering at the road through their binoculars, not moving.

"What's up?" Ethan nudged Scott's shoulder.

Scott passed him the binos. "Forty yards ahead. Center of the road."

Sergey still didn't move.

He pulled the binos up to his eyes and adjusted the focus, slowly sweeping the road from side to side. As he hit the center, he froze, his breath punched from his chest with a quiet gasp. Ethan dropped the binos and turned to Jack, his eyes wide.

Jack held out his hand.

"What the hell is that?" Scott glared at Sergey, still staring down the road, not moving, his body taut. Tension thrummed off him, waves radiating bitter rage. "*Who* is that?"

Sergey finally spoke as Jack took the binos from Ethan and looked through them. "From the uniform, he appears to be a prison guard. I cannot see the shoulder patch. I do not know which prison he was from."

"You mean he *was* a prison guard," Scott growled. "What the hell happened?"

Jack dropped the binos and passed them back to Ethan, his face pale and lips pressed into a thin line. Ethan didn't want to, but he took another look.

Ahead, forty yards down the road, a stake had been driven into the center of a pothole, lurching skyward. Fixed to the stake, the remains of a man hung from his wrists, nailed to the center of the post over his head. A tattered blue uniform hung off his body, partially burned and ripped to shreds. His stomach had been gutted, entrails pouring out, and his eyeballs had been plucked from his face. His lower jaw was gone, a gaping, red maw open to his throat. One foot was also gone, seemingly gnawed off by an animal.

"I do not know," Sergey finally breathed. "It is not a bear attack."

"No shit!" Scott snapped. "You said a prison guard. Just how many prisons are there in Siberia?"

Sergey hesitated. "Most of them."

"Could there be a breach? Could some prisoners have escaped from a facility?" Jack leaned forward, hanging over the front seat, putting himself between Scott and Sergey.

Exhaling, Sergey closed his eyes. "If that is the case, then we must hurry. We have to get away from here."

"Again, no shit," Scott grumbled.

"Scott." Ethan nudged his friend, shaking his head slightly. "Let's get the road clear. We have to move."

Sergey and Scott slid out of the jeep. Ethan turned to Jack. "Wait for me back in our jeep? You don't need to see this."

"If I help, it will go faster."

Jack and Scott caught the stake after Sergey and Ethan wrestled it from where it had been embedded in the near-frozen center of the pothole. Cursing and breathing hard, they carried it, deceased guard still attached, to the side of the road. Sergey searched the body and came up empty, but his lips thinned and his eyes darkened when he saw the black dolphin patch half-burned on the guard's right shoulder.

Scott said a quick prayer, and then they tossed the stake over the edge, into the ravine. There was nothing more they could do.

"What does the black dolphin mean?" Jack turned to Sergey. His blue eyes blinked above the dark fabric of his balaclava.

Sergey looked anywhere but at Jack. Biting the inside of his cheek, he glared into the forest over Jack's shoulder. "Black Dolphin Prison. Russia's worst. Our supermax, as you would say. Where our worst murderers are sent for life."

"Fuck," Ethan breathed, sharing a look with Scott.

"Why would a Black Dolphin prison guard be staked to a pole out here? Gutted like that?"

Sergey shook his head. "There is no good answer. None that is acceptable for us. We must keep moving."

"Sergey, what aren't you telling us?" Jack stepped closer, reaching for Sergey. His hand closed over Sergey's elbow.

Sergey wrenched away, turning back to the jeeps and their convoy. "We move! Now!" He strode off, moving fast.

Jack stared after him, frozen. Ethan rested his hand on the small of Jack's back and felt him tremble, felt the anger pouring off him. "Jack—"

"Let's go." Jack interrupted. "Whatever he's not saying has him spooked. Let's just get out of here as fast as we can."

Ethan nodded, and they jogged back to their jeep together. Sergey was already behind the wheel in his, and Scott was slamming the passenger door, rocking their vehicle on its snow-crusted wheels.

They were moving a few minutes later, Jack once again behind the wheel. Ethan couldn't rest any longer, not with the adrenaline from the discovery of the mutilated prison guard still swimming in his veins. And with worry for Jack, too. His eyes slid sideways, watching as Jack drove. He sat stiff-backed with his gloved hands squeezing the steering wheel hard enough to creak the old leather, his jaw clenched hard, the artery in his neck pulsing fast.

Ethan rested his hand on Jack's leg.

A moment later, Jack's hand dropped and covered his.

DARKNESS FELL EARLY IN the mountains, but the convoy pressed on.

"*We should push ahead*," Sergey said through the crackling radio, static almost washing out his words. "*The river is only a little farther.*"

"You want to cross at night?" Ethan frowned, dropping the handheld and waiting for a response.

"Da! *Of course!*" Sergey's harangued voice spat back through the radio. "*Is the safest time! Is coldest, so the ice is least likely to crack!*"

Slowly, Ethan exhaled. Sergey was right, but still. It was nearing the end of the winter season in Siberia—not that anyone could tell by the temperature—and the rivers were warming beneath the ice. What had been feet-thick ice roads across and up solid rivers months before were far thinner sheets. By now, the trucks and tractor-trailers were no longer using the ice roads over frozen rivers. What would the weight of their convoy do to the ice?

There was no other way around, though. They had to cross the frozen Angara river in-between the cities and towns that dotted its banks. And they had to move fast.

The snow that had fallen so gently earlier had turned into a snarling storm. Wind rocked the jeeps on their tires, the vehicles swaying like seesaws as snow pounded through the air. Their pace had slowed, and frustrations had skyrocketed. One jeep had almost slid off the road, its occupants cursing and shouting into the radio about the weather and the road for a good ten minutes until they were able to move again.

The weather was against them, as was time.

And the specter of the gutted prison guard hung on everyone's minds, and at the forefront of Ethan's. It was like a beacon signaling danger, a klaxon alert that had him obsessively keeping even closer to Jack. Even though he wasn't Jack's detail agent anymore, that urge, that need to protect him, had only grown stronger. He stayed near, moving as if they were a protective duo again, and his body was Jack's life shield.

He looked to Jack for the final decision. Push on to the river?

Jack nodded.

"All right," Ethan sighed into the radio. "We head for the river. We'll cross if we can do it safely."

Sergey's grumbling came back, but they both ignored him as the convoy started moving again.

An hour later, they pulled their jeeps off the road, following a track toward the frozen Angara. They parked along the snowy bank, their headlights shining on the rough river ice. Doors squeaked and slammed as everyone piled out, staring across the wide expanse.

Around them, a ridgeline encircled the river, dark peaks soaring and disappearing into the thundering snow clouds. At least with the ridge surrounding them, the wind had slowed. It wasn't howling as hard, the harsh bite softened to a sting.

Ethan and Jack trudged to the river's edge and stood beside Scott and Sergey. Scott had his face tucked into his zipped-up jacket, even though he was wearing his balaclava.

"Just like that winter in Afghanistan, huh?" Scott bumped Ethan's shoulder. "Tracking that opium dealer through the river valley."

Ethan snorted. They'd hiked sixteen miles up a frozen river, freezing their balls off as they tracked what the locals claimed was a solid source of terrorist intelligence, but what had ended up being a wild goose chase after an opium trader who had stiffed the villagers. Revenge by proxy, courtesy of the US government, according to the villagers.

"So," Sergey grunted. "Who is going to cross first?"

ETHAN WATCHED, HOLDING HIS breath, as the first jeep rolled onto the ice. Across the river, Aleksey and Anton waited with two LEDs propped up on sticks to guide the drivers across. The two had crossed first on foot, checking out the ice and radioing back danger zones and areas where the ice was too thin.

"*Is not great,*" Aleksey said, once he crossed. "*But it is only way.*"

"Stay slow," Ethan warned over the radio. "Don't make any waves beneath the ice."

The jeep slowed, almost crawling. Still, Ethan could hear the creaking of the ice beneath its tires. His stomach clenched, and he peered into the darkness, trying to pick out details that were too fuzzy in the falling snow, the outline of the jeep against the darkness smearing into night outside the halo of their taillights on the bank.

Jack stood silently at his side, and on the other side of Jack, Scott. Standing apart and alone was Sergey. Snow wrapped around him, wreathing him in solitude.

Finally, the first jeep made it across, sliding between the two LEDs and rocking up the snowy embankment. Turning, they parked and shined their headlights across the ice, trying to penetrate the snow-filled gloom.

"Next!" Scott waved for the next jeep to roll out, shouting at them to hurry their asses. He slapped the hood, and the Russian at the wheel gave him the finger and blew him a kiss as he slid onto the ice.

And on it went. One jeep after another, slowly, through the night.

After the first two, Ethan turned to Jack. "You should wait inside the vehicle. Stay warm." He called out to Sergey. "You too, Mr. President. You both need to keep safe and warm."

Sergey nodded once and headed for his jeep, keeping his gaze on the ice and their fellow drivers.

Jack watched Sergey go. "I'm going to talk to him."

Ethan nodded, but before Jack left his side, he reached out, stopping him with a squeeze to his elbow. "Good luck. I'll come get you when it's time." He dropped a kiss to Jack's balaclava-covered forehead, and, even though most of Jack's face was completely covered, he could see Jack's smile by the crinkle of his eyes.

SERGEY SLAMMED SHUT THE driver's door, shutting out the snapping wind and the blowing snow. The cold remained, the jeep as frigid as the night, and his breath puffed before him, a great billowing cloud obscuring his vision for a moment.

Leaning back, Sergey's eyes slid closed.

The pain—the wrenching, aching agony that lived in the center of his chest—twisted, sending a punch to his soul. He tried to breathe through it, but his eyes tightened behind his eyelids, and the sob that always threatened to burst from his lungs crawled too high, too fast, lodging in his throat.

Shakily, he exhaled. "God, Sasha," he whispered, his voice trembling. "This is *madness*. If you were here—" His throat closed, and he swallowed, breathing slowly. "You would *hate* this. You would be just like Ethan, trying to control everything. Try to make everything safe, as if you could tame the storm and the ice. I can see your scowl..." He tipped his head forward, and his eyes opened, blurring when he looked into this lap.

"You should be here," he whispered again. "Why did you—" He licked his lips and breathed in again. Anguish twisted the knife within him, and he imagined his blood pouring down his insides, sliding down his ribs, his heart crying the tears he could not shed. "Why did you not *say* anything?"

Squeaking hinges made him look up suddenly, made his eyes freeze dry as snow-sharp air slipped inside the jeep. A moment later, Jack climbed inside, sitting in the passenger seat and shaking off a layer of snow that had built on his shoulders.

Sergey looked away. He sniffed, trying to wipe his nose and pass it off like it was the weather.

Jack stared at him. Sergey felt it, felt the weight of his friend's gaze digging into the side of his face.

He kept staring into the darkness and tried to count the snowflakes that blew past. Anything to not think about Sasha, or imagine that it was him sitting beside him in the jeep.

ETHAN BLINKED HARD, TRYING to dampen his aching eyes. The cold seemed to sap away everything. Blinking was like closing his eyes over sandpaper.

Snow built up around the edges of his balaclava. Scott had ice hanging from the chin of his balaclava, where he exhaled and the moisture of his breath froze.

This was ball-shrivelingly cold. Colder than Ethan had been in a long time.

The jeeps kept moving, one after another. Most had made it across, their trips slow and uneventful. Even the creaking ice had become almost normal, the sounds of the frozen river and their drive almost like music. He could hear the dips and groans, the cadence of the crossing. It was almost predictable.

Until the sounds changed.

A crack, like the snap of a heavy whip, shot through the air. In an instant, he was alert, eyes peeled, spine ramrod straight. At the bank, he and Scott stared through their binos, watching the third to last jeep move over the ice.

"*Ice is bad, very bad!*" the driver shouted over the radio. "*Is cracking!*"

"Don't accelerate!" Scott shouted back. "Don't make waves beneath the ice! You'll make it worse!"

Tires revving, the jeep shot ahead, skipping over the ice. Behind them, a crack appeared, snaking almost to the riverbank. The ice groaned like an old wooden ship rocking on the ocean.

"Fuck!" Ethan shouted. Scott spewed into the radio, cursing the driver and his intelligence. Blistering Russian spat back.

Sighing, Scott glared at the dark crack in the ice, and then at Ethan. "Now what?"

"SERGEY. LOOK AT ME"

Flinching, Sergey shook his head, still staring out of the side window. Jack's voice was hard, like it had been the first time they'd spoken, testing each other's waters back in Prague.

"After all this time. After everything we've been through. Why *this*? Why now?"

He said nothing. Outside, snow billowed, flurries carving Sasha's face into the wind.

"What happened to 'you have my support, and my friendship, always'? Sergey, we were more than just world leaders. We were *friends*—"

"I cannot look at you, Jack!" His fist came down, hitting the steering wheel. "I cannot!"

"Why?" Jack hissed. "Say it to my *face*."

Slowly, Sergey turned to Jack, but closed his eyes as his vision blurred. He tried to breathe, but the knife in his chest was back, digging into his heart, trying to cut it out of his body. If only he *could* cut out his heart. It would hurt less than continuing on like this. "You remind me of him," he whispered, his eyes closed. "You remind me of him," he choked out again, his words breaking apart. *And you remind me of so much more.*

The heavy anger filling the jeep popped, vanishing with a fizz. He heard Jack exhale, heard him slouch back against the front seat. "I remember what it was like when I thought Ethan was dead."

"Do not compare. Please." Sergey grunted, turning back to the window, and tried to sniff away the burning behind his eyes. "You have a happy ending. I—" His lips clamped shut.

"I remember I wished I had died with him."

Even that desire had no comfort for Sergey. Every moment he wished for the pain to end, wished to just lie down and let the world pass over him, guilt flooded him from all sides of his soul. Guilt, and Sasha's voice, admonishing him about his responsibilities. *You are the leader Russia needs*, he heard in Sasha's voice, like they were sharing drinks again, relaxing in his apartment. *You need to bring reform to the rest of Russia. Your government, it can change things. You cannot give up.*

How had Sasha become the voice in his head?

A part of Sergey wondered if he had cracked. Was he so desperate that he'd reconstruct Sasha in his mind, keep his memories alive like a psychic voodoo doll? When would the voice in his head become a phantom that he saw? Would he start talking to shadows and corners?

Would he be happier if he did? Would he rather have Sasha back with him, even as a ghost or a phantom of his mind, than cling to sanity?

"He would not want that," Sergey croaked. "He believed so much in me. Wanted so much from me."

He heard the smile in Jack's voice. "Sounds like Ethan. He wants me to run for another term. Thinks I'm some kind of hero for the country. But I'm not Superman. I'm *just* a man."

And I am a broken man. Sergey rubbed his chapped lips together, the torn, frayed skin rough and catching, pulling in painful tears. "I keep reliving the last moments we had."

"The call?"

He shook his head. "At the air base. When he was doing his final checks. I chased him. I was angry. Shouting. I found out he intended it to be a one-way trip. We fought."

"Sergey," Jack breathed. "Is that how you left things?"

"He kissed me." His voice was lighter than a snowflake. "It is all I can think of."

His sniff broke the silence of the jeep after a moment, and then Jack's hand gripped his shoulder, slid down his arm, and found his clenched, trembling fist. Jack wrapped his hand around Sergey's and squeezed.

Slowly, Sergey opened his fist, capturing Jack's hand and squeezing back.

Sharp knocking on the passenger window made them both jump. Jack pulled his hand back as Ethan opened the jeep's door, standing in the way of the wind.

"Something's gone wrong. The last jeep cracked the ice. We may have to move the crossing if the ice is too badly compromised. Scott and I are going to check it out. We'll be back for you both." He said the last to Jack, staring into his lover's eyes.

Jack nodded. He grabbed his radio. "We'll watch from the bank." Jack followed Ethan without looking back, heading for where Scott was prepping Jack and Ethan's—*Sasha's*—jeep to scout the ice. Sergey followed slowly.

They'd unloaded everything, piling their gear and weapons on the bank and leaving the jeep as light as it could be. Scott had both doors wide open and the windows down.

Ethan passed Jack the binoculars, pointed out where the crack in the ice was, and then slid into the driver's side. He left the door open, as did Scott on his side.

Slowly, they crept out onto the ice. Creaking, the river sounded different than it had before. Maybe it was the wind changing direction, or the cold dropping the temperature of the ice. Sergey plunged his hands into his jacket and stood beside Jack, watching and waiting as Ethan and Scott drove forward.

"AHEAD IS CLEAR FIVE FEET."

Ethan didn't respond. He didn't need to. He kept his focus on the ice, the feet in front of their jeep illuminated in the headlights. Scott scanned ahead, scouring in every direction. To their left, the dark, jagged crack split the ice, gouging deep. If they stayed away from the spider webbing fractures, they'd be okay. They could still get the last two jeeps across. Or one, if they doubled up.

"You're looking good, looking good..." Scott kept up a steady stream of encouragement as Ethan slowly rolled forward, barely touching the accelerator. He kept it in first gear, kept the engine low and slow. "I think we're good, Eth—"

A teakettle whistle, the tell-tale, high-pitched scream of an incoming RPG, broke over the ice. Scott whipped his head toward Ethan, his eyes wide. "RPG!" he hollered. "Someone is shooting at us!"

"Where?" Frantic, Ethan twisted in his seat, trying to spot the incoming rocket. Did he accelerate and risk the ice fracturing, or slam on the brakes? "Where the fuck is it? I don't have eyes on!" He scanned the black night, trying to peer through the driving snow. Nothing. Whirling again, he turned back to the riverbank, searching for Jack on the snow's edge.

With a sick crunch, the RPG slammed into the ice just ahead of them and to their left, shattering the frozen river. Ice exploded, turning into windblown daggers swirling with the snow and slamming into their jeep. Their windshield shattered, thousands of pieces of glass raining into the cabin. Ethan flew forward, his forehead cracking against the steering wheel.

Beneath their tires, the ice crumbled into the rushing waters of the Angara, larger chunks breaking into smaller ones as they collided. The jeep rocked and rolled on the river's waves as frigid water sloshed around their ankles.

With a lurch, the jeep tipped forward, falling nose-first into the river. Scott cursed as Ethan gripped the back of the seat, clinging on tight. Raging waters rushed at their faces, foaming white and bitterly cold.

And then, the jeep screeched to a halt, suspended over the open waters.

Ethan glanced to his left and right, wide-eyed. The doors, open for the crossing, had caught on chunks of ice in the river, large sheets bumping and colliding before being crunched to smaller fragments and swallowed by the rapids. They had moments before the ice would no longer hold the doors and the jeep would plunge into the river.

"Gotta go." Ethan reached for Scott and shoved him sideways. "Climb!" Moving fast, he clambered onto the seat, standing on the worn leather as he hauled himself onto the jeep's roof. Snow pelted him, and the wind over the river was howling more fiercely than it had been on the shore. Ahead, he could make out the hazy halo of the headlights from the rest of the convoy waiting on the other side of the bank.

Scott crouched beside him. "It's a four-foot jump over open water to the ice!" he shouted over the wind. "If we miss, we're dead! The current will pull us under the ice!"

"If we stay in the jeep, we're dead too."

"Then don't miss." Scott's grumble belied the wide set of his eyes, the ring of white circling his irises. Ethan held his stare, one hand steadying his friend.

A rubber-band snap, followed by the clang and plink of metal striking metal blurred the world. *Bullets.* Someone was shooting at them.

Scott flattened himself to the roof. Ethan ducked and lost his footing, sliding onto the hood of the jeep, half-submerged in the river. His weight made the jeep groan, and the ice holding the doors creak and crack.

"Ethan!" Scott shouted. "It's breaking apart!"

"Jump, Scott! Now!"

Who was shooting at them? Who had fired an RPG at their jeep? Those questions had to wait until they weren't about to be swept into the jaws of the icy river. Ethan held his breath as Scott leaped, flinging himself as hard as he could from the roof, over the rapids, and landing in a slide on the ice, skidding to a stop feet away.

Ethan's turn. He didn't have the right height to make the jump. He couldn't climb back onto the roof, though. Someone was shooting at them, and he'd be an easy target back up there. He had to jump, and he had to jump *now*.

Inhaling, he pictured Jack. His smile. His laugh. The way he looked at Ethan.

Roaring, Ethan exploded off the hood, hurling himself through the air with no finesse. He pulled up his legs, trying to propel himself farther, and barely brushed the edge of the ice and the gurgling rapids before he landed in a skid on his belly on solid ice.

Scott scrambled to him on all fours, grabbing at his arms, his shoulders, and hauling him away from the fractured ice and their sinking jeep. Cracking shattered the night again, and the river groaned, and then another giant section of ice fell away, and then another, and then another, until most of the frozen river was gone.

They huddled on a patch of ice near the embankment, sheltered beneath a low-hanging pine.

Breathing hard, Scott pitched forward, resting his forehead against Ethan's shoulder. Ethan fumbled in his jacket, searching his pockets. One hand found the rings he carried, squeezing them tight. The other pulled out his radio.

Static and frantic voices choked their secured channel, Russian voices and Jack, calling his name. "We're all right," he croaked. "We made it to the other side."

"*Ethan. What happened? God, I thought—*" Jack broke off. "*Are you sure you both are all right?*"

Aleksey and Vasily ran toward them, sliding on their boots and shouting in Russian. "We're okay, Jack. We made it to the others." Sighing, Ethan pressed the radio to his lips, silently mouthing curses against the plastic.

They'd made it, but Jack and Sergey were stranded on the other side.

And someone was shooting at them.

ALEKSEY AND VASILY HELPED them off the ice, guiding Scott and Ethan to the rest of the convoy on their side of the now-rushing river. Giant chunks of ice hung in the waters. Slabs the size of small cars bobbed and rocked, crashing into one another and splintering apart, creating more ice chunks that clogged the rapids. There was no way to cross the river now, not with the ice grinding and crashing through fast-moving eddies and swift, frigid currents.

Ethan cursed himself and the world. Leaning against the front grille of Aleksey's jeep, he faced the opposite riverbank where he'd left Jack and Sergey. If he squinted, he could almost make out the halo of their headlights in the driving snow.

At least, with visibility dropping in the snowstorm, whoever had shot at them would have a hard time doing so again.

"*Where did the RPG come from?*" Jack, over the radio, was all business. "*Sergey's trying to spot something through the binos, but with this weather...*"

Aleksey hovered at Ethan's shoulder, gripping his rifle. "It came from that ridge," he growled, pointing to a crest above Jack and Sergey. "We saw spark up there, before impact."

A spark. The back blow from the rocket's launch, a fireball from the exhaust of the RPG. If it had been a spark to Aleksey, then it had to be some distance away. They had that, at least, on their side.

Jack still had to move, though. *Get out of there, now.*

Boiling frustration raged against his heart, clawed at the insides of his ribs. Fire raced down his arms, burned his muscles, and made his hands clench into shaking fists. Damn it, he was supposed to be with Jack, protecting him at all times. Now, someone had fired on them, destroyed their best way across the river, and separated him from Jack.

His only consolation, and it was a cold, thin comfort, was that Jack wasn't alone.

"*I cannot see shit in this snow.*" Sergey's grumbles erupted over the radio. "*Not a damn thing.*"

"We need to move. Get out of the area."

"*Agreed.*" Jack's voice made him close his eyes. Snow pelted his face, like daggers slashing his skin, but if he could, he'd run across the river and back to Jack's side. Didn't they do that in cartoons? Leap from ice cap to ice cap? Couldn't he? "*Do you think it was Moroshkin's men?*"

"With that kind of weaponry? I'd put money on it." Ethan stood still, staring across the river.

Sergey cut in. "*Whoever it is, we need to be gone before they come down to investigate!*"

He'd stay close, right on the riverbank. When the snow stopped, he'd be able to see Jack. That would be workable. Not ideal, but he could still see Jack, still know he was all right. "Get going. Keep a low profile. We'll shadow you on this side—"

"*No,*" Sergey interrupted. "*You will trap yourself between the mountains and the river. Head east. We will rendezvous at Ust'Ilga. A settlement, and where we turn north before Baikal.*"

Ethan bristled. Being across the Angara river was bad enough. Putting more distance between him and Jack was liable to send him over the edge. His stomach twisted, bile rising in the back of his throat. "I don't—"

"*I will keep him safe, Ethan.*" Sergey's deep voice rumbled through the radio static. "*I swear it.*"

Scott appeared at his elbow, frowning, his eyes pinched and hard. "The storm's getting worse. We've got to get moving, or we'll get stuck here."

They'd left behind the roads and were back to tracks and game trails. Getting stuck in the snow in the mountains—or worse, sliding down the side of a ravine—was not in the plans.

But leave Jack?

How bad would it be if he swam back across the river to him? Would he die after three or six feet in the frigid waters?

Groaning, Ethan slammed his fist down on the hood of Aleksey's jeep. Snow jumped from the metal, puffing around him. It was just supposed to be a quick recon of the ice, and now they were being pulled apart. *Again.* "Jack…" he said, speaking into the radio.

"*I know, Ethan. I don't like it either.*"

Maybe the shooter didn't know about Jack and Sergey. Most of the convoy was on the east side of the river. Ethan could keep whoever it was that shot at him and Scott on the ice focused entirely on him. If Jack and Sergey slipped away quietly. If he drew attention to himself. As long as Jack stayed safe, he'd do whatever it took.

"You guys head out. Move quietly. We'll try to draw the attention of our shooter." He nodded to Scott, still at his side, to spread the word.

"*It is a day's drive overland to Ust'Ilga. We will see you soon.*" Sergey spoke, and then the dim, almost non-existent light from Jack and Sergey's jeep, on the far side of the river, winked off.

Behind him, the convoy was revving engines and spinning tires. Snow sprayed when some of the wheels skidded out, sliding on the riverbank. A cacophony of noise, a distraction. Hopefully.

"Stay safe," he radioed back.

8

Northern Siberian Permafrost

A LOW HUM FILTERED through Sasha's fuzzy mind, a droning warble. Smoke stung his nostrils. His eyes burned.

Swimming through a dark haze, he struggled to make sense of the world. Molasses-slow, he watched his thoughts drip through his mind like fat drops of water, quivering before falling away. The Kara Sea. The missile, his ejection. Sergey's face, his smile. The *Spetsnaz* lieutenant. The forest. Sergey's laugh. Falling into the snow. The look on Sergey's face, just after he'd kissed him.

No. Not that memory. Sasha kicked, struggling, trying to pull himself out of whatever delirium he'd fallen into.

With a rush, like being plucked face-first from deep underwater, reality returned. Gasping, he popped open his eyes and flailed, struggling against something heavy that held down his arms and legs. He kicked, over and over, desperation crawling up the backs of his legs and making his palms itch. Where was he? Had he been captured? Did the *Spetsnaz* have him?

"*Aja biShindi.*"

A deep voice spoke, words and sounds that meant nothing to him. Blurry shapes moved nearby, a dark mass coming closer. Blinking fast, Sasha tried to focus, but his eyes kept burning, watering and overflowing.

"I will try again," the voice said, in Russian this time. "Hello. Welcome back."

Breathing fast, Sasha stared as the blurry shape took form, becoming an old man. A Siberian, with weathered, tanned skin, wide cheekbones, and narrow, dark eyes. His lips were thin and wrinkled, and thick lines around his mouth carved up his cheeks, disappearing into his hairline. He wore a dirty felt hat, dented on one side, and a long trench coat, the kind that would have been fashionable in Moscow in the 1980s. Buttons were missing, and the waist was tied with a frayed bit of rope.

"Who are you?" Sasha croaked. His voice cracked, and he coughed. "Where am I?"

The old man reached down and brought up a misshapen copper mug. He held it out. "Warm water. You need it." He held the cup to Sasha's lips.

He almost didn't drink. He tried to sniff the cup and the liquid within, but the man's dirt-crusted hands smelled of loam, pine, and black dirt. And something else. Something coppery that stained his fingers red and iron-brown. Slowly, Sasha opened his cracked lips. Warm water, fresh and clear, quenched his thirst.

"I am Kilaqqi. You are in my home."

Eyes darting left and right, Sasha finally focused on his surroundings. He was lying on the ground inside a yurt. Long birch poles formed a haphazard pyramid and were lashed together above his head. Canvas and old hides were wrapped on the poles, laid over each other in a hodge-podge assortment. The center was open to the sky, and tart, pungent smoke snaked lazily out of the opening. Heavy, oily smoke hovered just above where he lay, stinging his eyes. Reindeer hides covered him from his shoulders down, a thick pile that was almost smothering. The weight pinned his arms and legs. Across the yurt, blankets lay on the ground. A stave with a hoof rested on one blanket, next to a small drum made of old, stained hide.

"We found you in the snow." Outside, bells jingled and animals snorted. Voices sounded, calling and talking to each other in the same language he'd first heard Kilaqqi speak.

"You are a Siberian? A tribesman?" He coughed, and Kilaqqi held the cup to his lips again.

"We are reindeer herders," Kilaqqi said, smiling. "We have lived here for hundreds of years. Before Russia, before the Soviet Union and the Bolsheviks, and everything else."

Kilaqqi's words came back to him. *We found you in the snow.* He tried to sit up, but the weight of the hides and his body's weakness kept him pinned. "Where did you find me? You should not have brought me back here. It is too dangerous for you—"

"I know about the wolves that chase you."

"No wolves," Sasha snapped. "Men. Soldiers. *Spetsnaz* troops. Hunters."

"Yes, I know. We have seen their helicopter searching the forest for days now."

Sasha's next protest died on his lips. "You know what a helicopter is?"

Kilaqqi grinned. His teeth were old and worn, with gaps between them. "Of course. The children are taken to boarding school by helicopter every autumn and return when the snows melt in summer." He chuckled. "You do not know much about life in Siberia, do you?"

"They will keep looking for me."

"They already are. We waved to them yesterday. They flew off."

"They will be back."

"Not if these hunters only see Siberian tribesmen. We are easy to ignore, yes?"

Sasha swallowed. He stayed quiet.

"Right now, you must recover your strength. You were dangerously cold when we found you. We got you warm in time to keep your fingers and toes. And other parts." Kilaqqi chuckled.

"Thank you."

Kilaqqi stretched, his bones creaking, and went back to sitting beside Sasha's nest of reindeer hides. A fire smoldered in the center of the yurt, in a fire pit lined with black stones. He stoked it, adding pine needles and twigs, and then sticks and a small log. Last, he tore apart dried leaves and dropped them over the flames. The smoke turned sharp and bitter. A few seconds later, Sasha's nose twitched.

"It is a healing smoke," Kilaqqi said, eyeing Sasha's scrunched-up face. "I left the doorway to the underworld open, hoping that your lost soul would return."

Sasha stared at Kilaqqi, blinking slowly.

Kilaqqi smiled. "I thought, when we first found you, that it was the cold that had your souls out of balance. But when you warmed up, you were still missing something. One of your three souls was gone." He snapped his fingers, holding out his empty palm. Dirt stained the center. "I went to go find it. Down, into the underworld, across the river and into to the ghostlands. It is the land of the dead down there, in *Khergu*. Where the *Agdy* live. Evil spirits that can steal a person's soul."

Sasha said nothing. He'd never been one for religion, not the Eastern Orthodox faith of Russia, nor the western, individualistic Christianity. One of his fellow pilots had been a Buddhist, after falling for a girl during his time studying abroad in China. As a boy in school, he'd learned about the tribesmen of Siberia and their animist beliefs. Primitive, his teachers had said. Simple nature worship.

"I searched for your soul, but the reindeer came and told me there was nothing to find. The *Agdy* hadn't taken anything." Kilaqqi's dark eyes peered into Sasha, as if they knew his secrets.

"Then where is it?" Eyebrows raised, Sasha stared. The old man wanted to tell stories. Fine. He could listen.

"You cut it out of yourself."

Sasha stopped breathing.

"You cut out the parts of yourself you do not want. Threw them away, like you could get rid of them. But you cannot. They are a part of you. Forever."

He looked away and tried to breathe. Smoke stank like death and stung his nose. He closed his eyes, started counting in his head. Recited pre-flight procedures for his old MiG. Anything to not listen to Kilaqqi's voice.

"Cutting out a soul is no easy thing. What hate you must have within you, of yourself. You have hurt yourself—"

"Stop. Shut up. Quit talking."

"You can let it back in. It is out there, waiting for you."

"This is crazy talk," he snapped. "You're just a tribesman!"

Kilaqqi smiled and grabbed another dried leaf. He broke it over the flames and started to hum.

9

Southern Siberia

JACK AND SERGEY LURCHED over rough ground, keeping the Angara on their left as they headed south. Sergey stopped every hour or so to check the ice on the river. He came back each time with a frown and a shake of his head. "We keep going," he said. "We will cross when we can."

They moved slowly, and as quietly as they could. Jack kept a rifle in his gloved hands as he sat in the passenger seat, constantly scanning for anything around them. Any sign of the shooter, or that they were being pursued. The sun had just risen, turning the sky a muted, heavy lead.

The embankment ran out, and they turned into the mountains, putting more distance between the river and their jeep... and Ethan.

Ethan's absence was an ache in Jack's heart, a sense of loss that hovered around him. Where were their shared smiles, the looks they traded in silence as if they could read each other's thoughts? The hand that would slide into his during the drive, a simple act that made the world feel warmer? Sometimes he said things Ethan swore were on the tip of his tongue, and they'd laugh together, their worlds aligning like pages turning in a book. Being without Ethan, without that effortless love and care, was like a piece of himself was missing.

Sergey, silent and dour behind the wheel, did not make things any easier.

Not much had been said since their conversation at the river, when Sergey had nearly broken down but had gripped Jack's hand instead. Where was the Sergey who could talk to a wall and make it laugh? Befriend a lamppost, spin a yarn that captivated whole rooms?

Jack kept quiet, watching out of the window.

"Tell me how you and Ethan came to be lovers?"

He turned and stared at Sergey.

Sergey wouldn't look back. His jaw clenched, and he gripped the steering wheel, one elbow propped on the windowsill with his hand on his forehead. "I only know what the media reported. And all of it contradicted each other. I do not know what actually happened."

Slowly, Jack began to speak. He told Sergey about their friendship, about how Ethan was a breath of fresh air in a stilted world. How, even as the president of the United States, he'd become starved for human interaction and friendship. What Ethan had risked giving that to him, and how their friendship had grown, deepened, and become something more.

"Sound familiar?"

Sergey said nothing.

And then he told Sergey about the kiss. Ethan's hopeful, aching heart wishing for the best, and Jack, shocked and shaken and reacting without thinking. How they'd fallen apart, and then had come back together, ironically, to stand against Sergey in Prague.

Finally, Sergey reacted. Frowning, he shook his head, as if trying to understand. "You... didn't know this about yourself before Ethan?"

"No. I was never attracted to men before him. Generally, I'm still not." He hesitated. "I do know myself enough to recognize that I fall for someone with my heart first. That's how it was with him and me. I already had fallen for him, and then the desire started. Maybe if I had given it a chance before, the same thing would have happened with someone else. If I had been open to it."

Sergey scowled. His cheeks darkened, and his lips pressed together, a thin red line slashing across his hawkish face.

"What's this ab—"

"*Nyet*. No, no, I am done talking about this." His hands kneaded the steering wheel again. He refused to look at Jack.

"Sergey—"

"We come from different worlds, Jack!" Sergey snapped. "You know nothing!"

Jack's temper flared white-hot, racing through him in an instant. Cold fire, burning bright. "You're right, I know nothing about falling for a man for the first time. Nothing about trying to figure out a whole new sexuality. Make sense of a new world, or of choosing to accept the love of the best man I've ever known!"

"So *American*! You think you have all the answers—"

"You're *afraid*!"

"Maybe I just do not want it!" Sergey bellowed. He glared at Jack, his eyes dark and pinched. "Maybe I saw everything you went through and I want *nothing* to do with that kind of trouble!"

Sergey's words were like daggers, cutting into him. "*Fuck*, Sergey, he died for you and you can't even say that you cared for him!"

"He did not die for me!" Sergey's voice went high, strangled and thin. "He was determined to go on the mission! The mission *you* said was important! You made him go!"

"He gave you *everything* he had, every last thing so you could keep fighting! We'd be blind if it weren't for his sacrifice!"

"He should not have gone!" Sergey hollered. His slammed his foot on the accelerator, and the jeep jumped ahead, spitting snow behind their tires as they slipped almost sideways on the mountain track. "You should have helped me stop him!"

"Why? So he can still be here to follow you around? Wait for whatever handout you think would keep him interested?"

Brakes squealed, and the jeep shuddered to a halt, sliding on the frozen ground. Sergey threw open his door and leaped from the cabin, striding away.

Jack followed, jumping out and shouldering the rifle. He left his balaclava on the front seat. His boots disappeared in the snow as he shouted at Sergey's back. "At the very least, you could acknowledge that he meant *something* to you!"

"You think I do not love him?" Sergey spun, rage twisting his face into something ugly. Spittle flew from his lips. "Of *course* I do! He is the voice in my head! I see him in the snow and in the stars! I cannot be *free* of him!"

Jack froze. He stared at Sergey, breathing hard and shaking in the glow of the headlights, shin-deep in the powdery snow. Silence strained the frozen forest, the feet that separated them.

Shoulders heaving, Sergey dragged in breath after breath, swallowing gulps of frosty air. He looked away from Jack, into the forest, his hands on his hips. When he spoke, his voice was too deep, and it shook. "I—"

A blade sliced through the air, past Jack's cheek, and embedded in Sergey's shoulder.

Blood wept down the front of Sergey's jacket, staining the snow beneath him.

"Sergey!" Jack stumbled through the snow to him, just as Sergey's knees buckled. Jack fumbled, trying to catch Sergey and unshoulder the rifle at the same time.

He crouched low and peered into the trees. Thick pine trunks and low-hanging needles, coated in frost. Bushes and alpine brush, buried in drifts. Other than the quietly falling snow, nothing moved.

Sergey grunted as he pulled the short blade from his shoulder. Blood stained his hands and dripped from the tip.

"What are you doing?" Jack tore his gaze away from the trees, watching Sergey's blood splatter to the snow. Every first-aid course Jack had ever taken had said the same thing: leave a stab wound alone, and don't take the weapon out. The knife looked short, though, and homemade. Metal filed into a spike of some sort. Or a shank.

Sergey wiped the blade in the snow, cleaning the blood off. He peered at it, pressing his free hand against his bleeding shoulder. "Jack," Sergey hissed. "We have to get back to the jeep. Now!"

"What is it? Moroshkin's men?"

"Worse."

Turning, Jack found Sergey's gaze. His eyes were wide, and for the first time, terrified.

He nodded. "I'll cover you back to the jeep."

Sergey's face went bone white, the color of the snow that surrounded them, and his eyes darted over Jack's shoulder.

A moment later, the cold barrel of a gun pressed against the back of Jack's head, and a gruff voice barked, *"Uronit' vintovku!"*

10

Northern Siberian Permafrost

SASHA TRUDGED BEHIND KILAQQI, marching with the other tribesmen as they followed a herd of reindeer across the snow-covered plain. White blanketed the landscape, as far as he could see, and snow fell from the bleak, steel sky.

At least three hundred reindeer moved ahead, some with bells on their antlers or tied to a rope around their neck. Others wore harnesses, handmade from leather and hides, and carried the camp on their backs. In just an hour, the entire camp, and Kilaqqi's yurt, had been disassembled, the hides and old canvas folded and birch poles stacked and packed. They were on the move minutes later.

Kilaqqi had brought Sasha a set of clothes, a mismatched ensemble of old snow pants and a bright orange sweater with holes in the hem. A green hat with a yellow pom-pom and a stained bright-blue jacket rounded out the gifts of clothing. He was a walking eyesore, and as far from covert as he could be, but the clothes were warm, if smelly. They stank like wood smoke, like they'd sat around a thousand campfires and soaked up all the ash and embers.

"We are taking the herd south," Kilaqqi told him as they set off. "They have eaten the lichen in these parts. We have another feeding ground for them. They are eager to go."

After an hour, Sasha's legs nearly gave out. His thighs burned, days of trudging through deep drifts taking their toll. Kilaqqi gave him a steaming thermos and told him to drink. Strong, dark tea warmed his belly, and melted butter in the brew coated his tongue. Kilaqqi also handed him a stick to chew, which tasted vaguely minty and turned to pulp on his tongue.

He kept going.

They started walking again after breaking for a lunch of raw fish—caught that morning before leaving camp—and more twigs.

Sasha heard it first. He'd been primed to listen for the sound for days, the heavy thump of rotors in the air and the dull hum of the engine rumbling over the taiga. The *Spetsnaz* platoon was back.

He jogged to Kilaqqi's side, keeping his head down. "Those wolves you mentioned," he grunted. "They're coming."

"Keep with the herd. They've flown over us for days now. We should be no more interesting to them now than before."

Kilaqqi walked on, singing a song that the others picked up. Their low voices, some painfully out of tune, bounced off the snow and carried on the air. The reindeer snorted, a few stamping their feet at the sound.

Sasha stayed near a fat mare, grouchy and cantankerous. She snorted at the singing and bleated at the reindeer that passed her, bells tinkling from their antlers. Despite himself, Sasha grinned, and he rested one hand on her thick back, scratching at the fur between her shoulders. She grumbled but didn't shake him off.

The noise of the chopper drew closer, a pounding that vibrated Sasha's bones. The ground began to tremble, and the reindeer snorted and whined.

The fat mare gave Sasha a look, as if accusing him of causing the entire mess.

He dug his fingers into her fur, trying to still his hands' shaking.

When the chopper passed overhead, Sasha kept his head turned down, his face toward the snow. Still, he felt the roar of the rotors like a punch to his gut, and loose snow kicked up in a swirling storm, whirlwinds snaking through the herd and disrupting the animals. They snorted and whined again, and some tried to run. Others, a few with the bells, chased the spooked reindeer down and guided them back with nips to the butt. Kilaqqi and his fellow herdsmen waved to the chopper. If they were saying hello or telling the *Spetsnaz* to fuck off and get away from the reindeer, Sasha couldn't tell.

After the chopper passed, Sasha looked back, over his shoulder.

Hanging out of the cargo hold, his hand fisted in a gear strap and his boots braced on the run rails, the *Spetsnaz* lieutenant peered through his binoculars.

Sasha looked away quickly, but he heard the chopper bank and turn around, heading back the way they'd come: right for the herd.

His heart sank. "Kilaqqi! They are coming back!"

Kilaqqi stopped singing and stopped fussing with one of the reindeer, making faces at the animal as it jingled its bells, shaking its head back and forth. Standing tall, Kilaqqi stared down the approaching chopper in his flapping trench coat like a lone warrior from a classic film.

Sasha blinked, and then Kilaqqi was moving, shouting to his herdsmen and smacking the butts of reindeer around him. He made his way to the rear of the herd, where the reindeer bearing the camp's supplies were plodding along.

Kilaqqi pulled a rifle from the side of his reindeer's harness. It was old, with a wooden stock and an iron sliding bolt, but it looked nasty. He grabbed a shoulder bag with ammunition stuffed to the brim.

The others were grabbing rifles and shotguns as well, and arming their weapons.

"Here." Kilaqqi caught a rifle thrown his way. He turned to Sasha. "For you." He slapped the reindeer carrying his belongings, all of his worldly possessions, and the animal took off, snorting and running as fast as it could while carrying its load.

There was nowhere to hide on the open plain, no cover to be found. No snow trench to hurriedly dig. The men lined up with Kilaqqi, their rifles and shotguns armed and ready to fire. A line of men standing in the snow, facing down a charging attack helicopter. It was a bravery Sasha didn't have. "They will kill you!" he shouted, down on one knee. "We have to run!"

"No. We face our enemy." Kilaqqi sighted down his rifle, taking aim at the chopper. The roar had started again, the slash and cut of the rotors against the sky. Snow started to blow, kicked up and sprayed through the air, whiting out the world.

Perhaps, an opportunity. Sasha ran into the blinding snow, the driving flakes slashing at his cheeks. He ducked and rolled, took a faceful of snow, and then opened fire as the chopper roared overhead, lost in the swirling whiteout. He aimed for the fuel hatch, the rear rotor. He got two shots off from the old shotgun before the weapon clicked.

As he fired, so did the chopper.

Gunmen, *Spetsnaz* troops hanging out of the cargo hold and braced against the rails, opened up on Kilaqqi and the herdsmen. Visibility was low in the swirling snow kicked up from the rotor wash, but Kilaqqi and his men hadn't moved.

Or had they?

Shadows darted through the snowstorm, shapes moving in the gloom. Gunshots echoed, heavy bursts followed by metallic plinks and the snap of bullets striking steel.

Something fell, a loud scream and then the *whomp* of impact.

Sasha darted forward, sliding two new slugs into his shotgun. A body lay ahead, face-down and wearing a black uniform and helmet. He kicked the body over. One of the *Spetsnaz* troopers. Sasha grabbed his rifle and rooted through his pockets.

Overhead, the chopper was still roaring, still kicking up snow. Bullets flew through the snow haze. A man screamed. Shouts in Russian, and then shadowy figures seemed to slink through the whiteout. *Spetsnaz*, rappelling from the chopper.

Perfect. They'd just given him a fixed location.

Sasha's hand closed around what he'd been looking for. Gritting his teeth, a feral, wild surge flowed through him as he ripped the pins from the heads of four stolen grenades and hurled them toward where the chopper hovered. He dove to the ground and covered his head, burying his face in the snow.

He counted to three.

The chopper burst apart, shearing like a can wrenched in half. Flaming debris rained down on the snow as the lithe helicopter body pitched forward, plunging to the ground. Rotors chewed into the ice, splintering apart and flying through the air. Two *Spetsnaz* troopers went down, bits of broken helicopter and molten metal embedded in their necks. Burning fuel spread, slithering on the snow and catching fire. Finally, Sasha could see what was happening.

Kilaqqi and five of his men were still fighting, shooting and running. As he watched, Kilaqqi rose and took aim at a soldier dazed from the blast of the chopper, and fired. His trench coat fluttered, and the bloom from the crash lit up the sky behind him, silhouetting his form.

For a moment, Sasha saw the outline of a bear and a wolf, an eagle and a reindeer, standing beside Kilaqqi, all in a line, ghostly and ethereal. The animals were ferocious, as if they were each attacking in time with Kilaqqi and facing off against the *Spetsnaz* troops.

He blinked, and the spectral animals vanished. Kilaqqi ducked, and another man rose to fire on the *Spetsnaz*. One went down, crimson staining the snow beneath his body.

The *Spetsnaz* had lost four men. Three shot, and the one who had fallen before Sasha.

That left three more. Two troopers and the lieutenant.

Sasha scanned the makeshift battlefield, a mix of snow and flame and burning debris. Where was the lieutenant? He wouldn't go down that easy.

A snap cracked the air beside his head, and warmth rushed down his cheek. Cursing, Sasha ducked to the snow and felt the side of his face. His hand came away bloody.

Where had the shot come from? He searched the snowy plain. Saw Kilaqqi face down another trooper and win. Saw one of the *Spetsnaz* jog back toward the burning wreckage of the chopper and take a bullet to the back of the leg. Saw another herdsman line up for the finishing shot.

And then, he spotted a smudge of darkness in the snow, a man half-buried in a hastily dug snow trench. Easy to miss. Easy to pass right over. A line of fuel burnt between him and the man, shivering the air with heat waves. For a moment, Sasha doubted what he saw.

Another bullet cracked the air, a whistling snap that made the hairs on his arms stand on end.

Dropping to his stomach, Sasha lined up on the snow, sighting the dark smudge through his sights on his rifle, through the shimmering flames. He'd have one shot at this.

He inhaled, exhaled—

Another shot snapped past his cheek, stinging with the burn of metal slicing skin.

—and squeezed the trigger.

He dropped and felt his cheek.

Just a scratch.

Rolling away, Sasha waited for another shot, holding his breath. Had he done it?

He got to his feet slowly and saw the last of the soldiers go down, bleeding out on the snow. Kilaqqi was shouting to his men, rounding them up and taking their faces in his hands and looking into their eyes one by one.

Sasha ran across the snow, skirting the broken pieces of helicopter and the burning fuel. He kept his eyes on the man half-buried in the snow trench, the dark smudge of his body barely visible. Red spread through the snow beneath him, a stain that kept growing.

When he got there, he heard the man's rasping breaths. Dropping to his knees, Sasha hauled him from the snow trench and rolled him over.

His shot had pierced the man's shoulder. Blood drenched the snow on his front and back.

Dark, hateful eyes glared up at Sasha. Blood-flecked lips spat, lobbing a wad of spit into his face.

A long, thin scar curved down the man's face. On his black jacket, PALOSHENKO was stitched in white thread next to his officer rank.

It was him. The lieutenant.

Part of Sasha wanted to bury Paloshenko's face in the snow, smother him to death in the winter wasteland he'd hunted Sasha through. Force him to choke on frigid fear and emptiness. Or he could put a bullet in his brain, end it quickly.

Kilaqqi's shout made Sasha turn, though.

Riders approached, men doubled up on snowmobiles and waving automatic rifles in the air. Shots pierced the air, long *ratatatats* that spoke of the men's lack of training. These were not soldiers. These were thugs, bandits with weapons coming out of their ears. The riders broke into two groups, each circling to one side of the crash and penning them in the center.

He grabbed his rifle and ran to Kilaqqi's side, leaving Paloshenko to bleed. "What now?"

"I thought you would know." Kilaqqi stared at him serenely, as if they hadn't just downed a helicopter and killed a troop of *Spetsnaz* forces. Blood was smeared across his cheek and chin.

"I do not know who these men are." The hum and rumble of the snowmobiles grew, a high-pitched whine as they revved their engines and closed their circle around Sasha and Kilaqqi's men, like a snake constricting around its prey. Sasha whirled, spinning as fast as he could, his rifle raised, but there were too many men and snowmobiles zooming by. Snow arced from their treads, spraying in Sasha's face.

"These men we cannot fight."

Sasha whipped around, staring at Kilaqqi, his jaw hanging open.

"There are too many." Kilaqqi tossed his rifle to the snow and raised his hands. "And I have already lost enough men today." Scattered among the bodies of the troopers, some of Kilaqqi's herdsmen lay broken and bled out.

"I will fight," Sasha snarled. Turning, he raised his rifle and took aim.

A deep voice laughed behind him. Whirling, he saw one of the new arrivals had already crept up on him. Standing over Sasha, bulky and heavyset, the man wore a thick snow jacket and a full-face balaclava.

Before Sasha could swing his rifle around, the man slammed the butt of his own weapon into Sasha's stomach, and then his face. Bones crunched, and the world went black before he hit the snow.

11

Seattle

Jesus, customs took forever.

Sighing again, Doc switched his bag from his right shoulder to his left and crossed his arms. A family of five was making a mess of their entry to the US. One kid had drawn on the immigration form. Another was crying about their juice box. Of the three lanes that were open, moving people through customs and into the domestic side of Seattle's airport, that one had been the fastest.

No more.

Doc regretted his choice in line.

A few lanes over, Coleman, Kobayashi, and Park waited, pretending they didn't know each other. Wright and Ruiz were to his left, earbuds in their ears and looking bored.

Faisal stood in front of Doc.

Adam stood behind them.

Awkward.

He and Faisal had unofficially buddied up, staying near while deplaning from the London flight and moving toward customs control. They didn't talk, but Doc felt Faisal's gaze on him when he wasn't looking, and he, likewise, kept one eye on Faisal and one eye on the crowd watching Faisal.

When Adam had come up behind them both, standing way too close for a stranger and clearing his throat, Doc had thrown him a long glare.

And then the fidgeting began. Adam shifted from foot to foot. Folded and unfolded and refolded the dangling strap of his backpack. Scuffed the toe of his boot on the frayed carpet. Cleared his throat, again and again.

Finally, it was Faisal's turn at the counter. Doc stepped into the space he vacated, waiting behind the plastic flappers that kept the line pinned back away from the customs officers in their booths. He kept his head down, but listened as Faisal gave his name and passport over.

"Reason for your visit to the US?" The customs officer, a woman past middle age, with all the vibrancy and sour attitude of any government employee, looked over Faisal's entry form before laying his Saudi passport on the scanner.

"Visiting friends." Faisal smiled, but the woman ignored him. Her fingers slammed down on her keyboard, the clack-clacking of nails on keys like a rake against concrete.

Her keystrokes slowed. She frowned, staring at her screen. "You said you were visiting friends, sir?"

Doc's ears perked up. Behind him, Adam froze, breathing hard.

"That's right."

"Are you traveling alone, sir? We're going to need to ask you some questions—"

Fuck this. Doc pushed through the flappers and strode to Faisal's side. He wrapped one arm around Faisal's waist and leaned in close, dropping a kiss to his stunned cheek. "Hey, honey."

"Sir, who are you? What are you doing?" The customs official stood in her booth, glaring at Doc. She pointed back to the line. "You need to wait your turn, sir!"

"Sorry—" He searched her uniform, looking for the nametag. "Desiree. Thought I could help clear things up a bit with my fiancé." He tilted his head, resting it against Faisal's, and smiled. Below the booth edge, out of sight, he squeezed Faisal's hip, hard.

Slowly, Faisal's arm snaked around his waist. He smiled and dropped a light, feathery kiss to Doc's temple.

Desiree eyed them both. "You two are getting married?"

"Yes, ma'am." Doc beamed.

"Why didn't you fill out your form together?" Desiree waved Faisal's entry form in one hand.

"It said families could fill out one form. I don't know, I didn't think we qualified." Doc shrugged. "I just didn't want to do it wrong. But we're definitely family." Again, he smiled, pushing his cheek against Faisal's. God, Faisal had better be smiling, too, or they would be spending hours in a holding tank being interrogated by a grumpy cop with a beer gut and no hair.

Desiree pursed her lips again. Narrowed her eyes and glared at them both. Finally, she held out her hand for Doc's passport and killed the warning screen that had flashed when Faisal's was scanned, a string of codes Doc couldn't make sense of. Doc's passport passed easily, and she handed both back together.

"Congratulations. Welcome to the United States of America." She nodded them through, already impatient. "Next!"

Doc hurried Faisal out of the lane. As he did, he caught sight of Adam behind them.

Adam looked wrecked. Pale, his hair mussed and standing on end, his fingers sliding through his long strands too many times. Wide eyes, dark with hurt, like a puppy kicked for the first time.

Well, what the fuck did he expect? He was the one who was supposed to be helping Faisal, not Doc. Why wasn't he stepping up and doing what was right?

Sighing, Doc kept his arm around Faisal's waist as they walked through the concourse. Their next flight, up to Anchorage, Alaska, wasn't for another four hours. They had time to kill.

"You can let go now."

Doc squeezed Faisal's hip. "Let's keep it going for a little longer. Just in case they put eyes on."

Faisal stayed quiet.

"I'm starving. Jesus, that food on the flight was terrible. Let's get something to eat." He glanced Faisal's way. "Anything you need? Want?"

Briefly, Faisal's gaze darted over his shoulder, and Doc caught the twist and turn that Faisal aborted. "It would have been nice if he had stepped in." A tiny smile. "Not that I am not grateful for your help."

"Yeah, I know." Doc frowned, sighing as they kept walking. A restaurant on the right caught his eye, along with the sign in the window. "Hey, this place says they do kosher and halal stuff. Is that cool for you?"

"Yes. Thank you." Together, they headed for the restaurant, and Doc snaked a table on the far side. He took the chair against the wall, able to watch everyone who passed by and cover all corners. Faisal sat facing the concourse and searched the passersby, clearly watching for a certain set of shoulders and a messy head of brown hair.

12

Southern Siberia

SERGEY KEPT HIS EYES locked on Jack, their gazes fixed together. Jack had his hands up, but the man had already wrenched Jack's rifle away. Over six feet tall, with a shaved head, hulking muscles, and a face like a pit bull that had lost a dog fight, he was terrifying to look at. A faded skull tattoo lined one side of his neck. He didn't wear a jacket, just a thin, stained tank top. An eight-pointed star was tattooed on each shoulder. The edge of what looked like rays of a sun poked up above his neckline, beneath a tattooed dagger than seemed to run beneath his throat.

Prison tattoos.

Do not move, he tried to scream with his eyes. *Do not move, Jack.*

The man growled in Russian, "What brings two strange men into my wilderness, hmm?"

Jack swallowed hard. Sergey watched the rise and fall of his Adam's apple. Shit, Jack would be deaf to this. He didn't know Russian at all, save for the polite diplomatic phrases.

"We are passing through," Sergey replied, also in Russian.

The man circled behind him, slow, heavy steps through the crunching snow. "And who are you?" The tip of the man's rifle stroked up Sergey's cheek.

Sergey's eyes slipped closed, briefly. Thank God for small favors. "We are no one," he said, his voice shaking.

"And who is this? Who doesn't speak!" Turning, the man jabbed his rifle into Jack's face and pressed the bore hard against his cheek, smashing his face.

"A friend!" Sergey tried to stand, but the man grabbed Jack's hair, pulled him back, and shoved the rifle under his chin. Jack stared at Sergey, his eyes like saucers. "He is a friend! He speaks no Russian!"

The man threw Jack down face first into the snow. He paced again, circling behind them as Sergey shuffled to Jack's side. "A Russian and a foreigner in my country," he hummed.

"We will leave. You can go about your business—"

"My business is you," the man growled. He stood back, braced his legs, and pointed his rifle dead center at Sergey's forehead. "I have been tracking you for two days. Cut you off from your herd at the river. Led you away, down to me."

Dread sank within Sergey, pooling in the pit of his belly. They were already caught in this man's web. Desperation clawed out of him, a primal, base need to fight his way free and survive. The instincts of prey caught by a predator.

Had this been what this man's victims had felt like all those years ago? Terror, and an adrenaline-soaked dread, flooded him. His heart raced, pounding so hard his eyeballs ached. The need to run, to flee, to escape was blinding.

"We are no sport for you."

The man laughed. "Like this? Caught? On your knees in the snow?" He knelt and grabbed Sergey's chin, squeezing hard. "I hunted you here," he hissed. Another squeeze, and then he threw Sergey down in the snow beside Jack. "It's been a long time," he breathed, rolling his neck, "since I had a true hunt."

Sergey's eyes met Jack's again. He saw terror, the fear of not knowing a shred of what was happening, how fucked they truly were. He wanted to try and comfort Jack, but how? He shook his head, faintly.

"On your feet!" the man barked. "Now!"

Sergey scrambled, and he reached for Jack, helping him up. He stood in front of Jack, holding him back, and faced the man with his chin held high. "You will pay for what you do," he vowed, his voice finally not shaking. If not him and Jack, then Ethan would find this man, avenge their deaths. His men, too. Anton, Aleksey, Vasily. Ilya, if Ilya was still alive.

"I was told that once before." Grinning with broken, yellow teeth, the man raised his rifle again, sighting down the barrel. "They locked me up, threw away the key. Put me in a concrete box and said I'd never see another human being again. Stole the sun from me. I tried to chew through the walls once."

Jack's hand slid into Sergey's. He laced their gloved fingers together. Sergey squeezed back. *I'm so sorry, Jack. I'm sorry, Ethan.* There was a part of him that let go, though. A release. Like part of himself slipped away early, vanishing from his body. *Sasha... I will see you soon.*

The man rested his cheek against the barrel of his rifle. "Now," he growled. "Run."

For a moment, they both froze, Sergey's brain already set on being shot. He was turning out the lights, drawing inward, readying himself to die.

Jack tugged on his hand. His eyes flashed to the man, standing stock-still and grinning, his finger hovering over the trigger. He would shoot them in the back the first chance he got, when it was entertaining for him. They had one chance to flee.

Slowly, Sergey started backing away, holding on to Jack. His eyes darted to the right and left. They had to lose themselves in the trees. They had no weapons, no way to fight back. Blood still oozed sluggishly from his shoulder down his arm and dripped from his wrist into the snow.

They were ten meters away, though, and still moving backward.

Jack's shoulder brushed against the thick trunk of a pine.

"When I say, turn and run into the trees, Jack," Sergey hissed. "Stay low! Run for your life!"

Jack breathed in and out, his breath fogging the air. He gripped Sergey's hand. "We go together. Are you ready?"

Another step back. Sergey saw the man smile.

"Go! Now!"

Jack darted between the trees, ducking low, and ran. Sergey followed on his heels, leaping through the snow and zig-zagging between trunks and low forest brush.

A bullet slammed into a trunk, splintering the bark. Shards hit Sergey's jacket. Dirt scratched at his eyeball.

"Jack! To your right!"

He pictured the map they'd been using—folded, worn, and stained, lying on the front seat of the jeep—and the mountains they were winding through. The river to their right, the ridge rising to their left. They were penned in, trapped by Siberia and her unforgiving claws. Their only hope was to climb the ridge.

Jack scrambled through the snow, weaving through trees and starting up the ridge. He slipped, falling on his face, and came up sputtering. Sergey grabbed his arm and hauled him up, dragging him until he found his feet and pushed away.

The man stalked them, following at a steady pace. He fired up the ridge, the *whump* of bullets burying in snow and the thrash and rattle of bushes being hit enough to make Sergey's heart burst.

"Who is he?" Jack wheezed, slipping behind a trunk and pausing for a moment, heaving as he tried to catch his breath. "Who the hell is chasing us?"

Sergey waved at Jack, watching the man's dark shadow start up the ridge behind them. "We have to keep moving!"

"Who is he?" Jack repeated, his eyes flaring. "What aren't you telling me?"

"He's a prisoner!" Sergey grabbed Jack's elbow and shoved him forward, dragging him along as they ran. "Milos Degtyaryov, from Black Dolphin prison. It's where we keep the worst of our criminals. He's been there for two decades. He has no idea who we are, which is our only salvation!"

"What did he do?"

"They called him the Rybinsk Hunter. He *hunts* people, Jack. Stalks them like animals. Tortures them. It is sport to him!"

"He killed the prison guard, didn't he?"

"It looked like something he would do. He used to leave his victims for people to find. Gutted. Tied up. On display. It was a horror show."

"I don't remember this."

"You think Russia shared details of her worst crimes with the world? Especially when Putin was in charge? Ha! *Russia* barely knew at all. I was in FSB then. I saw the case files. We were all looking for this monster."

Finally, they were at the top of the ridge. Sergey stayed low. He beckoned Jack down, too.

A bullet whizzed over their heads. Another slammed into the dirt only a half meter away.

"Was there a riot? How did he break out of the prison?"

"No one can break out of Black Dolphin. It is not possible. Never, ever has it happened."

Jack flung his hand out, pointing down the ridge. "He's *right* there!"

"Something else. Something terrible, I think." Sergey started down the ridgeline, shuffling through the snow and bracing himself with one hand. He moved as fast as he could, risking a sudden drop-off. Branches slashed his face, his cheeks, and chin. Jack followed, almost on top of him. "I do not think he is the only prisoner hiding in these mountains."

"It was him at the river, wasn't it? How the hell does a prisoner get an RPG?"

"Prisons in Russia are not like prisons in America, Jack. If there is a riot, it is put down. Definitively."

"With an *RPG*?" Jack's voice went high as he hissed. Sergey didn't answer.

They moved fast, trudging through the deep powder. Sergey looked back once and saw Milos standing on the ridge.

The trees thickened, tangled with brush and warrens built by animals over the years. Sergey kicked through the brambles, the branches, and pulled Jack with him, keeping him close.

Another gunshot cracked the air, like a slap to their eardrums. He tensed, waiting for the impact.

Bark exploded off a trunk next to Jack's head.

Sergey pulled Jack away, spinning him around, and shoved him ahead. "Go!" They clambered through, trying to crawl over the thickened brush, covered in snow and hard frost.

Jack slipped, falling face-first with a hard smack.

Sergey froze. The snow Jack landed on wasn't powder.

Slowly, Jack slid on his belly down the ridge, picking up speed.

"Jack!" He lunged through the brambles and spotted it: ice. The brambles, the branches, the thick brush. It was creek debris. Jack had fallen on the frozen surface of a creek running down the ridge.

"Sergey!" Jack scrabbled, trying to find a handhold. His feet kicked and flailed, and he starfished out, but he kept picking up speed.

Govno, only one thing to do. Sergey ducked onto the ice, lying flat on his stomach with his arms in front of him. He pushed off, sliding down the frozen creek after Jack.

This side of the ridge was steeper than where they had been. Sergey slid for what seemed like forever, keeping his gaze locked on Jack. Jack's wide eyes found his, and he stared up at Sergey, his lips pressed together, his cheeks pale.

"Jack! Brace yourself! Cover your head!" Sergey shouted, watching the end of their fall abruptly rising to meet them: a hard stop at the bottom of the ravine, and a flat, frozen river, another tributary snaking through the mountains. "Keep your legs out! Stay on your belly!"

Jack threw his arms over his head and then plowed into the deep snow that had collected on top of the river. He skidded, but came to a stop half buried in the embankment, and in the middle of the ice.

Sergey followed his lead, covering his head and taking a deep breath before sliding into the snow beside Jack.

For a moment, neither of them moved.

Crack. A shot split the air, followed by a hiss and a whizz as the bullet flew too close. Ice crunched, and Sergey saw a spider line fracture out from a hole in the ice.

"Go! Go!"

He shuffled to his knees, slipping, and helped Jack up. The ravine was too steep to climb on either side, and they'd be fools to try. They'd be exposed, open to Milos. Instead, they jogged down the frozen river.

The snow cover thinned out as they moved until they were running on bare ice. Thin ice. Cracks and groans sounded with every footfall, a creaking that slithered up Sergey's spine.

His boots slid with every step. The ice was too slick. They had to get off the river. Ahead, the ravine seemed to end, the sheer walls they were trapped within falling away. They just had to get there.

Sergey slipped on his next step. Losing his grip, he tried to catch himself, but his other foot lost grip, too. He went down, landing on his back on the ice. His diaphragm seized, pushing up on his lungs, pushing all the air out of him. Gasping, he rolled to his side, struggling to catch his breath.

Jack kept going, but he turned back. "Sergey?"

Crack. Crack. Crack. Three shots, all in a row, louder than before. Ice chips flew, the bullets slamming into the river between Jack and Sergey. Milos had followed them along the ridge, past the frozen creek. He had the high ground.

Jack ducked, searching above.

The ice creaked. Groaned.

And cracked.

Whirling, Jack had just enough time for his panicked eyes to meet Sergey's before the ice fell out from beneath his feet and he plunged into the frigid water.

"Jack!" Roaring, Sergey lunged across the ice, sliding on his belly to the gaping hole fracturing the ice. The current moved swiftly below, and Jack had already been tugged away. Thrusting his arm into the freezing waters, Sergey stretched for him, trying to grab Jack before he was gone forever. His fingers brushed Jack's jacket, his hood. Frantic, he tried to grab hold, but the fabric slipped through his fingers.

Then, pounding. Looking down, he saw Jack pressed against the bottom of the ice sheet, kicking. Sergey could see him perfectly, his face against sheer river's ice, as he was dragged away by the current.

Sergey reached, straining as he threw almost his whole shoulder into the water. "Damn it, Jack! Grab hold!"

Jack's flailing hand slid against Sergey's wrist. He cursed, but held fast, squeezing Jack's arm until he felt his bones bend.

Another shot hit the ice, right where Jack was pinned. Damn it, if the bullet went through, Jack would bleed out underwater.

No. Gritting his teeth, Sergey braced his free hand on the ragged edge of the broken ice and hauled. The ice bit into his palm, slicing open his skin. On his shoulder, his stab wound throbbed, and a new pulse of warm blood dripped down his chest beneath his jacket.

Another pull, and he screamed through his clenched teeth.

Finally, Jack slid free from beneath the ice. His soaked blond hair appeared, and then the top of his head, his face, and Sergey hauled him out of the frigid water.

Jack coughed, spitting up water and hacking, heaving gasps as he tried to breathe through cold-shocked lungs. His body shook, violent trembles that made his movements uncoordinated and sloppy. He almost fell back into the river.

"Jack…" Sergey cupped Jack's face and looked him over. Jack's lips were blue. Not just a little blue, but deep, dark blue. His skin was paler than the snow, his eyes bloodshot. "Tell me your full name."

Jack tried, but he couldn't get the words out through his chattering teeth.

Crack. Another shot. This one ricocheted, the wild twang disappearing into the trees.

Damn it, they had to get Jack warm, and fast, but they couldn't stop. Not here, not now.

"We have to keep moving. We have to go!"

"C-c-cold," Jack managed to sputter. "C-c-can't m-m-move."

"Stay at my side. I will keep you warm." He gathered Jack close, pulling him up and tucking him beneath his arm. Instantly, the frigidity of Jack's body chilled Sergey, sliding through his jacket and around his ribs like a claw.

He wrapped his arms around him and ran his hands over Jack's shoulders. "Lean into me."

They set off, striding down the frozen river again. They just had to get to the break in the ravine, and then turn. In his mind, Sergey pictured their old map again, scanning and rescanning the terrain he'd nearly memorized. Angara river to the east, on the other side of the ridge. Ethan, and the others, across the river.

If they got across the Angara and kept heading south, there might be hope.

13

Middle Siberia

Braying laughter echoed against the inside of Sasha's skull. Cigarette smoke tickled his nose, made him cringe. The stench of too many vodka-soaked bodies crowded together made his eyes water.

Groaning, he tried to move, but couldn't. His hands were bound, tape wrapped around his jacket and his wrists. His ankles, too.

Darkness swam in front of his eyes, spotted with pinpricks of light. They'd put a hood over his head.

He lay on his side, and by the jostling and bouncing, it felt like he was in a truck. What sounded like a platoon surrounded him, raucous and hopped up on adrenaline and the high of victory. They weren't soldiers, though. They didn't speak like military men or address each other with ranks. Rabble-rousers. Thugs. The men who had circled them after downing the chopper.

His nose ached, but when he sniffed, he didn't want to black out from the pain. Not broken, then. His cheek throbbed, a dull pulsing that went down his jawline. He pushed at the inside of his cheek with his tongue. Puffy, tender, and sore.

"Kilaqqi?" He kept his voice low, hopefully not enough to rouse his captors, but if Kilaqqi was with him, maybe he'd hear.

Nothing.

Exhaling, he laid his head back on the wooden floorboards and let his body rock and sway with the rumble of the truck.

An hour later, the truck stopped. The men disembarked, clambering down from the tailgate and dropping to the ground. They grumbled and shouted to others nearby. More trucks idled alongside revving snowmobiles.

"C'mon," barked one of the men, kicking Sasha in the back. "On your feet, deserter!"

He shimmied to the tailgate, and then waited while the tape around his ankles was cut. They dragged him out, one hand gripping the back of his neck and forcing him to bend over at the waist, marching him away like he was a prisoner. Snow and hard-packed ice crunched beneath his feet.

Wherever he was, it was filled with people. Trucks drove past, rumbling, and men called out to one another, the rough language of street thugs and his rougher countrymen. Deep laughs, and what sounded like a fistfight.

Bandits? A *Bratva* nest? Had the mafia moved into the Sakha Republic? What were they doing with tribesmen?

"Where are the others? The others who were with me?"

"Shut your face, deserter!" The man gripping his neck shook him hard, and he nearly lost his footing.

Finally, a door opened before him, squeaky hinges and the sound of wood on wood. The man shoved him, and he stumbled into an open room, uneven floorboards catching the toes of his boots. He went down, landing on his knees.

He stayed silent. Clenched his jaw, and breathed through his nose.

"We picked him up with the tribesmen. They brought down that *Spetsnaz* chopper."

"Tribesmen?" A new voice spoke. Sasha's blood froze, and then burned, boiling in his veins. His heart pounded. He *knew* that voice.

"And him. He is military, must be. A deserter or something."

"Let us see who our stranger is."

The hood slipped over his head. He blinked, the sudden brightness of the room almost blinding him. Maps were tacked up on one wall, and tables had been pushed around the room in a ring, covered with papers. Photos were pinned to another wall.

He squinted, turning back to the man who had plucked the hood from his head. He was staring at Sasha, his mouth open, jaw hanging. "*Sasha?*"

"Ilya." Exhaling, he slumped forward, his muscles releasing their burning tension, the coiled need to fight. Ilya Ivchenko, head of the FSB. Sergey's best friend. And, when Sasha had worked in Moscow for Sergey at the Kremlin, his boss. Ilya had vanished after the coup, no sight or sign of him since. Sergey thought he'd been killed, and one day they'd find his bones in a ditch outside of Sochi.

But Ilya was very much alive, and in hiding in Siberia in what seemed like a thieves' den. Why?

Ilya went white at the sight of Sasha. Slowly, he crouched down, his wide eyes revealing more than Sasha had ever before seen on the man. Fear, and a quiet sort of pleading. "Sasha... Where is Sergey?"

His heart stilled. "You have not found him?"

Ilya shook his head. "You would never leave him... Unless—" His face darkened as his eyes narrowed. "What happened?" he hissed, gripping Sasha's shoulder.

"That American general! Madigan!" He swallowed hard. What did Ilya know? Where had he been? Why hadn't he made contact? Whose side was he on? "Madigan is in the Kara Sea. He released some kind of gas, a cloud that is in the atmosphere. If it ignites, the skies will burn. It is over Russia, and spreading around the world."

"A Tesla weapon?" Ilya's eyes darted over Sasha's face, seemingly searching. He squeezed Sasha's shoulder hard, digging his thumb into the soft skin and, beneath, into a raw nerve. "But *why* did you leave Sergey?"

"I flew over the Kara Sea!" Sasha barked, trying to twist away. "I volunteered! To help him! Get him information! Try and stop Madigan!" He groaned, clenching his teeth. "I was supposed to die."

Ilya released him, knocking him back on his ass on the wooden floor. He stood, staring down at Sasha. "You are the pilot from last week? Your jet exploded. Computers from here to Moscow picked it up."

He nodded, pulling himself back to his knees. Ilya, for all the time they'd spent together, was still FSB. Sill blood-loyal to the state. And, it seemed, to Sergey. They *were* on the same side.

"That is why the *Spetsnaz* were after you. They are Moroshkin's men."

"Madigan's men now. They tracked me down." He looked at the maps, the photos. The men standing clustered by the door, staring. Some had tattoos, spiders on their necks, and crosses. A Virgin Mary on one man's arm. They were criminal tattoos. "What is going on here?"

Ilya sighed. He beckoned Sasha to his feet. "This is my resistance movement. I built it from Russians who want Moroshkin gone. And," he said, nodding to the tattooed men by the door as he spun Sasha and cut the tape binding his wrists, "from men who have nothing to lose and everything to gain."

"Criminals?"

Ilya scowled. "That traitor Moroshkin has declared war on Russia, and on Siberia in particular for not supporting his coup. He is doing everything he can to destroy this place. It is total war."

"What about the people?"

"He does not give a damn about our people," Ilya growled. "Moroshkin sent his units deep into Siberia. They attacked all the prisons. Slaughtered the guards. Released the prisoners. Punishment for not supporting his government. I offered the thieves and the drug dealers a trade. Their support in exchange for their sentences. And they also have to track down the rest of the escapees. Murderers. Rapists. Terrorists."

No. Sasha's heart pounded again. Sergey, and Jack, and Ethan, and everyone else. By now, they would be deep in Siberia, deep in the middle of the blackest depths, where the darkest prisons were hidden from the world. "All the prisons were hit? Black Dolphin too?"

Ilya nodded. He hummed, his expression fierce. "Completely empty."

Sergey! Cursing, Sasha grabbed Ilya's arms. His hands shook. "Ilya, Sergey is there now. In Siberia!"

"What? Why? Last intel said he was still in the Caucasus."

Sasha's gaze darted to the criminals, too close for comfort. "The Americans came. They are helping. *Two in particular.* Close friends of Sergey's." He willed Ilya to understand, staring into his eyes. "There's a rendezvous on the east coast. Subs from America. Sergey is heading there now!"

"Through the worst band of murderers in the world." Ilya exhaled, tipping back his head and closing his eyes. "*Govno,* Sergey."

"We have to help him!" Damn it, Sergey wasn't supposed to be in danger. He was supposed to get to Simushir Island, meet up with the Americans. Get the help he needed, and then wait for the Americans to take care of everything. *Fuck, fuck!* He needed to be there, with Sergey. Aleksey and Anton were good policemen, former federal *polizei* from Sochi, but they weren't devoted to Sergey. Would they protect him the right way? Save his life?

And Jack. The American president. If he was murdered by an escaped Russian criminal…

"How can we help Sergey?" Ilya paced away, rubbing one hand over his face. "We don't know where he is. Siberia is a black hole. Millions of men have vanished and died there through the years. We cannot just search for one man. We will never find him!"

"I know his route. I helped plan it. I know where he should be."

"You know as well as I how useless plans are. This is not a parade route, Sasha. What do you expect, that you will wait on the road for him?"

"Yes."

Ilya sighed. "We're moving on Moscow soon. The time to strike against Moroshkin is *now*. He has weakened himself, splitting his forces over the pole. I cannot do the same. I cannot split my forces and send them into Siberia on a wild chase."

"But it is *Sergey*!"

"I *know* Sergey! I believe in him. You should too. You should think better of him! He can hold his own. He is a good fighter. And he is not alone, no?" Ilya scowled. "I can do more for him by retaking Moscow. Giving his country back to him."

"Are you sure you are not taking it for yourself?" Sasha snapped.

Two steps were all it took for Ilya to storm to him, fury crackling as he shoved Sasha back, sending him sprawling to his ass on the wooden floor again. "Watch your mouth," he growled. "Your *feelings* for Sergey are not an excuse to impugn our friendship. We were friends before you were *born*."

Heat flared through Sasha, a burn that scorched his soul. *Ilya knows!* Shame licked at his skin, left him exposed. How many others knew? How many others looked down on him, despised him? Thought him sick and deranged, a pathetic dog chasing its master?

Still… "I have to go to him," he breathed. "I have to."

Ilya's eyes closed. "You would be more helpful to me here. I could use you, Sasha."

"I *need* to find him."

"*Govno.*" Ilya scrubbed his hands over his face, through the unruly whiskers that had grown in on his jaw. "I can spare one truck. Some weapons. Fuel. But that is all."

"Thank you." He exhaled, his heart seeming to finally beat again. "Where are the others I was captured with? The tribesmen?"

Ilya turned to the one who had dragged Sasha in, a hulking man with a prison tattoo on his neck. The man grumbled something and stormed out.

"They were taken to a dorm for holding. They will be released now."

"They saved my life."

"We will give them food and blankets and send them on their way." Ilya gripped his shoulder. "Get over to Piotr. He'll get you clothes. A real jacket. Weapons. But, see me before you go."

LATER, HE SAT BEHIND the wheel of a small pickup truck, two rifles and a shotgun locked and loaded beside him on the bench seat. He had a new jacket on and a warm hat. Thick boots.

Kilaqqi had said his goodbyes already, and had left Ilya's compound with his tribesmen. "We must go and reunite with the herd," he said, smiling as he looked east. "And you have your own uniting to do."

"I am sorry," Sasha had stammered back to him. "For what happened to your people. You should have left me in the snow."

"Fear of what is to come is no excuse to not help another." Kilaqqi had touched his cheek, stroked his thumb over Sasha's swollen cheekbone. "Chew the roots I gave you three times a day. It will help with the pain."

He'd nodded and thanked Kilaqqi, and then watched him and his tribesmen walk away, leaving Ilya's den of thieves and returning to the snowy wilderness, back north to their herd.

He was heading south.

It was Ilya's turn to say goodbye. He leaned against the windowsill, staring at Sasha's profile. "You are a fool, Sasha," he growled. "But a loyal fool. Sergey is lucky to have you."

He squirmed, shifting in his seat. He revved the engine. Put the truck in first gear.

Ilya got the message. "Go on, go on. But!" He leaned close to Sasha, grinning wickedly. "When you find him again, give Sergey a big kiss and tell him it is from me, yes?" He winked.

Sasha slammed his foot on the gas. The truck spun, lurching forward, and Ilya dove back. His laughter followed Sasha.

"I will see you both in Moscow!" Ilya shouted. "*Udachi!*"

14

Seattle

"I CAN'T TAKE IT ANYMORE."

Faisal looked up at the breathy words, more grunted than actually spoken. He was sitting against the wall by the gate to their Alaskan flight, trying to be out of the way. Nearby, Doc lay propped against his backpack, his shades over his eyes, looking like he was asleep. Scattered throughout the rest of the gate's waiting area, the other members of the team slouched in their seats and tapped at their MP3 players.

And Adam hovered over Faisal, one hand clenching and unclenching on the strap of his backpack. He'd mangled it. Threads were loose, trailing down. The strap was fraying.

Sighing as if defeated, Adam folded himself down beside Faisal, his back to the wall and his body close. *Very* close. He pressed against Faisal from his shoulder to his knee, a warmth that went straight up Faisal's spine.

Faisal flipped a page in the magazine he was reading and suppressed his shiver. "What can you not take any longer?"

"Everything," Adam breathed. "This." He swallowed. "*Us*."

Faisal stilled. His lungs froze, and his muscles refused to move. Even his thoughts stuttered, circling around one, single word: *us*. "If you wish to end our relationship, then it will be concluded for the final time. I cannot keep doing this—"

"No!" Adam's voice was too loud, almost a shout. People turned their way, frowning. "*No*," Adam hissed again. He leaned into Faisal even more, digging his shoulder into Faisal's. "I can't take the *hiding* about us. Pretending like I don't know you. Or that I don't care about you. You're so Goddamned distracting."

He sighed. "Adam—"

"I can't keep anything straight anymore. I need to focus. I need to get us up there. Brief the team. Get ready for the rendezvous. But… all I am thinking about is *you*." Groaning, Adam buried his face in his hands. "The guys, they don't know anything about me. And now they've got a front-row seat to watch me come apart."

Faisal kept quiet. This was a side of Adam he didn't know well. Adam had been on his own when they first met, an independent operator detailed into the murky world of Middle Eastern intelligence. He hadn't had a team of Marines to lead, men he had to hide parts and pieces of himself away from, day in and day out.

"I need to do the right thing," Adam whispered. "I need to do the right thing for them. And for the whole world, damn it. You heard what's going on." Leaning back, he thunked his head against the wall and fixed Faisal with a wide-eyed stare. "I just don't know what's right anymore."

"Yes, you do." Faisal closed his magazine and set it on the ground. He started to reach for Adam, but then stopped, his hands stuttering in midair and falling uselessly to his thighs. "You have always known what right and wrong are, and stuck to your course, even when everything has been against you. This is no different."

Adam tried to smile, but it wavered and then turned aching. "Are you trying to tell me that I should stop hiding how I feel about you?"

His heart thundered, warmth flowing through his chest with every beat. "If you think that is one of your 'right choices,' then that brings me great joy, Adam. But, I believe the larger 'right choices' in front of you, at the moment, are how to prepare your team in the best way you can. Getting them to the rendezvous and preparing everyone for what is to come. Have you thought about how to tell them?"

Adam shook his head.

"You care for your men a great deal, Adam. You have always given away more of yourself than you keep, and they are no exception. Focus on what needs to happen. What you need to tell them. How they need to prepare. You cannot fight your conscience and this battle at the same time."

One of Adam's knees bounced up and down, fast. "If they find out about me, about how I feel about you, everything may come apart."

"It may." Faisal stared into Adam's eyes, watching as his fears multiplied, one panicked situation after another playing out behind his gaze. "Or, *in shaa Allah*, it may not. Your men may remember all the ways you have served them, cared for them, and led them. What you have given to them out of your heart. Remember, judgment leads a heart to regret, and a sour mind and an aching soul."

Finally, Adam smiled, watery and thin. "Not everyone sees the world the way you do."

"My faith guides me in everything I do."

Adam spoke softly, almost whispering, "*Al'ilaha 'illallah—*"

Faisal put his finger to Adam's lips. "Shhh, Adam. Don't." Adam had started to recite the *Shahada*, the statement of faith of all Muslims.

"You always stop me."

He sighed. "Those words have meaning. They can't be said idly."

Adam stared at him, his eyes pinched. "I don't say them idly."

"Adam—"

"I'm trying, Faisal," Adam breathed. "I'm trying."

"You are all over the place. Worried about your team, about the world, about me, and now you're thinking about the *Shahada*." He shook his head. "You don't have to be everything to everyone."

"I want to be everything for *you*." Adam's gaze flicked toward the gate's waiting area. The team had stopped pretending to not be interested in what was happening between the two of them. Only Doc, still supposedly sleeping, wasn't staring. Coleman's mouth was open, his jaw hanging. "And I want to be everything for them, too." He swallowed, looking down at the thin carpet.

Faisal shook his head. Serving too many masters was tearing Adam apart. His soul was fraying faster than he could bind the tears. "When was the last time you slept?"

Adam shrugged. "Saudi. Before we left. Maybe."

After the team arrived, Adam stopped sleeping in Faisal's bedroom. He'd crashed on the couch in the living room instead, but Faisal had heard him toss and turn all night long. He'd left his bedroom door open.

Faisal patted his thigh. "Rest. We have some time before the flight." He held Adam's stare after he spoke.

If Adam laid his head down, rested his cheek on Faisal's thigh, the wondering would be over. The team would know there was *something* between them, something deeper than they'd led them all to believe. If he did not, he'd keep spinning, his mind like a whirling dervish twirling out of control, dizzying anxieties sending him careening from worry to worry.

Fear strangled Adam's gaze, made his eyes shine brightly. *Yallah*, Faisal knew exactly what Adam was feeling. A lifetime of hiding, a carefully constructed web of obfuscation. Cutting a piece of yourself out and keeping it hidden, afraid to expose it to the light. Feeling it die, withering away slowly, but unable to do anything differently.

Being a gay Muslim was like walking around with a target on his heart. First, his fear of Allah. Did Allah truly hate him? Was he broken? Made wrong?

And after reconciling that, the fear of human hatred, and human *fatwas* that ordered his death.

He'd always imagined it was easier in America. That freedom was as effortless as breathing. Adam had shown him how wrong that was. Side-eyed glares, and a pervasive message, from the top of society to the bottom, that who he was was *wrong*. There were no explicit *fatwas* against being gay in America, but people thought nothing of saying, right to a gay man's face, that he was going to burn in hell for all eternity and that all gays were an offense to God's nature. And even in America, people were killed for being gay.

Coming out, in Saudi Arabia or in America, was like playing with a loaded weapon. Who would go off? Who was safe? Where would the pain strike?

Faisal couldn't quite figure out his uncle yet. Uncle Abdul had maneuvered his way into power, and then honed his children—and Faisal—

onto paths that could put them each on a rise to equal prominence. Most of Abdul's children had fallen away, but Faisal had never been able to shake the bone-deep gratitude that had filled the spaces between him and Abdul, the aching affection of an orphan searching for arms to hold him tight. How could he turn against his uncle after everything he had given Faisal?

How could he be anything other than who he was, either?

Where would they go from here? Would he be quietly shuffled aside, moved to obscurity and forgotten? Asked to leave the Kingdom? The thought made his stomach sour and his spine go cold. Leaving the Kingdom, the land of his family, the land of Allah… Arabia was his home. The desert was in his soul. Allah had revealed himself in those sands because of the primal power of the desert, the way life hung on the edge of a knife, taken or given with a single choice, a single act. How could anyone not be pressed against the divine in such a place? Feel Allah at every moment?

Imagining leaving, being banished from the desert, felt like dying.

Enough. Those thoughts were for later. Like Adam, he had to focus on what was before him. Everything else was too big, too large to fathom. Too large to battle, at the moment.

He'd given a choice to Adam, a way to break his swirling fears, the gnawing apprehension, and endless what-ifs. It was up to Adam if he was ready to embrace that.

He held his lover's gaze, staying quiet. It had to be Adam's choice, his free choice. The words of the Quran came to him: "*Allah will not change a person; they must grow what is in their own hearts.*"

Adam, I believe in you.

Taking a deep breath, Adam plucked up his backpack and set it off to the side. Turning, he carefully, cautiously leaned back, resting his head on Faisal's thigh. As he lay, he let out a shaky breath and closed his eyes.

Faisal beamed down at him and slid his fingers through Adam's shaggy hair. The longer look suited him, combed to one side instead of sticking into the air.

He closed his eyes and leaned back, resting his head against the cold airport wall. Barely whispering, he moved through the first lines of the Throne Verse, a prayer of protection, offering a *du'a* to Allah as his fingers slipped through Adam's hair, over and over. "*Allahu la ilaha illa huwa l-ḥayyu l-qayyum.*"

Adam rolled his head toward Faisal's stomach, pressing his face into his belly. "Are you praying?" he breathed.

"I am, for you."

"I remember praying with you, before." Adam squeezed his eyes shut and leaned into Faisal's stomach, inhaling as his nose found the divot of Faisal's belly button through his shirt. "I—"

"Shhh." Faisal stroked his fingers through Adam's hair again. "Rest. I am here. I will watch over you."

Nuzzling his cheek against the cotton of Faisal's shirt, Adam nodded, exhaling shakily. His eyes stayed closed, and within minutes, he was softly snoring, his open mouth pressed against Faisal's shirt-covered belly.

Faisal glanced to his side, where Doc lay. Doc was grinning, but he hadn't taken off his shades, and he still appeared to be sleeping. Knowing him, he'd probably eavesdropped on the whole conversation.

He chanced a look to the waiting area, to the rest of the team sitting at the gate.

Park and Kobayashi were staring, their eyes bugging out of their skulls. Ruiz had his fist to his mouth, covering a wide grin, his eyebrows arched high. Wright looked away, peering at the Burger King sign down the concourse. Coleman glared at the ground, his jaw clenching and unclenching, muscles bulging as the vein in his temple throbbed.

Breathing in, Faisal leaned back against the wall again and closed his eyes. He kept one hand sliding through Adam's hair, his fingers massaging his scalp and slipping through his smooth, dark strands. *Allah*, he prayed silently. *I place everything into your hands. Only you know the path before us. Keep our souls in your care for every beat of our hearts.*

15

Southern Siberia

"Jack!" Sergey stumbled as Jack went limp in his arms, no longer able to keep his feet beneath him. "Jack, damn you, keep going!"

Jack had stopped speaking an hour ago, instead mixing groans and whimpers and an endless, soft keen that fell from his frigid, blue lips. His shivers, once nearly violent enough to tumble Sergey to the ground, had stilled.

Sergey slid, his boots slipping on the slick snow as he tried to climb. He'd dragged Jack down the creek and out of the ravine, and they'd managed to stumble across a frozen beaver dam at a turn in the Angara. On the east side of the river, they'd kept going, climbing the ridgeline that stood between them and Ust'Ilga—and the others.

Since crossing the Angara, Sergey hadn't seen Milos's shadow stalking them. He looked over his shoulder and held his breath, but the man seemed to have vanished. He still flinched at every crack of ice, every branch snapping, every sound of the wilderness around them, imagining a bullet slicing through the air, or slamming into his back. Or Jack's back.

Falling to his knees, he turned to Jack, his friend already slumping into the snow. Seemingly automatically, Jack rolled into a ball, trying to burrow.

"No, no, no," Sergey hissed. "No, damn it." Burrowing was one of the last acts of a dying creature, nature's instinctual drive to curl up and expire. He pulled Jack close, rubbing his hands over Jack's arms, his cheeks. His skin was as cold as the snow beneath them.

Jack moaned and tried to chase his hands, pressing into the warmth of his skin.

"We are close, Jack. Just up this ridge. A little bit longer, and then, I promise, we will warm you up. A bit farther. Please. Please."

Whimpering, Jack tried to curl up again.

Sergey pushed to his feet, dragging Jack with him. Jack no longer tried to stand. He hung limply against Sergey's chest, his eyes closed. Frost crusted on his eyelashes, over his eyelids. Could he even open his eyes anymore, or were they frozen shut?

Only one thing left to do. Gritting his teeth, Sergey hefted Jack over his shoulders, holding on with both hands, and started to climb.

He stumbled more than once, falling to the snow. Jack's weight was like a cross he carried, and with every step, the weight seemed to double, then triple. The ridge seemed to extend to the horizon, a never-ending climb, a Sisyphean endeavor. His thighs burned. His legs quaked.

He closed his eyes and focused on putting one foot down in front of the other and dragging in breath after breath.

Somehow, unbelievably, they made it to the top. The ground leveled out beneath him, and he almost sobbed in relief. "Jack," he cried, squeezing Jack's thigh and shoulder where they lay across his back. "We made it!"

Silence.

"Jack?" Nothing, save the sound of his own breath, the rush of air over his cracked, dry lips. Was he carrying a corpse? Was it already too late? "Hang on, Jack, damn you, hang on!"

By his reckoning, and by his memory of the map, what he was looking for was close. Due north, along the ridge, on the east side. He set off, counting his steps to keep his mind quiet, to stop the screaming in his head that it was too late, that Jack was already gone.

Finally, he spotted it, buried in snow, the fence posts like small mountains rising from the powder. At the corners of the derelict *Chernaya Noch'* prison, empty guard shacks balanced precariously on rotten wooden poles, their roofs sagging from years of snowfall that had buckled the tin. Closed and abandoned decades ago, and with no one to care for the place, the decrepit prison had nearly been swallowed whole by Siberia.

Sergey stumbled down to the main fence. Long-rusted, the gate opened when he shoved his shoulder into it, pushing the chain links through the snow. Within the fence, the old prison yard, the ground where prisoners had stood in rows, calling out their names, crimes, and numbers every morning, was buried in snow. He trudged through the yard, toward the administration building.

He had to kick the door in, splintering the old wood down the center when the lock held. He kicked aside the shards and the rotted wood and slid into the old prison. Years and years ago, he'd transferred prisoners from Moscow to this place, political prisoners, enemies of the state, people who had angered the old regime. He and Ilya had first crafted their plan during the long train rides from Moscow to Irkutsk, and then the drives overland to the prison and back. A crazy plan, born of the desperate, dead eyes and broken souls of the people they transported. An ostentatious belief that they could make a different world. How young they'd been, and what dreams they'd spun. How had it all come together?

How had they lost everything they'd gained?

Like coming full circle, he was back at the prison that had broken so many Russian dreams.

Debris covered the atrium, the foyer. Broken benches, shattered glass, and animal carcasses. Something had lived in the foyer for a while, and had died there, too. He wrinkled his nose and turned left, down the officers' hallway. Jogging, he passed the warden's office and kept going, to the officers' quarters. The first door was broken, and the room was marred with black scorch marks, everything in it ash and twisted metal. The second door was locked.

"*Govno!*" He kept on, to the third set of quarters, and shoved his shoulder against the door.

It popped open. A dusty, frigid room appeared, like a time capsule from decades past. Two bunk beds in disarray. A closet toppled over, clothes and uniforms spilling every which way.

Perfect.

He set Jack down on the first bed, ripping back the covers and carefully sliding him from his shoulders to the mattress.

Jack didn't move.

No! He tore at Jack's jacket, his sweatshirt, his shirt, and his pants. Everything, until Jack was naked, and his pale, blue-tinged body lay still on the bed. Ice crusted and cracked as he removed Jack's clothes, a thin coating that had frozen around him on their escape. He flung the clothes across the room, as far as he could.

Faintly, barely, Jack's chest rose and fell.

Still breathing.

Relief crashed into Sergey, a physical blow that almost had him falling to the floor. A sob burst from him as he lunged for the old officers' clothes, the heavy, discarded jackets and sweaters on the ground. He grabbed everything he could, bringing it back to Jack and piling it around him, over his head and around his feet. He stripped the other bunks, four beds worth of sheets and heavy Siberian blankets, and laid them one on top of the other.

"Hang on. You are going to be all right. I swear it." He reached for his own jacket and pulled it off, then shrugged out of his sweater. Undid his pants. Slid out of his briefs.

He climbed into the bed beside Jack. Naked skin touched naked skin, and Sergey fought not to leap back, jump away from Jack's body. His friend was cold, cold enough to steal his breath away.

Sergey wrapped his arms and legs around Jack and turned him on his side until they were pressed together from shoulders to toes. He tucked Jack's head against his neck, briskly rubbed his hands over Jack's back. "Jack, Jack… Come back to me. Come back. Ethan is waiting for you."

Jack keened, almost wailed, and rolled against Sergey. He tried to speak, but his body started to shake, tremble almost uncontrollably. "E-E-Ethan…" he stammered. "T-tell h-h-him—"

"No! You will tell him yourself!" He squeezed Jack, pulling him closer, holding Jack as tight as he could.

Jack rested his cheek on Sergey's shoulder, exhaled, and went still.

"Jack!" Sergey shook him, grabbed his cheeks. Forced open his eyes. White stared back at him. "No!" He rolled them over, covering Jack's body with his, and pressed his lips to Jack's, breathing air into his icy mouth. "Not you too," he whispered, in between breathing into Jack. "Not you too. Jack!"

16

Ust'Ilga - Southern Siberia

ETHAN STARED AT THE snow-and-dirt-covered road leading to Ust'Ilga. His fingers drummed on the steering wheel, over and over. Beside him, Scott sat, also watching the road, still and silent. The rest of the convoy waited, parked on the side of the road, smoking and bullshitting as they waited for Jack and Sergey's return.

He lifted the radio to his lips, the one-hundredth time. "Jack, come back."

Like every time before, static was his only reply.

Exhaling slowly, Ethan closed his hand around the steering wheel, a tight fist that made the leather creak and the dashboard shake.

"It was a long drive after they got across the river. They could still be working their way here." Scott spoke softly.

"I know." He purposely unclenched his fingers, lifting them into the air and spreading them wide. "We've been down this road before. It's going to be okay." He didn't know who he was speaking to: Scott or himself. Who was he trying to convince?

But they hadn't seen or heard from their mysterious shooter since leaving the river. Not once had they been fired upon. Not once had they been attacked. Had it just been the river? A local obsessive about his privacy, his space?

Or had the shooter gone after Jack and Sergey instead?

What if it was Moroshkin's forces?

Damn it, he should have swum across the river.

"Jack, come back."

Static, and the warble of dead air, a high-pitched whine over their secured radio channel.

It's going to be okay. Jack is strong. He knows what he is doing. It's going to be okay. I believe in him.

His fist closed around the steering wheel again, clenching until his knuckles went white. *I believe in him.*

"Jack, come back."

17

Southern Siberia

WARMTH COCOONED JACK, wrapped around him, a fuzzy hold that enveloped him from head to toe. He sighed, relaxing into the gentle heat. He'd thought he would never be warm again.

His thoughts were honey-slow, fuzzy with exhaustion. His body ached, a bone-deep weariness that he felt in every nerve, every particle of his being.

But he was warm.

Arms wrapped around him, holding him tight. Slowly, his senses came back, touch and smell revealing the press of a body against his own, his cheek resting on a hard shoulder. His arms around another waist. Legs twined together.

Ethan. Smiling, Jack nuzzled into the warm body, pressing his lips to the skin beneath his cheek. His hips rolled, searching. Ah, yes. There it was. An answering hardness, matching his own. It had been so long since he and Ethan—

"Jack."

Desire fizzled, vanishing with a snap, leaving nothing but a frisson bursting off his veins, gone in a breath. *God, Sergey!*

Everything came back: their drive into the mountains, the argument. The murderer, Milos, stalking them up the ridge. Dodging gunshots. Sliding into the ravine. Running down the frozen creek. Falling into the ice.

Cold, unbelievable cold. Thinking he was going to die, when he could think at all. Snippets of time. Stumbling with Sergey, and falling to the snow. Fading in and out of consciousness as he dangled over Sergey's shoulders, listening to him scream with every step.

And then nothing. Until waking up with Sergey, naked body pressed to naked body.

Sergey must have stripped him to warm him up. Shared his body heat. God, Sergey had saved his life. And he'd—

Closing his eyes, Jack tried to pull back. Sergey's arms, and the mountain of blankets piled on top of them, kept him pinned. "Sergey, I'm sorry. I didn't know where I was."

"*Jack…*"

A note of pleading in Sergey's voice made him pause. Frowning, Jack found Sergey's gaze.

Raw desire bled from his friend, quiet desperation mixed with terror.

He blinked slowly, his thoughts coming together like trains crashing head-on in slow-motion. *Sergey is hard, too.* His cock pressed against Jack's hip.

He opened his eyes again. Looked up. "Sergey?"

Sergey's lips trembled, pressed together like he was trying to keep them closed, keep something back. His eyes gleamed, shining too bright, wet, and a flush rose on his cheeks, reddening his skin down his neck, across his chest.

And then he crumpled, collapsing in on himself like paper burning to ash, disintegrating into a million pieces. Sobs wracked through him, quaking his shoulders, ripped out of his chest. His hands shook and clung to Jack's shoulders as he folded in half, curling until his forehead touched Jack's. "I am not brave enough," he whispered through gritted teeth, between heaving gasps, anguished drags of air. "I am not brave enough."

"What are you talking about?" Jack reached for Sergey, cradling his cheeks, turning his face upward. Sergey's eyes closed. He wouldn't meet Jack's gaze.

"I am not a brave enough man," he breathed. "I am not like you. Or—" His face twisted, and a new sob ripped from him, choking his voice. "Or Sasha."

"Sergey…" Confusion strained Jack's voice, his thoughts. He shook his head, frowning. "Are you saying you're—"

"I do not know what I am!" He moaned again and turned his face away from Jack. "When you were sleeping, I imagined you were Sasha."

Jack sighed, breathing out what felt like every breath he'd ever taken. He remembered his shock, his utter confusion, when he'd first desired Ethan in a carnal, physical way. First thought about their bodies together, making love. "Is this the first time you've thought about another man this way?"

Silence strained the space between them. Sergey dug his forehead against Jack's, squeezing his eyes shut even tighter. "No," he finally breathed.

"No?" Shock stilled Jack, made him blink.

"I noticed men. Noticed how they looked. If they were attractive or not. Sometimes I wondered what it would be like. Two men together. But they were just thoughts! I thought everyone thought the way I did. Wondered, sometimes," Sergey whispered. "But you said you had never thought about it before you were with Ethan."

"No. I never did."

Sergey grimaced. "I remember growing up in the Soviet Union, Jack. I remember men disappearing for loving other men. And then, after the fall, nothing really changed. The new regime, same as the old regime. Just more money. More corruption. There was never a time when it was okay."

"So you hid what you felt?"

"I never knew what I felt!" Sergey hissed. "It was never a possibility! That world, that option, it just didn't exist. There was never the option! And I liked women. Women liked me. There was nothing wrong, *nothing*! Not until—" He sniffed and shook his head.

"Until what?" Jack's eyes narrowed. He had a suspicion about where Sergey was going.

Sergey didn't speak for a long moment. He shifted, pressing their foreheads together again. Jack heard the heavy gulp of his swallow. "If I could go back to any point in my life and have just *ten seconds...*" He trailed off. "I would have kissed him back. Held on, and never let go. Not have let him go on that mission. Damn the information. It wasn't worth his *life!*" Tears slipped from the corners of his eyes, down his cheeks, silently. "Or I would go further back. Tell myself to not be a fool. We could have had *time* together—" His voice cut off as his lips clamped shut, a shaky breath escaping from his nose.

"Is it... just Sasha?" Had Sergey fallen into the same realization that he had: that he could desire anyone if he fell in love with them? That his heart knew no limits on love and could grow to match what was offered to him.

Sergey chuckled once, a mirthless, dry crackle of sound. "No, Jack." His eyes slipped open, and he finally held Jack's gaze. "I have always thought you were a beautiful man."

Jack stared. Sergey looked like a man pushed over the edge, past all of his lines and limits. Red-rimmed eyes, a snotty nose, and dusky, tearstained, hollow cheeks.

"If things had been different, I may have fallen in love with you," Sergey said softly. "You... captivate me. You always have."

His chest went tight, and his lungs wouldn't drag in another breath. The warmth of Sergey's body, still pressed close from their hips down, turned searing. Neither of them were hard anymore, but their legs were still tangled together in a way that he had only ever lain with Ethan. Ethan, *God*, Ethan. His heart ached, desperate for Ethan's arms around him instead of Sergey's. Ethan's touch, and Ethan's love.

Sergey pulled away, sitting up and leaning against the wall next to the bunk, pulling some of the blankets over his lap. Dried blood flaked off his chest and down his arm, old drips from Milos's thrown blade. His wound had closed, though a wet, messy scab slashed his shoulder.

Jack sat up as well, sitting in the middle of the bunk, and wrapped a blanket around his shoulders. The air had a bite to it, a frosty nip. He was not Russian, and though Sergey could sit shirtless in Siberia, he could not.

"We are straight out of classic Russian literature, Sasha and me." Sergey tried to grin. He failed. "The man who loved the hero went away, and the hero learned, too late, that he did, in fact, love him in return." He shook his head, looked down at his lap. "So now I know. Now I must live with this." He sighed, sniffed, and scrubbed his hands over his face. "Live with knowing how much of a coward I am."

"Sergey—"

"No, no." Sergey waved him off. His head hit the wall. "Do not try and make me feel better. I do not want to. I need this. This feeling, my heart in a vise. Pulverized." He made a fist, squeezing slowly.

Jack stayed quiet. There would be a time and a place to discuss this, but it wasn't now. Not when Sergey was still blinking through tears, and the need to get back to Ethan was like a wolf howling in his heart. "We need to get going."

Sergey nodded. He closed his eyes. "There are clothes by closet. I threw yours over there. They were frozen."

Jack slid out of bed, padding naked to the pile of clothes on the cold floor. "That's sweet, Sergey, but you don't have to keep your eyes closed. I'm not a blushing virgin." He grabbed a pair of pants, a long-sleeve shirt, and a thick sweater, and pulled them on. He picked his way to the corner and pulled Ethan's sweatshirt from the frost-covered pile of his old clothes.

"From the back, you sometimes look like him. Only shorter," Sergey said, tacking on the end with an almost-smile in his voice.

"You Russians grow tall." Jack grabbed Sergey's clothes and brought them back to the bunk.

Sergey dressed quickly as Jack scrounged for a pair of boots. Outside of the blankets, their breath fogged in front of their faces. Jack shivered, trying to shake off the memory of freezing from the inside out. It clung to the back of his neck, making him shiver again.

Finally, Sergey stood, shrugging back into his jacket and tugging on his sweater's hem. He still wouldn't look at Jack. "I am sorry," he said, "for… what happened. I am sure Ethan will want to take a swing at me."

Jack laughed. "He will deeply thank you for saving my life." Sergey's eyes lifted. Stepping close, Jack cupped Sergey's cheek and looked into his haunted eyes. "You are going to be all right." He leaned forward and brushed his lips against Sergey's cheek.

Sergey's hand fell to his hip, squeezing as he exhaled, a breath of air ghosting over Jack's skin. A moment, and then he whimpered, turning in to Jack's touch, brushing their cheeks together.

Jack stepped back. "We do need to go. Ethan's probably out of his mind by now. I need to get back to him." Something didn't sit right, deep inside him, going this long without Ethan. It reminded him of the days when they were apart, Ethan still in Iowa and the two of them only able to see each other for forty-eight hours at a time. He'd missed Ethan then, soul deep. Somehow, between falling in love with Ethan and now, his life had been remade, reformed into something that required two hearts beating as one. Two souls in tandem with each other: his and Ethan's. Being without his other half felt like a piece of his own heart, his own soul, was missing.

And Sergey… His heart was missing a piece named Sasha, and Jack worried that that hole would never be filled.

"We should try to find a radio. Maybe get one working. It's a long way to Ust'Ilga by foot."

"Lead the way—"

Jack broke off, going silent as the walls trembled, dust rained from the ceiling, and a crashing boom bellowed from the far side of the prison complex, shattering the silence.

Sergey paled. "The gas tanks are on that side of the prison. They were never dug up!"

"Milos," Jack breathed. "He found us."

18

Ust'Ilga - Southern Siberia

LIKE THE FIREBALL BLOOMING on the distant ridgeline, flames ignited in Ethan's veins, crackling fury going off like a line of det cord winding straight to his heart.

"Jack. That's Jack." Conviction sat heavy in his voice as he jumped out of the jeep. Now was the time to act, to do, to go. It had been too quiet. Too damn quiet. They hadn't seen or heard a damn thing since the river. Whoever it was on their tail *must* have found Jack and Sergey. Tailed after them instead.

No longer. He and Jack had been separated for a day. That was a day too long.

He was going back to get his other half.

Scott followed, meeting him at the tailgate. "You don't know for sure," he said carefully.

Ethan flipped down the tailgate and reached for a stack of cases packed three high. He pulled them close, flipping the lids open, and pulled out the weapons one by one. First, an AK-47 with a grenade attachment. "If you were in trouble, with no way to reach out on the radio, what would you do?"

"Send a signal." Scott crossed his arms and frowned.

A five-inch caliber Barrett sniper rifle, a weapon that could make a man disappear in a puff of bone dust and a smear of blood, and could blow holes clean through armored vehicles. "Exactly. Something that could be seen for miles. Something that would draw our attention."

"Draw *everyone's* attention. Everyone around saw that. What if it's a trap? What if someone is trying to draw us out?"

Two handguns. "Not us. *Me.* I'm going."

"Ethan—"

"No, Scott." He slammed the tailgate shut. "I'm going. Alone."

"Like *fuck* you are—"

"One of us needs to be at Simushir when those subs arrive. Jack, me, or you. If it's not all of us together, then it's going to be just you."

Scott swallowed. He stayed quiet.

Ethan stared into Scott's eyes. Over half his life had been lived at Scott's side, through the Army and into the Secret Service. His best friend, a man he called a brother. And, before Jack, there'd been no man he'd loved more, either.

Theirs was not a relationship for goodbyes. "You need to get everyone to Simushir. You have to meet those subs. Get them up to the Kara Sea. Keep to the plan, Scott. I'm going to go find Jack."

Scott's face twisted in furious facial gymnastics. He looked away, shaking his head. "You drove here once. You know how to fucking drive back once you get him and Sergey."

"You have to move out tomorrow. No matter what. We're already delayed."

Silence, as Scott stared him down.

Somewhere, between national security and the safety of the world, between trying to prevent an apocalypse and looking into a man's eyes, there was a line in the sand called loyalty. Love, even. When did one outweigh the other? How did a man make the choice to cut the thread tying him to another in the name of saving everything?

"He's my assignment," Scott said softly. "You think I'd turn my back on my duty?"

Ethan smiled and reached out, gripping Scott behind the neck. "No. I know you'll do the right thing."

He shouldered the AK-47, slipped the two pistols into the back of his waistband, and hefted the sniper rifle before heading back to the driver's door.

"Hey." Scott appeared at the passenger's window as he shifted the jeep into first.

"Scott—"

"Relax, Prince Charming." Glaring at Ethan, Scott set a stack of blankets on the passenger seat and a duffel on the floorboard. "The med kit and blankets. You don't know what you're driving into." Scott sighed. "Be fucking careful, Ethan. Be real fucking careful."

He smiled, holding Scott's gaze for a long moment. He didn't need to say thank you. He never did.

"Go," Scott barked, slamming shut the door. "Hurry your ass back here with those losers. Damn presidents are always causing us trouble."

Ethan barked out a laugh. The jeep lurched forward as he guided it down the slushy mountain road away from Ust'Ilga, leaving Scott and the rest of the convoy behind. He pointed toward the flames licking into the sky, disappearing into the ridgeline's gloom and low fog.

Jack, I'm coming. Hang on, love. Hang on.

19

Southern Siberia

I<small>T WAS HOPELESS</small>. Ilya was right.

Sighing, Sasha slumped forward, his forehead hitting the steering wheel. He groaned.

He was a fool. A hopeless, heartsick fool. He should have listened to Ilya.

There was nothing. Nothing on the route Sergey and he had planned. No fresh tracks, no recent travel. No signs of life. Nothing at all. They must have changed their route. Gone a different way.

There was no sign of any escaped prisoners, either.

Siberia was huge. Two hundred escaped murderers could vanish forever. Disappear entirely. What were the chances of one of them running into Sergey's convoy?

He was buried in Siberia, twisted around the backwoods, halfway up a stunted mountain, and chasing after his broken heart's ghost. He was an utter fool.

Sasha rolled his head on the steering wheel, pressing his cheek against the cold plastic. He cracked his eyes open and glared out the windshield. What now? Should he slink back to Ilya? Join his attack on Moscow?

Continue to Simushir? Try to catch up with Sergey?

To what end? Desperate stumbling through the tundra had given shape to too many fantasies. Sergey, happy to see him again. Glad he'd survived. Welcoming him back into his life.

Why would Sergey do any such thing?

Emptiness, aching, gnawing emptiness, opened inside Sasha, a black pit of anguish, bottomless in his soul. Nothingness was like a vacuum, atomizing him to a billion tiny pieces. If he closed his eyes, could he blow away? Could he disappear into the snow?

What the hell was he going to do? His life, for the second time, had ended. Everything within it, everything he'd done, had crumbled to dust. He was, once again, rudderless. Wingless. Crashing down to earth in a spinning nosedive, screaming for the ground at Mach 3.

He closed his eyes. He was tired. Exhausted, physically, from everything. How many hours' sleep had he managed in the past week? Not enough for even a single night. And he was exhausted to his heart, his soul. How many times could a person completely restart their life? Say goodbye to the old and try to find a new way forward?

He didn't want to. He just didn't want to do it again.

Instead, he let out a breath and reached for the keys. He'd turn the truck off. Lower the windows. Lie down on the seat and let the snow fall. It would be night soon. Maybe he'd see the stars again. And, when he fell asleep, he'd see Sergey one last time.

His fingers closed over the truck's key, cold metal stinging his fingers.

In a nearby tree, birds leaped to the sky, screeching. He frowned.

And then he heard it. Like thunder, a rumble that crawled over the ridge and rolled down from the sky. A series of blasts, booms that shook his windows, shook the water in his canteen, making it splash against the metal as it lay on his dashboard.

He saw it, too. Roaring flame, billowing into the sky, a rising fireball that kept growing, bursting like a flaming geyser had appeared in the center of Siberia. He'd seen something like that once before, years ago on a flight line. A gas explosion, an eruption that grew with the vapor, ballooning larger and larger, feeding itself as it hungered for more fuel.

Something up on the ridge had exploded. Erupted.

And there wasn't supposed to *be* anything up on that ridge. Not according to the maps and the memories he had, poring over the route eastward while standing shoulder-to-shoulder with Sergey. Nothing was in these mountains.

Except for Sergey.

He reached for the stick, shifting the truck straight into second, and slammed on the gas. The truck lurched, spinning out on loose snow before roaring forward, climbing sideways across a game trail. Branches scraped his windows, and pockets of ice made his tires whine and the truck slide out. But he kept on, climbing toward the ridge.

He'd go as far as he could before he had to get out and run. And then he'd go as far as he could until he had to crawl. Whatever it took.

20

Southern Siberia

SERGEY POKED HIS HEAD around the corner of the prison administration building, trying to see the open spaces of the prison yard.

A bullet slammed into the concrete beneath his eye, spraying dust and ice into Sergey's face. He ducked back, turning in to Jack's arms.

Jack steadied him. "Did you see anything?"

"He is out there."

"Obviously, Sergey."

"He is somewhere in the yard. Maybe in one of the towers."

"So we find another way. We go back the way we came, try to find another way through the admin building—"

"There is no other way, Jack!" Sergey shouted, pulling free. "He set fire to the cellblocks! That way is shut!"

Jack glared. "What about the rear fence? What about a back way out of here?"

"Sheer rock. This place was built to have one entrance." Sergey pointed to the yard, and where the shot had come from. "And he is there!"

Jack threw his hands up. "Then what do you propose?"

Sergey stared at him. He breathed in and out, slowly. "You will run for the gate—"

"No. No way." Jack shoved Sergey against the cold concrete, pinning him with both hands. "I'm sick of this son of a bitch. We're going to get rid of him, and then we're getting out of here. Together."

Sergey glared and shook Jack off. "How?"

"How big do you think that fireball was? That explosion? Think! Ethan *must* have seen it. We're late, missing from our rendezvous. Do you think for one *second* that he won't be coming to check that out? He's on his way, I promise you that. We just need to hang on."

"And how do *you* propose we do that?"

Think, think. Jack closed his eyes. Took a breath. What would Ethan do? What choices would he make, right now? What did they have to work with? Themselves. Two rifles, pilfered from the prison officers' quarters. They were finally armed, but slowly being squeezed into a kill box. "Can we get to the roof? Higher ground?"

Sergey closed his eyes, exhaling as he rested his head against the concrete wall. Jack waited, biting his tongue. Sergey had crossed some line, somewhere deep within himself. This fatalistic pessimism wasn't his way.

But the heart had a way of tugging even the smartest person into twisted rationalities. How much hurt had Sergey accumulated in the past week? How much more in the last twelve hours? Would Jack think the same way, if faced with Ethan's loss?

No. He wasn't going down that road.

"Sergey," he prodded. "Can we get to the roof?"

"Yes," Sergey breathed. "If you don't mind a climb."

They scrambled back through the admin building. Smoke from the burning cellblocks, connected through a dark, collapsed gantry, stung their eyes. Jack coughed and pulled Ethan's sweatshirt up over his nose, trying to filter the worst of the smoke. The sweatshirt was still damp and cold, but he'd layered it over the sweater and clothes he'd taken from the prison officers' closet. His eyes watered, going hazy.

Sergey hauled open a side door after kicking apart the rusted lock. It opened to a narrow walkway, a tiny space cut into the rocky cliffs facing the prison. Hard, packed snow rose to their thighs, and they climbed up onto the walkway one at a time.

Halfway through the passage, a rusted ladder hung down the side of the prison, outside the burning cellblocks. Concrete walls kept the blaze inside, for now. Everything on the first floor was already in flames. Sergey pointed to the ladder. "That is your way up."

Jack eyed it. Black paint had chipped and flaked, revealing pockmarked metal and rust. Some parts had rotted almost completely through. "Will it hold?"

"One way to find out." Sergey grabbed the ladder and hefted himself up.

It creaked—metal groaning, rivets screaming—but held.

"Is good," Sergey grunted. He started to climb.

Jack glared up at him, but followed.

Ten feet above, Sergey placed his foot on one of the metal rungs and went right through it. The rung disintegrated, metal flakes and rust dust spraying down on Jack. He hugged the ladder, sputtering, as Sergey grabbed hold of the next rung, quickly pulling himself higher. "That one is bad," he called. "Watch out."

"Right."

They made it to the roof, Jack cracking through one rung after it strained under Sergey's weight. He slipped, but held fast with his thighs and his hands. He was near the top of the ladder when the rung went, and Sergey managed to reach over and haul him up the last few feet. They came over the roof's edge and landed in deep snow, rising to their shins, and beneath that, a packed ice layer that kept them from sinking all the way through.

Ducking low, they pulled out their rifles and made their way across. "Any idea where he is?" Jack whispered.

Sergey shook his head. He scanned the rooftop, his head on a swivel. Jack fought back a tiny smile. Sergey was back, finally. Back to being the FSB agent he was. They'd need that if they were going to get out of there.

The rooftop was covered in snow and ice, sunken in the middle and with deep drifts piled high on the corners. From there, they'd have a view of the entire yard, the front gate, and the fence line. If Milos was out there, they'd be able to find him. Take him out.

Like Ethan would do.

"You take that corner." Jack pointed to the south. "I'll take the other."

They moved slowly, keeping low. Snow tumbled beneath Jack's jacket, down his sweatshirt. His fingers stung, shocked by the cold of the rooftop and the chill of the metal on the rifle in his hands. Decades old, it had been practically an antique when the prison was still operational.

Finally, they arrived at their corners. Sergey lay down in the snow, propping his rifle on the lip of the roof's edge. Jack did the same, hissing as the cold hit his belly when his layers rode up.

He scanned the yard, the fence line. Peered into the guard shacks. Everything was quiet. Eerily so. The snow had stopped falling, but the world was still preternaturally silent. There was almost an expectant hush, waiting. Each breath seemed as loud as a gunshot. He wanted to wait to breathe, hold his breath forever.

At some point, breathing would become an issue. Smoke kept climbing from the first floor, belching skyward. His nose twitched and tickled. They had time, for now. But not forever. Milos had better make his move soon.

Milos was a hunter, Sergey had said. Stalked his victims. Weakened them, and then went in for the kill. Jack wished he'd paid attention, all those years ago, when his dad was trying to teach him about hunting. He'd never cared for it, and what little knowledge his dad had passed on had long since been replaced with song lyrics and congressional minutiae. What was the next move? What did they do now?

At the very least, he remembered being bored while hunting with his dad. Waiting for what felt like an eternity.

They'd stay put. Take their time. As much as they could.

He glanced down the roof, toward Sergey. Sergey glanced back.

Thump. Below them, something hollow sounded, like a soup can fired out of a tube. A dull whump, and a near-silent hiss.

Two dark canisters arced into the air, sailing over the edge of the roof. They landed in the snow, gentle puffs billowing out from where they lay.

"Go!" Sergey hollered. He waved at Jack, already scrambling to his feet. "Go! Grenades!" Panic lay in his gaze, and even from across the roof, Jack could see the whites around his eyes.

He couldn't run back to the ladder. He wouldn't make it.

Jack looked over the edge of the roof, toward the prison yard.

Bullets spat past his cheek. Milos was on the ground, just beneath them, firing upward.

"Jack! *Go!*"

Go where? He rolled back, escaping Milos's burst of fire, and scrambled on his belly, heading to the side of the roof. He peered down again.

The fire was worse on this side, flames licking out of broken windows. But deep snowdrifts lay against the building, blown by the winds. He could jump. Maybe.

"*Jack!*"

He *had* to jump. *Now.*

God, Ethan would throw a fit if he saw this. Taking a deep breath, Jack hauled himself up and over the side, sliding on his belly until he rolled over the edge. He clung to his rifle as he fell.

Freefall grabbed him, flinging him toward the ground. He thought he left his stomach on the roof. Primal thoughts screamed in his mind, desperate pleas that the snow be soft enough, deep enough, that he lived through the next moment. Ethan's face hung in his mind, Ethan's smile, the warmth of his arms.

Whomp. He landed on his chest, face-first in the drift. Snow puffed around him, like a snow globe gone crazy. He couldn't breathe; his lungs wouldn't work, wouldn't drag air into his body. He rolled, slowly, his arms fishtailing through the air as he struggled to physically drag oxygen into his mouth. Time slowed. The world lengthened, sounds distorted and stretched, like a rubber band pulled and pulled.

And then snapped. He sat up, gasping, heaving in breath after breath, his hands reaching for his throat, his chest, patting down his snow-covered jacket. He was alive. Somehow, he was alive.

Sergey. What about Sergey?

Jack stood, slipped, and trudged his way through the snow drifts. The fires still raged in the cellblock, licking through the windows. Black burns coated the concrete. Even in the snow, sweat started to prick at Jack's skin.

Had the grenades detonated? Was Milos still out there, just around the corner?

He kept going, pushing through waist-deep snow.

Ratatatat. Gunshots. A burst of fire, from the front of the building. He froze.

Twin booms sounded, blasts that exploded from the rooftop. Concrete and snow sprayed through the air, arching high before raining down on Jack, the yard, and into the center of the prison. He ducked as the cellblock groaned, burned concrete and metal moaning, the sound setting his teeth on edge. A moment later, the roof caved in, snow and broken, rusted iron crashing through the second story and into the flames. The fire hissed as snow from the roof collapsed into the center, flames twisting and trying to survive, and burn higher.

He rose slowly, peering through the broken windows. He could see the sky and shattered concrete, twisted bits of iron. The roof was gone.

Where was Sergey? What were those shots?

Damn it, running through snow was worse than running through a dream. He couldn't move any faster than a crawl, and his legs screamed, a burn that went from his hips to his toes. He tried to climb on top of the drift, but fell through, stuck with his fractional progress. *Damn it!*

Finally, he made it to the end of the building. The snow tapered out, and he stumbled the last few steps through ankle-deep powder. He leaned against the building, catching his breath, and then peeked around the corner.

In the center of the yard, Sergey was crawling on his side, a line of blood trailing him in the snow.

Milos stalked him slowly, a long, brutal-looking knife in one hand.

Jack raced across the packed snow. He slid on a patch of ice, but kept running, gripping his rifle tight. As he got to the edge of the yard, he bellowed, shouting at the top of his lungs. "Hey! Asshole! Over here!"

Milos turned and pulled a pistol from his waistband.

Jack, rifle already raised, fired.

The old Russian rifle kicked back against his shoulder and his shot went wide. Milos's shot was better, whizzing past him close enough to hum.

Jack ducked, running for the base of a guard tower at the corner of the yard. Rotten wooden posts held the tower aloft, a crisscross of old timbers. He crouched low, peeking through the beams as Milos turned back to Sergey.

He lifted his rifle and took aim, closing one eye as he rested his cheek against the stock.

Sergey stopped crawling. He looked up at Milos and snarled. Jack was too far to hear what Sergey spat, but he watched his lips move.

Milos laughed. He grabbed Sergey by the collar of his sweater. Leaned in, and lifted the knife.

Fuck, he had to make this shot. Had to save Sergey. He breathed in, sighted the center of Milos's back, and—

A blast roared through the yard, through the whole prison. The boom of a shotgun.

Jack jerked, looking up.

Striding across the yard, coming from the front gate, a man in a dark jacket, his hood pulled up, moved fast, holding a pump-action shotgun in front of him. Another rifle was slung over his shoulder. He pumped the shotgun once and took aim, his long legs spread wide as the stock rose to his chest.

Milos shouted as the second shot struck him, something harsh and guttural even in Russian. Blood wept from his shoulder, pouring down his left arm, hanging uselessly at his side. Gritting his teeth, he charged the hooded man, brandishing his knife as he ran.

The unknown man threw his shotgun in the snow, unslung the rifle from his shoulder, lifted it, and fired, emptying the magazine into Milos. Milos's charge stuttered, and he stumbled, falling to his knees as the bullets slammed into him, over and over. Finally, he pitched forward, face-first in his own bloody snow.

Jack didn't move. Who was this? He wanted it to be Ethan, God, he wanted it to be Ethan more than he'd ever wanted anything before. Ethan was his hero, he always had been, and of course he'd show up, save them both, kill Milos. Of course he would, he'd always be there, always.

But this man didn't move like Ethan.

He could pick Ethan out from a thousand people all dressed the same, all looking the same. The way he moved, the shape of his body. The way he stood, how he braced. The width of his shoulders, his back. The curve of his waist.

This wasn't Ethan.

Who was he?

The man moved toward Sergey, his rifle held at the ready, searching and scanning the yard for anyone else. Jack stayed down, hidden, and raised his own rifle.

Sergey lay on his side in the snow, propped up on his elbow. He stared at the man, his mouth hanging open.

Silence had once again fallen over the yard, a silence so complete Jack heard each of the man's footfalls, the crunch and slide of his boots. Heard him sling his rifle over his shoulder and crouch down beside Sergey.

And then, he heard Sergey's choked, breathless whisper: "*Sasha?*"

Impossible.

But… He watched Sergey push himself up and reach for the man. His hands shook as they neared the man's face, hidden by the hood.

The hood fell back.

Blond hair. Ice-blue eyes, staring down at Sergey, traveling over his body. Hands, reaching for Sergey's leg, where he was bleeding.

It *was* Sasha.

How the hell…

God, what now? After the emotional anguish, the self-torture Sergey had inflicted upon his heart, Sasha appeared out of the snow? How had he survived?

What the hell would happen now?

Jack stood and jogged to their sides, kneeling beside Sergey. Sasha's eyes flicked to him as he ran, but dropped back to Sergey. He snorted to himself. He was the third wheel, suddenly. Utterly inconsequential. Sasha hadn't even twitched as he approached, he was so entirely focused on Sergey.

Sergey didn't notice when he plopped down beside him, either. He just kept staring at Sasha, his jaw hanging open as his lips tried to form words that never came. One of Sergey's hands rested on Sasha's cheek. Touched him as if he weren't truly there.

Sasha's hands stuttered as he reached for Sergey. He froze, staring into Sergey's gaze. He, too, seemed to be struggling to find the right words, any words. And, Jack caught the edges of fear in his eyes, apprehension that he buried in the back of his gaze.

Jack leaned in, tugging at Sergey's pants on his lower leg, exposing his wound. A single gunshot, through his calf. Still bleeding, but slowing down. He pulled off his jacket and pressed it on Sergey's leg, leaning with all his weight.

Sergey's hand fell from Sasha's cheek, and he grimaced, groaning aloud. "*Govno!* Damn it, Jack! That *hurt!*"

"Of course it hurt. You're shot."

"Not that bad," Sergey growled. "Is just a nick on my leg." He scooted up, leaning back on his elbows. Looked at the snow. Finally, turned back to Sasha, still kneeling beside him, silent. "Sasha? How—" His lips moved, but nothing came out. "I heard you die," he whispered.

"I ejected."

"You said it was *madness* to eject in the permafrost! And that you would not even be able to if they fired at you at such close range! You would not have time!"

"I do not know how I did it. I was talking to you, and then—" Sasha looked away, down to the snow. "And it *was* madness. I should be dead."

"No," Sergey growled. He grabbed Sasha's wrist and pulled him close, until their faces were inches away. Fury crackled off Sergey, sparked from his eyes, made the air shiver between them. "Do not *dare* speak about dying again. You are not allowed to throw your life away! Do you hear me? I will kill you myself if you ever do something like that again! I *cannot*—" His voice, building to a crescendo, cracked, and he hissed, a quiet, sharp gasp. "I *need* you," he finally breathed.

Sasha stared into Sergey's eyes, breathing fast. His lips were open, his breath making tiny clouds that puffed between their faces.

Now, Sergey. Kiss him now. Jack's gaze darted between the two. He stayed quiet. *Sergey,* do *something. Tell him. My God, tell him. Don't wait.*

"I am here," Sasha whispered. "Always."

Sergey's expression curdled, and he let go of Sasha's wrist like it burned him to touch. "You promised that once before. And then you demanded to fly off and die!"

Everything within Sasha closed up tight. Jack watched walls fall behind his eyes, saw his spine stiffen. He pulled back, frowning at Sergey. "It was for you. So you could end this madness and go back to being president."

Sergey snarled, and he tried to pull away. Jack kept him pinned, leaning into his wound. Sergey sent him a withering glare before turning back to Sasha. "Do not do it again!"

"Sergey—"

A new voice broke over the yard. "Jack?"

He knew that voice. Relief flooded through him, followed by a sigh that came from his soul. He looked up and found Ethan standing just inside the broken front gate in the dim light of a distant pair of headlights. Ethan's gaze darted from Milos's broken body to the three of them in the snow. He had his rifle at the ready, pointed at Sasha's back.

"Sasha. Hold here." He grabbed Sasha's hands, moved them over his on Sergey's leg, and then stood and stumbled across the snowy yard to Ethan, a beaming smile stretching his face and making his cheeks ache.

Ethan stared at him, his eyes cataloging every scratch, every bruise, every soot mark Jack had picked up. His new clothes, scavenged from the Russian prison. Jack opened his arms. "Am I glad to see you, love."

Jack's smile must have let Ethan relax, at least a fractional amount. He lowered his rifle and wrapped him up, his hands sliding up Jack's neck and into his hair as he pressed their cheeks together, letting out a sigh. "We've got to stop meeting like this."

He kept holding on, smiling. He was safe, back together with Ethan. Ethan was in his arms. Sasha was alive. Sergey was going to be okay. The world still turned. The sky hadn't ignited yet. For the moment, everything was good. Relief made him giddy, made his stomach flutter and his blood quicken. "One of us," he said into Ethan's ear, "has very bad luck."

"I had a normal life before I met you." Ethan pulled back, but he cupped Jack's face. His eyes were smiling, even as they swept over his bruised cheek, his mussed hair standing on end.

"I guess we're just going to have to stick together, huh?"

"Guess so." Smiling, Ethan dropped a kiss to the end of Jack's nose. "Who is that?" He nodded to where Sasha knelt, his back to Ethan.

Jack sighed. Had it only been a few hours since Sergey had confessed his love, his desire for Sasha? Faced down a part of himself, and reconciled with his heart and soul?

Now, he glared at the prison fence, at the trees beyond, looking furious enough to chew nails as Sasha kept pressure on his wound. Sasha kept sneaking glances at Sergey, but Sergey never saw.

"Sasha. Sasha's back."

IT WAS TIME TO GO. Time to get back to the mission.

Ethan pulled out the med kit and wrapped Sergey's leg, hands, and shoulder as they filled him in on Milos, his criminal past, and how he'd hunted them. Sasha spoke next, grunting through what even Jack could tell was a condensed version of his time in the tundra. Finding the tribesmen, and then Ilya.

The news about Moroshkin emptying the Siberian prisons made Sergey snarl and growl again.

When Ethan was done, he confirmed what Sergey had already said: the bullet had gone straight through his calf and the cuts were shallow. Other than the pain, Sergey was going to be fine with some rest and fluids.

They piled into Ethan's jeep, Sasha sliding into the backseat with Sergey. Sergey kept to his sullen silence, slumping against the window as if he could escape, glaring out at the snow and refusing to talk as Sasha closed his eyes and rested his head on the seatback.

Five minutes after Ethan set out, Sasha started snoring.

And Sergey stared at him, frustrated fury melting away, replaced with naked longing.

Jack watched Sergey in the rearview mirror, sharing glances with Ethan. By the time they dropped off the ridge and Ethan wound his way through the track and back to the road to Ust'Ilga, Sergey had tugged Sasha, still sleeping, sideways, and was holding him in his arms. He buried his face in Sasha's neck and closed his eyes.

Ethan turned to Jack and arched his eyebrows.

"Sergey and I talked. He figured some things out."

Ethan slid one hand into Jack's, squeezing tight. "I'm glad. You two okay?"

Jack inhaled slowly. "I think so. It was a rough day, though." He squeezed back. "When we were running from Milos, I fell through the ice into the river. Sergey pulled me out. Brought me to the prison and kept me alive. Shared body heat with me."

Ethan's hand clamped down on Jack's, hard.

"I don't remember much after I fell in. He says I almost died."

Silence. Ethan breathed in and out, measured, deep breaths. He didn't let go of Jack's hand or loosen his grip.

"He had his realization then."

Slowly, Ethan nodded. He swallowed, and then lifted their hands, bringing Jack's to his lips. He pressed a kiss to the back of Jack's hand, letting his lips linger. "I'm glad he was there. He saved your life." He kissed Jack's hand again, and then his fingers, one after another. "I'm sorry I wasn't with you."

"It's not your fault." Jack slipped his hand free and cupped Ethan's cheek. "Nothing that happened is your fault."

"I shouldn't have left you at the river—"

"No." Jack shook his head. "No, don't do that. You couldn't predict what would happen. Milos. The RPG. It's not your fault when life hurls curveballs at us." He smiled, stroking his thumb over Ethan's scruff. "I should actually thank you."

Ethan frowned. "For what?"

"You gave me a crash course in weapons and tactics back in DC. How to shoot. How to react. How to keep my head when things go sideways." He smiled. "Without that—without you—I'd be a goner. You've made me stronger."

Finally, Ethan smiled. He glanced at Jack. Kissed his wrist, and then turned to his palm, dropping a kiss to the center. "I don't like you getting hurt. Being in harm's way."

"I know—"

"But..." Ethan glanced at Jack again. "'Badass Jack' is kind of hot."

He laughed, throwing his head back. "Kind of hot? Only kind of?"

Smoldering eyes raked over Jack, from his head to his crotch, and then back. "They're sleeping. I'll pull over right now."

He almost told Ethan to do it, a tightness in his blood pleading for exactly that. Him and Ethan, together again, finally. Body to body. Sweat-slick skin, moving together.

But he wanted more than a fumble in the trees and more than what he was capable of at the moment. Part of him wanted, but the rest of him was fading fast. Exhaustion had sunk its claws into him.

"I won't be any good. I might fall asleep on you."

Ethan barked out a laugh. "So inspiring." He grinned, and then held out his hand. "Sleep against me. You can lean on my shoulder while I drive."

Jack slid across the bench seat, collapsing against Ethan's side. He rested his head on Ethan's shoulder and smiled when he felt Ethan's lips press on the top of his head, against his hair.

"Love you," he said, lacing their fingers together when Ethan rested one hand over his belly.

"I love you, Jack."

His eyes slipped closed, and he fell asleep, safe in Ethan's arms as the jeep hummed over the road, bringing them down and out of Siberia and back to their mission.

Tensions Inside White House Skyrocket as the World Prepares for War

Sources within the White House report a tense, divided, and combative atmosphere as the world struggles to contain an explosive situation in Canada's northern territories. Russian General Moroshkin, the self-appointed leader of Russia following his coup against President Sergey Puchkov, continues to hold the territory he seized in Canada's Yukon and Nunavut territories. The U.S. has mobilized in support of Canada, pitting significant ground troops and air support against Moroshkin's invasion.

However, sources say that the White House's moves are scattered, and that senior advisors are kept out of the loop on key strategic decisions. An air of suspicion and mistrust has settled over the West Wing. Many staffers appear to be on edge and ready to snap, on the heels of former President Jack Spiers's assassination attempt.

21

Washington DC

"I STILL CAN'T BELIEVE he's gone..." Jason Brandt blinked fast as he bit his lip.

"It hasn't even been a week since President Spiers was attacked, Jason." Jennifer Prince leaned in, dropping a kiss to his cheek. She lay beside him in bed, her body pressed against his. "It's okay to still hurt."

Jason shook his head. "Where is Ethan? Ethan's been gone for too long. Why didn't he come back after the attack?" He scrubbed his hands over his face. "The president is in ICU. He's *brain-dead*. The truth about the clone of Mrs. Spiers is out now. And Ethan's... just *gone*?"

"Do you have any idea where he is?" Jennifer's thumb stroked along the center of his chest, over his sternum. "I really thought he'd be sitting by the president's bedside, day and night."

"The official statement is that he's in seclusion, mourning the events." Jason shook his head. "But that came from Pete, and Pete said it came from President Wall." He grimaced. It was still hard to say *President Wall*. No longer President Spiers.

And his boss, First Gentleman Ethan Reichenbach, was missing.

Jennifer stilled. She frowned, biting her lip. "You think..."

"I don't know what to think." He swallowed and rolled toward her, burying his face in her neck. Her hair smelled like sunflowers, like the shampoo she'd brought over and left in his shower one weekend. "I don't want to turn into Pete."

What had happened to them all? In two weeks, the whole world had changed. When had it begun? When had the slide into disaster and anarchy happened? Sochi? Earlier?

Or all the way back, to Madigan's betrayal, his attempted coup?

What had been Madigan's first act of rebellion? When had he first turned against the United States and started working for himself?

Madigan had shredded the world in one massive blow. President Jack Spiers, brain-dead after his miraculously-back-from-the-dead wife was revealed to be a clone, an assassin sent by Madigan to rip out the heart of the United States. And Ethan, missing after Leslie's reappearance. Not a word, not a hair seen of him since the attack on the CIA and Jack's hospitalization.

They had been *so* in love. He'd seen it, watched it. Hell, he remembered the gossip that had flown through the White House, back when Ethan was still the president's lead Secret Service agent. How close they were. How their friendship had been considered scandalous on one hand and proof of the president's everyman appeal on the other.

The way they'd hidden in corners of the White House, stealing moments to talk and laugh together. And then, after they were outed, how they had kept their love alive. Turning toward each other, always. They had been so *deeply* in love.

What the hell was this? It just didn't make sense. Was Ethan hurt? Wounded somehow, and in hiding? Was he so shattered, so deep in his mourning that he couldn't face the public? Where *was* he? Why didn't he reach out to his staff? They'd do anything for him, anything.

God, they all missed him. Barbara, the White House Social Secretary, hadn't stopped crying. Jennifer, White House Florist, had all but moved into Jason's office, bringing her floral designs with her. She said she didn't want to be alone in the crypt-like East Wing. And, truth be told, he was glad she was there.

President Wall had closed the East Wing. No journalists. No volunteers. No more press junkets or interviews. No meetings. They all still came in—at President Wall's invitation—but the place was a tomb.

Out of everyone, Pete Reyes, President Spiers's—*President Wall's*—press secretary had taken the news of Spiers's demise and Ethan's disappearance the worst. He hadn't led a press briefing in days. Hadn't left the White House in even longer. Whenever Jason saw him, Pete looked more and more disheveled with ever-darker red-rimmed eyes. He stank of tequila.

Jennifer stroked his hair and kissed his temple. "Pete's hurting. He's lost right now. You know he was with the president during his campaign. He worked with Spiers back in the Senate. We only worked with them a few months. I can't imagine how he feels. His friend was *assassinated*." She exhaled shakily, pressing her cheek to Jason's. "We should do more for him."

"He's so angry."

"He needs us." She kissed his ear and pulled back. Looked into his eyes. "We're his friends. We need to help him."

He nodded. Pete's rage, his anguish, were infectious. He could feel his own heart rising to meet Pete's bitter fury every time they neared.

It wasn't fair. It just wasn't fair. Why did the world have to be so cruel? Rip apart two men who loved each other. Break a country's back and terrorize the world. What was it Madigan wanted so badly, to do all of this?

"We need to get ready." Jennifer kissed his cheek and pulled away, sliding out of his bed.

"Why? Why do we even go in every day?" He rolled to his back, spreading out like a starfish. "What's the point?"

"It's our job," she said, stroking her hand over his feet as she passed, heading for the bathroom. "We're supposed to be there, on call. What if today is the day Ethan comes back? Won't you want to be there for him?"

Damn it. Jason rolled to the side of his bed and pushed himself up. He chewed on his lip, listening to the sound of the shower turning on and Jennifer slipping behind the curtain. She was right. He did need to do more. Help Pete. Help Pete's staff. Try and bring stability back to President Spiers's—damn it, President Wall's—White House.

It's what they both—Ethan and President Spiers—would have wanted.

"MADAM PRESIDENT, WE HAVE A SITUATION."

General Bradford strode into the Oval Office, followed by Director Mori and Paul Heng, Secretary of State.

Elizabeth shared a quick look with Levi, seated at the tables in the center of her office. Levi refused to leave her side, staying with her through every meeting, every moment she was in the West Wing. At the end of each day, she trudged upstairs to the Residence and slept in the Queen's Bedroom, one of the guest bedrooms down the hall from Jack and Ethan's.

Every night, Levi shoved one of the couches in front of her bedroom door. He slept there, curled up on the Victorian silk loveseat, knees bent and neck stuck at an odd angle, in his undershirt and boxers. He rewore his suit every morning, pilfering from Jack's shirts when his went too long and turned dingy.

Levi stayed seated, watching Bradford, Heng, and Mori stop in front of the Resolute desk.

"What's going on?" Elizabeth turned her laptop away and lowered the screen.

"We've lost contact with the SEAL team we deployed. They inserted twelve hours ago, and they were supposed to check in. They haven't. They've missed both their check-in windows."

"Have we lost them?"

Bradford frowned. "The Arctic is a nasty environment to operate in. Nothing goes right. But these guys are the best."

"The best that's gone silent." Her eyes narrowed, and she peered at Bradford. "We didn't just hand-deliver a team of our best operators to Madigan, did we? You know those SEALs were one hundred percent loyal?"

He glared at her and didn't blink. "These were our men," he growled. "*America's* men. Some of our best."

She sighed, long and loud, and rubbed her forehead. "Damn it. Keep me updated. I want to know the second they make contact. Don't give up on them just yet."

"I have no intention of giving up on any of our forces, Madam President."

"Ma'am, there's another problem." Mori cut in neatly, stepping forward and taking over as Bradford's face continued to flush, turning a deep purple that set off the rage in his eyes. "We've picked up communications between the Canadian government and the Russians. Between the embassy in Ottawa and Moscow."

"Shit."

Paul spoke up. He still had his pencil, and he flicked it against his palm, the eraser hitting his skin in a fast beat. "The Canadian prime minister's office is no longer taking my calls, ma'am."

She closed her eyes as the world swam before her. What was the record for a world leader destroying a nation? Would she set a new one, leading America to devastation in only a week? Would the Canadians truly turn to the Russians? Reorient the whole world? Allow the invasion of America to happen through their backyard?

"That's not the worst news, ma'am," Mori said slowly.

Elizabeth's eyelids opened with a snap. She stared at Mori, and then Bradford when both were silent. "What could be worse?"

Bradford cleared his throat. "Satellite imagery has picked up the Chinese launching their long-range naval vessels out of their northern sea base. We're tracking submarines, destroyers, and amphibious assault ships."

"An invasion force?"

"Yes, Madam President."

Oppressive silence filled the Oval Office. Not even a curtain twitched. Jack's photos, him and Ethan, sat behind her on the table by the windows. She could feel Jack's eyes boring into her back, staring at her, waiting for her to act. To save the day. Save America and the world. To do *something*.

"General, what is the status of our forces in the Pacific?"

"We've put the bulk of our forces against the Russians, off the coast of British Columbia. Pearl still has a fleet available. They're on high alert and waiting for orders."

"Have the fleet set up a defensive perimeter. I want a blockade to stop the Chinese. Do not let them cross Hawaii."

"Deny them passage through international waters?" Paul frowned. His pencil finally stopped snapping against his palm.

"If the Chinese are coming to help the Russians invade, then *yes*, I'll damn well deny them the entire Pacific if I can. Push them right back into their bases." She pinched the bridge of her nose. "General, we need to review civil defense measures. Contingency plans in the event of a ground invasion. I want a briefing on all your models."

Bradford nodded. He'd lost his purple rage, and instead, he was ashy, pale. Bags hung under his eyes, dark with lack of sleep.

She understood only too well. Were they presiding over the end of America? Was this what Rome felt like, before the republic was overrun?

"Paul, keep trying with the Canadians. Tell them I want to speak to the prime minister immediately. Director, see if you can get any more information on what the Canadians and Russians are talking about. Work your backchannels. General, keep an eye on the Chinese fleet, and get our forces in Hawaii out in front of them." She nodded to the group, dismissing them.

After they left, she collapsed in her chair, scrubbing her hands over her face.

"Madam President?" Levi spoke softly, and his footfalls over the carpet were gentle.

"Can you give me some good news, Levi?" Her hands fell to the chair arms. "Please tell me you have information on the mole."

His eyes pinched, and his expression went tight. He shook his head. "I've been going over Scott's notes. He went through the Secret Service again. Combed through all of us. I'm doing it again, to be sure."

She bit her lip, frowning.

"I'm starting with everyone on the plane when the president was in Russia for the funeral. Who could have smuggled the photos out of Russia and back to the US? Put them in his bag?"

When Jack had returned from Evgeni Konnikov's state funeral in Russia, photos of him overseas—in the private spaces of the Kremlin—had appeared in his duffel, marked with Madigan's signature: an M circled in red. Usually done in blood, but on the photos, it had been a red marker. A sign, a signal that Jack wasn't safe, not even in the White House. A dangerous warning from Madigan, something they all saw too late, putting the pieces together only after Leslie's attempt on Jack's life.

She peered at Levi, studying him. She trusted him, more than she trusted anyone else in the White House. He slept feet from her every night. Why hadn't she shared the last bit of information with him? Why was she holding back?

It was Madigan's last gift: a virulent distrust of everyone. It was like a virus, a palpable sickness that hung in the air. She saw it in the eyes of everyone who spoke to her. Could they even trust her? Could she trust them in return? This was no way to run a government or a nation. They'd crumble from within, fast, and Madigan or Moroshkin wouldn't have to fire a shot. Or ignite the sky.

"Levi," she said, sitting forward. She braced her elbows on the desk and looked him in the eye. "There's something else. Something I haven't told you."

Levi froze. He stared at her, not blinking.

"When Jack called, he told me there were more photos that Ethan had found at Madigan's old base. When Ethan found out the truth about Leslie Spiers."

"Photos of what?"

"Jack and Ethan, here in the White House. Surveillance-style photos. Someone taking pictures from inside. In the West Wing. Outside the Residence. In their private time, of their private lives."

Levi hissed and spun away, his hands clenching as he paced before the Resolute desk. She watched him, tracking his movements for two turns before she spoke again. "The people who have that kind of access to the White House are limited."

Levi nodded. He tipped his head back. "Unrestricted West Wing and White House access? It's not a long list."

"Can you run through the background of the White House staffers who have that level of clearance?"

"I already started. I'll take it deeper, though."

"What about executive staff? Advisors, officers, cabinet positions?"

"Looking at them, too. But—" He stopped. Pressed his lips together. "Who could have put the pictures both in the president's duffel and taken photos of him during off time? In private spaces?"

It was her turn to stay quiet.

He sighed, shaking his head. "It feels like a Secret Service agent," he breathed. "*We* have that kind of access. And it was mostly agents on the flight to Russia. It was a lean crew. But a big force of agents. Scott's orders."

She closed her eyes. Unease slid down her spine, and distrust choked her throat. "Who do we trust, Levi?"

Was Levi trustable, even?

"I don't know," he said softly.

WELBY'S EYES FLICKED DOWN the hall, watching as Levi slipped out of the Oval Office. He frowned. Levi's suit was rumpled, and his normally impeccable appearance was noticeably off. Like he'd been sleeping in his clothes, and not sleeping very well at that. Deep lines had burrowed into Levi's face almost overnight, two cratering frown lines across his forehead and two bracketing his downturned lips. It was strange to see Levi, normally upbeat and always ready with a smile, scowling all the time.

Though there hadn't been many smiles since the blast. Since the president's assassination.

Welby swallowed slowly and forced the memories out of his mind. He focused on the wall, on the butter-yellow paint and a dark handprint, a smudge left by someone leaning carelessly against the wall.

Levi headed his way, blinking hard. "Welby," he said, speaking low. "I've got to run down to Horsepower. No one goes in the Oval Office until I'm back."

Welby nodded. Levi moved down the hall, heading for the stairs taking him to the White House basement and the Secret Service's bunker.

His eyes darted back to the Oval Office. Levi had been spending a lot of time with President Wall. Granted, he'd become the new detail lead, the president's personal body man. But he rarely left Wall's side, and if he did, like now, he always left her behind closed doors, secured... and cut off from everyone else.

It was almost enough to make someone wonder. President Spiers and Ethan had been like that in the beginning, spending too much time together, and alone. But Ethan had never sequestered Spiers away. Kept him from everyone else.

What was going on?

"What the *fuck*?"

His thoughts were cut off by Levi's shout, coming from down the hall between the Press Secretary's office and the Cabinet Room. A thump, and then a crash, and Welby took off, running toward the noise. He had his weapon out, raised and ready to fire, before his first step.

A lamp lay on the floor, the shade crumpled and flaring skyward, like an old-time dress flipped back to reveal the hoop skirt and petticoats. A vase of flowers, white lilies and tulips—funeral flowers—had crashed to the carpet, water spilled everywhere, stems and crushed petals scattered over the tan rug.

And Pete Reyes had Levi shoved up against the wall, both his hands fisted in Levi's suit jacket. Pete's face was only millimeters from Levi's, and he hissed, fury shaking his voice and his words. "*Where is he?*"

"What the fuck are you talking about?" Levi tried to push Pete off.

Pete wouldn't budge. "Where is Scott Collard?"

Levi frowned.

Welby stuttered, freezing.

"He disappeared after the bombing at Langley. Ethan's *best friend!*" Pete shouted. "Where the fuck is he?"

"Personal leave!" Levi barked. He shoved at Pete again. "Last warning. Let me go. *Now*."

"Personal leave," Pete snarled. "*Bullshit!* Personal leave with Ethan, right? Both of them in 'deep mourning'? Hiding from the world?"

Levi's dark eyes flashed, and Welby knew it was over. Levi twisted, slipping his leg between Pete's before sweeping Pete's legs out from beneath him and hurling him to the ground. Levi leaned over and grasped Pete's throat, pushing him down and holding him there, a blatant show of dominance. "You don't know what the fuck you're talking about," he hissed.

Pete stared up at Levi. Lying on the White House West Wing carpet, stained shirt untucked, tie loose and rumpled, Pete looked like a drunk after a long night in Atlantic City. It was pathetic. Welby almost felt sorry for him.

"I know something's going on." Pete's eyes blazed. "I know it. I fucking *know* it, Levi. Where is Ethan? He wouldn't just vanish like this!"

Levi stood, shaking his head. Disgust flowed off him. "You need to take some time off and get your head straight. Accept what's what."

"Where's Scott Collard?" Pete stayed on the ground, on his back. "Where is Agent Scott Collard?"

Levi stepped over him. "Scott's with Ethan." He gave Welby a withering glare before he turned down the stairwell, heading to the lower level.

Pete closed his eyes, sighing. He didn't move. Didn't try to stand or pick himself up off the floor.

Welby held out his hand. "Come on, Mr. Reyes. Get up."

"Where is Agent Scott Collard?" Pete opened his eyes.

The bleakness in his gaze was a punch to Welby's gut, a hand that reached out and grasped his throat, choking him. Pete's bloodshot eyes had lost their bright sparkle.

Pete had been the perfect choice for Spiers's press secretary. He was just like the president, quick and sharp and more than a little mischievous. Pete had played with the press, and they loved him for it, the verbal give-and-take making the briefing room a lively, spunky place. He liked the press, enjoyed the game, and respected them... to a point. Pete had been like a rampaging tiger when defending Spiers and his relationship with Ethan.

When the president had joined the press briefings each Friday when he was trying to loosen up and be more approachable, the two together had been DC's best amateur comedy hour, playing off each other with so much warmth and respect.

This emptiness, the rawness, the desperation in Pete, was *wrong*.

Welby leaned down, helping Pete sit up. He opened his mouth, the line they had all been given about Scott's sudden personal leave after the blast on the tip of his tongue.

But it wouldn't come out.

Where *was* Ethan? Where *had* Scott disappeared to? Why was Levi keeping the president behind closed doors at all times, never leaving her side? Why hadn't a decision been made about President Spiers yet? Keep him on life support indefinitely, or let him go naturally? Where were his parents? The nation was on eggshells, waiting every day for news from the hospital. Why was everything so tight-lipped? Where was Ethan to do the Jackie Kennedy and help bind the nation together?

Damn it, they *needed* Ethan.

Where *was* he?

He held on to Pete's elbow as he helped him stand. Pete swayed on his feet, one hand on his head, and moaned. "Fuck, I wish I could sleep."

Welby squeezed Pete's arm until Pete turned to him with a frown.

"I don't know where Scott is," he breathed. "And I don't know what's going on either."

22

Sevoukuk, Alaska

"WHERE THE *FUCK* ARE WE?" Doc's backpack slid off his shoulder and hit the mud, splattering thick sludge over his boots and cargo pants.

The rest of the team stayed quiet, surveying their dismal surroundings.

"There are animal skins hanging from that… what the fuck is that? A jungle gym built by a drunk? Out of wooden poles?"

Doc was on a roll. Adam sighed. He felt Faisal at his side, the warmth of his body. He tried not to lean against him.

"Those are fucking bones!" Doc shouted. "Jesus Christ! What the hell kind of bones are those? Dinosaur bones? Loch Ness monster bones?"

"Fuckin' alien bones, Doc," Ruiz said, shoving his shoulder into Doc's and grinning.

Adam sent Ruiz a glare, and Coleman clapped his hand on the younger Marine's shoulder, squeezing hard enough for Ruiz to wince. Doc was enough of one mouth for the entire team.

"Whalebones," Adam finally said. "This is an Inuit village. They're subsistence hunters and fishers. They are still allowed to hunt whales as part of their tribal activities. They use the bones," he said, gesturing to what the team had thought were wooden beams, the outlines of structures that looked like homes, jungle gyms, and buildings, "to build. And yes, skins as well."

Doc glared at him. "Do they have a banjo or four?"

Adam fixed Doc with a hard stare.

Doc's mouth clicked shut.

"Wait here," Adam growled. "I'm going to get us some wheels."

"I will come with you." Faisal fell into step beside him.

A heavy silence, pregnant with a thousand unsaid words, choked-back chuckles, and quick, darting glances, filled the air behind Adam as he and Faisal walked away. Something heavy hit the mud, and Park cursed. Coleman's bark echoed behind them, bellowing at one of the team. "Shut your mouth!"

Adam breathed in and out. His heart hammered, racing so fast it ached. Was enough blood going to his head? He was dizzy, almost lightheaded.

"It will be all right," Faisal spoke softly. "It will, Adam."

"I wish I had your faith," Adam whispered. "What have I done?"

Faisal stayed quiet.

They trudged up the muddy road toward the center of town. Behind him, the propeller plane that had taken them all from frozen Nome, Alaska, turned around on Sevoukuk's single runway and started taxiing for takeoff. Sevoukuk was a forgotten spit of land on a forgotten island, far out in the reaches of the Bering Sea. Once part of the Navy in World War II, and then connected to the Cold War's efforts, the island had long been abandoned. The Inuit, accustomed to living on the island on their own, had taken to their newfound freedom with glee.

Sevoukuk was a mix of claptrap trailers and whalebone huts, hanging animal skins drying, and neon Goodwill donations. Snow clung to the sides of the mud roads, and heavy black waves broke along the rocky sea wall, sending below-freezing water spraying into their faces. Only a few hundred people inhabited the village.

Eyeballs tracked their movement, their long walk from the airfield to the town. Men sat in chairs around a trashcan fire, smoking. Their faces were wide and tanned, lined from exposure to the sun and the harsh winters above the Arctic Circle. Most had gray hair, though Adam guessed they were all in their forties. A harsh life, taken out on the body.

Four-wheelers sat in the road, parked in haphazard order like the drivers just stopped and hopped off. A line of beer bottles sat on a fence across the road. Shotguns leaned against the side of the chairs the men sat in.

Adam's hackles rose. He flared his shoulders, straightened his back. Faisal slid closer, just a hair.

"*Qanuippit?*" One of the men waved, smiling.

"*Ullukuut*," another said with a nod.

Adam's spine uncoiled. He smiled back. "Hey there. My friends and I are here to study some bears. The brown bear, and hopefully we can even see a polar bear." He grinned. "We're looking for some wheels. Do you have any ATVs that I can rent?"

The men shared long looks over the trash fire. "Bears are no camping experience. You boys are looking for trouble if you're going after bears."

"We're academics. We're just doing a field study. Nothing crazy."

"The other academics came with big helicopters. Lots of equipment. Lots of people." He stared at Adam, his eyebrows raised.

"Yeah, we're a smaller organization. Just looking for some basic research, really."

One of the men said something in their language, and the others barked out a laugh. Adam smiled with them. "We won't be here long. Just need a way to get around the island."

"You can have these." The oldest man pointed to the four ATVs in the street. Mud covered, they once were green and black, but were now a mottled shade of speckled brown. "They're even fueled up."

Adam dug in his pocket. "How much?"

The man waved him off. "Your money is no good here. Keep it. Search and Rescue will take it from you after they find your remains."

He smiled tightly. "Thanks. I think we'll be all right, though."

One of the others unloaded chains from the back of an ATV and started stringing them together, a make-do towing system that looked more dangerous than even Adam's team could come up with: Marines were the all-time masters of shitty, dangerous ideas.

"Don't worry about bringing them back," the old man said, grinning wide. "They have GPS. We'll go get them wherever you drop."

Were they still being kind, or were they playing with him? Adam just kept grinning. Playing a dumb American had worked for him more than once.

The men finished wrapping lengths of loose chains around the rears of the ATVs, and then gestured for Adam and Faisal to hop on the two leads.

"Thanks," Adam said, hopping on. Faisal slid onto his ATV and zipped up his jacket, almost to his nose. He'd gotten cold in Seattle, and traveling even farther north didn't make him any warmer. In Anchorage, he'd bought a thick, puffy jacket at the airport, and under that, he had the hooded sweatshirt he'd borrowed from Adam on the plane from Seattle.

"Good luck," the old man called. He winked and then waved when Adam revved the engine and pulled out, heading back to the airport.

Doc looked terribly unimpressed when they arrived with the ATVs chained together, but he kept his mouth shut. "Get these unchained," Adam ordered as he hopped off and pulled a map out of his backpack. For days, they'd been moving around the world to get to this island, and soon, to their rendezvous point. The questions from his team had started coming. Where were they going? And why? What was the plan?

And in their eyes, deeper, darker questions shone. He'd have to say something, and soon.

No. Mission first. He pushed everything away, grounding himself with the memory of Faisal's fingers ghosting through his hair.

He plotted out their route quickly and then went back to the team, waiting around the ATVs. "All right, we double up on these. I'll take the lead. We're headed fourteen miles east by southeast, to this cove between Sevoukuk and Sevoonga villages." He pointed to the map and the sheltered bay on the north side of the island. "We stop there."

Silence. He stared them down, waiting for them to question his orders. He'd given them reason to doubt him at the airport, with Faisal. When would everything start to unravel? When would they stop listening to him? When would the team crumble?

No one spoke.

"When we're there, start setting up camp." They each had a sleeping bag in their backpacks, a tarp, and the basics for living in the field. Doc had his med kit, and Coleman and Wright each carried a false-bottom bag of

Faisal's with their disassembled and untraceable weapons. "Full brief when we're settled in. I know you all want answers. You'll get them soon."

Nods, and then they broke apart, doubling up for the ATVs.

Adam saw his problem immediately.

Coleman grabbed Doc, hauling him by his neck over to one ATV. Wright and Park were fiddling with another, and Ruiz and Kobayashi on the third. He and Faisal were going to be riding together, it seemed. He passed Faisal his backpack and slid into the front of the ATV. Faisal hopped on behind him, settling in at his back, and his arms wound around Adam's waist.

Ohh, that was too close to familiar for comfort. Too close to having Faisal pressed against his back in a whole other way.

He revved his ATV and throttled hard, opening up the engine with a roar. His tires spun, and he spat mud and snow behind him in long arcs, sliding a bit before gunning forward. He kept going, speeding ahead, and listened to the roar of his teammates following behind.

Faisal laid his head on Adam's shoulder and held on tight.

When they passed the village and got over to the east side of the island, where it was rolling hills of mud and patches of snow, Adam dropped one hand and laced his fingers through Faisal's.

THEY SET UP CAMP on a flat patch of mud overlooking the bay. Black waves rolled up on the rocky beach, dark basalt boulders like something from another world. The sky overhead was gray and gloomy, a drab slate of mottled steel. Snow clung to the ground in patches, but mostly it was a sucking, oozing mud, frigid when it slipped through their boots. Down the island another two miles, there was a lagoon and an inlet, but they steered clear of those beaches. Walruses hung out there, and bears.

They cleared the snow and rocks from the ground, and then laid tarps out in a wide rectangle. They tied another to two logs they scavenged from the boulders and propped them up in the mud, making a rough lean-to. There was enough room for them all to sleep side by side, huddled close for warmth.

Faisal slid his sleeping bag next to Adam's. No one said a word.

Doc wheedled his way out of camp setup by collecting firewood and starting a fire. Faisal reassembled their weapons, all of their rifles and pistols. Adam unpacked his sat phone, and the rest of the team pulled out their extreme cold weather, ultra-thick neoprene dry suits. Designed for diving in freezing waters, Adam had ordered one for everyone before they left. Faisal had picked up the tab.

He pulled Faisal aside, stepping away from the camp. "Hey…" He kicked the dirt, rolling pebbles beneath the toe of his boot. "Uh, I thought you should know. East is that way." He pointed down the island, into the gloom. Faisal would need to know the direction of Mecca when he prayed.

Faisal smiled softly. "Thank you." He turned away.

"Wait." Adam grabbed his elbow, stilling Faisal. "Could you… could you come get me? When it's time to pray?"

"Why?" Faisal frowned as he breathed his question.

"I just want to be there. Be with you." He swallowed hard and kicked the dirt again. A tuft of moss rolled off the top of his boot. "I want to pray with you again," he finally whispered.

"In front of your team?" Faisal's eyes went wide. "What will they think? What will they say?"

"I don't care—"

"Adam, you're not even Muslim."

He looked away, glaring into the sea. "It helps, all right? Being close to you. Praying together. And—" He shook his head. "I need that right now."

Faisal stared at him as if he were a puzzle, a riddle he couldn't quite figure out. *Don't give up on me. Please, don't give up on me.*

Finally, Faisal nodded. "*Salat al-'Asr* is in a few hours. I will find you."

Adam smiled thinly. He headed back for the main campsite, and the small fire Doc had started.

"All right, everyone gather around." He rubbed his hands together, trying to warm them and find something to do with his nerves. This was it. The secret that had been burning a hole in his brain.

His team packed it in close. Marines weren't afraid of body contact, not when it was cold. Doc pushed himself into Coleman's side. The sergeant, a big man with shoulders the size of a semi-truck, rolled his eyes and wrapped one arm around Doc's thin body.

"You're probably wondering why we're out here in the middle of fucking nowhere." Everyone nodded. Doc snorted. "We've been detailed on another mission by Director Reichenbach. Yes, he's still in command," he said, as his guys frowned. "We're still on the hunt for Madigan. Even more so now."

He gave a quick rundown of Madigan's movements into the Arctic and his plans to pump the atmosphere full of methane hydrate, enough to ignite a firestorm that would burn across the world, incinerating everything on the surface. His team's expressions moved from shock to disbelief to dumbfounded rage.

"I thought we were coming out here to fight the Russians in Canada," Wright said. He shook his head, struggling to find something to say. "Why just us? Why are we here? What, are we swimming to Russia?"

Adam shook his head. "Madigan's still got people on the inside. In the White House, somewhere where his people learned about us. That's why Fitz was killed. Madigan is deep inside everything. They hit us, and they hit the president."

Stricken faces all around. His team looked torn between puking and tearing the island apart, the first step in ripping apart the world, looking for

Fitz's killer and the traitor who had betrayed everyone, from the president to their little team.

"We can't trust anyone. Not anyone in SOCOM right now. No one in DC. We're on our own, other than Reichenbach."

"Who is Reichenbach getting his orders from?" Coleman frowned and crossed his massive arms. "Has he gone rogue, too?"

Swallowing, Adam shook his head. "What the world has been told about the president's condition… is a lie." He took a deep breath. "President Spiers is alive. And he's not in the US. He's working with Reichenbach, or, more like Reichenbach and he are working together again. They've teamed up with the Russian insurgency, and they're headed up to the Arctic to take Madigan out. The plan is once Madigan is out, the deposed Russian president can take back his country and stop the Canadian situation before it gets worse. We're rendezvousing with them. With the president, Reichenbach, and the Russian insurgency."

Jaws dropped. Doc whistled. Coleman's eyes almost bugged out of his head. Ruiz shook his head left and right like he was trying to shake something off. Wright stared over the crashing waves, cursing under his breath. Kobayashi rubbed his hands over his face. Park stood still with his legs spread, staring down at the ground, his face hidden.

"Wait, rendezvousing with them? *Where?*" Doc spread his arms wide, gesturing to the emptiness surrounding them on all sides. "*How?* Are the Russians coming to America?"

Adam smiled. "It'll be amazing for you, Doc. Everything you love most."

Doc slumped and tipped his head back, groaning.

"I'm waiting for the call." He waved the sat phone. "We're a little early, but I don't think we'll be here more than two days. I want to inventory our food and water. We need to make it last. And get changed into your dry suits. When we go, we're going fast. Make sure you're ready. Weapons clean and ready to go, dry suits on. Doc, I want a rundown of your pack and a full inventory. Everyone, make sure you rest. This will be our last chance to catch our breath before we're on the move. We'll be going until this ends, one way or the other." He looked over his team. They stared back, no longer joking, no longer laughing. "Questions?"

Eyes slid sideways toward Faisal, standing aside from the group. Adam refused to squirm. He stared his team down, even though his stomach was shredding apart and his spine felt like it was liquefying.

"A word in private, L-T?" Coleman finally grunted.

He nodded. "The rest of you, get going. Sergeant?"

Coleman jerked his head away from the group, toward the boulder beach. Adam followed him down and tried to swallow his screaming heart.

23

Washington DC

WELBY WAITED UNTIL LEVI was out of Horsepower and back with President Wall in the Oval Office. When Levi went back in with the president, he had Scott's laptop under his arm and a stack of folders that he held in a tight fist.

Welby radioed for Keifer to take over his post, and then he slipped down to the ground level and headed for Horsepower.

He badged his way in, entering his code and ducking into the dim office. Some agents sat at desks, typing up reports on laptops. Intel agents interfaced with Headquarters on H Street. On the big screen, a gigantic digital map of the White House showed glowing dots moving around like ants, labeled with the codenames of the people the Secret Service were detailed to protect. Three agents racked out in the back, sleeping in the bunks against the far wall.

No one played basketball, like they used to all the time. The foam ball and plastic hoop were forgotten.

The air was heavy, filled with rancid bile. Failure. Recrimination. They'd let their president be hit, be taken out. It was their main job, and they'd failed.

Shame slicked up each of their backs like a painted stripe, a mark of failure. *Yes, I'm a Secret Service agent,* Welby imagined saying. *Yes, I was there when President Spiers was killed.*

I carried his body out of the rubble.

Welby headed for the front, for the big desk. For four administrations, Agent Hoffer had run the detail and sat at the big desk. Ethan had been his handpicked successor.

What had happened to them all? How had they gone from twenty years under Hoffer to cycling through three detail leads before one term was up? How had this happened? How had they all come apart?

He sat down, smoothing his tie. No one paid him any attention.

He logged into the system. At his fingertips was everything in the Secret Service surveillance archives. Hours and hours of tapes, all of the footage from the White House. For a moment, he didn't know what to search for. What was he even doing? What would he hope to find?

Ethan. That was the first question. Where was Ethan?

He hadn't come back to the White House after Sochi. Welby didn't blame him. How could Ethan have shared the White House with Leslie back in President Spiers's life?

On the flight back from Russia, he'd seen Ethan go to Scott's office on Air Force One, carrying a duffel bag. And then he'd heard him, sobbing like he'd lost everything. Like his heart had been destroyed.

Had that been the end? Was Ethan just *gone*? Had the president really died, and were he and Ethan already through, already broken up? After the reveal of Leslie's status as a clone and an assassin, the nation had turned their support back to Ethan, a near-overwhelming show of love and solidarity for the first gentleman they had once decried. Where had that kind of affection and support been before, when the two men needed it?

No, White House tapes wouldn't help him find Ethan.

Scott, then. The last he'd seen of Scott had been running through Bethesda Naval Hospital, running alongside Jack's gurney and the doctors as they rushed him into emergency surgery. Jack had come to, almost in a fit, just before the surgery. He'd screamed for Ethan. Tried to rise. Flailed when he was held down, like an animal caught in a trap. Even his eyes had been wild, inhuman. The memory haunted Welby at night and every time he closed his eyes.

What had happened that day, the president's last day?

He wound back the tapes until he found when he woke Spiers during the night, bringing him out of the White House and to Lawrence Irwin as Leslie had been taken down, captured for being the mole she was. He went further back, to the afternoon. President Spiers had spent the day in his West Wing study, sometimes reading. Sometimes staring into space. Sometimes holding one of the framed pictures of him and Ethan, gazing down at the glass like it was a crystal ball.

Before that, then. He rewound, and then stopped. Held his breath as he watched. He played the clip over and then rewound it again.

Spiers had gone down to Horsepower that day.

Welby watched him on the video knocking on Horsepower's door, wearing a sweatshirt that was too big for him, REICHENBACH stenciled across the back in blue. Ethan's Secret Service sweatshirt.

Welby watched Scott poke his head out and scowl at the president. Watched Spiers plead with Scott to talk to him. Christ, Scott had taken *that* tone with the president. Granted, Ethan was his best friend, but still.

He fished out a pair of headphones from the desk and plugged them in. Leaning forward, he zoomed in on Scott and the president, peering at them on the screen.

Welby pressed play again.

"Where's Ethan?"

Scott looked away.

"Please, Scott. Where is he? I've been trying to call him, but he's not answering."

Scott glared at the wall. "Why do you want to call him? Just to tell him it's over? Give yourself closure? Trust me, he knows. He doesn't need you to twist the knife any deeper."

"God, no!" The president ran his fingers through his hair and gripped the back of his skull. "That's not it at all! Scott—"

"Why are you wearing his sweatshirt?"

"Because it's the closest I can get to him right now. I'm falling apart, and I need him—"

"You can't just use him like that—"

"Damn it, Scott!" Spiers shouted, his hands fisted in his hair again. He spun, gasping, and glared at Scott. "Damn it, I'm not trying to use him! I'm trying to bring him home! I just told Leslie that I couldn't be with her because I love Ethan. And because he's it. He's the one for me. I want to grow old with him. Spend forever with him. I want everything with Ethan."

Scott stared, his jaw hanging open. After a moment, his eyes squeezed closed. "Goddamn it, Mr. President."

"Please," the president pleaded. "Where is he?"

"I don't know." Slumping, Scott leaned back against the White House basement wall and pinched the bridge of his nose. "He was staying at my place. I came home and he was gone."

"Gone?"

"Gone. Left his cell and his wallet." Scott's eyes narrowed as he chewed on his lip. "Irwin wanted to know where he was that day. I think he went to see him."

"Irwin. Lawrence. Okay. So… he's probably on a mission, then. Black bag. Compartmentalized." He squinted at Scott. "Right?"

"I guessed the same."

"Okay." Spiers closed his eyes, slowly pacing in front of Scott. "I'll talk to Irwin. See what's going on. I don't want to interrupt if… if it's something dangerous."

"Here." Scott dug in his suit pants. "I've been holding on to it. In case he calls or something. I don't know." He held out Ethan's cell phone.

The president took the phone and turned on the screen. "At least he's not deliberately ignoring me."

Scott stared, frowning. "Are you certain?" he growled. "Ethan loves you more than you know, and this is tearing him apart. If you're not absolutely certain, dead sure, about this, it will break him." Scott's jaw clenched. "He's like a brother to me. I don't want to see him like this again."

"I'm one hundred percent certain. It's him. Forever."

"When he gets back," Scott growled, "don't fuck this up, Mr. President."

Welby replayed the tape, back to the beginning, when Spiers first knocked on Horsepower's door. He watched the president pace, watched his frustration build, his face fall. Watched him declare his love for Ethan to Scott, his passion-filled cry that Ethan and Ethan *alone* was the one for him, the one in his heart. Christ, they loved each other so deeply. Ethan had been absolutely *gone* for the man. Seeing Spiers come undone for Ethan soothed that niggling part of Welby's brain that had always wondered if Ethan had given up too much. If he was too invested, and the president wasn't all in, all the way.

He seemed all in on the video, though. Desperate to find Ethan. He was wearing his sweatshirt around the White House, even.

And then:

"Irwin. Lawrence. Okay. So... he's probably on a mission, then. Black bag. Compartmentalized." He squinted at Scott. *"Right?"*

"I guessed the same."

Lawrence Irwin. President Spiers's deceased chief of staff. The same man who had called Welby that night and ordered him to arrest Leslie Spiers and bring the president down to the basement, to him. Irwin had been the one to discover her true identity. He'd investigated, tracked down her claims. He used a source, he'd said. Boots on the ground that had found the lab she'd been grown in. The base from which Madigan had trained her.

Boots on the ground. Ethan disappearing with Irwin, days before the truth about what she was came out.

It would be just like Ethan to throw himself into a mission, after heartbreak. He'd do anything for the president, absolutely anything. Even go to the ends of the earth, trying to find out if Spiers's back-from-the-dead wife was telling the truth.

If he could just talk to Irwin, he'd get everything. Where Ethan had gone, where Madigan's base had been. What happened, after finding the lab. But Irwin was six feet underground, buried days ago after giving his life to protect the president in the blast at Langley.

His sacrifice had been for nothing, in the end. President Spiers was still never waking up again. As good as dead. Already, people spoke about him in the past tense. Used phrases like *successful assassination attempt* and *former president*.

Levi's words came back to him, a vicious slap that smacked up the back of his head: *Scott's with Ethan.*

But, if Ethan wasn't secluded in mourning, and if he'd been on a black mission for Irwin somewhere in the world, then where, *actually*, was he? And where was Scott?

He watched the last moments of the video play again: Scott handing the president Ethan's cell phone in grainy slow motion.

PETE EXPECTED IT WHEN Jennifer and Jason showed up at his office later that morning.

News of his scuffle with Levi had made the rounds. Never underestimate the White House gossip factory. If you needed *everyone* to know something, fucking lightning fast, just drop word in the West Wing. Even with the reduced staff that they had, the ultra-tight security after Leslie, and after Jack—

No. Don't say it. Don't think it.

Damn it, in this den of loose lips, how could he not find what he was looking for?

What if there was nothing to find? What if Jack really was... *gone*? Ethan, too?

Pete sat slumped at his desk, his head buried in his hands, when soft knocks sounded on his door.

"Go away," he groaned into his palms.

"No. Not this time." Jennifer slipped into his office, her sundress swishing around her knees. "Pete... *Please*. Let us in. Let us help you."

He sat back, scowling. He wouldn't meet her gaze.

Jason hovered at the door, biting his lip. "Pete. What's going on? You're fighting with the Secret Service?"

He threw himself back in his chair, huffing, and gripped the armrests. His hands shook. "They're hiding something!"

"They're not hiding anything!" Jennifer perched on the edge of his desk and reached for his hands. "Pete, they're *not*. At least, not what you think. It's just the attack. Everyone's locking down. This is the White House. You know how it is. This is a crazy time."

He stared at her.

"Pete, everyone's on edge. We're practically at war. And you're running around throwing Secret Service agents into the wall?" She bit her lip and shook her head. "You're going to lose your job. Or worse. Do you *want* to be thrown in jail?"

"They need you in the press room. Dillon, he's being eaten alive." Jason sighed, slouching against the doorframe and crossing his arms. Dillon was Pete's deputy, a young Ph.D. student working his first job out of grad school. He was supposed to cut his teeth beneath Pete, but instead, he was stammering through updates as the world waited to see when war would break out over the North Pole and when the Russians would knock down their northern border. When missiles would fall on American cities. "We need you, Pete. We need you back."

Jennifer reached for him, resting one hand on his cheek. She turned his head until he had no choice but to look up at her. "We all miss them. Both of them. We're all in mourning." A tear slipped down her cheek, and she wiped it away with the back of her hand. "But we have to keep going. For them."

He closed his eyes. Leaned into her hand, her touch. Swallowed. "This *can't* be real," he breathed. "It can't be happening. They *can't* be gone."

She tried to smile, tried to give him some kind of comfort, but it was tight and strained, and her cheeks were wet with tears. "I wish it weren't."

What if there was nothing to find because there was nothing to hide? Was he one of those conspiracy theorists ranting and raving about the government always keeping secrets? Had he turned into one of those shaggy-haired guys, always muttering about secrets and subterfuge and glaring at shadows? Waiting for black helicopters to hover over his house?

He didn't want to say goodbye. He didn't want Jack's legacy to end in a bomb blast. *Assassinated.* His friend. *Assassinated.*

Pete breathed in. "I—"

Knocking at the door made him clamp his lips shut. He looked up.

Welby stood in the doorway, his piercing eyes burning into Pete, blazing even from across the room.

Pete stood. "What's up, Agent Welby? Everything okay?" Maybe Welby was there to escort him out of the White House. Not like he could blame the Secret Service, if they chose to do so. He straightened up and tried to tuck in his wrinkled button-down. How many days had he worn this shirt?

Welby's eyes darted from Jason to Jennifer. "It's about this morning."

He sighed. "I'm sorry for my behavior. I'm… I'm going to take Agent Daniels's suggestion. Take some time." He swallowed.

"Not that." Welby stared him down, not blinking. "Not that, Pete."

His blood froze, going quicksilver in his veins. Vindication, and a rush of relief, giddy joy, burst within him. He almost couldn't breathe. "What did you find?"

Welby looked from Jason to Jennifer again, pointedly. Both were frowning, confusion etched on their furrowed faces, their gazes bouncing between the two of them like watching a ping-pong match.

"They're solid. I trust them." He nodded. "What's going on? What did you find?"

Welby gave one last look to Jason and Jennifer before shutting the door behind him and crossing Pete's office. He pulled out a folded photo, printed from Horsepower, and set it on Pete's desk.

It was a surveillance image, Scott and Jack captured talking in the lower level hallway outside Horsepower. Jack had on Ethan's sweatshirt. Pete's heart clawed up his throat, screaming, as he gazed at the photo, at his friend.

"President Spiers and Agent Collard?" Jennifer frowned at the photo.

"This was taken the day the president was attacked. He and Scott talked… about Ethan. The president was trying to find him."

"Jack didn't even know where he was?" Pete's hands went to his hips. His friends always called that his thinking pose.

Welby shook his head. "*He* didn't. But Scott *did*. He said Ethan was staying at his place, but Irwin had wanted to see him. And then Ethan disappeared. And, Irwin was the one who sent someone to find out the truth." Welby pointed at the photo. "Irwin sent *Ethan*."

"Ethan found out about Leslie being a clone..." Jennifer deflated, exhaling and covering her hand with her mouth.

"Which means—" Jason rubbed his fingers against his thumb as if his thoughts were moving just as fast. "Jesus, Ethan couldn't have been in the States when she attacked Jack. He's not even here now."

Welby nodded. He turned back to Pete. "And what did Levi say? 'Scott's with Ethan'? Where? Overseas? If so, why did Scott leave the US? Why did he go to Ethan?"

His thoughts were going too fast, too many possibilities. Government secrets, government cover-ups. He'd always scoffed at the conspiracy theorists, but damn it, he really was one of those paranoid men. What was true? What was really happening?

"And," Welby said, pulling out another photo and unfolding it on Pete's desk. In this image, Scott passed Jack a cell phone. "Scott gave the president Ethan's phone. I pinged its location. Where do you think it went off?"

"*Not* a hospital in Bethesda?" Pete practically hyperventilated.

"It came back with its location blocked. Someone has put a scatter block on his phone, routing his data access through proxies across the globe."

"Couldn't his phone just be off?" Jennifer chewed on her lip, but hope shone in her eyes.

"The ping would come back different if it was off. Or out of power. It would come back as not found. Not scatter blocked. Not like this."

"So..." Jason paled, and he gnawed on his lip. "Where's the phone? Where's the president?"

Pete grinned, his cheeks burning. He tipped his head back, laughing, and pumped his hands in the air. "Yes, damn it, yes! There *is* something going on!" His fist hit his desk hard, sending the photos skittering across the surface. "Jack is *not* gone," he hissed. "We need to find out what's happening. Where he is. And why."

"And Scott and Ethan, too. Where are they? Why did Scott leave and go to Ethan?" Welby plucked the photos from the desk and folded them back into his jacket.

Jennifer spoke in the quiet that followed, spinning on Pete's desk, her dress shifting on the dark wood surface. "What if they're all together?"

24

Russian Far East

Finally, they'd left Siberia behind.

Descending from Siberia, the convoy had passed through the Sakha Republic, the tribal lands of Russia, and then into the Far East, some of the most distant lands of the Russian Federation. They'd also turned south, heading for Sakhalin Island and the Sea of Okhotsk. From there, it was only a boat ride to Simushir Island.

The snows had tapered out, and only patches of ice and muddy slush clung to the pockmarked and potholed roadways. It was just above freezing, hovering in the balmy spring temperatures of the upper thirties. The Russian members of the convoys had shed their jackets and sweaters and were just in shirtsleeves. Jack, Ethan, and Scott were still bundled up.

The miles wore on. Sergey insisted on driving most of the way, in the jeep he shared with Scott and Sasha. Rain slicked their windows, washing away the muddy snowpack. Dilapidated buildings and broken factories dotted the distance. Overhead, the sky was lead-colored, soaked with ever-present Russian rain. Vladivostok, and the region around the formerly grand naval port, had fallen into disrepair, abandoned to the winds and the rain. No wonder the regiments there had fled during the coup. A few mothballed squadrons of Sukhois and a handful of destroyers that nervously watched the Chinese, surrounded by daily reminders that 'New Russia' was a joke. Vladivostok was nothing like what she once had been, back in the days of the Soviet Union.

But bitterness about the "good old days" was what Moroshkin fed his troops with. The Soviet Union was gone. The oligarchic kleptocracy that had followed was gone, too, thanks to his anti-corruption purge. 'New Russia' was still trying to find herself. He'd tried to guide her forward, but…

Enough. Sergey couldn't keep thinking this way, his thoughts swirling down the drain of self-recrimination. *Think of something new.*

He scowled into the rearview mirror. Sasha sat in the backseat, his head tipped back, mouth open. He was snoring, just faintly.

If he wasn't so furious, so torn to pieces, so deeply, irrevocably conflicted, he'd probably think it was endearing.

Who was he kidding? Not himself, not any longer. His heart did soften at the sight, at just the knowledge that Sasha was back. Alive. Near to him again.

So close... and yet, so incredibly far.

No, don't think of this. Not this.

Sasha hadn't said a word to him since the temper tantrum he'd thrown leaving Ust'Ilga. Scott had offered up the front seat of their jeep to Sasha, and before Sasha could say anything, Sergey had jumped in. "He sits in the back!"

Scott had stared. Sasha had gone still.

"I thought you'd want to—"

"*No*. No, you will stay in the front." He'd glared at Sasha. "Someone who stayed when they said they would. Kept their word."

Sasha hadn't met his gaze or looked him in the eye since. Not once.

He'd grumbled something about Sasha also needing to catch up on his rest when they were on the road, but it had been a poor cover for his outburst.

He just didn't know what to feel, or what to think. Or how to do anything about something he didn't—*couldn't*—understand. Whenever he tried, his thoughts lurched to a halt, or plummeted into a blackness that eclipsed any of the self-hatred he piled on himself due to his failed presidency.

Sasha was *back*. The one thing he wanted, more than anything else. More than even being president again. Sasha, *alive*. And there with him.

But he wasn't with him. Not at all. And Sergey only had himself to blame for that.

He *wanted*. He *ached* with want. His bones burned with the pull of his desire, his body and soul desperate to go to Sasha, confess everything in the worst sort of babble, and beg for another kiss. Beg for Sasha's hands on him again. For Sasha to look at him that way that he used to.

But how? How did he even begin to reach out? How did he change fifty-two years of ingrained experience, a lifetime's worth of conditioning? If Sasha were a woman, he'd know what to do. Flirtation was his currency. He'd charmed both his ex-wives into and out of his life. But Sasha was no woman. And he didn't succumb to witty repartee or childish displays of machismo. He deserved more than that.

And even the thought, the impulse to act on his desire, had Sergey scurrying away, scrambling to find excuse after excuse to not act. He had no idea what he was doing. He would only screw it up, screw everything up. Hadn't he ruined Sasha's life enough? Sasha probably didn't even care for him the way Jack claimed he did. One kiss, one emotionally-fraught kiss, did not true love make. Jack was probably wrong.

After all, Sasha had *left* him. When he'd promised, *promised*, that he never would. What did that portend?

All of his thoughts were in disarray. He couldn't imagine it, even if he tried. And he did try. Behind the wheel as he drove, or when Scott insisted on taking a turn, and he sat slumped against the passenger window, glumly staring as rain-soaked Russia passed him by. He tried to picture going up to Sasha and saying something—anything—to confess the state of his heart. But even his imagined words fell flat, a senseless, rambling mumble, and he shamed himself in his own imagination. He tried to recall their kiss, tried to remember every moment, every touch and sensation of Sasha's lips against his own, his body pressed tight to Sergey's. Remembrance turned to dissection, and then brutal self-vivisection. Whatever had happened, it wasn't what he thought it was. Certainly, wasn't what Jack insisted. No, no, Jack was definitely wrong.

How could he be what Sasha desired? The idea was laughable. Fifty-two, the first Russian president to be objectively poor thanks to his commitment to anti-corruption. He had nothing to offer Sasha. No fancy house, no beautiful sports car. He'd been deposed. And he was too skinny. He'd always been rail thin in the FSB, a joke for his friends and colleagues. Too gray. Middle-aged. Sasha was young, in his thirties, and gorgeous. Well-built, broad-shouldered, narrow-waisted, and with a muscled body he took care of, maintained through dedicated exercise. Sergey could remember the last time he smoked more easily than remember the last time he purposely exercised. Sasha could have anyone, anyone at all. He'd never pick an old, skinny, poor man like Sergey. The whole thing was a joke.

He should be focusing on their mission. On the duties at hand. His responsibilities. One thing, and then the next, he'd always said. But *everything* had been consumed with Sasha, every action, every thought, every hope for the future. He was everywhere, in his mind, in his dreams, and before him, even. Slumped in the same jeep, softly snoring away.

Part of him wished he'd never realized the depth of his feelings. Of all that he was capable of. This, whatever it was he felt for Sasha, was different than falling for any of his other loves. His wives had been beautiful, wickedly smart, and dangerous. Emotionally and verbally. Talking to them was like navigating a minefield, and sometimes he plowed right in just to see the explosions. For all that, he'd enjoyed being with them. It had been fun, and he'd been loved, and he'd loved in return. Or at least he thought he had. The love he'd felt hadn't burned as deeply as this.

Never had he been this consumed, this wholly enraptured by another person. The kind of feelings he had for Sasha were different than what he'd had for his wives. They were more intense, and burned hotter, like he'd uncovered a new layer of love, something he hadn't known existed. Had he not truly loved his wives? He truly thought he had. But, set against the enormity of his overwhelming feelings for Sasha, it made him wonder. Was this just another part of what he'd banished, hidden from even his own soul for his whole life? Had he never opened himself up? Had he never found what he actually wanted? Did he, in fact, not know what loving another honestly was?

Was that what these crazy, fucked-up feelings were? The need to grab Sasha and never let go, shake him until tears ran down Sergey's own cheeks, never let him sacrifice his life again, and wrap his arms so tight around Sasha and bury his face in his neck. Kiss him, over and over. Explore his body, learning how to love another all over again, and in a brand-new way.

Sergey scowled into the rearview mirror. Sasha was still sleeping, slumped in the backseat. Still snoring. Still adorable. He wanted to crawl into the back with him and pull him into his arms again, like he had on the drive to Ust'Ilga. When they'd arrived, he had vanished from the jeep before Ethan braked, tumbling from the still-moving vehicle instead of facing Sasha when he woke in Sergey's arms. What did that say about his courage?

He sighed and propped his elbow on the windowsill, resting his head in his hand as he glared at the road. A rusted road sign ahead showed the miles to Vladivostok. Six hours away. They weren't going that far. Maybe half the distance.

If only he could speed up time. Anything to get out of the jeep, and get away from Sasha. If he couldn't go to him, then he'd run in the opposite direction, as fast as he could.

HOURS LATER, THEY FINALLY arrived at Sakhalin Island. The bridge had been bombed, but the tunnel was open, if jammed with cars. They plowed through, shoving abandoned cars out of their way when necessary and winding through the lanes.

They stuck to the northern half of the island, navigating between the tiny village of Nysh and the ghost town of Neftegorsk, decimated decades before in an earthquake and never rebuilt. Oil had hit Sahkalin big, but with the turmoil and the insurgency, Sergey told the others to stay to the narrow, rural mountain roads and keep away from the bigger cities. When disaster struck Russia, opportunists always crawled out of the woodwork. There would be oil smugglers and illegal drilling on Sahkalin. He could feel it in his bones.

On the east coast of the island, they found a cove and an old fishing boat tucked away for the winter. The jeeps had served them well, hauling them across the continent, but it was time to say goodbye. They hid the vehicles and siphoned the fuel out, pumping it all into the boat's tanks, and then into the spare canisters. They carted their weapons, food, and supplies onto the boat.

They worked fast, trying to stay out of sight. Jack and Sergey wore Ethan and Scott's borrowed balaclavas, but they were still taking a large risk being out in the open. It was the closest they had been to civilization since Volga.

In a few hours, they were ready to set out.

Sergey insisted on navigating. He sent everyone else away, down below to the main deck, except for Jack and Ethan, who disappeared with twinkling eyes and wandering hands to the forward cabin. He couldn't begrudge them their happiness, even though they were insufferable. All soft smiles and kisses.

In the main cabin, Vasily heated water for coffee, and Anton broke out two bottles of vodka. They were in high spirits, giddy with the conclusion of their drive, and still celebrating Sasha's return.

When they had arrived back at Ust'Ilga, Sasha alive and well in the jeep, their team had been elated. Joyous. Celebrating in the best Russian traditions, with cheers and shouts and long, emotional declarations from every man to Sasha. He'd been a favorite of the men, a steadfast and reliable right hand to Sergey. The perfect executive officer for an insurgency. Sergey let them celebrate, and skulked off alone to review the map and finalize their route.

The celebration of Sasha was still ongoing, apparently. That was good. Sasha deserved it. They would celebrate better without him, anyway. He stayed on the deck as the sounds of his men roared into the night, laughter and toasts and cheers, and Sasha's low rumble all mixing with the crash of black waves against the hull and the hum of the motor, churning on. Every time he caught Sasha's voice, his deep cadence, his heart sped up, aching for more, and he strained to hear what was said. And then, he chastised himself, furiously bullying his heart back into line. He was far too much of a coward.

It would never be more than what it was—a fractured dream.

IN THE FORWARD CABIN, Ethan slowly undressed Jack, peeling back each layer, dropping kisses to each exposed bit of skin. He pulled everything off, until Jack was naked, gleaming by the light of the moon shining through the porthole.

He washed Jack, dipping a rag in water warmed by Vasily and scrubbing at every inch of his body. He stroked every part, massaged Jack's muscles, and covered him in kisses until Jack was a writhing mess of overwrought nerves, his body loose and warm. He ran the rag over his own body quicker, focused and efficient, and then went to Jack on the bed.

He took his time loving Jack, worshiping him with his mouth. His tongue. He opened Jack leisurely, reveling in the taste, the feel of his lover. The connection, their love rebuilt through touch and breath and gasps, hands clasping for one another and fingers tangling in hair.

When Jack was ready, Ethan lay back on the flat, narrow bed, and Jack climbed on his lap. Lowered himself down, taking Ethan within his body with a sigh and a breathtaking smile. Ethan watched him move, watched the lines of his throat, his neck, his chest. Held his hips and stroked his waist, his back, his ass. Felt them connect, inch by inch, until there was nothing separating them at all any longer.

Jack moved slowly, rolling his hips and his ass over Ethan, until Ethan took over, moving deep within him, from root to tip with every stroke. He wanted to *feel* Jack, feel every micron of him. Press in and in until their skin let their souls slip within each other, merge, and become one.

He sat up, pulling Jack close as he thrust within his body. Kissed his chest, open-mouthed, as Jack's eyes rolled back in his head and his breath faltered, gasping Ethan's name with every press and rock of their bodies as he clung to Ethan, his fingers scratching up his lover's back, his cock rock-hard and pressed between their bellies.

Hands stroked, caressing skin and committing each other to memory. New marks. New bruises. Ethan's scar from the stitches Sergey had given him. Jack's bruises from the fall through the ice, mottled over his ribs. His faint black eye, courtesy of Leslie's blast at the CIA, just a week before. Old marks. Jack's star-shaped scar on his shoulder, the legacy of Ethan's shot fired to save his life. Their lives, as entwined as their bodies, as their legs stroking together, slipping together, wrapping around each other as they kissed and kissed, making slow love for hours.

When they came, Jack lay on his back, open completely to Ethan as Ethan pressed into him, holding his legs wide. Jack's arms wrapped around Ethan's back, around his neck, one hand sliding through his hair as he pulled Ethan close and kissed him through his orgasm, pouring his love, his ecstasy, into the meeting of their lips, the swipes of their tongues.

Ethan gripped Jack's ankles, drove deep into him, deep enough to touch the bottom of Jack's heart, and emptied his own heart into Jack's body, whispering *I love you* over and over.

Spent, they curled together, sweat and their fluids cooling on their skin, arms and legs intertwined, fingers laced together as they gazed into each other's eyes.

Neither said a word. They didn't have to. Their love said it all.

25

Washington DC

"THANK YOU FOR COMING DOWN, Madam President." General Bradford stood as Elizabeth strode into the Situation Room. Director Mori rose beside him, nodding to Elizabeth.

"News on the Chinese fleet?" She stopped behind Jack's chair, resting her elbows on the headrest. Levi shadowed her, standing almost too close, as if he'd have to jump in front of a bullet at any moment.

"No, ma'am. Our other situation." Bradford swiped an image from his tablet to the main screen along the Situation Room wall.

The Swedish weather satellite data appeared, the grainy black-and-white image with the bright fuchsia cloud extending from the Kara Sea and wrapping around eastern Russia.

Except, the cloud had grown. Ugly fuchsia swept across all of eastern Russia, most of China, the Korean peninsula, Japan, and into the Pacific. It was sweeping south, too, fingers of the cloud stretching to Central Asia, Pakistan, and India.

"Shit," she breathed. "It's growing fast."

"It will cover the northern hemisphere in days. The globe, soon after." Bradford swallowed. "If he detonates now, the death toll is estimated to be around four billion. It will only grow from here."

She sighed, dropping her head between her shoulders. *What's your play, Madigan? When are you going to blow the planet? When do you want to murder the entire world?* Slowly, she pulled herself up. "Thank you, General. Keep me updated."

Bradford and Director Mori both nodded.

She headed back to the Oval Office, Levi walking side by side with her. "Do you have the uplink set up?" she asked softly, turning her head toward his.

He nodded. "Let's do it in your private office." He took over the lead, badging the way into the president's private study. It still felt like Jack's. His papers, his clutter, were still all over the place. A leftover jacket over the back of his chair. She couldn't tell if it was Jack's or Ethan's. A picture of Ethan, red-faced and laughing like he was about to pee his pants, framed on Jack's desk next to the computer.

She waited while Levi pulled a sat phone from his jacket, turned it on, and passed it to her. Their eyes met and held, and then Levi went to the door, both standing guard and listening for anyone coming.

Taking a deep breath, she tugged a slip of paper from her pocket and punched in the number.

It rang, and rang, and rang. Cursing, she shared a nervous look with Levi, waiting out another long ring.

And then—

"*Captain Anderson,*" a gruff voice answered.

"Captain, thank God," she breathed, exhaling. "I thought something had happened."

"*It took us longer to surface, Madam President. We picked up some Chinese northern fleet activity. Stayed deep until they had passed out of range.*"

"Yes." She closed her eyes. "Looks like the Chinese are heading our way. Backing up Moroshkin's forces in Canada, most likely."

Captain Anderson was quiet. "*What are our orders, Madam President? We're out here off the coast of Russia. South of Petropavlovsk. Should we turn around and chase those Chinese?*"

"Not just yet. I need you to do something else. Head to Simushir Island, north of Bussol Strait. Make way for the north end of the island, to Broutona Bay. There's a flooded caldera there and an abandoned Soviet nuclear sub base."

She practically heard Captain Anderson blinking over the satellite connection. "*Madam President, what is our purpose at this base?*"

"You're meeting your contact there, Captain. Send a party to shore. They should be there soon if everything went well. Your contact is designated Phoenix One. They're connected to the Russian insurgency." Her eyes drifted to another framed picture: Jack and Ethan staring into each other's eyes, trying hard not to burst into laughter. She remembered that moment, that night. Sergey Puchkov's State Dinner.

"*And what am I doing when I meet with Phoenix One?*"

"Make contact. Provide any and all aid required. And then contact me immediately." Her hand squeezed the sat phone casing, hard enough to make the plastic creak and groan.

"*And if I can't make contact?*"

"Pray that you do, Captain. We need to find Phoenix One, and we need to find him now."

26

Simushir Island - Okhotsk Sea

Dawn broke over the sea, muted sunlight smearing over the horizon, painting the waters with smudged gold and faint periwinkle, wavering colors that bled into the fog-laden sky. Their stolen boat puttered on. Simushir Island loomed ahead, an expanse of loamy granite shrouded in mist and thick fog. Dark volcanic rock made the island seem menacing, and the peak of one volcano disappeared entirely into the leaden cloud bank. If ever there was a super-villain island, Simushir could be its twin.

Sergey yawned at the wheel, blinking hard. He'd been up all night, steering the boat on their heading and keeping them on course. Pouring more fuel into the tank when they ran low. The voices of his men in the main cabin had faded as the hours wore on, until all he heard were snores.

Sergey headed down, looking for leftover coffee. It would be cold, but it also would be caffeinated, and that was what he was in need of. He stepped softly, moving around his sleeping men. Aleksey had passed out halfway up the stair ladder, leaning against the railing, and right in the way. He made it around the sleeping policeman without waking him.

"Good morning."

Sergey almost jumped out of his skin. He whirled, eyes wide.

Sasha stared at him.

He sat at the built-in table in the corner of the cabin, next to the rest of their convoy members, all sleeping, some with their faces on the table, some leaning against each other. Vasily still had his hand on the vodka bottle. Sasha slowly batted his cup of coffee back and forth, sliding it across the plastic tabletop.

"You are not sleeping?" Sergey turned away, his shaking hands searching for leftover coffee.

"I slept the whole drive here." He heard Sasha's exhale. "I am still off. From the crash. From being on the run. I should rest, but my body..." He trailed off, going silent as he pursed his lips and picked at a broken bit of plastic on the table edge.

Sergey swallowed. "Is there any more coffee?" He watched Sasha from the corner of his eye, his gaze tracing over Sasha's body, his arms, down to his hands.

Sasha grabbed one of the men's mugs and poured the contents into his own, then slid his across the table. Plastic on plastic, a scratchy whine. "I could take over. You have been awake all night?"

Sergey snatched Sasha's coffee cup and headed for the ladder. He had to escape, back to the deck and the wheel. "I am fine," he grunted. "We are almost there anyway."

As he climbed, he could feel Sasha's heavy gaze hitting the center of his back. He wanted to squirm, wiggle away, slink over the side of the boat and disappear beneath the black waves. Turn around, go to Sasha and babble, just babble incoherently everything that was tearing apart his heart.

He cleared his throat and kept going, back to the bridge.

Sasha's coffee was as cold as the sea, bitter and biting. He choked it down, watching as Simushir grew closer. When he heard voices rising from the main cabin, he sped up the boat and let the roar of the engine drown out their words.

"HE WAS A GHOST when you were gone, Tati."

Sasha's whole body froze. Slowly, his eyes met Anton's.

Anton smirked, stretching his feet across the bench seat he sat on, across the cabin.

Sasha scowled. He rose, heading for the ladder.

"Tati, Tati. What are you doing? Sit down."

"Why are you calling me that name?" His hands clenched, and he glared at Anton. Tati was short for Tatiana, a woman's name. After everything, he wasn't going to stand for that. Not after drinking with these men for half the night, feeling a part of his soul stitch back together. It had been almost like he'd had friends again. Comrades. That warm, gut-full feeling of camaraderie. He'd missed it so much.

But he wouldn't be a laughingstock. Never.

Anton sighed. He nodded to Sasha, pointing to him. "Tatiana." He pointed above, to where Sergey had disappeared. "Onegin."

Shock slammed into Sasha, like a wave crashing over the side of the boat and drenching him in ice water. Tatiana and Onegin, two lovers doomed to forever be apart. It was Alexander Pushkin's greatest work, the seminal classic of Russian literature. Verses of the poem were recited in every bar, every night, somewhere in the Russian world. With each shot of vodka, the retellings grew more dramatic, the prose more sorrowful.

Anton spoke softly, his voice deep. *"Love's frantic torments went on beating and racking with their strain and stress. That youthful soul, which pined for sadness—"*

"Shut up!" Sasha stormed across the cabin. His fists shook, and a ruby haze washed across his vision. Fury flooded him, a bitter rush of ice that screamed, wailed. "Shut your mouth!"

Anton kept going, watching Sasha come closer. "*Tati, dear, with you I'm weeping for you have, at this early date, into a modish tyrant's keeping resigned disposal of your fate.*"

His eyes squeezed shut, and he turned toward the ladder, grabbing the railing. He almost propelled himself up, almost escaped, but froze. Sergey was up there. What was he escaping to, if he fled? More of Sergey's avoidance, his dark glowers, and his sulking anger?

He gripped the railings, kneading the metal. He almost felt it give, bend beneath his rage. If only. If only he could rip everything apart, and then rebuild it all the way things were supposed to be. Sergey, back as president. Him... anywhere else.

"I have been mocked before," he finally growled. "If you—"

"I'm not mocking you, Sasha." Finally, Anton stood. He came close, pressing his shorter body almost against Sasha's. He searched for the right words, frowning as his lips pursed, his mustache twitched, and his eyes narrowed. He sighed. "Tatiana and Onegin are a tragedy. Onegin figured out too late that he returned Tatiana's love. Tatiana had moved on."

Sasha turned away. He knew all this.

"Sergey lost himself after you were gone. He was a shell. A shadow. We already knew about you, and your feelings for him."

He whipped around, staring at Anton. Shame oozed from his pores, sliding along his skin. Everyone had known. *Everyone*. What had he done? How had he given himself away? He thought he'd hidden everything, dug a hole in his heart and buried his love beneath the crater. Shame rose within him like bile, trying to strangle him, suffocate him. His breath came fast, too fast, through his nose.

Anton reached out, gripping his arm. "Sasha, we've known from the beginning. Since the first night after Sochi. The way you cared for him. The way your whole world revolved around him. He was the center of everything for you. No one is that loyal unless they are truly in love."

He stumbled backward, almost hitting Aleksey on the stair ladder. His legs gave way, and he crashed onto the bottom step, sprawled on his ass as he buried his face in his hands. Acceptance was an impossibility. Something foreign. Something that didn't happen to someone like him.

Anton went with him, kneeling at his side. He wrapped one arm around Sasha's shoulders. He started reciting Pushkin's poem again: "*All for you, I drag my footsteps hither, yonder. I count each hour the whole day through, and yet in vain I squander the days that doom has measured out.*" He squeezed Sasha's shoulder, shaking him lightly. "Onegin's lines. But does that sound like anyone else we know?"

Swallowing, Sasha turned away from Anton. He wasn't going to discuss this. He'd rather never discuss it. Ever. It should have been buried in the hollow depths of his heart, forever.

Anton sighed. He released Sasha, clapping his hands on his meaty thighs and rising with a groan. "We are glad you're back, Tati. And I hope it is not too late." He squeezed Sasha's shoulder and returned to his seat, settling in and closing his eyes.

Was any of it true? For a moment in the snow, Sergey had seemed... awestruck. When he hadn't looked like he was about to puke, pale from seeing the ghost of a dead man before him. He'd touched his cheek. And then, he'd been furious, bitterly so. Lashing out, and keeping him at arm's length. Avoiding him, even.

Why?

You knew this would happen. You knew he'd react this way. It was only fantasies that had kept Sasha going, his dreams of seeing Sergey smile at him again. But, why would he? Everything, from the moment his resolve had failed and he'd kissed Sergey until now, was all of his own making. His own failure. Sergey's recoil, his disgust, was only natural.

He would keep his distance. Respect Sergey's wishes. Do what he could for Sergey, always, but keep away from the man himself. Whatever they'd had before, Sasha had destroyed it on the flight line at Volga.

Now, he had to pick his way through the pieces.

THEY DOCKED AT THE rotten remains of the Soviet submarine base, tying up to a broken pylon and side-stepping gaping holes in the wooden boardwalk. On the shore, sand shared space with tumbled gray boulders, like giants had stopped playing a game of jacks and abandoned the beach. Decrepit Soviet barracks squatted behind a broken fence, fallen down in most places. Once painted the gleaming, bright pastels of Soviet luxury, the buildings were more chipped paint and rust than anything else, windblown, with broken windows and caved-in roofs.

The sub base sat in a large caldera, a round depression blown out from a long-extinct volcano. Flooded, the caldera was a perfect deep-water pool, and Soviet engineers had breached a hole in the narrowest bit of land, creating an access point to the Pacific. It was isolated, protected, and obscure. All things that a covert nuclear sub base should be.

The rest of the island was a wasteland. Dark crags of granite and black earth, scrub grasses, moss, and loam. The caldera's twin volcano rose to the south, disappearing into the low-slung clouds. Oppression littered the island, the death and decay of the sub base casting a malaise over the land itself. Even the birds seemed off, squawking at the arrival of the humans like they were alerting some larger, menacing presence.

The island was undeniably Russian. If a land could be carved from the spirit of a people, Simushir could have been carved from a stoic, sullen Russian heart, and breathed to life with the dour soul of her people.

"Well, Jack." Sergey stood beside him on the beach, facing the Pacific Ocean. "We made it to Simushir. Now, it is time for you to do your part. Where are your submarines?"

Jack smiled. He squinted, looking out over the fog-covered waters. An entire ocean lay in the fog, and they were specks on an infinitely tiny dot, standing on an island that wasn't on most maps. Still, he saw a faint parting in the mist, a dark shadow cutting through the gloom. "I believe they are already here."

The rest of the convoy did a quick recon of the base, surveying the buildings for anything useful. Sergey ordered them to bring back enough firewood to last the whole night. Vasily and Aleksey disappeared, Vasily going on and on about finding birds' eggs and other food. Anything to get away from the rations and the scavenged tins they had been eating since Siberia.

Jack, Ethan, Scott, and Sergey waited at the pier.

They heard the boat first. A high-pitched whine, and the churn of a portable motor. Through the mist, they spotted a small inflatable fast boat carrying almost a dozen men cutting through the water. As they got closer, Jack picked out the sub captain, and the executive officer, along with a heavily armed security detail.

What a sight they must be. Unwashed, unshaven, and standing on a rotten pier. Jack slapped his best smile on his face and strode forward after the small boat docked and the commanding officer disembarked. His rank insignia showed *captain*. Jack held out his hand.

Elizabeth had sent the captain and commander of Pearl Harbor's submarine squad to him. Normally, submarines were manned by commanders. This man, though, had proven himself to be the best among his peers, and had risen to command the fleet of fast-attack hunter-killer submarines.

Hunter-killer submarines did exactly that. Hunted their prey in the depths of the ocean, and then vanished again. The men who led those missions were made of steel, predators who worked in the shadows. Hunter-killer subs were the sharpest knives brought to a back-alley fight, and their commanders were the best at slitting throats. This man would be no different.

The captain was tall, taller than he'd expect would serve on a submarine. He carried himself like a man used to authority, a man with power. He had a lean face and deep-set eyes the color of cobalt that flicked over the caldera, the desolate base, and their party, taking everything in in a fast, periscope-like sweep. His gaze was firm, as if he was accustomed to taking no crap. But, his eyes narrowed when he saw Jack, and his jaw dropped, just a hair. It was enough of a reaction for Jack to know he'd thrown him completely. Beside the captain, his executive officer froze as well, his gaze darting from Jack to his captain and back again.

"Mr. President?" the captain finally breathed. He blinked. His gaze flicked behind Jack, first to Ethan and then to Sergey, and finally to Scott.

The captain's name tape read ANDERSON. Jack nodded. "Hello, Captain Anderson. You were sent to rendezvous here by President Wall."

Captain Anderson nodded. Jack watched the pieces fall together behind his eyes. "Phoenix One. You're Phoenix One."

Jack nodded.

"Good call sign." Captain Anderson took Jack's hand. His grip was firm, and he gave a wry, tight smile. "I am relieved that you're alive, Mr. President. I'd also like to know just what the hell is going on."

AFTER LISTENING TO A quick and dirty summary of the high points, Captain Anderson insisted on taking all four of them back to the sub. "President Wall instructed me to let her know as soon as I made contact. Now I understand the urgency."

"I need to talk to her, too. We need an update on the situation in Canada, and General Moroshkin's movements."

"Shooting has stopped for now, but the Chinese are sending a fleet across the Pacific. We ran beneath them on the way." Captain Anderson frowned, deep lines furrowing his lean face. "Things are changing by the minute."

"And only getting worse." Jack held his hand out to Ethan, beckoning him down to join them on the pier. "Captain, may I introduce Ethan Reichenbach, director of the black team assigned to take out Madigan." He watched Anderson carefully as Ethan joined them.

Captain Anderson smiled wide and gripped Ethan's hand. "Mr. First Gentleman, it's an honor."

Ethan nodded, and Jack spotted a hint of a flush above the growth of his scraggly facial hair. He still wasn't comfortable with compliments, with any kind of attention paid to him. "We're putting a bunch of pieces together for this mission, Captain. My team, your subs, Russian intelligence. It's going to be a patchwork."

"We'll make it work." Captain Anderson shook Scott's hand and then introduced his own executive officer and the head of his security detachment.

As he spoke, Jack spotted Sergey scowling and looking around, searching for someone. "Where is Sasha? We need him," Sergey grumbled. He lifted his radio, snapping in Russian. Sasha's voice came back, and in a minute, he appeared at the beach, jogging from the direction the rest of the convoy had disappeared to, searching for supplies.

"Where have you been?" Sergey grunted, looking past Sasha as he fisted his hands in his pants pockets. "We need you."

Sasha stared at Sergey. "I did not want to intrude."

"You have the intelligence, no? You flew that damn mission." Sergey walked away, heading for Jack, Ethan, and Captain Anderson.

Jack and Ethan shared a long look as Sergey introduced himself to Anderson and his men. Anderson's executive officer had wide, saucer eyes, and he fumbled his greeting as he shook Sergey's hand. The shock of finding two world leaders—one supposedly dead—on an island in the middle of nowhere had yet to wear off.

"President Wall is waiting." Anderson hesitated, and then frowned at Jack.

"She *is* the sitting president," he said, answering the question in Anderson's eyes. "The world needs to think I'm down and out. I'm a ghost, Captain."

Anderson nodded and smiled tightly. "Mr. President," he still said. "It would be my privilege to take you aboard *Honolulu*."

Ethan and Scott followed Jack into the boat, and then Sergey and Sasha squeezed on board as well. With everyone, it was a tight fit, and Sergey ended up mashed beside Sasha and leaning against the inflatable sidewall.

They took off with a roar, the motor carving a deep wake behind their fast boat. Freezing spray blew over the bow, splashing their faces and wetting their lips. Next to Ethan, Jack turned his face into the wind and closed his eyes. He could taste the sea, smell the weight of salt in the ocean. Simushir was colder than the mainland had been, and even though the wind was cutting and frigid, the sea-salt air was like ambrosia, honey-sweet to his soul. They'd made it. They'd made it to the rendezvous. One step closer to taking out Madigan.

Ethan wrapped his arms around his waist, holding him from behind, and Jack leaned into him. He watched the dark, fin-like sail of the *USS Honolulu* draw closer, rising out of the ocean like a sea monster from legends of old. Sailors stood on the bridge at the top of the sail, watching their approach. Beyond *Honolulu*, three more dark towers rose from the churning waves, a triangle of submarine sails, deadly and dangerous. Elizabeth's fleet, as promised.

Beside them, Sergey shuffled closer to Sasha, his hand jerking back and forth as if he didn't know if he should reach out or not. Finally, he rested his hand on Sasha's back. "You are not all right?"

Sasha looked grim. His lips were pressed in a hard line, and he gripped the rounded edge of the boat. "I am a pilot," he said. "Not sailor. Boats make me…" He trailed off, but the hard swallow he gave conveyed the message.

Sighing, Sergey rubbed his hand up and down Sasha's back. He frowned and looked away, over the ocean's swells, and missed it when Sasha turned his wide, confused eyes toward him.

Ethan spoke into Jack's ear, softly. "They haven't figured anything out, have they?"

Jack shook his head.

And then, they pulled up alongside the submarine. Their little boat maneuvered next to the huge, rounded black hull, sliding right alongside a set of bouncing buoys. Long and narrow, the sleek curve of the submarine looked like a whale hovering on the surface of the ocean before diving back down. The sail rose high on the forward section, and down the spine of the sub, sailors scurried along a narrow walkway, catching and throwing lines back and forth from their fast boat. Low waves broke over the back of the sub, washing the hull with frothy sea water.

Two sailors lowered a rope ladder to the boat and the captain went up first.

"Captain on deck!" one of the sailors shouted. Anderson turned around and helped Jack out of the boat first, followed by the others.

Jaws dropped as the sailors recognized Jack. Anderson gave them a heavy look, the full weight of his authority in his glare, and they snapped back to their duties in an instant.

"Mr. President, welcome aboard the *USS Honolulu*."

THEY MADE THEIR WAY to the captain's cabin quickly, crowding the five of them, plus Anderson and his executive officer, into the cramped space. Along one wall, six display screens showed the status of the ship and her departments, their position, and data from all the sensors on board. A narrow desk squatted between two built-in chairs, and above the desk, the captain's bunk was stowed and folded against the wall. Three red phones, the ship's radio, and a dizzying array of communications switches sat on the wall above the desk. Even with everyone shoved into every possible space—Ethan and Jack sitting at the desk, Sasha and Sergey huddled against the wall, Scott leaning on the cabin's door, arms crossed—it was a tight fit.

Anderson called to the radio room for a secured signal to the White House Situation Room. Minutes later, one of his screens flickered, and then the White House seal flashed. Anderson swung the screen out in front of Jack, and in an inset video, Jack's filthy, bedraggled image appeared, staring back at the screen.

A moment later, the image flickered. Elizabeth sat at the head of the table in the Situation Room, her hands clasped in front of her. Her jaw clenched hard, like she was bracing for terrible news.

When she saw Jack, she smiled wide and let her head droop forward for a moment. "Jack... I'm glad to see you in one piece. I must have been absolutely crazy to agree to this plan of yours."

"Yes, Madam President." Jack grinned back at her.

"Is everyone with you all right?"

Jack nodded, and Ethan leaned into the video feed.

"Ethan." Elizabeth's smile wavered as her eyes glittered, and she couldn't speak for a moment. "I'm glad to see you both." Her eyes flicked away from the screen, and she nodded to someone out of sight.

Levi appeared beside her. "Where's Scott?"

Scott grunted and leaned in, grinning.

"Y'all can hurry it up and come back anytime," Levi said. He gave them a tired smile and backed away.

Elizabeth got down to business. "Jack, we've got a situation here."

She briefed them on Moroshkin's movements in Canada and the nervous ceasefire that had settled over the region. Canada's refusal to talk to them anymore, and Russia's direct communication with the Canadian government. NATO's silence. The advance of the Chinese fleet across the Pacific, and her defensive line at Hawaii.

When she finished, Jack leaned forward, balancing his elbows on his knees as he exhaled. "Back channels to Canada aren't working?"

"They aren't saying a word to us. CIA and NSA are tracking comms between Canada and the Russians. It's tapered off for now. We're in wait-and-see mode."

"We've got to do something about the Chinese fleet." Jack's gaze flicked to Anderson. "You have four subs with you?"

Anderson nodded.

"Elizabeth, let's split this fleet. Send two subs up the backs of the Chinese. If they make a move at Hawaii, Anderson's subs can be there waiting for them."

Anderson chimed in. "My guys can sprint back and catch up to their present position in under a day. They'll never know they're there."

Elizabeth nodded. "I agree. Let's do it." She pulled a tablet across the table and sent a picture over the secured link. "Jack, here's the latest from the Swedish weather satellite. The cloud is growing. It's already estimated to kill over four billion people if it ignites now. Every hour it grows, more lives are at risk."

The black-and-white photo showed a river of fuchsia, spreading out like spilled ink from the Russian Arctic and starting to sweep around the globe. "Most of Russia, China, and starting to touch Canada and the US." Jack glanced at Ethan. One of Ethan's hands rose, settling on the small of his back, a silent show of support.

Sergey crossed the cabin and leaned into the feed, glowering at the data. "Damn the man," he growled. "Almost all of Russia will be incinerated in this blast!"

"We're not going to let that happen, Sergey." Jack held his friend's glare when Sergey turned to him. "We're going to stop him."

"Jack, what's your plan?" On-screen, Elizabeth sat back, lacing her hands together.

All eyes turned to him.

No pressure. He exhaled slowly and leaned back into Ethan's touch. "I want to take two subs up under the Arctic ice. Captain Anderson's and another. We'll make our way beneath the polar cap to Madigan's location. Based on Sasha's recon flight, we have a great idea of what we're up against. One sub and one destroyer. It was surfaced through the ice a week ago."

"What kind of sub?" Anderson frowned. "There's a difference between a fast attack boat and an SSBN." A hunter-killer, or a mobile missile launcher.

Jack turned to Sasha. Sasha shrugged. "A dark sub. Black."

Anderson arched one eyebrow. "Would you be able to recognize it if you saw it again?"

Sasha thought it over, nodding his head from side to side. "*Da.* Yes."

"Jack, I thought you said the pilot went down during the mission?" Elizabeth leaned forward.

"We recovered Sasha on our way." Smiling, Jack gestured to Sasha and pushed the screen toward him.

Clearly uncomfortable, Sasha managed a tight smile and looked like he wanted to make his six-foot-plus frame disappear into the cheap wooden paneling.

"What can you tell us about Madigan's position, son?" Anderson folded his arms and hovered over Sasha, staring down his long nose. "What kind of intel were you able to get on this overflight?"

Taking a deep breath, Sasha launched into the report on his flight, from the moment he took off until the moment he ejected. His approach over the ice-covered Kara Sea. Finding Madigan's position, and the two ships in the ice. The sub, its sail poking through the frozen sea. Explosions beneath the ice, and open holes. Burning RusFuel stations and oil derricks.

Their defenses, and how many times he was fired upon. His evasive maneuvers. Finally running out of time, and sprinting for deep Siberia while making what he thought was his last call to Sergey.

As he finished, Sasha turned toward Sergey, holding his gaze as he relayed his side of their final call. Sergey stared back, eyes wide, lips pressed into a thin line.

"Damn, son," Anderson breathed. "That takes a lot of guts, volunteering for a one-way mission like that."

"It was the right thing to do," Sasha rumbled. "For Russia, and for the world."

Jack heard what Sasha didn't say: that he did it, all of it, for Sergey.

Ethan spoke in the silence that followed. "Sasha can reconstruct everything that he saw. Draw us a map. Give us actionable intelligence on the size and strength of Madigan's forces."

Anderson frowned. "Week-old intelligence."

"It's the Arctic, Captain. Everything is measured in glacial epochs there. Nothing moves fast. Not men, not machines, not nature." Ethan shook his head. "After helping Moroshkin's coup, he must have moved what's left of his forces in bulk to the Arctic in one go. Anything else would be a logistical nightmare."

"You said something about your team?"

Ethan nodded. "Yes. My team closed in on Madigan. Found his base in a derelict tanker off the coast of Saudi Arabia. Uncovered Madigan's assassination plot." He looked at Jack, swallowing. "Found out the truth about the attacker in the nick of time."

Silence hung in the cabin. Jack held Ethan's stare. He reached for Ethan's hand and squeezed.

"I sent my team to these coordinates." Ethan reached for another of Captain Anderson's screens and called up the GPS, punching in longitude and latitude. "We need to go and pick them up."

"And then what?" Elizabeth, again, over the secure link. "Jack, *you* are not seriously thinking about going into the Arctic. We lost a SEAL team deployed off Franz Josef Land. Now *you* want to go in? You're the *president*—"

"No, Elizabeth, I am *not* the president. I'm the *former* president. Right now, I'm just a man. A man supporting a government operation, your and Director Reichenbach's operation: capture or kill Madigan before he commits an act of global genocide." He looked Elizabeth in the eye, across the thousands of miles that separated them, and squared his jaw. "We've come this far. I'm not leaving Ethan's side. We're doing this together."

Sergey spoke quickly, sliding across to Jack and Ethan's sides. "As representative of the true and authentic Russian government, I will join with you in this. You require Russian authorization to operate in our territory, which I am glad to extend to my friends in the United States. We would appreciate your help in taking care of this terrorist we have in our polar region."

Elizabeth closed her eyes and bowed her head. "Captain Anderson," she finally said, slowly looking up. "This is your boat, and this would be your mission, with Director Reichenbach attached to your command. In your professional opinion, can this be done?"

Anderson pursed his lips. One boot scuffed at the deck as he frowned, as if the corrugated steel and rubber had done something out of line. All eyes were on him, in the cabin and over the uplink.

If Anderson nixed the idea, Jack was on thin ice going forward. And, he'd been beneath the surface once already.

He wasn't the Commander in Chief. He wasn't in the chain of command, not since he'd walked out of Bethesda and had given the keys to the White House to Elizabeth. He couldn't order anyone to do anything. Anderson, so far, had been deferential and respectful to his former office, and possibly to how he viewed Jack as a man. But all that could change in a moment.

"Madam President, if you're asking me if I can get two subs under the ice and sneak up on this bastard, the answer is yes. I can get us there. Now, what will we face?" He blew out slowly, and a low whistle echoed through the cabin. "Strange things happen under the ice. Waters that go down deeper than you can believe. Subs can hide in those depths. Is there one Russian sub under Madigan's command? Or two? Or more? What about combat? How is your team, Director Reichenbach? Are we inserting them on the ice? We left Pearl with provisions for arctic operations, but what about your men? Are they ready for this?"

"They're ready." Ethan crossed his arms. "I trust my lieutenant. He knows what to do. He'll do whatever it takes."

"Mr. President." Anderson flicked his eyes to Jack. "You've just come across the entirety of the Russian continent, a country gripped in civil war. You managed to sneak through territory that has been blacked out to the world since the coup began. You launched an intelligence gathering mission from inside hostile territory—" He nodded to Sasha. "—and successfully retrieved critical, actionable intelligence. All of this is incredible work. Beyond incredible." He took a deep breath and squinted. "You should stop here, Mr. President. You've already done enough. The world thinks you're dead."

Jack smiled. He licked his lips, looking down at the decking for a moment. "Captain, you and I are about the same age. We grew up watching old men become the worst kind of politicians. Breaking promises, sending our friends out to fight wars in distant countries. Screaming at the other side when things didn't go right. Refusing to take responsibility for anything. Always pointing the finger. Always, always, someone else's fault. And America suffered. The world suffered. Our country lost itself, and we watched it happen, growing up in the shadow of so many failures." He sighed. "I think that's where Madigan was born. Somewhere along the line, too many promises were broken. He went through four wars. Watched his people suffer and die, and came home to the same old garbage."

Shaking his head, Jack stood slowly. "I swore I'd be different. I swore, every single night, that I wouldn't go down that path. I'd take responsibility. I'd show up. I'd make the hard calls, and live with them. I swore on my wife's sacrifice that this crazy, desperate world she was taken from wouldn't be what we had to live with. That there was something *better* in the future, for all of us."

He thought back to his heroes, to the legacies of men and presidents who had shaped his worldview, and his presidency. Men who knew sacrifice, on so many levels. Men who gave their all to the nation. "When was the last time a president truly sacrificed for our nation? For the world?" He swallowed, memories of his short tenure in office flashing in his mind. Building outreach, reaching to other nations, trying to rebuild the world community. Taking the lead in aid after the blast in Nairobi, and stitching the global community even closer together. Facing down the barrel of a gun, and feeling cold steel bite his skin. Ethan rushing to his rescue. Standing together with Sergey and striding forward, leaving the ghosts of both nations behind. Feeling it all come apart, like water slipping through his fingers, as Sochi fell and the woman he thought was Leslie, his long-dead wife, lay in his arms.

Choosing Ethan. Choosing to stand and fight, to strike back, to bring back to Madigan what he had taken from Jack: his own life. "I will lay down my life to stop Madigan and to save America, and save the world. He thinks he's already beaten me, that I'm already down. But I am the *one* thing he won't see coming."

Silence. Not even a breath moved the air. Distantly, Jack heard the hum and splash of waves rolling against the sub's smooth hull, a gentle lap that permeated the background.

Anderson peered at him. A new light shone in his eyes. Something had lit deep within the man, some core that Jack had tapped. "Respectfully, Mr. President," Anderson said slowly. "How's your combat training?"

"He's received Secret Service training." Scott jumped in, speaking from his slump against the door. "Tactics, weapons, advanced drills. I've seen him in combat, too." Scott looked Jack dead in the eye, shadows of Sochi in both of their gazes. "I wouldn't have smuggled him to Russia if I thought he couldn't survive."

Anderson's eyebrows arched to his hairline. "I'd like to hear that story sometime," he said. Sighing, he scrubbed one hand over his mouth and peered at Jack, as if trying to divine the future in the depths of his gaze. Measure Jack's soul by the light in his eyes.

It was all on Anderson. Submarine captains were confident to the point of cocky, but rock-solid in their measured, precise risks. Aggressive, but not reckless. Surety lived in their bones, as much as salt flowed in their veins.

"If anyone can do this, Madam President," he finally said, softly, "it's the people in this room."

He held Jack's gaze as he spoke, unblinking.

Jack smiled, nodding to Anderson as Ethan slipped his hand into Jack's and laced their fingers together. Jack squeezed back until his bones ached, until, if he squeezed any harder, Ethan and he would become one, bones and blood fusing together.

This was it.

Time to save the world.

THEY SPENT HOURS SKETCHING out their battle plan. Courses plotted up to the Arctic and beneath the ice. The best vector for approaching Madigan's location. Sasha helped them draw a finely detailed map, to the grid square, of Madigan's forces and position.

Anderson offered them each the use of his shower. "It's not much. We run tight water rationing on board. Our de-sal plant can only do so much each day, and the bulk of that water goes to the reactor cooling system. But, you can each get wet, soap off, and rinse. And shave." He grinned. "I can scrounge up some fresh uniforms for you as well."

A sponge bath didn't really count as bathing, not compared to a shower with soap, and falling into the ice didn't count either. Jack stank, badly enough that he'd gotten used to the odor. A dignified president, even a former president, he was not. "We'd be grateful, Captain."

He went first, followed by Sergey, and then Ethan, Scott, and finally Sasha. They gave their clothes to a young seaman in exchange for fresh navy uniforms, blue combat fatigues. Jack kept Ethan's sweatshirt, holding on to the grimy, stained fabric.

As they were dressing, he watched Ethan smuggle something from his old jacket into the pocket of his new uniform top. Ethan wouldn't look at him, no matter how much Jack tried to catch his gaze.

Jack hoped the seaman took their old, disgusting clothes and threw them straight overboard.

After, Anderson met up with them again. He already looked haggard, worn weary just at the thought of their mission ahead. "Would you like to spend the night on the sub, Mr. President? I can move my officers around this evening. Give you and your men bunks on board."

"We'll be crowding you soon enough, Captain. We'll spend the night on the island and stay out of your hair until we're underway. We've got to connect with our people back there, too. Sergey's men need to keep fighting."

Anderson nodded. He most likely wouldn't be sleeping for another two days. "Fair enough. I'll send you back to shore with the supplies we brought from Pearl." Food, clothes, blankets, weapons, and fuel. Elizabeth had filled the subs to outfit an army. "We've got a lot of work to do to get ready to be underway. We'll be able to raise anchor just after dawn."

Jack nodded. "Send a boat to pick us up. We'll be ready."

27

Simushir Island - Okhotsk Sea

ALEKSEY, ANTON, AND VASILY, three former federal policemen and the unofficial officers of Sergey's convoy, had rounded up the men and started fires by the time Jack and everyone else made their way back to the island. Cheers rose when Ethan and Scott brought up crate after crate of food, blankets, weapons, and the rest of the supplies. Three of the men had shot a deer while surveying the west side of the island. Already skinned and gutted, it slowly spun on a homemade spit over a roaring bonfire. Smaller fires were scattered on the narrow beach, some occupied, some burning low to embers and left abandoned.

The sun slipped beneath the rise of the volcano, turning the gunmetal sky dark granite, and then to deep black when it disappeared behind the island. From horizon to horizon, a billion twinkling lights stared down at the beach. A tiny sliver of moon crept through the sky, but the majesty of the night belonged entirely to the stars. They winked overhead, scattered like diamonds thrown across the inky fabric of space, the carpet of time. How many of those stars were already extinguished? Were they only seeing ghosts, spectral flashes that had already passed from the universe?

There was something there, in that thought, that Sergey couldn't put his finger on. Something about time passing, and the end of all things. Death, and what was left behind. Unsaid. Undone.

And, always, there was Sasha.

He'd never thought much about the stars before Sasha. They were there. Pretty to look at. Political, once he'd moved into Russian politics. Space was a place where nations could further extend themselves. Russia and the United States, always pushing for more. Russia's space program hadn't been as grand as it once was for decades, but it was there, and he'd kept up with their advances. Signed leases with other countries to blast their rockets into orbit. Cut ribbons at a new launch pad. Welcomed home Russian cosmonauts from their tours at the International Space Station.

Sasha always looked up at the stars.

He'd wanted to be a cosmonaut before his Air Force career came to a bloody, violent end. Serve Russia in space, proudly wear the Russian flag on his sleeve as he lived aboard the International Space Station. Fly a ship into space, even.

What had he thought, staring up at the stars over Moscow, over the Kremlin, knowing that his dreams had come to an end? What color, what shape, what form did his pain, his anguish take?

Had he ever mourned for the life he'd lost?

Had he felt like Sergey had felt, bereft and broken, lamenting the loss of a life he hadn't even lived? All of the what-ifs and the hopes, the dreams and the fantasies, gone forever with finality's severing blow, a finite slash across their lives.

But Sasha was alive. He was still alive.

Maybe one day he could become a cosmonaut. Perhaps he still could fly into space. His Air Force career had been exemplary before the attack. His work at the Kremlin after, even more so. Why could he not follow his dreams again?

Could Sergey follow his?

Could he cross the sand, sit beside Sasha in front of the fire, and confess everything to him? Despite all of his fears, and everything stacked against him? Could he speak aloud what lived in his heart?

He'd probably be shot down, sent crashing to the earth like a fighter squaring off against Sasha in his MiG. Why was Sasha even single? He was brilliant and beautiful, eye-catching like a priceless jewel cut from a forbidden gem. Caring. Loyal. Dedicated. Sasha had no business being single, and Sergey had no business thinking he was the man who could change that.

But he had to face this. Had to confront what had grown in his soul, and what he had only realized when Sasha had ripped himself away from Sergey's side. The ache from that, from Sasha's leaving, still festered, a scab on the bottom of his heart.

He'd survived a career in the cutthroat FSB, survived Putin's regime, worked his way up through the deranged and deadly ranks of Russian politics, and completed an anti-corruption purge decades in the making. He'd never been a coward before. He wouldn't start now.

Slowly, he made his way across the beach, his boots digging into the fog-damp, dark sand. His men were scattered around the fires, some already snoring, others staying up and relishing in the simplicity of nothing. Finally, they were at rest, at least for the next few hours. They were safe on this island at the end of Russia, practically at the end of the world. Even Scott had parked himself beside a circle of low embers and fallen asleep, wrapped up in his jacket with his arms crossed over his chest. His snores bounced over the old base, snorts that could rival a bear.

Jack and Ethan were lounging together at a fire farther down the beach, and through the flickering flames, he spotted Jack's brilliant smile and saw him tip his head back, laughing at something Ethan had said. Ethan, too, seemed relaxed in a way Sergey had never seen, leaning on his side and propped up on his elbow, gazing at Jack like Sasha stared at the stars: with wonder, with adoration, with raw, aching love.

And Sasha sat alone, huddled close to his own fire as he gazed upward.

Sergey had no idea what to say. His heart thundered as he moved closer, a physical ache against his ribs. It must be trying to escape. What was he thinking? He couldn't do this.

Breathe. He kept walking, slipping through the sand until he hovered in front of Sasha's fire.

Slowly, Sasha's gaze lowered to rest on him. He stared, silent.

How did he even begin? "Sasha," he started, grunting through his clenched throat. He tried to clear it and looked away. He couldn't hold Sasha's ice-blue gaze any longer. Those eyes were going to cut out his heart.

"Sasha, we need to talk," he finally managed.

"We do not," Sasha rumbled. "I know my place. I know what I did was wrong. I will not ask anything from you, other than this: please, let me keep fighting for you, Sergey. For your Russia."

"What you did—" He frowned, and then sank to his knees in the sand beside the fire, just out of Sasha's reach. "Do you mean kissing me, or do you mean leaving?"

Sasha frowned and cocked his head to one side. He blinked. "I will never apologize for doing what is right for you. We needed that intelligence. I had to make that flight."

"There could have been another way." Scowling, Sergey fisted his hands in the muddy sand, clenching rough grains in his palms. He felt them slip through his fingers, cold and damp. "Some other way that did not involve you risking your life. We could have done this together!"

Sasha looked away quickly. "No. My way was best. It had to be done."

"Sasha, *please*—" Sergey clamped his lips shut with a sigh and stared at Sasha's profile in the flickering firelight. Orange flames danced over his pale skin, casting him like a golden god from an ancient myth. His shoulders rose and fell, faster than before. The only sign of Sasha's nerves. He could be like a statue sometimes.

"So, you are saying kissing me was what you did wrong?" He watched Sasha carefully, almost frantically.

There. Sasha's jaw clenched, the muscles from his temple to his neck straining, bulging outward. His pulse leaped, bounding beneath his jaw. He shook his head. "It will not happen again."

The words wouldn't come. Sergey wanted to shout, bellow at the top of his lungs what was in his head and his heart, but what he felt couldn't be translated into words, and when he tried, everything got choked in the hollow of his throat. Now, *now* was the time to act. To say something. "What if..." He hesitated. "What if I want it to happen again?"

Sasha froze, going so still so suddenly Sergey wondered if time had stopped, if the earth had ceased its rotation. Sergey tried to breathe, but his lungs wouldn't work, and he mouthed over old air as he struggled for something, anything to say. He'd made a mistake. He'd made a *terrible* mistake.

Between one blink and the next, Sasha moved, twisting and turning to Sergey. He quivered, his entire body a wordless question. His wide eyes darted over Sergey, from the sand beneath his knees to his burning gaze. His hands clenched as his jaw hung open, speechless in a way Sasha never was. Beneath his borrowed black undershirt, his chest heaved, rising and falling in a too-fast rhythm.

"After you left..." Sergey fumbled, and he cursed under his breath. His hands dug into the damp sand again, fisting around grains that slithered away from him. "You changed everything, Sasha. What you did—" His breath blasted from him.

"I have been a coward my whole life. I hid from what I could have felt, burying it until I forgot I even was capable of this. I forced myself to not think it, never, not ever. And then you came along, and I did not even know that everything within me had changed. You were like the final piece of a puzzle I never knew I was building. I did not even know it was complete until you left, and everything came apart." Swallowing, Sergey tried to get a grip on his rambling. He wasn't making sense. He took a breath. "Jack calls it bisexual," he said slowly. "He says that is what I am. How I feel. That I can love both." He glanced up, finding Sasha's gaze.

Sasha looked absolutely *devastated*.

Sergey felt a punch to his gut, a brutal blow that knocked the air from his lungs and made him dizzy, made his ears ring like an alarm had gone off inside his skull. He was wrong. Jack was wrong. Sasha didn't feel that way for him.

"No," Sasha breathed. "No, no, no, Sergey, you cannot! It is impossible. You *cannot* be this way!" His voice rose, until he was begging, pleading for Sergey to take it back. "Not you. Please. Not you, Sergey."

"What are you saying? I cannot love another man?"

"No! *You* cannot!" Sasha ran his hands through his hair, gripping the blond strands as he groaned. "You are the president! You are our country's *only* hope. *You* are the one who can bring us out of the dark ages. Fix everything. Give us a new country, and a real place in the world."

"You give me too much power—"

"No! I do not. You already purged the corrupt oligarchs. No one has been able to do this, and you did. You are bringing equality to Russia, the promise that all Russians are safe in your nation. These are things Russia needs!" He swallowed hard. "You must take back Moscow, and you must throw out Moroshkin and this rebellion. And then you will lead us again, Sergey, further into the future."

"If that happens—"

"It *must* happen."

"*If* that happens, then I want you by my side." He held out his hand, reaching for Sasha. "With me."

Sasha's jaw dropped again. His eyes went glassy, a shine that fractured the blue in his gaze. "You cannot be weak. They will eat you alive," he whispered. "Moroshkin built his followers by claiming you and Jack were too close. They joked about you and him as lovers, and it was not even true. What do you think they would do to you if you really were with another man? You *cannot* be weak."

"Weak?" Sergey tried to laugh, shaking his head. "I am already weak. Weakened by cowardice. By shame. By want." He stared into Sasha's wet gaze. "I broke when you left. A part of me flew off into the skies with you, and I want that back. I already love you, Sasha. I'm already weakened by this, by these feelings. I want to be strong again." He turned his hand over in the sand, palm up, and slid it toward Sasha. "Strong *with* you."

"Sergey…"

"We can do all those things together. We can bring Russia into the future, side by side. There is more work to be done, yes, and we can do it—"

"You're deluded by Jack! Russia is *not* America! If you are in love with a man, they will never accept you! Never let you be president. You could never do what needs to be done." Sasha shook his head, snarling. "Russia will never accept you and me."

"You are wrong." Desperation colored his voice, made his words shake. This was not at all what he'd imagined would happen. Not even close.

"I am *not* wrong. I know how little our country accepts men like me, Sergey." His voice turned sharp, cutting.

Sergey scooted forward until he was right in front of Sasha. "Tell me this one thing, Sasha. Do not hide behind duty and loyalty. You will tell me the truth. Do you care about me at all, or is this just a way to push me off, this talk of Russia and her future, all of her needs?"

Sasha reached for him with one shaking hand, resting his palm against Sergey's thin face. Sasha was warm, his hand rough. "You can build a new future for us all. Make Russia a true home for people like me. This is no small thing." He trembled as he touched Sergey, and let out a breath, almost a gasp. "And… I care for you so deeply that it hurts—"

"Then—" Reaching out with both hands, Sergey clasped Sasha's face, bringing him close, until their foreheads touched, rubbing together. "Sasha, please. *Please.*" Everything in him ached for Sasha, yearned for the man, for the connection he could feel quivering just beneath their skin, electric zings where they touched. He wanted to know, and be known. Love, and be loved. Hold Sasha, and face the future together. "Please," he whispered.

Sasha squeezed his eyes closed and shook his head, his cheeks brushing Sergey's palms. "Russia needs you to be—"

"Then let us leave. As soon as Madigan is dead, and Moroshkin, too. We will go, far away. Where it can be just you and me, and nothing can come between us."

A lone tear slipped down Sasha's cheek. It crashed into Sergey's thumb, sliding down his skin. "Russia needs *you*," Sasha breathed again. "And I will not be the man who took away Russia's best hope for her future. Who took you away." His hands rose and covered Sergey's. "Russia needs *you*. I am nothing compared to all of that."

Sergey's heart screamed, burned to its core with anguish and agony. Fault lines appeared in his soul, cracks that went all the way through him, through his past and his present, and stretched into his future. The choices in his life had led to this moment, and he'd do anything to make it different. Anything to change the world, and all the fates, and allow the two of them to close the gap between their shaking lips and steal another kiss for themselves.

One kiss from Sasha was all he would ever have.

His eyes slipped closed, and his hands fell from Sasha's cheeks. He fell forward, pitching into Sasha, and ended up pressing his face into Sasha's shoulder, his chest. His lungs burned, and he heaved, trying to drag in breath after breath. All he did was pull Sasha's exquisite, indefinable scent deep within his soul: musk, cold air, and the glow of the stars over Moscow, painted and brushed over his body.

Sasha's arms wound around him, dragging him closer, pulling him flush against his body as he lay back on the sand. Side by side, almost intertwined, Sasha pressed his lips to Sergey's hair in an open-mouthed moan. It was almost a kiss, aside from the groan, the wave of pain falling from Sasha.

Sergey wrapped his arms around Sasha's waist, finally stroking the body he'd dreamed of ever since Sasha had left his side. Strength, so much strength, wrapped in layers of soft cotton and starched blue canvas. Hardened muscles, shaking beneath his palms. Sasha's thighs gripped him, wrapped between and around his legs and held him fast. His hips pressed against Sergey's stomach, and, *oh*—

"I should go," Sergey whispered. He had no right to feel Sasha's body like this. Or, maybe he should stay, endure the torture of having who he loved so close, and yet unreachable. "I should—"

"Not yet, Sergey." Another open-mouthed press, and another mournful moan. "It is selfish," Sasha breathed over his hair. "But let me hold you for one night."

One kiss. One night in Sasha's arms.

He turned his face into Sasha's chest and breathed in, reliving every memory he had of the two of them together. Every smile. Every laugh. Every single moment of crystalline happiness.

One night beneath the stars.

28

Simushir Island - Okhotsk Sea

"You can't see anything like this in DC." Jack sat on the sand, his arms wrapped around his knees, and stared up into the night sky. "It's breathtaking."

Ethan gazed at Jack. "Yes. It is."

Starlight and firelight painted diamonds over Jack, carving brilliance over his cheekbones and curling around his smile. Flickers of flame danced up his skin, like the fires in Ethan's heart, his soul, coming alive and caressing his lover. A river of stars stretched overhead, and the black ocean reflected their glimmer, an endless wash of sparkling perfection. The whole world seemed to revolve around this one point, this one island. Somewhere, far away, distant decisions placed the world's fate on a deadly axis, but there, on the sand-strewn beach beneath the jewel-studded sky, Ethan saw only perfection.

His heart burned, searing in his chest, suddenly too large for the cage of his body. Jesus, he loved Jack. He'd never known it was possible to love someone this deeply, this entirely. His whole world had been remade, and even himself, reborn into a new man. A man who shared half a life, and half of his soul, with the one person who meant everything. With Jack.

He reached for the pocket on the front of his jacket. Dipped his fingers within, and touched two rings, sitting over his heart.

They'd survived everything. Finding each other through the winding paths of each of their lives. Accepting the spark, and growing their friendship, and then their love. Protecting that from the world. Protecting each other from the world.

How many times could they have called it quits? Thrown in the towel, said it was too much, too strange, too difficult to be in love with each other? They'd kept going, kept loving, in spite of it all.

And then Jack had tripped over Madigan's hate, over a grenade dropped in his heart in the shape of his dead wife. It was the perfect attack; resurrect an unfinished piece of Jack's life, a hole in his heart that hadn't had the chance to mend.

But the trap had failed. Faced with Leslie again, Jack had finally found the closure he'd been robbed of. Discovered the hole in his heart had been filled with healing. With Ethan. "I'm not the same man who married her," Jack had breathed earlier, resting in Ethan's arms as the sun set on the cold sand. "I'm someone new. What I dream for is different. Who I love has changed. What I want, more than anything else in the world, is to be with you. Forever. No matter what."

He'd held Ethan's hand while they watched the fire burn, watching the logs turn to cinder and ash. "Once, I wanted her back. I wanted her back from the dead, like magic. But... that was a selfish dream. I would never wish that on her, or anyone. Captured and held for so many years? No. It's better that she's gone. At peace. I loved her, and we were good together. But in the end, she gave me the greatest gift of all. The confidence to start down the path that led me to you."

Facing Leslie had revealed to Jack that his love for Ethan truly was bone-deep. Something that lived and breathed in his soul. Something that couldn't be broken and couldn't end, he'd said. "I was never more certain of anything in my life than coming back to you. Choosing you, Ethan, over everything."

It was Ethan's turn. Time to show Jack just how deeply he felt. How much Jack meant to him, and what he dreamed for the two of them, every single moment.

Fears he'd once had melted away, slithering from his heart and his soul like mist burned away by the sun. There was nothing in the world that could stop their love. Nothing at all.

He slipped the smaller ring from his pocket, palming it before Jack saw. It had dulled a bit, bouncing across two continents. The black titanium had smudges from his fingers where he turned the rings over and over, imagining their future. But the diamonds gleamed, a perfect circle all the way around the band. An eternity circle, for a love without end.

Jack grinned down at him, catching Ethan's stare. "I meant the stars are breathtaking," he teased. A flush crept over his cheeks and stretched down his neck.

"I know." Ethan smiled. He lay on his side, propped up on one elbow beside Jack. "You're just more so to me."

Jack laughed.

Ethan reached for him, for his left hand, and gently pulled Jack's fingers to his lips, pressing a lingering kiss to his knuckles.

How was it possible to feel this much love for someone? His heart felt like ten hearts, or a thousand, all beating as one, all burning incandescent with love for Jack. He rested his cheek on the backs of Jack's fingers, breathing him in.

He pulled back and looked into Jack's eyes. Stared into his soul. Slipped the ring onto Jack's finger, slowly. "Marry me," he breathed. "Marry me, Jack."

Shock slammed into Jack, seeming to snap through him like a bolt of lightning. His eyes blew wide and his jaw dropped, and he gasped, a ragged pull of shaking breath. His hand clenched down on Ethan's, squeezing tight. His gaze flicked from the ring to Ethan and back again. "Ethan—" He choked on his words, and his lips moved soundlessly, struggling to speak. "Ethan," he whispered, his voice cracking. "Ethan, my God…"

Jack tumbled sideways, crashing into Ethan on the sand. He tore his hand from Ethan's hold and grasped his face, cupping his cheeks and brushing their noses together. "Yes, yes, yes," he breathed, his voice wavering. "A thousand times yes, Ethan."

Ethan pressed his lips to Jack's and tasted salt as Jack moaned into the kiss. Jack's hands wound around Ethan's head, gripping him like he was afraid Ethan would disappear. "Where did you—" Jack tried to say, in between kissing Ethan, nonstop. "How did you get a ring?"

Smiling, Ethan brushed his thumb over Jack's cheek, chasing away a tear. "I had them made before Sochi. I've carried them with me since."

Jack curled forward, pressing his forehead against Ethan's. "Ethan…"

"Shhh." Ethan kissed his eyes, his cheeks. "That's the past. And we're stronger for it. Our love has been tested by fire. Nothing can tear us apart. Not now."

Jack shook his head "Not ever. I never want to be without you."

Ethan kissed the ring that rested on Jack's finger. "You never will."

Jack beamed, his face brightening like spring bursting over a winter wasteland. He squinted at Ethan and cocked his head to one side. "You said you had 'them' made."

"I had a set made. I thought they could be wedding rings. I wanted them to match. I want to wear the same rings."

"Do you have the second ring? Yours?"

Ethan nodded, and he pulled it out of his pocket.

Jack plucked it from his fingers. He reached for Ethan's left hand as he kneeled, balanced on one knee, grinning his thousand-watt smile. "Ethan Reichenbach," he started, his eyes glittering. "I love you more than I can ever say. Will you make me the happiest man who's ever, ever lived? Will you be my husband? Will you *marry* me?"

Ethan thought he'd experienced the absolute height of happiness moments before when Jack had said yes, but a new joy burst through him at Jack's words. A new light that raced through his veins and set up a home in his heart. Perfection. Certainty. Nothing was as right as this moment.

He tried to speak, but his throat closed, and his eyes watered. He nodded, pressing his lips together when Jack slid his ring onto his finger. Jack clasped his hands, threading their fingers together. Both rings gleamed, matching promises for the whole world to see.

They met in the middle, lips caressing slowly as their bodies slid together. Jack melted into him, and Ethan laid him back on the sand, covering Jack's body with every inch of his own. Time fell away as they kissed, as their bodies molded together, a perfect fit.

Ethan slid his hand down to Jack's hip, squeezing. "Into the sleeping bag," he breathed, kissing down Jack's neck. "I'm not giving those subs a free show."

Jack chuckled, his breath stuttering at Ethan's nibble on his neck. "Make love to me."

He ran his nose up Jack's neck, breathing in his scent, and sucked at his earlobe, the curve of his jaw. "Are you sure?" Ethan had taken Jack multiple times now, but Jack hadn't taken Ethan since they'd been back at the White House.

"I love it," Jack breathed, like he was confessing. "I love having you inside me. Love when you make love to me. I want it all the time. Want you all the time."

Fuck, he nearly came at Jack's words, shivering from the tips of his hair to the soles of his feet. His cock, already rock-hard, throbbed, begging for Jack's body. He'd make love to Jack every day, every hour if he could. Worship at Jack's body for the rest of his life. Make him scream with pleasure, shiver and shake and tremble apart, delirious from their lovemaking.

They scooted into the sleeping bag, ditching boots and shirts and pants in a haphazard array, leaving them lying in the sand like flagrant evidence. Ethan snaked a tube of lotion he'd swiped from the supplies Anderson had given them from the pocket of his pants.

Jack rolled on top, straddling Ethan and rocking his hips, his hard cock pressed against Ethan's. Ethan's hands roamed over Jack, into the curve of his lower back, and grabbed his ass, squeezing his cheeks. He dipped his fingers within Jack's cleft, stroking over his puckered hole. Jack moaned, sucked on Ethan's bottom lip, and pushed his ass into Ethan's hands.

Lightning crackled through him, burning him from the inside. He popped the top of the lotion and squeezed a dollop into his palm. He tried to warm it, but the lotion was cold when it hit Jack's skin. "Sorry," he breathed.

Jack shook his head and spread his legs. Bowed his back. A shiver snaked up Jack's spine. "Keep going."

In minutes, Jack was panting, hanging his head between his shoulders as he hovered above Ethan's lap. Ethan's fingers disappeared inside Jack's body, kneading and stretching his asshole as his balls quivered, tickling against Ethan's own. He rubbed his cock over Jack's slick hole, sliding over his opening, over and over. Each time, Jack shivered and his eyes rolled back. The top of the sleeping bag clung to Jack's sweaty, shaking shoulders.

"Roll over, love." Ethan kissed Jack's chest, nibbling on his skin.

Jack slid off, and they shimmied into position, Jack lying on his front, propped up on his elbows as he arched his back, his ass offered up just for Ethan. He spread his thighs as wide as they could go in the sleeping bag.

Ethan's eyes nearly crossed, nearly whited out with static, bells ringing in his ears. They'd never made love this way. He'd never taken Jack from behind, and Jack had never taken him this way. He loved kissing Jack when they made love, loved Jack's legs wrapping around him, feeling the soft hairs on his thighs grip his sides. Loved wrapping his own legs around Jack. Loved riding Jack, and Jack riding him. Feeling Jack's hands slide over his chest, or disappear into his crotch. Stroking Jack, when Jack rode him, until senseless, rambling mumbles fell from Jack's lips.

But, Jack was stunning like this. Flushed clear down the curve of his back, his ass red from Ethan's hands and spread wide, his body trembling. He was open, slick and waiting for Ethan.

Ethan's mouth went dry as he leaned over Jack, gripping his hip when he pressed a shaking kiss to his pale shoulder blade.

His cock found Jack's hole, and his thighs pressed against Jack's. Jack rocked back, trying to take him, trying to push Ethan inside him. Ethan nipped at his shoulder. "Slow. I want to feel you spread apart around me."

Jack whimpered, his head falling forward.

The head of his cock breached Jack, slipping just inside his tight hole. Jack moaned and arched his back again, trying to push, trying to press, and he rubbed his cheek against Ethan's. Ethan kissed his jaw, his neck, his bounding pulse. Wrapped one arm around Jack's chest and held him close, Jack's back molded to his chest, his body. He didn't move.

He waited, kissing Jack over and over.

Slowly, Jack's body swallowed his cock, his hungry ass clenching and pulling Ethan deeper, dragging him within his own body.

Ethan's world imploded when he bottomed out, pressed deeper within Jack than he'd ever thought possible. His hands roamed over Jack, from his hips to his chest and up to his hair, mapping his body and keeping them flush and locked together.

Jack rocked his hips, slid his ass over Ethan's cock, taking charge as Ethan kissed every inch of Jack's skin he could reach.

And then, he took over, deep, fluid rolls of his hips into Jack's body. He mouthed over Jack's hair, kissed the curve of his ear. Ran his hand up Jack's neck and turned his head, his fingers grasping Jack's blond strands as they kissed over Jack's shoulder, sloppy and all tongue. Jack's Adam's apple jutted out from his arched neck, and breathless pleas and Ethan's name mixed with his grunts and groans.

Sweat rolled down their skin. Their hot breaths turned the sleeping bag humid, turned the air within the cotton confines an almost scorching heat. There was no hiding what they were doing, not to anyone watching, but the top of the sleeping bag clung to the backs of Ethan's shoulders, keeping them enveloped in their private cocoon.

Jack's arms shook, almost violent trembles while he held them both up. Ethan grabbed his wrists and folded Jack's arms beneath his chest, laying Jack on his front. He went down with Jack, holding him, enveloping him completely.

Jack gasped, thrusting his ass back to meet each of Ethan's hot slides. "More," Jack panted. "Harder, Ethan."

"Kiss me."

Jack twisted and their lips met, another sloppy, tongue-filled kiss. Ethan lit off like a firework. His hands grasped Jack's hips, and he rested his forehead on Jack's shoulder and thrust into him, hard and deep. Harder than he ever had, almost recklessly pounding into Jack.

Jack arched his back and wailed, shouting Ethan's name as he shook, as his body trembled, and as his ass clamped down on Ethan's cock, his desperate thrusts. He humped the sleeping bag, rutting wildly into the cotton and the sand beneath. "Ethan, Ethan—" Jack gasped. "I'm—"

He felt Jack's orgasm tear through his body, felt the clench of his ass, the shake and shiver of his muscles as he thrashed and groaned. It kept going, a relentless wave that never stopped. Jack shouted and writhed, like a boat rocked on an endless, rolling storm, and he backed up on Ethan's cock like he wanted more.

Ethan buried his face in Jack's neck and thrust deep, fucking Jack through his own orgasm. Jack squeezed him dry, his clenching ass yanking Ethan's orgasm from him in a blinding wave. He kept moving, kept driving into Jack, until they were slick with come, covering their legs, Jack's skin, his skin. He couldn't stop, didn't ever want to stop. He'd make love to Jack forever, live in the juncture of their bodies with him for the rest of their days.

Eventually, he slowed, but stayed buried within Jack. Jack moaned and kissed Ethan's hair over his shoulder. "Ethan," he breathed. "*God...*"

"I think they heard that on the subs." Ethan grinned and kissed Jack's shoulder blade, his cheek, and the edge of his wide smile.

"I think they heard that in space." Jack arched his back and squeezed his ass around Ethan again. "I can never get enough of you."

Ethan kissed the corner of Jack's beaming grin again. "That's a relief. I would hope my fiancé likes our lovemaking."

Laughing, Jack wiggled until they separated, and then shimmied and squirmed until they were lying side by side, gazing into each other's eyes. His cheeks were flushed, lit by a radiant glow, contentment oozing from his bones. He slid his fingers through Ethan's chest hair. "Jack Spiers-Reichenbach," he sighed. "That sounds good. Really good."

Shock jolted Ethan like he'd touched a live wire. His thoughts went sideways, smeared apart, and he stared at Jack, his mouth hanging open. "You want to take my name?"

"Of course I do. I want the whole world to know." One thumb brushed over Ethan's nipple. "I want the world to know I'm yours." His eyes gleamed, joyous in the way that he'd been after he'd kissed Ethan on the White House lawn in the back of the ambulance. Proud. Proud of Ethan, of their love, of his choices. Happy. So fucking happy.

Ethan smiled back, until his cheeks burned, aching. "Ethan Spiers-Reichenbach sounds good, too," he whispered.

"Sounds perfect, love." Still smiling, Jack kissed him, soft and sweet.

Their hands rose, cupping cheeks and sliding through sweat-slick hair. Their bodies pressed close again. Beside them, the fire burned low, turning to smoldering coals, as they made their own heat that lasted through the night.

IN THE MORNING, THEY grimaced at the sticky mess they'd made. There was no hiding what they had been up to all night long.

"We need showers again."

Ethan poked his head out of the sleeping bag. Dull fog hung in the predawn air, low over the sand and the beach. Others were rising, huddled around reignited fires and slowly waking up. "Cold saltwater is all that's available, love."

"I am not Russian enough for that."

Ethan managed to drag his scattered clothes into the bag and shimmy into his pants and undershirt. Cold, the uniform clung in all the wrong places, and Jack tried to keep his distance, rolling away as Ethan dressed. Their stomachs ached, by the end, from laughing.

He grabbed a metal bucket from their supplies and filled it with seawater, and then brought it back to their campfire. Jack did his best to restart the fire from inside the sleeping bag, poking it with sticks and turning the coals over. Ethan finished the job, and in minutes, the fire roared and the bucket of water started to steam, resting half in the coals.

Jack scrubbed down with the warm saltwater first and then dressed. Ethan stripped, washed, and redressed, right as Scott headed over.

"Morning." Scott sipped at his battered tin mug, the same one he'd used since they left the forest and the Volga river valley. Burned coffee stench hung in the air. "Have a good night?" His eyebrows rose, almost to his hairline, and he hid his grin behind his mug.

They couldn't keep their guilty smiles contained. Scott snorted.

And then he froze, staring at their hands. Wide eyes flicked first to Ethan, and then to Jack, and finally, he beamed. "Ah, he worked up the nerve to ask!" Scott grabbed Ethan and pulled him in for a huge hug, slapping his back. "Proud of you," he murmured into Ethan's ear. "*Fucking* proud of you."

When Scott pulled back, he turned to Jack, offering his congratulations and a handshake. "Congratulations, Mr. President. You're a damn lucky man." He gripped Ethan's shoulder. "This guy is something else."

"I am." Jack smiled, laughing at the flush Ethan felt rising on his cheeks. "I really am the luckiest man on the planet."

"And don't forget it." Scott's voice was teasing, but his eyes had a sheen to them, a hardness, an unspoken promise. He held Jack's gaze until the moment almost became uncomfortable, and then grinned. "Vasily's up and bitching about breakfast. Come and get your burned coffee and your smoked deer."

CAPTAIN ANDERSON SENT A boat to pick them up, and the final batch of supplies. They carried the crates up to Aleksey as Sergey briefed them on their next mission. The rest of the men, Sergey's resistance, had to carry on. Take the boat and go south, to Vladivostok. Get into the fallen military city and take control of the naval base. Get in contact with Ilya. Take a plane and supplies to his men, and join the fight to retake Moscow.

Anton, Aleksey, and Vasily nodded, and then shook Sergey's hand and brought him in for a back-slapping hug. They said their goodbyes to Sasha next, standing apart from Sergey. Anton grabbed Sasha's face and stared at him. Said something in growling Russian that had Sasha closing his eyes.

Jack, Ethan, and Scott thanked the men for everything they'd done. There was too much to say and not enough time. Jack promised to visit them in Moscow after they retook the capital.

And then it was time to leave.

Jack, Ethan, and Scott boarded first, followed by Sasha. Sergey came last, after staring at the decrepit base, the rotten wooden beams, and the chipped paint. He stood out on the thin beach, a dark outline as the sun broke over the horizon, turning the foggy sky a sodden steel-gray.

"Sergey," Jack called. "Let's go."

Nodding, Sergey trudged down to the boat, and Jack got his first real look at Sergey that morning. He opened his mouth, and almost reached out, but Sergey headed for the opposite side of the boat, facing the breaking waves and the beating wind as he crossed his arms and closed his eyes.

Jack turned to Sasha, trying to find answers.

Sasha stood at the bow, his once-proud shoulders slumped, his rigid spine buckled almost in half, everything about him screaming defeat. A man beaten down, wounded in his soul. A man who had lost everything.

He took in the distance between Sasha and Sergey, the way they orbited each other like magnets rejecting the attraction. The way they kept their backs to each other, as if looking hurt too much, cut too deep.

Jack leaned into Ethan and closed his eyes as the boat set off for *Honolulu*.

CAPTAIN ANDERSON PULLED THEM up to the Control Room, the Conn, as soon as they boarded.

"Our people have been scouring the map Lieutenant Andreyev recreated," he said, nodding to Sasha. "There's something else going on up there."

"Like what?" Jack frowned. The map Sasha had drawn had been digitized, scanned and displayed on a dozen computer screens around the room. Red circles surrounded Madigan's drill holes, creating an oval on the ice.

"These holes they blew. If these positions are accurate, or even close to accurate," he said, eyeballing Sasha, "then these aren't random. They are trying to structurally weaken the ice sheet."

"Why?" Ethan, standing behind Jack, frowned.

Anderson sighed. "Unclear, based on what we have. To gain access to the waters beneath is our first guess, and gain it in a big way. Clear out a major section of the ice sheet." He pointed to the black sail, the dark fin of the submarine sticking out of the ice. "We know this is an SSBN. A *Borey*-class ballistic missile submarine. She carries twenty cruise missiles that can strike anywhere in Europe."

"Or ignite the gas." Jack groaned and scrubbed one hand over his face. "Are they clearing the ice so they can launch?"

"They don't need to. Those cruise missiles can punch through that ice pack, especially at that depth and thickness. So why are they blasting the glacier apart? Is there something under there? What are they trying to get to?"

All eyes turned to Sergey.

"The Arctic has been a Russian graveyard for centuries. The Soviets buried everything there. Secrets, enemies..." He sighed, his expression twisting. "It... was also a dumping site for nuclear waste during the Cold War. Almost twenty thousand containers of radioactive material dumped in the Kara Sea alone. Fourteen decommissioned reactors. And nineteen scuttled nuclear vessels."

"Nuclear waste?" Jack breathed. Behind him, the Conn went silent, every man stilling.

Sergey nodded, once.

Anderson's jaw clenched, hard enough to see his pulse pounding in his temple. "Could he be pulling something up? Something that's in line with his plans?"

"He wouldn't be carving up the ice if he didn't need to." Ethan pointed to the map, to the red circles outlining a rough ovoid shape in the ice. "What's the size estimate of this? Can we project what it could be, based on what he's clearing?"

"A little under four hundred feet." Anderson frowned. "About the length of this sub."

"Sergey!" Sasha barked.

Again, everyone looked to Sergey. He'd gone pale, ghostly white, and his eyes bulged, shock pouring from him. "*Nam pizdets*," he breathed.

"What is it?" Jack growled. "Sergey, what is under that ice?"

Sergey struggled to meet Jack's gaze. His eyes bounced over the Conn and finally settled on the map, on the red circles in the ice. He read the coordinates again, whispering the longitude and latitude. "It *is* a sub," he finally grunted, "named K-27. Illegally scuttled in the eighties in shallow water off the coast of that island." He pointed to Novaya Zemlya, a finger of ice-covered land curving into the frozen Kara Sea. "Its reactor is still live. It can be brought back online. Or worse."

"Worse?" Anderson stared hard at Sergey.

"The right technician can restart the nuclear reactor," Sergey said, choosing his words. "And then they can take it further. Turn the reactor critical."

"A nuclear reactor on a naval submarine can be weaponized," Anderson said carefully.

Sergey held one hand to his gaunt face. "Yes. Naval reactors, in your nation and mine, use highly enriched uranium. Bomb-grade uranium. The most powerful of which was put into this sub, into K-27. But it couldn't be controlled. Could not be contained. There were many accidents. Many people died. That is why the sub was scuttled. It was too dangerous when it was operational. Now? After degrading on the ocean floor for decades?" Sergey scoffed. "If Madigan is going after this, he can get his hands on a nuclear weapon many times the size of the bomb you dropped on Japan."

Silence.

"That's how he's going to do it," Jack finally said. "That's how he's going to ignite the gas cloud permeating the atmosphere. A nuclear blast at ground zero. Fallout will spread around the globe. He's going to triple his devastation, make it nuclear." Jack snorted. "No simple ignition for him. And his fingerprints will be erased. He can shift the blame." Jack jerked his chin to Sergey. "To Russia, or someone else, and say they sent the planet back to the stone age. It's exactly what he wants. He can still be the hero of wastes afterward. King of the ashes of the world."

"But he's up there." Scott frowned. "Why would he blow the world and stand next to the blast? Won't he be cooked when the sky ignites?"

"The one area that's safe from his disbursement into the jet stream *is* the Arctic." Anderson called up another screen, showing the growing fuchsia cloud stretching around half the globe. The Arctic and the ice pack north of Madigan's base were clear. "And if he's got a Russian SSBN, with his own crew loyal to the cause," Anderson said, tapping the map and the dark sail sticking up through the polar ice cap, "then he can just go under the ice and wait for the fallout. Come out by Iceland or Alaska. Kick-start his new world order wherever he wants."

"All right." Jack met everyone's gaze, one by one. "Now we know: this is how he's going to do it. He'll blow when he's able to get K-27 up from the sea floor and weaponize the reactor. He's had a week's head start." He swallowed. "Our job is to stop him. If K-27 is still on the bottom of the ocean, it stays there. If he's got her up, the reactor stays cold. If he's got it online, we shut it down. No matter what. We take him out. This is how we stop Madigan. This is how we save the world."

29

Washington DC

LEVI AND PRESIDENT WALL ducked out of the Oval Office and headed down to the Situation Room, their heads together as they talked fast and low, as if sharing national secrets.

Welby stared them down, watching every single step. What was going on? What were they hiding?

Time to find out.

He ducked into the Oval Office, waving to the president's secretary, Mrs. Martin, as he entered. He waved a manila folder as he pushed open the door. "Got to drop off a new brief."

Mrs. Martin didn't even bat an eyelash. "Have a good day, Agent Welby," she said, as he entered the silent, empty Oval Office.

He took a few steps in and swallowed. The power of the office still stopped him in his tracks, even now, years after he'd become an agent. The fate of the world had been shaped within these curved walls, so many times over. For good or for ill, decisions had been made by men and women in this office that had impacted the lives of billions. He took a shaky breath.

What he was about to do was treasonous.

His stomach had burned a hole through itself, and he'd tied himself in knots, agonizing through the long hours of the day and night. They needed answers.

But he'd never crossed this line before.

Damn it, he needed to move, and fast. He was already on borrowed time.

Welby headed for the Resolute desk and started pulling out drawers. Nothing worthwhile in the top two. Notepads and folders, pens and sticky notes. A candy bar. A card, from Ethan to Jack, something sappy and silly at the same time. He put it back, carefully.

His thumbprint opened both of the locked lower drawers, and he held his breath when he tugged them open. Dozens of file folders. The president's laptop. Top Secret briefs.

And, another laptop, resting on top of a burned briefcase.

He hauled the briefcase out and set it on the desk. It was a wreck, soot-covered, torn on one side, and water-damaged. The handle had been ripped off. Both locks were broken.

Perfect.

Inside, most of the papers were damaged, burned on the edges, or blackened with smoke and soot. Debris filled the inside of the case, gravel and dust. Blood stained one corner. The briefcase had sat in a pool of blood and soaked up enough of it to make Welby look away from the rust-drenched corner.

Lawrence Irwin had carried his briefcase with him into Langley, before the blast. Welby remembered that night. He remembered every moment of what happened, a picture-perfect clarity set in Imax quality in his mind. Waiting in the SUV, equal parts bored and on edge, wondering what was happening within Langley. Why had they taken Leslie Spiers into custody? Was she working with Madigan? What would they find during the interrogation?

And then, the blast. He and his team racing into the still-burning, still-collapsing building. Tearing through concrete and debris, searching for the president as fires roared and smoke billowed around them.

Pulling back blocks of concrete, adrenaline tearing through him faster than a Formula One racecar. Finding Irwin's broken, bloody body. And then the president lying beneath him in a spreading pool of blood.

President Spiers had seemed so light, so fragile, when he scraped him off the ground. Floppy like a doll in his arms. Limp, too limp. He'd carried him over the shattered remains of the CIA's headquarters as helicopters and rescue workers and firetrucks arrived, sirens blaring, lights flashing. People shrieked, crying for help.

He'd carried the president's broken body, staring down into his pale, empty face.

Assassinated.

The word hung like cobwebs in his mind, like a whirlpool that sucked down all other thoughts. It had been *him* on duty, *him* that night. *He* had let his president be attacked. *Assassinated.* He had let the nation down. He had let the president down. And, he had let Ethan down.

Or had he?

Desperation redoubled his efforts, and he clenched his jaw as he rifled through Irwin's briefcase. Where would Irwin have sent Ethan to search for proof of Leslie Spiers's betrayal? Out of the whole world, where would he have gone?

One folder caught his eye. Bright-red Top Secret borders lined the edges, and a giant seal warned him away from the contents. "*Operation: Vigilant Fury*" was the codename.

He snorted. *Vigilant* was President Spiers's Secret Service codename. What could be better for a Top Secret operation to hunt down Madigan? The government did not have the best sense of humor, but they excelled in irony.

He flipped the file open.

Photos, dozens of them, from prison breaks around the world. Satellite imagery over South America, the Maghreb, and Somalia. Dossiers from a dozen military officers, one from a man named Noah Williams, supposedly dead sixteen years prior. Welby's eyes narrowed. Leslie Spiers was supposed to be dead, too. He knew how that had played out.

Intelligence reports. Memos and intelligence analysis and mission briefs from a Marine Corps strike team sent to Ethan. Pages and pages of reports, each one detailing more of the team's actions and missions.

Ethan must have run the strike team, secretly. In addition to being Jack's first gentleman, he must have been running a black strike team, working hand in hand with Irwin. No wonder Irwin turned to him. They were *already* hunting Madigan together.

And the Marines. Were they the missing piece he needed? They must be the ones Ethan had turned to when he needed to follow Leslie Spiers's tracks.

Who were they?

Welby dug deeper. The mission briefs had been signed by an "*AC, LT1*". Not good enough. He needed a name.

Finally, at the bottom of the file, he struck gold. A sheet of paper, torn from a notepad, with scribbles of Irwin's that he should have thrown away months ago. "*LT Adam Cooper, SOCOM. General Bell, Commanding Officer. Possible team lead. Check background. Current disciplinary action? Investigate connection to F.*"

He had a name. A place to start searching. Finally.

Welby put everything back into the briefcase, exactly as he found it, and slid it back into the bottom drawer.

He took the *Operation Vigilant Fury* folder with him, hidden inside the manila envelope. He clenched the paper with Lieutenant Adam Cooper's name on it, tight enough that his hand shook.

One step closer to the truth.

EXCEPT LIEUTENANT ADAM COOPER was a ghost.

Welby slammed down the phone in Pete's office and groaned. Across the desk, Pete stared at him, his wide eyes almost bulging from his skull. "Nothing? Again?"

"Not a damn thing," Welby growled. "Irwin and the CIA must have scrubbed him from the system when they brought him on board. His record is a shell. I can't get any working information for him. No current posting. No current duty assignment. Nothing."

"What about this?" Pete spun the scrap of paper and jabbed his finger in the middle. "His commanding officer was General Bell at SOCOM. Can you get in touch with him?"

"I tried. The general is 'unavailable'. And his secretary has no idea who any Lieutenant Adam Cooper is. Never heard of him. Which is bullshit, because if he was in disciplinary trouble, then his secretary would have run the paperwork. She *has* to have heard of him."

Pete sighed and threw himself back in his chair. He ran his hands through his hair and laced his fingers behind his head. "You searched all the military databases, right?"

Welby nodded.

Pete gnawed on his lip, staring at Welby. "I've got a person," he finally said slowly. "It's not, you know, *entirely* legal. But I've used them in the past to track down sources. People I need to find when they've gone to ground. If I need them for a story, or if I need them to shut their mouth."

Welby's eyebrows skyrocketed.

"You think being press secretary is just throwing press junkets all the time?" Pete scoffed. "This is one of the dirtier offices in the West Wing. And I've never been afraid of getting into the mud." He swallowed. "Not for Jack."

"I don't need to hear any more." Standing, Welby smoothed his tie and headed for the door. "I'd hate to have to arrest you because of something I overheard." Never mind the treason he just committed himself.

He turned the doorknob. "But, I expect you'll let me know?"

HIS CELL PHONE BUZZED a few hours later. Welby glanced down at the screen. A text from Pete had popped up. *Get here asap.*

Welby pocketed his cell phone and turned back to the shift brief. Levi was talking through the elevated threat assessments, and what they all needed to watch out for. Tasking agents rotating off shift with intel work in Horsepower. Reassigning other agents, and moving their posts around. Changing the West Wing procedures. It was a big shake-up, and Welby couldn't see the reason why. Why move agents? Why have them hunting for intelligence? That was H Street's job, for the intel desk jockeys at Headquarters.

He escaped as soon as the brief ended, slipping out the back. On the way out, he saw the confusion on the other agents' faces, too. What was up with Levi? Why these changes?

Unease slid down his spine, drumming along each one of his vertebrae with a deeper, darker worry.

He pushed his gnawing anxieties away as he slipped into Pete's office. Pete stood at his desk, his back to the door, on the phone. As Welby entered, he waved him in, thanked whoever he was talking to, and hung up.

"What did you get?" Welby crossed his arms and hovered in front of Pete's desk.

"A few things." Pete pulled his keyboard close and started pounding at the keys. "Okay, first, my guy looked up Adam Cooper. Turns out, he's been using his civilian ID to move around. Him and a bunch of other MAMs flying on the same route."

"Military age males?" Welby frowned. "That's not unusual. That's anyone from fifteen to fifty. About half the population of airline travel is in that range."

"Not on this route." Pete spun his monitor toward Welby. A flight route lit up, one red line bouncing from Riyadh to London, London to Seattle, Seattle to Anchorage, Anchorage to Nome, in the far reaches of western Alaska, and then to Sevoukuk, a tiny village on St. Lawrence Island in the Bering Sea. "Only eight men flew this itinerary, and all together, all on the same day. Adam Cooper, six other American men, all in the Marine Corps, and one Saudi national."

"A Saudi?"

"Faisal al-Saud. His passport was flagged in Seattle. Someone came forward and said al-Saud and he were getting married in the States, and the immigration officer let them through."

"Who the hell is Faisal al-Saud? Why is he connected to Lieutenant Cooper?" Welby's brow furrowed, and he stared at the red lines on the monitor as if he could read the lieutenant's intentions in each hop.

"Dunno." Pete shrugged. "I looked up what I could. He's an orphan. His parents were killed in those big bombings the Kingdom had twenty years ago. His uncle adopted him, raised him. He's a quiet prince in the royal family. The only thing that stands out is that he's reported to be the royal head of the Saudi Intelligence Directorate."

"Shit..." Welby cursed and leaned forward, bracing his palms on the edge of Pete's desk. "Is that good news or bad news for us? These flights originated from Riyadh. What the hell was Lieutenant Cooper doing in Saudi Arabia anyway?"

Pete shrugged again. "The only thing we know for sure is that Lieutenant Adam Cooper landed on St. Lawrence Island yesterday. And Ethan wasn't with him."

"Did you track Ethan's passport? Find out where he was?"

"No." Pete shook his head. "He must have been using a burner. Irwin could have gotten him one from the CIA. Ethan's most recent passport scan was his last official trip with the Secret Service. Ethiopia."

A shiver crawled up the back of Welby's neck, ringing his throat until his scar burned. Ethiopia. He remembered gasping for breath as his throat filled with blood. Hands holding him down on the conference table in Air Force One as the surgeon leaned over him, shouting at him to keep still. He swore one of those hands had belonged to Jeff Gottschalk. He'd held Jeff's hand, clenched so hard he thought he broke it. He thought he was going to die on that table, bleed out at thirty thousand feet, all over the seal of the United States.

He took a breath, but Pete jumped in, speaking first. "So. Lieutenant Cooper is in Alaska. Hanging out in the Bering Sea. Moroshkin is invading Canada. You think he's making a move against Moroshkin?"

"He's headed the wrong way for that. He's thirty miles off the coast of Russia. Canada is a long way from Lieutenant Cooper right now. No, he's pointed at Russia."

A light went on in Pete's eyes, an almost mad gleam. He spun his monitor back around as he pounded at his keyboard again. "Take a look at this." He spun the monitor back.

A gaudy, flashing webpage blinked back at Welby, a mess of translation protocols converting Russian web text to broken English. "Looks like… a message board?"

"Yes. A Russian conspiracy theorists' website. They run a message board and yak about all the same things our conspiracy nuts do. Aliens. Government cover-ups. Secret military installations. HAARP. Chemtrails. All of it."

Welby stared at Pete. "Why do we care what Russian nuts are talking about on some badly managed website?"

Pete held up one finger and then pounded away at his keyboard again. A new page came up, a thread of messages. He scrolled to the second message. Pictures filled the thread, groups of hard-looking Russians swarming around a convoy of rugged jeeps that had seen far better days. Some of the men wore full-face black balaclavas. Everybody carried automatic rifles.

"This group of men was seen moving across Russia. First in the west by Volga, and then they reappeared on the east coast, north of Vladivostok. There are unconfirmed reports of sightings in Siberia."

"Looks like a gang of Russian thugs." Had Pete really lost it? Had he chased a rabbit down a crazy hole? Maybe Levi was right, and Pete really did need time off. Hell, maybe he did, too.

"Look closer." Pete pushed the monitor across the desk and started slowly scrolling through the thread. Picture after picture came up and passed, scene after scene of dark-clad Russians clutching weapons and riding in jeeps.

And then—

"Wait!" Welby's hand shot up.

There, striding alongside a balaclava-wearing man, his face turned to the side and cast in half shadows, was *Ethan*.

"You see it too?" Pete breathed. "Tell me I'm not crazy."

Welby shook his head, back and forth, over and over. "It can't be him." The denial was automatic, a knee-jerk gut-check. "There are thousands of people who look alike. This must just be an uncanny double. It's not him."

Pete scrolled again. A new picture, Ethan turning toward the camera this time, and calling to someone behind him.

Welby hissed. He reached behind him and pulled one of Pete's chairs close, collapsing to his ass when his knees buckled.

"I thought the same thing when I saw them," Pete said softly. He sat on the side of his desk, one leg dangling. "It couldn't be him, I thought. No *way*. Why would he be in Russia? With some kind of gang? But…" Pete swallowed. "If Lieutenant Cooper is in Alaska, hanging out on an island within spitting distance of Russia, and Ethan might be *on* the east coast of Russia… I mean, it can't be a coincidence, right?" He trailed off. "C'mon, man. Tell me I'm not losing it."

"It's him." Welby clasped his hands together and fisted them in front of his mouth, covering his lips. "It's him," he repeated. "And I know who the guy next to him is, too."

Twelve years he'd served at Ethan's side, from the day Ethan graduated the Secret Service Academy at Rowley until his transfer to Iowa. Welby had been an agent one year longer, but he'd still been a newbie when Ethan had joined the DC field office, and then the White House. Twelve years of operations together. Twelve years of moving with Ethan, watching him on the protective detail. Watching him with his protectees, how he moved with them.

And then, seeing how different he was with President Spiers. Ethan had always been a consummate professional, a man of clean lines and exacting standards. He'd rocketed up the ranks of the Secret Service because of his discipline, his no-nonsense behavior, his determination and dedication to the service. Professional at all times, even with the most difficult assignments, the most pain-in-the-ass protectees.

Until President Spiers. Until he and Jack came together like sparks catching flame.

With him, Ethan had made protections personal. Welby had seen it, even before the truth came out. Ethan had become compromised. He cared about Spiers. He stood too close. Kept the president in his body space, inside his shadow. Moved his own body in tandem with the president, like they were connected. Like they were a team, a unit, a pair. He'd protected Spiers like he was protecting the most precious thing in the world, and after, when everything came out, Welby realized that had been *exactly* what Ethan had been doing.

The man in the pictures, striding alongside the man in a black balaclava, moved the same way.

Twelve years he'd been at Ethan's side, and he could pick out Ethan's style of protection in an instant. He could see the way Ethan breathed and moved with the man in black, reacted to him almost before the man in black even made a move. A matched set, a unified team. A partnership closer than any he'd ever seen.

"It's President Spiers," Welby breathed. "The president is alive."

30

Washington DC

"WHAT THE FUCK IS going on, Levi?" Snarling, Welby pinned Levi to the wall in the tunnels below the White House. He'd called in a report, asking Levi to come check out something suspicious. Something he didn't want to say over the radio.

Given Levi's turn toward obvious paranoia and isolation, he'd gambled that it would work.

It did. Levi came down alone, and Welby jumped him.

"Welby?" Levi's eyes went wide, and he struggled against Welby's hold. Levi against Pete was an unfair match. Pete never stood a chance. But agent to agent, Levi against Welby? One of them would have to bleed to end this.

"*Spiers is alive*," Welby hissed. He leaned in close, breathing against Levi's cheek. "Ethan's *with* him. *I know the truth.*"

Thrashing, Levi tried to shake him off. Welby kneed him in the gut and spun him around, slamming him face-first into the concrete wall. "So, here's the question!" Welby roared. "Are you working with him or against him? Where the fuck were you the night of the bombing?"

Levi hadn't been at the White House when the blast went off at Langley. He hadn't been with Welby, either.

"What the fuck is this?" Levi snarled, his face smashed to the wall. "What about *you*, Welby? Are you working for Madigan? Trying to find out information to pass on to him?"

"How fucking *dare* you!" Welby twisted Levi's arm, hard. Levi tried to kick Welby's legs out behind him. Welby slammed him into the wall again. "Every time I close my eyes, all I can see is the president's broken body. *Tell me he's alive!*" Welby's voice rose, bellowing. "Tell me he's with Ethan, and they're still fighting Madigan. *Tell me!*" He shuddered, and then dragged in a ragged breath. "Tell me we're on the same side," he breathed.

Levi thrashed and then went limp, sagging against the wall with a sigh. He rolled his forehead against the concrete and groaned. "Luke…" he groaned, using Welby's first name. "Jesus Christ, I want to trust you. I fucking do. I hate this. I hate not trusting anyone."

"Why don't you trust us, Levi? What's going on?" He kept Levi pinned.

"There's a mole," Levi whispered. "Another one. Someone in the White House. Someone close to the president. Pictures from Evgeni Konnikov's funeral ended up in the president's duffel with Madigan's signature on them. Pictures of Ethan and Spiers were at Madigan's base, where Leslie was made. There's someone on the inside." He glared over his shoulder, looking Welby dead in the eyes. "Is it you?"

Welby blinked. His heart hammered. "No. It's not me."

Levi breathed hard, his nostrils flaring. "I think it's an agent. Someone with our level of clearance."

"It's *not* me." Welby let Levi go and backed away. "Levi, it's not me."

Levi turned and leaned against the wall. Defeat poured off him in waves. He stared at Welby, eyes wide. "I want to believe you."

"Then do." Welby spread his hands and held them up as if surrendering. "Trust me, Levi. I want to help the president and Ethan. I want to bring them home. Why are they in Russia?"

Levi doubled over, blowing out as he braced his hands on his knees. "Fuck, how do you know where they are?"

"Pete and I have been trying to track everything down. Lieutenant Cooper and his team. Ethan, and how he found out about Leslie. Where Scott went after the blast. They're all together, aren't they?"

Levi leaned back against the wall, thunking his head against the cold concrete. "They will be soon. Luke, who else knows? Who else knows what's going on?"

"I don't think we do know what's going on. But it's just us. Pete, me, Jason, and Jennifer."

Exhaling, Levi closed his eyes. "At least you didn't tell another agent."

"You really think another agent has turned? Now? After everything?"

"I'm fucking terrified of it." Levi held Welby's gaze, and Welby saw the naked fear in Levi's eyes. Raw, aching worry, the kind that Welby lived with. The kind that pitted his bones and turned his guts to barbed wire tied in knots.

"Trust me, Levi." Welby dropped his hands. He looked at Levi, really looked at the younger man. Levi looked destroyed. Torn apart and put back together wrong. Sunken, bloodshot eyes, and deep bags on his face. His shoulders, normally ramrod straight, were slack, and he leaned forward like a someone had sliced the strings holding him up. Everyone knew when Ethan had put Levi on his team guarding President Spiers that Levi was on the fast track. Everyone knew Levi would inherit the detail from Ethan, after Ethan's fifteen-to-twenty glorious years running it.

How plans changed. Levi was supposed to have another fifteen plus years before he had to command the detail, the White House Secret Service. And he was supposed to trust his people, not go it alone.

"I want to trust you," Levi breathed. "Your background came back clean. Twice."

"We're on the same side. Let me help you."

Levi swallowed, and then slowly, with halting, grinding words, told him everything. Jack's plan to stay dead to fool Madigan, and his and Scott's spine-meltingly terrifying journey to smuggle themselves into Russia. Madigan's plot in the Arctic. Jack, Ethan, and Scott joining Sergey Puchkov's insurgency and racing across Russia to meet with American subs. And Jack's plan to head to the Arctic himself, with Ethan's team and a pair of subs, and take Madigan on.

When he finished, Welby couldn't breathe. He turned away, pacing, and tried not to faint. Tried to stop the world from spinning off its axis. "Fucking hell," he finally whispered.

"You see?" Levi laughed bitterly. "None of that can get out. Fucking *none* of it. Their *lives* depend on it. And everyone else's, too. They're trying to sneak in and stop Madigan, when even a SEAL team failed, Luke. And the fucked-up thing is? This could be our only hope. A president everyone thinks is dead, a Russian insurgency, and Ethan and Scott."

"I'll take those odds." Welby turned and faced Levi, his hand on his hips. "I've served with Ethan and Scott for over a decade. I know what they can do. I'll put my money on them, every time."

Levi looked away. Welby watched him swallow hard. "What is it?"

Closing his eyes, Levi dropped his head. "Scott," he said softly. "There's no background check on him. I can't find it. Everyone else has one… except him."

31

Bering Sea

THEY SPENT THEIR FIRST day onboard *Honolulu* running through familiarization briefings and exercises, learning emergency procedures for fires on board, explosions, and man overboard situations. Jack's head spun, too much information coming at him too fast.

The executive officer and the navigation officers gave up their two cabins, hot racking with other officers while Jack, Ethan, Sergey, and Sasha were onboard. Jack and Ethan moved into the executive officer's cabin, and Sergey and Sasha moved into the other. Scott volunteered to hot rack with the chiefs in the Goat Locker, sharing their bunk when they were on duty and getting his butt out of it when they were off. In the forward compartment, hammocks had been pulled out in anticipation for Adam's team in the torpedo room, the same place SEALs crashed when they were hitching a ride on board a submarine. It was going to be a tight fit, with everyone crammed inside.

Finally, they arrived off the coast of St. Lawrence Island, deep in the Bering Sea and pointed down the gullet of the Bering Strait. Captain Anderson sent a boat out again, motoring to the northeast side of the island, and a small cove Ethan pointed out on the map. Ethan, the executive officer, and a team of security personnel went out. Jack watched from the bridge on top of the sail, trying to keep his breakfast down. Black waves crashed over the top of the sub, whitecaps that rolled over *Honolulu's* back. On the surface, the sub rocked and rolled with the ocean's currents, the seesaw motions exaggerated in the bridge. Icy spray blasted him in the face, and fierce winds whipped down the length of the sub. Sergey, Sasha, and Scott stayed below.

Jack almost wished he could join them.

He watched Ethan's boat head toward shore, bouncing and tumbling on the roiling waves all the way to the beach.

Minutes after Ethan landed, they set out again, this time carrying another eight men. He picked them out one by one: Lieutenant Cooper and his men, and one extra. An Arab, slim and tall, who stayed at Adam's side, looking cold and miserable and zipped up in a thick jacket. Was this Prince Faisal from Saudi Arabia? Had he joined Adam's team, journeyed halfway around the world to help? What an alliance they were creating.

Jack spotted Doc clinging to the edge of the boat, leaning over the side like he was hurling his guts overboard. He rested his cheek on the inflatable rubber, but he bounced with every wave and roll of the ocean. In moments, he was hurling again, chunks blowing into the water as another of Adam's Marines held on to his belt to keep him from going overboard.

And then they were back, clambering on board and disappearing into the sub. Jack scrambled down to greet them, alongside Captain Anderson.

When Adam saw him, he smiled wide and held out his hand. Jack pulled him in for a tight hug. "Good to see you, Mr. President," Adam grunted, pulling away. He nodded to his team, and Jack shook each of their hands and returned their smiles.

"I'm glad to see each of you," Jack said. "Let me be clear. We are going to get this son of a bitch. We're going to take him out, and we're going to find whoever it was who killed Corporal Fitz." He watched Adam's men grit their teeth, saw their jaws clench. "We'll make them all pay."

Hoots and hollers followed his words, and then the executive officer offered to lead Adam's men to the torpedo bay, their new home.

Adam and the Arab hesitated, hanging back.

Jack held out his hand. "Jack Spiers."

"*Alhamdulillah*, Mr. President. I am glad to see you well. We have spoken before. Faisal al-Saud. *Bismillah,* it is a distinct honor to meet you at last." Faisal took his hand and shook it, more firmly than he would have expected.

"Faisal has been an invaluable aid to our mission, every step of the way." Adam swallowed. Jack watched him fidget, watched him slide closer to Faisal. "I consider him a member of my team."

"As do I, then." Jack nodded to them both. Behind Adam, Ethan came down the ladder, shaking saltwater from his hair and wiping the drips from his face. "Get settled in. We'll update you all soon."

Nodding, Adam and Faisal followed their team, heading forward.

Anderson passed Ethan a towel. "Mr. President, our transit through the Bering Strait is going to be delayed."

"What's going on?"

"The Bering Strait is one of the most difficult passages in the world, Mr. President. It's just about one hundred feet deep where we can cross, sometimes as low as fifty feet. We need to make the passage submerged, but that requires exact precision. This storm is getting worse. Ice drifts are banging around on the surface, and the currents are strong. We're going to wait for a few hours. The weather report says this will pass soon."

Jack and Ethan shared a look. "As long as it's not too much of a delay."

"We'll make up speed under the ice cap." Anderson smiled. "Since we're treading water, I'd like to ask you both to join me for lunch. It would be an honor, and I'd be a poor captain if I didn't treat my dignitaries with the respect they deserve."

Jack laughed. "Captain, you've done an admirable job with what we've handed you." He looked at Ethan, who nodded. "We'd love to join you."

32

Kara Sea – Madigan's Base Camp

"GENERAL."

Cook's deep voice boomed down the hallways of their command ship, the Russian destroyer *Veduschiy*. Parked in the Kara Sea after breaking through the ice, the *Veduschiy* had been ensnared once again. She was affixed to the ice and the ice to her. She wasn't going anywhere.

She wouldn't need to, ever again.

Madigan watched Cook storm into the destroyer's command center. The dim lights and the red-and-blue glow of the displays cast harsh shadows over his already lean and dangerous features. Even in the darkness, his eyes gleamed, a predatory intensity that couldn't be contained.

The past few days had been hard for the man. He needed to give Cook a win, or an outlet, at least, for the roiling bloodlust that had spiked within him. The discovery of Paloshenko's failure and the loss of the MiG pilot had nearly made Cook snap. "What is it, Captain?"

"We've received a message, sir. From our contact." Cook scowled, ferocious anger rolling off him. His arms trembled, the strength in his muscles desperate to lash out, to destroy. "Jack Spiers is *alive*," Cook spat. "He's not on life support in America. He's on a mission to the Arctic." Cook slammed down a tablet, their contact's message scrawled across the screen. "He's coming *here*."

Jack Spiers... Despite himself, Madigan grinned. He chuckled under his breath and reached for the tablet. Jack's whole mission was there: two subs heading for the Arctic, Lieutenant Cooper's team, Ethan Reichenbach, Scott Collard, and Jack.

"Jack, Jack, Jack..." He hadn't thought Jack had it in him. The senator from Texas was all smiles and blond hair, a pretty-boy politician who talked a big game but liked to settle for negotiated agreements and bilateral partnerships. He'd made his name in negotiation, in making everything a win-win for all sides. He didn't know how to play in the big leagues, and that had been Madigan's golden ticket.

Jack, he'd thought, would be the easy target. Fifteen years of planning. Fifteen years of painstakingly setting up his people and waiting for the right moment. And then America had elected a blond floozy, a feel-good candidate after successive years of bad politics.

Jack was supposed to be *easy* to eliminate. The world should already be his, united under his rock-solid grip on global security amid a planet recovering from the ashes of a nuclear holocaust.

He'd underestimated Jack. Or, at least, had underestimated the people around Jack. Ethan Reichenbach, his surprise lover, who had come back from the dead for him.

Madigan remembered Reichenbach well. A serious man. A boring man. He'd been too uptight for Madigan's tastes, and he'd decided not to approach and recruit him, not when Reichenbach was in the Special Forces, or later when he rose through the ranks at the Secret Service. Maybe he'd made a mistake in that. Maybe he should have worked harder to turn Reichenbach to his side.

No matter. Eliminating a target was just as good as turning them, in this case. Jack was already supposed to be dead, and Ethan out of commission somewhere, mourning his everlasting love. Instead, they were heading for him, together again.

Two birds with one stone.

"Let them come," he said, smiling back at Cook. Cook's glower, if possible, grew worse, his cheeks darkening to an almost dangerous maroon, his eyes sharp as knives. It was men like Cook, Madigan thought, who birthed the legends of werewolves. Men with fearsome beasts caged inside them, ready to rip another man apart in a bloodthirsty rage. "Read it again, Captain. Our man is right there with them. Retask him. Have him keep his cover going. Keep him in for the long haul. No matter where they go, or how far they get, keep him right there. Right next to their jugular. This mission of Jack's does nothing to hurt us. Instead, they'll be coming right here, and we can take our time eliminating them once they've arrived." He grinned. "Wouldn't you like that? Wouldn't you like to take your time? Make it hurt?"

Finally, Cook's scowl softened, turning almost interested, like a mollified animal. A shark that had been promised a meal.

"Where are we on raising K-27?"

Cook straightened and visibly switched tracks within his mind. "The divers report that the hull is intact and the keel is undamaged. They can raise the sub as one piece and bring her up to the ice."

"Excellent. Have them begin immediately."

"Already done. She'll be off the ocean floor in four hours. Rising steadily after that, until she's through the ice."

Madigan nodded. "Which means we need our nuke tech here, asap." He slid the tablet back to Cook. "Work it out. Make it happen."

"Yes, General."

"And we need to prep our people around the world. The time is near. How are we doing with our transmission?"

"The satellite transmitter is online. We're bouncing the signal through three hundred proxies before broadcast. Even if someone's looking to trace it, it will just look like a streaming signal bouncing from one of three hundred different locations."

"Good. Begin the broadcast. I want everyone ready. When we light this up, I want our people to be the first ones out on top of the rubble."

Finally, Cook smiled, an almost feral, wild thing. He nodded, but said nothing, and slipped back into the shadows of the destroyer.

White House Scrambles to Avoid War on Multiple Fronts

The White House is scrambling to contain two explosive situations rapidly coming to a head. Russian forces have not retreated from their positions in occupied Canada, and while hostilities have ceased for the time being, sources within the intelligence community report that Canada has cut off communications with the United States. The White House has been frantic to reestablish communication with Ottawa. One West Wing source says, "…[this could be] the end of American hegemony in North America. If Canada turns to the Russians instead of the US, [the US] will find herself very, very alone in the world."

News of the Chinese sending a fleet of warships toward the Pacific coast of the United States has further strained the already beleaguered White House.

Additionally, scattered reports suggest the White House is also attempting a high-level military operation, possibly in the Arctic. When questioned, multiple senior advisors insisted they had no knowledge of any activities taking place in the Arctic. However, several officials did say that President Wall has been unusually circumspect, even keeping information from her National Security Staff, and preferring to meet exclusively with one or two "trusted advisors" only.

33

Washington DC

AT FOUR FORTY-NINE in the morning, Elizabeth heard a bump outside the Queen's Bedroom door in the White House Residence.

She crawled out of bed, moving slowly to the doorway. She wore one of Ethan's large undershirts, borrowed courtesy of Levi's pilfering in Jack and Ethan's bedroom, over her underwear. They were not the clothes in which to fight off an invasion.

Taking a breath, she leaned against the doorway, listening through the wood.

Levi's voice, cursing softly under his breath, hit her ears. She opened the door.

Levi huddled on the couch in his boxers, rubbing at his shin. He had his weapon in one hand. The coffee table was on its side, three feet away.

"You all right?" She leaned over the back of the couch, where it blocked the doorway, and smiled at him.

"I'm fine." Levi managed a tiny grin. "Sorry I woke you."

"What happened?"

Shaking his head, Levi looked away. "I think I had a nightmare," he finally breathed. "Came up swinging."

She stayed quiet, listening to the sounds of the White House, the creak and hum of the old house's bones. Carefully, she climbed over the back of the couch and settled down beside him. "You too, huh?"

"Nightmares seem to be the name of the game, right now."

Elizabeth leaned back, sighing. "The Chinese fleet is due to hit our blockade off Hawaii soon. God only knows what will happen then. Are we about to have a war on two fronts?" She pinched the bridge of her nose. "Or is it three fronts?"

Levi de-cocked his pistol and set it down. He rubbed his hands together and shook his head. "I don't know who to trust. If I trust the wrong person, it's game over." He swallowed and turned to her. His dark eyes caught the reflection of the moonlight. "But what if I already have trusted the wrong person? What if I can't see it?"

She frowned, studying him. Deep in his gaze, fear bubbled, a grating, grinding anxiety. It wasn't like Secret Service agents to be woken by nightmares. What had spooked Levi this deeply? "Something happen?" she asked, her voice soft.

Levi turned away. His hands rubbed over themselves again. He shook his head but didn't speak for a long moment. "I've hit a dead end investigating the Secret Service," he breathed. "I need another angle. Another way to approach this. I'm going crazy looking at my own people."

"Have you looked into Corporal Fitz's murder?"

Levi turned to her and frowned.

"Corporal Fitz was murdered right before the *Vinogradov* was sunk. He was a member of Lieutenant Cooper's team. The one Ethan was running."

Levi buried his head in his hands and groaned.

"The number of people who knew about Lieutenant Cooper and his team can be counted on one hand. We need to know who said something and to whom. How did Lieutenant Cooper's team get exposed to Madigan's people?"

"You're gonna want to call General Bell up to Washington," Levi growled. "I can't get ahold of him. He's blowing me off. But he's one of those people who knew. And he's an asshole, too."

She arched one eyebrow.

"Ethan and I went down there when Ethan and President Spiers were setting up the team. We had to go talk to General Bell at SOCOM to get Lieutenant Cooper transferred over to Ethan's command. He… wasn't happy to see Ethan. At *all*. Wanted nothing to do with him. Accused him of being illegal." Levi snorted. "I wanted to punch him right in his smug mouth."

Leaning back, Elizabeth covered her eyes. "So there's one who wasn't fully on board the 'Team Jack' train." She sighed. "All right, I'll summon him to Washington. When he gets here, meet with him personally. See what he has to say about Cooper and his men." Levi nodded, but his shoulders stayed taut, clenched like he was waiting for a blow. She reached out, resting one hand on his arm. "I know it's hard, Levi," she said softly. "But we have to keep looking, even at our friends. If someone is out there, waiting to hurt us, then we need to root them out. Dig them out before they get a chance to do anything. Betrayal… it's the worst kind of pain when someone you know twists a knife in your back. Let's catch them before they have the chance to plunge it in."

34

Bering Sea

Laughing, Captain Anderson reached for Jack's glass. He refilled it with sweet tea and passed it back, still smiling after retelling one of his favorite training stories. He had a reputation as a captain who could turn shit into gold and break hard-luck curses. He took on board officers and men who needed a little extra polishing and delivered fine sailors to the fleet after a deployment on his boat. The job, though, came with its share of hair-raising stories, which were only funny in the retelling.

Anderson sat back, stretching one arm along the wall behind his seat. They were in the wardroom, alone in between shifts. The rest of the officers had already eaten and cleared out. Anderson sat at the head, in his seat, with Jack and Ethan sitting on either side of him.

"Captain, I'm impressed you recognized us on that pier." Jack smiled. "We looked like an escaped chain gang, and we smelled worse. How did you know it was us?"

Anderson smiled. A new light shone in his eyes. "It's impossible to *not* recognize you, Mr. President. You're the media's favorite subject. Then, and now."

He rolled his eyes. "The media. They, almost more than anything else, make me want to run away and hide on some lonely island."

"Truth be told, Mr. President," Anderson said carefully, "I never paid much attention to the media about you and Mr. Reichenbach. It was your private life they were trying to dig into. I didn't care for it. But—" Anderson pointed his finger at Jack. "I'll tell you who did listen to the media. Who listened to every single thing that came out about you and Mr. Reichenbach." His eyes narrowed as he leaned forward, bracing his elbows on the edge of the table. "My son."

Something in the room changed. The lightness, the fun, the laughter, fled and seemed to take all the oxygen with it. Jack's gaze darted across to Ethan.

"I was in port after a long exercise. My wife had been emailing me and emailing me about how our son had been acting up. He's sixteen, so, typical teenage stuff, I thought. Mouthing off. Being a brat. Slamming his door. I thought he was just going through phases, but she told me it was getting worse.

That he was getting depressed. He'd sit in his bedroom and listen to music at full blast, and when she went in to yell at him to turn it off, she'd find him crying."

Under the table, Ethan's foot slid alongside Jack's.

"So, when I got home, I tried to talk to him. He wasn't having any of it." Anderson shook his head, seemingly lost in his memories. "My dad was hands-off with me, and I don't really know how to do it any different. I was hands-off with him. It was right before Christmas." His gaze landed on Jack, eagle-eyed. "You both made big headlines at Christmas."

Jack's lips thinned. He breathed in deep, through his nose, and stared at Anderson.

"I remember getting the paper and seeing you both on the front page, dancing together at the White House. Didn't think anything of. Until." He wagged his finger again, pointing at Jack. "Until I walked into my son's room that night and I saw him staring at that picture of the two of you like it was the most amazing thing he'd ever seen.

"He'd cut it out of the paper. When he saw me, he hid it. Crumpled it up and buried it under his pillow. I tried to stop him, but he was frantic. Hyperventilating. Started crying and saying he was sorry, he was so sorry."

Jack's jaw trembled, and he covered his mouth with one hand as his eyes burned. He blinked fast.

"Turns out," Anderson said slowly, "he was figuring a few things out about himself. Like how he was attracted to other boys. You'd become a hero to him, Mr. President. Someone he could look up to."

That was it for his heart. Jack took a shaky breath, and a tear slipped down his cheek. He tried to stifle his tears, but failed. Ethan reached across the table and grasped his free hand as Jack shook his head. "I didn't do anything."

Anderson squinted at him. "You were a man my son could look at and see himself in. Someone who followed his heart, and was brave in the face of everything and everyone standing against him." Anderson looked down at his lap. "He thought I'd be all kinds of upset. Thought that because I was military, I'd be against you, and thus, against him. We had a long talk that night. Almost all night long, in fact. I told him exactly what I thought of you, Mr. President. And you, Mr. First Gentleman." He nodded to Ethan.

A slow smile unfurled over Anderson's face. "Now, my son emails me every single day. He's my best bud. I know about his friends, his hopes, his dreams. His homework. I know about the boy he wants to ask to prom." Anderson chuckled, and then went quiet. He looked Jack dead in the eyes. "I have you to thank for that, Mr. President. You gave my son hope when he was lost. Gave him someone he could admire. Someone he needed." He held up his glass, a silent toast.

Tears slid down Jack's cheeks, searing his skin. He smiled at Anderson while clenching down on Ethan's hand and wiping away his tears with the other. "I'm proud of your son," he finally managed. "I know what it's like, facing down what feels like the whole world to be who you are."

"Mr. President, if there is *anything* I can do for you, I will. Anything."

"Please, call me Jack." He was about to shake his head, to say that Anderson had already done more than enough when the thought went off like a rocket in the back of Jack's mind. He looked down at his and Ethan's hands. "Actually," he said, smiling wide as he wiped the last tear from his cheek. "There is something I'd like to ask you, Captain." On the tabletop, he laced his fingers through Ethan's. Ethan's ring gleamed, catching the light and scattering halos around their joined hands. "Ethan and I are engaged," he started, "and we're on a boat at sea." His smile turned soft. "And you're the captain."

Ethan sucked in a breath. His eyes went wide. "Jack... Are you sure?"

"More than sure, Ethan. Let's do this. I want to be Jack Spiers-Reichenbach. I want to face Madigan as your husband."

Anderson set down his glass and turned to Jack. "I've never performed a marriage at sea. It's not really in the job description for a submarine captain. But... I think I can figure out what to do." Smiling, he added, "It would be the highest personal honor to marry the two of you."

Silence. Jack bit his lip. Ethan stared at him, his jaw hanging open, but joy tumbled from his gaze.

"If we're going to do this, we should do it sooner rather than later. We won't have time once we get into the Bering Strait, and beyond that, we're at war." Anderson glanced at his wristwatch. "In fact, the best time would be now." He looked from Jack to Ethan. "If that's too soon, I understand—"

"No, it's perfect." Ethan spoke, and he rubbed his thumb over the back of Jack's hand. "We're both more than ready."

"Is there anyone on board who you want to serve as witnesses? Or best man, even?"

Their eyes met. "I'll get Scott," Ethan said.

"I'll get Sergey."

Anderson stood. "Meet me in my cabin when you've got them."

SCOTT TOOK ONE LOOK at Ethan when he showed up at the mess hall and threw his fork down on his tray, right in the middle of his applesauce. He sighed as he stood, holding his coffee cup like he might throw it at Ethan's head. "What now? What have you done?"

Chiefs from the sub's different departments sat with Scott. They had been eating, ribbing each other in the way that enlisted guys loved to. Back in the day, Scott bled Army green through and through, a salty, hard-edged noncommissioned officer. Even though this was the Navy, not the Army, being back with enlisted men was almost like a field trip for Scott.

The chiefs eyeballed him and Scott as he approached, walking unsteadily. Was the sub tilting? Was it turning over? Or was that just him and his jelly legs? He felt like a baby horse, all knock-kneed and unstable.

What must he look like, to put that look on Scott's face?

He took a breath and exhaled. Took another. "I need you to come with me," he finally grunted.

Scott's face twisted into the look of grinding frustration with Ethan that only Scott could make, only after their decades of friendship. "What did you *do*?" he groaned, gesturing with his cup. "Everything was *fine* yesterday! You guys were *crazy* on that beach—"

"The captain is going to marry us. I need you to be my best man."

Scott's jaw dropped. A moment later, so did his coffee cup, crashing to the deck.

JACK RAPPED ON SERGEY'S door as politely as he could. A half second later, when it didn't open, he slapped at it with his open palm, over and over and over again.

"*Govno*! What the hell?" Grumbling, within. "Son of a bitch..." Sergey, bitching up a storm. Jack smiled and leaned back, bracing his hands on either side of the doorframe.

"What the fuck do you want?" Sergey growled as he ripped open the door. His scowl was terrible, and nothing he'd ever turned on Jack before. As his eyes landed on Jack, his expression shifted, smoothing out until he merely frowned. "Jack? The hell are you doing?" He took all of Jack in, from the way he bounced on his toes to his face-splitting grin.

Jack's cheeks ached. He glanced behind Sergey, into his shared cabin with Sasha. Silence and tension strained the air, enough to make a tuning fork sing. Sasha was lying on the bottom bunk, and had been facing the wall, but he rolled toward Jack when he heard Sergey say his name.

"I'd like to invite both of you to join me." It was hard to speak around such a beaming grin. He leaned in and then back, almost rocking off the doorframe.

Sergey's eyes narrowed. "Why? What is happening?"

"My wedding. And I'd like you to be my best man, Sergey."

SERGEY, SASHA, AND SCOTT crammed into the captain's cabin, taking their places on opposite sides of the cramped, tiny space. Sergey and Sasha huddled together, trying not to touch or look at each other as they stood side by side. Jack buzzed in front of them, practically vibrating.

Across the room, Ethan and Scott hovered by the door. Scott kept a running commentary going, bitching about Ethan's hair, his day-old scruff, the gray in his temples and his beard. "You're sloppy," Jack heard. "Damn it, your collar isn't even straight."

Grinning, Jack turned to Sergey. "Well? How do I look?"

Sergey looked him up and down and scrunched up his face. He wagged his hand in front of him as if to say *so-so*. "Is just a borrowed navy uniform, Jack." He shrugged. "You look better in a tux."

"We're fresh out of tuxes on board, Sergey." He reached for the buttons on the uniform top. "Ethan, let's ditch the jackets. Black undershirts okay?"

Ethan nodded, but behind him, Scott rolled his eyes, and almost hurt himself in the process. He took the uniform top Ethan shrugged off, folded it, and then tossed it on the desk next to Jack's. "Not like your wedding should be formal or anything," Scott grumbled.

Anderson chuckled from where he stood, in the corner and out of the way as he finished buttoning up his dress uniform top. Behind him, the executive officer stood ramrod straight, silently staring at the scene before him like he was watching a train wreck in progress and couldn't look away.

Anderson had changed into his service dress blues, his official uniform for important functions. Ribbons marched proudly across his chest, his gold braid sat perfectly, and his buttons gleamed. "Are we ready?"

Jack turned and met Ethan's gaze. He couldn't stop smiling.

Ethan held out his hand. Pure joy fell from his eyes, solely directed at Jack.

Jack laced their fingers together and stepped forward, standing before Anderson and facing Ethan. Their gazes locked.

"Let's begin." Anderson clasped his hands before him. "I'm, uh, going off the cuff for this one." He raised his eyebrows. "So, bear with me."

Time fell away. The hum and buzz of the sub faded, disappearing into the background. All Jack felt, all he saw, all he heard, was Ethan. Ethan's hands in his, his thumbs stroking over his palms. Ethan's eyes, his gaze fixed on Jack's, filled with a brilliance to rival the sun. He swore he heard Ethan's heart, beating in time with his own.

"We are gathered today with Jack and Ethan and their friends to celebrate the union of their marriage." Anderson cleared his throat. "It's an unusual gathering, to be sure. The Russian president, and a Russian Air Force officer." He nodded to Sergey and Sasha. "A Secret Service agent." Another nod to Scott. "And a Los Angeles-class fast-attack nuclear submarine. This must be the presidential equivalent of eloping."

Jack laughed, loud and clear, and even Sergey and Scott chuckled. Ethan leaned in, kissing his cheek through his smile.

"Let us bow our heads together for a moment and bless Jack and Ethan as they begin their journey. Bless them with a long and loving life, full of the same joy and desire that we've already seen in them. Bless them with unconditional love for each other, for all time, and that their love remains strong and true from this day to their last. Bless, also, those who would wish Jack and Ethan their best, but cannot, sadly, fit into this tiny cabin."

More laughter. Jack threaded his fingers through Ethan's, holding him tight. Anderson's voice seemed to fade and return, rising and falling in time with his heartbeat. The words were a distant thing, something removed from the reality of Ethan, his soon-to-be-husband, standing before him. Ethan. His husband.

"I'll be honest," Anderson said. "I have never seen a couple change the face of the world as much as these two men have. Their love has redefined our entire planet. You both have consistently dared the world to change. To grow. To accept what is before them: two people in the deepest kind of love.

"And the world did change for you. Your love changed the world, continues to change the world, this very moment. Your love knows no boundaries, no limits. Yours is a love that poets have written about, great playwrights and bards of ages past. Yours is a love that will continue to redefine the world, long after this day has passed into history."

Ethan's face flamed a deep burgundy, blushing hard as he listened to Anderson speak. Jack chuckled and cupped his cheek, and then leaned in and pressed a delicate kiss to his cheekbone. Ethan leaned into his kiss, smiling.

"Jack and Ethan," Anderson said, turning to each of them individually. "From the moment you met, from the first moment your eyes landed on each other, there was a spark between you both. A spark that grew into a flame. A flame that grew into friendship. A friendship that grew into love. And now, you place the fires of that love into each other's hearts, where each of you will care for it together for the rest of your days."

Tears pricked at Jack's eyes. He blinked fast, but one slipped free, trickling down his cheek. Ethan smiled and wiped it away with his thumb. He kept his hand on Jack's face.

"Jack, please repeat after me."

He spoke after Anderson, repeating the vows that would bind him to Ethan. "I, Jack, take you, Ethan, to be my husband. To have and to hold, in sickness and in health, for richer or for poorer. I promise my love to you forevermore."

As he spoke, Ethan seemed to stop breathing. He stared at Jack, his lips parted, his eyes filled with tears. His hands squeezed Jack's, and when Jack finished, he burst into a glowing smile as the first tear slid down his cheek.

"Ethan, please repeat after me."

It was Ethan's turn next, and he spoke after Anderson, his low voice gravelly and grinding on the words. "I, Ethan, take you, Jack, to be my husband. To have and to hold, in sickness and in health, for richer or for poorer. I promise my love to you forevermore." Jack mouthed the words along with Ethan, around his smile. When Ethan finished, Jack leaned in and sneaked another quick kiss.

"Whatever lies ahead, good or ill, you both will face it together, and together, nothing will ever stand in your way. Remember, always look to each other first. The tides will rise with your love, and carry you ever onward, away from the rocks and the shoals, and out of troubled waters." Anderson smiled wide. "In all the days to come, from this day forward, you each will take your place at the other's side as husbands."

Ethan beamed and Jack laughed again, a happy, bright, ringing laugh.

"Let the ship's log record that at this date and time, and by the power given to me by the United States government, I now pronounce Jack and Ethan Spiers-Reichenbach married. You may now kiss your husband."

They came together, hands on faces and lips sliding over lips, capturing each other, holding fast as the clapping started. Ethan twisted and dipped Jack, holding him low as he kept their kiss going. Laughing around the kiss, Jack twined his fingers through Ethan's hair, sliding his hand up the back of Ethan's neck. They kept kissing; they could keep kissing until the sub went sailing off the edge of the world, as far as Jack was concerned.

"All right, all right," Scott groused. "Take that back to your cabin. Jeez."

When Ethan pulled Jack up and finally broke their kiss, all Jack saw were smiling faces. Anderson held out his hand, giving them both a firm handshake. Ethan turned to Scott, and the two of them bear-hugged, a fierce grapple that looked almost painful.

Jack turned to Sergey.

Sergey's eyes were wet, but he smiled wide at Jack and held out his arms. "Jack, *pozdravleniya*! Congratulations! You two are made for each other." He kept smiling, but his gaze hollowed out, and Jack saw him glance sideways at Sasha.

Sasha smiled tightly and grunted his congratulations, shaking Jack's hand. He kept his distance from Sergey, not even looking his way.

And then, Ethan was back at his side, slipping his arm through Jack's. "Hey, husband," he breathed into Jack's ear. "Want to get started on our honeymoon?"

35

USS Honolulu

Sasha STORMED OUT OF Captain Anderson's cabin as soon as Jack and Ethan ducked out, laughing their way down the hall to their borrowed cabin. Scott and Anderson were cracking open a bottle of bourbon and joking about how it was about to get noisy in Officer's Country, the part of the boat with the officers' cabins. The executive officer, still looking shocked as to why he was even in the cabin, much less at sea with the formerly dead—now married—American president, finally opened his mouth, cracking a dry joke about checking trim levels with the diving officer to make sure they stayed at even keel for the next hour or ten, what with the pounding the forward section was about to get.

Roaring laughter followed, and Sasha fled.

Sergey followed, shoving past Scott on his way to the door.

In the passageway, Sasha turned away from their shared cabin, heading for the rear of the boat. His shoulders were tight, taut beneath his borrowed uniform, his broad frame almost filling the width of the empty passage.

"Sasha!"

No response, aside from the stiffening of Sasha's spine and the quickening of his steps.

"Sasha, damn you! Stop!"

Sasha came to a perfect halt, falling to attention in a half second. His jaw thrust out, sharp enough to cut, and he stared straight ahead, not blinking. When Sergey stopped at his side, he watched Sasha's nostrils flare and heard the heavy hiss of his angry breaths.

He swallowed. They hadn't said a word since the beach, since Sergey had woken up alone in the cold sand after falling asleep in Sasha's arms. Part of him was furious, again. He was more than tired of Sasha's love of leaving, his constant disappearing act.

Another part of him just wanted Sasha back.

"What can I do for you, Mr. President?" Sasha growled. He kept his eyes averted, staring straight down the passageway.

"Sasha—"

"Lieutenant Andreyev, sir," Sasha spoke through gritted teeth, practically spitting his words. His shoulders shook, and his hands made fists at his sides. "I serve the Russian Federation, Mr. President. I will do what is best for Russia—"

"Damn it, Sasha, stop! Stop this!" He stood in front of Sasha, forcing their gazes to meet. Sasha closed his eyes. "Did you see what just happened in there? Jack and Ethan, they *married* each other!"

Sasha's jaw clenched, seemingly hard enough to crack a tooth.

"Did you hear what the captain said? How they changed the world with their love? It is true, Sasha! They knew what they wanted and they followed it. No excuses."

"They are *American*—" Sasha started to spit.

"No. They are just human. *Men*. Two men in love. No different than you or I could be."

Sasha's face twisted, misery making him ugly for a moment until he forced himself back to rigid blankness.

Sergey stepped close to Sasha, close enough to feel his body's heat and the rise and fall of his chest with each heaving breath. "They never let anything stand in their way," he breathed. "The world changed for *them*. If it happened for them, it could happen for us. Do you see how happy they are?" He took a shaky breath. "I *want* that. I want that kind of joy. That kind of love."

"Please…" Sasha whispered. His expression fell, losing his stoic, hard edge, and turning to raw anguish.

"I want to give *you* that kind of happiness." Sergey kept going. He lifted his hands, reaching for Sasha's shoulders, but hesitated. "I want to *love* you, Sasha."

Sasha's trembles turned to shudders, but he kept his eyes clenched shut. He shook his head. "The country needs you," he breathed. "Needs what you can do for Russia—"

"Do not make this about me choosing between Russia and you, Sasha—"

"That is *exactly* what this is! You *must* choose Russia. You must! I am *nothing*, Sergey, I am not worth—"

"You are *everything* to me!" Sergey shouted. He grabbed Sasha, and Sasha's eyes whipped open. "And I choose you! Do you hear me? I choose *you!*"

Sergey's hands rose, cradling Sasha's strong jaw, his sharp face. "We can do it all together, Sasha. We can change Russia together. What better way than by the two of us at the top?" He stroked Sasha's forehead, pushing back a lock of blond hair that had fallen over an eyebrow. "After everything, do you honestly think I would be stopped by people telling me no, no, you cannot love this man? After everything I have done?"

Sasha said nothing. He stared at Sergey, his blue eyes searching Sergey's gaze. Sergey let him look, and he poured his love outward, trying to convey his agony at being ripped away from Sasha's side, the anguish he'd felt believing Sasha was gone. The desire that burned in his soul and lived in his blood, aching to reach out for Sasha. The dreams he had, of Sasha's smile, his rumbling laughter, of just him, happy. Happy and in love. Hopefully, in love with Sergey.

Sergey stroked his thumb over Sasha's cheek. "I choose *you*."

Sasha exploded. Fury crackled over his face as he shoved Sergey back. Stunned, Sergey hit the bulkhead, and his shoulders crashed into the cabin door behind him. His mouth dropped and he reached for Sasha. "Wha—"

Sasha slammed into him, wrapping his arms around him, covering Sergey's body with his own. His hands roamed over Sergey, grabbing his hips and sliding up his sides, over his ribs and up his neck, running through his hair. He pushed Sergey back, throwing him against the bulkhead again when Sergey tried to push off and grab Sasha in return. Stunned, Sergey opened his mouth, protest ready on his lips.

Sweeping in, Sasha plunged his tongue into Sergey's mouth, slipping it along Sergey's until their lips joined, bodies surging together.

Sergey grabbed him, grabbed his broad shoulders, his arms. He pulled Sasha in, hands scrabbling to get him closer, kiss him deeper.

"What the *fuck* is going—"

Beside them, the door Sergey had slammed into whipped open, and Senior Chief Wilson, a bulldog of a man, built like a brick shithouse and with a perpetual rottweiler's scowl on his face, glared into the passageway.

Sergey and Sasha broke apart, barely, and froze. They stared at Chief Wilson, kiss-red lips quivering as they panted together.

Chief Wilson stepped back in his cabin and shut the door.

Sergey's eyes flicked to Sasha's. He cupped Sasha's face. "Come with me."

STRAINED SILENCE FILLED THEIR cabin when they stumbled through the door. Sasha went in first, and he stood in the center of the tiny room, keeping his back to Sergey.

Sergey watched his shoulders shake, his hands tremble.

Govno, Sasha was gorgeous. Even encased in a borrowed uniform, his rugged beauty could not be hidden. The curve of his biceps, almost straining the material. His blond hair, trimmed close to his head. Strong features, his aquiline nose, his jutting, harsh chin. Sasha seemed carved from marble, a statue of men from days of old come to life.

He stepped behind him, close enough to touch, but didn't. "What is it?" he breathed over Sasha's shoulder. He rested his forehead on Sasha's trembling shoulder, exhaling. "Do you not want this, Sasha? If I am just pushing you to something you truly do not want—"

"I do want this. You." Sasha exhaled, hard. "But, I have never—"

Sergey frowned. "What?"

Sasha turned his head, and his cheek brushed over Sergey's. His stubble caught on Sergey's skin, an almost-burn. "Never with someone I cared about. Or wanted." Slowly, he spun, facing Sergey. Took Sergey's hand in his own roughened palm. "No feelings, ever. That is how I survived."

Leaning in, Sergey pressed his forehead to Sasha's. "I am sorry, Sasha." As he spoke, his lips dragged over Sasha's, almost a kiss.

Sasha shook his head. He reached for Sergey, both calloused hands cradling his neck. "*Krasivyy...*"

"I am not." Sergey held his waist, his thumbs massaging the tops of Sasha's jutting hip bones. His waist was narrow, the point of a deep V at the end of his torso. Muscle corded beneath his palms, abs and obliques that were as thick as his forearm. "I am old. Too skinny. Gray. Wrinkled—"

Sasha kissed him, shutting him up. "You are beautiful to me," he murmured against Sergey's lips. "So beautiful."

And then they kissed, slowly. Lips slid softly, learning a new lover. Tasting each other as hands rose, stroking skin and clothing-covered chests. The curve of Sasha's pecs pushed against Sergey's fingers, his chest heaving with deep, shaking breaths. Sergey's fingers went to Sasha's top first, undoing each button with shaking fingers. Sasha's hands covered his as he reached the last button.

He pushed the uniform top off, stroking his palms across Sasha's chest and over his shoulders. Beneath his touch, Sasha shivered, and his eyelids fluttered. The top fell to the floor, crumpled. He went for Sasha's undershirt next, lifting it slowly over his tight, pale skin, his taut muscles, and over his head. Sasha's nipples hardened beneath his hands. Red splotches appeared on Sasha's hairless chest and around his neck as Sergey gazed at him. Perfection. Sasha was perfection. Full, broad shoulders, thick and dusted with a smattering of freckles. Had he gotten those when he was a boy? Or when he was older, working shirtless on the flight line beside his jets? His skin was light as the moon, soft like cream, and as Sergey watched, goose bumps rose beneath his gaze.

"If one of us is beautiful, that man is you." Sergey stroked one hand down the center of Sasha's trembling chest and down his flat abdomen.

"I want to touch you," Sasha breathed. "But..." At Sasha's side, his hands trembled, clenching and unclenching, as if he were holding himself back, straining against his desire.

Sergey reached for his own uniform. "Then touch me, Sasha. I am yours." He started on the first button.

Growling, Sasha tore his hands away and ripped his jacket open. Buttons flew, peppering the cabin walls with hard, fast plinks. He peeled it off Sergey's shoulders, shoving it halfway down his arms, and then grabbed him around his waist, hauling Sergey close. Sasha curled over him, bending him backward. Sergey's arms stayed tangled in the uniform, and Sasha bunched the fabric behind Sergey with one hand, keeping him trapped.

Gripping the back of his skull, Sasha kissed him, his tongue sliding over every one of Sergey's teeth before tangling with Sergey's.

Sergey's hips jerked, grinding against Sasha's as he groaned. His cock was already hard, and it somehow grew even harder at Sasha's dominance, the way he seized control of Sergey's body. His hip brushed against Sasha's cock, straining his uniform. He *wanted*, so badly. Days ago, had he been confused? Had he thought that he didn't want this? What a fool he'd been. He needed this, needed Sasha.

Through the kiss, Sasha yanked the uniform top from his arms, releasing Sergey's mouth only long enough to rip his undershirt over his head before pulling Sergey back. His wide palms gripped Sergey's hips, almost bruisingly tight. Their skin met, naked chest to naked chest, and Sergey moaned into Sasha's mouth. His hands rose, running up Sasha's muscled back as Sasha sucked on his tongue like he would a cock.

Pushing him back, Sasha maneuvered Sergey until he backed into the bunk along the wall. His legs hit the edge, and he collapsed, falling to his ass on the thin mattress. He came face-to-face with Sasha's crotch and his cock, straining against his blue uniform.

Sergey reached for Sasha's pants, but Sasha slapped his hands away and dropped to his knees. He stripped off Sergey's boots and then his own.

He hesitated, looking into Sergey's eyes.

Yes, more. Sergey reached for his own belt, his shaking hands fumbling with the buckle. He should say something, tell Sasha how much he was enjoying this. His hard cock, of course, was one signal, but he should tell Sasha. He opened his mouth, right as Sasha yanked down his uniform pants and briefs and swallowed his cock, all the way to the base.

Whatever he was about to say vanished, lost in a breathless string of curses, a mixture of Russian and English and Ruslish. He fell back, hands flying to the bulkhead, the mattress, the perfectly tucked sheets. He fisted the scratchy wool blanket, balling it up, as Sasha sucked him, swallowing his head and sucking like a vacuum before rising and twirling his tongue around the tip of his cock. Sasha buried his nose in Sergey's crotch, swallowing around the head before rising with a sloppy, slurping moan. Spit dribbled down his dick, down Sasha's chin, and over Sasha's hand as he jerked Sergey when he wasn't deep-throating him.

He was slick, coated in Sasha's saliva. Sasha's other hand grabbed Sergey's ass, gripping one cheek in a firm squeeze. He scraped his fingers over Sergey's skin, around his hip, and down his thigh, until he pulled Sergey's legs farther apart.

More. He needed more. Sasha's mouth wasn't enough; he wanted them to be together. Reaching down, Sergey grabbed Sasha behind the neck and tugged, dragging him up his body. Sasha rose like a tiger, sleek and powerful and pressing his chest against Sergey the whole way up, dominating him again as he pushed Sergey to his back on the bunk, slipping out of his pants as he moved. Over him, above him, Sasha surrounded him on all sides, his arms pinning Sergey, his broad shoulders enveloping him as he leaned down and ravaged his mouth.

Sergey's hands dragged down Sasha's chest, down around his waist, and finally buried themselves in Sasha's crotch, in his fine, curly hair. Sergey hesitated, but then wrapped his hands around Sasha's hard cock.

Sasha groaned around his open-mouthed kiss. His arms shuddered, and he almost collapsed as Sergey stroked him.

He didn't know what to do or how to hold Sasha. Everything was backward and in reverse. Was he stroking too hard or too soft? Sasha captured his lips in another kiss, and his questions melted from his brain.

And then, Sasha pulled back. Staring down at Sergey, he seemed to focus, the fire in his eyes banking, just slightly. Just enough to chain back the unrestrained passion that had exploded from him, that he'd unleashed on Sergey as he'd manhandled him across the cabin and dominated him into the bunk. Restraint, regret, and retreat. Each paraded through Sasha's eyes as he gulped.

No. Sergey ran his hands through Sasha's blond hair, gripping the strands tight. He pulled Sasha close. "Look at me," he breathed. "Look at me, Sasha."

Something jumped in Sasha's eyes as Sergey yanked on his hair, a white-hot spark. He hovered over Sergey's lips, staring into his gaze.

Slowly, Sergey closed the distance between them, kissing Sasha slowly, greedily, all tongue and teeth, with his eyes wide open. *I want this*, he tried to say, speaking through his gaze. *I want you. I want* everything *about you.*

He felt Sasha's hands in his hair. Fingers pressed against his scalp. And then, an answering pull, Sasha jerking his head back, but keeping their eyes locked together, their almost savage kiss continuing. *Yes. Yes, Sasha.*

Slowly, Sasha lowered himself down onto Sergey, his strength covering Sergey from head to toe. Their cocks brushed, and Sergey jerked, rocking his hips up and sliding his cock against Sasha's.

And then, they were pressed together, oh so tightly.

Perfection. Yes, this was what he needed, what he wanted. Perfection rolled through Sergey, a wave crashing against his soul, followed by searing, roaring flame, enough to blind him and white out his vision. Everything clicked into place suddenly, as if he'd been trying to solve a Rubik's cube and could previously only see one side. His life came into focus with a snap, a clarity that stole his breath away. This was *exactly* what he wanted. A hard body on top of his and a cock pressed against his own.

He held Sasha's stare as he thrust up, rolling his cock against Sasha's. Again, and again, harder, gazing into Sasha's eyes. Sasha thrust back into him, pulling Sergey's hair until his neck arched, and Sasha dropped kisses and suckling nibbles on his skin like falling bombs. Sergey wrapped his legs around Sasha's hips, squeezing him tight, and Sasha gasped as his eyes blazed. He never took his gaze off Sergey's, never even blinked.

It was more than fucking, more than making love. It was baring everything about himself to Sasha and letting Sasha into the deepest parts of his soul. He opened himself completely to Sasha, hanging on as Sasha drove against him. Sweat beaded on their skin, and his thighs slid along Sasha's sides, gripping and squeezing in time with Sasha's thrusts. He met Sasha's thrusts, drove their bodies together, tried to touch every inch of Sasha's skin. His hands moved from Sasha's hair to his face, down to his neck, and then cupped his jaw.

He saw, in Sasha's eyes, his desire, his passion, and even, deep in his ice-blue gaze, his love, tangled and twisted around an aching, gnawing fear. "Sasha…" Heat built through his body, wave upon wave, spreading from his cock. His heart, too, burned, opening, unfurling before Sasha. Lightning sang throughout him, sizzling into his soul. He kept chanting Sasha's name and staring into his eyes, his hands digging into Sasha's back and his straining muscles.

Sergey hung over a precipice, his body about to come apart, split in half with the force of his orgasm, and then reform, be rebuilt in a brand-new way. Sasha was going to destroy him. Destroy his old life, and then resurrect him. He welcomed it. "Sasha." He shuddered, panting. "I am yours. Yours, Sasha."

Gasping, Sasha thrust hard, grinding his cock against Sergey's. His eyes blew wide and his lips moved, nearly soundless whispers falling from him, curses in Russian and English that tumbled over Sergey's body. "I want to watch you come," Sasha growled. He nipped at Sergey's lower lip. "I want to make you scream."

Govno, yes. He fought to keep his eyes from rolling back in his skull. "With me." He wanted to see Sasha come apart, feel his release on his skin. Hold Sasha as he trembled, as he shouted, as he clung to Sergey, strung out on love.

Sasha gazed down at him. "Sergey…" He captured Sergey's lips, devouring him, kissing his soul as he drove them together faster, harder.

Sergey's orgasm crept up on him, building in his soul before blasting off, his body burning like a shooting star, like a fighter jet screaming through the skies under Sasha's control. He shouted, a wordless bellow as his body clenched around Sasha, and his release spread between them, hot on their skin.

Sasha gasped, and his body curled like a bow over Sergey as he gripped Sergey's skull, staring into his eyes. Love, fear, passion, anguish. So much mixed in Sasha's gaze, tumbling, crashing, smearing into each other. "I—" Sasha started.

And then his eyes went wide and he buried his face in Sergey's neck as he exploded, as his orgasm crashed through his body, making him tremble and shudder in Sergey's arms.

Sergey held him through it, stroking his back, his neck, his hair, and pressing his lips to Sasha's temples, the corners of his eyes. A new feeling cracked open in his chest, a burst of warmth, of radiance, of awe. How had they gotten to this point? He and Sasha, strangers in the world a year before, now clinging to each other like they were lost men, holding fast to the one other person in the world who meant everything. "Sasha," he panted, pressing his cheek to Sasha's hair. Sasha still trembled in his arms. "There is nothing to fear. We will make this work. I promise."

36

USS Honolulu

"You know, Doc, you actually *can't* feel the motion of the ocean in a sub."

"Fuck. *Off.*" Doc, head buried in his folded arms, growled at Wright. "I feel it. And I've already puked my guts out ten times."

Wright and Park, bracketing Doc on either side of the bench, laughed. They were in the mess hall, the whole team—minus Doc—scarfing down real food before their mission began. Kobayashi held out his fork, a piece of chicken stabbed on the tines, right in front of Doc's buried face. "Smell anything?"

"I swear to fucking God, I will puke on every one of you. Every fucking one. Except for Faisal."

They all laughed. Wright and Park went back to rocking into Doc's side, gently swaying him on the bench as Ruiz almost snorted corn up his nose, trying to eat and giggling at the same time.

Faisal smiled. He reached out and took Doc's hand, dragging it across the metal table.

Park and Wright both arched their eyebrows. Ruiz whistled. "Doc, you got something special going on with Prince F? Getting a little sugar-sugar?"

Doc tried to pull his hand back, tried to jerk out of Faisal's hold. "Hell no! Give me my hand back! I want to live, and if the L-T sees, that ain't gonna happen!" He kept his face buried in his elbow on the table, but kept trying to jerk away weakly.

Faisal didn't let go. "Calm down," he chuckled, turning Doc's hand over. "I am only looking for a pressure point." Searching, he found the spot in between Doc's thumb and fingers and pressed down firmly. After a few moments, Doc's shoulders relaxed and he sighed, visibly relaxing as he almost melted into the table. "*Alhamdulillah.* See?"

"What kind of ninja Arab genie thing is that?" Ruiz held out his hand, flopping it in front of Faisal. "Do me, Prince F."

"It's a Chinese pressure point, not an Arab one." Faisal grinned. "Definitely not from a djinn. And not ninja, either."

"Close enough." Ruiz wagged his hand. "C'mon. Maybe I'll get rich like you if you rub off on me."

Kobayashi and Wright groaned and rolled their eyes, and Park collapsed sideways into Doc, giggling and snorting like a toddler.

"You are incorrigible." Faisal plucked Ruiz's hand from the table and held it in his own. He traced the line down the center of Ruiz's palm.

"My momma always did say I was a cutie." Winking, he grinned at Faisal, a megawatt smile that could have flashed across a million television screens.

"Incorrigible, dumbass, not adorable." Doc grabbed his spoon, blind, and beat Ruiz with it, never sitting up. "Means you're impossible. Which you are. Can I study your brain? I want to know how you live with only two brain cells. I could hook up a light bulb to your skull. When your two cells bounce together, I bet the bulb lights up."

More laughter. Faisal joined in, shaking his head as the men kept their playful bickering. Ruiz had a nasty scar curling around his forearm, and he complained of stiff fingers when it was cold. Faisal pressed halfway down the scar, gently rubbing, and waited.

"Damn!" Ruiz jerked, and he stared at Faisal like he'd been burned. "The hell? My fingers feel all tingly!"

Faisal nodded. "This should help with your pain."

Ruiz stared at him and then smiled. Not a sarcastic smile or a sharp smile, but something honest. Something that said thanks.

At the end of the table, Adam sat down with his tray in front of Coleman. Coleman sat apart from the others, watching like a hawk. His dark eyes flicked to Adam.

"I've been thinking about what you said," Adam said carefully.

Coleman raised his spoonful of applesauce, swallowed it all, and then dipped his spoon into the sludge again. He never blinked.

Adam swallowed. "You're right. I do need to get my head straight. Stop being all over the place. So… Here it is." Inhaling, he glanced down the table again, watching Faisal gently tease Ruiz and Park as Doc brandished his knife and fork in both hands, his head still down.

On the island, Coleman had dragged him down to the beach and read him the riot act, a blistering tirade about how he was scattered, divided, anchorless. How he was blowing in the wind, and if he was going to have any hope of leading the team through what they needed to do, he needed to unfuck himself. Figure his shit out, and fast. Find his true north, and start navigating right. No one trusted an aimless leader, and that was exactly what he seemed.

"I love him," Adam said, turning back to Coleman. "I'm in love with Faisal. We were together before I joined the team. Before I took command. I ended it, but that was a mistake. We're working it out." He took another breath, squaring his shoulders before his sergeant. Time to lay it out there. Get real. "He means as much to me as this team does. Each and every one of you matters to me. Deeply." He shrugged and gave Coleman a tiny smile. "It's just a little different with him."

He'd heard about the love an officer was supposed to have for his men, for his team, throughout officer training. But he'd been a lone operator, a solitary Marine right out of training, and that had led him traipsing down the path of conspiracy, of secrets kept from his own government, and of Faisal. Transferring and taking charge of the team had capsized his already bruised and battered heart. He'd been in love with Faisal, but had tried to drown that love while he struggled to lead his team. He'd been an out of control yo-yo ever since, wild swings sending him everywhere but where he needed to be.

But now, seeing his team and Faisal all together, everything clicked.

Coleman raised another spoonful of applesauce to his mouth.

"We will do this. All of us, together. We will kill this bastard, and then we will all go home." Adam leaned forward, his hands turning to fists on the tabletop. "All of us."

Swallowing, Coleman lowered his spoon and set it on his tray. He reached for his water glass and raised that instead, holding it out for a toast.

Adam smiled and raised his glass, clinking the plastic together. "I'll need you, Sergeant, like always."

"Fuck off!" Doc leaped to his feet and jumped Park, bending him half over the table as he pretending to stab him with his fork. Ruiz and Kobayashi howled, and Wright tried, weakly, to pull him off, but he was red-faced and laughing far too hard to be helpful.

Coleman arched his eyebrows at Adam, and a tiny smile tugged at his lips. "I don't think there's any hope for them, L-T."

MUCH, MUCH LATER, WHEN most of the team was snoring in hammocks strung around like a crazed chimpanzee swing gym, Adam slipped into the torpedo room, back from his final pre-mission briefing with Ethan, President Spiers, Captain Anderson, and the Russian president and his officer. Even President Wall had been there over a secured satellite uplink to the White House. His mind spun, dizzy from the intel, and a part of him wanted to scream. K-27, a nuclear submarine being weaponized to ignite the skies. Waves of fire that would burn across the world.

President Wall and her Secret Service bodyguard, Agent Levi Daniels, had gone ghostly pale when the Russian president told them about K-27. "As if things weren't bad enough," President Wall had breathed. "Now he can weaponize a nuclear submarine."

"His people, the ones we *know* defected, turned traitor, and joined him—" Daniels's voice had gone thin, and he cleared his throat, not looking at the screen or at any of them crowded around the Captain's table in *Honolulu's* wardroom. "Madigan doesn't have a nuclear tech. He doesn't have someone who knows how to weaponize that reactor. Maybe he got a Russian nuke tech from Moroshkin?"

"We proceed as if he has full capabilities," President Spiers had said.

Christ, it was too much. Adam just wanted it all to end.

And, after... Well, he knew exactly what he wanted after the mission was over. What he'd always, always wanted.

Ruiz snored loud enough to wake the dead. Kobayashi was as quiet sleeping as he was during the day. Park was still awake, flipping through a rumpled magazine he'd swiped from the mess hall. Wright and Coleman chatted softly in the corner, Wright clutching a picture of him and a blonde chick, her face half-hidden behind his bare shoulder as they posed in front of some monument in DC. Doc lay face-down in his hammock, his arms hanging over the sides, almost brushing a bucket someone had placed beneath him. A piece of rope stretched from the bucket's handle and wrapped around Doc's waist, tied in a knot. When he stood, the bucket would follow him, every step he took.

Knowing Doc, he'd keep the bucket clattering behind him just to fuck with the rest of the guys, and especially whoever had tied it to him.

Adam wound his way to a hammock set apart, respectfully distant from the gaze of the team and their antics. A slender shape rested in the canvas, curled beneath a green wool blanket. He squatted next to the hammock and leaned in. "Hey."

Faisal rolled over and smiled. "Hey, yourself. How did the briefing go?"

Adam blew out a long exhale and arched his eyebrows, bobbing his head as he shrugged.

"That well?" Faisal chuckled softly.

He didn't answer. Instead, he nodded to the hammock. "Any room in there?"

Faisal squinted at him but said nothing.

"These can hold dudes up to four hundred pounds. You and me together aren't even close to that. Scoot. Make room." Adam waited as Faisal slid to the side, and then he clambered into the hammock. They almost tipped, and Faisal made a wild grab for the bulkhead to steady their sudden swinging plunge. Adam snorted but scooted close to Faisal once the hammock was stable. He wrapped his arms around Faisal's waist and buried his face in his neck, breathing deeply.

Faisal ran his hands through Adam's hair. Pressed his lips against Adam's forehead and his messy hair. "What are you doing?" he breathed.

"Making a choice." Adam's lips moved against Faisal's skin, a kiss with every word. "No more hiding. I can't operate like that. I can't be torn in half." He sighed, nuzzling Faisal's jaw, the warm skin beneath his ear. "I love you, *habibi*. That love gives me strength. I won't hide it. I won't hide who I am. Not anymore."

Faisal's exhale, over Adam's head, was shaky. He felt Faisal's pulse beneath his lips quicken. Felt Faisal's arms tighten around him. "*Habibi...*" He swallowed, and Adam kissed the burnished gold skin, the rise and fall of his throat. "*Bismillah*, are you certain?"

"More certain than I have been for years." He squeezed Faisal's hips, stroked one hand over the small of his back. "I'm sorry, Faisal, for—"

"Shhh. *Maa shaa Allah*. It is all in the past."

Squirming, Adam shimmied until he was face-to-face with Faisal. He held his gaze, the soft sheen of his eyes reflected in the dim lights of the torpedo room. A red glow hung in the room but didn't fill the shadows. One curl of ruby light tickled down Faisal's cheek. It looked too much like blood. He wanted to brush it away. "Promise me something."

"I will promise you anything, *habibi*. In this life, or the next."

He cupped Faisal's cheek, covering the streamer of red. "Promise me you will be careful. You will be safe."

Faisal frowned.

"We're going to do this. Take Madigan down. I want you at my side, like we used to be. But… I can't lose you. I can't see you get hurt. I *can't*." Adam licked his lips, shaking his head. "You have to stay safe."

Faisal reached for him, cupping his cheek in return. "*In shaa Allah*, I will be safe. And you will be as well. *Subhanallah*, we will all be relaxing by my pool in one week, drinking mango juice and eating *luqaymat*."

Adam smiled. "I thought we went naked when we were at your pool. That was your rule, if I remember right."

Faisal winked. "That is for you and me alone. Your team must wear their swimming suits. I won't share you."

Laughing, Adam nuzzled his nose against Faisal's, exhaling softly. "Be careful, *habibi*," he said, becoming serious again. "You are everything to me." He held Faisal's gaze, staring into his eyes. "I'm fighting this fight to go home," he breathed, barely whispering at all. "Home to *us*. I want our life back. I want to be by your side every day, from now until the end of time."

"I do, too," Faisal whispered. "I pray for that every night. *In shaa Allah*, Adam, we will have it."

"*In shaa Allah*." His lips moved against Faisal's. "*Barakah Allah*."

37

USS Honolulu

THE BERING STRAIT LAY dead ahead.

Tension strained the dark Control Room. Dim running lights cast the crew's faces in half shadow and made their eyes gleam as they stared at their controls.

Captain Anderson stood just before the periscope stand, his arms crossed. His eyes darted over every control panel, over every person. The contact evaluation board, mounted ahead of him and scattering soft blue light, tracked targets and ranges to anything picked up within *Honolulu's* detection range. Trailing behind *Honolulu*, their partner, the sub that had stayed with them from Elizabeth's fleet, *USS Bozeman*, followed.

Depth, speed, angle, and trim displays crowded space with fire control consoles and weapons. Behind the periscope in the center of the Conn, the navigator hovered over his plotting table, furiously calculating their course and checking it against the computer display. Transparent charts lay over the plotting table's crimson light board, marked up with grease pencils. On a submarine, redundancy and double, even triple checks, meant the difference between life or death.

Ethan couldn't turn without bumping into someone. He stayed still, pressed against Jack's side, and tried to be out of the way. That was nearly impossible. A dozen men were crammed inside what looked like an airline cockpit shoved into a large bathroom. Stacked from the deck to the low, curved overhead bulkhead were display screens, gauges, bundles of cables and wires, consoles and toggles, emergency equipment, and more. The Conn was stuffed full, jammed to practically bursting.

Honolulu had submerged, and beneath the ocean, her movements were smooth as glass. If he didn't know they were underwater, he wouldn't have guessed.

One of the helmsmen, a young enlisted man, exhaled shakily. A bead of sweat rolled down his temple.

The Bering Strait was one of the most difficult crossings in the world, even during peacetime. A shockingly narrow undersea canyon filled with a jungle of undersea mountains and craggy valleys, the clearest passage was barely deep enough to slip a sub through fully submerged. Sneaking through the Strait into Russian waters, beneath a storm, and entering an Arctic war zone with two heads of state on board was insanity by any definition.

And they were headed right down the center.

Nerves radiated from the three men seated at the diving station. The helmsmen and planesman sat behind commercial airplane-style control yokes, each linked to the rudder and the diving planes, controlling the boat's course and depth. Behind them, the diving officer, Lieutenant "Roller" Whipple, sat, double, triple, and quadruple-checking their every move, and taking over when needed. The engine room telegraph also squatted between the three men, the old-school turns like a rotary phone telegraphing to the engine room to give the captain the power he needed.

Roller was young and had earned his nickname the hard way, Anderson said. He'd rolled the sub through the ocean like a sea snake for months, barely able to keep *Honolulu* at the right depth and trim when he first came on board. More than one officer had puked when he was at the helm.

Senior Chief Garcia kept an eye on him from his own station, manning the ballast control panel. He was in charge of the boat's dive and surface, keeping the sub buoyant while submerged, and her levels trim and even. Above him, two bright-red Chicken Switches hovered on the control panel. If all hell broke loose, he yanked those switches and high-pressure air forced out the water in the buoyancy tanks in one explosive rush. If that happened, *Honolulu* would blast out of the water, rising like a torpedo fired from her own tubes. Except, under the ice, she'd slam up against the ice sheet, and if it wasn't thin enough to give, she'd smash into a billion pieces and sink to the bottom of the Arctic Abyss.

Captain Anderson pulled down the handset for the boat's intercom and flipped to the main channel. "All hands, this is the Captain. We're preparing to enter the Strait. From here on out, there are no drills. Once we reach the other side, we're at war."

Sergey hovered at Jack's side in the dim light, standing beside Sasha. Something had changed between them, from the day before to now. Instead of turning away from each other, they now turned toward each other, standing inside each other's shadow. Sergey kept one hand on Sasha at all times, and Sasha tried to keep Sergey within the breadth of his shoulders. It felt like Ethan was looking into a mirror.

"Captain," Navigation officer Lieutenant Commander Jacinto said, "seven minutes until Little Diomede. Turn in nine minutes. New heading will be three-three-six degrees to Herald Canyon." Jacinto was a thin man, almost gangly, and he folded over his plotting table like it was a toy he couldn't let go of. Calculated precision and dead seriousness were etched into the lines of his face, a steel-hardened exactitude that submariner navigators required.

"Diomede will pass to port?"

"Yes, Captain."

Captain Anderson nodded once. "Ocean depth?"

"Ninety-six feet, Captain."

"Roller, make your depth eighty feet. Slow to six knots."

Roller's wide eyes bulged like a King Charles spaniel. He responded immediately. "Eighty feet and six knots, aye aye, sir." His jaw kept moving, a manic, mechanical chewing. Three packs of nicotine gum were stuffed in the front pocket of his uniform top.

Ethan exhaled, nice and slow, as *Honolulu* crept through the Strait. Anderson kept his gaze locked on the displays, his eyes flicking from depth to trim to angles and back again. "We're passing through the shallowest part now," he murmured, leaning close to Jack. "Our keel is just over ten feet above the ocean floor. If a wave breaks over the surface, we flash our skirts to anyone out there. We're close enough to throw a rock and hit both Russia and the US. We are feet from either nation."

Jack swallowed. He stayed silent.

"Ocean depth ninety feet, Captain."

Anderson's eyes flicked back to the screens. His jaw clenched.

"One-minute warning." Behind them, the navigator called out their course and bearing again. "Turn in forty-five seconds, Captain." Big and Little Diomede were two rocky outcroppings of bird shit and dust in the middle of the Bering Strait, two and a half miles apart from each other. The borders between Russia and the United States ran down the exact center of the waters between the islands.

Jack leaned into Ethan. He slipped his hand through Ethan's, lacing their fingers together.

"Five, four, three, two, one, and *mark*."

"Helm, five degrees left rudder. Heading three-three-six degrees. Keep the turn gentle," Anderson growled. "If you turn us too sharp, we'll roll and expose our port side out of the water."

Roller didn't blink as he repeated his orders. "Five degrees left rudder, heading three-three-six degrees, gentle turn, aye aye, Captain."

Slowly, the Conn tipped sideways, a gentle bank as the sub turned, moving out of the Strait and into the Russian Arctic. Ethan looked to Jack and met his gaze. In the darkness, Jack's eyes gleamed, a shine that made the blue of his eyes look like stars burning in the night sky.

"This is it," Jack breathed. "We're at war."

THEY DIDN'T KNOW WHAT would be waiting on the other side of the Strait. During Anderson's brief, the captain outlined every possible scenario, from empty polar seas all the way to Madigan to a silent *Akula* lying in wait, a Russian hunter-killer submarine of their own. What did Madigan have at hand? What had Moroshkin taken over the pole with him to Canada? What elements of the Russian Northern Fleet had defected during the coup, and who had simply pointed their boat as far from Russia as possible and tried to flee the calamity? No one knew the answers. Unknowns stacked against their operation, giant question marks that could spell disaster.

Beyond the Strait, geography opened up a triangle of terrible waters. Undersea mountain ranges of plunging ice thrusting downward from the polar ice cap created caverns and jungles nearly impossible to navigate. Shallow waters and shoals narrowed the potential routes to one: Herald Canyon, to the starboard of Wrangel Island, a barren rock in Russia's desolate Siberian Sea.

Herald Canyon was a notorious ice maze. Even in summer, the ice never completely melted, and the shift and slam of the bergs and the ice sheets sent slabs of ice deep into the waters. The ocean floor was shallow, still a part of the continental shelf off of Russia. A flat plain that rose and rose, trying to pin submarines like butterflies to the bottom of the ice, trap them and strangle each boat out of its depth.

The deepest pass through Herald Canyon was the Wrangel Trough, an ancient riverbed that had once cut through the Siberian Plains when the Sea had been a steppe that linked Russia to America millions of years ago. Successfully navigating through the Wrangel Trough would turn them into salmon swimming upstream, dodging the shallows and the plunging ice, squeezing through passes barely large enough for their hull, and praying that they were alone.

Under the ice, sonar, *Honolulu's* eyes and ears, barely worked. The Arctic wreaked havoc on sound and sonar. In the open ocean, American submarines could pick out the sound of a toilet flushing on a cruise ship and the footfalls of a guard walking a perimeter, the hushed whispers of a drug deal going down. Sailing into the Arctic was like putting a blindfold on and earplugs in, and spinning someone around until they were dizzy. Mazes of ice jungles, floating icebergs with keels that plunged hundreds of feet into the waters, ice sheets that rumbled and crunched, and wild sea life all created an undersea opera of acoustic chaos. Sonar displays looked like snow on an old television set. Making sense of the undersea world was a nightmare. The mix of fresh water from the ice and saltwater in the depths bounced sound waves like a hall of mirrors. And when the sea floor dropped out beneath them, sonar reflections and refractions bounced off the bottom of the ice and into the depths.

At best, they could see the bottom of the ocean and the bottom of the ice and figure out a way to navigate through the pinched corridor.

Ethan and Jack hung behind the navigator and the plotting table. Ethan kept one hand on the small of Jack's back, and his eyes fixed to the sonar display. He held Jack for his own sanity. Planning this mission out, they'd always talked about what to do once they got up on the ice. When they were already *in* the Arctic. They'd never thought about how dangerous it would be to even get there. What if they slammed into an ice keel? Or got trapped in the twisting ice canyons and narrow passages with no way out?

What if an *Akula* found them and blew them to bits when they were pinned? It would be a long, dark dive to the bottom of the Arctic Abyss, and when the sub hit crush depth, those waters would burst in, freezing them while they drowned, suffering twice over at once.

Ethan swallowed hard and scooted even closer, wrapping his hand around Jack's hip. Somewhere, there was a beach with their name on. A real honeymoon destination. Not slinking through Arctic waters with seventy feet of hard ice pushing down on them.

The maze of ice canyons kept them deep. The sonar array mapped the bottom, sending a picture in waterfall lines of blues, yellows, and reds to the main display. Pictures emerged from the scratchy colored lines, sound bouncing back and painting what was in front of them like there were headlights in front of the sub. The colors signaled depth and range. Blue was good. Blue was open waters and clear range. Yellow was a warning. Red, and then shades of pink, was full-on pucker time.

Red filled the screen, the bottom of the ocean close enough to drag their hands through. Boulders rose in furious magenta, seeming to pass to their right and left as the helmsman breathed like he was giving birth. Just watching, Ethan wanted to yank back on the control yoke and get them away from the bottom. Good thing he wasn't driving. He'd slam them into the ice roof. The planesman, in charge of keeping them trim and level, had balls of neutron steel, keeping the *Honolulu* flat and steady and right between the ocean floor and the ice as he stared at the screens. He didn't blink.

Something rose in the sonar's display, dead ahead. A craggy protrusion, jutting up from the sea floor, almost like a log broken in two, snapped over some giant's thigh.

"Sonar, Conn. What is that ahead?" Anderson never took his eyes off the screen.

The sonarman, Petty Officer "Boomer" Michaels, responded, "Not clear yet, Captain."

"Nav, anything on charts?"

"No, sir."

"Helm, plane up to avoid. *Gently*," Anderson growled. "We've got *feet* to maneuver here. Thickness of the ice overhead?"

"Ninety-two feet."

The nav officer whistled. The corners of Anderson's eyes clenched, a slight squint.

They planed over the jumble beneath them, slowly gliding through the frigid waters. As they passed directly overhead, the sonar image cleared up, and everything snapped into perfect focus.

"My God," the executive officer breathed.

It was another submarine, broken in two at her midship. She'd sunk to the bottom of the ocean and rested like a child's toy tossed aside, split in half and forgotten.

"Conn, Sonar. Looks like an *Akula*-class. Torpedoes brought her down. It's… a new wreck, sir. No signs of settling or sea growth."

All eyes flicked to Sergey and Sasha. A downed Russian sub, cracked in half, in their own waters.

"Our country has never sunk a Russian sub up here," Anderson said softly.

Yet hung unspoken in the air.

What were the Russians doing? They weren't on the path that would have taken them to Moroshkin and his fleet, and they had been heading away from Madigan's position. A sub on the run, making a break from Murmansk to the Strait? Why had they been shot down? Had they come to warn the Americans?

Anderson's voice rang out. "One minute of silence. Mark."

Sergey bowed his head, grief washing over his features. Sasha stayed by his side, a solid presence, and Ethan watched Sergey lean into him, like a sapling blown in the wind.

When the minute mark passed, Anderson nodded to Sergey. "To your men," he said simply. The submarine service was something unique. Ethan had heard about it, the jokes and tales passed back and forth to kill time in all branches of the military. But submariners were a breed apart, men who lived beneath the ocean and bent nature to their will time and time again. Camaraderie in those men crossed national lines, enough to honor the Russian ghosts they sailed over.

Sergey nodded to Anderson. "Still on patrol," he said softly, finishing the Russian toast.

"Conn, Sonar. Ice ridges ahead. The ice is plunging, but the bottom opens up, too. We've hit the slope."

Anderson nodded, and Ethan felt the Conn exhale, collective relief from a dozen men shaking out of their skin.

"What's the depth, Boomer?"

"Two hundred sixty feet and dropping, sir. Fifty thousand feet until we reach the Continental Shelf. First ice ridge closing in eighty feet."

Anderson steered the boat beneath the first ice ridge, gently diving her to a new depth. Some of the raw tension had fled as the ocean floor dropped away. The men didn't hold themselves like a thousand volts were passing through their bodies anymore. They'd started to blink, to look like humans again.

And then the second ice ridge came up, steeper and deeper than before. And the third, like a knife trying to gut them.

In minutes, they were back to navigating their way through an underwater maze, dodging cleavers of plunging ice, underwater spires that seemed as tall as skyscrapers, and blind alleys that led to choke points. Anderson kept diving the boat deeper into the dark depths, until the first groan sounded along the hull.

At Ethan's side, Jack exhaled shakily and scooted closer. Ethan welcomed it. Across the Conn, Sergey was pale, almost translucent. He could see a thick ring of white around the entirety of Sasha's eyes.

"Conn, Sonar. I'm picking something up…" Boomer's voice trailed off. In his corner, he frowned at his screen, shaking his head.

"What is it?"

"It doesn't make sense." Frustration strained Boomer's voice. "It could be our own echo. Or it could be an organic. I'm not getting clear signals. It's irregular, but that could be the ice."

"How close is this mystery object?" Anderson growled as he made his way to Boomer's screen.

"The signal is bouncing off the ice, Captain. What I can hear, I can't understand, and from what I can see, I can't get a good bearing. It could be all the way under the North Pole."

Anderson glared at the screen. A snow of noise, of barely comprehensible lines, dots and dashes streamed across the display, and on the far-right side, a faint, barely there pulsation. Like a shooting star, there and then gone. And there again. Natural sounds were random, noise that could numb the brain. Machines, on the other hand, were reliable. Predictable. Rhythmic. His lips pressed together. "You see *something*, Boomer."

"Yes, Captain. I think I do."

"Keep an eye on it. I want to know the instant this thing twitches."

Boomer nodded, and Anderson moved back to his position in the center by the periscope stand, his eyes flicking over every station, every screen.

"Captain, another ice keel ahead. Range, three thousand yards. This one is massive, sir." Boomer squinted at his screen. "And, if that object exists, it's beyond the ice keel, sir. Or it's our reflection coming off this huge sheet of ice. If you turn into the dive, I can get us a better picture. Or, we'll know we're looking at our shadow." Boomer had his hands over his headphones, and he hunched in front of his display, trying to divine meaning from the mess on his screen. Overhead, the navigational display showed a thick red band plunging down from the ice, dangerously close and angled on their starboard side.

"Helm, five-degree turn to starboard. Heading zero-seven-zero. Ahead slow." Anderson glared at the screens, and around him, his men became tense again, windup toys keyed to the last screw.

Boomer kept listening and kept staring at his screen, frowning hard.

Ethan closed his eyes and let out a breath. He tried to uncoil his muscles, tried to physically relax. His body felt like a spring, coiled and ready to burst. He thought he could hear the noises coming through Boomer's headphones, popping, humming, hissing noises that made his bones itch. Beneath all of it, a deep, rumbling thrum and patter, almost like a heartbeat.

"Boomer, what the hell are we hearing?" Anderson's bark broke over the Conn. "Is this our own echo?"

Ethan's eyelids snapped open. At his side, Jack tensed, his body going rigid as they felt the raw intensity of the Conn ratchet up, and smelled the stink of adrenaline letting loose into veins. On the sonar display, a shattered mess of red lines appeared in the dead center, incomprehensible, but close. *Damn* close.

Anderson was silent for exactly one second. Ethan watched his eyes narrow, his lips flatten.

"Emergency deep! Take us down to the depths! Dive, *now*, Roller!"

The deck slanted immediately, Roller plunging the ship into a steep dive.

"Captain!" Boomer's voice was like lightning, crashing over the deck. "Contact! Jesus Christ, it's a Russian attack sub! Hostile contact, designate Sierra One!" He piped the sonar noise he was hearing up to the captain as the displays went red, solid lines of cascading maroon flashing as alarms wailed. From the speakers, Ethan picked out a sizzle, the sound of an electrical plant on a nearby submarine, water rushing over a hull, and a rhythmic swish of a turning propeller. On the nav display, a flattened oval appeared, crimson bright and taking up almost the entire space between the ice keel and the ocean floor below.

The silhouette of a submarine.

"Dive!" Anderson shouted. "Get us underneath that sub! Make your depth two hundred sixty-five!"

"Captain, ocean depth is two seventy-three!"

"Two hundred and sixty-five feet! Do *not* overshoot!"

At the helm, Roller's eyes went even wider, bulging like he was a character in a bad cartoon. His planesman went white as a sheet, not even breathing, but he moved automatically as the alarms wailed and shouts broke over the deck.

"Conn, Sonar!" Boomer hollered over the klaxons. "It's an *Akula*-class sub! They're turning toward us!" A new alarm sounded, a high-pitched wail. "They're flooding their torpedo tubes!"

"Engines ahead full!"

"Captain, we're going to hit bottom!" The nav officer gripped the railing behind the periscope until his knuckles went white.

"No, we won't," Anderson growled. "Weapons, get me a firing solution on their position. I want torpedoes going up their bearing when they fire. Helm, get us the hell out of here. Point us to the Makarov Basin and run like hell." He turned to Chief Garcia. "Make the boat ready for depth charges. Deploy countermeasures." His gaze turned to Jack, and then to Ethan. "Stand by to brace for collision."

Ethan grabbed Jack and the nearest handhold, clinging to both. Jack, in turn, clung to him, his hands wrapping around Ethan's waist. The deck pitched hard toward the bow as *Honolulu* kept diving toward the bottom of the ocean. Ethan scrambled, almost lost his feet, and the men sitting at the diving station nearly toppled over. Their seatbelts held them fast, but one of the watchstanders wasn't so lucky. He tumbled and rolled, sliding on his ass down the length of the Conn before slamming sideways into the damage control board.

A low, quaking thrum rumbled through the Conn, like a train rushing past them a handsbreadth away. Every surface rumbled. Display screens shook, the whole sub vibrating, a Martini being shaken. Jacinto's grease pencils leaped from the plotting table and hit the deck. They kept rolling, down the steep angle and into the darkness.

"She's right above us!" Boomer shouted. "She's covering my scope!" The *Akula* filled the sonar display, an almost solid magenta wash eclipsing their underwater world.

"Torpedoes in the water! Inside five hundred feet!"

"Chief, countermeasures!"

Chief Garcia's hands flew over his board, almost fast enough to blur. "Deployed, Captain!"

"Depth!"

"Two hundred forty feet, captain!" The diving officer clenched his jaw. "Two hundred fifty! Two hundred sixty!"

"Level off!"

"Torpedoes inside three hundred feet!"

Ethan caught Jack's gaze, caught the fear pouring out of Jack's eyes. In their depths, Ethan saw the same in his own gaze, reflected back at him. He didn't want it to end like this. Not twisting apart in the ocean, crushed by pressures as he froze and drowned. After everything, not like this. Jack's hold around his waist tightened enough to bruise his hips. Ethan had one hand on the handrail, and with the other, he cupped Jack's cheek.

"Countermeasures deployed! Jammer ineffective! Torpedoes still on target! Range, one hundred fifty feet!"

Anderson glared at Chief Garcia. "Sound collision alarm."

Garcia grabbed a large switch over his board and hauled it down. At once, a new klaxon wailed through the ship, an awful screech.

"Brace for impact!"

Ethan held Jack's gaze and pushed their faces together. "I love you," he whispered against Jack's lips. "I love you."

Booming crashed behind them, and Jack's eyes squeezed closed. The sound of a thousand bubbles popping, and a hiss like an anaconda hovered over their heads, and then a second boom sounded. Darkness veiled the Conn like a curtain as the lights flickered. The whole world shook. Ethan bucked, losing his footing, but kept an ironclad grip on his handhold and on Jack. They rolled to port, falling sideways against the plotting table and almost on top of it, before shuddering and rolling back.

When would the water crash over them? When would they draw their last breath?

Tearing metal screeched and groaned, a crescendo of shrieking that seemed to rake up the inside of *Honolulu*. The lights winked out, plunging the Conn into pitch black.

"Torpedoes detonated, Captain!" Garcia's booming voice broke over the alarms. "Countermeasures successful, but we still took damage."

"Damage control?" Anderson's voice, rising in the darkness. A moment later, the battle lights winked on, and the alarms fell silent as Garcia's hands flew across his board.

Lieutenant Harvey, at the damage control station, responded. "Emergency Reactor Scram, sir. The shock of the blast knocked the reactor into safety standby." A hum, and then emergency lights flickered and rose, casting the Conn in a sickly, almost hospital-like glow. "Flooding reported in the engine room and the battery compartment."

"Get that saltwater out of there before the batteries start venting chlorine! All drain pumps reroute to the battery compartment. Damage control teams to the Engine Room. Secure collision alarm. Chief, dial up the pressure in the hull. Let's slow that leak. And get the reactor back online."

"Captain, we've got another problem!" Roller's eyes were locked on his display, and he leaned over his helmsman, his hands on top of the younger man's, physically trying to haul the control yoke over to help the helmsman steer. "Rudder is jammed. We're pointed eighteen degrees to starboard, sir, and I can't unstick it. Not from here."

"Conn, Sonar." Boomer's voice shook. "Approaching Makarov Basin. Distance to Sierra One two thousand feet."

"Jacinto, adjust our bearing to compensate for the rudder. We can't fix it now." Anderson strode to the weapons station and leaned over Lieutenant Munoz. "Weapons, do you have a track on that bastard? Did you get a bearing?"

Munoz nodded, breathing hard. "I got two curves as Sierra One passed." An almost flat triangle flashed on his screen, a complex trigonometry problem that put the Russian sub at the apex, dead in Munoz's target. "We can light her up."

"Sound battle stations. Flood torpedo tubes one and two. Set torpedoes for short range attack. Enable seekers at one thousand feet and step them up to fifty knots."

Man Battle Stations! Man Battle Stations! clanged through the ship. Munoz's hands flew over his board, setting up the torpedoes as Anderson ordered. Deep inside *Honolulu*, Ethan swore he could feel the torpedo tubes opening, water rushing in to fill the dark launch tubes.

"Tubes one and two ready, sir."

"Make sure our torpedoes hit them and don't get scrambled by the ice," Anderson barked. He backed off Munoz and went to his position by the periscope. "Confirm your solution and shoot."

The deck beneath Ethan's feet shuddered as the torpedoes launched from *Honolulu*'s belly. Two new sonar pings blazed across the screen.

"Close the outer doors and reload." Anderson's voice rang across the Conn. "Flood tubes three and four. Helm, ahead full. Those bastards are going to shoot up our torpedoes' wake, and I won't be here for them when they do. Get us out of here and under the ice." Anderson's gaze flicked over the Conn, finally landing on Jack and Ethan. "We're going to lose them under the ice cap, Mr. President. Get in deep water and under fast ice. We'll run like hell."

"What about *Bozeman*?" Jacinto spoke, still gripping the edge of his plotting table. His hair stood straight up, mussed after the tumble and rumble during the torpedoes' detonation just behind *Honolulu*.

"*Bozeman* was behind us in Herald Canyon. With the noise we just made, she definitely knows about Sierra One. Commander Roberts is good. He'll hunt them down while we keep going." Anderson took a breath and turned back to Munoz and Boomer. "Range?"

"Twenty seconds left on torpedoes one and two. Fifteen. Ten."

"Boomer, sonar on audio."

"Aye aye, Captain."

Audio filled the Conn, a bubbling, hissing undersea warble that changed in a split second. A smear, like greased bacon sliding on a pan, and then a cannon shot, a rumbling boom, and a lion's roar, and then another. Ethan felt like he was in some kind of nightmarish delirium, where lions roamed in an undersea world. Had he fallen down a rabbit hole?

And then, the sound of a crystal chandelier crashing to the ground, thousands and thousands of shards of glass bursting apart, like all the glass in the world was exploding in the same moment. The sonar display went off like fireworks, crackling lines and bursts of color, exploding sounds in all frequency ranges.

"Ice." Anderson frowned. "Did we hit Sierra One?"

"Can't say." Boomer worked the controls, staring at the screen. "Getting a lot of reflection off that ice keel, and the ridges in the thick cap beyond it. Sierra One picked the perfect place to hide, Captain. I'm having a hard time making anything out, especially with all that ice detonating."

Anderson's lips pursed, but he said nothing. He glared at his screens and then turned to Jack and Ethan. "We survived," he said, his voice low. "More than what our Russian friends on the bottom of the ocean can say."

Again, all eyes flicked to Sergey. He stood by the weapons station, grasping the handrails behind Munoz's chair. Sasha hovered beside him, one hand seeming to disappear on his back. Sergey looked drawn, exhausted by more than the physical exertions of the battle.

Sasha looked ready to puke. He stared at Sergey like Sergey was the center of his world, the axis he revolved around and the only thing he was still standing for.

"Maintain course across the Arctic Abyss." Finally, Anderson exhaled, his shoulders sagging just slightly as he pinched the bridge of his nose. "Boomer, what's the ice look like?"

"Fast ice, Captain." Boomer's voice was still shaky. His hands trembled over his screen, but he kept going. "We're under the cap. No ridges or keels on my scope."

Anderson nodded. "How's our rudder?"

Roller spoke through clenched teeth. He and the helmsman were both holding on to the yoke, their arms and shoulders straining as sweat dripped down their faces. "Struggling. We're pushing twenty-three knots, sir. We can't keep this up for long."

"Boomer, find us a polynya. We need to surface, and fast."

FAST ICE WAS AN Arctic submariner's dream.

The hardened ice cap above, more than eighty feet thick, was solid, firm enough to withstand the drifts and slams of ice that built up from Siberia and pushed into the Arctic Ocean, pressing over the top of the world on its way to Canada. Nearer to Siberian shores, the crash of ice sheets slamming into the polar ice cap sent deep ice ridges down into the seas, blades the size of city blocks that a submarine could slam into, or shear herself apart on.

But over the top of the world, the bottom fell out beneath *Honolulu* as she passed over a triplet of plunging basins. The Makarov Basin, the Polar Drop, and the Nansen Basin, where the ocean floor was a terrifying seventeen thousand feet or more beneath them. Ancient undersea mountain ranges divided the basins, soaring ridges that rose up and tried to tickle *Honolulu*'s belly. They were in such deep waters that even with the thick ice above and the mountain ridge below, *Honolulu* sailed through the waters with open seas above and beneath her.

It was ball-shrivelingly terrifying. If anything went wrong beneath the ice cap, they'd plummet to the bottom and vanish from history forever.

Fast ice also went on for what seemed like an eternity, even more so with a stuck rudder and two straining helmsmen. Anderson rotated men in to hold the shuddering yoke stable as each team drenched themselves with sweat, struggling to hold a steady course.

Finally, Boomer shouted that the ice above was thinning and that he'd found a polynya, a section of ice-free waters in the middle of the vast Arctic. Or, almost a polynya.

"Brash ice and slurry, Captain." Floating icebergs and slushy ice like a melted snow cone.

"We can punch through." Anderson turned to Roller, back at the helm. "Bring us to a stop under that opening. Roll into the jammed rudder, and then reverse engines and push her into the current. I want us dead in the water. Keep us trim."

Roller nodded and popped another three pieces of nicotine gum into his mouth. His jaw never stopped moving, a manic chewing that made him seem like a hamster. But, he brought the boat to a standstill, just inches off the center of the polynya.

"Well done, Roller. Take us up to periscope depth."

"Periscope depth, aye." Roller's biceps shook, but his hands were steady on the control yoke, working in tandem with the planesman.

Ballast blew as an alarm rang three times. *Honolulu* began to rise. Anderson stood by the periscope well, and when it rose, he ducked down and swept in a circle, scanning the ice above. He pulled back. "Mr. President. Care to take a quick look?"

Jack ducked down and pressed his eyes to the scope. Floating ice chunks the size of small cars bobbed in the seas, colored from soot black to gem-like turquoise to arctic white. Swells sent slurry over *Honolulu*'s rounded black deck, leaving trails of ice like snow covering a driveway. The bob and weave of the ocean returned, the roll and sway of the deck beneath his feet as the sounds of a million ice cubes cascading against the hull plinked and rattled through the Conn. Jack stepped back.

Roller moaned, his head in his hands. "I hate the swells."

Anderson clapped Roller on the shoulder as he made his way toward the central hatch, leading to the bridge on the sail. "Have Commander Ross meet me on the deck. X-O, bring the presidents up once I secure the bridge. Boomer, keep a steady lookout. Call at the first sign of anything that isn't an organic."

The executive officer helped Jack and Sergey into life jackets as Ethan and Sasha hovered nearby, pale and looking like they'd regretted eating breakfast. Of the two of them, Sasha looked worse. He kept both hands on the railing and seemed to struggle to keep his stomach down. Ethan, as always, was rock-solid and focused entirely on Jack.

"Be careful," Ethan breathed as Jack passed, heading for the hatch leading to the bridge. Jack nodded and kissed his cheek. Behind him, he caught Sasha's furtive clasp of Sergey's hand, his tight squeeze, and Sergey's small, radiant smile in return.

He waited for Sergey on the ladder, just beneath the open hatches leading out to the bridge. Biting salt air whipped down into the tower, and above, a circle of battleship-gray sky hung low, almost close enough to touch.

"Congratulations," he said, leaning his shoulder into Sergey. "I'm happy for you. And proud of you."

Sergey smiled slowly. He kept his eyes ahead, fixed on the ladder. "Sasha would want me to say that I have no idea what you are speaking of." His eyes flicked to Jack. "But I will say thank you. And, that I needed your kick in my ass. It is the best thing you have ever done for me, Mr. President."

Laughing, Jack started to climb again, through the sail and onto the small open bridge. Water drained from the base of the bridge, but slurry ice still made the deck slippery. Below-freezing water slicked over the hull in rushing sheets. Mist and swirling fog rose from the hull like curling smoke, the heat of *Honolulu* turning the frigid Arctic waters to steam. Around their slushy breach in the ice cap, a bitterly frozen white wasteland stretched as far as the eye could see, as if the whole world were frozen. Beyond that, fog descended, blurring the horizon into a canvas of smeared lead and dirty snow.

Biting winds blew off the ice sheet, swept up the side of *Honolulu*, and snaked around his neck and down his spine. He shivered, curling around himself as memories of frozen water closing over his head and his face pressed against the cold, slick underside of a frozen river went off like torpedoes in his mind.

Sergey stood beside him, close. He wrapped his arms around Jack, rubbing his hands briskly up Jack's arms. Anderson and his executive officer filled out the rest of the small bridge, both of them surveying the fog-shrouded landscape. On the deck, crewmen in life jackets and foul weather gear scurried down the rounded hull, heading for the jammed rudder. The damage was obvious from the sail. A deep gouge had ripped a chunk of the rudder clean off, and debris had jammed into the gears and spaces of what was left. It would not be an easy fix.

"Contact," Anderson said as he peered through his binoculars. "Looks like a research station. Maybe two. Oil exploration site, maybe?"

Sergey nodded. "There are many in these parts. RusFuel has contracts for the Arctic."

"I'm not seeing any movement. No signs of life." Anderson squinted at Sergey. "What was their status before the coup?"

"Operational. Spring and summer are the prime seasons for exploration. We had just started getting their first reports of the season in Moscow."

One eyebrow arched high on Anderson's thin face. "Looks like nobody's home now." He passed the binoculars over.

"How far are we from Madigan's position?" Jack's breath fogged in front of his face as he spoke.

"October Revolution Island is down that bearing." Anderson pointed into the fogbank, but Jack couldn't see anything. "The middle of three arctic desert rocks that Russia claims. They form the entrance to the Kara Sea."

"How solid is the ice between here and Novaya Zemlya?" Sergey used the Russian name for Severney Island, the crooked finger of land that sheltered Madigan inside the Kara Sea.

"Packed in. Siberia's been pushing larger ice sheets into the Arctic every year. It's solid for hundreds of feet, and then tapers to brash ice in parts."

Sergey hummed. Jack watched him. "What are you thinking, Sergey?"

"Those stations arc all the way into the Kara Sea. We could use them. Hop our way down closer to Madigan's location."

"We go overland, and *Honolulu* moves under the ice? See if we can get a good look at Madigan before we make our move?"

Sergey nodded.

They both turned to Anderson.

Anderson sighed, like a man being told to do the impossible with a shoestring. "We're not up to an undersea dogfight. Not with this." He jerked his chin toward the busted rudder. "Until we get ourselves repaired, the overland route is the next best option. We'll stay here to support you while you recon."

"Thank you, Captain.

"Don't thank me yet. I can get you from *Honolulu* to the ice cap, but from here to the station it's an hour's walk in the Arctic. You'll need to bundle up."

JACK KNEW, FROM THE moment Sergey suggested their excursion, that they wouldn't be going alone.

Ethan instantly joined the mission. Sasha, too. Ethan briefed Scott and Adam, and then Adam rounded up his team and got them all geared up and waiting in the mess hall in six minutes, well before Jack had struggled into his thick neoprene dry suit and snow-white arctic military pants, jacket, hood, and gloves. Together, the whole team looked like a cross between polar bears on hind legs and a troop of Marshmallow Men.

On the bobbing hull of *Honolulu*, Adam gave a quick brief of their mission. Doc listened doubled over, his hands on his knees, his skin as white as the snow slurry washing over the bow. They split the mission gear between everyone, checked and rechecked their arctic gear. And then, it was time to go.

Anderson had a small team ferry them from the deck of *Honolulu*, through the slurry ice, and to the edge of the glacier. Sasha and Ethan shoved shoulders until Sasha put his foot down and insisted on disembarking first. He clambered out of the small boat and onto the ice sheet like a cat setting its paws on an uncertain surface.

The ice held.

Ethan hopped out, and then Scott and Adam, and after Adam's team set up a perimeter, Ethan and Sasha pulled Jack and Sergey out of the small boat. On the ice cap, Faisal looked wide-eyed, gazing at the snow that surrounded him on all sides. He was bundled up tight, his jacket zipped up above his nose, and thick goggles covered the rest of his face. Together, they strapped crampons to their boots and roped a safety line around each of their waists. Adam's team linked into their small groups. Sergey and Sasha moved together, and Jack, Ethan, and Scott tied themselves into one unit.

"We're all here, Captain. Ready to head out." Jack spoke into the radio Anderson had fitted him with. Adam had patched him, Ethan, Sergey, and Sasha into his team's radio and passed out a set of throat mics and earpieces for them all, but Anderson had given Jack a separate ship-to-shore portable radio. It would only work while *Honolulu* was surfaced through the ice. "We're moving to the RusFuel station."

"Repair estimates are three and a half hours, Mr. President. I've got a team standing by in case you need them, but the cavalry won't be moving quickly if you get into trouble. Keep your eyes and ears open. You're in the Arctic now. This place wants you dead, and that's before you find the son of a bitch. The wind, the snow, the cold. They're all racing to see what kills you first. And, Mr. President, remember this. If you think it's a polar bear, shoot first. Don't let them get too close, or you'll be a bloody smear on the ice before you even get near Madigan."

"Thanks, Captain." Jack grinned as Ethan rechecked his rifle, and Sasha put his in the ready position. "I'll call you when we get there."

38

North Kara Sea

OCTOBER REVOLUTION ISLAND WAS one of the last solid rocks on the planet, before the Arctic waters and the sea ice encased the island and its two neighbors. It was the most northern-flung scrap of dry land, covered in frigid sand and frozen tundra and hugging the same high Arctic circles as Franz Josef Land and Svalbard. For most of the century, it had been encased in sheets of ice, glaciers that crept off Siberia and plowed right over the island. Wind-burned lichen and frost-covered scrub grass tried to grow. Seals and walruses sometimes beached themselves on the glacier. Polar bears occasionally padded through the ghostly, snow-packed fog. It was as far from livable as any human could get on the planet. It might as well have been the moon.

The sea ice ran right up to the glacier that surrounded the island. A solid glacier, but, deceptively, not smooth. A hundred feet beneath them, the heaving ocean beat against the underside. Just like the ice keels stabbing into the depths, ice sails soared into the gloomy sky. Pressure ridges from crunching ice sheets pushed together, creating mountains that stretched like never-ending walls. Crevasses arched away in long lines, gaps that opened to the black waters below, so deep down that they looked like dark slits falling away to nothingness. A bad step and a slip into one, and their bodies would never be found.

Picking across the ice sheet to the RusFuel station took over an hour. They leaned into the katabatic winds as snow flurries blew twisters between their bodies. The safety line linking them together in groups turned from a nuisance to a silent comfort. Stepping across narrow crevasses and walking along the rippled edges of ice made Ethan's heart pound until his head ached, beating like a bass drum.

Ethan stayed at Jack's side, almost hovering, and Sasha stayed by Sergey. Adam's team fanned out in a diamond formation, keeping Jack and Sergey in the center. Ethan watched Adam and Faisal, watched how they moved together, stayed together, operated as one.

Red flags marked the edge of the RusFuel station, stakes with bits of plastic flapping back and forth. Against the snow, the red flags looked like spilled blood, virtually a river of it, twisting and twining through the ice.

The station had the bare look of a Wild West outpost. It had clearly been built for efficiency, not for looks. At first glance, it seemed like a spaceship from the set of a bad 1950's sci-fi movie. A central, wind-worn red building on stilts squatted in the center of a grid of shipping containers. Flags marched in straight lines, marking out walking paths between the main building and the shipping containers. A fleet of snowmobiles sat parked next to the central building, the seats and saddles covered in snow. On the other side, a generator sat, cold and offline, beside giant barrels of what should be fuel.

On top of one of the shipping containers near the main building, a geodesic dome—a giant golf ball, hollow on the inside—sat beside a dizzying array of antennas, masts, and satellite dishes.

The station was dark, and the air silent. No hum of a generator, no rattle and clank of a diesel engine churning out electricity.

"Looks like nobody's home." Ethan called for a halt. He ducked to one knee and peered at the station, searching for something. Movement. Signs of life. Signs of a struggle. Anything at all.

Adam's voice broke over their radio, into his earpiece. *"I'll take my team in for a closer look, Director."*

"Go for it."

He waited, weapons ready, with Jack, Scott, Sergey, and Sasha as Adam and his men crept up on the station, circling it from all sides before moving in. In their arctic suits, they blurred into the landscape, until they looked no different than a passing snow flurry. A haze of movement against the endless white wasteland.

Adam called it in. *"Station is clear. No one's here. Power's offline. It's creepy in here, sir."*

"We're coming in."

They moved in, Sergeant Wright holding the door for them, and they took their first steps into the RusFuel station.

As he entered, the hairs on the back of Ethan's neck rose. It was cold, as cold inside as it had been outside. No one had been in there for a long time. He peered around the empty central room of the main station. Half-filled glasses of tea sat on tables next to unfinished, stale toast. Papers still lay in open folders. There were no signs of violence, no signs of a struggle. Overhead, bare fluorescent bulbs hung dark and cold. One hallway led away, presumably to the dormitories, also dark. "Where is everyone?"

"Could they be out doing surveys? Or at an oil rig?" Jack looked hopeful.

Sergey shook his head. "Always, a station has an operator on-site at all times. To keep the power on." He lifted one hand, pointing to the dark lights.

"Evacuated after the coup?" Adam stood in a loose circle with them, Faisal at his side, as his team spread out, poking through the station's remains. Over Adam's shoulder, Ethan watched Ruiz take a drink from one of the glasses, make a face, and spit the slushy tea back into the glass.

"If they were evacuated, then why are snowmobiles still here?" Sasha shook his head. "Russians do not leave equipment behind. Not like you Americans."

Adam frowned and opened his mouth, but Wright's voice stopped him. "Hey, L-T! Come check this out."

They trooped over to Wright. A map of RusFuel drill and research locations hung on the wall, tacked at an angle. The map was in Russian, but they got the gist. "Looks like we're... here." Wright plopped his finger down on a yellow RusFuel symbol seemingly in the middle of endless white space marked "*Arctic*". Sasha grunted and nodded when Wright looked to him for confirmation. "These stations will take us south. Right to where we want to go." Wright dragged his finger along an arc of yellow RusFuel symbols, heading south into the Kara Sea, on the ice cap and stretching toward Novaya Zemlya. "All the way to Madigan."

"I saw stations destroyed when I flew over. Burning." Sasha set his jaw and glared. "Madigan destroyed many. These." He pointed to the stations nearest to Madigan's position, halfway up Novaya Zemlya and on the sea ice.

"Well, he didn't get this one," Wright snapped and turned his attention to Adam. He flicked a polite glance to Ethan and Jack. "We can use this station as a base for now. It's close to *Honolulu*, we've got four walls and a roof, and wheels. Well, treads. Snowmobiles. We should recon to the south. Check out the next station."

Adam nodded. "Sir?" He glanced from Ethan to Jack.

"Do it," Jack spoke first. "Take your team out and report back what you find. We'll remain here. Try and find some answers."

Footsteps from down the hallway made them all spin on their heels. Sasha and Ethan had their rifles up to their shoulders a second before Adam and Wright. Around the main room, the rest of Adam's team took up firing positions, each dropping for cover or flattening to walls as they watched and waited.

Sergey's voice broke through the darkness. "I found the safe, and the weapons locker—" He turned the corner to the main room and stopped dead, his arms full of rifles and fingers stuffed with plastique explosives.

Sasha dropped his rifle first, almost exploding as he cursed and growled at the same time. Deep Russian rumbled from him as he snapped at Sergey, pointing his finger and shaking his head. Sergey's eyebrows climbed up his forehead.

Scott chuckled.

Adam's team slowly dropped their weapons, all of them glaring at the Russian president. "We head out in five," Adam snapped. "Everyone be ready."

THE TEAM SET OUT on snowmobiles, everyone taking one, except for Faisal, who sat behind Adam and pressed his face between Adam's shoulder blades for the ride. They left enough snowmobiles for Ethan and the others to follow later.

Adam's GPS pinged twenty minutes after they set out. He called the team to a halt and sent Coleman, Park, and Kobayashi in to check it out on foot. Five minutes later, Coleman radioed back the all-clear signal and they came in on the snowmobiles.

It looked almost the same as the last station, except bigger. The central building was larger. Another grid of shipping containers sat in the snow and ice, with heavy drifts built up against the north and west sides. Red flags flapped in the wind, staking out the perimeter and the walkways, and, at this station, down the length of a smooth ice runway. At one end of the runway, a small Russian Beriev propeller plane rested on skis. The plane had spent its whole life in the Arctic.

Behind the main station, a hole had been blown in the ice cap, a perfect circle down to the ocean. The ice cap was thinner by this station; only thirty feet or so, at best guess, looking down the crevasses they passed.

A winch hung off a steel girder, drilled into the ice cap next to the blast hole, and a thick suspension cable ran from the winch to a commercial mini-submarine, a technical submersible designed for underwater drill operations. The sub, built for maybe four people, was staked to the ice and snow by a thick, frost-crusted chain.

There was no movement. No sound. No signs of life.

They crept in slowly, parking the snowmobiles across the runway and slipping in over the smooth ice and windblown snow. Adam sent Coleman and his team around the back and put Wright out by the runway, watching the horizon and keeping his eyes peeled for any unwanted visitors. Together, he, Faisal, Doc, and Ruiz breached the main building at the same time, running up the stairs and throwing open the doors, shouting at the top of their lungs for anyone inside to drop to the ground.

No one answered. The station, like the previous one, was abandoned.

Except, Adam spotted a half-full mug on the edge of a table. Coffee gently sloshed up the sides of the mug, like it had just been set down.

He caught Faisal's gaze.

"SOMEONE IS HERE. WE'RE going to find them." Adam briefed his team in the main room, speaking softly. "Wright, is the perimeter set?"

Over the radio, Wright answered back. "*Just finished, L-T. Lasers are up and running.*" Static cluttered his words.

"Good." Invisible, anyone crossing Wright's perimeter wouldn't even know they had tripped the laser. "Anything going in or out, we'll know."

"What's the plan, L-T?" Coleman set his jaw, staring with narrowed eyes at Adam.

"We need to find out who's here. If it's one of Madigan's men, we grab him. Get every single thing out of him. If it's a RusFuel guy, we figure out what he knows. What he's seen. And why he's hiding. Whose side he's on."

He sketched out a basic map on a piece of paper, the layout of the station, the outlying buildings, the shipping containers, the ice hole behind them, and the runway. "Coleman, take your team and search the shipping containers and the drill hole. What's in there? What do they have on-site? Ruiz, Doc, you two search the generators, the antennae farm, and the snowmobiles. Any footprints? Anything jacked with the equipment? Check everything over. Wright, you check the plane. See if anyone is hiding in there."

"*Roger that, L-T.*"

He turned to Faisal. "You and I will check the main building. Offices, dorms, labs, everything they've got here." Nods all around. "Report back updates on everything you find."

More nods, and then Adam dismissed the team. They broke apart, Coleman taking Park and Kobayashi with him to the shipping containers, and Doc and Ruiz heading for the generators and antenna farm. Antennas, satellite dishes, and geodesic domes crowded on top of one of the shipping containers, covered in snow and dripping with icicles.

Adam hefted his rifle and gestured down the first dark hallway. Like the other station, the lights were dark, generator power offline. Faisal clicked on the flashlight mounted to his rifle and followed Adam.

"THIS IS BULLSHIT," RUIZ grumbled as he scanned the snow, searching for footprints outside the station.

"What is?" Doc rammed the butt of his rifle against the frozen lock on the shipping container behind the generators. It snapped and fell to the snow. Ruiz followed him inside, scanning the container with his flashlight.

"L-T keeping Prince F inside the station. Why can't any of us be inside the station? Where it's *warmer*."

Doc picked his way through the dark shipping container. Cables lay in bundles, and chains wrapped around thick wooden spools. Tools hung on one wall. He grabbed a crowbar. "Okay, first of all, that station is creepy as fuck. I don't want to go down those dark hallways. Fuck no." He turned and pointed the crowbar at Ruiz. "And second of all, you're from fucking Minnesota. Faisal is from Saudi Arabia. Who do you think is doing better in this shitshow?"

Ruiz scowled. "You don't think he's giving Prince F all the good stuff? Better treatment and all that?"

"I think he's fucking Faisal, yeah. Is that better treatment?" Doc shrugged. He banged on the sides of the first drum he passed. Thick booming echoed back like it was full of liquid. "I thought you liked Faisal. Would you be bitching more if Faisal were given a mission on his own? Sent out here?"

"How would I know he knows what the fuck he's doing?" Ruiz grumbled. "He ain't trained with us. And, naw, I don't hate him. But he ain't one of us."

"You're just jealous of the new baby." Doc winked and slammed the crowbar into another drum. Another heavy echo. "So where else should he be? Where would he be doing the best he can *and* be out of our way?"

Ruiz said nothing.

Doc smirked over his shoulder. "L-T's trying to do everything for everyone. Making sure we all don't go flying off the handle about Faisal and keeping Faisal alive. I mean, c'mon. The nephew of the Crown Prince of Saudi Arabia, *here*?" He shook his head.

"Fuck, Prince F is that important? I thought he was just another prince. They have five fuckin' thousand."

"Nah, he's big shit. Maybe the next king, even." Doc swung his crowbar against the next drum as Ruiz whistled.

This time, the drum rang loud and clear.

COLEMAN SPLIT HIS TEAM up at the shipping containers. He sent Park down one row and Kobayashi down the third. He took the middle. None were locked, and after cracking through the ice built around the handles, they swung each container open and looked inside.

Coleman found more snowmobiles. A bright-yellow arctic construction vehicle on treads. Parts for drilling, long, long lengths of pipe that would be right at home on an aircraft carrier, and drill bits the size of a minivan. Pistons and engine parts that could have gone on a tank. Whatever the station's purpose was, it was *big*.

He pressed his throat mic and radioed his team. "Found anything?"

Static nearly drowned out Park's response. "*Nada, Sarge. Just equipment. I think I see you, Kobayashi.*"

"Kobayashi?"

"*I just flipped you off, Park. Nothing relevant, Sergeant.*" More static.

He set off for the next container. More drill equipment.

His radio chirped again. The static over the line was worse than before. He could barely hear Park's voice, tinny through the connection.

"*Park to Coleman... approaching ice hole... something... gotta see...*"

"Park? Park, come back?"

Nothing.

Coleman tried Kobayashi. "Kobayashi, come back. Kobayashi?"

Static and dead air.

He took off, jogging down the long line of snow-blown steel boxes toward the ice hole. His finger curled around the trigger.

"WRIGHT? WRIGHT, COME BACK. Shit, I can't raise anyone." Adam pushed on his earpiece like that would make the signal clearer. All he could hear was static, endless wails and warbles. "Where the hell is this static coming from? We should have a clear signal."

They'd wound their way through the complex, back to the dormitories. A long line of empty, mostly unmade bunkbeds. Pictures of wives, girlfriends, and porn stars were pushed into the metal grates of the bunks and tacked on walls. People had been there. Had lived there. Where had they gone?

"Unless there's something else in the air." Faisal leaned his rifle against the wall and dropped his backpack. He sat on the edge of a bunk.

Faisal pulled his laptop out of its protective sleeve and powered it on. The battery stuttered and the screen flickered, but it finally powered up. Faisal grinned. "I will do an RF sweep. See what else is out there."

Adam nodded. He poked around the rest of the dorm, using the barrel of his rifle to open locker doors and flick through the RusFuel technicians' clothes and jackets. Their shirts were stained with sweat and dribbled sauces, and stank like vodka. Definitely a Russian station.

"Adam…" Faisal's voice hardened. When Adam turned back, he saw Faisal frowning at his screen. "The frequencies here are jammed almost to the max. The C-band is off the scale."

"C-band?"

Faisal looked up. "It's the band for satellite transmissions. Whatever is going on there is bleeding into everything."

"Let's go find out what it is."

HIS FIRST THOUGHT FOR finding whatever satellite was transmitting with enough power to clutter the airwaves was the antenna farm on top of the shipping container Doc and Ruiz had gone to investigate.

"No," Faisal said. "None of those dishes would be capable of this kind of power. From what I saw, most of the masts and receivers were damaged anyway."

"Then this is something different? Something new?"

Faisal nodded. "It will be somewhere with a clear line of sight to the sky."

Adam's eyes rolled upward. He stared at the ceiling.

Faisal stayed in the station while Adam clambered to the roof. There weren't any ladders to help him up. He jumped from the top of an oil drum to the sharply angled overhang, and then pulled himself up by grabbing onto the edges of the corrugated steel sheets and sliding on his belly. The overhang tried to block the harsh winds roaring off the ice sheet from pushing too hard on the station. For Adam, it was a frigid obstacle, chilling his body as he slid over the frozen metal. Finally, he swung his feet over the edge and jumped down to the flat roof of the main station.

He peered around, turning in a slow circle with his rifle up. Nobody home.

He scanned the snow.

Footprints, from the edge of the roof to the center. Something squatted in the middle of the roof, covered with a thin piece of parachute silk. It rustled in the faint wisps of wind that slipped around the protective overhang, shuffling like dry sand.

Adam slowly crept toward the center, keeping his head on a swivel, searching for anything. Static hummed in his ear. His molars ached, and the hairs on his arms stood straight up, quivering like he'd been zapped with electricity.

A sound split the air, almost like a shout. He whirled and raised his rifle, scanning right and left.

What was that? A bear? What did a polar bear shout sound like, anyway? He shuffled toward the edge of the roof, his rifle still up and ready to fire.

Over the edge, he could see almost the entirety of the station. The antenna farm and the doors of the shipping container wide open. Rows and rows of more shipping containers. The ice hole. Snowmobiles. The plane. A smear against the endless white, lying in the snow at the edge of the runway caught his eye. Wright, keeping watch after searching the plane.

He scanned the station again. Someone kneeled next to the ice hole, peering into the darkness, but from his vantage point, he couldn't see which of his men it was. They wore the same arctic uniforms, all white from head to toe, an almost seamless blending into the snow and ice.

Must have been a bear. Or the wind. Radios were down, but no one had raised an alarm. His team was still searching.

He had his own search to complete. Adam turned back toward the roof and took a step. He tripped, stumbling for a few steps before falling to the roof. He curled to his side as he landed on his shoulder. Wincing, he lay there for a moment, letting the sting fade.

When he opened his eyes, he saw it. A thick black cable, rubber coated, stretching over the roof and toward whatever was in the center. Snow had covered it completely. His eyes tracked the cable, and like a maze being revealed, he suddenly saw the rise in the snow where the cable had been buried, purposely hidden. Another cable stretched from the center of the roof beneath the parachute silk, and another. And another, like the spokes of a wagon wheel radiating outward. The ends went over the edge, dropping toward the runway.

Peering over the roof, he traced the cables through the snow, following the rise, the disturbances where they had been buried and concealed. They wound around the snowmobiles and disappeared into the lines of shipping containers.

Adam frowned. What the hell were those?

He peered across the station. He couldn't see his team. Whoever had been at the ice hole was gone now. Doc and Ruiz, at the antenna farm, were silent. A little strange, but Doc knew when to get serious on an operation.

He headed for the center of the roof. Whatever the cables were doing, somehow it was connected to whatever was under the parachute silk. He ripped it away.

Six cables came together at the base of a thick steel needle, like a syringe for a giant, that pointed toward the sky.

Jesus, this was the satellite. Some kind of crazy, cutting edge satellite transmitter, low-profile for black missions. He'd seen things like it before, back when he was working in the field, but they'd never been this huge or this high-powered. Standing next to it, Adam felt like his organs were vibrating, like his spleen was trying to duke it out with his liver, and the winner would punch through his stomach to escape his body.

But how were they transmit—

His gaze traced the black cables, radiating out from the satellite. Of course. The cables, lying in the snow, *were* the antenna. One giant antenna spread around the station.

Whatever this was, it *wasn't* RusFuel tech. Russian state-owned scientists did not work with technology that still had the stink of DARPA on it. Which meant—

"Hey!" Doc's shout broke over the station. "*Hey!* I need some fucking help over here!"

Adam sprinted to the edge of the roof. Below, Doc dragged Ruiz behind him through the snow, trailing a line of blood that stretched from Ruiz's head to the antennae farm. "What the fuck?"

"Someone fucking jumped us!" Doc looked up, and Adam saw a gash on his temple and a smear of blood coating the side of his face, all the way down to his chin. "We were opening up the oil barrels and someone fucking jumped us!"

"Ruiz?"

"Out cold." Doc dropped to his knees, breathing hard. He grimaced, swaying like he was about to faceplant.

"I'm coming down. Hang on." Adam scrambled to the edge of the roof and slid over on his belly. There wasn't anything beneath him except snow and ice, six feet down. Jesus, he hoped it was a soft landing. Adam let go, pulled his knees in close, and dropped.

"L-T!"

He landed on his side, powdery snow puffing up around him as his hip hit a hard chunk of ice. Coleman's voice made him scramble to his feet. He limped toward Doc and Ruiz and saw Coleman jogging toward the pair as well. "Sergeant?"

Coleman's eyes were wide, wider than he'd seen before. Coleman wasn't a man easily rattled. He'd been Adam's right hand from the moment he'd taken over as team leader. Unflappable. Solid as steel. Adam had borrowed his strength, his determination, more than once.

"Park and Kobayashi are gone." Coleman dropped to Ruiz's side and rolled his chin, peering at the gash in Ruiz's temple. Blood oozed from the wound and over the back of his head.

"Gone? What do you mean *gone*?" Adam knelt beside Doc and took his face in his hands, shaking him gently when Doc wouldn't focus on him.

"They were checking out the ice hole. I couldn't hear anything over the radio. I went to join up with them, but they both vanished." Coleman's gaze hardened as he poked at Ruiz's blood-covered head.

Adam's gaze flicked over Doc's shoulder to Coleman. Coleman's jaw clenched hard, a vein pulsing across the center of his forehead. Even though he knew it was useless, he tried the radio again. "Wright, come back. Anything on the perimeter?" The laser tripwire hadn't gone off, but still.

Nothing but static. "Park? Kobayashi?"

More static.

Slowly, Adam turned back to the station. The still, silent station. *Faisal*.

"Get inside," he growled. "Everyone get inside, now."

COLEMAN CARRIED RUIZ FIREMAN-STYLE while Adam helped Doc stumble up the stairs and into the main station. Faisal met them at the door, helping Adam carry Doc the rest of the way in, and then clearing one of the tables off for Coleman to lay Ruiz on.

"He's dazed. Maybe a concussion." Adam crouched down as Doc breathed deep, bent over as he sucked in large gulps of air. His eyes were squeezed shut, but he nodded to Adam.

"I'm okay," he grunted. "I'm okay. Just need some air."

"Can you treat Ruiz?" Behind Adam, Faisal had taken over, putting pressure on the gash and trying to wipe away the blood that matted his hair and covered one half of his face.

Doc nodded slowly. "Yeah. Yeah, I can."

Adam went to Coleman as Doc joined Faisal. His sergeant paced like a caged tiger, his jaw clenching as he stared out over the icy expanse and the eerie stillness of the station. A barren world had swallowed two of his people. Where had they gone?

Someone—or some*ones*—was here with them. And unless RusFuel technicians were deadly serious about their drilling, Adam would put money on their mystery guest being one of Madigan's men. They must have taken the station. The techs were most likely dead.

So where were the bodies?

If he was getting rid of bodies in the Arctic, throwing them down a deep, dark hole would be the perfect place. "What did you see at the ice hole?"

Coleman shook his head. "Nothing. It was like they were never there. No signs of a fight."

"Did you hear anything?"

"Not a damn thing. Fucking radio." Coleman squeezed his rifle hard. The plastic casing groaned.

He had to see for himself. "Stay here. Guard the others."

"L-T—"

"Stay *here*." He forced Coleman back with his gaze. "Someone's out there, and we've got wounded in here. You need to guard them. I'll go check it out." He looked back to Faisal. Faisal held Ruiz's head while Doc rubbed at the gash, cleaning the blood away. Ruiz was still out.

Coleman glared. "Yes, sir."

Adam ducked out of the station and stayed low. He scanned the ice. Nothing. Nothing but windblown desolation. The open doors of the shipping containers Coleman had gone through banged in the wind, the hinges creaking and groaning as steel clanged against steel. On the ground, he picked out the disturbance in the snow, the buried cables he'd traced from above. Someone had gone to a lot of trouble to cover every inch of those cables with loose snow. Thanks to the ice cap, they couldn't go very deep, though. This part of the Arctic was essentially a desert. The snow blowing in the air was the same snow that had fallen twenty, fifty years before. Old snow, dry like sand. Maybe an inch of new snow fell each year. Probably less.

The antenna farm lay to the left, and the ice hole to the right. He headed to the right, jogging low from the station to the submersible, staked to the ice. The suspension cable swayed above, creaking in the winch.

It was just like Coleman said. There was nothing at the hole. No signs of a struggle. No shuffled snow. Nothing at all to suggest that two of his men had vanished at this spot. He edged his way around, checking every inch of the frozen ground as he made his way toward the antenna farm.

On the far side of the hole, just as he was about to turn away, he finally spotted something: about eight feet down, smeared against the side of the ice, was a streak of bright red.

Fresh blood.

HE HEADED FOR THE antenna farm next, moving fast through the line of snowmobiles to the open shipping container. Doc and Ruiz had been inside, Doc said, checking out the oil drums.

A crowbar lay half-inside the doors. Blood clung to one end. Snow stuck like dust, the dry flakes crimson.

Oil drums lined one side of the container, all the way into the black depths. Chains and tools hung on the other side, clanging as the winds slipped into the open container. Spools of cables and rope turned the darkness into a maze. Three drums in, a lid was partially pried off.

He grabbed the crowbar and went to the third drum, prying the lid the rest of the way off. He tossed it aside.

The drum wasn't filled with fuel or oil.

Thick rubber suits were stuffed inside, and on top of those, heavy masks with thick seals stared up at him, like alien faces. Badges with blank indicators. A Geiger counter.

Radiation suits. He was looking at radiation suits. His briefing with Reichenbach and the others came flashing back: K-27, the nuclear sub, the weaponized reactor, and the potential for a nuclear blast that would kick-start the fires in the sky, and the chain reaction that would decimate the world. Madigan needed this equipment, nuclear technology to restart the reactor in K-27. Did he have a technician, too? Or was he just going to flip the switches and hope for the best?

A noise in the darkness, like a boot scraping over cold steel, made him turn. He whirled around, raised his rifle to the darkness, and crouched low, hovering behind the drum. He could feel the presence of another person, the way his senses screamed that he wasn't alone. The way his blood quickened, his pulse raced. The way his stomach clenched and refused to let go. Someone else was there with him. But who? One of his own? Or the attacker?

His eyes scanned the container, the sides, the tools and parts hanging on the wall.

Realization slammed into him. Those weren't tools or parts for oil drilling. He'd seen enough intelligence briefings on nuclear reactors, on dirty bombs, on components to always be on the lookout for, to recognize what he saw.

Time to go. He had to get back to the others. Adam backed out of the container, keeping his weapon trained on the dark shadows, the plunging blackness behind him. He could feel eyes on him, a hot, heavy stare like a predator lying in wait.

He ran across the ice, zig-zagging his way back to the main station. As he thundered up the stairs, he saw Coleman through the windows, watching his approach. Coleman's gaze was sharp, tracking every one of Adam's steps.

He spoke as soon as he stepped into the station. "Sergeant, we have a problem—"

"Actually, *you* have the problem, Lieutenant Cooper."

Behind Coleman, a new voice rose. A head appeared, and then shoulders. A tall man with dark hair and a lean face stood behind Coleman, his hands hidden. From the way Coleman stood, Adam guessed there was a rifle digging into his back. Coleman's weapon lay on the table. Ruiz still lay where he'd been, unmoving with gauze covering half his head. Doc was nowhere to be seen.

Adam raised his rifle, pointing it at the center of the new man's forehead. A blink later, and he remembered the man's face, the last time he'd seen him: on a report of the officers who had fled with Madigan from South America, joining up with him after murdering their colleagues at the base in Paraguay. Captain Martin, Army Special Forces. Even from his official Army photo, he'd looked like a creep. Deep-set eyes, dark and gleaming, like he had a secret that would destroy you and he couldn't wait to tell the world. Lips that seemed to perpetually smirk, a pair of sharp cheekbones.

"Drop it," Adam growled. "Or I'll shoot you in the head."

"I think that would be a mistake, Lieutenant."

Adam spun, pointing his rifle to another new arrival, a man stepping from the shadows in the back of the room. Fuck, there were more of them. How many of Madigan's men were there?

He recognized the new man immediately: Captain Ryan Cook. Madigan's hand-picked right-hand man. The Butcher of Baghdad. The new one, after Saddam. He'd made a name for himself in the ranks. Official estimates put the number of Iraqis and Arabs he'd murdered at just over three hundred. Unofficial chatter and barracks gossip tripled that.

Cold sweat broke over Adam. His heart raced, blood pounding loud enough to drown every thought but one as his vision went rage-red. All he saw was Cook and the hostage he held.

The barrel of Cook's weapon dug into Faisal's temple, and blood dripped from the corner of Faisal's mouth, down his chin. One eye was bruised, turning black. His mind screamed, over and over. *He's got Faisal. He's got Faisal. Not Faisal. No.*

"Let him go," Adam growled. A note of pleading had crept into his voice.

The front entrance to the station banged open. Boots thundered toward the main room. Adam's gaze darted to the entrance, but he kept his rifle fixed on Cook.

Six men in arctic gear stormed into the station. More of the soldiers who had fled with Madigan from South America. He picked out each of their faces. Recalled their service records. Special Forces. Weapons specialist. Interrogator. Commander of a black site.

One of the men had Doc, shoving him forward until Doc fell to his knees with his hands laced behind his head. He'd been beaten. One eye was swollen shut. His lip was split, and his teeth were stained with blood. Another man dragged Wright in by his uniform and threw him face-down to the deck. Wright didn't move.

"Drop your weapon, Lieutenant," Cook ordered. "We have your men. We have your lover." He grasped Faisal behind the neck and shoved him to his knees, digging his weapon against Faisal's skin. "You're ours."

"*Fuck* you!" Adam spat. "I'm not fucking yours. I'll never join you."

Cook looked him dead in the eye, grinned, and turned his weapon to Ruiz. He squeezed the trigger.

The blast echoed through the room, a single shot that slammed into Ruiz's neck. His body jerked, and blood arched in a short spray, then pooled on the table beneath him and dripped to the floor. So much blood, flooding from Ruiz, fleeing his body. He bled out, gone in seconds.

"Stop! Stop!" Panic seized Adam, clawed at his heart. He saw Coleman's eyes slip closed. Heard the rasp of Doc's breathing. Where was Park? Kobayashi? Had Cook killed them too? How many more of his team would be murdered?

Cook turned his weapon back to Faisal, pushing the barrel into his cheek as he grasped Faisal's chin, holding him from behind. "It's been a long time since I've murdered an Arab," Cook purred. "Do you know how much I love killing Arabs? Their blood is so sweet. I swear, it smells like oil. Oil and cold hard cash. Like fucking roses to me. God, I love the smell of a dead Arab." One thumb stroked over Faisal's face, lewdly. It pushed into Faisal's mouth, forcing his jaw open. Cook jammed his weapon between Faisal's lips. "I've never killed a prince before."

"Stop! Jesus fucking Christ, stop!" Tears blurred Adam's vision, but he kept his gaze locked on Faisal. Faisal stared back, not blinking. It wasn't supposed to go like this. The mission wasn't supposed to go sideways like this, his team picked apart and murdered at a ghost station, miles away from Madigan. Have their legs cut out from beneath them before they even started? He wasn't supposed to watch his people die.

Ethan's words, seemingly from so long ago, came back. *Stay away from Cook, Adam. Stay the fuck away from him. I mean it.*

I'm so fucking sorry. His eyes slid closed as he dropped his rifle and threw it to the side. It clattered, the plastic hitting the bare flooring of the station like a guillotine falling. "Don't kill my people," he choked out. "I'll do anything you want. Just don't fucking hurt them."

COOK HAD HIS MEN secure Adam's team in the center of the station under guard. Four of his men went back outside while Cook took Adam down the hall. He explained what Adam needed to do, the price he had to pay to keep his men alive.

Adam closed his eyes. His whole life, every choice he'd made, narrowed to this point, this moment. Every decision, every compromise he'd made within himself. From agreeing to bring Faisal on his mission to accepting Ethan's mission back in Tampa. Back, further, to when he'd taken over the team, and they'd gone to Ethiopia on a simple support mission for a presidential visit. And further than that, to the night he'd met Faisal, the first moment he'd laid eyes on him and his heart had imploded, like a star going supernova.

Ethan, forgive me. If you were in my shoes, what would you do? I'm not strong enough to face this. "I'll do it," he rasped. "But, I need to see Faisal first."

"You aren't making any demands. You'll do this, or we'll put a bullet in your prince's head."

"I'll do anything you want." Adam held up his hands, trying to reassure Cook. "*Anything.* Just, *please.* Let me see him. Only him."

Cook stared at him, a flat, level gaze. Adam had looked into the eyes of mass murderers and terrorists, killers who dreamed in blood and rejoiced in death. Even those men, evil men with hearts of darkness, had something in their gaze. A spark of life, some evidence of a soul. Gazing into Cook's eyes was like staring into the abyss, into a black scream that swallowed his heart. His bones itched, and all he wanted to do was run, get away, escape under his bed like he was five years old. The fear he felt was primal, an animal's instinct to escape a predator. Almost like Cook wasn't even a man.

Reaching out, Cook grasped him by the throat and hauled him back to the main room. Adam held Cook's wrists as he struggled to breathe, tripping as he stumbled behind him.

Cook threw him down beside his team in the center of the room. The tables had been cleared out, and two of Cook's men, soldiers from the SOCOM base in South America, had their weapons trained on his team. Wright lay on the deck, his head in Doc's lap. His breathing was shallow, and he seemed woozy. Coleman kneeled beside Doc, supporting him. His jaw was chiseled from hardened granite, clenched so hard Adam thought he heard teeth cracking. Neither man looked at Adam.

Faisal was the only one who crawled to Adam's side and pulled him off the floor. Adam climbed Faisal's arms, pressed their bodies together. He grasped Faisal, held him close, and buried his hands in Faisal's hair as he breathed in beneath the angle of his jaw. "Faisal, I'm so sorry."

"What have you done, Adam?"

He shook his head, keeping his face buried in Faisal's skin. Breathed in Faisal's scent, the spices, the sweetness. God, how he loved Faisal, every part and piece of him. Every curve, every plane of his body. How had he thought he could ever live without him? "I'll do anything to keep you alive. You, and my team."

"But—"

Adam pulled back. He kissed Faisal sweetly, holding his face in both hands. "No buts."

Faisal swallowed.

Adam watched the rise and fall of his Adam's apple. Wanted to kiss it, one last time. "I love you," he breathed. "Faisal, I love you so Goddamn much. I… I've been working on something. I want you to hear me out, okay? Don't stop me. Just listen." He took a breath, slowly, as Faisal frowned.

Adam spoke softly, reciting the words of the *Shahada*, the Islamic statement of faith, as he stared into Faisal's eyes. Faisal jerked, and he opened his mouth as if he wanted to stop Adam like he'd done so many times before. Adam shook his head, and he pressed three fingers over Faisal's lips. He kept speaking until it was done.

In the eyes of Islam, and beneath the gaze of Allah, he was now Muslim.

Faisal's eyes gleamed as he stared at Adam, shaking his head. "Why?" Faisal whispered.

"Because I love you, and because I want to share everything with you. This life, and the next. Live with you forever and for eternity in the next world." He reached into his jacket, beneath his layers, and pulled out his dog tags. Slipped them over his head. He tried to meet Faisal's gaze, but couldn't. "I wanted to memorize the first two chapters of the Quran for you," he breathed. "I've been working on it. It was going to be my gift." He tried to smile. "This isn't a good substitute, but it's all I have right now." He held up his dog tags for Faisal.

Everything clicked in Faisal's mind. Adam watched realization slam into him, and Faisal went from confusion to terror in a half second, blind panic as he reached for Adam, grasping him by his arms. "No. *No*, Adam, *please. In shaa Allah*, there is another way."

"I wanted this to be a happy day." Adam bit his lip. Tears once again blurred his vision. He tried to blink them away, but they cascaded from the corners of his eyes. "I wanted to spend this life by your side. I'm not going to live through this, though." He swallowed. "I'll wait for you, Faisal. I'll wait for you at the gates to the garden. I won't enter paradise without you."

"Adam, *please. Please—*"

"I'll pray for you every day. And sometime in the future, far, far from now, I'll see you again." He held out his hand, clenching his gift, his Marine Corps dog tags, the sum of his identity in his life. "If you accept. If we do this. If we join together for eternity." His throat closed, almost choking him, and he struggled with the next words. "Faisal… will you marry me?"

Fat tears streamed down Faisal's cheeks. His hands shook where he grasped Adam's wrists, his arms. His mouth hung open, soundless whispers falling from his lips. Slowly, he nodded.

Adam had researched Islamic marriage before. First, when he wanted to torture himself when he imagined Faisal marrying a beautiful Saudi woman, or three beautiful women. He wanted to know what it would look like, what it would sound like, when his heart finally shattered.

But as he read, he imagined asking Faisal himself. Imagined how he would do it. The *mahr*, the gift he could get for Faisal, the first offering he'd make as a prospective groom. Faisal had everything he could ever want, and could buy anything in the world, so what could Adam possibly offer?

His love, his life. His heart joined to Faisal's. Together for eternity, accepting what had grown inside him from when Faisal had first shown him the path of his faith, deep in the sands of the desert. The whispered words of the *Shahada* were his true gift. The recitation of the first chapters of the Quran was going to be a historical touch. What a poor man could offer to his beloved when he had nothing else to give but his heart and soul.

"I give you this *mahr*, Faisal, in the hopes that you find it pleasing to your heart." He offered his dog tags again, as if he'd slip them over Faisal's head. It was all he had, but in giving it, he'd give Faisal a piece of his soul. His world, the purpose he'd thrown himself into before Faisal had entered his life.

A sob choked Faisal's voice as he nodded and squeezed his eyes closed. "Everything you give to me pleases my heart," he whispered between sobs. He tried to breathe, tried to drag in deep gasps of air as Adam slipped them over his head.

Cook's footsteps banged on the deck. He was coming back for Adam.

"Faisal, say it. Please, say it." Adam scooted close and pressed their faces together. Memories flickered through his mind like photographs falling to the floor. The night they met, the music playing beneath the tent on the beach, and the sweet honey taste of *luqaymat*. Peaches on Faisal's lips, the warmth of his skin, *Subhanallah*, Faisal was always so warm, like he carried the sun within his soul. Feeling sand beneath his knees and sliding through his fingers. "Please. I want this. I want to be by your side for all eternity. *Please, Faisal. Maa shaa Allah.*"

Faisal's soaked cheeks pressed against Adam's, and his snot slicked Adam's skin. Carefully, he whispered, *"An kah'tu nafsaka a'lal mah'ril ma'loom." I give myself away in marriage to you.*

Adam exhaled, pressing kisses to every inch of Faisal's skin. Over his cheeks, his eyes, into his hair. *"Qabiltun nikaha,"* he breathed. *"Qabiltun nikaha." I accept you in marriage. "Jazaa ka Allah u khaira. Allah u akbar. Allah u akbar."* He kept kissing Faisal, kissing each tear that streamed from his eyes, following the salt trail to his lips. *"Ana bahibak." I love you.*

Faisal couldn't speak. He tried, but sobs stole his voice. His lips moved, and Adam tried to read what he said, feel the shape of his words as his lips pressed against his skin. Promises of love, of eternal devotion.

"You're done." Cook's voice echoed behind him. His hand grasped the back of Adam's neck. "Time to get to work."

"I'll wait for you," Adam said. His voice cracked. "I'll wait for you at the gates of paradise."

Faisal reached for him, lunging as Adam was yanked back by Cook. *"Ana bahibak."* He spoke in Arabic, sputtering as his sobs restarted. *"Ya rouhi. Enta habibi ya hayati." You are my soul. You are my love, the love of my life.*

Adam stumbled as Cook dragged him to his feet and shoved him back. He kept his eyes on Faisal. *"Ya rouhi,"* he breathed. *"Ya hayati."* Faisal's face crumpled, and fresh tears flowed down his cheeks.

He had one last thing to say. "Faisal," he called. "Take care of my team. Love them like you loved me."

The last thing he saw was Faisal's shaky nod, and his lips mouth *ana bahibak* one last time as he clenched Adam's dog tags in his fist.

Cook shoved him hard out of the main room, sending him sprawling on his back down the dark hallway. Kicks followed, vicious blows to his chest, his stomach, his jaw.

Allah u akbar. Faisal's face, smiling down at him. The first time he took his hand and laced their fingers together. *Allah u akbar.* Desert sun beating down on him, turning the world into a strange, otherworldly thing, reality only a mirage, a shimmer before his eyes. Faisal's laugh, the sounds of his voice. *Allah u akbar.* His lips, whispering poetry against his skin, promises of love that would last until the stars burned themselves out and the universe grew cold and still. *May Allah bless you, Faisal, for how you loved me when I could not even love myself.*

One last kick slammed into his chest, and the world went black.

39

North Kara Sea

CAPTAIN ANDERSON'S VOICE BROKE over the radio as Jack and the others waited in the first RusFuel station.

"*Mr. President, I've got bad news for you.*"

Jack keyed the radio on as Ethan leaned in, frowning. Sasha and Sergey sat beside them, Sasha mechanically cleaning weapons as Sergey chattered at him in Russian. From the way Sergey gesticulated, and how Sasha smiled softly every now and then, Sergey was either telling one bad joke after another or sharing his dreams of their future.

Scott leaned back in a chair, his arms crossed, and snored.

"What's going on, Captain?"

"*Sonar has picked up Sierra One again. She's come over the pole and is hanging out in deep waters. Bozeman took damage coming through Herald Canyon and had to go back through the Strait. We're alone up here. We've got to move, or we'll be sitting ducks. Easy targets for their torpedoes.*"

"How are your repairs coming, Captain?"

"*We're better than we were before.*"

Not fully repaired, though. Jack exhaled. "Get your people out of harm's way, Captain. Stay safe."

"*Safe is blowing those bastards out of the water. We'll get it done, Mr. President. They'll be on the bottom of the seafloor soon. Once we go under, we'll be out of radio contact until we surface again. Come hell or high water, Mr. President, we'll find a way to get to you.*"

"Thank you, Captain." Jack watched Ethan check the bolt on his rifle, unload his magazine, check it, and reload. One of Ethan's rituals, something he did to prepare himself. Cycle his thoughts and prepare for what was to come. He held one hand out to Ethan, laying it flat on the table.

"*Stay safe, Mr. President. We'll contact you as soon as we can.*" The radio cut out.

Ethan laced his fingers through his own and squeezed.

WHEN THE RADIO CHIRPED again, Ethan almost dove for it. He'd started to pace, slow, looping steps from one end of the station to the other. Jack watched him silently. Adam's silence had started to gnaw on his mind, too.

"Director Reichenbach, this is Lieutenant Cooper. Come back."

Ethan pressed his throat mic and spoke. Relief strained his voice. "Lieutenant, good to hear your voice. We were starting to get worried."

"Sorry, sir. There was some interference at this station. Some radio equipment one of the techs had that wasn't ever turned off. We just got it taken care of."

Ethan nodded. "What's your status, Lieutenant?"

There was a pause, and a warble in the signal, a brief flicker of static. *"We're all clear, sir,"* Adam said. *"Station is secure. You guys should head down and join us."*

Ethan's gaze flicked to Jack. He turned to Sergey, who nodded.

Jack smiled. "Tell him we're on our way."

40

North Kara Sea

SNOWMOBILES ROARED OUTSIDE THE RusFuel station. Adam lay on his belly, drooling blood onto the floor of the radio room. One eye was swollen shut. At least two ribs were cracked. Breathing felt like he was being squeezed in a vise, or getting bear-hugged with a bike chain. His hands were secured behind his back, and his boots were taped at his ankles.

He heard Cook's men order his people to the center of the main room, down the hall. Heard the pull and tear of duct tape. His people, being restrained.

Ethan would be here soon. He'd ride in, and he'd save the day.

Adam had to believe that. He clung to the thought, whispering it over and over, praying as his lips moved through the puddle of blood beneath his chin. *Allah, guide Ethan. Protect him, shield him. Protect him from what I have done.*

He just needed Ethan to hesitate. To see that all was not right. Question why he wasn't waiting outside for them. Cook would most likely ambush Ethan and the presidents, and Sasha and Scott.

But if he jumped in front of Cook's rifle. If he took the bullets meant for Ethan. If he died to save the presidents. Ethan would then have time to turn the tables and save the day. Save his people. Save Faisal.

He could die and make up for his betrayal, the way he'd slid a knife into Ethan's back with his transmission. *Allah, please, let none of my people die because of me. Shield them. Protect them. In shaa Allah. Please, please.*

And then, he'd wait for Faisal. He'd wait fifty, sixty, seventy years. More, even, gladly. Maybe Faisal would find someone new, another lover to care for him for the rest of his years. It was still too new, thinking of Faisal moving on when they had only just married minutes ago. But Faisal should be happy. He deserved to be happy, to be loved. Of all the people Adam had ever met, Faisal deserved joy, love, and life more than anyone else. If he had to share Faisal in the garden, play the part of second husband, or hover in orbit around whatever love and life Faisal rebuilt for himself in the years to come, content to only gaze on Faisal's smile and the brilliance of his soul, well—

It would be worth it. It would all be worth it.

The door burst open. Cook stormed across the radio room, his boots creaking the bare wooden flooring. "Time to go." He hauled Adam up, grabbing him by his arms and dragging him out. Adam's broken ribs jarred, and agony scorched across his side, like a blazing fire igniting in his nerves. He clenched his teeth, straining, but refused to shout.

Adam twisted when they passed the main room. He spotted Doc and Coleman, lying on their sides with their hands and ankles taped together, Wright taped up but still lying on the floor, and Faisal, staring at him with his huge tawny eyes. Love and sorrow poured from Faisal's gaze, like a waterfall that would flow across the floor and sweep Adam away in a rescuing tide.

Doc and Coleman's gazes, on the other hand, were hard and bitterly cold. If looks could kill.

Cook dragged him out of the station and down to an array of parked snowmobiles. Four of Cook's men were revving their engines, eager to go. Equipment sleds had been lashed to the backs of three snowmobiles, laden down with parts and tools that Adam had seen beneath the antenna farm. Nuclear reactor components. Radiation suits. Masks.

"Get down." Cook threw him onto the back of one of the sleds. Adam landed in a skid, and his head banged against something frigid and hard, wrapped in parachute silk. A slender steel radial jutted into the air from the folds of the silk, and beneath him, thick lengths of rubber cable lay neatly coiled. The satellite. It had been Cook's, and Madigan's.

Cook shoved Adam's head down and looped a thick chain through his elbows and then the sides of the sled, securing him as a prisoner. Shit. Adam tried to jerk, twist away, but stabbing pain from his ribs stole his breath away. Gasping, he flopped to his back.

And then he saw it.

The oil drums, the ones actually full of fuel, had been dragged out and placed beneath the stilts of the station. They were packed in beneath the main room, all side by side.

Captain Martin squatted beneath, messing with one of the barrels. Adam's breath quickened, fast pants that made his agony bloom, but he didn't once think about the pain. *Please, Allah. Please, no.*

Martin jogged back to the snowmobiles, and Adam's worst fear was confirmed: on the front of the barrel, fixed to the explosive plastique he and his team had carried in themselves, a timed detonator counted down, square numbers flashing brightly.

"No!" he bellowed. Thrashing, Adam jerked against the chain holding him back, kicking his legs and rocking from side to side. The sled wobbled, but all he did was make noise. "No!" he shouted again. "You said they would live!"

Cook grinned. He straddled the snowmobile ahead of the sled Adam was chained to. "I never said that. You did. You bought your own lie."

"You motherfucker!" He kicked again, pounding his taped-together boots against the side of the sled, against the cables, against the crazy satellite, anything he could reach. Rage boiled in his blood, stole his breath. He flung himself as far as he could, trying to reach Cook on the snowmobile. He'd strangle the bastard. Knock him down and break his neck. Something. Anything. Anything to stop what was to come.

The chain jerked him back. He fell to his side, landing on his broken ribs. Pain lanced through him like he'd been stabbed, staked to the sled, run through by a hot poker.

Cook laughed and gunned the snowmobile's engine. "I told you, Lieutenant. You're ours."

Engines roaring, Cook and his men set out, snow arcing behind their snowmobiles as they skidded over the ice cap. Adam rolled and watched the station shrink, turn to a dark dot in the gloom. *In shaa Allah*, he whispered. *Ethan. In shaa Allah, please be careful. I am so sorry.*

Wind from the drive pelted Adam's face, his exposed cheeks, and dry snow and chips of ice flew through the air like razor blades, slicing his skin. He welcomed the agony, and the flare of his ribs twisting inside him. Pain was all he deserved now.

ETHAN AND SASHA RODE ahead on their snowmobiles, taking joint lead in a diamond formation. Jack and Sergey followed behind. When they'd set out, Sergey and Jack had shared a small, private smile and a long look as Ethan and Sasha jockeyed, again, for the point position, the vanguard protector of their little party. In some ways, Sasha and Ethan were cut from the same stubborn cloth.

Scott seemed content to perpetually bring up the rear. Jack saw him watching Ethan, tracking his movements everywhere he went, on the ice and at the station.

It was nice having Scott also watching Ethan. Protecting him. Ethan would throw himself across a crevasse for Jack to walk on without a second thought. Jack just wanted Ethan to be protected with the same fervor and force that Ethan gave him.

The RusFuel station appeared on the horizon, a dark shape in the gloom. Bitterly cold, cutting katabatic winds flowed off the glacier, sweeping down the ice cap, and swirled through the team. The winds did nothing to pierce the fog, the arctic smoke that crept over the open waters and built cloud castles above the ice caps. It was like being lost in a dense soup made entirely of ice that slapped them silly and a cold that bit into any exposed skin.

Jack stayed close to Sergey and kept Ethan's broad shoulders in sight. If he got lost, only a polar bear would be able to find him.

Ethan edged ahead of Sasha on the final stretch, taking point. Jack and Sergey shared another quick look. Sergey shook his head, the trim of his jacket's hood flaring as they rode.

And then, Ethan slid his snowmobile to a stop, braking hard. Sasha overshot him, but swung around and headed back. He stopped nose-to-nose with Ethan as Jack, Sergey, and Scott joined them.

"What's up?" Jack breathed hard and ran his tongue over his cracked lips. Even with his jacket zipped up to his nose, the dry air was sapping him.

Ethan shook his head. He pulled his pack around and dug his binoculars out. "Something doesn't feel right."

Sasha grunted. He revved his engines. "It is too quiet. You Americans are usually louder than this."

"Adam should be out here. He should have a perimeter set. Should give the all clear signal for us to come in."

"It's cold as fuck, Ethan." Scott leaned over his handlebars and spoke through his jacket. The thick zipper muffled his voice. "He called it in. We're good." Leaning back, Scott glared at Ethan through his goggles. "I'd be pissed if you made me stand guard out here in the fucking wind."

Ethan tried to smile. One corner of his mouth quirked up briefly. Jack stayed silent as Ethan looked at him. Their gazes locked. He could see Ethan weighing his gut against Scott's words, judging his instincts against what he'd been told.

"Sasha and I will go check it out," he finally said. "Scott, you stay here with Jack and Sergey. Keep watch."

Scott sighed. "You're the boss." He sat back on his snowmobile and pulled his rifle over his shoulder, holding it low and ready across his lap.

Sasha and Ethan had their rifles out already, hanging across their chests in quick release harnesses. Ethan checked his rifle's chamber while Sasha revved his engines again.

All right." Ethan nodded once to Sasha. "Let's go."

"FUCK, COLEMAN, HURRY!" DOC shook his wrists, trying to help Coleman along. Coleman's fingers were bloody, his nails torn from scratching at the duct tape, trying to peel it away. Warm blood slid down Doc's fingers. "Faisal, how are you doing?"

Faisal sat beside Wright, picking at the tape binding his hands. "Slowly."

"What the fuck was all that Arabic you and the L-T were talking? Did he give you a plan or something? Tell you what was going on?" Doc glared over his shoulder at Coleman as he spoke, as if that would hurry Coleman along.

Faisal swallowed. "No, he did not."

"So what the fuck was all that?"

"It was... personal." Beneath his fingers, Wright seemed to be slowly coming to, blinking hard and breathing deeply.

"Personal? What the fuck?" Doc shook his head, scowling at Faisal. "He *should* have been communicating with us. Trying to get us out of this situation. Or tell us some part of his plan. You're a distraction, Faisal—"

"It was the last time I was going to see him!" Faisal snapped, shouting. "We had to—" He clamped his lips shut and looked away, blinking fast. "He does not plan to survive this."

Silence. Until Wright moaned, and Doc turned his attention to him. "Wright, you okay?"

"Yeah... yeah, I think so. Fuck, they hit me hard." He turned his head and coughed, sounding like he was hacking up a lung. "What the fuck is going on?"

"They shot Ruiz. Park and Kobayashi are gone." Doc and Coleman shared a look as Doc spoke.

Faisal kept picking at Wright's tape. He had a strip loose. If he got more, Wright could pull the rest apart.

"They took the L-T," Coleman finally growled. "He surrendered. I think they made him do something, but I don't know what."

"What the fuck? Why'd he do that?"

Faisal ripped away another piece of tape. His nail bent back, breaking, and pain rocketed up his finger like he'd been stabbed. "I believe you can break free, Wright. Try now."

Wright grit his teeth and heaved, hauling his arms apart. Seams tore and then ripped, and the duct tape split in two. His hands were free. He undid his ankles and then Faisal's hands, and then crawled to Doc and Coleman. "Why the fuck did he give up?"

Doc and Coleman's eyes slid to Faisal, silently.

Snarling, Wright turned away. He stormed across the room, kicking a chair out and flinging a table over. "They took our fucking radios! All of our weapons!"

Doc and Coleman scrambled to their feet. "We don't have time for that shit, Wright. We've got to go. *Now*." Doc grabbed his pack, dumped by one of the tables, and tried to shove as much back into the bag as possible. "They took all our C4, too, and I heard them moving those oil drums. What the fuck do you think they're doing?"

Wright's lips thinned. He and Coleman headed for the doors at the rear of the station, glancing right and left. "Zero contacts," Coleman grunted. "I don't see anything."

"Nothing." Wright glared at Coleman. "How do we get in contact with Reichenbach? We've got to report in."

"One thing at a time," Coleman growled. Together, they pushed out of the station, heading down to the ice. Doc followed, Faisal on his heels.

Doc dropped to his knees and peered beneath the station, between the stilts. He cursed. "Motherfucker. They rolled the oil drums under there. Our C4 is all over the barrels."

Coleman and Wright went pale. Their eyes widened. "The whole station is going to blow."

"We've got to get the fuck out of here." Doc jumped up and turned to the snowmobiles. Empty ice greeted him. "Fuck!"

Faisal's eyes darted over the station, the shipping containers, the fuel drums, the ice hole, the submersible—

The sub. *Allah u akbar*. He swallowed. "We need to get inside the sub," he said, stepping forward. "We can use it to escape."

"We need to go after the L-T—" Coleman started.

"*How?*" Wright said, his voice going shrill. "We've got no gear, no equipment. Zero intel. What the hell can we do?"

Coleman stepped forward, snarling as pressed into Wright's face. "We can't just abandon him—"

Faisal grabbed Coleman's jacket, tugging him back. "I want to find Adam just as much as you do. *Maa shaa Allah,* we will. But right now, we have to survive. We must get away before this station blows up."

Doc took off first, heading for the ice hole. Coleman stared back at Faisal, his expression sprinting from rage to frustration to defeat and back again. "We can't leave him," Coleman growled.

"I will never leave him," Faisal breathed. "But he wants you to live, Sergeant. That is why he did what he did. Do not make his sacrifice be in vain."

Doc managed to get the sub door open and crawl inside. "It's all in fucking Russian!" he shouted, his voice tinny and echoing in the sub's belly. "I don't know what fucking buttons to push!"

Coleman cursed as Wright slid inside the sub, belly-flopping through the round opening. "Get in," Coleman grunted, nodding to Faisal as he reached for the sub's thick docking chain, wrapped around a metal stake driven into the ice.

"Together." Faisal helped him unwind the chain, the frozen metal biting into his skin, so cold it felt like knives were flaying his palms open. Coleman hissed beside him, gritting his teeth with every yank on the metal. Each link was the size of Faisal's thigh.

"Get in, Faisal," Coleman snapped. "If that thing goes, you can't get caught in the blast."

"Neither can you." He heaved the final twist of the chain off the stake. Overhead, the winch groaned, the cable slipping, and the sub started to swing toward the center of the ice hole.

Wright lunged out of the opening and reached for them both. Faisal grasped his hand, holding tight. Coleman followed, grabbing the sub's round hatch opening with his bare hand. He strained, digging his heels into the ice as he struggled to hold it close. Wright hauled Faisal through the hatch, almost throwing him in before turning to Coleman.

"C'mon, big guy." Faisal scrambled out of the way as Wright and Coleman came hurtling through the hatch, tumbling to the sub's deck. With four men, the submersible seemed tiny all of a sudden.

Doc sat at the controls, cursing more than Faisal had ever heard. He hovered behind Doc, eyeing the array of knobs and controls and the hard angles of the Cyrillic alphabet.

A rumble started, and then a blast, like thunder cracking over their heads. Furious flames roared into the sky, swallowing the station whole and blasting debris across the ice. Burning metal and fireballs of diesel screamed for the sub, for the open hatch.

"Holy fuck!" Doc hollered. "Shut the hatch! Shut it now!"

Coleman leaped first, slamming the hatch closed and pulling the lock. They swung over the hole, battered by debris and flames, the ruins of the station plinking against the sub's hull like hail. They swung crazily, a pendulum pushed too hard.

"Get us out of here, Doc!" Wright bellowed.

"The fucking buttons are all in Russian! What should I push? I don't know, how about that one?" Doc sputtered, shouting half to himself and half to Wright, and jammed his finger down on one of the buttons. They started to rise, winching upward toward the crane hoist.

"*Other way!*"

Doc jammed his finger down on the button directly below the first.

The winch unspooled the entire length of cable, and they plunged straight down, deep into the blackness of the ice hole, tumbling end over end. *Adam, ya hayati. I will wait for you at the garden of paradise as well. We will be together again.*

ETHAN SLIPPED QUIETLY OVER the ice, his rifle up and ready to fire. Sasha mirrored his movements, padding down the length of the runway. Nothing moved at the station. In the mist, it was as eerie as a ghost town. The winds whistled through the steel containers, over the ice, under the wings of the propeller plane, and around the ugly confines of the main building.

Where was Adam? Where was his team? Where was Faisal?

Something was wrong. He knew it, deep in his gut. Adam wouldn't leave the station unsecured like this. Would never let Ethan drive Jack up to a location without a perimeter and a guard, a welcome party stationed at least a klick out.

He cocked his head, listening. Through the wind, he thought he heard a shout. Maybe—

The world came apart before he finished his thought, erupting in a fireball exploding outward from the center of the station, spreading up and out.

Heat blazed, searing air slapping Ethan across the face. He squinted, covering his eyes, and ducked down. Shipping containers burst apart as the explosion engulfed them. Corrugated steel, debris from the station, and shattered glass flew through the air, slicing the fog like knives. Shards of metal embedded in the ice, slamming over a foot deep into the cap. Broken chain whizzed by Ethan's head. The ice sizzled when it landed, hissing and turning to steam.

Fuck, he hated being right. Ethan dove, landing on his belly on the ice and moved fast, sliding away from the inferno that the station had become. He tried to find Sasha, but smoke and steam and flying debris blocked his sight.

Adam, were you in there? What had happened? Why had Adam called them to this station? An ambush after the call? Or…

Swallowing, Ethan crawled down the runway as a flaming shard of steel slammed into the ice behind him, swaying back and forth like a knife plunged into a cutting board. Almost like it had been aiming for his back.

ONE MOMENT, JACK AND Sergey were sitting side by side, straddling their snowmobiles and softly talking about their lovers, and their seemingly new quest for point position and strongman on the team.

The next, the station exploded, flames roaring through the arctic gloom.

"Ethan!" Jack revved his snowmobile and shot forward, gunning the engine hard.

"Jack, wait!" Scott followed a moment after Jack, jetting over the ice.

Sergey stared at the fireball, the rising inferno. Dread pitted his heart, made a bottomless pit in his chest. His hands slicked with sweat within his gloves, his body racing from too-cold to searing heat as the sounds of the Arctic, the whistling winds, the shifting ice, faded away. Time slowed, reality replaced by a honey-slow haze as he watched the black smoke plume curl and rise.

Sasha, no. Not now. Not like this.

Reality snapped back like a gunshot behind his head, and he leaped into gear. Sergey slammed down his accelerator and followed Jack and Scott into the inferno.

ETHAN HEARD THE ROAR and grind of snowmobiles approaching. He rolled over, leveled his weapon, and waited.

"Ethan!" Jack's voice rang through the smoke and fog, shouting at the top of his lungs. "Ethan, where are you?"

"Here!"

The nearest snowmobile engine sputtered and choked off, and he heard the heavy machine lurch to a halt. Then, footsteps pounding over the ice. "Ethan!"

He rose and saw Jack's shape through the gloom. He took off. Jack saw him, and he ran toward Ethan, reaching for him with both hands when they got close. "What happened?"

"I don't know." Behind Jack, two more snowmobiles arrived, Scott already half off his and chasing after Jack, and Sergey standing up, searching for Sasha. "We need to find Sasha. He was checking the plane."

They ran together down the length of the runway, heads swiveling as they headed for the parked Beriev. Ice cracked and hissed, turning straight into steam around them, sizzling as the station burned. Black, heavy smoke rose into the steel-gray skies. The stench of burning diesel clung to his throat, the back of his tongue. Jack stayed next to Ethan, one hand on his back.

"I'm okay, Jack. I'm okay."

"What happened?"

"It blew as we approached. If we hadn't stopped, if we'd just gone straight in—"

"Did you see anything?"

Ethan shook his head. "I don't know where Adam or his men are."

Jack said nothing.

"There!" Sergey's shout made Ethan look up. His heart clenched, and Jack let out a curse beside him. "*Govno*, Sasha..."

Sasha lay face-down on the ice, beneath the Beriev's wing, not moving.

Sergey got to Sasha first. He rolled him carefully, cradling his head in his hands. "Sasha," he said softly. "*Zvezda moya.*" My star. "Open your eyes."

Sasha's eyelids flickered. He rolled into Sergey's hold, groaning.

"You are okay," Sergey said. He nodded, smiling down at Sasha. "You are okay."

Sasha's eyes darted from Sergey to Scott, and then picked out Jack and Ethan and the burning station. "I was checking the plane. What—"

A new roar blasted over the remains of the station. They ducked down, shielded behind the Beriev. Overhead, a massive dark shape screamed out of the smoke over the burning station. Sleek and devastating, giant fifty-foot rotary blades made spirals out of the smoke as a massive helicopter banked and veered their way, straight above the runway. The pulse and pound of the chopper's blades shook the air, made the ice tremble beneath their feet. Ethan's bones shook, rattled inside his body.

"Fuck." Sasha spoke first. He scrambled to his feet and knelt in front of Sergey, as if he could protect him. "It is a Halo. Soviet design. The largest, strongest helicopter ever built."

Ethan's stomach tried to roll itself up, tried to turn tail and run as the Halo screamed toward them. It was far bigger than Marine One back at the White House. As long as a commercial airplane. He'd seen a Halo lift an already-massive Chinook troop transport beneath its belly in Iraq, years ago. The Halo had carried away the Chinook as if it were a child's toy dangling beneath it. The Halo was more beast than machine. A modern-day dragon.

Scott and Ethan raised their rifles and took aim. Firing on the Halo was laughable, but it was all they could do. "Jack, behind me! We've got to get out of here!" Ethan squeezed his trigger after he spoke, and bullets spat from his and Scott's rifles. Sparks winked off the Halo's frame, the hardened steel fuselage, their bullets smacking into the chopper and sliding away. Their shots were cute against the mammoth machine. Cute and ineffective.

He could hear Jack's breathing, hear his fast inhale-exhale behind him. Feel Jack's fingers grip his waist.

"Everyone into the plane!" Sasha barked. "Now!"

"You want to fly away?" Sergey sounded like Sasha had suggested a trip to the moon. "They are in the runway!"

Sasha ripped open the doors to the Beriev. "Get in!"

Sergey stopped arguing. He slid inside the plane, plopping into the copilot's seat. Jack followed, hovering behind Sergey as Scott and Ethan kept firing at the Halo.

Ethan's gaze darted sideways. An oil-soaked, burning shard of steel had embedded in the ice, ten feet away. Enough to cover behind, maybe get a different angle on the Halo. He took a breath, and then another, and then took off. He heard Jack's voice shouting his name, but he kept going. Behind his footsteps, ice exploded, bullets from a large-caliber weapon chewing through the ice cap. The Halo had a door gunner.

He spun when he got to the burning steel, dropping to one knee and lining up his shot between the jagged, flaming points of twisted metal. The Halo had turned to track him and continued on its spin, a slow, lumbering twirl over the runway. Perfect. The rear rotors were just coming into view.

Scott opened fire the same moment he did, their synchronized shots slamming into the rear rotors and blade assembly. More sparks, and the sound of plinking metal. Were they doing anything?

And then, the Halo jerked, like a string tied to its back had been pulled. She jerked again, twisting off course. The rear rotors groaned, and then a new rhythmic warble sounded, a terrible noise. Something that sounded like rotor trouble.

Grinning, Ethan kept firing, and the Halo veered off, disappearing over the burning station and into the black smoke smothering the sky.

Time to go. He jogged back to the Beriev, sweat from the heat of the burning steel pouring down his face. Sasha ran around the plane, spinning the dual propellers and tearing off thick wads of padding wrapped around the nose.

Jack glared at him but said nothing as he held out his hand, helping Ethan into the cabin. Scott followed, and then Sasha, clambering forward into the pilot's seat. "This plane has spent days cold soaking, maybe weeks," he snapped. "Even with the engine blankets, procedure says at least three-hour warm up before pre-flight."

Sergey stared at Sasha. "We do not have three hours."

"I know." Sasha flicked a series of switches on the dashboard. His hands trembled. Beneath their feet, the Beriev started to rumble. He reached for the throttle controls in the center of the cockpit, grasping the heavy handle. "Hold on."

Sasha shoved the throttle forward, as far as it would go.

41

Washington DC

THE DOOR TO THE Roosevelt Room closed with a hard click. Levi turned the lock, securing the room and its inhabitants.

"What the hell is this?" General Bell growled, glaring at Levi. "I didn't come up on the first Goddamn flight to DC to be babysat. Where's the president?"

"You're not meeting with the president." Welby, standing at the far end of the table, spoke. "You're meeting with us."

Seated on either side of Welby, Pete and Jason squared off against General Bell. Pete looked more menacing than Jason: jaw clenched, a deep scowl on his face, laser-focused eyes that burned with wrath. Jason squirmed as if he were sitting in front of his high school principal.

"And who the hell are you?" Bell snarled.

"You should remember me." Smiling, Levi gripped the back of the chair at the head of the table. He stared Bell down. "I was the one who wanted to punch your lights out in Tampa. Only, the first gentleman held me back."

Bell inhaled deep and straightened, tugging on the bottom of his uniform jacket. His lips pursed like he'd sucked the sourest lemon. He said nothing.

"General, the president called you here because you are one of five people, outside of Lieutenant Cooper's team, who knew about their assignment. Who knew where Lieutenant Cooper and his men had been detailed."

Bell stared, his gaze hard. "Even if that *were* true," he said flatly, "I couldn't confirm it. I don't know who the hell you people are."

"Call us true patriots." Pete's hand hit the table. A smack cracked through the room.

Levi spoke again. "President Wall has put me in charge of investigating a traitor. A mole. General. Madigan still has his people inside us. Like a cancer."

"There are lots of moles." Bell snorted. "You don't get to Madigan's rank without building a cult following. He's got a thousand men who will die for him. Nearly everyone under his command. He served for many years. Led our forces in combat. He's built loyalty the hard way, with blood, sweat, and tears."

"Are you one of those men, General?" Welby finally spoke again.

Bell took his time answering. His face twisted, like he was disgusted with the question. "No," he finally growled. "I may have my issues with the government, but I believe in this nation. In her soul. I believe she's still alive. Madigan's already written her off, and he appointed himself judge, jury, and executioner."

Levi let out a breath. "Glad to hear that, General. 'Cause I'm asking for your help."

Bell's eyebrows launched straight up, almost to his tightly buzzed gray hair.

"One of Lieutenant Cooper's men was murdered right before everything went to hell. Before the *Vinogradov* sinking. Before the coup in Russia. It caused the team to go to ghost protocol. Because of that, they were scattered and couldn't track Madigan, which let him slip away from Somalia and into Russia, and then help Moroshkin with his coup." Levi squeezed the head of the chair, almost bursting the stuffing from the seams. "That team was one of our best weapons against Madigan. They tracked him around the globe and pinned him to his base in Somalia and the Middle East. But that all went to shit when one of their guys was murdered in his apartment, with Madigan's calling card left at the scene."

As he spoke, General Bell stiffened, straightening almost fast enough to snap his spine. His expression, disgust mixed with snobbish disdain, melted, and his face hardened to stone. Levi watched him carefully.

"Who was killed?" Bell finally asked. His voice was softer than it had been and had lost its edge.

"Corporal Chad Fitz."

Bell blinked. He said nothing.

"Someone knew who these men were, General. Someone knew Lieutenant Cooper was working for Ethan. Working with the White House. We need to find out who knew and how. Find out how they were able to take out a member of a Top Secret black team."

"You're forgetting one thing."

"What's that?" Levi propped his hands on his hips and fought not to sneer. He remembered their last meeting, when he'd wanted to wipe the floor with Bell, smack his smug attitude right off his face.

"Lieutenant Cooper's team also knew about themselves. That's eight more people who knew. Seven, with Corporal Fitz deceased. Seven more potential breaches."

He exhaled. "I had considered the possibility. We're not strangers to betrayal here."

Bell made a noise, something between a grunt and a snort. "What do you propose?"

"These men served under your command, General. You may not have liked Lieutenant Cooper, but he was one of yours. You *know* these men, and you know the military. Agent Welby and I run the White House Secret Service. We know the White House." He headed for Bell, stopping in front of the older man. "Let's work together. Dive deep into the files, into the backgrounds of everyone. Who knew what, when, and why."

The lines around Bell's eyes were deep, furrows that had built up over years and years of service to the United States. Levi held his narrowed gaze, watching the general work something out within himself. Shadows of emotions played in the depths of his eyes, and his weathered face twitched.

"If you want to do this now, as we're squaring off with the Russians in Canada," General Bell said carefully, his voice low and gravelly. "Then there *must* be a reason. Lieutenant Cooper was a shit show, but he had the makings of a decent officer. If he and his team were truly as effective as you say—" Bell shook his head. He looked Levi dead in the eyes. "You haven't said what happened after Cooper and his men went ghost."

Levi stared back, silent.

"They're back in action. And something else." Bell stepped forward. "Something that has you scared."

"Will you help us or not?" They were standing so close that his breath, his words, brushed over Bell's face.

Something shifted in Bell's eyes. "I don't leave my men behind. Never. And I don't let anyone get away with their murder." He pulled out a chair and sat down, his back stiff and straight, hands laced together on the tabletop. "Where do we begin?"

HOURS PASSED. THE WALLS of the Roosevelt Room filled up, covered with papers tacked to the wainscoting and taped over glass frames and oil canvases. Profiles of personnel in the White House, senior staffers who had access to the West Wing and Air Force One. The list of individuals who traveled to Russia for Evgeni Konnikov's funeral. Stacks of Secret Service files.

On the opposite wall, Lieutenant Cooper's team. Pictures of each man were tacked in a line. Sticky notes littered the wallpaper beneath each. Information from their files. Bad habits. Foreign contacts. Any possible connection to Madigan.

Beneath Lieutenant Cooper's picture, the top sticky note read *Faisal al-Saud???* The name had been circled, over and over again. Doc had two demotions under his belt, and a string of nights spent in the brig for recklessness. He had bad attitude written all over his file. Coleman was divorced, his bank account almost empty. Most of his money went to his ex-wife and three kids living in California. Ruiz had come into the Marines with a Green Card, served for his citizenship, and then tried out for special operations. He still had family in South America. Almost all of them. Wright had served five tours in the Middle East, volunteering for one after the other. Park was three college courses away from his bachelor's degree.

Pete flipped through Kobayashi's file as Levi and General Bell went through the short list of White House staffers with the right combination of clearances, access, and who had been on the trip to Russia. Himself. Welby. Scott. A smattering of other agents from Alpha and Charlie shifts. Pete. Jason.

Levi's stomach had tied itself in knots days ago, and the list only pulled those knots tighter. Scott's name screamed from the short list, Technicolor-vibrant, like a cartoon *POW* that tried to punch him in the face. Scott's was the only file they didn't have. The only background Scott hadn't ordered. He couldn't process the thought. Couldn't draw the line from A to B without detouring into the tangle of his heart. Scott was one of his best friends, and Ethan's absolute best friend. If Scott had turned and was working against Jack...

Levi didn't know how Ethan would survive that. Or how he himself would. The thought of Scott's betrayal made him vomit. He'd already emptied his stomach the day before, overcome with sinking, drowning vertigo, his thoughts a cascading series of screams. *It was Scott. No, it can't be Scott.* The signs pointed to—

No. Not Scott.

He tucked the sticky note with Scott's name behind his own on the wall. He wasn't ready to face it. Not yet.

Jennifer had slipped in a few hours before, bringing food. She'd set up her phone as well, and music played softly in the background. She sat beside Jason, reading through files with him and holding his hand on the tabletop.

"Kobayashi is the most put-together of them all." Pete waved to the file before him. "Smart guy. Started in the Navy before transferring to the Marines. Worked on aircraft carriers. I guess he wanted to do something more exciting than babysitting nukes all day, though."

"Nukes? Was he a security guard?" Welby frowned, looking up at Pete.

Slowly, Levi twisted his head. Pete's words hit him slowly, like a wave rolling in off the sea, a Doppler shift in the words as meaning caught up to the vowels, the consonants.

"No, he was an actual nuclear technician. Worked on the reactors and everything." Pete shrugged and scrubbed his hands over his face. "Top marks in his military schools. When he reenlisted, he opted to transfer to the Marines, though." He flipped the folder shut. "Nerd who wanted some adventure. He's clean."

Levi blinked. "Can you... say that again?" he said slowly. "Kobayashi is a *nuke tech*?"

42

Kara Sea

TEARS FROZE ON ADAM'S cheeks, rivers of ice that cascaded down his face. He watched the fireball rise, the black plumes of smoke curl and belch into the dark sky. *Faisal...*

He'd killed them all. Faisal and his men. Doc. Coleman. Wright. Ruiz. Even Park and Kobayashi. He was responsible for their deaths. And… God, Ethan. Had he arrived? Had he brought the presidents to the station, delivered them to their deaths? Why wouldn't he trust what Adam had said over the radio?

He was scum. Worse than scum. A murderer. A traitor. There was a circle of Hell reserved just for him, a permanent place of agony and torment. He knew, without a shadow of a doubt, that his punishment would be to watch, endlessly, the station erupt. The fireball rising into the sky. Feel the tear as his heart ripped in two, as it tore again, shredding itself to tattered ruins in his ribcage.

The sled he was riding on jerked, bouncing over the ice. He rocked with it, his body limp. His head slammed against the metal frame. Ahead, the snowmobile engines whined and then slowed, revving down. They braked and came to a stop, and Cook clambered off his snowmobile. Others stopped nearby—Cook's men, officers who had joined Madigan, turned against the United States. Adam hated every one of them.

He was *just* like them.

Cook strode toward him, speaking into his radio. Adam didn't hear the words, but he caught Cook's grin as the radio dropped away from his lips.

"Just kill me." He barely recognized his own voice. Empty, and hollow, like a corpse had spoken. He shuddered out a breath. He was already dead inside. "Kill me. I won't do anything else for you, you sick fuck."

The radio chirped in Cook's hands, and a voice broke over the air. "*Halo inbound. Combing for survivors.*"

"Shoot on sight." Cook spoke into the receiver. "Kill anything that moves. Nothing walks out of that station."

Adam grit his teeth and snarled, trying to lunge for Cook. "Kill *me*!" he bellowed. Fresh tears welled in his eyes, dripping down the ice tracks that covered his cheeks. "Do it!"

Cook laughed. "No. No, Lieutenant. I'm not going to kill you. That would be too easy." He cupped Adam's chin like Adam was a boy. "This hurts, doesn't it? It's going to hurt for a long, long time. I'll make sure of that. Remind you every day of what you've done. You sold *everyone* out, Lieutenant. You killed them *all*." He winked. "Good job. You're doing great. You're part of our team already."

Cook reached over Adam for the parachute silk-wrapped satellite. "Let's get this set up," he called, marshaling his people. They grabbed the long rubber cables, shoving Adam aside, and then jogged across the ice. Cook placed the satellite array in the center of their circle and angled it, pointing just off-center to the sky. He swapped what looked like a battery out of the main casing with a fresh one from his jacket and tossed the old one.

"Let's go."

Adam watched him and his men walk back to their snowmobiles. He rolled his head, tracking their movements. His breath caught on his cracked lips as he spotted the mammoth outline of a warship over Cook's shoulder. Beside the warship, the black, fin-like sail of a submarine poked up through the ice cap. Broken blocks of turquoise and translucent ice and brittle snow tumbled around the sail and the black hull. Men moved over the ice, some heading for a derelict smattering of shipping containers and tents, and what looked like an Arctic shantytown. Others lounged on scrappy chairs, smoking cigarettes as they laughed, rifles balanced with easy familiarity across their laps.

An array of snowmobiles rested beside the warship, next to an empty helicopter ice pad, orange spray-painted in a circle with a giant H in the center. Red flags and more spray paint marked the ragged edges of broken ice, a manmade lead the destroyer had carved entering the sea. Tumbled ice broken apart like boulders lay in heaps along the lead, dropping off to the waters below. The ice was thinner than before. Only eight feet, maybe.

He closed his eyes, exhaling. Madigan's Arctic base. The heart of his plan to poison the skies and burn the world. What was left of his ragtag prisoner army. His Russian warships. K-27, his nuclear trigger.

Cook's snowmobile and sled started forward, slower this time, heading straight for the warship. He watched the dark hull grow larger, looming above them, until they parked by the stern.

Cook twisted around in his seat and grinned at Adam. "Welcome to your new base, Lieutenant."

43

North Kara Sea

THE BERIEV HURTLED DOWN the ice runway, engines roaring. Ethan clasped Jack's hand, hard enough to make Jack's bones shift. Seated behind Sasha and Sergey, Ethan saw more than he wanted to out of the front of the plane. His heart clambered into his throat as his stomach went into open revolt.

"That Halo is back!" Scott shouted. "Coming back over the station. She's moving behind us!"

Ethan craned his neck, trying to see. The Halo moved through the billowing smoke like a monster rising from the depths. "We've got to move!"

"Can this go faster?" Sergey leaned closer to Sasha.

"Soviet piece of shit," Sasha snapped. The controls shook violently in his hands. He strained to hold the yoke, and his legs were pressed hard on the foot pedals for the rudder. "This plane is garbage!" He slammed his fist on the instrument panel, punching it until a glass dial shattered.

"It's what we have." Jack leaned forward. "We just have to go. *Now*."

Bullets chewed the ice behind them, gouging holes in the runway. Chunks of ice hit their plane, like hail slamming into a tin roof. Scott dove back from the window.

"*Da*." Sasha grit his teeth and gripped the control yoke. The plane rose, jerking upward in a stomach-lurching jolt, and screamed just over the burning station. Flames curled around their wingtips and swirled in the wash of their propellers.

"They're coming around." Scott was back at the windows, going from side to side in the cabin of the Beriev, watching for the Halo. "Coming behind us, again!"

Dull thuds sounded, like rocks being thrown at their hull. Sasha growled. Sergey's face went white.

"Tell me about the gunner!" Sasha shouted over his shoulder. "Was he using gun mount?"

"*What?*" Ethan shouted, shaking his head. "What the hell are you talking about?"

"Was he using fixed gun mount in the door? Or was it just man and a rifle?"

"Gotta move!" Scott's bellow interrupted their shouts. "He's getting closer!"

Ethan scrambled to recall. He'd been on the ice, flames licking his arms. The Halo overhead, firing after him, turning his way... "Just a man. He was leaning out of the opening. No mount."

"Perfect." Sasha jerked the yoke hard, veering the plane in a tight, screaming turn. The Beriev's engines wailed, and the whole frame shuddered, jerking violently like it was about to come apart at the seams. The move might have been perfect in a MiG, but it was going to rip them to shreds.

Sergey grasped the window frame, his seat edge, the controls above him, and then Sasha's arm. "We are not in a fighter jet!"

Sasha leveled them out. Ethan looked up.

They were headed right for the Halo, coming in at a sharp angle and close enough to count rivets on the massive beast. The door gunner, a vicious looking man with a long beard and a shaved head, grinned wide and swung his massive rifle toward them. It would have been right at home mounted on a tank. He aimed for the cockpit.

"Duck," Sasha growled. "Duck now!"

"What the fuck are you doing?" Sergey sputtered. "Sash—"

Sasha grabbed Sergey by the back of the neck and pulled him down, tugging him until he was face planted in Sasha's lap. Muffled curses rose from Sergey, but he stayed low when the glass shattered and bullets slammed into the metal airframe. Berievs were built like steel bulls, their noses reinforced to withstand the inevitable Soviet crash. Or, in this case, bullets.

Ethan grabbed Jack and pulled him down, twisting his body over Jack's as they lay on the cockpit deck. He joined Sergey, cursing Sasha's choices. "You're going to get us killed!"

"Almost there," Sasha hissed. Bullets continued to plink off their hull and slam into the airframe. One wing creaked like it wanted to tear itself off the plane and flee. The frame shuddered, absorbing bullet after bullet.

Sasha jerked the controls to the max, twisting the old Beriev almost straight up, shooting over the nose of the Halo. The engine wailed. One propeller rattled and broke in two, the pieces flying away. The roar of the Halo, the twin gas turbine engines, boomed through their smaller plane, deep enough to rattle their organs. Busted glass rained down through the broken cockpit windows, and then the Halo's rotary blades were far, far too close, filling Ethan's sight.

They bucked, skidding wildly through the air as they passed over the Halo and then fell, almost in a mad tumble, half from the broken propeller and half from the turbulence kicked off from the Halo's rotors. *We're not flying. We're falling.* Ethan pulled Jack close, trying to brace for the seemingly-imminent crash and protect Jack as best he could. Ice-cold wind whipped through the cockpit.

Sasha leveled them off and slowed their speed. The engine sputtered, and the plane listed to one side. Silence strained the Beriev, save for Sasha's deep, harsh pants. The winds leveled out until it was just the breeze from their flight.

Sergey bolted upright. His face was purple, twisted with rage, and he lunged at Sasha, grabbing him by his jacket. Bitter Russian flew, in time with each shake Sergey gave Sasha.

"Holy *shit*. They're going down."

Scott's voice made Sergey pause. He glared back, his eyes red-rimmed and furious. "What?"

"The Halo. It's fucking going down."

Ethan scrambled to his feet and pushed his face out of the busted side window. Below them, the Halo was plunging, spinning faster and faster as it dove out of control. Smoke poured from its shattered cockpit. They watched it slam nose-first into the ice cap and burst apart in flames.

Everyone turned to Sasha, staring. They hadn't fired a shot. There wasn't a way to, not in the sealed Beriev.

"What… did you do?" Sergey asked slowly.

"Target fixation." Sasha tried to exhale. His hands were still shaking. Sergey grabbed them. "Is problem with Russian gunners. Door mounts break all the time. Russian gunners think they can shoot without them. But the mounts stop gunner from swinging around inside the aircraft and—"

"Shooting their own pilots in the back." Ethan exhaled and slumped against the bulkhead. "Jesus Christ, you got their gunner to shoot their own pilots?"

Sasha nodded, once. "I thought would work."

"What would you have done if it *hadn't* worked?" Scott's grumble hung in the silent cockpit.

Sasha shrugged.

Sergey opened his mouth, a fresh tirade on his tongue.

"Okay." Jack interrupted Sergey before he could begin, clamping one hand down on his shoulder. "We made it out alive. What's our next step?"

"Our plan got shot to shit." Ethan closed his eyes briefly. *Adam, where are you?* He rejected the niggling voice in the back of his head that said the only logical answer was that Adam and his men were inside the station when it blew. There wasn't anything logical about this. "We can't fly anywhere in this busted plane."

"No." Sasha scowled at the display. He leaned forward, his frown furrowing. "Actually, we cannot fly much more at all."

The engine sputtered, groaned, and then died, a sad little whine the only farewell it made. For an instant, everything was silent. They glided, almost weightless in the Arctic air.

Sasha looked at Sergey as alarms rang out in the busted, bullet-riddled cockpit. "We are going down."

44

Kara Sea – Madigan's Base Camp

COOK SHOVED ADAM FORWARD, pushing him through the dark hallways onboard the old Soviet destroyer.

The ship should have been mothballed years ago. Paint had long ago chipped, and bare metal had turned to rust. One flickering light worked in each hallway. The ship was cold, power mostly offline. Their footsteps echoed like bells, his and Cook's and two of Madigan's criminal army as they paraded toward Command.

Light poured from a hatch ahead, dull, but brighter than the dim gloom of the hall. Voices rose and fell, some in Russian, but most in English. He could barely make out the words.

Adam stumbled, and Cook shoved him hard against the bulkhead, digging his cheek against the rotten metal. "There's something you should see," Cook said slowly, almost hissing into his ear. "Come with me."

He dragged Adam by the back of the neck, bending him over at his waist with his face pointed down until they reached the hatch. The voices were louder, but Adam couldn't parse out what was being said, not bent over and twisted around Cook's grasp. He tried to fight, tried to shake Cook off, but Cook just squeezed harder, until spots floated in front of his eyes and the world started to go dark.

And then Cook threw him through the hatch. He landed in a sprawl on the deck, face mashed to the cold steel.

Voices stopped. He felt eyes on him, gazes peeling back his skin. What were they looking at? Was he supposed to perform? Be their circus freak? He looked up, glaring.

And found himself face-to-face with Kobayashi.

Reality stuttered to a halt. The world, even, seemed to stop spinning, stop turning. His thoughts froze and then shattered, like an iceberg crumbling to dust. He tried to add it all up, put two and two together. He tried to breathe, but everything was too slow. A gong must have gone off somewhere; he could barely hear, save for the deafening roar of his world falling, ending. A scream sounded, somewhere far away, a roaring, wailing bellow. He stared into Kobayashi's eyes and watched his teammate slowly smile.

"Hey, L-T," Kobayashi said. He threw his hands out like he was celebrating. "Surprise."

The world restarted, reality snapping back like the launch of a fighter jet off a carrier. He throttled from incomprehension to blinding fury in half a heartbeat. He lunged, diving at Kobayashi.

Hands grabbed the back of his jacket, holding him back. He strained forward, choking himself. He'd kill Kobayashi, kill him with his bare hands. Like a rabid dog, desperate for the kill. He pictured it, imagined it, holding Kobayashi down and choking him, strangling the air from his lungs

His throat burned, and he backed down a half step, coughing hard. The shout, the bellow, died. God, it had been him. He'd been making that noise, that inhuman wail.

Kobayashi chuckled. He reached out and ruffled Adam's hair.

Adam lunged again, snarling. Rage consumed him, burned his soul, ripped through his heart like a nuclear reactor. He'd mourned Kobayashi. Wept for him, and all his men. He'd loved Kobayashi as an officer loves all his men. Hell, Kobayashi had been his easiest, the Marine he could count on to always be squared away. Betrayal opened beneath him, an endless black void. He was falling, toppling end over end, untethered to reality.

"You killed Park!"

Kobayashi nodded. He shrugged. "I had my orders: get here. Had to move quickly, especially since K-27 is already up." He gestured to the windows lining one wall. Directly across from the destroyer, the ice cap had been blown away in a nearly perfect oval. Red flags and spray paint marked the ragged edges of the massive hole. Dark Arctic waters sloshed against the blown edges of the ice and, in the center, the rusted, algae-covered sloping hull of K-27, risen from the depths. She hovered more out of the water than in, an unnatural sight for a submarine. Gigantic poles, what would have been used as drill pipe on an oil rig, had been slammed into the ice in a circle around K-27. Strung between the poles, and diving beneath her hull, was a massive industrial net, buoying the once-sunken sub. She wasn't floating on her own; they'd raised her part of the way and winched her up with the net. Just enough clearance to access the reactor, if Adam had to guess.

Red colored his vision, like a bloodlust out of control. He bared his teeth, growling, spewing nonsense, threats and promises to rip Kobayashi's throat out, dance in his intestines, bathe in his blood. "When did you turn? When did you decide to betray us?"

Kobayashi laughed. "I've always been against you. You think I transferred into your unit after you stormed the West Wing with Reichenbach by chance?" He shook his head. "God, you're naïve. Even for an officer, you're fucking stupid."

"Everyone was vetted," he hissed. "Everyone's background was checked." It had been a scouring, a wildfire through the ranks. Anyone and everyone who'd had contact with Madigan was ripped aside, investigated like they'd been abducted by aliens.

Kobayashi shook his head. "Madigan wrote the book on decentralized counterterror missions. Black communications. Off-the-grid operations. What makes you think what we did overseas wouldn't work against our own government?" He winked. "We're everywhere."

Adam spat at him. A fat glob landed on Kobayashi's cheek. "You killed them all! Did you ever fucking care about them?"

Cook kicked out the backs of Adam's legs, sending him to the deck as Kobayashi wiped the spit from his face. Squatting, he smeared his spit-covered hand down Adam's cheek. "*You* killed them all," he said.

"You killed Fitz. And Park."

"Park, yes. Fitz wasn't me." Kobayashi rose. "You'll have to excuse me, L-T. I've got work to do. We're restarting the reactor on K-27."

COOK DRAGGED HIM FROM Command. Adam fought Cook every single step. He kicked, thrashed, tried to body-slam Cook and break away. Cook threw him into the bulkhead, slammed his head against the hatch entrance. Kicked him when he slumped to the deck. The two men with Cook watched and laughed as Adam coughed up blood and saw triple.

"*Captain, we've got a problem,*" Cook's radio chirped. "*Survivors at the station have taken out our Halo.*"

"What?" Cook turned to the men with him. "Take him to the brig." He strode away, barking orders into his radio for a team to assemble at the snowmobiles, ready to ride.

Adam watched Cook stride away as the other two moved in, each grabbing him under one arm and dragging him away. Survivors. There were survivors. Who? Ethan? The presidents? Doc, Coleman, or Wright?

Faisal. Please, please, let it be Faisal. In shaa Allah, *please.* The thought was an ugly one. He shouldn't put Faisal over everyone else… but he couldn't help it. There were a thousand reasons why he should never have gotten together with Faisal, a thousand damnations he could heap upon his shoulders. But what was done was done. He was already finished.

He eyed his captors, the two criminal soldiers carting him to the brig. They were African, busted from a Sudanese prison. One had a sick-looking scar down the side of his face. The other's arm was twisted and scarred, ravaged with burns. The first carried his weapon in a thigh rig. The other had a knife sheathed on his belt in the small of his back.

Survivors at the station. He had to help them. He'd do whatever he could, anything he could, to right what he'd done.

All he needed was the right moment.

45

Washington DC

She watched Secret Service Agent Levi Daniels slip out of the Roosevelt Room and walk down the West Wing hallway. He rubbed one hand over his furrowed forehead and breathed out slowly as if he was in pain.

Perfect.

Luli Fan was an exemplary graduate student. She earned straight A's in her Georgetown graduate courses. She'd landed a prestigious fellowship out of Yale, her undergraduate school, which took her to Georgetown and DC. She'd applied for and received an internship in the White House, in the West Wing. She worked in the environmental affairs policy division and loved penguins. She lived alone with one cat and loved peppermint ice cream. She watched four shows on Netflix and kept up with her parents, who lived in California, outside of San Francisco.

Her father was a very bad man, at least according to the government in Beijing. He'd stolen low-level military information, plans about the construction of their submarine bases built inside tunnels and hidden away from American spy satellites. He'd traded the information for a new life in America, for himself, his daughter, and his wife.

Luli Fan's father, then, was easy to manipulate. All it had taken was a few careful threats, promises of extraction back to China and a description of the exquisite tortures that his wife and daughter were sure to face. Perhaps even a trip to the North Korean prison camps for him, to be reeducated on loyalty.

Luli Fan's father folded like a bad hand at a Vegas card table.

Yue Ying, of the Central Military Commission in China, took the next flight to Washington DC and let herself into Luli Fan's apartment.

Luli Fan had been selected for this mission, and if she came through, then her loyalty, her commitment, would be richly rewarded. The Chinese government would take the bounty off of her father's head, for starters. And she'd be a wealthy woman at the end of the week.

All Luli Fan needed to do was stay out of sight. Stay unconscious and sedated and lying on her bed for the next week. Yue Ying would take her place. In another life, they could have been twins. The same light to their eyes, the same angle of their smile. Luli Fan had been picked for this mission because of her spooky similarity to Yue, a combination of genes and environment that had produced an almost identical twin, despite different families, different lineages.

Now, Yue was inside the White House. Inside the West Wing. The clothes she wore were Luli's, along with Luli's blue White House badge. She could move freely around the West Wing. Go to any office. Talk to anyone.

And who she wanted had just walked down the hall.

She slipped the trigger-loaded syringe into her palm and followed Levi Daniels.

He went down the hall, past the Cabinet Room, and turned. Padded his way down the staircase to the lower level. She followed, pretending to check her phone as she bounced down the stairs. If asked, she'd say she was on the way to the mess for a fresh cup of coffee.

No one asked. The lower level was quiet. Few people moved around, their faces buried in their phones.

Levi Daniels headed for the Secret Service bunker, but hesitated. His head tipped forward and his shoulders slumped. He turned away, heading instead for the entrance to the garage.

Yue followed him, and once there, kept to the shadows. She paralleled him down the line of cars, keeping low.

When he stopped outside a black SUV, she struck. Moving fast, she slid over the hood of the car beside Levi and rose, silently, behind him.

He stiffened, sensing something, and started to turn.

Too late. She stabbed the syringe into his neck. The trigger depressed automatically, flooding his body with the sedative.

"What the—" His hand flew to his neck, bumping the empty syringe. He whipped around, but the sedative had already started working. His legs gave way, and he pitched forward, falling against her. Yue caught him as his eyes slipped closed, and he fell unconscious.

She pulled out her phone. Hit the speed dial. After one ring, the line opened with a click.

"Colonel Song. I have Agent Levi Daniels."

46

USS Honolulu

CAPTAIN ANDERSON WAITED BENEATH the forward bow hatch, watching water drip from the circular seal.

"Docking complete, sir." Heavy bolts from *Honolulu* clamped down on the airlock between his boat and the civilian sub he'd found floating beneath the ice cap. Boomer had picked up a faint S-O-S in Morse code, coming from someone banging against the side of the sub walls.

He'd sent over one of his divers.

After his diver had boarded, Boomer picked up a new message in Morse code. *Americans. Bringing in to dock.*

Who was inside the sub? How had they gotten there?

Water continued to drip slowly, the last drop from their docking being squeezed out. Above, he heard the mini sub's airlock cycle open. He gave the nod to his chief, who started rotating *Honolulu*'s hatch. Along the hallway, lights flickered. Creaking rumbled through the hull.

Honolulu was barely holding together. Sierra One had wounded her, badly, before *Honolulu* put six torpedoes in Sierra One's side and sent her to the bottom of the Arctic Abyss. Before that, though, Sierra One's torpedoes had chased them under the ice, pressing them farther and deeper into dangerous waters and icy ravines. Pressed between underwater ice blades and the torpedoes, there'd been nowhere to go but down. Underwater blasts rocked *Honolulu's* systems and pressures from the Arctic Abyss crunched her hull, ripping open stress fractures in her plating. Water sloshed on the lower decks, too much for the bilge pumps to suck out to sea. Their shocked and shaken reactor was underpowered, damaged, and the engines were barely able to make ten knots. They were limping, wounded, and nearly broken.

A shivering, wet body tumbled through the open hatch, almost falling to the deck. Anderson steadied the man, helping him to his feet. He recognized him: Doc, the corpsman from Ethan Reichenbach's Marine Corps team.

"Captain, I've got four in here!" His diver, Petty Officer Swanson, called from above. "They're hypothermic. The seal on this submersible leaked on them. There's freezing water in the hold."

"Chief Liu is here." Anderson passed Doc to Chief Liu, his own corpsman, and *Honolulu*'s sole medical provider. He arched his eyebrows up the hatch, meeting Swanson's gaze. "I already gathered the hatch leaked." Water dripped onto his shoulder.

Liu wrapped Doc in a blanket and passed him down the hall. They'd converted the wardroom to a sickbay. Their injured were already there.

The next two clambered down into *Honolulu* on their own. Sergeants Wright and Coleman, the enlisted leaders of the Marine team. Both were shivering, and their eyes were hollow and red-rimmed. Their lips were blue, and their teeth chattered.

Last out was someone he didn't remember. An Arab, tall and slender, and bundled with extra layers of clothes. He was pale, and his lips were tinted blue, but he was in better shape than the others. Anderson stopped him. "I'm Captain Anderson. I don't recall your name."

The man flinched. "Faisal, Captain." He licked his lips. Closed his eyes. Exhaled slowly. "Faisal Cooper."

Cooper? That was the name of the Lieutenant leading the Marine team. He frowned.

"Lieutenant Adam Cooper and I were… close," Faisal breathed. "I was attached to his team as a special advisor."

"And where is Lieutenant Cooper? How'd you guys get in that sub?"

Faisal looked down the hallway. His jaw clenched hard, and a vein pulsed in his temple.

Oh. Anderson breathed out. He crossed his arms, pursing his lips. "Where is the president? Where's the rest of your team?"

Faisal shook his head. "I don't know. We were separated and ambushed at one of the stations. The president and the others never arrived."

It was Anderson's turn to bow his head and glare at the deck.

Faisal's voice was soft, but roughened when he spoke. "How did you find us?"

"We were coming back to the rendezvous. We took out that Russian sub over the pole. She's down in the Nansen Abyss, and no one will ever find her or her crew." A part of Anderson twinged at that. He was, in his soul, a submariner. Any sub going down was a haunting reminder of their own fragile predicament, how their lifesaving boat could become a tomb from one second to the next. "Boomer picked up your SOS."

Faisal almost smiled, weakly. "Doc insisted on banging on the hull. I thought Sergeant Wright was going to strangle him after a few hours."

"It saved your life."

Faisal nodded. Silence strained the air between, filled only with *Honolulu's* rattle and uneven hum. "What now, Captain?" he finally asked.

Anderson squared his jaw. A broken ship, an exhausted crew, President Spiers missing, and their assault team shattered. Any commander would call it in, retreat and regroup and lick their wounds before launching a stronger assault.

They didn't have that luxury. They were running out of time.

"We have to keep going. Find Madigan, and get back in the fight. We finish the mission, no matter what."

47

Kara Sea

SASHA DID HIS BEST bringing the powerless plane down. He'd kept them gliding until the end, until the plane tipped nose-forward and plunged the last twenty feet into the ice cap. Jack and Ethan, sitting behind Sasha and Sergey, held hands and stared into each other's eyes. Ethan mouthed *I love you* in a constant loop. Behind them, Scott strapped himself to the jump seat in the rear and kept a steady spew of curses flowing at the top of his lungs.

When they crashed, the Beriev tipped onto its left side, snapping the wing clean off. The nose crushed instantly, shorn metal and engine parts exploding outward and scattering across the ice.

Jack, Ethan, and Scott bounced in their seats, rattled against their restraints, but stumbled from the wreckage with just bumps and bruises.

Sergey wasn't as lucky. The nose had crumpled, exploding inward and outward and compacting the cockpit almost right on top of Sasha and Sergey. Sergey had slammed forward, his head smacking the instruments. He sat slumped in his seat, blood oozing down his face, unconscious. Sasha hovered next to him, bleeding from his nose, trying to rouse his lover.

Ethan physically checked Jack over when they stumbled from the wreck, running his hands through Jack's hair, down his neck, and cupping his face. He looked deep into Jack's gaze.

Jack grabbed his wrists. He tried to smile. "I'm okay, Ethan." Nodding, Ethan kissed his forehead, letting his lips linger.

In the distance, the high-pitched whine of snowmobile engines broke the heavy silence that covered the ice. "We've got company," Scott growled. "Get behind the plane!"

They took cover, shielding behind the right wing and engine, and pulled out their rifles. Ethan laid out spare magazines in front of him and Jack. "Remember how to reload?"

Jack nodded. "I've had some practice." He looked up. A line of snowmobiles appeared on the ice, racing toward them. Six men in mismatched uniforms, each armed to the teeth. Jack spotted nasty-looking rifles and bandoliers of bullets.

Ethan frowned. "You shouldn't have to know these things."

"I'd rather be at your side, in everything, everywhere, than sit on the sidelines and pretend I'm safe."

The first bullet flew over their heads.

"They're here!" Scott fired over the wing, trying to hold the new arrivals back.

"Sasha, how's Sergey?" Jack shouted toward the silent cockpit. Sasha hadn't said anything to them on their way out. He'd been pale, ghostly white, and focused solely on Sergey. "We've got company, Sasha! What's going on?"

Bullets erupted from the cockpit, spraying through the shattered windows toward the snowmobiles. They were wild, with no real aim. Sasha, firing blind. "Keep them away!" Sasha barked. "I am trying to pull him out!"

"Easier said than done," Scott grumbled. "They've got a lot of firepower."

Swallowing, Jack refocused on the men attacking. They'd stopped their approach, Scott and Ethan pinning Madigan's men back about sixty yards out. Some covered behind their snowmobiles. One hefted a giant machine gun on top of his snowmobile saddle, balanced on a tripod.

"Fuck. Ethan, two o'clock!" Scott shouted.

"I see it." Ethan swung right and took aim at the machine gunner.

Jack spotted another gunman sighting in on Ethan. He lined up, put the gunman square in his reticle, and fired.

The gunman fell backward.

"Two down," Ethan called. He threw Jack a tiny, sad smile. "Thanks."

And then, Ethan's eyes went wide as stared over Jack's shoulder. "RPG!" he hollered. "Nine o'clock!"

SASHA WHIPPED AROUND AT Ethan's shout. "RPG!" Ethan bellowed again.

Fuck. An RPG would destroy the plane, and them along with it. Sergey still hadn't woken up. His head lolled on Sasha's shoulder, and the most Sasha had gotten out of him had been a feeble moan when he'd slapped him.

Two of Madigan's men were still loading the RPG while the other three laid down suppressive fire. Ethan and Scott tried to fire back, but they couldn't get a fix. Sasha saw Ethan rise again, trying to fire. Bullets slammed into the wing in front of his face, sparking against his cheek. He dropped back.

They had moments, only moments before their plane lit up like a firework.

He searched the cockpit, trying to find something, anything to fight back with. He had no shot from the crumpled, sideways cockpit, no way to target the fighters. Damn it, if he didn't get Sergey out of there, they'd both die. But Sergey wasn't moving. And he wasn't going to leave Sergey.

His frantic gaze landed on the pilot's ejection handle.

Perfect.

He ripped Sergey's harness away and caught him before he tumbled out of his seat. Manhandling him, he maneuvered Sergey across the central terminal, until Sergey straddled his lap. He tucked Sergey's face against his neck. "Hold on, *lyubov moya.*" *Hold on, my love.*

Sasha wrapped one arm around Sergey and gripped his rifle. He reached down and jerked the ejection handle with the other.

The top panel of the Beriev blasted off with a bang. It clattered across the ice, snaking away from the crash, and a split second later, the pilot's seat blasted out of the plane, screaming sideways over the ice, straight for the line of Madigan's men.

His second ejection was worse than the first. At least in the first, he'd gone straight into the air. This time, Sasha skidded half a foot above the ice cap. The wind tore at his skin. Ice blistered off the cap, slicing his face. Snow pelted his eyes, and he squeezed them closed as he roared. He held on to Sergey as tight as he could, both arms wrapped around his love.

Do not forget to shoot. Gritting his teeth, Sasha extended his rifle behind Sergey's back and fired blindly on Madigan's men.

ETHAN, JACK, AND SCOTT watched, jaws hanging, as Sasha rocketed across the ice, blasting away at Madigan's men. His shots were wild, unfocused, but he took out one of the attackers and stunned the others. Everyone stopped and stared as he shot through their line, blasting a hundred yards down the ice cap.

"Fire! Now!" Ethan rose up and started shooting. Scott joined him, and then Jack. In moments, the RPG shooter was down, and then a fourth. "Two more!" Ethan shouted.

They were a tricky last two, though, crouched behind their snowmobiles and firing sparingly. Battle-hardened, if Ethan had to guess. Conserving their ammo. Playing it safe.

"Reinforcements arriving," Scott growled. "I see one inbound on a snowmobile."

"I don't have a shot yet." Ethan kept his sights fixed on his last target. "Jack?"

"I've got him." Jack squinted through the scope, watching the new arrival draw closer. He saw the man raise his rifle and take aim. Jack's finger started to squeeze the trigger.

Ethan's target jerked. Blood sprayed over the ice and snow, a fan of red. He fell sideways.

Jack froze, finger half-squeezed. "My target took out his own man!" He watched the new arrival sight in on the last attacker and fire, right as Madigan's man turned toward him. "He just killed the other one, too."

"What the fuck?" Scott grumbled.

"I'm not taking any chances." Ethan motioned to Scott. "Lay down cover fire. Keep him pinned."

Scott nodded and fired at the mystery man. Bullets chewed the ice in front of and behind his snowmobile, forcing him to stop and dive for cover. Scott kept firing, keeping him pinned as Ethan edged away, jogging wide over the ice and slipping through Madigan's destroyed attackers. He signaled to Scott to stop firing and then ran the last ten yards to the mystery man's position.

The man rose slowly, peeking over the saddle of his snowmobile. He had his rifle in his hands but kept it low.

Ethan came up behind him and shoved his rifle against the back of his skull. "*Freeze*! Drop it! Now!"

The man's hands came up slowly. His weapon fell sideways to the snow. "Ethan…"

Ethan's blood froze. His stomach sank, dropping beneath the ice cap. "*Adam?*"

Slowly, Adam turned. His beaten, bruised face stared up at Ethan, one eye swollen shut, lip and cheek busted and oozing blood. He trembled as he knelt in the snow.

"I'm sorry," Adam rasped. His teeth clenched, and a tear rolled down his cheek. "You told me to stay away from Cook. I'm sorry. But he was going to kill them all. He shot Ruiz right in front of us. And—" He couldn't finish. Adam's voice cut out, his lips quivering as another tear slid down his cheek.

Realization crashed into Ethan, harder than the plane slamming into the ice. "The others?"

Desperate hope burned in Adam's gaze. "Is Faisal with you? The radio said survivors…"

Slowly, Ethan shook his head. He dropped his rifle.

Adam's face twisted, anguish destroying him as the truth slammed into his soul. Ethan watched him crumble from the inside, curl in half and topple to the snow. He buried his face, pressing his bloody cheek against the ice cap as he wailed. Tears streamed from his eyes, freezing when they hit the glacier.

"We are Allah's, and to him we shall return. *Ya hayati…*" Adam whispered wetly. Spit and blood dripped from his face.

Ethan spotted Sergey and Sasha lying farther down the ice cap, flopping free from the ejection seat, and Scott and Jack striding toward him and Adam, their rifles up. He waved Scott and Jack over and then crouched down.

Once, Adam had held him when he thought Jack was gone. Adam and Faisal, both. It was a debt he'd never wanted to repay.

He grabbed Adam's shoulder and hauled him close, wrapping him up in his arms. Adam's face pressed against his chest, tearstained, snot-covered, and bloody. Adam's hands rose, grasping Ethan's arms. Buried against Ethan, Adam let it all out, wailing, screaming, bellowing his agony, his fury, the loss of the love of his life.

Ethan held him through it, holding him on the freezing ice as Scott and Jack watched silently.

WHEN ADAM WAS ABLE to breathe again, he spilled his guts, telling them everything. What had happened at the station. His team going missing, one by one. Cook threatening everyone and murdering Ruiz. Threatening Faisal. His capitulation.

Being taken to Madigan's base.

Seeing Kobayashi and K-27 above the ice, and the scope of Madigan's army. Fewer men than they had all estimated before, from all of the prison breaks. Madigan must have lost some of his men in the coup in Russia, and then more in the move up to the Arctic. But still enough fighters to be a problem. A big problem

They were all silent, absorbing the information. Fury blazed in Jack's eyes. Ethan watched him carefully.

He helped Adam up and passed him to Scott. Scott helped him walk, supporting him as they headed for Sasha and Sergey. The ejection seat lay on the ice, and, next to it, two bodies, tumbled free, not moving.

Ethan walked ahead of Scott and Adam, next to Jack. "This is coming apart fast, Jack. We've lost everything. Adam's team. Adam himself. He won't be effective now." He glanced ahead, to the still forms on the ice, but said nothing. "We've lost the element of surprise, too. Madigan knows we're here."

Jack nodded. "Adam made that call to lure us in and changed everything."

Exhaling, Ethan nodded. "Cook had his team. Threatened to execute them one by one unless he complied."

"What Adam did was the worst thing that could have happened. Madigan knows we're coming. And they've raised K-27 already."

Ethan shook his head. "No, Kobayashi's betrayal was the worst. He set Adam up for failure. For heartbreak. What kind of choice was Adam forced into?"

"It's something we need to be ready for. But why did Kobayashi wait? Why didn't he shoot us in the back of the head on *Honolulu*? Or at the first station?"

He shrugged. "I can't understand it, Jack. I don't see the rationale. But there has to be one. He got his orders from Madigan. Everything Madigan has done, from the first moment until now, has had a reason."

"I'm afraid to find out what that is."

Ethan glanced over his shoulder, looking first at Adam, and then at Scott. "Adam did say that Kobayashi didn't kill Fitz."

"I know," Jack said quietly. "You know what that means."

Someone else was working with Madigan. Someone in Tampa? Another supporter of Madigan's at SOCOM? Ethan's blood chilled as he counted who knew about Adam's team, and who knew the men's identities. One name stood out from the rest: General Bell. He'd hated Ethan on sight, and his contempt for Jack had been obvious. Was that a sign of his switched loyalties?

Something Jack said tugged on his brain. "Jack, I don't know what I would have done in Adam's shoes. If it had been Scott, or you… I can't watch you die. I couldn't watch someone kill you. If that means I'd make the same choice Adam did, then that's what I'll live with."

"Ethan." Jack stopped and faced him. He reached for Ethan's arms, his elbows. "We have to think larger than ourselves right now."

"What are you saying? Adam should have let them all die?" He didn't want to follow that thought down its path. Didn't want to think about what Jack was trying to say.

"The stakes are the highest they'll ever be, Ethan." Jack squeezed his elbow. "I don't ever want to be without you. I don't want a single moment to go by without you at my side. But this is, quite literally, the end of the world. If we have to make the tough call…"

Ethan clenched his jaw. He looked away, squinting into the fog. "I don't know if I can do that."

"If it comes down to me or the world, Ethan—"

"You *are* my world. You're *everything*. I can't—"

"My life is not worth billions, Ethan." Jack reached for him, cradling his face. "You are my whole world, too. My everything, forever." He licked his chapped lips. "But this is bigger than us. You have to be able to let me go. It's what I want if it comes down to that."

His chest went tight and his heart hammered, thundering. He couldn't breathe, and he couldn't look at Jack. "I can't talk about this—"

"Ethan—"

Movement, farther down the ice, saved him. Sergey sat up slowly, grumbling and reaching for Sasha.

"Sergey's moving," Ethan grunted. "Let's go." He took off, jogging toward Sergey and Sasha's crash and leaving Jack to catch up.

When he got to Sergey, he saw the Russian president scowling at Sasha. Sasha lay on his back, spread-eagled on the ice, and stared back at Sergey, grinning like a madman. It was the first time he'd seen Sasha really smile. On his harsh and normally dour features, the wide smile made him look unhinged.

Sergey glared at him, glared at the ejection seat, and then squinted back toward their crashed plane, a football field's length away.

He turned his dark glower back to Sasha. "Let's *not* do that again."

Sasha grabbed his jacket and pulled him close, kissing him full on the lips. "We lived." He shrugged. "I did not think we would."

When Sergey pulled back, his scowl had softened just a bit. He looked from Ethan to Jack and then to Scott and Adam as he slumped against the wrecked ejection seat with a sigh. "Now what?"

"WE'VE LOST THE ELEMENT of surprise."

Ethan squatted and etched a quick map in the snow. Their plane crash and the burning station behind them. Ahead, Madigan's Arctic base.

Adam quickly sketched out what he'd seen. The destroyer, and opposite that, K-27, risen from the sea. Off to the side, the black upthrust of a submarine's sail soaring through the ice. Snowmobiles. The empty helo pad.

"It's about forty miles southwest." He pointed toward the base, into the gloom. "There's a lead here. Broken ice where Madigan's destroyer chewed through the ice cap. It's starting to freeze over, but it's rocky ground. We could hide in there."

"Forty miles, climbing over broken ice?" Jack shook his head. "There's no way."

"We are not all young men." Sergey frowned, glaring at Adam and Sasha both.

"So, they know we're here. When those assholes don't report back in, someone's going to come looking for them." Scott jerked his chin toward the dead, still lying among the snowmobiles. "We need to be gone when they get here. I don't see any other places to hide." He turned, scanning the flat, empty horizon.

"We need to go on the offensive." Jack frowned. "How do we strike his base? Where are his weak points?"

Silence.

"We need to take back the element of surprise." Ethan rose and turned to Madigan's fallen men. "He's expecting us to be dead, right? Let's be dead."

48

Washington DC

Slowly, awareness came back to Levi. He blinked, shapes swimming in front of his face. Darkness and light, patches of black and gray, and then a blinding white blast. He tried to roll away, grunting.

"He's coming to."

"Excellent."

Alarms rang in his brain, shouts for him to move, get out of there. Dread slipped up his spine, trying to whisper something in his ear. He squinted, trying to make out what was in front of him.

His eyes focused. Colonel Song's face hovered before him.

Levi wheeled back, scrambling away from the man. His hands were locked together, closed in his own handcuffs, and he fell to his side as he tried to get away. His back hit metal, his handcuffs clanging against something hollow.

He'd never met Colonel Song, but Ethan had told him all about the man, and had described him to a T. Mysterious, slippery, untrustworthy. A mysterious helper in Saudi Arabia. Not an ally. Not an enemy, on that day, but who knew about the future? Ethan hadn't liked Song, not at all. But Song had disappeared after Ethiopia, Levi thought. Ethan had even tried to get ahold of him during the hunt for Madigan. He was like a ghost. According to the Chinese embassy, he didn't exist.

"What the fuck do you want?" He scanned his surroundings. He was in the back of an empty industrial van. Bare metal interior. Metal doors. No seats. He lay on the floorboards, backed against the rear doors. It was a van to murder someone in, according to every Hollywood movie he'd ever seen.

A woman spun in the front seat, looking into the back. Bright light streamed behind her, almost blinding him. He frowned. "Luli?"

She smiled. "No. Luli has nothing to do with this. She was a useful entry to the West Wing, but that is all."

His gaze darted from her to Colonel Song. "What's going on?"

"I need you to deliver a message for me, Agent Daniels." Colonel Song's voice was deep and smooth. He spoke calmly, like he didn't have a Secret Service agent handcuffed before him.

"Can't you pick up the phone?"

The corner of Colonel Song's mouth quirked up, briefly. "As I told Mr. Reichenbach, I prefer more direct channels. You must pass a message along to your president, Elizabeth Wall."

"What message?"

"We need to meet."

LEVI BURST INTO THE Situation Room in the middle of General Bradford's briefing. The door banged against the wall as he shoved it open, a dull crack breaking through the room.

All eyes flashed to him. General Bradford's jaw snapped shut as he glared, throwing a poisonous look at Levi that would have made a lesser man wither.

Elizabeth rose from her seat and went to Levi, meeting him halfway to her. The others seated at the table didn't know what to do. Some rose with the president. Others stayed seated, scowling at Levi and Elizabeth in turn.

"Levi..." She grabbed his shaking hands, wrapped one arm around his shoulders, and steered him to the back of the room. He was rumpled, far more than normal. Shirt untucked, tie loose. He kept rubbing his neck and rubbing one wrist. His eyes were wide, wild. "What's going on?"

He blew air through his lips, a forceful exhale. "What isn't?" He shook his head. "Madam President, we walked them all into a trap."

"What?"

"One of Lieutenant Cooper's team was a former nuke tech. Kobayashi was transferred to Cooper's team after the first White House attack, and whoever made the transfer erased their footprint. We just walked Kobayashi into the Arctic alongside Phoenix One. We gave Madigan *exactly* what he needed: a nuclear operator." His lips clamped shut. Pain leached from him, wounded fury and anguish.

"Jesus..." Her thoughts swam, and she closed her eyes, covering her mouth with her hands for a moment.

"Madam President? Would you like to return to the brief?" General Bradford's voice slapped the back of her head. "The Chinese are not slowing down, and they're nearly on top of our blockade."

Heavy silence filled the room after he spoke.

Levi leaned in close. "Madam President, there's more. And you're not going to like it."

She met Levi's gaze. For the first time, she saw naked terror in his dark eyes. Endless, aching terror.

49

Kara Sea – Madigan's Base Camp

Cook glared over the ice, his arms crossed, radio clenched in one fist, and watched six snowmobiles speed toward him.

He'd sent a team of three Serbs and three South Americans out to take care of whatever survivors there were. That had been over an hour ago. He'd lost contact after they'd engaged, after reports of the survivors holed up by the plane, three firing on the team, and then—

Nothing.

On top of that, Lieutenant Cooper had disappeared. The two men he'd put on guard, Sudanese fighters who'd made names for themselves as hardened war criminals, were in Cooper's cell with broken necks. So much for the brutality they'd promised. Cooper was supposed to eat his own intestines for his last meal, choke on his own blood before slowly bleeding to death.

Cook left their bodies there. They didn't matter.

But finding Cooper *did*.

Where had he gone? What had happened to his men?

Who was coming back now?

One of the snowmobiles pulled right up to him. The driver wore the same mismatched uniform and winter jacket and face mask as all the criminals did: a hodgepodge of Russian, African, and Latin American military uniforms, none of the pieces matching. They said they looked intimidating, showing the different countries they'd fought and killed in.

Cook thought they looked stupid.

He stared down at the driver, waiting as he pulled to a stop. Behind him, a body lay draped over the back of the snowmobile. Brown hair, white arctic jacket, filthy and stained. Blood-spattered.

Slowly, Cook smiled. He grabbed the dead man's hair and lifted his head. Cooper's pale, bloodstained face gazed back at him. His eyes were closed, but blood matted one side of his head, thick and oozing. Gunshot to the temple, if he had to guess. There was enough blood for it. "What happened?" He dropped Cooper and turned to the driver.

The driver stared him straight in the eyes as he tugged down his face mask. "We took out the survivors. Dropped them all. Found this one making a run for it on the ice and put a bullet in his head."

Cook nodded. "Who were they?"

"President Spiers and his fuck toy. That crazy Russian president, and some kind of bodyguard of his."

The other snowmobiles waited, ten yards away. Draped over the back of each snowmobile lay a body in arctic gear. Circles of blood marred the backs of the white jackets.

"What happened to your radios?"

The driver pulled his handheld out of his jacket. A bullet had smashed the receiver. There was a hole clean through the case.

Cook nodded. "Bring them to me. I want to—"

Cook's radio spat static, and then Kobayashi's voice fell from the speaker. *"Captain. The reactor is back online. Should I begin weaponization now?"*

"I'm on my way. I need to see it." Cook glared at the driver as he dropped his radio, his eyes flicking from Cooper's slumped body to the other riders. "General Madigan will want to see the bodies. You know where to take them."

"Yes, sir."

Cook peered into the driver's eyes. "What's your name?"

The driver grinned, almost wolfishly. "Scott. My name is Scott."

"Scott? I don't remember you. Where did you come from?"

"Colombia." Scott leaned back. "Got popped running high-value shipments for the cartels into Miami. But at least the prison was warm. And I did good business inside. 'Prison Banker', they called me." He grinned. "It was a hell of a lot warmer there than here."

"If you don't like it here, why'd you join?"

"I like my freedom better. I wasn't about to stay in that prison after you emptied it. Fuck that."

Cook grinned slowly. "You'll be warm in no time. We're almost through with our mission. See me later." Nodding once, Cook straddled his own snowmobile and throttled the engine. He waited, though, watching.

Scott nodded. He waved to his teammates and revved his engine, guiding his snowmobile toward the *Veduschiy*. The others slid into a line, passing by Cook as they wound their way around the destroyer.

Cook stared after them, and then switched the channel on his radio and raised it to his lips.

"ALHAMDULILLAH, I DID NOT think that was going to work." Adam slid off the back of Scott's snowmobile and crouched behind him, keeping low by the stern. He mumbled something that sounded like Arabic, closing his eyes as he kissed his gloved fingers and touched his chest.

Ethan, Jack, Sergey, and Sasha moved in beside them, parking by the stern and out of sight, tucked in close to the destroyer's rear loading ramp. On each of their snowmobiles, one of Madigan's dead lay, dressed in their own white arctic outerwear. They'd changed into the mismatched uniforms of Madigan's men on the ice cap, keeping their dry suits on underneath everything. That had been a level of cold Jack didn't want to experience again. He'd caught Sergey's eye, shadows of his harrowing plunge beneath the ice in both their gazes.

Jack scanned their surroundings. Coming around the back of the destroyer, they'd entered the inner spaces of Madigan's Arctic base. The destroyer, *Veduschiy*, rose to their right. Dead ahead, rising from the cracked surface of the ice cap, was the dark sail of Madigan's submarine. Both ships had been on Sasha's map.

Scattered between Madigan's two ships, a slumland shantytown had sprung up. Tents and cargo containers and homemade scrap lean-tos squatted beside snowmobiles, arctic crawlers, ice diggers, and cannibalized bodies of old Soviet airplanes. Anything that Madigan's criminal army could use as living space had been rolled onto the ice and lay in a tangled, twisted scatter. Ratty tarps stretched between the tips of cargo containers and shorn steel walls, fluttering in the wind. Fires burned in barrels, and weapons leaned against the drums, keeping warm.

Off to the left, the rotten, rusted, slime-covered hull of K-27 hung suspended half in the Arctic waters. Just like Captain Anderson had speculated, Madigan had blown the ice in order to raise K-27. Frigid waves lapped over the ice cap, freezing into a new lip that circled the hole. The net Adam described strained and creaked, stretching the length of a football field beneath the sub, down the center of her hull. It must have been a commercial fishing net, something Madigan had taken from the Russians in Murmansk.

K-27 was already up. Kobayashi was already inside restarting the reactor, according to Adam. Their options were growing ever more fractional by the moment.

"Holy fucking shit..." Ethan's whispered curse drew Jack's attention. He whipped his head around, searching for what had made Ethan react.

He found it a moment later.

Strung up on the side of the port bow, dangling by their necks from chains tossed over the side of the *Veduschiy*, twelve bodies hung, limp and lifeless. Each wore the distinctive operator's uniform of a Navy SEAL.

"The team Elizabeth sent in..." Jack swallowed. He closed his eyes and bowed his head. How many had Madigan slaughtered? How many had he killed already, and how many more did he plan on murdering? Where did his bloodlust, his madness, end?

Who could stop such a man, determined and deadly as he was?

Standing on the ice beside the gruesome *Veduschiy* and bracketed on two sides by twin submarines—one a dangerous relic of Soviet history, and the other a gut-punch representation of Madigan's amassed power—Jack felt small in a way he hadn't had for years. Presidents, as a rule, didn't feel small.

Not even facing down the UN, or Congress, or the press, or even in his election campaign. Here, he felt small as a human being and small as a man.

What they were doing was ludicrous.

Madigan had broken the back of the world, had broken the back of America, and here he was, standing beneath the corpses of the best military personnel the United States could offer and still thinking he could make a difference. He and Sergey, two middle-aged men. Ethan and Sasha, men too devoted for their own good, with hearts and souls too big for this world. And Scott, a beacon of eternal friendship, of fidelity, enough to make him want to weep.

What could they possibly do, in the face of what they were up against?

Dejection wasn't something he was used to feeling. That sinking, hollow feeling, the bottom of the world dropping out from beneath him. An aching void of hopelessness that swallowed his soul. Those were unnatural feelings, and his bones itched, trying to shake it off. But his soul was screaming, shrieking that he'd already failed, he'd already lost, and he was just too dumb to realize it.

Ethan. He needed Ethan. Jack looked up and found Ethan's gaze.

Ethan's eyes were begging, pleading with Jack, desperate for a shred of hope.

He slid off his snowmobile and padded to Ethan's side. Ethan held him close, drawing him in, as if he, too, needed to lose himself in Jack's arms. They were still huddled by the stern of the *Veduschiy*, away from the blowing wind and the bare desolation of the ice cap. K-27 lay across the ice, and they could hear the muted sounds of Madigan's men making noise in their shantytown. Sergey and Sasha stood nearby, but for the moment, they were alone.

Ethan exhaled into Jack's neck, kissing his jaw. "When this is over," Ethan started, whispering. "I'm going to take you to a beach. Some faraway island where it's just us and the ocean. Perfect water, crystal clear, as far as you can see. Warm white sand forever. We'll lie in the surf, and I'll make love to you for days."

Jack grinned. "Sounds perfect," he whispered back. "Exactly the honeymoon I want with you."

Ethan's hands stroked up and down his back. He leaned into Ethan, listening to his breath drag in and out, his heart beat its steady rhythm. "I love you."

Scott coughed. "We need to get moving." He almost sounded apologetic. "Are we going in, or what?" He slid the bolt back on his rifle, checking the chamber.

Ethan stepped back. He looked into Jack's eyes, cradling his cheeks. "Not all of us."

"Ethan—"

"Scott, you and Jack will stay here. Guard the snowmobiles. We might need to make a fast getaway, and we'll need them ready."

"Ethan!" Frustration cracked like a whip inside Jack. "We're not splitting up. Not now!"

"This isn't for you, Jack," Ethan said softly. "You're not a killer. You're not a murderer."

The next part of their plan was simple and direct. Breach the destroyer. Adam said it was undermanned. Empty, dark hallways, few crew, and the elements of Madigan's army that were on board were lax in their security. Adam had escaped after all. They were hoping to sneak inside, use subterfuge, where the SEALs and their direct assault had failed.

Breach, and then take down the destroyer. They still had half of the C4 plastique explosive from Adam's team, and what Sergey had scavenged at the first RusFuel station. Place the charges below the waterline, and then blow it all. The ship would sink, and locked in the ice, she'd break apart and crack in half. Her sinking would shatter the ice cap, too, and destroy K-27's careful raising. With no anchor points holding the net beneath her belly, K-27 would, hopefully, plunge back into the dark sea.

In the confusion that followed, they'd take out everyone they could. Eliminate Kobayashi. Eliminate Cook, and Cook's men, his fellow officers from South America.

Find Madigan. Put a bullet in his head.

Oh, Jack wanted to do it. He wanted to be the one to do it. Pull the trigger while looking Madigan right in the eyes. Part of him recognized that wasn't the healthiest thought. But, after everything, who could blame him? Madigan had been at the center of each of the worst days of his life. Losing Leslie, almost losing the White House, and losing Ethan. Vengeance tasted sweet to his soul, so delicious he could practically taste it. He hungered for it.

Ethan was right, though. He'd fired in self-defense so far on the mission. He'd killed one fighter, the man trying to take out Ethan. That, he hadn't processed yet. He'd hit pause on his emotions. In the moment, he'd been focused on saving Ethan, protecting him in every way. If that meant another man died, so be it.

He could do the same for Ethan within *Veduschiy*. "Ethan—"

"*No*, Jack."

Ethan didn't ever use that tone with Jack, that final, definitive, commanding tone. But Jack knew that when Ethan did, his words were law. Jack felt his soul draw up short.

"I can't do what I need to do in there if you're with me. I'll be too focused on you. Always keeping one eye on you. It could kill me, Jack. I need you to stay here. Guard our escape with Scott." He tried to smile. "Do this for me."

Jack closed his eyes and exhaled. "Don't think I don't see how you're putting me and Scott out here. I know what you're doing."

"Guilty as charged." Ethan kissed his forehead, letting his lips linger on Jack's skin.

"I'm holding you to our honeymoon." Panic lapped at his spine, a frantic need to hold on to Ethan, to not let him go. "An empty beach. You and me."

"You and me." Ethan breathed the words against Jack's skin, kissing him again. He stepped back.

Behind Ethan, Jack spotted Sergey and Sasha standing close, heads together. Sergey kissed the back of Sasha's hand, over and over, gazing into Sasha's eyes. Sasha cupped his neck, fingers sliding through Sergey's thin hair.

"We'll check out that shantytown. Try and get more weapons. Stay out of sight." Scott gnawed on his lip, watching them ready for the breach.

Ethan nodded. "Stay safe. Both of you. Watch for our signal."

Adam carried the backpack that Ethan had smuggled under his stolen parka. He'd dumped everything except ammo and the explosives. All they'd need.

Russian destroyers had a cargo ramp on their stern. It was down, and had scraped and gouged the ice cap as the *Veduschiy* bobbed on the sea. Now, the ramp was practically a part of the ice itself, a permanent fixture joining the ship to the bleak landscape.

Adam nodded, and then Sergey and Sasha grunted their response. Something heavy hung over the group, something that felt like goodbye. Jack couldn't breathe. Couldn't let go of Ethan.

Ethan stepped back. He turned away and motioned to the others. "Let's go."

50

Washington DC

"I *DEMAND* TO SEE the president, and I am not moving one inch until I do!"

Welby and General Bell, back at work again at the crack of dawn in the Roosevelt Room, shared a confused stare over the table.

The voice rose in the hallway again. "As the majority leader of the Senate Select Committee on Intelligence, I demand to speak with the president!"

"Fuck," Welby breathed. It was too early for this. He waited, listening to the sounds in the hallway. Any moment, Levi would give Senator Stephen Allen a piece of his mind. Senator Allen might find himself banned from the White House if he wasn't careful.

Instead of Levi's firm voice, Agent Walsh's stammer filtered through the door. Walsh was a junior agent, a young guy fresh from the academy. He'd joined the White House when Scott had staffed up the force after Ethan moved into the Residence.

"Sir, I-I don't know what to tell you, Senator, sir. You're not on the president's schedule—"

"I don't *need* to be on the president's schedule!" As he strode to the door, Welby heard Senator Allen sigh. "Son, do you know who I am?"

Welby burst into the hall. Walsh whirled, his wide eyes pleading with Welby to take over. "Senator Allen. We do know who you are." He spread his legs and squared his shoulders, making himself a physical barrier to the West Wing.

It was hard not to know who Senator Allen was. The main Republican leading the charge against President Spiers, Senator Allen's remarks after the attack on Langley had been somewhat less than respectful. Not a man in the Secret Service hadn't bristled at his words. Gossip from the agents at the Capitol was that they had stripped him of all his usual Secret Service perks. No heated SUV, warm coffee, morning paper, or even a hello for him from his detail.

"And you are?" Senator Allen's eyebrows arched high.

"Special Agent Welby, second-in-command of the White House Secret Service."

"Finally, someone useful. Could you radio someone in charge, please?" Senator Allen sighed again, shaking his head. "Unbelievable," he hissed.

Welby ran his tongue over his teeth as he drew himself to his full height. His knuckles cracked as he clenched his fists. "Senator, there are procedures for visiting the White House and the president. You will need to go back to the Capitol—"

"There are procedures for running this country, too!" Senator Allen snapped. "Procedures that this president has refused to follow! We are on the brink of war with both Russia and China, and President Wall is stonewalling Congress and our committee! She has completely abrogated her responsibilities, and I'm here to find out what is going on. Get to the bottom of this *insane* administration."

"Senator—"

"Son, you do *not* understand." Senator Allen stepped forward, crowding Welby. His voice dropped, and he spoke to Welby like he was sharing state secrets. "I *have* to see the president. If I do not, then we're going to remove her from office." He pulled a folded sheet from his jacket pocket. "I have the signatures of a majority of the House of Representatives here, ready to invoke the Twenty-Fifth Amendment."

Welby's jaw clenched. "You don't have the authority."

"We have *every* authority. It's sponsored by the Speaker of the House." He arched his eyebrows again. "Do you really want to fight me on this? Explain to *former* President Wall why she's being escorted from the West Wing? Tell her that you refused her the opportunity to save her job?"

Behind Welby, the door to the Roosevelt Room slowly creaked open. General Bell stood there, staring at Senator Allen, his chin raised. He said nothing.

Welby fumed, quietly steaming on the inside. He couldn't show it, though. He'd never give the senator the satisfaction. He spoke into the microphone clipped to his sleeve. "Watchman requests ten-twenty on Intrepid." They'd kept Wall's code name from when she was Secretary of State.

The comms officer in Horsepower came over the line. "*Uhh, Watchman, Horsepower. We don't have a ten-twenty on Intrepid.*"

He turned away before Senator Allen saw the naked shock that he couldn't hide. "Say again?"

"*We don't have a ten-twenty on Intrepid. Intrepid was in Crown last night.*" Crown, the Residence. "*This morning, there's no location data. We thought it was a bad receptor, and we were going to check on it after Intrepid came down to the West Wing, but—*"

His stomach plummeted as if he'd leaped from the top of the Washington Monument. "But?"

"*Sir, she hasn't come down. She's late.*"

"Excuse me," he said, shoving past Senator Allen.

"Hey!" Senator Allen bellowed. "Hey! I am talking to you!"

General Bell's voice rose behind him as he ran. "Senator. General Bell, commander of SOCOM. Would you like to join me for a cup of coffee?"

He couldn't think about that right now, about General Bell and Senator Allen together. Welby kept going, walking at a steady pace until he turned the corner, out of Senator Allen's sight. Then, he took off, sprinting for the Residence, shouting into his wrist mic. "QRT to Crown! QRT to Crown, now!" Heart hammering, he drew his handgun, shoved through the double doors of the West Colonnade, and sprinted across the Cross Hall. He took the red-carpeted grand staircase steps two at a time, flinging himself around the U-bend.

"What's Agent Daniels's ten-twenty?"

"*Uhh... we don't have a ten-twenty on Agent Daniels, sir.*"

Behind him, feet pounded on the marble, agents in body armor wielding assault rifles following him up the stairs.

He ran down the Residence's central hallway, banging doors open and clearing rooms one by one. His chest grew tight, his breath rapid, as each one came up empty. His palms slicked with cold sweat, and he almost lost his grip on his weapon. *No, no, God, not again. We can't have failed again.*

By the time the quick reaction team thundered up the stairs, he'd cleared the floor, and the truth was sinking in: the president was missing.

He slammed his fist against the wall outside Ethan and the president's bedroom. Brass candle holders along the wall clattered, and an ivory candlestick toppled to the carpet. It rolled toward Welby's feet and brushed his shoe.

Dread pooled inside him, a waterfall of sickening terror. Had he trusted the wrong man? Had he placed his faith in the wrong person? He leaned against the wall, pressing his forehead to the cream and buttercup striped wallpaper as the QRT agents spread throughout the empty, silent residence. Their commander hovered behind Welby, waiting for orders.

His eyes slipped closed and let out a soft sigh as he slumped forward. "Where are you, Levi?"

51

Kara Sea - Madigan's Base Camp

ETHAN AND ADAM LED the breach. Sergey followed, and Sasha brought up the rear.

They moved fast, winding through the groaning ship silently, rifles up and ready to fire. Deep in the bowels, they heard the creak of the ice scraping over the hull, crunching and sliding as the ship bobbed in the swells. Water lapped, a rhythmic slap and clap. The air was frigid, biting. The metal hull acted almost like a refrigerator. Their breath fogged in front of their faces. Only a few lights worked, flickering red bulbs in steel cages set every ten yards. Dark shadows clung to the bulkheads, the hatches.

Inside, the *Veduschiy* was almost decrepit. Water dripped from leaky pipes. Rancid puddles, covered in frost and a thin layer of ice, pooled beneath joints and junctures. Mold raced up the rivets. Rust and rot chewed through bulkheads and hatches. Broken machinery lay abandoned in dark, dank hallways. Like everything from the Soviet period, the ship was a study in contrasts: a statement of power, a promise of violence and viciousness, but hobbled by crippling ineptitude.

And yet, the Soviet Union had still been a devastating superpower, responsible for bringing the world to the brink of destruction more than once. Underestimation was a dangerous game, as they'd learned the hard way.

Adam froze and spun to the right, peering through an open hatch that led to a ladder, rising within the ship.

"Contact?" Ethan breathed behind Adam, keeping his voice as low as possible. Even whispers carried too much of a risk. Their radios were useless now, after Kobayashi's betrayal.

Sasha and Sergey waited a few feet behind them. They moved as one, Sergey's FSB expertise dovetailing into Sasha's military training. Back to back, covering each other's blind spots, working as a team. In this, at least, they were united. Action. Purpose. They still had other areas they needed to work on.

Adam squinted into the darkness. "I thought I saw—" He shook his head. "It's nothing."

Ethan nodded. "Move out."

Down they went, to the center of the ship, to the engine room. He memorized each turn and how many steps they'd taken. When they blew the engine room, they'd have to book it, fast.

At the engine room, they stacked against the hatch, Ethan in the breach position, followed by Adam, Sergey, and Sasha. The hatch was open, and they hung in the shadows beyond the entrance, peering within. Low red lights mixed with the old green glow of eighties technical screens gave the room an eerie glow. Dials flickered, the bulbs within on their last legs.

Ethan's belly button clenched. The ship, everything about it, was creepy. Apprehension made his blood pump, made his ears ring. He exhaled slowly.

"Zero contacts," he breathed over his shoulder. He didn't see, or hear, anyone inside. "Breach on my count." He held up three fingers, against the glow of a red-caged bulb. Then two. Then one.

Ethan stormed into the engine room and turned left. Adam followed on his heels and turned right. They snaked around the bulkheads, rifles up and sweeping in arcs before them. Sasha and Sergey followed, hot on their heels, sweeping and trailing their movements.

The engine room was massive. Cavernous, the hollow space swallowed them up. Their footfalls echoed, clanging on the grated metal deck. They'd entered on the upper level, onto a catwalk ringing the engine room. Beneath them, in the center on the lower level, sixteen overpowered diesel engines stretched in rows, massive cylinders bigger than Ethan on each engine. The Soviets had loved to build large; anything worth building was worth overbuilding.

Most of the engines were cold and offline, save for two that rumbled away, keeping the ship at minimum operations. The stench of diesel and stale saltwater almost gagged him. He blinked fast, his eyes stinging. Clearly, spilled fuel wasn't a concern of the Soviets. The ship's steel was marinated in it.

A rickety metal ladder stretched from the catwalk to the lower level. Ethan motioned to Adam and then to the ladder. He and Adam headed down.

Sasha and Sergey stayed above, circling slowly on the catwalk, keeping watch.

They moved fast, ducking beside a row of engines and pulling out a block of C4. Adam peeled off the sticky back and stuck several to the incoming fuel lines, hoses as thick as Ethan's chest. They scrambled to the hull, ducking behind broken machinery burned black in a fire decades before, it seemed. The sounds of the waves were stronger down there, a heavy beat against the metal hull. The frigid ocean kept the engine room almost frosty, and no doubt bled heat away when the ship was fully operational. Adam slapped more C4 on rusted joints, shorn rivets, and rotten, rusted sections of the hull. Last, he flipped the arming switch on the remote detonators, a simple radio receiver that waited for the right signal. Ethan had the transmitter in his jacket pocket.

Adam signaled he was good to go; all C4 placed. Ethan nodded, and started back toward the ladder, picking his way through the dark engine room.

Above, on the catwalk, metal creaked, long and loud. He froze.

He heard Sasha and Sergey freeze as well, their soft footfalls go still.

A rubber band snap whipped through the darkness.

Ethan's blood turned to ice. *That was a gunshot.*

Sasha groaned. A body slumped to the catwalk above, rattling the grates.

"Sasha!" Sergey ran across the catwalk, not at all stealthy. Ethan shrank into the shadows, ducking behind an engine, and watched Sergey's shadowy body kneel by Sasha's prone form. He reached for his front pocket, for the transmitter.

All at once, the overhead lights flicked on, blinding him. He dropped low, squeezing his eyes shut as the bright lights stabbed his eyeballs. Bullets slammed against the engine casing he hid behind, impact sparks raining down on him. Adam cursed, and Ethan spun away, searching for a way out. Adam tried to follow, but bullets sparked the deck between them, and he dove back. He was pinned.

Overhead, lining the catwalk on three sides, a dozen of Madigan's men stood, their rifles pointed down at Ethan and Adam. Another group had their rifles trained on Sasha and Sergey. Sergey tried to fight back. He got a kick in the face for his efforts. He landed face-down beside Sasha, blooding pouring from his split lip.

More men stormed in through the hatch they had used, blocking any hope of escape.

Ethan ducked as a bullet whizzed by his ear. He slid behind one of the massive engines, tucked between two giant cylinders, and reached for the transmitter again. A block of C4 stuck to the engine just feet from him. He could see another six blocks within ten feet.

He palmed the transmitter. A flick of the switch cover, and then a press of the button was all he needed. *At least Jack can get away.* He swallowed and closed his eyes. *Goodbye, Jack.*

"Drop it!" The barrel of a rifle pressed against his temple, digging into his skull. "Drop it now!"

His eyes flew open. One of Madigan's men snarled at him, hatred burning from his gaze as he held Ethan's stare. This was one of Madigan's handpicked officers. One of his South American men. He wouldn't hesitate to shoot Ethan, drop him at the slightest twitch. Already, his finger was half-squeezed on the trigger. Ethan was millimeters away from death.

He hadn't flipped the switch cover yet. If he tried, he'd be dead before he even got it open.

Slowly, he lifted his thumb off the switch.

In one move, Madigan's officer slapped the transmitter from his hand and slammed the butt of his rifle against Ethan's skull.

He slumped to the deck as darkness swallowed the world.

52

Russian-held Canada

"WHAT THE HELL IS going on, Levi?" Elizabeth's strained voice leaked from behind her hands. She'd buried her face in her palms and leaned forward, balancing her elbows on her knees as the private charter jet started its descent. "What are we doing?"

Levi sat across from her. He chewed on his lip, watching the lines on her forehead furrow and the crinkles around her eyes deepen as she screwed her eyes shut. He reached out, resting his fingertips on the edge of her knee. "What we have to do," he said softly.

"But *this*?" Her hands slid down her face until they cupped her mouth, as if keeping in words she wanted to say. "I can't shake the feeling that we're making the wrong choice."

"You didn't have a choice." Levi looked away, staring at the clouds passing by as they descended. It had been nothing but clouds, an endless void of leaden gloom all the way from Maryland to Canada. They'd slipped out of the White House in the middle of the night, dodging the monitors and the security checkpoints like Ethan used to do. Elizabeth had lain in the back of his SUV as they drove together up to Maryland.

Colonel Song and Yue Ying picked them up in a sleek private jet. One fabricated flight plan later, and they headed first for Niagara, and then turned north, sprinting across the border into Canada, just barely skimming over the treetops and below the radar ceiling.

Hours later, they finally came in for their landing. Colonel Song and Yue Ying stayed up front in the cockpit. Elizabeth stared silently out of the window for the whole flight. She looked at nothing, but her gaze was heavy. Levi watched her weigh her choices deep within her soul.

Colonel Song came out of the cockpit and sat across the aisle from Elizabeth on the long cream couch that stretched the length of the jet. He crossed one leg primly and stared at her.

"What happens now?" she finally asked, frowning. Outside the window, the bleak Nunavut landscape appeared: drab, frost-covered scrub and barren rock. In the distance, dark Arctic waters lapped at a fog-shrouded shoreline. Beneath them, two concrete runways lay at acute angles. A single hangar squatted at the juncture of the runways. A few forgotten bush planes sat parked beside the hangar, their propellers spinning slowly in the breeze.

Jeeps bearing a Russian flag painted on their doors waited in a line at the end of one of the runways.

"When we land, we will meet with General Moroshkin." Colonel Song spoke, carefully, deliberately. "We will meet in the hangar."

"And then?"

Colonel Song stared at her. "That will depend on you." He stood, smoothed his suit jacket, and headed back for the cockpit. "We land in five minutes." The cockpit door clicked shut.

Elizabeth buried her face in her palms again. Dark, wavy locks shook free from the clip holding her hair back. Levi pushed one curly strand back, tucking it behind her ear.

"If this doesn't work, I'll be the biggest failure of a president the United States has ever seen," she breathed. "Or the world. I'll be a traitor. Benedict Arnold… and Elizabeth Wall."

"And if it succeeds," he said softly, "you'll be the president who saved the entire world."

53

Kara Sea - Madigan's Base Camp

Ethan's world went from pitch black to screaming pain, a whirlwind of blows and kicks as he came to.

Arctic air bit into his skin, his chest, arms, and face. He'd been stripped of his stolen jacket and his dry suit had been cut away. His exposed skin puckered, slapped with the sub-freezing temperatures.

Another kick to his stomach. Groaning, Ethan tried to curl into a ball.

A chain, wrapped around his neck, bit into his skin and hauled him back. He went flying, dragged across the *Veduschiy's* deck.

He tried to get to his knees, but kicks and punches rained down on him, and the chain kept dragging him left and right, knocking him off-balance. He saw the world in snatches: the deck of the *Veduschiy* and Madigan's men circling him. Criminals with rotten teeth and tattoos swirling over their necks and fists, grinning wickedly as they punched him over and over again. Men with jaundiced, bloodshot eyes, almost feral as they kicked and beat him, rejoicing in their bloodlust. He smelled blood, and tasted copper in his mouth, on his tongue. Spat, and saw red stain the deck.

The chain strangling him looped over a long launch tube, the gun barrel for the *Veduschiy's* massive five-inch caliber guns. A Sudanese man with rotten teeth held the end, and he grinned every time he hauled on the chain.

Ethan collapsed to his side, coughing, and tried to roll to his stomach. He spotted Sergey and Sasha kneeling on the deck, side by side, weapons pressed to the backs of their skulls. Both stared at him, their expressions grim even by Russian standards. Blood soaked the right sleeve of Sasha's jacket.

"Sir!"

The voice came from off to the right. He turned and got a fist to the face for it. But he spotted Adam, kneeling with his hands locked behind him. Two guards stood over Adam, weapons trained on his head. Ethan met Adam's gaze, for a split second. Desperate fear hung in Adam's eyes.

Footsteps rang over the deck, and the wild, endless beating slowed, and then tapered off. One last criminal remained, holding him by the slack in his chain and punching him in his stomach, his ribs, over and over.

"That's enough."

Ethan collapsed, falling in a heap to the deck. He tried to breathe, tried to drag in freezing air, but his lungs were seizing. He only managed quick, wet gasps. A part of his brain went wild, primal panic trying to take over.

He lay on his belly, his temple pressed to the cold steel. A pair of boots stopped in front of him, with another man standing behind the first.

"Ethan Reichenbach." The voice spoke again, deep and rumbling. The man almost sounded amused. "You never fail to be predictable." He knew that voice. He'd know it anywhere. He'd committed it to memory, sworn an oath to his soul that he'd wipe the man off the planet.

Slowly, Ethan pushed himself to his knees. Shuddering, he glared up at the speaker. "Madigan. You're fucking insane." Behind Madigan, Cook winked at Ethan.

Madigan laughed. "No, I'm just ahead of my time. The world is headed for a collapse all on its own. I'm simply speeding up the process. Taking control of what's to follow." He grinned down at Ethan. "You should remember, from your time in the Army. Destabilize. Destroy. Seize the initiative and take control." Madigan spread his hands. "This is nothing different. Only the target has changed."

He swayed on his knees. "You're targeting your own country. Our country. The world."

Madigan shook his head. "And this is why I decided not to recruit you. You've been on my radar for a while now, Reichenbach. You stood out in your Special Forces unit. A regular killer. You knew when to get things done. Had a reputation for efficiency." He grinned. "I liked that. But then you left and joined the Secret Service." Madigan moved, slowly circling Ethan. His boots scraped the frigid steel. "I kept my eye on you. Thought you might come in handy, especially when you rocketed up the ranks. But." Madigan sighed behind Ethan, disappointed. "You are terribly, disgustingly naïve. You think you're loyal, but you're just a dog chasing after a bone, slobbering because you think it's the right thing, what you're supposed to do." His circle complete, he squatted in front of Ethan. "Your bone is rotten, son. You're feasting on the remains of a failed state."

Ethan shook his head. "You are fucking insane. America isn't a failed state."

"Isn't she? She's lost her power in the world. Lost her respect, her standing. We once controlled economies, countries, had armies stationed in every hemisphere. When we lifted our fingers, the world jumped to where we said. We had true power. True might. We forged this world into our own image, crushing whatever and whoever stood in our way. Communism. Fascists. Terrorists. Radicals. And you know who really had that power? I did. *I* toppled governments. *I* created insurgencies. *I* destroyed and rebuilt whole countries while you were sleeping."

He stood, gazing down at Ethan with disgust. "And president after president ruined the world I built. Your leadership can't even stand firm in the face of a single enemy. Now, Spiers has finally sold America out, hopping into bed with the Russians, the Saudis, with anyone who will hold his hand and help him through the hard choices. He won't do what's right. He's not strong enough, and he never will be."

Blood rage blinded Ethan, and he snarled, lunging forward. The chain jerked him back. He fell to his ass, sprawling on his bound hands as he choked, struggling for air.

Madigan held up his hand. The chain stopped pulling, but the frozen links still bit into his skin.

"*I* built this world you live in. *I* emboldened the Caliphate to destabilize your president," he purred. "*I* put Al-Karim on his path. Sent the Middle East into a tailspin. I waited for each president to fail to take charge, and fail to take care of the problem. Like a festering wound going rotten, Al-Karim helped pull the world down. And your president wanted to *talk* about it. Endless summits with his allies." Madigan looked at Sergey, his lips curling in a sneer. "And selling America out to her enemies. He made false promises to the world that America was for them. This world your president tried to create? It's a sickening parody of peace. This isn't what I spent my whole life fighting for!" Madigan's voice rose to a shout. "So, I will rebuild this world," he hissed, "under *my* control."

Silence hung over the deck, heavy. Ethan felt the freezing wind slice against his cheek, curl through his hair. He still could barely breathe. "What do you want with me?" he choked out.

"With you?" Madigan snorted. "Nothing." He turned to Cook. "What's Kobayashi's status?"

"He's ready to weaponize the reactor. All safeguards have been taken offline. It will take him about two hours to complete the process."

"Excellent. Tell him to begin immediately. Send out the signal to our worldwide forces. They need to be ready. And bring me the ship's radio."

Cook nodded and stepped to the side. Madigan turned his attention back to Ethan.

Squatting, he reached for Ethan's chin, gripping him hard as he twisted Ethan's head from side to side. "There's nothing that I want from you, Reichenbach. You're a dog trailing after its owner, and you're too stupid to realize it. No, I don't want you. I want your owner."

Swallowing, Ethan glared at Madigan, gritting his teeth. "You'll never get Jack."

"Do you remember the early days of the Iraq War? When the handcuffs were off, and we could pry information from those raghead terrorists by any means necessary?"

A cold chill that had nothing to do with the wind tap-danced down Ethan's spine. He tried to drag in more air, more breath, but couldn't. His heart hammered, pounding against his ribs.

"Do you know what I learned about torture, Reichenbach?" Madigan gripped his chin and pulled him forward until their faces were inches apart. "It's completely ineffective against the subject," he said as if whispering a secret. "But completely effective if the *subject* is witnessing their loved ones being tortured." Slowly, he grinned. "There is not a single thing that I want from you. But I want Jack Spiers, and *you're* going to help me get him."

Ethan spat, blood-soaked spittle spattering Madigan's face.

Madigan nodded to the Sudanese man holding the end of Ethan's chain. The man yanked, and then kept pulling, hauling the chain until taut, choking Ethan. He kept going, yanking Ethan to his feet, and then off his feet, until Ethan dangled in the air, inches off the deck, twisting and thrashing wildly as the chain noose strangled him.

Somewhere, Adam shouted again, screaming his name and cursing at Madigan. Between Ethan's blinks, he saw Adam try to break free. Saw the men guarding him grab him and pull him back, beat him down to the deck viciously. Nearby, Sasha shifted, putting his body in front of Sergey's, as if he could shield him from Madigan and what was to come.

He gasped against the chain choking him. He couldn't breathe, couldn't drag in even the small wisps of air he'd managed before. His feet kicked, toes reaching for the deck, desperately trying to take the pressure off his straining throat. Stars burst in front of his eyes, colors exploding as the world darkened at the edges of his vision. *Jack.* He closed his eyes, drawing forth every memory of Jack he could: Jack smiling, laughing, gazing at him with love in his eyes. Sweaty and tousled after making love, and waking up in each other's arms. Always, back to Jack's smile.

"Drop him."

He hit the deck hard, limp and boneless as the chain rattled. It loosened just enough for him to drag in a small breath, his lungs pushing painfully at his bruised and battered ribs. Ethan pressed his forehead against the deck, coughing and gagging as spit and blood dripped from his lips. *Get out of here, Jack. Go. Take Scott and go. Get away from here, before it all goes up.* Failure stung his soul, but all he could focus on was Jack. The world paled, always, beside Jack.

Two men came up behind him and hefted him to his knees, holding him up, restraining him.

"Is everything ready?"

"Yes, sir." Cook, again, striding toward Madigan. Ethan watched as Cook passed Madigan a handheld radio.

His blood chilled when he saw what else Cook had with him: a stun baton, a thin pipe, a bucket of water, and a blood-and-oil-stained rag.

Cook tossed the pipe to the men restraining Adam. Blood dripped from Adam's lip, and his eye was swollen shut again, but he was back on his knees, glaring at Madigan and Cook. His eyes followed the pipe, though, and he fought back as his captors grabbed him and pinned him down. One of the men forced Adam's mouth open, and another slid the pipe between his lips and yanked it to the back of his jaw like a bit. Adam tried to shout around the pipe, but the men holding it jerked him hard against their bodies. One of them drew a knife and pressed it against Adam's throat.

"No interruptions." Madigan winked at Ethan. He held the radio up to his mouth and pressed the button. Overhead, loudspeakers on the *Veduschiy* clicked on, whining and crackling for a split second before settling into the open channel. "Jack Spiers," Madigan said. His voice boomed out of the speakers, echoing across the ice cap. "I know you're out there. I have something that you want."

Madigan nodded to Cook. He held the radio out toward Ethan, still holding down the transmitter.

Cook smirked at Ethan and swung the stun baton, like a batter winding up for a swing. Electricity crackled off the twin prods at the end, snapping in the freezing air.

He clenched, trying to gird himself for the impact. Cook slammed the baton into his bruised and battered stomach. Electricity crackled through him, lightning bursting through his veins and his muscles. He went rigid, teeth gritted, and shrieked, jerking as Cook kept the prod buried in his belly.

"How does this sound, Jack? Do you like what you hear?" Madigan waved to Cook, and Cook pulled back. Ethan sagged in his captors' arms, limp. "I've only just begun."

54

USS Honolulu

"CAPTAIN, I'VE FOUND A LEAD. It doesn't look natural, though..." Boomer's voice trailed off. "Our sonar is still jacked, but this looks like the remains of an icebreaker chewing through the cap. Most of it's frozen over again. I'd say... maybe a month ago."

"What icebreakers would be chewing through the ice up here within the month?" Anderson shared a long look with Faisal, Coleman, and Wright. They'd been invited to the Conn after leaving the wardroom-turned-sickbay. Doc had chosen to stay behind for the moment, clutching a bucket as he heaved. "Bring it up on the main screen, Boomer. Nav, plot me a course to the lead."

A chorus of *aye, Captain*s rang out as Anderson headed for the plotting table. His navigator hunched over his charts, checking the computer's course and heading against his own calculations. He passed the final bearings to Anderson.

Faisal watched it all as if he were in a bubble, as if the world were happening around him, and he was stuck in slow-motion. Numbness seeped into his soul and circled his bones.

He had to be realistic. Adam was almost certainly *gone*.

He thought he'd prepared himself for the possibility of a life without Adam. Thought he'd guarded his heart, gave everything up to Allah and put his trust there. What would be was Allah's will; he had no illusions otherwise. Adam and he... Only Allah knew the duration of their days. He was ready, he told himself, for what would come.

But he'd thought that meant Adam would leave. Walk away, again, and live out the rest of his life apart from Faisal.

He hadn't once thought about Adam's death. He hadn't thought Allah would be that cruel. To bring them back to each other—had it only been days since they'd lain together in a single hammock, whispering promises into each other's skin—and then tear Adam from his heart again?

Part of him wanted to pray, to wail, to plead with Allah that this wasn't the end. To demand answers, yell and scream until the clouds parted and he stood before his creator himself. Petulant fury raged in his soul, just like it had when he was six years old, and his uncle had come home instead of his parents.

The last time he'd prayed, Adam had been beside him, their movements in sync, their words whispered together in the cold hollows of the torpedo room. Adam had looked sideways at him, sneaking glances and smiles in between the verses. They'd held hands as they bowed low. Adam had stroked his thumb over Faisal's palm. His voice had sounded so sweet, reciting the *Fatiha* in rolling Arabic.

He didn't want to let that memory go, let it become just one blip in a long line of prayers. If he'd known how much those moments, those breaths, those whispered words would come to mean, he'd have paid more attention. Kept every moment in his memories, like capturing fireflies in a jar. Had Adam smiled at him six times, or seven? When he kissed Faisal's nose, why hadn't Faisal kissed him back? Why had he ducked his head and shifted away, coy instead of playful, focused on prayers instead of the gift that was beside him?

He couldn't let it go, not yet. He wanted to always hold onto that feeling, the memory of Adam beside him, their souls so close they were almost one. He wasn't ready for his next prayers to be alone.

To be without his husband.

He held Adam's dog tags in one fist, clenched over his heart. Was this all he'd ever have of Adam? Would they ever find his body? He should try to find him, bring him back to Saudi. He'd ask his uncle for space in the royal cemetery, a plot beside his. He'd wash Adam, whisper the prayers in his ears, and wrap him in his shroud. Sit in mourning and pray for him for forty days, or, in the old ways, for an entire year. Or for ten years. Or a hundred. For the rest of his days.

The promise of paradise, and a life forever at Adam's side in the next world, was too distant a dream for the immediacy of his shattered heart.

Speak the name of the one you love in your heart and in your prayers. He swallowed. *Adam, always Adam. Always and forever.*

The diving officer called to the captain, and Anderson ordered an 'all stop', and then a slow rise to periscope depth. He felt *Honolulu* shift beneath his feet, the whoosh and hiss of air slipping from the ballast tanks.

Coleman shifted, pressing in behind him. "You okay?" he murmured into Faisal's ear. "Need to talk?"

Faisal shook his head. "No, thank you, Sergeant."

Anderson kept calling out orders. "Raise the masts. ESM sweep. Extend and open up the radio antennas. If there's anything out there, I want to hear it."

Coleman raised his eyebrows. In the dim light of the Conn, his eyes gleamed, dark shadows and blue-green shine piercing Faisal. "He and I talked, before—"

"*Please,*" he said, closing his eyes. "Not now. *Yallah,* I can't—"

"*Conn, Radio!*" A voice broke over the intercom, one of the crewmen shouting. "*We're picking up a transmission!*"

"Put on the speakers."

Shrieks of pain erupted over the speakers. Deep, throat-tearing screams, ragged and gut-wrenching. And then shuffling. A scuffle, or a man being restrained. The sound of a chain being pulled, and then choking sounds, a man gasping, struggling for breath.

"*Hold him back, hold him back. Tilt his head.*"

Madigan's voice broke over the radio. "*Are you familiar with waterboarding, Jack? I perfected it years ago. And so did the good captain.*"

Water being poured. A man, choking, struggling for breath, gurgling as his gasps quickened, faster and faster until he just sputtered. And then silence.

No one breathed. Anderson's eyes were wide, circlets of white ringing his irises all the way around.

Nothing but the sound of water pouring slowly, endlessly, over the radio.

A chain released, heavy plinks echoing on the transmission. Something thudded. A man gasped and coughed, hacking and vomiting as he spewed up water like he was coughing up a lung.

Faisal closed his eyes and looked down. Memories flashed through his mind, streaks of light like tracer rounds piercing the darkness behind his eyelids. Years ago, with Adam, them together in another world.

Madigan's voice came next. "*How much longer will you hold out, Jack? How much longer will you listen to the love of your life suffer?*"

"Jesus Christ," Anderson growled. "That's Ethan Reichenbach." He whipped around, growling to the radio room to turn the transmission off the main speakers, and then grabbed the intercom handheld and pulled it down. "Patch me into the ship-to-shore radio. Jack Spiers is still out there, and damn it, he needs our help."

55

Kara Sea - Madigan's Base Camp

JACK'S WHOLE BODY SHOOK as he held himself up, leaning his entire weight into his palms as he slumped forward. In front of him, a steel sheet haphazardly stuck into the ice cap formed a wall for one of the Arctic shantytown camp huts. Only a scattered handful of Madigan's criminal army seemed to still be around, and they were near the center, huddled around barrel fires and drinking vodka. He could hear their shouts and cheers in the silent spaces between Madigan's transmissions and Ethan's screams and cries of pain.

Ethan. God, Ethan… Had he really told Ethan to let him go, let him die in order to save the world? Had he really condemned Adam for caving in the face of losing his team and the love of his life? Watching the people he loved be murdered, one by one? Had he really thought he could somehow withstand the same? That he was made of sterner, more hardened material, his soul girded with patriotic passion, ready to embrace sacrifice for the good of the world?

Ethan's screams shredded his convictions, made a mockery of his lecture on the greater good.

He wanted to tear across the ice cap, run guns blazing toward Madigan. Fire into the sky like some kind of deranged action hero and bellow at the top of his lungs, demand Madigan meet him for a pistol duel at high noon. Everything in him wailed, desperate to rescue Ethan, to put a stop to his torture, to just give in and give Madigan what he wanted.

Tears streamed down his face as he trembled and heaved. Vomit stained the ice between his feet. Beside him, Scott clenched his rifle so hard his arms and shoulders shook, and his face turned purple, his eyes almost incandescent with pure rage.

The *Veduschiy*'s speakers hissed as Madigan opened his broadcast again. *"Are congratulations in order, Jack? I see a ring on Reichenbach's left hand. Are you wearing one too?"* His voice dripped with condescension, with hateful mockery. *"Are you going to let your husband die?"*

Ethan's voice broke in, and Jack's heart leaped to his throat. He spun, staring at the *Veduschiy* as Ethan spoke. His voice cracked, sounding choked, but he forced his words out. *"Jack will never surrender."*

"*Everyone has a breaking point,*" Madigan purred.

"*Get out of here, Jack!*" Ethan shouted. "*Get far away!*" His voice cracked again, and a wet thump echoed over the transmission. Ethan groaned. "*Go,*" he grunted. "*I'm with you all—*" Another wet thump, and then a kick, and Ethan's voice faded to pained grunts and groans.

"*Turn yourself in, Jack. Your plan has failed. We stopped your people from blowing up this ship. You're not sinking anything today. Surrender and I'll let your husband live.*"

Jack turned to Scott, tears blurring his vision again. Scott gazed back, his entire soul tearing apart in the depths of his eyes. Surrender was anathema to everything Jack knew, everything Ethan and Scott stood for in their professional lives. If they surrendered, that would be it. Madigan would win. The world would die.

But Ethan would live.

You are my whole world, Ethan had said. *You are my everything.*

If he didn't turn himself in, seven billion people might have a chance of surviving. Maybe he and Scott could storm K-27. Or blow the net, and send her back to the depths. Maybe they could cobble together a plan, scrape a victory out of the disaster their mission had become.

But his world, after Madigan and after Ethan, would be bleak and empty.

He wasn't strong enough for this. Wasn't strong enough to listen to Ethan suffer and die, all for his moral convictions. Damn it all, he was just a man.

He blinked, and tears cascaded down his cheeks. He looked at Scott again.

Scott saw the decision in his eyes. "Jack," he breathed. "Ethan—"

"*Honolulu to Phoenix One. Honolulu to Phoenix One. Come back.*"

Jack's jacket squawked, his secured ship-to-shore radio blurting out Captain Anderson's message. He and Scott dove down a darkened alley, hiding between a torn-apart shipping container and an old, broken plane fuselage. No one shouted, and no one came running.

"*Honolulu*, Phoenix One," Jack breathed back into the radio. "Christ, am I glad to hear you."

"*We picked up Madigan's transmission. We know he's got Reichenbach. What's your status, Phoenix One?*"

Jack's eyes squeezed closed. He exhaled. "Ethan led a team into the *Veduschiy* to blow the ship. The plan was to crack the ice cap and sink the *Veduschiy* and K-27. They must have been captured. I've only heard Ethan's voice."

"*Where are you now? Can you get to an extraction point for us to pick you up?*"

Jack pressed his lips together and bowed his head. Ethan's voice, telling him to run, to get away from there, replayed in his head. Anderson was offering him just that: an escape.

He couldn't live with himself if he walked away from Ethan again. He'd sworn to Ethan to always be by his side, to have and to hold, in good times and bad. To turn to each other, always. To never, ever let go of each other.

Run, and survive as a shell of a man?

Surrender to Madigan?

There was a third option.

"Captain, if you're in range for an extraction, you should be in range for a torpedo strike. Do you have a bearing on the *Veduschiy*?"

Silence, for a moment. Then, "*Yes, Mr. President. We can launch against the* Veduschiy. *Isn't that where Reichenbach is being held?*"

Jack nodded to himself before speaking. "Yes. And it's where I'll be, too."

"*Mr. President—*"

"Captain, you need to launch your torpedoes against the *Veduschiy* and K-27. Sink both of these ships to the bottom of the ocean. You're the only hope we've got now."

"*Mr. President—*"

"These are your orders, Captain. I have to do what I have to do. The world is in your hands now." He waited. Anderson could call his bluff, tell him he wasn't the damn president, and he wasn't going to listen to his orders.

Finally, Anderson came back. "*Yes, Mr. President. We have to maneuver to a new position to get a fix on both. We can launch in six minutes.*"

"Perfect. Launch as soon as you're able." He swallowed. "Captain Anderson, thank you. For what you're about to do. For saving the world. And for what you did for Ethan and me."

Captain Anderson's voice turned rough, gravelly over the radio. "*It was an honor, Mr. President. It's been a privilege.*"

"Six minutes, Captain." Jack nodded again. "Phoenix One out."

He turned to Scott. "Scott… I *swore*, when we left the US, that I would get you back to your family. I swore that you'd see your daughter again."

Scott looked away, blinking fast as he clenched his rifle.

"You have to get out of here. This ice cap is going to blow and take everything down with it."

"I can help—"

"You've done enough." Jack rested his hand on Scott's arm, squeezing gently. "You've done far more than enough, for both me and Ethan. Above and beyond the call of your duties to your job, to your president, and to your friends." He smiled, but it wavered. Scott's expression darkened further. "Go. Survive, Scott. It's what Ethan and I both want."

"I'm not abandoning you guys," Scott growled. "When this thing blows, Madigan's people will be running around like a kicked ant pile." He hefted his rifle. "I can pick them off."

"From outside the blast radius." Jack squeezed his arm again. "Take your snowmobile and get away from here."

Scott turned away, gazing over the ice cap and into the gloom. "What about you?"

Jack's gaze fixed on the *Veduschiy*. "I will always choose Ethan."

56

Russian-held Canada

GENERAL MOROSHKIN STRODE INTO the empty, windblown hangar and stopped dead. His jaw dropped as he stared at Elizabeth, standing in the center of the barren space. His eyes dragged over her as if staring at a ghost.

Blustering, he whirled and came face-to-face with Colonel Song. "What is the meaning of this?" he bellowed. "You said I was meeting a representative of your government! That you had an alliance proposal for me!"

"That is exactly what this meeting is," Colonel Song said calmly, ignoring Moroshkin's furious, dark expression. "I represent my government. I have been sent directly by my president to negotiate in these matters. And we do have an alliance proposal for you."

"Unless it is a *complete* surrender from this American—"

Elizabeth interrupted Moroshkin's tirade, speaking over his growl. "General, the only one who will be surrendering today is *you*."

Moroshkin slowly turned, his eyebrows arching almost clear of his forehead. Behind him, Colonel Song's lips pressed to a thin line as he glared at Elizabeth.

She pressed on, dragging in a slow breath through her nose. She kept her hands clasped behind her back. "General Moroshkin, as we speak, your country is on the verge of annihilation."

He snorted, waving one arm at her. He turned away, heading back for the entrance. Colonel Song blocked his path.

"The man you put your trust into, former General Madigan, duped you, General. Did you never ask him what he wanted with your ships up in the Arctic? Were you never once curious?"

Moroshkin froze. She watched his shoulders tighten, watched his uniform stretch across his back. "For resources exploration," he growled. "He says United States has advanced procedures for finding oil beneath the ice. He offered to search, in exchange for half profit. He will do the same once we take Canada's Arctic, as a deterrent against the United States."

She shook her head. "General, you've been lied to. The United States military possesses no advanced military or naval tactics for oil exploration."

He snorted at her again, but she kept going. "Madigan fed you a lie and used your greed to steal ships from you. Ships that he is using to engineer the end of the world as we know it."

Moroshkin's eyes narrowed. He said nothing.

Elizabeth unclasped her hands, letting them swing forward. She held out a tablet, the screen displaying the Swedish weather satellite data. Violent fuchsia overlaid nearly the entire northern hemisphere and streaked into the southern. "These are satellite photos of the Arctic. They show the dispersal of methane hydrate into the atmosphere, into the jet stream. Do you see how over half the world is covered? This is from hours ago." She pointed to each country she named. "The United States. Europe. Russia. China. And Canada. Each completely covered. Madigan's plan, we've discovered, is to saturate the jet stream with enough of this gas to ignite a firestorm that would cascade through the atmosphere. Scorch the earth. It would be like a nuclear blast rolled into an airborne tsunami wave, burning across the planet. We uncovered a saying of his, what he motivated his troops with. 'A new dawn is coming'. Have you ever heard that from him?"

Moroshkin said nothing.

Elizabeth zoomed in on the scan. "Madigan is operating out of the Kara Sea. Deposits in the ice, and from your undersea oil wells, have fed him a limitless supply of what he needs. He's almost ready to ignite everything."

Moroshkin paled. His lips pressed together.

She looked him dead in the eye. "Have you ever heard of K-27, General?"

He whipped away, pacing. "Nonsense! This is nonsense! Madigan is my ally. He came to *me*. He would not turn on me!"

"General, Madigan has turned on everyone." She held out the tablet, offering it to him. "Look at the data, General. Madigan plans to burn the world down. He wants to kill us all. The only safe spot on the planet is right above Russia, just north of the Kara Sea. Not Canada, and not where we are right now. He's going to incinerate every single one of your troops in Canada."

He glared at her, and then snatched the tablet from her hands. He scrolled through the series of images, from the start of the gas cloud to the present, his glower growing darker, and he spat curses under his breath.

"You were sent to Canada as a distraction," she said. "And to keep you away from Madigan's plans."

Moroshkin's shoulders slumped. He closed his eyes, his fingertips pressing against the glass screen.

Colonel Song stepped forward, holding out his own tablet. Made of clear glass, it had holograms floating above the surface. It was far more advanced than hers. He poked one of the floating holograms, and a projection rose, playing through Chinese satellite data showing the growing cloud, and then an animation of the atmosphere lighting up. A wave of fire rolling over fields and mountains, bursting towns apart like film of early nuclear tests from the fifties and burning the earth to ruins. Finally, a clip of the Chinese president, speaking to his security council. The clip had a Russian translation already overlaid, followed by an English one. *"We must stop this global destruction,"* the Chinese president said, *"by any means necessary. Madigan is our enemy now. He is the world's enemy."*

The clip ended and the projection faded back into Colonel Song's tablet.

Moroshkin's heavy breathing filled the hangar. He clenched Elizabeth's tablet in both hands, bending the case as his hands shook. He stared at the dented and rusted hangar walls. Wind whipped through gaps and cracks in the steel, whistling a tuneless, eerie call.

She crossed to Moroshkin's side. Her heels clicked against the cold concrete, as loud as hammer blows. "We have a common enemy. Madigan is a danger to us all. A danger to the world."

"A common enemy means that we are united." Colonel Song stepped forward as well, bracketing Moroshkin on the opposite side of Elizabeth. "For the moment."

"What do you propose?" Moroshkin finally growled. "What is it you want to do?"

Elizabeth stepped in front of Moroshkin and stared him down. "Turn your ships around, General. Put your fastest jets in the air and boats in the water. Send your subs back under the ice. Get your forces back to Madigan and *stop* him." She swallowed hard. "We had a team going up there, but we've lost contact with them. We're blind in the Arctic right now. General, yours are the only forces that are close enough to put a stop to this madman."

Moroshkin looked up, into her eyes.

57

Washington DC

Pete tapped his foot in time to the beat pouring from Jennifer's phone. "What station is this? It's pretty good."

"An online one I follow." Jennifer smiled at him as she took a sip of coffee.

Beside her, Jason furrowed his brow as he compared a handwritten list to a stack of folders. "Jen, I don't see your name on this list."

Jennifer and Pete frowned. "What list are you working on?" Pete shuffled through the madness of files in front of him. They were back at work in the Roosevelt Room again, sifting through files of West Wing personnel. General Bell had vanished, as had Welby and Levi. Pete grumbled about their dwindling numbers, and he'd locked the door to keep anyone else from entering.

"This is everyone who was on the flight to the Russian state funeral. The trip to Moscow." Jason frowned at Jennifer. "You were on the flight. We sat together."

"You asked me out when we landed." Jennifer grinned.

"Yeah, but you're not on this list."

"Well, that's dumb." Jennifer shrugged. "I was there. I had to take care of the flowers President Spiers gave at the funeral." She frowned and pursed her lips. "Is there anyone else missing?"

Pete stood and shuffled through his papers, scattering sheets right and left. "Where did you get that list, Jason?"

"From the original manifest."

"Yeah, but who gave it to you?"

Jason swallowed. "Welby gave it to me."

In the background, the song changed, the fast beat mellowing to something soft and smooth, almost bluesy. Almost like a farewell.

Pete's gaze locked with Jason's. "Tell me honestly: do you think we can trust the Secret Service?"

"Hey, *you* brought Welby into this—" Jason shoved back from the table, holding his hands in front of him.

"Yeah, but the info we're getting from them isn't accurate! If Jennifer isn't on the list, then who else is missing?"

"You want to accuse the guy we've been sitting next to for two days?"

"Where the hell is he now?" Pete spread his arms wide, shouting. "Or Daniels? They've both vanished! And the whole reason we're in this mess is because of the *lies* the Secret Service put out there!" He threw a folder onto the table. Papers skittered wildly, spreading across the polished mahogany surface.

"Okay." Jennifer stood, slowly pushing back from the table. She dropped a kiss on Jason's head. "You guys need a break. I'm going to go get some lunch and bring it back. Take a break until then." She grabbed her phone. "Seriously, guys. You're starting to see bogeymen everywhere."

Jason smiled at her, his lopsided, dopey smile, as she ducked out.

In the hallway, she looked down at her phone. The last song played remained on the screen. The broadcaster would have set it to play on an endless loop, one long broadcast from the online radio station she'd been listening to for the past three weeks straight.

The song was called "A New Dawn Rises."

Her phone buzzed. A text message popped up. *The signal was sent. You in position?*

[Heading to rendezvous now.]

She hurried through the West Wing, entered the Residence, and moved fast across the Cross Hall. Her heels clacked against the marble, the sounds bouncing off the tall ceilings and crystal chandeliers.

In ten minutes, a van would arrive at the gates. Florists, delivering flowers for her weekly order. Or at least, that was what their credentials said. In twelve minutes, they'd be parking beneath the East Wing, where she'd meet them at the loading dock. From there, it was eight minutes from the loading dock back to the West Wing.

They'd move faster once they started firing. And without Welby and Levi Daniels, the Secret Service agents left behind were all younger, less experienced agents who quaked in front of a senator and had only been called in when the White House needed to staff up in a hurry. Young, inexperienced, and easy to intimidate.

They were insignificant.

She ducked into the East Wing and headed for the elevator that would take her to the garage. She didn't fidget as she waited for the elevator, watching the light as the car descended from the second floor to the first. When it dinged and the doors opened, she stepped inside smoothly. No one watching would have any idea what she was about to do.

The elevator doors started to close.

A hand grasped the sliding brass door. The doors slid back.

Jason grinned at her, his hands in his pockets, shoulders slumped, and shirt rumpled. "Mind if I tag along? Pete's going crazy in there." He shrugged. "I'd rather be with you."

Jennifer pasted her wide, bright smile on her face, the one that had first lured Jason in. "Sure!"

Down they went, into the garage. She fished her keys out of her purse. "I have a floral delivery on the way, too. I'm going to check it out before we go, okay?"

"No prob."

The doors dinged and opened to the dim, cavern-like depths of the underground garage. Dark shadows clung to the cars. Down a long aisle, a rectangle of light bled into the darkness, the ramp rising into the daylight.

A blue van rumbled down the ramp and rolled into the garage. She waved. It drove toward her.

The driver stopped and looked her in the eyes after he rolled down his window. She walked toward him. "Hi! Thanks for agreeing to this special delivery. We really need to try and bring some cheer into the White House. Everyone has been so down since the attack." As she spoke, she motioned to his hip, and his holstered weapon.

The driver withdrew his weapon slowly and held it out to her, below the windowpane. A silencer was already screwed into the barrel.

"Thanks so much," she said, reaching for the weapon.

She whirled around, facing Jason, and pointed it at his chest. "Sorry about this, Jason."

Shock blasted across his face, followed by betrayal.

She squeezed the trigger twice. Jason fell to the ground, limp, and his head cracked against the concrete. Twin pools of blood spread from his chest, above his heart.

"You missed," the driver growled.

"Shut up." She passed the weapon back to him. "He wasn't supposed to follow me."

"What are we going to do about him?"

"Leave him there. He won't matter in ten minutes anyway." She slapped the side of the van and the rear doors burst open. Twelve men poured out, each wearing the coveralls her normal delivery florists wore. Bins and buckets of roses and tulips, lilies and sunflowers came out of the back of the van, too. The men dumped the flowers on the concrete.

Weapons poured from the bottom of the buckets. Subcompact rifles and handguns, magazines and clips. Enough ammo to lay siege to an installation, shatter a building's foundation, and kill everyone inside. Or to take the West Wing of the White House.

Jennifer grabbed a subcompact rifle and held it close, low and ready, her finger over the trigger. "Up the stairs, down the East Colonnade, through the Cross Hall, and into the West Wing. Head for the elevator to the PEOC. The bunker." Her team nodded.

These were her brother's men.

Her twin brother had died years before during a "training accident", according to the government. When she'd asked for more information, tried to find any information at all about how he died, door after door had been slammed in her face. No one had wanted to talk to her about her brother.

A personal visit from General Madigan had set the story straight. Her brother had been a hero, fighting in the shadows, in the black spaces off the edge of the map. Leading missions so dark only an elite few knew about them.

Years ago, her brother had a led a mission into the dark heart of the Middle East. He'd never returned, and the government had erased all knowledge of him. A stock letter, with a typo, was all she had left of his life, telling her he'd perished in an "unfortunate training accident".

Until Madigan had come to her. Given her the truth. Told her what really happened, and how the United States had abandoned her brother to die and then abandoned him again to be forgotten from history, stricken from the record and denied his rightful honors as a hero. Rage had nearly killed her for two years, but Madigan kept checking in on her through his people. Helped her when she needed it. Guided her when she was lost.

Doors opened before her, acceptances to Georgetown, and a position at a top DC think tank, a consultancy that worked with the off-book segments of the military. Through it all, she'd trained when she could, meeting contacts in underground gyms and country escapes. She'd learned to shoot in the West Virginia backwoods, under the tutelage of a Special Forces sergeant who specialized in training individuals, no questions asked. She had purpose again.

One day, out of the blue, an invite to a prestigious floral design course in Paris appeared, alongside an advertisement for a position as a White House floral designer. Her path unfurled before her like a rose in slow bloom. She would be the spider at the center of the blossom, waiting to strike.

During the first coup, she'd sheltered in the East Wing, huddled in Barbara's office as she longed, with all the fire in her soul, for the end of Jack's government, and of Jack Spiers himself. As hard as Barbara prayed, weeping softly in her shaking voice and huddled with Jennifer, Jennifer begged for the exact opposite. Downfall. Destruction. A new dawn in the world. It had been so close.

And then, setback.

She'd almost quit. Almost put a bullet in her brain, determined to join her brother at last. Madigan was gone, on the run and in hiding, and their world, their dreams, were at an end.

Until a man came to visit her one night with a message from Madigan. One of her brother's men, he said. And they had work to do. Stay in place. Keep your cover. Report back. Wait for more orders.

Her next orders came much later, from the lips of a Marine who worked for Ethan Reichenbach. One of the select members of the elite team responsible for hunting Madigan.

They laughed all night long at that, sharing drinks before tumbling into bed. She saw him every time he was in DC with his team, working operations and missions for Reichenbach. They shared intel, and her bed, and he passed everything to his contact at Madigan's side.

Soon, she'd see him again. He'd sent word that he was headed out on one last mission, one last operation embedded in Lieutenant Adam Cooper's team before their new dawn rose.

When the world was in ashes and the fire burned out in the sky, they'd find each other in the rubble and wreckage, and make their way by the flaming light of the new dawn.

But first, she had her own mission. Her own part to play in the revolution. Jennifer led her team out of the underground garage, stepping over Jason's unmoving body. They snaked up the silent East Wing stairwell. All she needed now was for Barbara to poke her head out.

The East Wing was a ghost town. Only key staff remained. With Ethan Reichenbach presumed missing and the government in crisis mode, there wasn't much for a social secretary and floral designer to do. Her team padded through the empty hallways, slipping silently down the East Colonnade. She led the stack by the door to the Residence, outside the Grand Visitors Foyer separating the East Wing from the Residence.

Her team, her brother's men, each looked her in the eye. She nodded back to them.

This was it. Time to strike.

58

Kara Sea - Madigan's Base Camp

JACK DROVE HIS SNOWMOBILE across the ice, out in the open, toward the *Veduschiy*. He could feel the pressure of a hundred pairs of eyeballs on him, watching his every move. He stared at the frozen, bullet-riddled bodies of the SEAL team Elizabeth had sent. Their corpses banged against the hull like deathly windchimes, frozen chains wrapped around the men's bodies rattling and scraping against the destroyer's old steel.

When he arrived at the *Veduschiy's* loading ramp, a team of Madigan's soldiers was waiting for him. Americans, not criminal thugs. Soldiers who had abandoned their posts to join his army. They smirked at Jack as he slowly walked up the ramp, his hands held over his head. A dozen rifles were pointed at him. Two men stripped him of his own weapons, his rifle over his shoulder and his pistol in his waistband.

A familiar face walked down the ramp to meet him. "Hello, Mr. President." Kobayashi grinned and pointed his pistol at Jack's head. "Won't you join us on the main deck?"

Kobayashi led him through the dark hallways and cramped hatches, winding him up through rotten ladders until they came to a rusted door that opened to the top deck. Frigid wind whipped over the hull, whistling along the metal surface. Kobayashi shoved Jack through the hatch. He stumbled but caught himself.

Ahead, a crowd of Madigan's men, easily a hundred or more of his army of traitors and criminals, stood gathered around the bow of the boat, beneath the barrel of the destroyer's immense long guns. To the right, he spotted Sasha and Sergey, kneeling with their hands behind their back. Sasha practically covered Sergey's body with his own, trying to shield him. Sergey's eyes were closed, his forehead resting on the back of Sasha's neck. Jack met Sasha's gaze. Grim determination, and what looked like an apology, stared back at him.

To the left, Madigan's men restrained Adam, pinning him back by his arms and holding him on his knees. A dirty pipe had been shoved in his mouth, and blood dripped from the corners of his lips where it dug into his skin. Hot, angry tears stained Adam's face, tracks of dirt and sorrow running down his skin.

And, in the center of the crowd, Ethan lay in a soaking, shivering heap. A rusted chain wrapped around his neck, looping over and over, and then rose, thrown around the barrel of the destroyer's long guns, and dropped to the hands of a grinning member of Madigan's army.

Jack met the man's maniacal, vicious stare. *You're going to die.*

Where the chain looped around Ethan's neck, dark bruises and tears in his skin bloomed. Rivulets of blood trickled down his bare chest. Burns and angry welts marred the skin over his abdomen, and the skin over his ribs, from his back to his sides, was discolored, vivid aubergine, ugly olive, sickly yellow.

Silence reigned on the deck as Jack slowly walked forward. Ethan's eyelids fluttered, and as he sucked in ragged, short breaths, his wandering gaze fell on Jack.

Jack watched his eyes widen, watched him struggle to his knees, trying to form words as he shook his head. Despair poured from him, falling from his watering eyes.

He smiled, trying to put all of his love, all of his happiness, into his gaze. "…All the way, Ethan," he said softly, completing their promise, the words Ethan hadn't been able to get out over the radio. *I'm with you all the way.*

Ethan pitched forward, curling in on himself, as a sob burst from him and his eyes squeezed closed. Tears ran down his cheeks, mixing with the blood on his face, and rained pink droplets to the cold steel beneath him.

"Touching, Jack." Madigan smirked, crossing the deck to face Jack. Cook shadowed Madigan's every move. Jack's stomach lurched. Vivid crimson stained Cook's hands, his sleeves up to his elbows, his pants, and spattered across his face. He held a blood-soaked rag. *God, Ethan's blood.*

Jack's eyes locked onto the rag. His mind roared, replaying Madigan's transmission of Ethan's waterboarding. Ethan's screams, his thrashing, the sounds of him drowning. And then silence.

Jack swayed, the world around him seeming to tilt, seeming to swirl into a vortex. Was someone screaming, or was that just his mind, the roar of his own rage, his soul on furious fire?

He looked Madigan dead in his eyes. "You wanted me. Now you have me. Let Ethan go."

Madigan nodded to the man holding the end of Ethan's chain. Shrugging, the man let go, and the chain pulled free from his hands, rising over the barrel of the long guns and then crashing to the deck, steel crashing against steel. Ethan didn't move.

"What do you want from me?" Jack shook his head. "What's this obsession of yours?"

Madigan threw his head back, laughing loudly. "Jack, there is nothing I want from you. Not a single thing. You have no power here. No leverage to negotiate. No possibility of securing your release. No," he stepped forward, crowding Jack. "I wanted you here because I wanted to look you in the eyes and watch you realize that you have lost. You've failed. As the *president*. As a *man*. You've failed, Jack."

Jack swallowed hard. *One minute, forty-five seconds.*

"You've been living on borrowed time ever since you and Ethan interfered in my last mission. It wasn't personal before that, Jack. I didn't care about you. You were Leslie's ridiculous husband, the one thing that held her back from joining me fully."

He froze. *Leslie?* Memories flashed, images of Madigan's clone, the thing that he'd believed was his wife, preying on his emotions. No, not the clone. Madigan wasn't talking about the clone. He was talking about his wife. His *real* wife, before she died.

"She was on the verge of joining my team. I recruited her myself. All she kept talking about was you. What you would say, what you would think when she left you and your marriage and joined my unit. You were a nothing attorney who still acted like a college boy, and she could have done so much better. I was sick of hearing about you. When she died, I thought, 'at least I never have to hear about Jack Spiers again'." Madigan chuckled, shaking his head. "Imagine my surprise when you ended up the poster boy for the Republicans trying to rebrand their image."

Trembling settled over his body. Madigan squinted at him. "You never saw it, did you? You were only picked for the nomination because you weren't a threat. You were soft. Malleable. Attractive enough to sweep the votes of people who didn't care about policy. You were the safe choice, Jack. And, just like Leslie did, the world chose to bide their time with you until they didn't need you any longer."

Madigan's words hit him like bullets. His hands shook, his arms, his whole body. He tried to breathe, but his chest was too tight. His eyes slipped closed.

No, Madigan wasn't going to rewrite his history.

"No one expected anything from you. Which made you the perfect target for my coup. No one could be disappointed in a man they expected nothing from. You are an *insignificant* president and an *insignificant* man. Always in the wrong place at the right time."

Jack opened his eyes. Stared into Madigan's.

Maybe it was all true. Maybe he had been about to lose Leslie, and maybe his rise in his party was only because he'd been a moderate, a man dedicated to building bridges across the aisle for the length of his career. Maybe he was seen as weak, and every criticism from Congress, every attack in the press, every dark thing whispered about him by his detractors was true.

But he'd also found Ethan. Had fallen in love with him, and found the man who'd unlocked the depths of his soul. Found the love of his life.

That was true. Their love, their life together. What they built. What they shared. The vows they made, first by their choices and their actions, and then by their rings and words. Their love was the foundation of his life, the very definition, the meaning of his life. Beyond politics, beyond the presidency, beyond even the world; Ethan was everything that made his days worth waking up for.

In the length of his entire life, he could point to one unwavering truth: he loved Ethan to the depths of his soul. And Ethan loved him in return. And if that was the worth of his life, if that was what all he had, well—

He was the wealthiest man who had ever lived.

Jack grinned. "Wrong place at the right time?" He nodded, counting down in his head. *Five... Four...* "I can live with that."

He imagined the torpedo streaking in under the ice cap, silent in the dark waters. He could almost feel it, thrumming through the ocean. Closer, closer, any moment now. He stared into Madigan's dark eyes.

Deep beneath their feet, in the bowels of the ship, two torpedoes struck the hull under the ice, right on her midline. She shuddered, quivering like her hull was a gong that had just been rung. For a moment, there was silence.

And then the *Veduschiy* heaved, rising up in the air, tossed from the sea, before crashing back down. A torrent of freezing water shot high, massive waves rising over the deck. Madigan's men tried to run, but most were swept off their feet as the waves broke over the bow, knocking them down and sending them careening toward the railing and the side of the ship. Shouts rose, everyone searching for a handhold, scrabbling fruitlessly to hang on.

Water pounded down on them, scouring Madigan's men off the *Veduschiy's* deck. Shrieking, they bowled over the edge and plummeted to the hard ice below, where their bodies broke, snapping in half or smearing to paste against the glacier.

The man who had held Ethan's chain, who had strangled him, screamed as the waters swept him off his feet and slammed him into a steel gun cage. His spine cracked, the snap loud enough for Jack to savor, and he flopped over the side of the *Veduschiy*, plunging to the ice, limp and broken.

The bridge, rising over the top deck in a tower of rusted steel, crumpled, folding in on itself as rivets popped and blew, and girders collapsed. Metal groaned and screamed, torn apart as the *Veduschiy* slammed onto the ice cap. Another wave crashed over the deck, soaking Jack and spinning him around. Shouts turned to warbles, shrieks to rumbling whale song as he flailed under water, almost swept away.

Jack dove for Ethan, gritting his teeth as he clung to the deck through the pounding wall of water crashing on top of him. Madigan's men swept away before his eyes, but he pushed forward, grabbing Ethan and holding on with his fingers, digging into a deck plate with all of his strength. Ethan's weight tore at him, and he screamed as his arm pulled hard. God, it felt like it was going to rip out of its socket.

And then the wave subsided, and he hauled Ethan close. Shivering, blue-lipped, and pale as a ghost, but alive. He palmed Ethan's cheeks, ran his fingers through Ethan's soaked hair, and unwound the chain from his neck. Rusted links pulled chunks of his skin away, and more blood trickled from his wounds.

Metal shrieked, the ship ripping apart like a toy twisted in half. Her keel was blown. Her back had broken. Her two halves groaned as they were pulled apart by the waves.

She'd split in half, and the *Veduschiy* was going down.

Beneath their feet, the bow tilted, slowly tipping backward as it began to sink into the black, frigid waters.

Somewhere, Madigan was shouting, trying to bellow orders in the madness, but most of his men had already been washed overboard. Jack spotted Cook hauling Madigan away, escaping from the chaos and the destruction.

"Jack…" Bloodstained tears rolled down Ethan's cheeks. "You said— You shouldn't have—"

He kissed Ethan's temple. "I can never leave you, no matter what's at stake. *You* are my world, Ethan. My everything."

Ethan pitched forward, into his arms. Jack grabbed him and helped him stand. Already, the deck beneath their feet was dangerously slanted.

Adam had managed to shake free from his captors at the first blast. Jack saw him beating one of the men who had restrained him, the pipe that had been in his mouth raining blows on the man's face and head, over and over, turning his captor to a bloody pulp.

Sasha had thrown himself over Sergey when the wave crashed, but now one of Madigan's last fighters hauled him away, trying to strangle him with the loose end of Ethan's chain. Sergey worked his bound arms beneath his feet and in front of his body, and then tackled the fighter, looping his arms around the man's throat as Sasha rolled away. Coughing, Sasha pulled the chain off his neck as Sergey slowly strangled his attacker. Sergey's arms strained, shaking, and he grit his teeth, screaming the last few seconds until the man went limp and slumped to the deck.

Adam threw his captor over the railing and turned to Jack. Blood covered half his face, and he clenched the pipe in one hand. Sergey grabbed two guns and a knife off the man he'd killed. He cut Sasha's restraints, and then Sasha cut his, squeezing Sergey's shaking hands after. Jack watched them, watched Sergey close his eyes and sway into Sasha's hold before they joined Jack and Ethan.

Sasha sliced through Ethan's restraints, and Ethan wrapped his arm around Jack's waist, leaning hard against him.

The remnants of Madigan's army in the shantytown raced toward them, firing blindly at the sinking, broken *Veduschiy*. Giant fissures opened in the ice cap, cracking and snapping, broken apart by the *Veduschiy*'s blast. Spider lines stretched all the way to K-27.

K-27 rolled, rocking on massive waves that bounced her practically out of the black water and onto the ice.

They shuffled away, trying to keep their balance. The deck tilted wildly, and they grabbed for anything to keep them upright.

The stern half of the *Veduschiy* sank quickly, the ocean bubbling as half of her was swallowed by the waves. Screams and cries filled the air, men struggling to escape and metal shearing apart. Bullets cracked overhead and slammed into the steel hull.

A second boom split the air.

K-27 rose, riding what looked like a geyser, and fell, slamming into the cracked ice cap. Her rotten hull shattered, metal splintering and bursting apart, cracking open like dropped eggs all over the fractured ice. She started to slide, her heavy stern pulled down by the water. Her hull scrapped along the ice, shearing sodden, decrepit steel from her frame. A million nails scratched across a chalkboard, steel gouging into ice. The ice cap splintered, breaking apart beneath K-27's massive frame, plunging her stern deeper into the sea. And then, K-27's nose tipped upward, standing high in the sky, as if in farewell, as she slipped down, her mangled hull sinking into the water before her nose finally disappeared beneath the ice.

Ethan barked out a gasp as Jack buried his face in his neck. "Holy shit," he breathed. "I can't believe—"

The ship bucked hard, knocking them off their feet. Ethan lost his balance, but Jack and Sasha grabbed him, supported him on both sides.

The last of the stern disappeared beneath the roiling water, feet from where they clung to the *Veduschiy*'s bow railing. Dark waves lapped at the deck. They had moments before where they were standing would be engulfed by the ocean

"Got to move!" Adam grunted. He hauled himself to the railing, scrambling across the nearly vertical deck. "We have to jump!"

Beneath the ship, broken ice churned in the dark, freezing water. Ice that had frozen to the *Veduschiy*'s hull had broken away, shattered from the blast. If they jumped now, they'd be plunging into below-freezing water.

Jack eyed Ethan. His dry suit was ruined, the top half cut away and his chest exposed. Those bruises most likely covered broken ribs. Could he survive a jump into the Arctic Ocean?

The remains of the bow lurched. He grabbed the railing, now nearly vertical, and hauled Ethan alongside. Gurgling waters swallowed the *Veduschiy*'s bow.

Either way, they were going into the sea.

Sasha and Sergey appeared at the railing alongside Jack and Ethan. Sergey set his jaw and climbed over the railing, holding on with both hands. They were maybe fifteen feet above the water and sinking fast.

Sasha helped Jack maneuver Ethan over the railing. Ethan still clung to Jack, leaning heavily on him, but he held himself up while Jack and Sasha clambered over.

Twelve feet to the freezing water. Churning waves roared, soaking them with frigid spray that stung like knives. The bow section was nearly vertical. Jack felt his hands slip. Felt Ethan's body shake violently, straining to hold on. The ocean roared, the *Veduschiy's* steel frame shuddering.

"Jump as far as you can!" Adam bellowed. "Swim away, or you'll get sucked down with the ship!"

Jack looked at Ethan. Was he strong enough to swim clear? He gripped Ethan's hand, lacing their fingers together. Ethan squeezed back as he closed his eyes. They'd get through this together.

Beside them, Sergey did the same, grasping Sasha's hand as he stared at the waters below.

Jack's chest heaved, breaths coming hard and fast, almost too fast. His body tightened, his bones puckering as his stomach folded in on itself.

"Jump! Now!" Adam roared. "Now!" He let go first, throwing himself off the railing and into the waves.

Sergey and Sasha jumped together. Twin splashes rose beside Adam's.

Jack caught Ethan's gaze. Ethan stared back, exhaustion and terror-laced apprehension tangling together. His body kept shaking, trembling against Jack's side.

"I've got you," Jack breathed. "Always."

Ethan nodded.

Jack gripped Ethan's hand and took a breath. They leaped.

Freefall snatched him and Ethan and threw them down. For a moment, there was just the icy wind blowing past them, ruffling their hair and whistling past their ears.

Then, impact. Below-freezing water grabbed Jack, tearing at his skin and shredding his muscles. His lungs seized, shocked by the punch of the cold. He wanted to gasp underwater, reflexively drag in a shocked breath to satiate his terrified body. Lightning seemed to race through him, stiffening his muscles until he could barely move. His mind went flat, thoughts hammered away as if he was being sucked down a vortex, a whirlpool. Beneath him, the dark mass of the broken *Veduschiy* plummeted to the depths, metal talons from her broken body reaching back for him, trying to drag him down with the ship. He felt the pull, the yank.

Ethan's grip on his hand slackened.

No. *No.* Jack kicked with everything he had, straining for the surface. Fractal light shimmered above, rolling diamonds in deep turquoise waves. Ethan's hand opened completely, going slack, but Jack gripped his wrist as Ethan's body drifted beneath him, limp and weightless. Kicking again, Jack grit his teeth and screamed, struggling to pull them both free. Bubbles rose around him as he strained against the tug of the *Veduschiy*'s grave.

And then, like a rope snapping, he shot upward, free from the *Veduschiy*. He hauled Ethan with him, shoving him above him, kicking as fast as he'd ever kicked, up toward the light—

They broke the surface together, Jack gasping as Ethan bobbed motionless by his side. Bullets and shrieks filled the air, and the creaking, shattering ice. "Help," he tried to croak. His voice shattered, weak as his body started to shake.

"Jack! Here!" Sergey's hand stretched out, inches from Jack's face.

It seemed miles away. He lunged, grasping Sergey's hand as he hauled Ethan close. "Help him, Sergey!"

Sasha and Adam appeared by Sergey's side, helping to haul them both from the waters and onto the ice. Hundreds of broken bodies littered the glacier and bobbed in the waves—men who had been holding them all hostage only minutes before. He recognized some of the American soldiers-turned-traitors who had met him at the loading dock. He didn't see Kobayashi.

Jack shivered, rolling into Adam as Sasha and Sergey laid Ethan out and checked his breathing. His lips were blue, his skin nearly translucent. A moment later, Sergey began chest compressions.

Jack crawled to Ethan's side and grabbed his hand. He pulled it to his lips, kissing each of his knuckles as Sasha breathed into Ethan's mouth. Sergey resumed chest compressions, cursing softly in Russian.

Sasha leaned down for another breath. His lips locked with Ethan's, and then Ethan sputtered, coughing against him. Sasha pulled back and rolled Ethan to his side as he coughed up what seemed like half of the Arctic.

Jack grasped Ethan and pulled him into his arms, trying to warm him. Immediately, Ethan started to shiver, and Jack ripped off his jacket, wrapping it around Ethan. Sasha helped, layering Ethan's bare chest with what they had. Jack gazed into Ethan's eyes, trying to pour his own body's warmth into Ethan's skin while the whole world seemed to fall apart around them. The sounds of chaos, of anarchy. Of breaking ice and shattered ships, and Madigan's army trying to flee. Snowmobile engines roaring away, and bullets flying through the air. Adam and Sasha huddled nearby, each clutching a rifle they'd scavenged from the dead. More rifles lay between them, a small stack. Together, they sheltered behind a chunk of the *Veduschiy*, what looked like a blown-off bulkhead. It was some cover, at least, from the chaos around them.

Sergey knelt beside Jack, one hand on his shoulder.

"Where is the other sub?" Sasha's growl made Jack's spine stiffen. He and Sergey twisted around, searching over the ice. The black sail that had thrust up through the ice cap alongside K-27 and the *Veduschiy* was gone.

"They might be going after *Honolulu*. Captain Anderson fired on the *Veduschiy* and K-27. I ordered his attack."

"So that is what happened." Sergey smiled weakly. "I thought we were finished."

Ethan pushed himself up, leaning against Jack. "Jack—"

Bullets chewed the ice in front of Sasha and Adam. Chunks flew, peppering their faces. Jack and Sergey rolled over Ethan as Adam and Sasha fired back, ducking behind the bulkhead as shots sparked off metal.

"Who's shooting?" Jack shouted.

Two figures stalked across the ice, firing on their small shelter. Blood streamed down the sides of their faces. One, with a long, curved scar running down the length of his face, threw his rifle away and pulled out a knife. He stopped and pointed it toward them, gaze leveled right at Sasha.

Jack cursed when he recognized the second man: Cook.

A bullet whizzed past Jack's head, a whistle-buzz that made him flatten to the ice.

If Cook had survived, then had Madigan escaped as well? Where was he? The rest of Madigan's army had splintered, escaping across the ice and firing on each other, long-submerged inter-army hatreds seeming to explode with the loss of their commanders.

Jack searched the ice cap, looking everywhere.

There. Behind Cook and the others. A snowmobile screaming away, heading north. A single rider, a man with broad shoulders, wearing the same olive-colored jacket Madigan had been wearing on the *Veduschiy*. The hood fell back—

Madigan. Jack cursed.

Fire roared in his blood, a primal need flooding him to the depths of his soul. Madigan could *not* get away. After everything, after all that he'd done. Madigan could not escape again.

He grabbed Sergey's arm. "Madigan!" he shouted into Sergey's ear. "He's escaping! Going north!"

Jack saw Sasha's gaze flick toward Madigan, and then back to Jack and Sergey. "Go," he grunted. "We will handle these men. Go get him!" He shoved two rifles toward Jack and Sergey and then turned back to Cook.

Ethan. Jack cupped the side of his face. Ethan still shivered, but some color had returned to his skin. "I have to stop him."

Swallowing, Ethan nodded. His jaw clenched tight, and he tried to hide the panic, the terror, and the desperation in his gaze. "Be careful."

"I'm with you all the way." He pressed a quick kiss to Ethan's icy lips. Their words, their promise to each other, enlarged, filling the spaces between them. In this life, and the next, Jack would be with Ethan until the very end.

Sergey pointed to a snowmobile abandoned in the snow, its driver shot dead and lying across the saddle. He squeezed Sasha's shoulder, and then Sasha laid down covering fire as Jack and Sergey sprinted for it. Sergey shoved the body away, and Jack straddled the snowmobile. "Get on!" he shouted. "Madigan is getting away!"

Sergey jumped on and gripped Jack's waist. "Go!"

Engine screaming, they roared away, chasing Madigan.

59

USS Honolulu

THE CONN LOOKED MORE like a traffic accident than the command center of a warship. Flashing and flickering lights pulsated, barely clinging to power. Alert-red and fading-green tried to shine from damaged displays. The plotting table flickered and died. Shouts rose, sailors hollering damage reports and status updates almost faster than Captain Anderson could keep up.

Almost.

Right after they had fired on the *Veduschiy* and K-27, a second submarine had dropped from the ice—the SSBN Sasha had detailed on his map. They hadn't been able to fire on her.

The Russian sub had sunk into the depths, descending far too close for a submariner's comfort. A *Borey*-class ballistic missile submarine, she'd turned on a dime and pointed straight at *Honolulu*. With both of them hovering in the depths, it was as close to a Mexican standoff as two submarines could get.

And then, she'd blasted *Honolulu* with a high-pulsed active sonar ping through the waters. Pure sound waves, sonic energy, burned through the sea, louder than a train horn. At such a close range, the ping was a roar, a weapon all on its own, a spear that slammed into *Honolulu*'s hull. Her metal buzzed and hummed, screaming through the decks and the bulkheads as if cymbals had crashed together. Fluorescent bulbs fizzed and popped as electronics consoles exploded, shattering glass across the deck. Lights flickered wildly.

In submarine warfare, there was only one reason for an active ping: locking on to an enemy vessel's coordinates for an immediate strike. The prelude to an annihilation.

Anderson opened his mouth, and the Conn fell silent instantly. "Helm, left full rudder and give me everything you've got!" *Honolulu* was still limping, barely powered, and her rudder hadn't been fixed. Left full rudder was only a quarter of a turn. "Take us down to two hundred feet, now!"

Honolulu shuddered and shook as she sluggishly responded, lurching to one side as she plunged into the depths. She left a trail of bubbles behind her, a churned wake.

"Conn, Sonar!" Boomer's voice went high and tight. "Torpedo in the water aft! Torpedo in the water aft!" A bright beacon appeared on the flickering overhead screen, a visual representation of the torpedo chasing *Honolulu*.

"Fire a noisemaker!"

"Aye, sir!" Lieutenant Munoz, weapons officer, jammed the button for torpedo countermeasures. A canister shot from one of the torpedo tubes, and as it entered the water, a seal burst and the chemicals within created a raging bubble storm. Hopefully, enough to draw a torpedo's attention.

"Second torpedo in the water!" Boomer's voice went higher. "Third torpedo in the water, Captain!"

"Two hundred feet, Captain." The diving officer's voice shook as he called out *Honolulu's* depth.

"Helm, right full rudder! Drop us down to three-fifty! Make it loud!" Anderson gripped the railing as *Honolulu* plunged deeper and twisted, arching away from her original course. More water churned, a turbulent wake as she groaned and shifted hard. Anderson heard the rudder creak right through *Honolulu*'s hull.

If they dropped low enough, the thermocline could shield them from the torpedoes' passive sonar, and if their wake was loud enough, the torpedoes could mistake the churning for *Honolulu*'s own rudder and engine noise. He watched the fathometer, the depth gauge on *Honolulu*, tick off the feet as they plunged.

"Three hundred feet, Captain!"

The hull screamed, popping and crunching. They'd taken heavy damage fighting Sierra One beneath the ice and were in no position to be in a shootout with another Russian sub.

"The first torpedo hit the noisemaker, Captain! It detonated!"

"And the others?" His fingers clenched down around the railing. They had maybe a few more moves.

Silence, as everyone waited for Boomer's response. The ocean hummed beyond the hull. Lights flickered and danced across nervous faces and wide eyes.

"All detonated, Captain. All torpedoes are a miss." Relief rang through Boomer's voice, and muted cheers rose. "Captain, they didn't follow us."

Anderson frowned. "What are they doing?"

"If I had to guess..." Boomer's voice trailed off. His guess was a calculated interpretation of his sonar array, his screens and what they painted for him. "Sir, they're starting a launch."

"More torpedoes?"

"No, Captain. RSM-56 Bulavas. Cruise missiles."

"Shit." Anderson cursed as he stalked forward. "Helm, bring us back up to ninety feet. Weapons, make ready your torpedoes."

Lieutenant Munoz paled. "Captain, we took a blow to the forward torpedo bay in the last battle. If we launch torpedoes, we could blow the bow off and flood the boat."

"We don't have a choice." Anderson's gaze locked on to Munoz's wide eyes. "We have to stop them from launching, or those cruise missiles will ignite the atmosphere, and everything that the president has done here will have been for nothing."

Munoz nodded once and spun back to his console. His hands shook as he armed six torpedoes, more than would normally ever be fired.

As the boat rose and the deck tilted again, Anderson spared a glance for the last four members of the strike team. Faisal stared back, his dark eyes somber as if he'd already accepted what Anderson feared, unspoken in the center of his chest: they most likely wouldn't make it through this. Doc slumped beside Faisal, a practiced indifference hanging on his thin frame. But his face was pinched, drawn with more than just his endless seasickness. On either side of Faisal, Sergeants Coleman and Wright stood with their legs spread and arms crossed, jaws clenched tight. Classic Marines, stoic to the last, to the very end.

60

Kara Sea – Madigan's Base Camp

AFTER THE TORPEDOES SLAMMED into the *Veduschiy's* hull, Cook shepherded Madigan through the emergency hatch and down the midship external ladder.

On board the sinking *Veduschiy*, he watched Madigan drop the last few feet to the ice and scramble away as the hull of the *Veduschiy* chewed through the edges of the glacier.

Two of Madigan's criminal army had raced across the splintering ice cap on snowmobiles, the first to arrive from their shantytown redoubt.

Madigan shot both in the forehead. They tumbled backward, falling sideways, lifeless as the snowmobiles petered out. Madigan climbed on one of the snowmobiles and barked orders into his radio to their remaining sub.

Those orders echoed in Cook's earpiece as he disappeared back into the bowels of the *Veduschiy*.

He had to buy Madigan time.

Cook headed for his cabin, stumbling through the tilted hallways and holding on with both hands. There was something he had to get.

He'd taken over the executive officer's cabin on board, a palatial space compared to his jail cell. The metal walls made the room frigidly cold, almost like he was back home in the cellblock of Z Unit. There was a narrow bunk built against the cabin's hull, but he'd always slept better on hard concrete or steel. He rested on the floor.

His guest had been handcuffed to the bunk, anyway. After his failure, he was lucky to be alive. Madigan had insisted on keeping him alive, and Cook had insisted on keeping him under watch. But now, he'd serve a purpose.

Cook spun open the lock and shoved the hatch to his cabin open.

His guest was already up, standing beside his bunk and bent awkwardly as he strained against the restraints. His shirt was bloodstained, the rough stitches on his chest and back oozing blood. A knife lay on the floor, tossed from Cook's shelves. He'd obviously been trying to reach it.

Well. It had been his, after all.

Cook grabbed the knife and ripped it from its sheath. He stalked across the cabin and cut through the man's restraints, then spun the knife around, offering him the handle.

The man's dark eyes flicked from the handle to Cook's face. He said nothing.

"There's someone here you have unfinished business with," Cook growled. "A pilot."

Reichenbach and Spiers had survived. Lieutenant Cooper had escaped. The Russian president, too.

And Puchkov's constant companion—the mysterious fighter pilot who had overflown their base the week before.

Lieutenant Paloshenko, Siberian *Spetsnaz*, took the blade from Cook. His fingers wrapped around the handle slowly. "I will slit his throat," he growled, his vowels rolling in his deep Russian accent. He raised the blade, pointing it in Cook's face. "And then I will slit yours. You will face me."

He grabbed Paloshenko and shoved him across the wildly tilted cabin, through the hatch. "Fucking move, before this whole ship is underwater."

61

Washington DC

"SENATOR, GENERAL, IN HERE!" Welby ushered General Bell and Senator Allen into Horsepower and left them behind, racing across the bunker-like room to the weapons lockers.

Alarms wailed, sirens and old-fashioned alert bells clanging in the hallways. Horsepower's main screens were red, the offices of the West Wing highlighted and blown up on-screen, showing the details of Jennifer's attack. She and her team had stormed into the West Wing by the Press Briefing Room. She'd shot up Pete's office, the empty Cabinet Room, and then made her way down the hall toward the Roosevelt Room and Oval Office. The first wave of Secret Service had held her and her team off long enough to evacuate the Roosevelt Room.

Welby had Pete to thank for that.

He'd been in Horsepower, reviewing footage on all cameras, searching for any sign of Levi and President Wall leaving the premises. Damn it, but Levi was too good. He'd been trained by Ethan, and Ethan knew all the tricks. Hell, he'd used them all to date President Spiers. If Levi had been the one to smuggle President Wall out of the White House, he'd covered his tracks personally.

He'd been grinding through another playback when his phone had rung.

"Welby."

"*It's Jennifer.*" He'd never heard Pete's voice shake like that. Even over the phone, he heard Pete's panic, sensed his terror. "*It's fucking Jennifer.*"

"What?"

"*Jason just called me. She met a group of guys in the East Wing garage. They had guns. She shot him. He's bleeding out down there!*"

His chair flew back when he stood up and crashed into the far wall. He'd barked orders to his men, calling for the video feeds to be pulled up. Nothing but snow and static on the East Wing cameras—someone had destroyed them already.

But he'd spotted her leading a team through the Residence, almost to the West Wing.

His palm hit the alarm switch as he shouted for the agents to grab their weapons and initiate intruder procedures. "Pete, we're coming for you."

They'd barely managed to evacuate Pete and the rest of the offices in the West Wing before Jennifer had blasted her way in.

He'd found General Bell and Senator Allen in the empty Vice President's office. Wide-eyed, Senator Allen had hovered behind General Bell. Welby had to shout at him twice to get him to move, to run in front of him down the hall to the stairs that would lead them to the ground floor.

Welby watched the monitor as he shed his jacket and strapped on a flak vest. He'd had no time to grab one before running to rescue the rest of the staff. "Where is she going?" On-screen, Jennifer moved quickly down the hallways, slipping past the Oval Office. She didn't seem to care about the president's spaces.

Pete appeared beside him, his hands laced behind his head. "Holy shit," he breathed, watching Jennifer. "Holy fucking shit."

"How did we miss this?" Welby slammed three new clips of ammo onto his belt and checked the clip in his weapon. He'd fired six shots already.

"God, she has total access to the White House. The Residence, everything, because of her stupid fucking flowers!" Pete grit his teeth, almost screaming. "She wasn't on the manifest for the flight to Russia. She came onboard at the last minute, something about the flowers, she said. They needed to be tended in flight. Not like other times, where they could just be put in water. She insisted on coming. I thought she just wanted to spend time with Jason. And I thought she was cleared. I thought she was listed."

"What's Jason's status?"

"He sounded fucking bad on the phone." Pete's voice shook. He scrubbed his hands over his face, watching Jennifer kick down one of the doors to an unmarked room in the West Wing.

"Oh fuck," Welby hissed.

Pete echoed him. "Fucking hell, not that."

Welby shouted over the din of agents loading up and strapping on their flak vests. Forty agents had assembled in Horsepower, and more held down the rest of the White House and surrounded the West Wing. "Listen up! Our target has just led her team to the elevator entrance to the PEOC!" Behind him, Jennifer laid her palm on the keypad, and the reinforced steel doors to the presidential elevator slid open. "She's entering the elevator and descending to the bunker!"

The PEOC, the Presidential Emergency Operations Center. All cleared West Wing staff had access to it, in case they were the last line of defense, and they were the ones who had to get the president down to the bunker. Pete frowned. "What the fuck is she doing down there?"

"Nothing good." Welby nodded to his men. "I want two teams to work on breaching the bunker from the East Wing. Try and drill through the vault doors there."

"Sir, it's—"

"I know it's reinforced, and I know it's meant to withstand a nuclear blast. Do what you can. We have to get in there. Get creative." He jerked his head, sending two teams out the door. "The rest of you are going to secure the West Wing. Post up triple strength around the Situation Room. Escort Senator Allen there, too." Most of the staff had retired to the Situation Room, and the Speaker of the House was on a secured connection from the Capitol. The national security staff were in there as well, along with General Bradford and CIA Director Mori.

The agents filed out. As they went, each laid their palm over a picture taped by the door. It had appeared right after the Langley blast, both a reminder and a testament. A way to honor their fallen, and a promise to do better.

Each agent touched a picture of President Spiers and Ethan Reichenbach, their former boss, dancing arm in arm at the White House Christmas Ball.

Welby spared a glance for General Bell and Senator Allen as the senator was escorted from Horsepower. General Bell had to know what it meant. Did Senator Allen?

By the shocked look on their faces, both men registered the impact. Back in the war, when Welby had served, he and his men used to slap a picture of the World Trade Center in New York City before battle, reminding them why they were there and what they were doing.

He turned away, listening on the radio as his teams checked in.

"Agent Welby." General Bell stood behind him, unbuttoning his dress uniform jacket. "I'm coming with you." He reached for one of the flak jackets hanging in the weapons locker.

"Sir—"

Pete interrupted. "I'm coming too." He mimicked General Bell's movements, slipping the flak jacket over his head and securing the straps around his chest and under his arms.

"Sir, with all due respect, you *cannot* come with me. This is the White House and this is a Secret Service operation—"

"Son, I co-wrote the book on urban warfare, and that includes fighting within urban structures. That bunker is secured so that there is only one entrance in or out, and that's through the elevator. You sent the rest of your team away, but you're strapping up for a mission, which means you're about to do something that you know is ri-god-damn-diculous. And no matter what you think, you can't do it alone. I *know* what you're planning." General Bell arched one eyebrow at him. "Am I on the right track?"

Welby hesitated. Could he trust General Bell? He still didn't know. Pete hovered as well, watching him. If he couldn't trust Bell, could he trust Pete? Pete was friends with Jennifer. How had he missed who she was? *What* she was?

He closed his eyes and took a breath. Paranoia had seized Levi, taken hold of him until he almost blew apart.

If he'd learned one thing from Ethan, and from President Spiers, it was that they were stronger together. Everyone, always. He locked eyes with General Bell, and with Pete, and then nodded. "All right. We need all the explosives you can carry."

"HOLY GOD, WELBY, WHATEVER you're doing, make it fast."

Word spread quickly that he was on the move, attempting a breach. The teams at the East Wing entrance weren't having any luck. Agent Beech had taken command in the Situation Room. He was within, protecting General Bradford and Director Mori. He also had a front-row seat to what Jennifer was up to in the bunker.

They'd established a live feed from the PEOC to the Situation Room. Standard procedure, in the event of a national emergency. Now, a means to watch Jennifer and her team. Agent Beech was now his eyes and ears.

"Status? What's going on?" He listened as he and General Bell laid a final brick of explosives around the base of the reinforced elevator doors. There was no way they were getting them open. Pneumatic locks had shut, all but permanently sealing the elevator from the outside world. Pete waited at the corner, keeping watch down both hallways branching off the Oval Office.

"Jesus Christ, one of the guys with her pulled out fucking body parts from his bag. A severed hand and an eyeball. The hand fucking matches the president's prints. Jesus fucking Christ..."

His blood went cold. He stopped breathing. "President Wall's?"

"No. President Spiers's."

It can't be. No, no, it can't be. He breathed hard, his thoughts racing. Spiers was with Ethan, and they were somewhere else, somewhere far away from here. Or were they? When was the last Levi had heard from them? He hadn't said. What if their mission, whatever it was, had failed?

A chill settled over his body as a different thought slammed into him, nearly toppling him over.

What if the hand and eyeball were cloned?

Jennifer had unrestricted access to the White House, even the residence. They'd had recent experience with clones—too recent—and the early reports were that Captain Leslie Spiers's DNA had been stolen from Army databases. Madigan had stolen the blueprints to her identity.

Could Jennifer have done the same? Stolen Spiers's DNA from the Residence? A full-body clone was a massive undertaking, on the fringes of medical science, even. But... body parts were made all the time.

What could she do with President Spiers's hand and eyeball?

The answer came over the radio. *"She's calling up the nuclear launch protocols. President Spiers's palmprint still has access. She's able to get into fucking everything."*

Welby cursed. If he'd been waiting for final proof that President Spiers was still alive, that was it. Levi and President Wall hadn't canceled his clearance or his access. They were expecting him to come back. "We need to go. Now." He waved General Bell and Pete back, jogging around the corner. They huddled by the shot-up door to the Roosevelt Room.

General Bell held the detonator in his hand. He passed it to Welby. "It's your house."

Welby shot him a glare and grabbed the detonator. He pressed the trigger.

A deafening boom burst from around the corner. The walls shook and the floor trembled. He heard doors fly off their hinges and wood splinter, glass shatter from portraits and paintings. Walls creaking and plaster cracking. For the second time in a year, the White House was crumbling under attack.

He waited, counting five seconds for the rubble to settle, and then popped up. "Let's go." He drew his weapon and clicked on his flashlight, holding it crossed below his grip.

They picked their way through the dark, smoke-filled hallway. Power had been cut to the White House, and the blast sprayed plaster dust and debris into the air. They moved like shadows, sidestepping broken furniture and paintings and over destroyed walls that been ripped apart.

Welby finally smiled, relieved for a half second, when they spotted the elevator. "It worked."

They'd blasted a hole in the flooring beneath the elevator's locked-shut doors. A dark opening yawned in front of the elevator, and the steel reinforced barrier surrounding the elevator shaft had cracked. Welby shined his flashlight through the tear.

He had a clear line of sight to the elevator cables.

"We're in," he called over the radio. "We're going down to the bunker."

"Better fucking hurry. She's trying to crack his verification launch code. She's got two of the six digits already!"

62

Kara Sea – Madigan's Base Camp

Ethan dragged himself across the ice, kneeling behind Sasha and Adam. His hands shook as he grasped a rifle, but he hefted it to his shoulder. He recognized Cook, and his sneer, as he sighted in on the man.

Sasha cursed as one of the men pointed a knife his way and shouted in Russian. "Paloshenko. *Spetsnaz* who tracked me in Siberia," Sasha spat. "Should have put a bullet in his brain."

They kept firing until their rifles ran dry. They'd scavenged them off the dead; they had no ammo, no way to reload. Adam snarled and ducked beneath the bulkhead they were using as cover. Three bullets slammed into the metal, making dents by his head.

And then, Cook's rifle clicked. He was out of ammo, too.

Sasha rose first, flinging his weapon aside and charging for Paloshenko. He bared his teeth, growling like an animal as he ran. He ducked low, his arms spread wide, and threw himself at Paloshenko as the *Spetsnaz* officer braced himself and swung down with his knife. The blade flashed, flying over Sasha's shoulder, and both men went down to the ice in a long skid.

Red smeared behind them.

Cook kept his focus on Ethan and Adam. He threw his empty rifle aside and pulled out a handgun. Two bullets slammed into their shield, in-between Ethan and Adam's faces.

"How does it feel, Adam?" Cook shouted. Wind whipped his words away. His voice strained, shouting over the chaos surrounding them. "How does it feel to have killed your team? You might as well have blown them up yourself!"

Ethan grabbed Adam's wrist, holding him back. Adam's eyes burned, rage igniting his soul. He shook beneath Ethan's touch.

"Jack used your pain, Ethan." Cook's voice dropped, a dangerous bellow. "He didn't come to save *you*. He came as a distraction! He would have let you die!"

It was Adam's turn to grab him. Ethan held Adam's gaze as his own hands shook, trembled against Adam's hold. It wasn't true. Cook didn't know Jack. He was just trying to get under Ethan's skin.

Cook hadn't seen the look in Jack's eyes on top of the *Veduschiy*. When Jack saw him on the deck, barely hanging on. Why *had* he held on? Why had he fought Cook's torture? They had been as good as defeated. Out of options. All he'd wanted, all he'd wished for, begged for, as Cook held him down and waterboarded him, was for Jack to get away. To be safe, somewhere far, far away when the world went up in flames.

And then Jack had come to him. A part of his heart had collapsed at that, seeing Jack there, surrendering to Cook and Madigan.

But they were together all the way. Jack had come back for *him*.

A third bullet slammed into the bulkhead, denting the metal by Ethan's temple. A click followed, and then another.

Cook was out of bullets.

Ethan's eyes flicked to Adam's. Their gazes locked.

Adrenaline surged through him, liquid steel that flooded his veins, pumped iron into his muscles. His bones were wreathed in titanium, his strength returned to him in a rush that set his body on fire. For the moment, he was invincible.

By the look in Adam's eyes, so was he.

"Together," Ethan said. "We do this together."

Adam nodded.

They rose, Adam vaulting over the broken bulkhead as Ethan scrambled around it. They charged Cook, bellowing as they ran.

Cook met them in a boxer's stance, parrying Adam's wild punch but missing Ethan's. Ethan ducked and slammed his fist into Cook's belly, doubling him over. Adam jumped behind Cook, sweeping his feet out from beneath him and dropping him to the ice. As he fell, Cook tackled Ethan, dragging him down.

They landed in a heap on the ice, grappling and snarling. Ethan clawed at Cook, trying to shove him off, but Cook had the advantage. He rose over Ethan, gripped his neck in both hands, and slammed Ethan's head against the ice.

"No!" Adam charged Cook, trying to tear him off Ethan. He wrapped his arm around Cook's neck and squeezed. Cook reached for him with one hand, and Ethan managed to drag in a ragged breath.

A gunshot split the air, cracking like a whip.

Adam staggered backward, stumbling away from Cook. A red stain bloomed on the front of his jacket.

Cook turned back to Ethan, grinning wildly. He gripped Ethan's throat in both hands, leaning his whole body's weight into his grasp as he straddled Ethan's body. He seemed to be searching for something, his fingers feeling out the bones of Ethan's spine through his skin.

Ethan's legs kicked, scissoring wildly beneath Cook's crouch. His superhuman strength, a gift of adrenaline, faded, leached away by the ice and his weakened body. His vision dimmed, growing dark around the edges, and all he could see was Cook's mad grin and the insane light in his eyes, staring down at Ethan's last moments.

PALOSHENKO WENT DOWN HARD, Sasha on top of him. His knife sliced through Sasha's jacket, through skin. Sasha felt his muscle open up, felt warm blood flow down his back.

They skidded, grappling for the upper hand. Sasha twisted, rolling into Paloshenko's arm and slamming it down. He flattened Paloshenko's hand against the ice, dragging it beneath their skid. Paloshenko bared his teeth and growled in Sasha's face, but refused to let go.

Fine.

Sasha slammed his head into Paloshenko's, bashing his skull back against the ice. He moved fast, driving a one-two series of punches into Paloshenko's ribs before grabbing his blade open-handed and ripping it away. Blood wept from his sliced hand, but in a single motion, Sasha flipped the blade around and slammed it into the center of Paloshenko's palm, thrusting it into the ice.

Paloshenko roared. He thrashed beneath Sasha, kicking hard and swinging his hips, unbalancing Sasha just enough to throw him sideways. Sasha rolled away.

Paloshenko pulled the knife from the ice and through his palm, slowly. Blood dripped from the blade and ran down his hand, down his fingers, staining the glacier.

Shoulders heaving, Paloshenko stalked toward Sasha. Sasha waited, hands loose and ready. Lunging, Paloshenko swiped the blade down across Sasha's face, his chest. Sasha ducked, and then ducked again as Paloshenko kept coming, kept lunging and ducking away, trying to slice him clean through from his throat to his groin.

Sasha ripped his jacket off. He held it by its sleeves, the fabric loose between his arms.

Paloshenko's eye twitched. He roared and charged, swinging fast and furious at Sasha.

The blade nicked Sasha's cheek, sliced down his jaw.

Sasha spun, rolling into Paloshenko's hold, and wrapped his jacket-covered hands around Paloshenko's arm. Caught, Paloshenko struggled, cursing, but Sasha twisted the jacket, tightening his grasp.

His back was to Paloshenko, their bodies aligned. Paloshenko wrapped one arm around his neck and started to squeeze.

Sasha grabbed his hair and yanked him forward, lifting Paloshenko's feet from the ice as Sasha doubled over.

Roaring, Sasha flung them both backward, his momentum sending them both into the air before slamming back down to the ice, landing hard on Paloshenko's back.

Crack!

Paloshenko gasped for breath, stunned and flailing on the ice. His legs went limp and loose, no longer kicking, no longer thrashing. Sasha scrambled as Paloshenko struggled to roll over and tried to drag himself away, reaching out with his bloody hand and pulling his broken body by the furrows of the glacier.

Sasha plucked the knife from where it had fallen on the ice. He stalked back grabbed Paloshenko, rolled him to his back, and stared down at the man.

Broken, bleeding, and shivering, Paloshenko glared back up at him. Fury and hatred burned in his eyes, black pools of emptiness that wanted to swallow Sasha's soul. How many had he killed, hunting for Sasha in Siberia? Kilaqqi's men hadn't been the only ones to pay the price for Paloshenko's merciless hunt. Kilaqqi, a man who gave everything he had to a stranger, only because he could. And Paloshenko had tried to murder him. Before that, even, Paloshenko had served with Moroshkin and had joined in his coup. Had taken Sergey's government from him.

Wanted to take Sergey's life from him.

He slammed the blade into Paloshenko's chest, into the center of his heart, and watched his empty eyes go dim, and the hatred flare out of his gaze.

ADAM TURNED TOWARD THE gunshot as his blood stained the front of his jacket. He pressed his palm over his wound, ignoring the pain as his eyes caught on the man who'd fired.

Finally.

Standing behind him, swaying in the wind, stood Kobayashi. Blood covered one side of his face, matted his hair. His eyes were glassy, unfocused, but he blinked fast and sneered at Adam. "Lieutenant!" he shouted. "You've lost! It's over!"

The rage, the all-consuming, world-ending fury he'd felt when he realized Kobayashi was working *against* him, was working *for* Madigan, roared through his soul again. Kobayashi had played him, had played them all. He'd killed Park.

Had helped Cook and Madigan set up the ambush at the RusFuel station.

Had helped kill Faisal, the love of his life.

Adam started for Kobayashi. The rest of the world blurred: the glacier, the roiling seas and the cracked ice, Cook and Ethan, scrabbling and snarling, Sasha and Paloshenko, wrestling in a pool of blood. Even the gunshot in his belly, bleeding down the inside of his jacket.

He murmured softly, prayers for the dead that he hadn't yet spoken. Prayers for Faisal, and prayers for himself. *Soon, I'll be with you,* habibi. "Pardon my sins which are many and accept my deeds which are very little. Allah, forgive Faisal, and forgive me, for what I am about to do. Faisal is blessed, Allah. Bring him among the guided ones, raise him up, and let him by your side. Lord of the two worlds, forgive us, and make Faisal's grave wide and full of light." He swallowed. "Tell him I love him."

He kept stalking toward Kobayashi. Kobayashi's eyes widened, and he fired again at Adam.

The second shot grazed Adam's shoulder. He kept walking.

Kobayashi fired again. This time, his shot went wide. He squeezed the trigger again.

His weapon clicked.

Out of ammo.

Adam smiled, a wild, feral baring of his teeth. He burst forward, racing the final feet that separated him and Kobayashi, and tackled Kobayashi to the ice. Howling, Kobayashi tried to get away.

Adam was bigger than Kobayashi, taller, stronger, even while shot. He manhandled Kobayashi, throwing him down and straddling him, pinning his arms beneath Adam's knees. He ground Kobayashi's face into the ice, slamming his skull again and again. Blood pooled beneath Kobayashi, from his nose and his temple, and the back of his head. Bone crunched along the side of Kobayashi's skull, like cracked eggshells beneath Adam's fingers.

Adam's arms tingled, though, and his hands grasping Kobayashi's hair slackened. Blood loss was a bitch, stealing his strength when he needed it most. He could feel his blood pumping out of him.

He scoured the glacier, searching for something, anything to help him. He was weakening, and he needed to end this, now.

A chunk of broken ice the size of a basketball rested only a foot away. Shorn from the ice pack, it had sharp, jagged edges, and had probably been frozen solid for a hundred years.

Perfect.

Staggering, Adam scrambled for the chunk of ice. He hefted it in both hands and turned back. Kobayashi tried to slither away. Adam stumbled after him, heaving the ice chunk over his head on trembling arms.

Kobayashi screamed and threw his hands up, trying to block Adam's blow. Adam dropped to his knees, using his body's fall to help drive the ice down, slamming it into Kobayashi's face, and then again, into the side of his skull. Kobayashi's arms fell away as he went limp, motionless on the blood-drenched ice.

Adam pitched sideways, collapsing beside him. He tried to breathe, to keep drawing in slow, shallow breaths. Crimson spread beneath Kobayashi, reaching across the glacier to him. He splayed his hand out, resting his fingertips in the spreading pool.

Kobayashi's eyelids fluttered. "I... wasn't... alone..." he croaked. His chest rattled as his body trembled, and Kobayashi's last breath slipped from his lips.

Adam closed his eyes and rolled to his back. *Faisal. I'll see you soon, ya hayati.*

ETHAN STRUGGLED TO BREATHE, gasping against Cook's hold around his throat. Cook's hands were massive, both circling his neck, all the way around to his spine. The crime scene photos from Cook's jailbreak flashed in his mind: the young guard had had his spine broken, an internal decapitation by someone ripping out his vertebrae.

Cook's fingers closed around the knobs of his spine as if searching for handholds. His nails dug into the open cuts on Ethan's neck, the wounds where Cook's chain had already broken his skin, almost down to his muscle.

He thrashed, trying to throw Cook off. It was no use. He might as well have tried to move a mountain. His own hands wrapped around Cook's neck, squeezing, but his strength was gone, bled out of him through Cook's torture and their escape into the freezing waters. Cook would kill him long before he could even make Cook dizzy.

Still, he couldn't just give up. Ethan kept squeezing, even as the world started to darken around the edges of his gaze.

"Ethan!" A voice shouted over the ice pack, a hoarse bellow.

A voice he would recognize anywhere. A voice that had been with him for nearly his whole life. A man he trusted to his bones.

"Ethan!"

The rumble of a snowmobile engine, running at the engine's redline, screaming almost out of control.

Gunshots, wild firing, chewing the ice beside him. Cook looked up, glaring, and his grip slackened momentarily. Ethan sucked in a partial breath before Cook's hands closed again.

Scott, be ready. I only have one shot at this. Ethan let go of Cook's throat and slammed both his palms against the underside of Cook's jaw, shoving his face upward.

Cook's hands closed tighter around his throat, choking out all his air. He felt bones twist in his neck, his trachea start to collapse as Cook's fingers gripped the edges of his vertebrae. Moments, he had moments. Ethan pushed, heaving with all his might, straining through gritted teeth as he pushed Cook up, up, up—

A shotgun blast boomed, echoing over the glacier. And then another. A third. Cook's head exploded, half his face melting away as Ethan held his chin high, pushing him up for Scott's aim.

Blood and bone and bits of brain poured down on Ethan, coating him. Cook's hands went slack around his throat.

Ethan gasped, dragging in breath after breath as he shoved Cook's corpse sideways.

Footsteps pounded over the glacier, and then Scott slid beside him, grabbed him, pulled him close. "Holy shit!" Scott shouted. "Ethan! Jesus, Ethan!" Scott's hands went everywhere, searching for wounds.

Coughing and hacking, Ethan nodded, slapping at Scott's shoulder. His body burned, his ribs ached, and his lungs felt like they were still filled with water. Like he was still drowning, even doubled over on the ice. "Adam," he choked out, through his bruised and bloody throat. "Adam was shot."

Scott cursed, but clambered to his feet. He gave Ethan his shotgun and jogged to where Adam lay. Nearby, Sasha, pale and unsteady, trudged back toward Ethan, one bloody hand pressed to his shoulder. He collapsed to his knees in the snow and pitched over on his side.

Ethan gripped Scott's shotgun and looked north. His eyes followed the tracks Jack and Sergey had made with their snowmobile until their trail disappeared into the gloom. He couldn't help Jack now.

What Jack had to do, he had to do on his own.

His eyes slipped closed as he swallowed. *Jack... Be safe. Come back to me.*

63

USS Honolulu

"Range to the sub?" Anderson's voice went taut as his jaw clenched. The crew was wound tight, the atmosphere in the Conn heavy enough to sink the boat. The world hung on what they did next. On whether they were successful or not.

Boomer called back, his eyes glued to his sonar display. Sweat stained the back of his shirt, and rivulets ran down the sides of his face. "Range, ten thousand feet, Captain. She's staying close to the ice. I'm getting a ton of refractions. Multiple target points and ice reflection." His display jumped, flickering between showing five subs and then one, and then three. Back to a single sub.

"Lieutenant Munoz, flood tubes one through six and prepare to launch your torpedoes."

Clanking echoed through *Honolulu*, the damaged torpedo doors on the bow struggling to open fully. The ship creaked and groaned as the hull strained. "What is my target, sir?"

In submarine warfare, the unwritten rules said to always fire on a submarine's propellers. Disable her. Break her rudder. Leave her dead in the water. Leave her unable to complete her mission. But don't break her back. Don't send a hundred men to their deaths.

Those rules didn't apply here. "Target her midline. Crack her in half. Break her open like an egg, Lieutenant."

Munoz said nothing, but his hands flew over his control board, priming his torpedoes with coordinates to the center of the Russian sub.

"Conn, Sonar. She heard us flood our tubes. She's flooding four of her own."

"Roller, we're going to need to maneuver after we fire. Be ready." A submarine was not a jet fighter. Evading torpedoes and trying to swim away like a dolphin wasn't what they were designed for. He'd used up almost all his tricks. But if he could swim his way out of this, make a break of the depths and save his crew, he'd give it his all.

Roller nodded, chewing gum almost fast enough to blur his jaw.

"Weapons ready, Captain." Munoz exhaled, holding his trembling hands over the firing board. "As soon as we fire, she's going to send her torpedoes up our solution."

"Roller, when we launch, take us down, emergency deep. I want us rolling beneath her. Try and scramble her torpedoes. If we hit the thermocline and kill our propellers, those torpedoes might turn their attention back home."

"Aye, Captain."

Anderson nodded to Roller and turned back to Munoz. He opened his mouth, ready to give his next order. Behind him, by the dark plotting table, there was a blur, a deep clap followed by a grunt, and then footsteps.

A pistol cocked and jammed against the side of his head. "Not one more fucking step," a voice growled. "You're *not* taking out that sub."

Everything stopped. His crew stopped breathing. Everyone's gaze turned to the center of the Conn. Even *Honolulu* seemed to still, as if holding her breath while her captain stood with a gun to his head.

They had a traitor on board. Had been carrying him the whole time, from the start of the mission. One of Madigan's men, embedded in Lieutenant Cooper's own team. President Spiers's words of warning, his reason for fleeing Washington, his subterfuge getting to the Arctic. It had all been for nothing. Madigan had been right by Spiers's side the *entire* time.

Anderson's eyes flicked sideways. He stared into Sergeant Wright's steady gaze. Cold fire and dedication burned back. The kind of soul-deep dedication that belonged to a martyr. There'd be no reasoning with Wright.

Behind Wright, Coleman slumped sideways, falling to the deck. Blood seeped from his chest, staining the deck bright red, a klaxon of color even in the dim lights. Fury blazed from his eyes as he glared at Wright. Faisal and Doc kneeled beside him, trying to press on his chest as Coleman coughed up blood.

"Disarm those torpedoes." Wright dug the barrel against Anderson's skull. "*Now.*"

Anderson said nothing.

"I said, disarm those torpedoes!" Wright roared. His fingers squeezed the grip of his pistol as his face twisted, murderous wrath in the harsh curve of his lips.

Anderson stared him right in the eyes and stayed silent.

"Fine," Wright growled. "You and your crew are not going to stop us."

In one move, he pivoted to Lieutenant Munoz and the weapons station. Anderson lunged, trying to tackle him, but the time it took to squeeze a trigger was much less than the time it took for him to get to Wright.

Wright fired, almost emptying his weapon into Munoz. Bullets slammed into Munoz's chest, turning his body into a bullet-riddled sack of meat, and then flew through him, shattering the weapons control console. Sparks flew as glass burst and displays shorted out, whining and going dark.

Anderson tackled Wright to the deck, just as Roller shoved the control yoke hard, plunging the boat downward, straight for the depths.

Everything and everyone not strapped in tumbled end over end, careening out of control. Sailors rolled down the deck, slamming into stations and bulkheads. Munoz's body hit the deck hard with a sick splat. His corpse bounced off the periscope stand and continued to slide. Crimson blood slicked the deck, drops racing down the slick surface. Coleman, too, went sailing down the deck and banged off the plotting table. Doc rolled like a gymnast, clear across the Conn and slamming into Boomer's sonar station.

Anderson braced his feet on the periscope railing and grabbed hold of Wright, fisting his hands in his uniform. Wright had dropped his pistol, and it clattered down the deck with everything else, sliding through Munoz's blood and bouncing off people and bulkheads. It disappeared into the darkness by the plotting table and went silent.

Wright wrapped one leg around Anderson in a classic grappling move and grabbed Anderson's hair. He hauled Anderson's head back, opening up his face, and slammed three punches into his cheek, his nose, his eyes. Anderson's world went white, bursting with stars as pain nearly blinded him. Grunting, he slammed Wright down on the deck, leaning his weight against his forearm as he pressed it across Wright's throat.

The boat creaked and groaned, and the hull popped with rifle-shot cracks. The hull was squeezing, clenched in the fast-rising pressures of the depths. How deep had they gone? A steep dive, over twenty-five degrees down angle. They could go hundreds of feet in seconds. It had already been too long.

Each breath seemed heavier, weightier, the pressures of the sea pushing inward, squeezing *Honolulu* like a balloon about to pop.

"Level the boat!" Anderson roared. "Bring us up!"

Roller clawed his way up the deck, crawling through a river of spilled blood before climbing back into his seat. He grabbed the controls and jerked, bringing the boat to level.

Wright wrapped both his legs around Anderson and twisted, flipping Anderson on his back and breaking his chokehold. He reared up, sitting on top of Anderson as he pummeled him in the face, over and over.

Roller roared and charged, leaping from his station toward Wright.

Wright twisted and grabbed Roller out of the air, gripping him by his throat and slamming him to the deck. Roller hit hard and didn't move. He lay face-down, still.

Anderson blinked blearily up at Wright. *It can't end like this.*

THE PISTOL WHISPERED UNDER the plotting table, into the darkness beside Coleman.

Faisal snatched it, plucking the weapon out of its bloody slide.

Coleman struggled to breathe, gasping for air. Wright had drawn his concealed weapon in the dark, pressed it to Coleman's back, and fired a shot into his right lung. Blood frothed at Coleman's lips, flecking over his pale skin. Faisal had clung to him during the wild tumble, slingshotting the two of them beneath the plotting table. He kept pressure on Coleman's gunshot, trying to stop the burble of blood spilling between his fingers.

Coleman's eyes darted to the pistol he held. He reached for Faisal, one shaking hand grabbing his jacket. He pulled him close.

"Go. You know what you have to do." He shoved Faisal, pushing him away.

If he left Coleman, he might bleed out. Bleed to death, cramped beneath the navigation station of a broken submarine beneath the ice cap.

Faisal grabbed Coleman's hand and pressed it over his own wound. He spoke fast, whispering in English in Coleman's ear. "Allah, I beseech you in your mercy. Protect this man. Keep him in your sight and your care."

He rose, gripping the pistol in his hand. The weapon was slick, drenched in blood. Droplets fell from the barrel, striking the deck as he slipped behind Wright, moving in the shadows. He kept praying, turning to Arabic. "Allah, remove all fear from my heart. Guide my hands and protect these men from the vileness of this enemy."

He raised the pistol and sighted the back of Wright's head. Time slowed, elongating between breaths. He saw Adam in his mind, saw his smile, the tousle of his hair. The way he tipped his head back and laughed. How his brow furrowed when he struggled. Their love had been hard fought, hard won, a dangerous gambit between men who had everything to lose by taking a chance on each other. How had they found each other? How had they come so far, loved so deeply?

How had it all been ripped away?

He knew how. He knew *exactly* how.

Yallah, Wright had played them this whole time. From the very beginning. From the first moment he'd met him, after Ethiopia. How long had Wright served with Adam? How long had he been betraying him?

And at the station, when they'd escaped before the blast. Wright had supposedly been beaten outside, and then dragged in and dumped on the deck. He'd recovered fast for someone beaten unconscious. He must have been faking it. *Wallah,* he'd been working with Cook at every moment. Would he have left them there to die in the blast, if they hadn't escaped? Had he stayed with them, a silent betrayer lying in wait, to ensure that the final nail had been hammered into their coffin? Into Adam's coffin?

Fury swept through him, the scorch of the midday desert sun stabbing his soul. He'd been happy. He'd been so happy, and he and Adam were making it work.

It wouldn't end like this.

He exhaled. In his mind, he prayed. *Allah, deliver me from what I am about to do.* He'd never killed in raw, aching wrath before. Never in bloodlust and vengeance. Never had he truly desired another man's death.

Adam's smile hovered in his mind again. His skin, pale against the Saudi sun and sand. His cheeks, blooming with new freckles whenever they were in the desert for too long. Ana bahibak, *Adam.*

"Wright!" he bellowed as Wright reared back, preparing to slam his fist into Anderson's face again. Blood poured from Anderson's nose and dripped down his face.

Wright whirled, glaring into the darkness.

Faisal stepped into the light, into the green glow of the submarine's displays. "For Adam."

He squeezed the trigger. He squeezed again, and again, and again. Over and over, until the weapon clicked.

Bullets slammed into Wright, first into the center of his forehead, then the side of his cheek, his neck. Lower, into his chest, his heart. He shook, rocked with the blow of each gunshot, trembling over Anderson as his blood sprayed.

Finally, he slid sideways, falling to the deck with his eyes still open.

Silence filled the Conn.

Anderson rolled over and pushed himself to shaky feet. Faisal raced to his side, supporting him with one shoulder.

"Status," Anderson barked, spitting a wad of blood to the deck. "How much time left before those cruise missiles launch?"

The crew lurched back to their stations, sliding into their duties on autopilot. Still, they stared with wide eyes at Munoz's destroyed console, the blood-slick and body-littered deck.

Boomer's voice shook hard when he spoke. "Cruise missiles launching in less than a minute, Captain."

Anderson closed his eyes. He exhaled, and then looked at Munoz's destroyed console. "Nav," he said, his voice catching. "Plot a course for the dead center of her hull. Ramming speed."

64

Over the Canadian-US Border

THE TV WAS ON in the back of Colonel Song's plane, breaking news streaming live over the air. TNN's reporters scrambled for new information, any information to explain what was happening.

All around the nation, pockets of anarchy had broken out. Scattered police officers had turned on their colleagues. Splinter cells on military bases had activated, firing on their fellow soldiers. And in Washington DC, the White House was under attack. Again.

Unknown perpetrators had penetrated the West Wing, reports said. Information was sketchy at best. The White House was on lockdown. Senators and generals were inside.

But no word on President Wall, or her status or condition. Was she a hostage, they wondered? Was she even at the White House?

"Oh God…" Elizabeth stared at the screen as she gripped Levi's hand. "It's Madigan. He's started his attack. His followers. These are his followers."

"I'm trying to get through to the White House." Levi dialed every number he could. It was useless. White House protocol locked down communications and shut down cell phones when under attack.

Colonel Song eyed them both. "If Madigan has truly launched his attack, then we are already too late."

"No. No, I won't give up hope yet." Elizabeth held a fist in front of her face, bouncing it off her pursed lips. "We're still here, aren't we?"

"For now," Colonel Song said.

65

Washington DC

ONLY A WHISPER OF sound whistled as Welby, General Bell, and Pete slid down the elevator cables in the three-hundred-foot shaft leading down to the PEOC. Cold concrete, damp earth, and hot steel hit their noses, the stench of an underground bunker buried in Virginia clay.

Welby and Bell slowed their approach as they reached the roof of the elevator, and then helped Pete down as well. Pete swung his backpack around and pulled out the last bricks of C4 with shaking hands.

Bell peeled the stickyback off and placed them where Welby pointed, around the elevator vent, and flicked the embedded trigger switches, activating the close-range detonator transmitters. All three men clambered back up the cables, moving clear of the blast radius.

Welby spoke softly, holding the detonator. "When this blows, we drop back down and breach. Grenades first. Take as many of her team out as we can. I'll go first and give the signal when it's clear for you to follow."

Pete's eyes were wide, thick circles of white ringing his irises. He nodded, jerking his head up and down.

Bell gave Pete a long stare but nodded once to Welby.

He jammed his thumb down on the detonator.

Fire bloomed beneath them, blasting the roof of the elevator down into the car. The vent spat downward, shattering against the steel cage. The doors were propped open by design, held in the bunker for the president. Debris roared from the elevator, cluttering the car's floor and the bunker's entrance.

"Go!" Welby slid down the cables first. He braced on the edge of the elevator car and peered through the smoke, the dust of the explosion. Steel plates and fluorescent light bulbs swung in the car, next to a gaping hole, just wide enough for a man to squeeze through.

He grabbed the three grenades clipped to his belt. Pulling the pins, he lobbed them through the hole and jumped back, right as gunshots blasted up from the bunker. Bullets whizzed by his legs and slammed into the elevator shaft. More plinked off the elevator's steel walls.

He counted down the seconds as the grenades rolled into the bunker's hallway. Shouts and guttural orders echoed from the bunker, Jennifer's men scrambling in the face of three surprise visitors.

But the bunker was small, just the footprint of a quarter of the West Wing. The concrete walls and iron pipes made a cave, a perfectly sealed blast room. It was the one thing that had always given him the heebie-jeebies about the bunker. It was the perfect place for a grenade ambush.

The Secret Service operated under the belief that there never would be an ambush against the bunker.

Until today.

He listened as the grenades detonated, their blasts magnified by the confined space, the concrete and steel-reinforced walls that wouldn't give. The blasts had nowhere to go but deeper into the bunker, around the corners that he pictured Jennifer's team hiding behind. Bits of metal, super-heated, and roaring flames would be spearing into her soldiers. By the cries and shrieks he heard, a chunk of her men were down.

Bell dropped beside him. He pulled two grenades from his own belt and lobbed both into the bunker. They skittered, spinning across the floor, and disappeared into the smoke and gloom.

Fewer voices called out the grenade warning. Fewer shouts. But more moans. Her forces were down.

They waited for the detonation, counting the seconds. Silence, after the blast.

Welby's met Bell's gaze.

Time to breach.

Welby dropped to a kneel holding his weapon out, his finger already half squeezing the trigger. He kicked aside the shattered grate and dropped into the elevator, landing crouched in the debris. Spinning, he slammed his back against the wall, covering behind the slim doorframe, and waited for Jennifer's team to fire.

Beech's voice whispered in his ear piece. *"All we see is smoke. She ducked out of sight at the first grenade. We saw five men go down in the blast. No visual on current targets."*

He couldn't respond. Not in the silent, smoky bunker. Slowly, he slid forward, peering around the frame of the elevator car.

Smoke and dust choked the air. Debris from the grenades. Bodies on the floor. Men, twisted and unnatural.

He ducked out, clearing right and then left and flattening along the wall. Still no movement. No shadows in the gloom. Looking back, he motioned for Bell and Pete to follow.

Bell came first, lowering himself more slowly through the hole. Pete jumped like Welby had, but stumbled on the landing.

Welby covered them both as they joined him outside the elevator.

The elevator was the dead end of a T intersection. To the right and left, short hallways led to support facilities. A tiny dorm room. A lavatory. A spartan kitchen. Two empty rooms, nicknamed the crying rooms by the staff. Ahead, the central hallway led to the bunker's operation center, a cramped space stuffed with computer systems, enough monitors to make anyone go blind, server racks set up in a maze, and communications equipment that even Welby had never seen. It looked like a strange mixture between a junk shop and what an alien spacecraft should look like. Like Air Force One had burrowed underground and compacted to the size of a bedroom.

Jennifer was at the end of the hall. On the main screen, President Spiers's code to unleash the nuclear launch safeguards flashed. The code was less secure than the handprint and retinal lock. Handprints and retinal locks were supposed to be the Cadillacs of the security protocol.

Four of the six digits had been entered. A brute force cyberattack cycled through the final two digits.

They were almost out of time. With each digit uncovered, the possibilities decreased exponentially. As he watched, the fifth digit flashed, plugging into the display. Only one digit left to go.

"Jennifer!" he bellowed. "We know you're down here!"

Scuffling, just ahead. He spun, his weapon raised. Behind him, Bell fell into the rear, covering. Pete clung to Welby, breathing hard.

"Why do you want the nuclear codes, Jennifer?" If he could get her to respond, he could get a bead on her.

More shuffling, like soft footsteps, to his left. Welby spun again, trying to peer through the smoke.

Her voice came from the right. "In moments, this world will end. And when it does, we will be in control of the world to come. These weapons guarantee that control."

"Sounds like a shitty world!" Pete shouted. "I don't want any part of that!"

Welby spared a withering glare for Pete. Pete swallowed hard, his jaw snapping shut with an audible crack.

"Pete, you were supposed to be killed in the first attack," she spat. "You and your big fucking mouth."

"You lost then and you're going to lose now!" Slowly, Welby slipped forward. He had a target on the left and Jennifer on the right. *Come on, Beech, what do you see?*

"You can kill me, Agent Welby. I'm glad to die. But it won't change anything. We've already won."

The last digit flashed, locking into place. An alarm blared, and the monitors all flashed the same alert. *Nuclear safeguard offline. Launch protocols active.*

"Shit." They were out of time.

"*Fuck, Welby, the codes have been breached!*" Beech's panicked voice rang in his earpiece. "*Get her, now!*"

What the fuck did Beech think he'd been doing? Gritting his teeth, Welby swung to the left, spraying bullets down the side of the bunker, hoping he'd hit someone. He whirled, turning to his right, and caught Jennifer dashing for the main display.

Gunshots roared, bullets sizzling past his head. Instincts screamed for him to duck, to take cover, but he kept going. He heard Bell behind him, spinning and firing on Jennifer's men hiding in the hallways, waiting to ambush them. Pete, stepping forward, firing on the teammate she'd hidden to the left, behind a rack of servers. Pete was just disciplined enough to not go full auto, but he still emptied his clip into the man and into the servers. Sparks flew, scattering around the cramped bunker. Overhead, lights flickered and spat, fluorescent bulbs exploding in a shower of sparks.

Jennifer raced forward as the first bullet slammed into Welby's shoulder. He kept going, firing as he ran.

A bullet plunged into his back.

She punched the orders to activate nuclear warheads. Across the country, silos were screaming online, warheads cycling into active mode. Silo covers were sliding back, revealing their deadly cargo. She was launching now. A nuclear blitzkrieg. He had to stop her.

Two bullets slammed into him, into his thigh. He stumbled, but pushed on.

One of his shots shattered an elbow. Another blasted her hip. Jennifer fell forward, bracing her upper body on the console.

Steps away, he was steps away. She clawed herself up, her fingers racing over the command controls. Presidents weren't coders. They were push-button junkies, and the bunker had been built to accommodate that. Procedures for firing nuclear warheads, and potentially ending the world, were easy to enter, once the code was active. Targets selected automatically, the major population centers of nations on a touchscreen console.

Jennifer selected cities across all of the United States. Her hand hovered over the launch key.

Welby threw himself against her, slamming her fully into the console. He grabbed her remaining arm and ripped it backward, tearing it from its socket. She screamed and kicked behind her, trying to sweep his legs out from beneath him.

He spun her, grasping her throat and slamming her back against the console. Both her arms hung useless; one shot at the elbow, one dangling dislocated from her shoulder. She glared up at him, smoke staining her pale cheeks, blood flecked across her blonde hair. Once, he'd thought she was beautiful.

Welby pressed the barrel of the weapon to her belly and pulled the trigger, emptying his clip into her. She trembled and shook beneath his grasp with every shot, the bullets passing through her and into the control station. Circuit boards fried and the system whined, crashing offline. *Access Lost* flashed on the main monitor. *Reenter nuclear activation codes.*

"*You did it!*" Beech shouted in his ear. "*Jesus Christ, you did it! Welby, holy fuck!*"

Beech's voice warbled like he'd fallen underwater. Welby heard footsteps running behind him, heard someone shout his name.

He stumbled, falling to his knees, and then pitched to his side. He still held Jennifer's throat in his iron-clad grip. She came with him, and he stared into her eyes, watching as she shuddered, as she breathed her last breath. As her eyes rolled back in her head, and she went limp in his hand.

He let go, and she flopped away, falling to the bunker's concrete floor like a ragdoll.

Hands grabbed him, tried to steer him down. Roamed over his body, searching for his wounds. He closed his eyes. Saw Ethan, his colleague, his coworker, a man he'd spent twelve years beside. Saw President Spiers, a man he'd thought he'd failed. Had thought he'd let die.

He saw both of them dancing at the White House, twirling beneath the chandeliers of the ballroom, a golden glow wreathing their movements, catching their radiant smiles. Around and around they went, spinning and dancing, laughing and smiling. Happy. So very happy.

Mission accomplished, Mr. President.

His eyes slipped closed.

66

USS Honolulu

On THE SONAR SCOPE, the Russian sub appeared dead center, a growing tower of endless red that filled the screen.

"Distance, two hundred feet, Captain." Boomer's voice had stopped shaking. Steel filled his words instead.

Anderson leaned into Faisal, gripping the younger man's shoulder. The collision alarm wailed, a deep klaxon blaring through his boat. His crew were at their best in this moment, facing their end, plowing toward this Russian sub of Madigan's intent on destroying their world. They were the last line, the very last line of defense.

To their side, Doc had hauled Coleman into his arms, and he sat leaning against the shot-up remnants of Lieutenant Munoz's weapons station. Coleman still dragged in shaky breaths, his head resting on Doc's shoulder.

"Distance, one hundred feet, Captain."

"It's been an honor," Anderson said, his voice catching. "Every last one of you are heroes." He met each sailor's gaze, nodding to the men under his command.

And then—

Impact.

Time snapped, racing from too slow, the waiting that came before their collision, to too fast, the gut-punch crash of *Honolulu* slamming into the belly of the Russian sub.

Honolulu crunched, the sound of a heavy battering ram slamming into the side of a car. Rivets popped along her hull, and then steel bent and tore, her frame twisting and tearing into ragged pieces. Sonar winked off, the sensors in the nose of the ship pulverized on impact.

They held fast to whatever they could, grasping railings and handholds and gritting their teeth. Anything not bolted down flew across the Conn and slammed into the bulkhead. The plotting table wrenched free from its bolts, toppling over. Wax pencils whizzed through the air.

The explosions started.

He'd evacuated the forward compartment, moving his crew to the middle of the boat. The torpedoes in their tubes were still armed, still hot and ready to ignite. There was no way to fire them, not with a busted ship and a destroyed weapons console, not in time for them to have mattered. But ramming the torpedoes into the belly of the Russian sub was enough to set them all off.

Chain reactions ignited, booming explosions roaring from *Honolulu*'s bow. He felt the shudder of the torpedoes bursting apart. If his closed his eyes, he could feel the flames. Alerts flashed across the control boards, but his crew silently turned them off. *Flooding in the forward compartments. Reactor scram. Hull integrity compromised. Collision.*

Hissing followed, the rush and swirl of water pouring into *Honolulu*. The lights winked out, plunging the Conn into pitch-black darkness. Emergency lighting struggled online, fading fast. Only a few lights stayed on, flickering like mosquito traps buzzing in the night.

Water foamed over the deck, sloshing around Anderson's shoes. The sea was invading, roaring into their home, their sanctuary. In his whole career, he'd never lost a boat. Never even sprang a leak. Now, they were going to sink to the bottom, entombed forever in the Arctic.

Collapsing steel roared, metal shredding metal. It sounded like they were flying right through the sub, like the crunching, crushing metal was right outside the Conn. He heard the final sound, every submariner's worst nightmare, the hiss and fizz of a hundred balloons leaking air. The sound of a sub venting oxygen into the sea.

Honolulu was dead.

Anderson closed his eyes.

A jerk wrenched him sideways. He stumbled and nearly fell, but Faisal held him up. Another jerk, and then a bone-rattling shudder, like *Honolulu* had been dropped in a cement mixer. "What's going on?"

His crew was blind and deaf to the outside world, sitting in front of dark consoles, but still, they scrambled to answer. Boomer struggled to listen to his headset, still plugged into the small rear sonar array. He'd spun the array as far as it could go, pointing it down and forward, trying to get any eyes and ears on what was happening.

"Captain, something is sinking to the bottom. Something big."

Half of *Honolulu*, most likely. He swallowed. "Anything on the Russians?"

Silence, for a beat. "Captain… it *is* them. The Russian sub, she's what is plunging to the bottom. She's snapped in half, all the way to her sail."

"What's our depth?" He wasn't feeling the crush of the sea, the rise in pressure that came with the dead man's drop to the bottom.

"We're… holding steady. No, dropping. Dropping eight degrees, Captain." Boomer spun in his chair and stared at Anderson. Through the darkness, his eyes gleamed like stars, like planets lit up in the night sky. "Sir, we're free from the sub. That shaking, that was her tearing free."

Free from the sub. Anderson rocketed forward, pulling out of Faisal's hold. He gripped the railing. "Blow the ballast!" he roared. "Blow it now! Now! Now!"

Chief Garcia lunged for the Chicken Switches, the bright-red toggles that controlled the air in *Honolulu*'s ballast tanks. Her forward tanks were gone, crunched in the collision. Hell, her forward half was gone, by the sound of everything. The Russian sub had ripped free and torn half of *Honolulu* with it, but that was her ticket to freedom.

Air whooshed out of the stern ballast tanks, blasting into the sea with the roar of a freight train. Lurching, *Honolulu* leaped forward, rising like the cruise missile the Russian sub never launched. She rocketed for the ice, seven thousand tons of metal racing for the surface.

"Brace for impact!" Anderson roared. "Sound collision alarm!"

For the second time in an hour, men and machines tumbled in the Conn. Anderson held on to the railing and to Faisal, holding the young man tight. Faisal, in turn, gripped him, their feet locked together, barely staying upright as the deck tilted almost vertical. They both gripped the overhead handles, hanging like subway riders on a train out of control.

Boomer's voice rang out, shrill and tight. "Ice cap is ten feet, Captain! We're going to punch through!"

If they still had their bow, the curved, reinforced nose of their boat, they'd punch through with just some dents and a story to tell back home. But missing their bow? With half their ship shorn off? They'd be lucky if they didn't pulverize against the ice. Anderson squeezed his eyes closed. His thoughts went straight to his son. *I never got to tell him I married the president and the first gentleman.*

They hit the ice like a car slamming into a crash test wall. It barely slowed them down. They all turned into test dummies, flying forward and back, thrown from their chairs, their perches. Anderson hit the deck hard, rolling into Faisal. Metal screamed and collapsed, shredding again. Lights winked off, *Honolulu*'s power plant giving up the ghost for good. Even the battery battle lamps winked out. But, above all that, the unmistakable sound of ice shattering, cracking apart, breaking before them, drowned out everything.

Honolulu shuddered and rocked, and then the sound of metal sliding on metal tore at their eardrums. Anderson cursed, and everyone covered their ears.

Slowly, inexplicably, the trembles stilled. Movement stopped. They couldn't even feel the bob and sway of the sea.

Anderson exhaled shakily. He called out the names of his crew, waiting for grunts and groans, answers in the darkness. Everyone accounted for. An absolute miracle. Would he be so lucky with the rest of his crew? Hands grabbed him, helped him stand. Flashlights winked on. He saw Faisal's blood-covered face, inches from his own.

"Let's get the hell out of here," Anderson growled. "Abandon ship. Security detail onto the ice first."

Wherever they were, whatever had just happened, they were surfaced within Russian territories, in Russian ice. What would greet them outside? A firing squad? Or something else?

Doc struggled to hold Coleman up. Coleman's skin was pale, almost the color of ice. Anderson pointed Faisal toward his surviving crewmates and then strode out of the Conn.

He would lead his crew onto the ice, into whatever awaited them there.

67

Kara Sea

JACK CHASED AFTER MADIGAN, redlining the engine on his snowmobile. Sergey clung to his waist, leaning forward as they tried to push the snowmobile just that much faster.

Something rose on the ice ahead. A beacon, a strobing light spinning in the low-hanging gloom. Beside the beacon, a red mound squatted on the ice. It looked like a tent. Snow had blown against one side. It had been there for a while.

"His escape!" Sergey bellowed in Jack's ear. "The ice is thinning out here. That Russian sub of his! It will pick him up here!"

"No, it won't." Jack throttled the engine, pushing the snowmobile as hard as he could. Beneath his hands, the machine shook, trembling as it flew across the ice, blasting over crevasses and almost skidding out of control.

Madigan reached the beacon first. He slid to a stop, jumping from his snowmobile and drawing his weapon. Kneeling down, taking cover behind his snowmobile, he opened fire on Jack and Sergey.

"Hold on!" Jack bellowed. He jerked the snowmobile to the left and then to the right, zig-zagging fast across the ice. Ethan had told him once, racing through the training grounds at the Secret Service training center at Rowley, that a zig-zag pattern was the best way to survive someone shooting right at you. He jerked hard to the left again as bullets slammed into the ice.

A shot whizzed by his head, a whistle followed by a wet smack. He turned hard to the right, but the bullet had already landed.

Sergey tumbled from the back of the snowmobile and hit the ice, rolling over and over in a long slide. Red stained the ice beneath him until he came to a stop. He didn't move.

Jack whipped around. "Sergey!" Nothing. No movement.

For a moment, he was torn. Go to Sergey? Or finish this, once and for all?

Where was Madigan going? If that sub appeared, he'd be gone again, in the wind. Their best chance to put him down was here and now.

Jack spun back toward Madigan and gunned his engine. He leaned low over the snowmobile and zeroed in, riding a straight line. Bullets slammed into the snowmobile's frame, his treads. It jerked beneath his hands, shuddering violently. A few more seconds, only a few more seconds.

He slammed on the brakes and leaped free, feet from Madigan, before Madigan's final shots tore through the front controls, the windscreen, and shredded the saddle. Jack hit the ice hard, rolling as he struggled for the breath that had been knocked from him. He moved as he gasped, rising to his knees and unshouldering his rifle.

Ethan. Be like Ethan. Move like Ethan. He raised the rifle and fired, chewing through the ice surrounding Madigan.

Madigan rolled behind his snowmobile, ducking low.

Jack's rifle clicked. Empty. He cursed.

"Jack!" Madigan shouted. "We seem to have similar problems!"

"Come out, Madigan!" He kept his rifle up, as if he could still fire. "I'll put a bullet in your ass."

"Jack, Jack… so unpresidential." Slowly, Madigan stood. He turned toward Jack, holding his arms wide. He tossed his own weapon to the side. It slid on the ice, disappearing in a puff of loose snow. "What would the American people say if they saw you now?"

"They'd ask me why you're still breathing."

"Then shoot me, Jack. Why haven't you?" Madigan's eyes gleamed, taunting him.

Jack flung his empty rifle sideways and charged. Madigan braced himself, dropping low as he threw his hands up.

They crashed into each other, falling and sliding along the ice. Madigan wrapped his legs around Jack, wrestling him down, pinning him on his back. Fists rained down on Jack's face, Madigan's days as a brawler in the military roaring to life.

Jack thrashed beneath him. His thoughts coalesced, falling back to days he'd spent with Ethan, training at Rowley, wrestling in the White House gym. Ethan, pinning him down, and him, wanting to kiss his way out of it. Ethan, snapping at him to pay attention, to try harder.

Jack scissored his legs, sweeping Madigan off-balance. They scrambled to their feet, circling each other, fists raised.

"I can't believe I sat at the same table as you," Jack spat. "You were in my Situation Room! On my National Security Council!"

"You were a joke president no one believed in. A pretty boy candidate who turned out to only be after his own self-interests in the end." Madigan grinned. "Just like every other politician. Looking for a piece of ass and a power fuck. Can you really blame me? Blame us? You were *such* an easy target."

"You murdered thousands of people." Nairobi and the nuclear blast. The criminals he'd released, and the havoc they'd wrought. Secret Service agents at the White House. Military personnel. Civilians in Russia during the coup.

His wife, all those years ago, on a mission Madigan had sanctioned and had planned. "You killed Leslie!"

Madigan's grin grew wicked. "But I brought her back to you, Jack."

Roaring, Jack charged, throwing himself at Madigan. They met in a grapple, hands grasping each other's shoulders. He kicked, slamming his boot into Madigan's knee.

Madigan buckled, crying out, but kept his feet. He hobbled sideways and grabbed Jack's throat.

Jack gripped Madigan's thin gray hair with one hand and made a fist with the other. He hauled Madigan close, dragging him in, and then pummeled him, pummeling his fist into Madigan's chest, his ribs. *This is for Ethan.* Over and over, until his hand burned, until his knuckles were slick. Until pain shot through his fist each time he buried another punch in Madigan's stomach.

Spinning free, Madigan released Jack and stumbled backward, gasping. He doubled over but glared at Jack, murder in his eyes. "I always hated you," he hissed. "I picked your presidency because I hated you. I wanted to watch you die."

Jack spat. Blood stained the ice. "You disappointed me while you were on my staff, Madigan. I always knew you could never accomplish anything." He grinned, holding his fists high. "I'm still alive, aren't I?"

Roaring, Madigan charged. As he moved, he reached behind him, into his waistband. He sprang at Jack, a wild haymaker flying for his head. Jack ducked, but when he came up, Madigan spun behind him.

Madigan wrapped a rope around Jack's neck, pulling tight. He twisted the ends around his hands and crossed his arms behind Jack's head, heaving.

Jack's hands flew to his neck as he gasped for air that wasn't there. He tried to pry his fingers between his skin and the rope, tried to wedge something, anything in there to relieve the pressure. Madigan jerked, grunting behind him, and squeezed his arms, tightening the rope.

"I always win in the end, Jack," he snarled, right in Jack's ear. "Why do you think I was on your staff to begin with? This world? The one you think is yours? It's mine!" Roaring, Madigan heaved Jack into the air, throwing his strength into a final crush of his arms. "I made this world!"

The world dimmed around Jack's gaze. *Ethan.* His eyes fluttered. *Ethan, what do I do? What do I do now?*

Sunny days, dusty days, afternoons spent beneath a shade tree at Rowley. Sparring with Ethan, and then with Scott, round after round. Scott always went easy on him. Ethan, when Jack had pushed him, pushed back.

He came down from Madigan's heave and found his feet. Kicking back, he looped one ankle around Madigan's leg and swept forward, knocking the older man down. He went down with Madigan, throwing his body weight backward onto Madigan's chest.

The rope slackened. He dragged in a breath, and then another as he rolled on top of Madigan, pinning him to the ice.

Madigan's hands grasped at his jacket, tearing at his throat, his face.

Jack grabbed one of his hands and Madigan's elbow and twisted, snapping Madigan's joint. A crack split the air. Madigan shrieked and tried to draw his hand back, but his arm flopped toward the ice, useless and bent backward.

Harsh pants, their heavy breathing, and deep grunts filled the air. Jack leaned forward, both hands circling Madigan's throat. Madigan's one hand rose, scratching at Jack's face, trying to gouge out one of his eyeballs. Tried to claw across his cheek.

Jack shook him off. His hands squeezed, strangling Madigan. Madigan gagged.

"Jack… You can never be free of me," Madigan croaked. His one arm grasped at Jack's sweatshirt—Ethan's sweatshirt—and tried to pull him down.

He leaned all his weight onto his left hand and reared back with his right. He let loose, a single punch flying down, slamming Madigan's skull into the ice. "That is for Leslie!" he shouted.

Another punch, heaving Madigan against the ice once more. Bones crunched. Madigan's eyes went wide. Blood appeared beneath Madigan's skull, slowly spreading like a halo. Dazed, Madigan struggled, but his grip went slack on Jack's sweatshirt as his strength seemed to wane. "That is for Ethan!" Jack roared.

He dropped his hands Madigan's throat again, tightening, clenching until his arms shook and he felt each bone shift in Madigan's neck. Felt the fragility of his spine.

He stared into Madigan's eyes, into his dark, panicked gaze. Madigan's one hand grasped at Jack's sweatshirt, at his shoulder, flailed against his chest.

"And this is for me..." Jack twisted, wrenching his hands sideways. A brutal snap broke over the ice, and Madigan's expression went blank, his eyes suddenly empty.

Jack pitched forward, curling his body over Madigan's. For a moment, he didn't move. He didn't breathe.

And then he howled, spit and blood pouring from him. His cheek pressed against the glacier, freezing him down to the center of his soul. What had he done? God, what had he done?

Ethan's voice filled him, flooded his heart. *You did what you had to do. What had to be done.*

Still, he scrambled back, crawling away from Madigan's limp and lifeless body. He stared at the corpse of the man who had shadowed his every move, had shredded his presidency, and had shaped his life in ways he could only pretend to understand. What in his life was his own? What had Madigan shaped?

His eyes closed, and he tipped his head back. Ethan. Ethan was his own. Ethan was the foundation of his world, the anchor to his soul. Ethan was the answer to a question he'd always asked, and always wondered. Ethan was everything.

He turned his back on Madigan and stumbled away.

Across the ice, Sergey pushed himself up, rising on shaking arms.

Jack broke into a run. "Sergey!"

He slid on his knees the last feet, grabbing on to Sergey as he came to a stop. He ran his hands over Sergey's body, and then found the gunshot wound straight through Sergey's shoulder.

"I am all right. Is just a graze." Sergey snapped. "Is always this shoulder." Gritting his teeth, he sat back, groaning. "Always, always, this shoulder. Shoot me in the other shoulder, please. I am tired of this one hurting!"

Jack laughed, relief going off like a warhead inside him. "I'll shoot you if it will make you happy."

"*Govno*, no, fuck off." Sergey shoved him. "You are nothing but trouble." He wagged his finger in Jack's face. "Nothing but trouble, Jack!"

"Ethan says the same thing."

Sergey snorted. "I bet he does." Jack helped him stand, throwing Sergey's arm over his shoulder.

Together, they limped to Madigan's snowmobile. "You know, we have matching gunshot wounds in our shoulders now."

Sergey snorted. "Gunshot wounds to make us BFFs, Jack?"

Jack started to respond, but his eyes caught on Madigan's corpse. Whatever he was about to say fell away.

Sergey stared at Madigan's broken body, splayed out on the ice. "You did the right thing, Jack." He pressed his cold lips to Jack's temple, a careful kiss. "You did the right thing."

Swallowing, Jack looked away from Madigan's body and guided them to the snowmobile. "Did we do it? Did we actually stop Madigan in time? Save the world?"

Sergey peered at the sky. "I see no flame. No end of the world." He opened his mouth, and then froze. He turned to the sky again. "What is that…"

They both turned north, watching as wave after wave of planes, fighter jets, heavy helicopters, and troop transports zoomed over the ice, low enough to blow them off their feet.

"They are Russian!" Sergey shouted. "They are Russian forces!"

"What Russians are to the north? Do you have a base at the North Pole?"

Sergey shook his head. "No. It is Moroshkin. From Canada."

68

Kara Sea

Anderson threw his shoulder into the central hatch on the sail leading to the bridge and shoved it open. Normally, the hatch was round. Today, it was shaped like a flattened football. Half the sail was crushed.

He clambered into the sideways-leaning bridge. *Honolulu*'s remains had come to rest on her side, her broken body all the way out of the water and on top of the ice. Behind them, a roiling mess of black water bubbled like a volcano's cauldron. Shattered pack ice lay in heaps, sheets as big as houses tossed twenty feet from the ragged hole. *Honolulu*'s corpse lay like a whale beached after a storm, lost in the flotsam and wreckage of some great, angry swell. A long scrape of broken ice lay gouged behind her, shattered propeller blades and shorn-off hull plates littering the ice.

Her forward half was gone. Of the twelve Tomahawk bays she had left port with, two remained, their square lids crumpled and crushed. Forward of that, everything was missing. Ragged steel and dangling metal stretched in every direction, the remnants of *Honolulu* bleeding out onto the ice.

A roar zoomed overhead. Anderson ducked, raising his rifle to his shoulder. Jets buzzed his sub, triads of them, over and over, a fleet of jets. Then, planes, helicopters, troop transports. Like an air show or a flotilla lift, hundreds of aircraft swarmed above, filling the steel skies with thunder and roaring wind.

He spotted the Russian flag emblazoned on the aircrafts' sides.

Squawking from his jacket nearly gave him a heart attack. He'd forgotten all about the ship-to-shore radio he'd stuffed in his pocket, a frantic hope that he'd hear from President Spiers again.

This time, it was heavily accented English barking at him. A Russian helicopter circled overhead. "*American submarine, American submarine, do you copy?*"

"American submarine *Honolulu* responds. We read you. We are declaring an emergency situation. Mayday, Mayday, Mayday, over."

"*American submarine* Honolulu. *You are in Russian territory. We will assist you in leaving Russian territory at your earliest possibility. We thank you for your assistance in this internal affair. We will take from here.*"

Anderson dropped the radio, chuckling as the helicopter moved off, joining the rest of the airlift and landing farther across the pack, near two other gaping holes in the ice. Russian soldiers poured from the dozens of helicopters that landed, screaming across the remains of the ice pack and tackling men in torn and ratty uniforms who tried to scramble away. Madigan's criminal army. They were arresting the remains of Madigan's criminal army.

He looked at the two gaping holes in the ice, to his left and his right, and the fractures and spider lines that stretched between them. Two ships that had once rested there. Two ships he'd sunk.

Anderson leaned forward, dragging in a deep, frigid breath as he closed his eyes.

They'd done it.

THE CREW OF *HONOLULU* poured out of the hatches, keeping close to her banged and battered hull. Russian soldiers across the ice pack were rounding up Madigan's army, herding them into holding areas and shooting the ice beneath their feet if anyone tried to make a break. Jets continued to buzz overhead as heavy transports circled.

Chief Liu had thirteen of *Honolulu*'s crew laid out on tarps on the ice, tending to their injuries. Broken bones and concussions; they were lucky. They were damn lucky. Two bodies were still inside, though. One a hero. One a traitor.

Faisal crouched with Doc, tending to Coleman. Doc had pilfered Chief Liu's supplies, taking morphine and a kit for a collapsed lung. He'd released the pressure in Coleman's chest and set up a one-way valve, then poured quick clot into his wound. Coleman lay in Doc's lap, buzzed on morphine, his eyes closed. Doc struggled to stay awake, one hand resting over Coleman's chest.

A snowmobile with two riders buzzed in from the north, screaming over the ice. Their engine whined like a jet's, like it was racing one of the fighters overhead.

Faisal watched the snowmobile roar away, bypassing *Honolulu* and heading for a small group huddled by one of the ragged holes in the ice. He squinted.

Three men sat on the ice, bloody and exhausted, while another tended their injuries, pressing bandages to wounds and starting IV lines. The men held their own fluid bags, leaning on each other to stay upright. From the back, he saw blond hair, and brunet—

One of the men turned.

Even with the bruises, even through the blood, Faisal would recognize him anywhere.

He took off, racing across the ice, sprinting faster than he'd ever run before. *Allah, please, please. All glory is yours, always, but please, Allah, please. Just this once. Please.*

His wild tear caught the attention of the Russians. Soldiers broke away from harassing the remnants of Madigan's army and chased him instead, sliding across the ice. Some shouted. A few opened fire, bullets sparking at his feet. He didn't care. He kept running.

The Russians shooting his way got the attention of the group he ran for. Heads turned.

He saw Ethan's jaw drop. Saw Scott smile in relief. Sasha just stared at him, his usual dour expression somehow darker, the furrows on his lean face deeper.

Adam froze. His gaze shattered, and he scrambled to his feet. Limping, he staggered forward, dropping his IV bag. Scott came to his side, helping him stand and pulling out his IV line. Faisal's eyes picked out the blood over Adam's hip, a wound that still oozed through his bandage.

But Adam was alive. He was *alive*.

Faisal flew at him, leaping the last few feet and throwing his arms and legs around Adam. Adam caught him, staggering back, and would have fallen if it weren't for Scott's bracing hold.

"Adam!" Faisal shouted, shrieking, out of control. "*Yallah*, Adam! Adam! Adam!" His hands cupped Adam's face, stroked down his bruised and battered cheeks. He couldn't stop saying his name, repeating it over and over.

Adam sank to the ice, dropping to his knees as he held Faisal tight. He buried his face in Faisal's neck, breathing in deeply, ragged breaths that sounded like screams. "You're alive, you're alive..." His hands gripped Faisal, running over his back, squeezing his shoulders, his hips, sliding up into his hair. Touching him everywhere, as if making sure he was really there, alive and in one piece. "The others? Is everyone—"

"Coleman is shot. Doc has him stabilized." Faisal looked down into Adam's eyes. Rage pulled at his heart. "Wright... He was with Madigan."

Adam's eyes slipped closed, and he curled forward, pressing his forehead to Faisal's chest as his expression cracked, anguish pouring from him.

"He's gone." Faisal wrapped his arms around Adam again. Even to his own ears, his voice was hard, rough in a way he never was. "You're hurt." He pulled back enough to get his hands on Adam's abdomen, lift his jacket and poke at the wound. A gunshot, clear through, above his hip.

"I'll live," Adam breathed. His face was wet, his eyes were dazed, but he stared at Faisal like he was the sun. "*Allah u Akbar*, you're alive..."

"*Habibi...*" Faisal cupped his cheeks again and pressed their foreheads together. "*Ana bahibak*, Adam. *Ya rouhi, enta habibi hayati.*" *You are my soul, the love of my life.*

ETHAN ROSE AS JACK and Sergey zoomed across the ice. Scott puttered between him and Sasha, trying to plug every wound with gauze and bandages.

He'd demanded a med kit from one of the Russian soldiers, and so far, he'd opened nearly every little paper packet, searching for the right bandages amid the unfamiliar Cyrillic script. Sasha had a thick eyepatch pressed to a wide cut on his neck, and forty pieces of tiny gauze covering his sliced palm.

Ethan's eyes met Jack's as Jack braked and slid off the snowmobile. Elation and exhaustion warred in Jack's gaze. Weariness, too. And, buried in his eyes, fear. Shame.

His hands shook when Ethan went to him. "Madigan is dead," Jack breathed, burying his face in Ethan's neck. "I—" He shuddered, leaning into Ethan.

Ethan held Jack tightly, resting his cheek on Jack's hair. He kissed the curve of his ear, stroked his back. "I'm sorry," he breathed. "You did the right thing. But I know it hurts."

There was a difference in distance when taking another's life. Jack had fired on Madigan's men, had taken a few of them out. Had shot a man trying to kill Ethan. But he'd never killed personally, right up close, watching the light fade out of another man's eyes. Even with a man as vile as Madigan, a man who deserved to die, what Jack had done would still leave a mark on his soul.

"I'm here, Jack," he breathed. "I'm with you all the way."

Jack's arms tightened around his waist, and his hot breath ghosted over Ethan's skin, trembling. He pulled back. "We did it," he said, swallowing slowly. "We actually did it. We saved the world."

"Again."

Jack smiled. "Again."

"You know what this means?" Ethan's hands stroked up Jack's back again, smiling through his own pain, his own exhaustion. "We get our honeymoon. You… me… an empty beach…"

Beaming, Jack caressed his face, cupped his cheeks. "Music to my ears." He leaned in, kissing Ethan.

The kiss stretched on and on, Jack cradling his cheeks as Ethan's hand slid into his hair, cupped the back of his head. He pulled back, dropping kisses to Jack's cheeks, his eyelids, the center of his forehead. "I'm so proud of you," Ethan breathed. "You did this, Jack. You turned this into a victory. You are my hero, Jack. You're the whole world's hero."

AS ETHAN WENT TO Jack, Sasha headed for Sergey.

Silently, Sergey opened his arms, and Sasha folded into his hold, resting his forehead against Sergey's temple. "You did it," Sasha murmured. "Now you must go back to being Russia's president."

"Just because Moroshkin's forces are here cleaning up Madigan's trash does not mean I am safe. We can still make a break for it, Sasha." He kissed Sasha's temple. "I just want to be with you. No more people shooting at us.

No more plane crashes." He pulled back, mock glaring at Sasha. "You are forbidden from flying again. Two crashes in two weeks. *Nyet*. No more."

Sasha stepped back, away from Sergey. "Sergey—"

A new sound roared overhead, thundering jet engines and the bellow of troop transports rumbling up from the south. Helicopters, chewing through the air in a long line, with teams of men sliding down ropes and hitting the ice. Thousands of men, Russian policemen this time, the black-and-blue uniforms of the federal police forces and of the FSB. They swarmed the ice, racing to Moroshkin's men and forcing them to their knees, arresting Moroshkin's traitorous forces. Still more took over guarding the remnants of Madigan's criminal army.

Sergey's jaw dropped. "Ilya…" A smile broke over his face as he tipped his head back and laughed. "Ilya, you son of a bitch! You did it!"

A lone helicopter broke away from the southern fleet, zipping over the ice as if searching for something. It banked hard, circling over Sergey and the group before starting its descent fifty yards to the north. Snow blasted over the ice, whipped up by the propeller blast, stinging their faces. Sergey raised his arm, squinting at the chopper as three men hopped out.

Ilya strode toward them, flanked by Aleksey and Anton. All three were smiling, and Ilya opened his arms to Sergey as he drew near.

"*Yobaniy nasos*," Sergey growled, beaming. He grabbed Ilya and pulled him into a bear hug. "You son of a bitch. What have you done?"

Ilya grasped his shoulders, pulling back just enough to look Sergey in the eyes. "Mr. President, I am pleased to inform you that Moscow is once again yours."

Anton and Aleksey cheered as Sergey shouted, wordless screams of relief and joy that burst from the center of his chest. He grabbed Ilya's face and pressed their foreheads together, smiling at his friend. Beside him, Sasha tipped his head back and sighed up to the sky, his eyes closed. Sergey pulled him close, hugging him as tears pricked the backs of his eyelids.

Jack and Ethan joined them. Ilya saluted Jack, and Anton and Aleksey pumped his hand, smiling and congratulating him over and over. "Message from your embassy, Mr. President," Ilya said, pulling out a folded piece of paper and handing it to Jack. "I was told to deliver this to you when I found you."

Sergey read over Jack's shoulder.

Traitor found. White House secure. Canada has taken out the trash. Come home, Phoenix. Signed, President Elizabeth Wall.

69

Russian-Occupied Kara Sea

Ilya ARRANGED AN IMMEDIATE transport for them off the ice and back to Moscow.

Anton and Aleksey staked flares in the ice, guiding heavy transports fitted with skis onto a spray-painted runway. In less than an hour, the ice pack looked like a metropolitan airport, albeit one encased in a winter wonderland.

Five body bags were loaded onto a cargo jet, only Munoz's in a place of honor. Madigan, Cook, Kobayashi, and Wright's were stored out of sight. Jack turned away, not watching as Madigan was carried on board. He stared over the gaping maw in the ice sheet where the *Veduschiy* had sunk. There were more American ghosts beneath the ice. More heroes they had to recover.

Jack had Anderson and his crew evacuated to the embassy in Moscow on the first flight out. A security detail stayed behind, along with the engineering team, first shutting down the reactor and then blowing the command and control systems, stripping *Honolulu* of her technology.

Jack shook Anderson's hand as he climbed up the cargo ramp. "You did it, Captain. You saved everyone."

"They were your orders, Mr. President." Anderson saluted sharply. "The whole plan was yours. And... what you went through...." Anderson squinted. His gaze flicked to Ethan, exhausted and leaning against Scott, still breathing shallowly, still blood-covered, and wrapped in Jack, Sasha, and Scott's jackets. "Like you said: when was the last time a president truly sacrificed for America?"

He returned Anderson's salute as his guts folded in on themselves. He'd hear Ethan's screams and the sounds of his waterboarding in his nightmares for the rest of his life. "None of this should have happened. I was only doing what had to be done."

"That's what makes you a good man." Anderson followed his men into the jet, the last one to board. The ramp rose, and then the plane started to taxi away and lift into the gray skies, disappearing into the leaden gloom.

They were next. A sleek transport waited for them, something that promised a fast flight back to Moscow.

Sergey, his bloodied arm in a sling, pulled Jack close before they boarded. "My people will take you straight to your embassy."

"We'll be headed stateside as soon as we get there. I'm sure the news has already broken. I need to get back to the US." Jack smiled at his friend. "But we'll be talking soon, I'm sure. Congratulations on getting your country back."

Sergey let him go with a rueful grin. "I will miss you, Jack. Being with you every day… It was good." He shrugged. "When it was not horrible."

Jack laughed. "Take care of yourself. And good luck. I'm happy for you."

He and Scott helped Ethan on board, each of them supporting a shoulder. Ethan was still too cold. Hypothermia threatened to pull his temperature even lower. His chest rattled with every breath, and dark bruises stretched over his abdomen, his ribs. Ethan's neck was a raw, bloody mess. Bruises in the shape of chain links looked like stamps on his skin next to open wounds that still oozed. Jack helped him lie down and pillowed Ethan's head in his lap. Scott laid a blanket over Ethan and sat at his feet, resting one arm over Ethan's shins. Seconds later, Scott started to snore.

Faisal and Doc carried Coleman's stretcher on board. A Russian flight medic took over, but Doc still buzzed around Coleman, checking everything the Russian medic did until the medic forced Doc into a jump seat and buckled him in. Doc tried to protest, but he dropped off, falling asleep as he reached for Coleman.

Faisal helped Adam on board next. They sat side by side, wrapped in a single blanket, their hands laced together. Adam rested his head on Faisal's shoulder.

The ramp closed, and the engines rumbled as the plane's propellers started to spin. Ice crunched beneath their skis. Pressure pushed them back in their seats, the plane accelerating down the slick runway, and then they were airborne, soaring into the skies. Jack peered out of the window, watching the ice cap fade away, the remains of their battle, their desperate last stand to save the world.

There was still so much to do. Environmental scientists would have to be flown in, an international team that could reverse the damage Madigan had wrought. Sergey promised an exclusion zone around the Kara Sea, and with no one to ignite the gases at their source, where the concentration was highest, the chain reaction that could burn through the planet wouldn't occur.

He rested his head against the cool glass as wispy steel clouds surrounded the plane, enveloping them and carrying them away.

Back to reality.

His fingers slid through Ethan's hair. His other hand rested on Ethan's chest, holding his hand. What would happen now? What would the world's reaction be? Could anyone ever understand what they had done? What they had experienced? The reasons behind the choices he had made?

What waited for them back home? Respect? Recrimination? Revulsion? If he had to put money on it, he'd bet on the worst.

Across from them, Adam cleared his throat. He caught Ethan's gaze, and then Jack's. "When we land in Moscow…" He licked his lips. Swallowed. "I'm not going to the US embassy." He squeezed Faisal's hand. "I'm going to the Saudi embassy with Faisal. I'm going home."

Ethan nodded. He looked up at Jack.

"Lieutenant Adam Cooper." Jack smiled. "I accept your resignation from the United States Marine Corps, and I thank you for your exceptional service to our country."

Adam's face crumpled, and he turned into Faisal's neck, hiding as he gasped, as he sniffed, as tears streamed down his cheeks. Faisal held him through it, pulling him close. He mouthed two words to Jack and Ethan over Adam's trembling body: *Thank you*.

Jack's fingers slipped through Ethan's hair, until Ethan's eyes closed and exhausted snores fell from his lips.

No matter what, he and Ethan would be together. Married now, bound together for the rest of their lives. His wedding ring gleamed, diamonds shining in the dark titanium channel, a promise that looped around his finger. Eternity. Forever. Perfection.

AFTER JACK AND THE others left, Sergey became a whirlwind, slipping right back into the presidency and working side by side with Ilya. Moroshkin's men were taken into custody, as were Madigan's.

"Where is Moroshkin?"

Ilya's expression turned sour. "We haven't found him. I will interrogate Moroshkin's senior leaders when we are back in Moscow. We will find the bastard."

"He brought his men back when we needed them, Ilya. He came home in the end."

Ilya snorted and shook his head. He'd never shared Sergey's more idealistic ideas.

Finally, it was time for Sergey to fly back to Moscow, take the reins of his government back and make a statement to Russia and to the world. Begin the process of unifying the country and healing the wounds of the coup. But he wasn't going back alone.

He found Sasha helping Anton and Aleksey as they processed Moroshkin's men and prepped them for transport back to Moscow and to Lubyanka Prison.

"Time to go, Sasha. Ilya has a chopper for us."

Sasha stared at him, not saying a word. His eyes traced Sergey's features, the long lines of his body.

Finally, he spoke. "Let me help Anton and Aleksey a little more. I will fly back with them later."

Ilya shouted to Sergey, waving him over to the helicopter waiting to ferry him away. The engines were warm, the blades already whirling at full blast.

"Hurry." Sergey smiled, and he reached for Sasha's bandaged hand. "I want you with me in the Kremlin. I have been dreaming of it."

Sasha nodded and gave him a thin, weak smile. "You must focus on what you need to do. You are the president, Sergey. Your duty is to the Russian people. They need you now, more than ever."

"Together." Sergey squeezed Sasha's hand. "We will do it all together. You and me. The way it should be."

"*Ya lyublyu tyeba,*" Sasha breathed. *I love you.* He squeezed once and then let go of Sergey's hand. He looked down. "Go. Before Ilya has an aneurysm."

Sergey's smile almost split his face. "*Zvezda moya*, I will see you soon." *My star.*

He jogged away, to Ilya and the helicopter waiting for him. He climbed on board, slipped a headset on, and turned back to Sasha.

Sasha watched him rise, their gazes locked until Sergey disappeared into the clouds.

70

Moscow

THE KREMLIN WAS A war zone.

A horde of barbarians had moved in, it seemed. Carpets had been torn up, golden chandeliers lay in ruins on the floor, paintings had been ripped down and their canvases torn. Statues had been lined up in the grand halls and used as target practice. Not a single room had escaped some form of wild destruction. The parliament buildings, too, had suffered. The council chambers and inner offices had been torched. Sergey's private office had been ransacked and burned.

Power had been cut to the Kremlin as part of Ilya's attack plan. Nothing worked. It would take months to repair the damage.

The presidential apartments were no better. Bullet holes ringed the walls, gouged through paintings and sculptures. One leg on his hideous, gaudy gold dining table had snapped, and the table had toppled over like a dead golden cow, legs stretched straight in the air. His bed, an ornate four-poster that had been luxurious even for the czars of old, had been sliced and diced, the mattress shredded, the velvet curtains around the bed torn down. Carpets had been burned. The red couches he, Sasha, and Ilya had lounged on for so many nights had been broken, stuffing thrown around the sitting room, their wooden legs used as fuel in the fireplace.

He did what he could, pushing debris to the side and rolling up the burned Turkish rug. Blankets and sheets in a tucked-away linen closet were, thankfully, unscathed. He pulled them down, and the few pillows that had escaped destruction. Sergey laid everything out in front of the fireplace in the sitting room before starting a roaring fire, the only source of light.

He found two unbroken glasses—mismatched, of course—and a half-full bottle of whiskey.

It had been hours. Hours since he'd left the Kara Sea, and hours since he'd come back to the Kremlin. He'd addressed the nation, reassuring the Russian people that their government was back in power, back at work for them. Ilya had, helpfully, of course, left him a four-foot-high stack of reports and folders to pore through. His first day back at the Kremlin sprinted from six to ten to twelve to eighteen hours.

And still no sign of Sasha.

Before he and Ilya dropped from exhaustion, he'd asked Ilya to check around, see where he'd gone. All of the transports had returned from the Kara Sea hours before. Maybe Sasha was resting. Or seeing Dr. Voronov, who'd driven right up to the Kremlin gates like it was any other workday.

Sergey sipped his whiskey and watched the flames flicker in the fireplace. Exhaustion tugged on his aching bones. Christ, he was old. A month-long insurgency, and two weeks on the run with Jack. He felt like a submarine had run him over. Everything hurt. Every piece and part of him ached. Even his hair. Even his toenails. His shoulder ached. All he wanted was to curl up with Sasha and sleep for a decade. Perhaps make love again. Explore Sasha's body slowly, like he'd yet to. They'd been too wound up, too strung out on *Honolulu*. Too little space, too little time. Too much they still had to say. A desperate fumble, like they were still schoolboys sneaking into a hall closet for a furtive grope and rub. He wanted more. So much more. What did Sasha taste like? What did he sound like, writhing in ecstasy? What would Sergey's name sound like falling from Sasha's lips as he came?

Would Sasha take him? He could picture it. Their bodies, rocking together. Sweat-slick skin and kisses pressed to shoulders. Sasha's hands running down his skin. Him, pushing Sasha back. Watching his chest heave, that splotchy flush staining his pale flesh. Straddling him. Seeing that look in his eyes, that one that made Sergey feel like he was the sun, and Sasha the moon. Their lives were orbits of each other. Gravity and inevitability had pulled them together. It had only been a matter of time.

What would their future look like? They'd keep their love quiet, at least for a while. Rebuild Russia together. He'd wake up every day with Sasha by his side, listen to his ideas and his dreams all day long, until they tumbled back into bed together. Was this what Jack experienced? Was this Jack's life in Washington DC, living with Ethan in the White House?

How could he be so lucky?

Knocking broke his reverie, heavy pounding against the thick wood. "Finally!" He rose, carrying his whiskey with him as he sauntered to the entrance. He'd dressed down, flinging away his suit jacket and unbuttoning his dress shirt. His suit pants were rumpled from the day that never seemed to end. But he didn't care. "Sasha, *zvezda moya*, these apartments are also yours now, you do not need to knock—"

He opened the door.

Ilya stood in the doorway, stiff. He squinted at Sergey.

"Ilya?" He frowned. "What are you doing? Where is Sasha?"

Ilya pressed his lips together. His eyes slid sideways. "He is not in the Kremlin. He's not even in Moscow."

Reality seemed to flush away, his hopes, his dreams vanishing in an instant, torn out of his heart. Unsteady, Sergey leaned into the thick door, stumbling as he shook his head. "No, no, no, he said he was coming back with

Anton and Aleksey. You must go talk to them. They will tell you where he is. Go, Ilya, go to—"

Ilya grabbed his hand and stopped his wild gesturing. "Sergey. I already spoke to them. Sasha told them he was taking a different flight. I checked everything. No one remembers seeing him." Ilya exhaled softly. "He's gone."

You must focus on what you need to do. You are the president again, Sergey. Your duty is to the Russian people. They need you now, more than ever.

Sergey squeezed his eyes closed as his breath left him, rushing out in a great whoosh. Curling forward, his forehead hit the door. *Sasha, you fool. It is you I need now, more than ever.*

He should have seen this coming. Sasha's fanatical dedication to Sergey's presidency and his dreams of what could be changed. He was a Russian's Russian; Sasha would have made a fantastic Communist. Sacrifice for the state. Live an empty life. Give up all your dreams. Take nothing for yourself. He should have seen this coming from the night on the beach. Sasha's stricken expression, as if him returning Sasha's love was the worst possible thing that could happen in the world.

"That answers my next question." Ilya's voice was soft but gruff. "When did you…"

He wouldn't keep this from his friend. Sergey waved him in, plodding back to the sitting room and the roaring flames. Ilya stared at him when he sat in the middle of a nest of blankets that had obviously been made for two. "How do I answer that?" Sergey closed his eyes. "While hunting Madigan with Jack. After Sochi, when we were building the insurgency. Here, in the Kremlin. A thousand different times. A thousand different ways." He tipped his head forward, letting it dangle between his shoulders.

"It was obvious to me how he felt. The way he looked at you. You are the center of his world."

"And he became the center of mine." Agony stabbed him deep in his heart. Sasha was *gone*. Again. "Ilya, what must you think of me? This is an old man's middle-aged crisis, yes?" He swallowed hard. "Tell me I am delusional. Tell me I am mad. Tell me I was taken in by a pretty face. Tell me this is *nothing*." He slammed his fist against his chest. "Tell me I should not feel this way."

Ilya stayed quiet. His eyes lingered on Sergey. "I think," he finally said, "you have not gotten close to anyone in a long time. Not even your wives. I was there for both." Ilya leaned forward, pushing into Sergey's shoulder. "If he was the one who got your blood pumping again…" His hands spread wide as he shrugged. "Who am I to judge, if he makes you happy?"

"I was happy." His voice was barely a whisper. He stared at the flames. "I thought—"

I thought I was in love.

No, he *was* in love. He'd already fallen in love with Sasha, had embraced that love, and he'd thought Sasha had finally, *finally* embraced his own love in return. *Ya lyublyu tyeba.* Hadn't Sasha said it? The last thing he said to Sergey. *I love you.* The first time… and the last time.

He should have heard it for what it was. A goodbye, and not a promise of happiness to come.

The fire blazed, almost too hot to endure when combined with the roar of his own shame, his own soul's furious wailing. He burned from the inside, his heart going off like a nuclear reactor gone critical, a meltdown of what felt like his entire world. His anchor had come undone; he was adrift at sea.

What now? What did he do when faced with the loss of the one person who meant everything to him… *again*? What did he do when Sasha kept cutting out his heart and taking it away with him?

Well, Sasha would keep it this time. Keep Sergey's heart and all of his dreams, all of what they could have become.

Sasha was gone. And this time, he wasn't ever coming back.

Final Day of Congressional Hearings Set to Begin for President Jack Spiers

The final day of congressional hearings of President Jack Spiers is set to begin on Capitol Hill today. For two weeks, lawmakers from both the House and the Senate have conducted an extensive investigation into President Spiers's actions from the day of the Russian coup in Sochi to his return to the United States from Moscow, following a questionable joint US-Russian black strike on former General Porter Madigan's terrorist camp in the Arctic. The joint strike led to the death of Madigan and the disbandment of his terrorist army just prior to the launch of what has been described as "a devastating terrorist attack against the world."

Investigators have questioned whether any of the actions taken by Presidents Spiers and Wall were constitutional. The White House and President Spiers both claim that Presidents Spiers and Wall were working in "close cooperation" during the entire operation. Who was in charge of the strike, and who ultimately authorized the mission, are critical questions for the investigators, who have struggled to unravel President Spiers's and Wall's murky chain of presidential succession. President Spiers claims he surrendered his presidency to then-Vice President Wall under the Twenty-Fifth Amendment.

Under the Twenty-Fifth Amendment, a president may voluntarily surrender his duties only after notifying the Speaker of the House of his decision. Such notice was not given by President Spiers. However, the Vice President may also assume the office of the president provided that a majority of the Cabinet or the House of Representatives affirm that the president is unable to discharge his duties. Vice President Wall ascended to the presidency after the Cabinet was briefed about President Spiers's injuries in the Langley blast, injuries which turned out to be fabrications. Their signatures affirming President Wall's ascension to the presidency, and the invocation of the Twenty-Fifth Amendment itself, have been challenged as fraudulent, with several Cabinet members publicly complaining that they were misled.

President Spiers's legal status during the events of the previous month is a critical concern. If Spiers was legally the sitting president, then his actions with the Russian insurgency would have legal basis. However, if he is determined to not have been serving as the sitting president at the time, which he himself maintains that he was not, then congressional investigators suggest he has broken the Logan Act, a law that forbids private US citizens from conducting diplomacy on behalf of the United States government. Jack Spiers, private citizen, would have had no legal grounds to offer support to the Russian insurgency or lead them to a rendezvous with US naval assets.

Republican congressional investigators have repeatedly raised the question of whether Spiers's actions violate the Espionage Act. During the course of his Arctic strike, the Russian president, a former FSB officer, and other Russian and foreign nationals, "entered and transited" on a US nuclear submarine. US nuclear submarines remain Top Secret installations and have been deemed "vital and essential" military equipment by Executive Order. The foreign nationals were reportedly in the command center of the submarine, exposed to America's highest technological inner workings. Several congressmen have called for charges of treason to be brought against President Spiers.

The hearings are unprecedented in American politics, bringing both chambers of Congress together in a patchwork of investigations. Due to overlapping and deeply specialized issues, a bicameral special investigations committee was established, comprised of members of the House Judiciary Committee, the Senate Select Committee on Intelligence, and the House Committee on Oversight.

In the final day of hearings, Senator Stephen Allen, famously hostile to President Spiers, is set to take the floor and address President Spiers directly.

71

Washington DC

JACK'S PALMS SLICKED WITH cold sweat. He breathed slowly, in and out, as representatives and senators took their seats at the crescent-shaped dais. They stared down at him, sitting alone in the center of the chamber at the long inquisitor's table. In the gallery, well behind him, Ethan sat with Scott and Levi. He could feel Ethan's gaze, a warmth in the center of his back, like Ethan was the sun trying to shine just for him.

One more day. Only one more day.

And after... well, it was best not to think too far ahead of himself.

He'd known, as soon as he gave the reins to Elizabeth, as soon as he slipped out of that hospital, that his choices would come back to haunt him. He'd been compromised by everything—by his aching, bleeding heart, his wounded soul, and his broken dreams—and he'd absolutely put Ethan over the United States. He would *always* put Ethan over the United States. Over *everything*.

But that wasn't what presidents did. It didn't matter that, in the end, they'd saved the world.

Now, his choices were being picked apart by bureaucrats, by lawyers and congressmen who hated his guts. Who'd railed against him, and had called him an abomination. A traitor to the party, and even to the nation.

His hands shook as the proceedings were called to order, and he was reminded that he was still under oath. He laced his bruised and scabbed fingers together, trying to hide their trembling. His thumb played with his wedding band, rolling the diamonds and dark metal around his finger.

"Senator Allen, you have the floor." The chairwoman turned the proceedings over.

Jack turned and locked gazes with Senator Allen.

Silence.

"Mr. President..." Allen began, shaking his head. "I can't believe we're here. I cannot, for the life of me, actually believe that we are right here. Sitting in this room, having these discussions. Over the past two weeks, we have already established the facts surrounding your actions. My questions to you will be brief. I expect your complete forthrightness."

Jack swallowed.

Senator Allen leaned forward, glaring at him. He lifted a sheet of paper and peered down his glasses. "Mr. President, were you or were you not incapacitated in Bethesda Naval Hospital for three weeks following the attack at Langley?"

"I was not."

"Did you or did you not delegate your presidential powers to then-Vice President Elizabeth Wall and conspire to leave the country?"

"I did."

"Did you or did you not join with Russian President Sergey Puchkov and the Russian insurgency in the Russian Caucasus?"

"I did. But not to fight in their insurgency." *I went to find Ethan and put us back together.* "I went to forge an alliance with President Puchkov and join forces to take out Madigan. He posed a grave threat to not just our two countries, but to the entire world."

"And did you forge this alliance with President Puchkov?"

"I did."

"Mr. President, according to article two, clause two of the United States Constitution, the Treaty Clause empowers the president of the United States, and *only* the president of the United States, to chiefly negotiate agreements and treaties. In the *US vs Curtiss-Wright* verdict, Justice Sutherland wrote, and I quote, '...the president *alone* has the power to speak or listen as a representative of the nation... The president is the *sole organ* of the nation in its external relations and its *sole representative* with foreign nations.' The president *alone*." Allen's eyes flicked off the page, glaring down at him. "So, if you were not the president at this time, as you insist you were not, then what were you doing forging an alliance with the Russian president?"

Jack pressed both hands flat against the surface of the table, the polished oak and mahogany gleaming in the light of a hundred flashing camera bulbs. "Title three, chapter four of the United States Code also specifies that the president may delegate certain functions of their authority to another. It is under this specific law that I was able to open negotiations with President Puchkov."

"Title three, chapter four. 'The Duties of the President of the United States', specifically the delegation of duties." Allen seemed prepared for the answer. "You're saying that you delegated some of your powers to then-Vice President Elizabeth Wall?"

"No. I'm saying President Wall delegated a specific set of powers to *me*. In connection with her government, and with her full blessing, I approached President Puchkov and asked for our two governments to work together."

"President Spiers, you are saying that you did not violate the Logan Act?"

"No, I did not." Jack leaned into the microphone, his voice booming around the room. "And I will remind the senator that the proper address is President Spiers-Reichenbach."

Senator Allen's eyebrows shot straight up. He set his paper down, smoothing it as his lips pursed. "Let's talk about your marriage, President Spiers-Reichenbach. In the middle of this catastrophe, in the middle of what the White House describes as the 'potential end of the world', you found time to plan a wedding?"

Red-hot fury bubbled in his chest. His eyes narrowed, and his hands shook on the tabletop. His wedding ring gleamed. "Before entering what we both understood to be a mission with an almost certain probability of death, yes, we decided to marry."

"This was a rash decision? Made in the heat of the moment?"

"Absolutely not."

"Did you take time away from important military matters for your wedding, Mr. President? How much of an impact did this wedding have on critical operations?"

"I would say none. It was after a quick lunch with the captain. We were delayed transiting the Bering Strait. The entire ceremony took four minutes. If we had not chosen to get married, then lunch would probably have continued for another half hour."

Murmurs from the gallery. The silent representatives and senators seated at the dais glared at the crowd.

Allen continued. "Are you aware, President Spiers-Reichenbach, that you are being accused of violating the Espionage Act? And if charges are brought against you, the punishment could be life in prison, or even death?"

"I am aware." His voice shook. His eyes strayed again to his wedding ring.

"What do you have to say for yourself?"

Jack inhaled slowly, dragging air in through his nose. "Did I work with Russian President Sergey Puchkov? Yes. Did I bring him and other foreign nationals aboard a US nuclear submarine? Yes. Were foreign nationals exposed to classified information, including movements of our forces, plans and procedures, and sensitive military tactics? Yes. Were we 'at war or in a time of conflict'? Yes." He swallowed. Those were the high points. Conviction on any of those charges would mean multiple life sentences as a starting point. "But we were *not* at war or in conflict with President Puchkov's Russian insurgency. President Puchkov was, and remains, an ally.

"The world grows more complicated every day. People we thought we could trust turn out to be traitors. Nations that have long been in opposition to the United States became close friends. I had a choice to make: did I trust the people I allied with? Did I need their help to execute the mission? Senator, presidents shape the future every day with the choices we make. Sometimes we choose right. Sometimes we choose wrong. But in this situation, I firmly believe that I made the right choice. President Puchkov has proven his personal and political trustworthiness multiple times over."

Jack licked his lips. In for a penny, in for a pound. "President Puchkov helped recover several of our assets when Madigan published Top Secret intelligence cables online, outing the identities of undercover intelligence officers operating in dangerous and risky environments. Where we were unable to recover all of our people, President Puchkov ordered his agents to assist. Because of his actions, five of our officers who would have been killed were saved. They were exfiltrated from their operations, flown to Moscow, and immediately transferred to US control."

Gasps rose around the room, from the gallery and the dais. Anyone not on the Senate Select Committee on Intelligence had never heard the details of the recovery of their intelligence officers overseas after Madigan's leak. He and Sergey had vowed to keep it private. Eyes bulged almost out of their sockets. He could practically hear the headlines screaming across the internet, screeching over social media and blaring out of the TV.

"Prior to the coup, our two nations were developing joint plans to seek out and destroy Madigan after the sinking of the *Vinogradov*, and as an extension of our already close cooperation in the Middle East, combating the remains of the Caliphate. President Puchkov has also spent time in the White House Situation Room. He was instrumental in saving American lives during the hijacking of oil tankers in the Strait of Hormuz in early spring. He ordered a Russian destroyer to sail in-between a terrorist vessel and one of our aircraft carriers moored in Bahrain, shielding our forces from possible destruction.

"President Puchkov has also personally saved my life on multiple occasions. In Sochi, during the coup. In Russia, while we were transiting to the rendezvous, and in the Arctic. He has been, and always will be, a close friend to me and to the people of the United States. He has proven through his actions that he is an ally to us and a friend of the world." Jack closed his eyes and took a steadying breath. "He was also with me when Madigan died."

The chairwoman of the committee leaned forward, speaking over the sudden shouts and calls from the gallery. "Madigan's death is not the subject of this investigation."

Jack said nothing as the chairwoman called for order, over and over again. Some of the loudest cries since he'd returned had been questions about Madigan's death. How had it happened? Who had killed him? What were the circumstances? When would the autopsy be released?

The whole federal government was tight-lipped about Madigan's death. Who actually knew what he'd done? Not even Jack knew the answer to that. He'd testified in a closed hearing before the Senate Select Committee on Intelligence. But those walls were famously silent, and words spoken in those chambers often never saw the light of day.

Senator Allen chaired that committee. He'd led the questioning there, keeping Jack sweating for almost a full week as they picked through every single moment of what he'd done.

The chairwoman turned the floor back over to Senator Allen, once she wrangled control back from the gallery. Cameras flashed. Bulbs popped. The hum of video recorders filled the air. Jack stared at the maze of wires before his table, power cords to a hundred different video cameras, fifty different microphones.

"President Spiers-Reichenbach," Allen began. "Whether or not your actions were legal or illegal—and that is something this committee will decide—you have *absolutely* violated the public's trust in you. You bring up defenses to each of the possible charges levied against you, Mr. President, and the common theme running through them all seems to be that you think you can dictate what is true and what is not true at your whim. Whether you *are* or *are not* the president. The presidency is an elected office, one that cannot be disposed of because you feel like taking a break. Whether you *are* or *are not* incapacitated, or just decided to play hooky. Whether you *are* or *are not* guilty of espionage because you happen to like the Russian president."

Jack felt suddenly small, exposed in the glare of the cameras, like a fish alone in an empty bowl with a thousand eyeballs staring in at him.

"The office of the president, and the immense duties and responsibilities therein, do not personally belong to you, President Spiers-Reichenbach. You are merely holding the office. The presidency belongs to the people of the United States. And, Mr. President, the people of the United States deserve the truth from their leaders.

"Our leaders *must* be accessible. They *must* be trustworthy. If our leadership is not accessible, honest, and accountable, we run the risk of our nation sliding into a degradation of democracy and a despairing illusion of freedom. Mr. President, you have *not* been accessible. You have *not* been honest. And you are now being held *accountable*." Allen fell silent, staring at Jack. "What do you have to say for yourself?"

The chambers fell into an absolute silence. Even the press of cellphone keys, the tap of manic fingers on screens, ceased. A thousand eyeballs, again, fixed on him, and through the television, a hundred million more as well. Jack's heart hammered, pounding against his ribs. Expectancy hung in the air, alongside the hum of microphones and whirl of cameras.

Jack stared down at his hands, at the twinkle of his wedding ring. The world seemed to tilt, tip over sideways. His stomach wrenched, a gut-punch to the center of his soul. He'd been a lifelong public servant, had built a career out of wanting to do the right thing. Wanting to make the world better. But everything he'd done was dissolving, every choice he'd made washed in bitter recriminations. His actions were being picked apart by people who hadn't been there, who hadn't seen what he'd seen, or felt what he'd felt. Who hadn't had to weigh the world against the love of his life and make a choice with a gun to his heart. Who didn't have to live with choices that could break a man in two. Grief, aching, swelling grief roared through him. The recitation of his sins, the public indictment of his character, was like a claw gouging his soul, hollowing him out with every word.

He breathed out carefully. "Senator, this world is complex. Tumultuous and challenging in ways that defy logic and defy emotion. Situations are quick to evolve, and quick to turn disastrous. Threats lie in every shadow. Friends can be hard to find. It's a painful world, when you get right down to it. But, to my bones, Senator, I believe in this world. And I believe in this country, in these United States. I have always dreamed of serving this nation. I have always wanted to give everything that I could give to make her stronger, more beautiful, more inclusive, more equal, more prosperous. In short, everything that I could to make her a more perfect union. I have devoted the entirety of my adult life to this nation, and I have done so with joy.

"In the past eighteen months, America has faced a threat from Madigan that it has never faced before. A former general, a man so intimately acquainted with our intelligence and terrorist-fighting capabilities that he was able to remain one step ahead of our considerable forces at all times. A man who had sown a network of like-minded anarchists and conspirators across the world. A man who planned not just the destruction of our nation, but our world. Our way of life. A man who wanted to rip America from her pedestal and replace our shining light with a despot's vision of a totalitarian utopia.

"I chose to take extreme actions to stop this madman. In turn, he chose to take extreme actions against me. Cloning my deceased wife. Attacking the heart of our nation's intelligence and government. In his quest to destroy me, others paid the ultimate price."

Jack swallowed, pressing his lips together as his voice trembled. He took another breath, his hands flat on the table again. His wedding ring gleamed, sparkling as if it were a beacon signaling to his heart. *Ethan... You are my everything.* He wanted, more than anything, to turn around and catch Ethan's gaze. See him smile. Borrow his strength.

"I have no misgivings about the choices I made. I have no doubts that extreme measures were required to root out this cancer of a man. In order to preserve the American way of life, the beacon of liberty in our great world, sacrifices must sometimes be made. *I* was willing to pay that price. *I* was willing to be that sacrifice and lay down my life for this nation and this world. Every choice I made was for the American people. I would gladly have died for everyone in this room, and everyone watching. More than once, I was certain that my next moments were my last. In some way, it's a terrible blessing that I am here now. I lived to face this hearing."

A few dark chuckles rose in the gallery. The dais was deathly, gravely silent.

Jack leaned back and stared at Senator Allen. He'd done what he'd done. Made his choices. Chosen to love Ethan, and follow that love wherever it took him. Chosen to fight back, to not take what Madigan had thrust upon him and

Ethan. Chosen to stand up and work together with Sergey to right their crazy, tilted world.

But most of all, he'd chosen Ethan, time and again. And he'd never regret that.

Senator Allen stared back and said nothing.

"President Spiers-Reichenbach." The chairwoman took over, leaning close to her microphone. "What are your intentions? Do you plan to invoke the Twenty-Fifth Amendment and reclaim the presidency?"

Jack's eyes unfocused, the chambers before him going blurry. This was it. The end of the line. Grief roared through him again, a silent scream. "No, Madam Chairwoman," he choked out. "I do not. My intention is to return to private life and let the presidency remain in the extremely competent hands in which I left it. President Elizabeth Wall has my full support as president of these United States."

Silence. Profound, eternal silence, broken only by the whirr and click and flash of cameras capturing his gasp, the way he looked down and tried to hide his face. The tear he couldn't quite blink away sliding down his cheek.

"If there are no further questions," the chairwoman said, looking to Senator Allen.

Allen shook his head.

"We are adjourned." Her gavel slammed twice, and the chambers erupted in a roar, shouts and questions beating down on Jack from every direction.

ETHAN, SCOTT, AND LEVI worked their way to Jack's side, shoving through the crowd. Secret Service agents from California had been brought in to cover Jack, agents who had no relationship with him, the White House, or the ongoing investigations into President Wall, Levi, or Welby. They stood stone-faced by Jack's side, twin statues that never said a word.

Ethan pulled Jack close, wrapping one arm around him as Jack tucked his face against Ethan's neck and breathed deeply. Ethan's scent—soap, cotton, and their love—flooded him, brought him back from the edge. He was careful when he wrapped his arms around Ethan in return. Ethan's ribs were bandaged, and one arm was in a sling. His throat was still a mess of vivid bruises and hideous scabs. He could still see the mark of each chain link where it had wrapped around his neck. Pictures of his injuries were on the front page of every newspaper, alongside Jack's bruises and his battered face, his split and swollen lip and black eye.

Cameras kept flashing, and the shouted questions grew louder. Questions about them. Questions about Madigan. Accusations. Tirades. Blistering critiques.

"Let's get out of here." Ethan guided Jack behind Scott, heading for the secured exit away from the mob.

A staffer from the dais slipped through the crowd, heading their way. Ethan jerked Jack behind him, turned toward the staffer, and made himself large, spreading his shoulders and glowering.

The staffer, a rail-thin man with large, thick glasses, rolled his eyes. He waved to Levi and whispered in his ear.

Levi frowned. He turned to Jack as the staffer ducked away.

They escaped the chambers, into a private hallway tucked in the bowels of the Capitol. "What was that about?" Scott asked, his hands on his hips.

"Senator Allen asked to speak to the president." Levi still couldn't use Jack's first name, no matter how much he asked. "In private. Away from everybody." He nodded down the hall. "If you want to meet, he's down there."

Jack squeezed Ethan's hand. "Maybe he wants to gloat. Maybe he wants to describe in detail what my life in prison for espionage will be like."

"You don't need to listen to that shit," Ethan growled. "Let's just go—"

"No, I want to hear what he says." He was exhausted, run through from everything. From having to defend himself until his throat bled from speaking. For once, he wanted to hear another person speak, say something, anything that wasn't an accusation against him. He could hope, at least.

Ethan looked less than convinced. But he followed Jack down the hall, and when Jack kept hold of his hand, he followed Jack into the private meeting room.

Senator Allen was already waiting inside. His eyes widened when he saw Ethan at Jack's side, and then dropped to their joined hands.

Jack braced himself, but Allen said nothing.

"Well?" Jack was done being polite. He wasn't the president any longer. And he wasn't in the chamber either. "You wanted to talk?"

Senator Allen licked his lips. Looked down. Ran his tongue over his teeth as he stared at the carpet and pursed his lips. His mouth moved slowly, as if he was trying out his words before he spoke. "I... wanted to thank you for your testimony," he finally grunted. "You spoke well, Mr. President."

"Hopefully it keeps me out of prison." Ethan's hand squeezed down on his, so hard it almost hurt.

Allen's chin lifted. "I don't know what will happen. The committee is divided. Bitterly so. We're going to deliberate through the weekend. I, uh—" He swallowed. "I'll give the White House a call. Let President Wall know the decision before it hits the media."

Jack's jaw dropped. What world was he in? What alternate reality had he stepped into? "Senator... you have never liked me."

"No." Senator Allen shook his head. "I never have. You were too young. Too inexperienced. You're a Millennial, and my generation has never liked yours. I was against your nomination from the moment it was suggested."

The senator's words hit him like bullets, echoes of Madigan's words all over again. He was suddenly back in the Arctic, standing in front of Madigan's sneering face. Then, staring down at his dead eyes, his broken, empty expression, after he'd killed—

Jack clamped down on Ethan's hand and stepped closer to him, seeking his strength.

"But," Senator Allen continued. "I respect you. Especially now. I was there. I saw the stakes at the White House and in the Situation Room."

"What Jennifer did wasn't in the hearings."

"No. Her actions will remain locked behind closed doors. Hers and President Wall's, when she left the country and brokered a treaty between China and Moroshkin." Allen shook his head, suddenly seeming twice as old as his seventy years. But, he strode across the room and offered a handshake. "Thank you, President Spiers-Reichenbach, for your actions."

Stunned, Jack took his hand. They shook, and Senator Allen smiled at him. "I'll do what I can," he said softly. "There's a lot of anger in the committee. But I'll do what I can." He dropped Jack's hand, nodded once, and headed for the door.

When it clicked shut, Jack turned to Ethan and collapsed into him, burying his face in Ethan's neck again before the storm broke in his soul. Sobs tore through him, wracked his body. Ragged wails muffled in Ethan's suit jacket. Everything he'd done had left him empty, a shell of a man, but Ethan's arms and Ethan's soft voice whispering in his ear brought him back, each and every time.

"It's going to be all right, Jack," Ethan whispered, stroking up and down his back. "You're going to be all right. You did the right thing. You made the right choices." He kissed Jack's hair, his temples. Wiped his tears away with his thumb. "I'm here. I'm with you all the way."

"That's the only thing that matters," Jack breathed, his voice shuddering. He squeezed Ethan's hips, breathed out against his neck. "You and me. Together." He wanted to say it, wanted to promise Ethan he'd be with him all the way, too, forever and ever. Raw terror held him back, a visceral fear that ate away at the bottom of his heart. "What if—"

"Then I'll buy a house right next to the prison and visit you every day." Ethan kissed his hair again. "I'll never stop loving you, Jack. I'll never stop being here. I am with you all the way."

He curled into Ethan again, both fists grasping his suit jacket. "I'm scared."

Ethan kissed him again and held him close, but said nothing. What could Ethan say? There was nothing they could do. Their lives were, again, held at the mercy of others. Their lives, and his freedom. *You are being held accountable.*

Some nights he wished he'd died in the Arctic. Wished the torpedoes that had slammed into the *Veduschiy* had destroyed the ship and them too. He would have died holding onto Ethan, and that, at the end of the day, was all he wanted. A life, however long it was, beside Ethan for each and every day. Not this nightmare that loomed before him, the specter of prison and a life apart from Ethan. Would he even be able to take it? How long could he last? When would the agony, the loneliness, the aching heartbreak eat through his soul?

Madigan's face flashed in the darkness behind his eyelids. *You'll never be free of me.*

His stomach lurched, and if he had eaten anything that day, he'd have vomited, thrown it all up in a moment.

Even from beyond the grave, Madigan was still haunting him, still controlling his life. Still turning it to wreckage and ruins, rubble that he had to live with.

THEY SLIPPED OUT OF the Capitol and into waiting SUVs, dodging the press and a mob of people. Some shouted encouragements. Others jeered, promised to see him locked up for the rest of his life. Jack, his eyes red, kept his face down as he climbed into the SUV with Ethan, Scott, and Levi.

Ethan held his hand, lifting it to his lips and pressing kisses to his knuckles, his wedding ring. His thumb stroked over Jack's palm. Scott and Levi stared out the windows, frowns fixed firmly to their faces.

They wound through DC, stopping at the InterContinental Hotel. The press hounded them again as they exited and headed for the entrance. Scott nodded from the backseat.

Some intrepid members of the press managed to slip into the InterContinental's lobby. They chased Jack and Ethan to the elevators, where burly security guards held them back.

Everyone thought they were staying at the InterContinental. Two presidents couldn't occupy the White House at the same time. Jack and Ethan had gone to the Residence to pack a bag each, taking suits and jeans, shirts and their mementos. Jack's teddy bear, Ethan's photo book. The rainbow coffee mug, still sitting beside the coffee maker. Leslie's folded flag. Jack still wore his broken watch, and he'd worn Ethan's sweatshirt from the day of Leslie's blast until the day he stepped foot back on American soil, greeted by President Wall and a mob of reporters at Andrews Air Force base.

They rode the elevator up a few floors and then back down, disappearing to the basement and the secured employee parking garage. The doors opened, and Scott and Levi waved from their SUV. Different than the first, and not government black, the SUV slipped away from the hotel every day with Ethan and Jack lying down in the backseat. They left the stone-faced Secret Service agents at the hotel, a part of the ruse.

An hour later, Scott pulled into his driveway. He and Levi turned around. "We know this is your last night here in DC. Is there anything you want to do?"

Tomorrow, before dawn, they were flying out to Texas. Finally, Ethan was going to meet Jack's parents. Maybe it would be the last time Jack would see his parents, too. Inevitability and terror hung over them like a guillotine, coloring every thought, every word. Would they be able to do this or that again? Was this the last weekend he'd be able to hold Jack's hand? Kiss him freely without prison bars in the way?

Jack's smile was faint, but it was still there. Exhaustion tugged on him, a weight that hung on his soul. He'd aged in the past few weeks, growing weary before the committee during the hearings. "I just want to spend time with my friends. Thank you, Scott, for letting us stay here."

"We're happy to have you." Scott reached back and squeezed Jack's knee. "Even Stacy is glad. She is happy you both are back. And that you brought me home, too." He winked.

Ethan caught Scott and Levi trading looks and smothering grins as they got out of the car. He wrapped his arm around Jack's shoulders and kissed his temple. "I think they're planning something," he whispered.

Scott pushed open his front door.

A roar of cheers rose, hoots and hollers and whistles. What sounded like a stadium of people clapping. Across Scott's front entrance, two banners hung crookedly. *Congratulations* blared in rainbow colors, alongside a statelier *Just Married*.

Jack's jaw dropped as he stepped into Scott's house. He spun, trying to take it all in.

Every member of the Secret Service White House team was there. Even Welby, looking grouchy in his full-leg cast as he sat on Scott's couch, his crutches propped nearby. Pete was there too, his arm looped through Jason's as he helped him stand. Barbara, who'd found Jason bleeding out in the garage and pressed her floral cardigan against his wounds, keeping him alive until the ambulance arrived, stood on Jason's other side. Jack's staff, from Diana Ramirez, his White House counsel—who'd first put together the argument that Ethan and Jack could live together as the first couple—to Director Mori and General Bradford. Even General Bell, standing and smiling in his gruff way.

President Elizabeth Wall stood off to one side, holding a glass of champagne out for Jack.

Jack shook his head, tears filling his eyes. His lips trembled, and he covered his face with his hands as the tears started to fall. Ethan wrapped him up as the cheers rose again, a roar of clapping that went on and on.

Finally, he was able to speak. Ethan kept a hand on his back, and Jack threaded his fingers through Ethan's. "Thank you," he breathed. His voice still shook. "Thank you, from the bottom of my heart. Every one of you helped me. Every one of you believed in me… even when I didn't believe in myself. And that is a gift that I will never forget. I don't know what is going to happen. But I will always love each and every one of you." His lips trembled again, but he forced out, "Thank you," and smiled for his friends.

The party lasted for hours, every guest staying until they'd spoken to Jack and Ethan and congratulated them on their marriage. Thanked him for what he'd done. Expressed hope for the outcome of the hearings. Liz, Scott's daughter, bounded for them, wrapping first Ethan and then Jack up in giant hugs. Even General Bell, who saluted Jack crisply when Jack approached. "Mr. President," he said, only dropping his salute when Jack returned it. Bell turned to Ethan and held out his hand. "Mr. First Gentleman."

Smiling, Ethan took his hand, shaking firmly.

Bell turned back to Jack. "Thank you for putting that monster down." Nodding, he moved off, back into the crowd.

Jack's hand clenched on Ethan's, shaking hard. He turned away from the party, closing his eyes as Ethan held him. For now, the nightmares were still too close to the surface. Madigan's ghost was tenacious, haunting Jack at every moment. Ethan did what he could, staying by Jack's side, and always, always being there when Jack turned to him. "I'm with you all the way," he murmured in Jack's ear.

SCOTT FOUND LEVI IN his backyard, squinting up at the stars as he played with a plastic champagne flute. He sauntered to his friend, his hands in his pockets. He'd ditched his jacket and tie hours ago and had rolled up his shirt sleeves. The summer night was cool, but compared to the Arctic, it was a sauna.

Levi pressed his lips together and looked away. He frowned, glaring at Scott's fence line. Licked his bottom lip, over and over. "I gotta ask you something, Scott," he finally said. "When I was leading the detail, I went through everyone's background checks again. But I never found yours." He looked up, right into Scott's gaze. "Where is your background check? You hiding something?"

Scott snorted. He tipped his head back, laughing. "I *know* you're not accusing me of working with Madigan. I *know* you're not."

Levi looked like he wanted to puke. "I didn't know what to think. I still don't." He shook his head, grimacing. "C'mon, man. You know what this looks like."

"Yeah. I do. I also know what it looks like to run your own background investigation. That's why I gave it to Harry."

Levi blinked. "Inada?"

"Yeah." Scott jerked his thumb, gesturing back to the party. "We can go ask him. He's here. I asked Harry to run a deep dive on me and on Director Triplett. I wanted it to be aboveboard. I needed everything to be tight. No possibility for anything shady. And Harry was the only guy I trusted at headquarters."

Levi doubled over, breathing out in a great whoosh as he started to laugh. "Jesus Christ, man…" He shook his head. "You couldn't leave that in a damn memo?"

"Well, I kinda left in a hurry." Scott laughed and grabbed him, pulled him close. He wrapped his arms around Levi, groaning as Levi squeezed him tight, hard enough to crack his back. "I'd never turn, Levi. I'd never turn against my friends."

"I know," Levi breathed. "That's why I couldn't believe it. I never said anything." Pulling back, he glared at Scott. "But you owe me, like, seven meals. Cause that's how much I threw up, worrying about you."

Scott chuckled and pulled him close again, steering him back inside his house. "Deal. We can start here. Stacy made her brown sugar sliders. I swear, I want my last meal to be these things."

"Keep eating them, and they will be." Levi grinned, Scott slugged him in the shoulder. Their eyes met, relief rejoicing in the depth of Levi's gaze.

ELIZABETH JOINED JACK AND Ethan in Scott's study as the party wound down. Her Secret Service detail was more than happy to stay for the duration, but she had to get back eventually. She was getting experienced in sneaking away from the White House and avoiding the press.

Still, she sat with them both, sharing another glass of champagne. Jack had finally relaxed, shedding his jacket and tie, and he sat practically in Ethan's lap, one leg thrown over Ethan's on the brown leather couch. He seemed to revel in his status as a private citizen for the night, loose in a way that Ethan hadn't seen since the early days of Jack's administration. Ethan, too, had shed his suit jacket and his sling, and had unbuttoned the top buttons on his dress shirt.

"So," she said, smiling. "Have you thought about what's next for you both?"

"I'm trying not to think about it. Orange isn't my color."

Elizabeth shook her head. She refused to believe that the committee would bring charges against Jack, and told him so every time they met. "I have a few suggestions."

"Elizabeth, I'm not invoking the Twenty-Fifth Amendment." Jack held up his hands, grinning. "It's yours. You wanted it. No backsies." The three of them laughed, shaking their heads at the presidency being described in schoolyard terms.

"Elections are just over two years away." She sighed, blowing air out of her rounded cheeks. "The Unity Party has a lot of work to do, especially without their head."

"I still believe in our party. I still believe it's the way forward. Our generation—" Jack motioned between Elizabeth, Ethan, and himself. "We needed a new party. The old ways weren't working for us. The old battles weren't our battles. We always cared about different issues. I can't believe it took this long."

"We needed someone like you." Elizabeth tipped her champagne glass to Jack, and Ethan slid his hand over Jack's thigh, stroking his leg through his suit pants.

"What are you suggesting?" Ethan stepped in when Jack seemed content to just sip champagne and ignore Elizabeth's growing smile.

"Well, a few things. First, I never filled my Secretary of State position. I hear you're pretty good with diplomacy, Jack."

Jack almost spewed champagne across the room. Coughing, he leaned forward, hacking up a lung as Ethan slapped his back. He glared at Elizabeth. "Very funny. You think I could survive a Senate confirmation hearing? I just escaped Congress. I'm not heading back there anytime soon. You'd have to drag me."

Elizabeth shrugged, then winked. "I'm sure that could be arranged."

Jack shook his head. "Next."

"Well…" Her lightness vanished, and she scooted closer. "I was thinking about something more along the lines of Ethan's role. Something off the books. But something that we need, now more than ever."

Jack leaned back against Ethan's chest and stayed quiet. He peered at her.

"You know as well as I do that it's a brave new world out there. Madigan showed a lot of people how vulnerable we can really be, and just how to strike at us. NATO crumbled when we needed them. Even Canada was willing to listen to Moroshkin. Russia looks like she could be a good ally, but even our best intelligence estimates put her recovery at five years, minimum. Our friend Sergey has a lot of work cut out for him."

Jack nodded. He'd kept up with the presidential daily brief. As a former president, he was legally entitled to receive it. The mass of terrorist threats, the dramatic rise in chatter, and overt and covert plans against the United States, had risen like a tidal wave. The world smelled blood in the water. Sharks were coming from every corner of the globe.

"I was thinking we needed a back channel. Someone who can speak when our government can't. Cloakroom diplomacy. Fully empowered by me, of course," she said quickly. "But also backed up with a sharp dagger." She looked at Ethan. "I want to keep your strike team. Add in a diplomatic element. Maybe we can put some of these threats to bed. Or nip them in the bud before they even begin."

"My team disbanded." Ethan shook his head. "I transferred command authority back to General Bell. Lieutenant Cooper resigned from the Marine Corps. Sergeant Coleman and Doc are on extended leave. Even I don't know where they are."

"We'll build you a new team if you both accept. I believe this is important. And in this new world, I think we need something like this. Asymmetrical diplomacy for an asymmetrical world. We need options open to us, both the cloak and the dagger, and a quick shift capability. Exactly what you did with President Puchkov."

"I might hang for what I've done." Jack wasn't kidding, and he wasn't speaking metaphorically.

"You won't." Elizabeth stood. She set down her champagne flute. "The world needs that kind of moral courage now, Jack. And the world still needs *you*. Think about it."

He waved to her, a half smile on his lips, and then sank back against Ethan when she left, taking half the party with her as the Secret Service agents on duty headed back to the White House.

"What do you think, love?"

"I think," Ethan said, dropping a kiss to Jack's temple, "that you get to decide what you want to do with the rest of your life. It's whatever you want to do."

"Well… Whatever *we* want to do for the rest of our lives."

Ethan smiled slowly, until his cheeks hurt. They were a *we*, together forever, for the rest of their lives. "I'm happy being by your side. It's where this all started, isn't it?"

Jack laughed, a champagne giggle. His cheeks flushed. "By my side… beneath me… on top of me…"

"Oh!" Ethan tipped Jack sideways, pushing him into the couch. He held Jack's hands over his head as he dropped down. His ribs ached and his shoulder twinged, but not enough to stop him from spreading out on top of Jack and dropping kisses to his neck, down his throat, and across his collarbone.

Jack's laughs turned to moans, and his legs wrapped around Ethan as his hips rocked up, his cock thrusting against Ethan's. "I just want this forever," he breathed, arching into Ethan's touch. "I love you so much."

"I love you," Ethan whispered, capturing Jack's lips. Their kiss stretched on and on, and neither man noticed Scott quietly shutting the study door. "And you have me. Forever."

Jack's fingers went to Ethan's shirt, working quickly down the long line of buttons. "Make love to me. Don't ever stop."

The party rolled on without them as Ethan painted Jack's body with love, breathed life into his soul, and held him through all of his tears.

72

Riyadh, Saudi Arabia

ADAM PLUCKED AT THE long sleeves of his snow-white *thawb*. The garment was long and far looser than anything he'd ever worn before. Like a dress, or a muumuu, even. The gentle Riyadh breeze wafted up the long, loose hem. Even though the wind was hot, goose bumps rose on his calves.

Being in Riyadh in summer felt like he was on the surface of Mars. Heat blasted him, as if the sun had turned its whole focus on the desert city. Shimmering heatwaves reflected off the ground, the buildings. Even at the king's palace, with its stately palms, jewel-encrusted courtyards, and industrial air conditioning, the heat still roasted their every move.

Faisal ran his hands down Adam's chest, smoothing his *thawb* after straightening his collar. The ends of Adam's *keffiyeh* dangled over his shoulders, loose knots tickling in the soft air.

The king had summoned them both to Riyadh. King Faisal al-Saud, the man for whom Faisal was named, the ruler of Saudi Arabia, and the head of Faisal's family.

First, Uncle Abdul had been summoned to the palace, shortly after Adam and Faisal landed in Riyadh, sent from Moscow by the Saudi Arabian embassy. Uncle Abdul had been white as a ghost when he stormed into the airport and found them, bruised, bloody, and bedraggled, and barely hanging on. To Jeddah they went, back to Uncle Abdul's villa, along with an army of physicians.

It was in Jeddah they told Uncle Abdul about their marriage.

He'd paced for hours, and then prayed through the entire night. They heard his low voice, the groans and warbles of his Arabic filling the villa. Prayers to Allah, for guidance, for wisdom. For peace. For answers. For help.

Adam and Faisal had clung to each other all night long, every hour repeating the vows they'd made. Faisal wore his dog tags, the metal cool against the warmth of his golden skin.

"No matter what," Faisal whispered against his lips. "We will stay together."

"I'll go wherever you will go. Anywhere." If they were banished. If Faisal was cut off. If they had to resettle somewhere in Europe, or in Malaysia, or Jordan, or Egypt, or Morocco, or even Australia. Somewhere, they would try and have it all: their faith and their love. Would one always have to be subsumed for the other?

No matter what, anywhere they had to go, he'd follow at Faisal's side.

In the morning, Uncle Abdul, ashen-faced, had said, "I must inform the king."

He was on a plane to Riyadh that afternoon.

A week passed.

Doc texted them one afternoon. *Hey asshole. Where did you disappear to?*

He hadn't told Doc and Coleman. They'd been transported to the US embassy while they were unconscious, and they'd woken up at Bethesda Naval Hospital when they were back in the States. He'd never gotten a chance to say goodbye.

[I went home with Faisal. To Saudi.]

No shit? For how long?

[Forever.]

Silence, for hours, and he'd thought that was the last he'd ever hear from Doc.

Coleman's busting out of here in a few days. You got some spare rooms in one of your sugar daddy's palaces? We both wanna be somewhere warm after that shitshow in Santa's hellhole.

He hadn't expected that. Faisal found him struggling to hold back tears as he sat on the dock, the same one he and Doc had shared a beer on when he'd finally admitted the truth about him and Faisal.

[If we still have anything after his family is done with us, then yeah. Please come.]

Good luck, L-T

And then, they'd been summoned to Riyadh.

Faisal's hand shook, trembling as he paced. Adam grabbed him and pulled him close, threaded their fingers together. They stood in the center of King Faisal al-Saud's palace, waiting in the jeweled gardens for their summons to the terrace. Sapphires and rubies and emeralds inlaid in mosaics twinkled overhead and beneath their feet, scattering rainbows across tiles of white marble and turquoise waters, and the palms that shaded the garden. Roses burst in wild bloom, and bees buzzed from flower to flower.

Anyone could see them embracing. Anyone could see as Adam cradled Faisal's face in his hands and stroked his cheeks.

"I am afraid," Faisal whispered. "I don't want to be banished. I don't want to lose the last of my family."

"You will always have me." Adam tried to smile, but a part of him squirmed, his mind screaming that Faisal would only lose his family because of him. Because of what he'd done.

What if the worst happened? What if the king annulled their marriage, or declared it invalid in the eyes of Allah? What if they brought in an imam to rip apart the whole thing, and then arrest them both? Or, more likely, arrest Adam. He could disappear into the Saudi judicial system, die in some dank, dark dungeon, and no one would ever know. Maybe Faisal would one day receive a bill for his death.

Or maybe he'd just disappear.

What if there was a woman, some bride the king had picked out for Faisal? They could shred his marriage to Faisal and remarry him to their handpicked bride in one fell swoop.

Adam closed his eyes. Should they have even come back?

Faisal pressed his trembling lips to Adam's. Now they were in truly dangerous territory. Anyone could be, and probably was, watching. They could explain away the closeness, the touching. But not a kiss.

He kissed him back, wrapping his arms around Faisal's waist. If this was the last kiss, then he wanted it to be good.

Footsteps padded whisper-soft across the marble. A low cough broke them apart, sent them scattering like lightning had struck. A thin aide to the king stared at them both. "The king will see you now."

Walking through the garden felt like he was walking to his death. Did death smell so sweet? Sweat dripped down the back of his neck, but it wasn't from the heat anymore. His sweat was ice-cold and stank with fear. He'd faced terrorists, traitors to his nation, and torture, but facing Faisal's family was what was going to do him in.

Faisal's hand slipped into his. He laced their fingers together.

Ahead, King Faisal sat on a divan, an aubergine pillow dusted with gold thread. Lilies floated in a pond beside him, shaded by a thick palm. Tulips grew in clumps, a rainbow of grid squares interspersed with white marble tiles, like a checkerboard of flowers and negative space. Beyond, more roses grew, thickets of sunset orange and blood red next to royal purple and delicate peach.

Uncle Abdul knelt on a hand-woven rug in front of the king. He stared at them, his expression betraying nothing.

King Faisal motioned to twin rugs laid before him, next to Abdul. He spoke in Arabic. "Join us."

Faisal bowed low, and then folded himself down before the king, sitting beside his uncle. Adam copied his movements, doing what he and Faisal had practiced. He wasn't as smooth as Faisal, but he didn't fall on his face, either.

The king peered at them both, silent. He was old, weathered from years in the desert, a long life in Riyadh. Flypaper-thin skin seemed painted on his bony hands, protruding from beneath his thick robes. When he finally spoke, his voice was rich and deep, melodious in a way that made Adam want to weep. "*Hafeed* Faisal." Even though Faisal wasn't his direct grandson, he used the honorific. "My namesake. I have watched you grow from a boy to a man. My pride in you rose like the sun climbing over the desert. I chose your uncle to succeed me as king, and he tells me he has chosen you, out of all of his children, to succeed him as well. Do you know why this is?"

"No, Your Royal Highness," Faisal whispered. "I never wanted to become king."

King Faisal smiled. Wide gaps stretched between his square teeth. "One reason why it should be you. No one should want to be Saudi Arabia's king. It is a thankless job, and more difficult every day. I am old and weary of this role."

Adam tried to glance sidelong at Faisal, but Faisal's eyes remained fixed on the rug threads.

"I am old, *hafeed*. Your uncle, even, is old. We are old men in a young world." King Faisal sighed, his breath like desert wind. "Do you know our history, *hafeed*?"

Faisal nodded.

"Allow me to share a different telling of our tale. Two hundred years ago, our family made a deal with *Shaytan*. We gained power over these lands, but looked the other way as the Wahhabis seized control of our dynasty's mosques and education. Strict devotion to Allah. What could be the problem? A simple life of prayer and supplication. We were a finger of sand the world had forgotten, and our grandfathers could not see the future."

Faisal shifted, his spine curling forward.

"There is nothing more dangerous to this Kingdom than the Wahhabi and Salafi clergy, *hafeed*."

Adam stopped breathing. He looked up, breaking protocol, as his jaw dropped.

The king kept speaking. "*Yallah*, I have tried, Faisal, to pry free the claws of the Wahhabis. They are like raptors who have dug into their kill. They are not easily broken. Their rabid fundamentalism is no longer quaint. Salafi and Wahhabi leaders push for generations of our young Saudi men and women to become extremists. To embrace hatred and division, and reject the world. The Caliphate was born of these beliefs. Of desperate men yearning to return to the dark ages.

"A life of prayer and supplication is no longer what the Kingdom needs. We need a strong people. Educated. Our graduates can read the Quran, but cannot compute. We train no engineers. No scientists. These clerics, they try to block all of my education reforms. They do not reform their curriculum. They twist our sacred texts into hate. I sack them as fast as I can, but new clerics rise. They are a cancer in this Kingdom." King Faisal shook his head. "Our Kingdom is changing, *hafeed*. The Middle East is changing, faster than we can keep up with. Our people hunger for more engagement with the world. We need a stronger, diversified economy. Private investment. Flow of ideas. We import workers, but not their ideas. We must be more open. Women must be offered the choice to learn, and to work, or our economy will collapse without the input of our whole population. We hover on a precipice. We must strengthen our Kingdom... before we are gone."

Faisal looked up, into his great-uncle's gaze, frowning. They'd never expected these words. If anyone heard the king speak this way, he'd be attacked in the streets. Effigies of him would burn as riots called for his head.

King Faisal sighed, the breath in his body rattling his bones. He leaned forward and rested his hand on top of Faisal's head. "You have been careful, *Alhamdulillah*. They would have killed you if they had known."

Adam saw Faisal's eyes squeeze closed, saw him swallow hard. He wanted to reach out, grasp his hand, thread their fingers together and never let go.

King Faisal cupped Faisal's chin. "*Hafeed*, I left Wahhabism the night your father and mother were killed. *Ibn akh* Omar, your father, my nephew, was murdered by Wahhabi extremists who had been taught religious hatred right here, at home in the Kingdom. I won't lose two family members to these *shaytans*."

Banishment. It's going to be banishment. Adam looked down as the tears started falling down Faisal's cheeks. Damn it, if there was one thing Faisal prayed for, it was to *not* be banished. He loved his home. He loved the Arabian Peninsula. He loved his uncle, and spending time with the family he had left. Especially in the past year, when he and Uncle Abdul had grown closer in his own absence. Damn it, this was going to kill him.

Banishment, and losing his future Kingdom. A high price to pay for a marriage. Doubt filled Adam, rising up in him like vomit, almost choking him. Words pushed at his lips, wanting to come out. He'd take it back, all of it, if Faisal could stay. If he could have everything he wanted. He'd make it easier on everyone.

Damn it all to hell, this was why he'd left in the first place.

"*Hafeed*," the king said softly, watching his great-nephew's tears spill down his cheeks. "Tell me. *Subhanallah*. What do you want?"

Faisal shuddered and closed his eyes. "I want…" he began, his voice shaking. "*In shaa Allah*, I want *everything*. I want to be your *hafeed*, and *ibn akh* Faisal, and husband to Adam bin Cooper. I want Adam to be of the House of Saud. I don't want to go," he breathed. "I don't want to leave my family. I want to be *loved* by my family, exactly as I am."

The king cupped Faisal's wet face with his bony hands. He leaned forward, kissing Faisal's forehead. "*Hafeed*, you are deeply loved. *Ana bahibak, hafeed* Faisal. You are loved for *everything* you are."

Faisal tipped forward, falling into the king's lap as he sobbed. Uncle Abdul and Adam shared a look and then leaned in, resting their hands on Faisal's shaking back. Adam felt Faisal's muscles tremble as be sobbed, raw, aching, soul-tearing sobs that he'd stuffed deep down inside of himself for years.

All those nights he and Faisal had stayed up talking, wondering about Faisal's family. Wondering about what would happen, if they ever found out about their love. Had they ever expected this? Ever dreamed that Faisal would be welcomed with acceptance?

The king stroked Faisal's *keffiyeh*-covered head, murmuring softly. "I left Wahhabism, *hafeed*, and searched for something different. What could bring our Kingdom into the world? What reforms could I make, faced with everything against us? The Wahhabis are a sickness inside the Kingdom, Iran breathes down our neck, the rest of the Middle East preying on us, vying for our power and our control. We are the home of the Prophet, peace be upon him. The home of Islam.

"After your father died, I was lost. Had Allah abandoned the Kingdom? The House of Saud? Trapped by hatred on one side, and silence on the other." King Faisal brushed Faisal's tears away with his thumbs. "When *ibn akh* Abdul came to me years ago, asking to speak about you, I knew what we had to do."

Faisal's eyes went wide, and every muscle in Adam's body tensed, ready to spring into action. Was this where the machete came out? The firing squad? What if all these pretty words weren't what they seemed?

"*Ibn akh* Abdul and I went back to the foundation of the Quran. To the roots of Islam. We turned deep into our faith. Asked questions. Why was the message given to the Prophet, peace be upon him? Why did he receive the blessings? We asked imam after imam, brought dozens in to speak at the palace. They spoke of us being Allah's chosen. Being the ones to unite the world in a great caliphate. But only a few spoke about the heart of Islam: Islam was given to us to fight oppression and to empower people. The basis of the Quran is to seek justice and love for all. To oppose oppression and tyranny. And here, I have become one of the oppressors. A king who enslaves his people." He shook his head. "*'Remember when you were few and oppressed to the ground'*, the Quran says. The soul of a Muslim is supposed to delight in protecting the vulnerable. Helping the downtrodden. Who is more oppressed than *mithli al-jins*?"

Mithli al-jins. The Arabic word for homosexuals, for men who loved other men.

Adam stopped breathing. He saw Faisal's jaw snap shut.

"We read the Quran again, from cover to cover, *ibn akh* Abdul and I. We looked for everything, anything to do with *mithli*. The Wahhabis, the Hanafis, the Salafis, all of them, they say the Quran forbids it. Forbids you from existing. That *mithli* should be purged from the earth."

Adam slid his hands down Faisal's back, to his husband's waist. Monarch or not, if one sideways word fell from King Faisal's lips, he would rip Faisal from his hold in an instant.

"The Quran says *nothing*," King Faisal breathed. "It only speaks of the Prophet Lot, and condemns the rape that occurred there, as all sexual violence should be condemned. But the Prophet Lot is not *the* Prophet, peace be upon our messenger. *Our* Prophet never speaks of forbidding *mithli*. Not once. There is no law in the Quran dictating how love may be condoned or condemned. We turned to the Prophet's example, peace be upon him, to guide our thoughts and actions, as the Prophet's example must always be emulated, he who is of Allah.

"The Prophet loved *mithli*. He welcomed *ghayr uli al-irba min al rijal*, men who felt no attraction for women, to work in his home. Not a single *mithli al-jins* was ever persecuted. Ever condemned. We have gotten it all *wrong, hafeed. Yallah*, everyone is *wrong*. The Prophet, peace be upon him, and Allah *love* you. Just as *I* love you. *Subhanallah*."

No one breathed. No one spoke.

Uncle Abdul rose and crouched before Faisal, pressing his forehead to Faisal's as Faisal's tears continued to fall. "You pushed us to find the hidden truth. To find a deeper faith. To truly follow the Prophet's path, peace be upon him."

"I thought you were furious, Uncle," Faisal whispered. He reached behind him, groping for Adam's hand, and then yanked Adam forward until he was kneeling beside him at the feet of the king. "*Wallah*, you prayed all night long…"

"We are afraid." Uncle Abdul's voice shook, and his gaze darted from Faisal to Adam and back. "You're not safe here. Not now. Not yet. We have more work to do."

Fear filled Faisal's eyes. "You are sending us away."

"You must prepare for your future." The king sat back, dropping his hands into his lap. "The future king must follow in the footsteps of his *'Am*." His uncle, Uncle Abdul. "First, an ambassadorship. And then, Riyadh's governorship, when *ibn akh* Abdul takes my place as king. And, one day—" King Faisal smiled slowly. "You will serve the people with Allah's blessings, fulfilling the Prophet's promise of love and justice in your reign as the first *mithli* king of Saudi Arabia. You will guide our Kingdom to adapt to *true* Islam. Authentic Islam."

"An ambassadorship?" Adam watched Faisal struggle for words, struggle to draw in a breath around the tears that still cascaded down his cheeks. "Where will you send us?" No matter where it was, it was still away from the Kingdom, away from the Gulf, away from the family who had just opened their hearts to him. It wasn't fair. Adam's heart ached for Faisal, his husband who deserved everything but always had to settle for less.

King Faisal smiled. "Bahrain."

Faisal gasped, and he rocked back, his hands rising, covering his face as fresh tears poured from his eyes. Sobs shook his body again as he pitched forward, falling into Adam's arms.

Bahrain. The only country in the Middle East where homosexuality was legal. Where they could be together, without fear. Without looking over their shoulders every moment of every day.

Where only a sixteen-mile-long bridge separated the tiny island kingdom of Bahrain from the east coast of Saudi Arabia.

They would be closer to Riyadh, to Faisal's family—*their* family—than ever before.

And they could be open about their love. No hiding. Not anymore.

"The ambassadorship to Bahrain is a vitally important one, *hafeed*. You will be interacting with the Americans daily, and with their operations in the Gulf. Their Gulf headquarters is there. You will be involved in multinational defense planning. A key member of the Gulf security team." The king smiled again. "*Bismillah*, you are more than ready for this."

Faisal nodded, but didn't speak. Sobs still tore through him as he clung to Adam. Even Adam didn't know what to say. Where had this come from? Never, not in their wildest dreams, had they imagined such acceptance. He'd been ready to pack his bags and move anywhere, and try and console Faisal's broken and bereft heart after.

Now, he was going to be the husband of the Saudi Arabian Ambassador to Bahrain.

"There is one more thing we must do before you move into your new ambassadorship." The king's expression softened, as did Uncle Abdul's. "*Alhamdulillah*, we must bless your marriage. You will perform *nikah* again, here, with your family."

"*Yallah*, Your Royal Highness...." Faisal shook his head, sniffing. His hand gripped Adam's, and he leaned into him, as if he'd fall apart if Adam weren't holding him up. Adam stroked his back. "There is no imam that would bless our *nikah*."

"There is, *hafeed*. Do not despair." The king turned, finally, to Adam.

Adam swallowed, stiffening under the king's full focus. He still held Faisal in his arms, and his skin crawled, the exposure making him want to reflexively escape, run away, flee. Years before, he'd been banished from Faisal's life. Now, he cradled him close and listened to the Saudi Arabian king plan their wedding.

"Adam bin Cooper... al-Saud," King Faisal said, the corner of his lips quirking up. "*Ummun to billah.*" *May Allah bless your marriage with goodness.* He held out his hand. Adam leaned in, grasped his hand, and pressed a kiss to his thin, weathered skin. As he pulled back, King Faisal took his hand and drew it to his lips, kissing him in return. "*Nahn eayila*, Adam bin Cooper al-Saud."

We are family.

73

Shipunovskaya, Russia

SHIPUNOVSKAYA, IN THE NORTHERN Arkhangelsk Oblast, was a weary, shitty place.

Sergey drove twelve hours north from Moscow, straight up the M-8. For the first time in too long, he was alone. No bodyguards. No staff. No Ilya.

No Sasha.

As he drove, the plains of Moscow gave way to thick forests, and then the northern hinterlands, the farming and logging lands of Russia's wild north. Half-hewn forests rose and fell next to the road, and decrepit logging trucks rumbled by his sedan, rough logs balanced precariously on the back of rusted flatbeds. Children sometimes rode on top of the great piles of logs, waving to him with their hair flapping wildly around their heads. He grit his teeth and waved back, keeping his recriminations to himself.

Legislation to ban children on the backs of logging trucks would be added to the next session of the Duma.

Pastures opened between the trees, full of bored cows chewing on grass as they waded through ankle-deep mud. Overhead, the sky was the same steel gray as the Arctic. He was practically driving all the way back.

When he got to Shipunovskaya, he rolled through the dreary, drab town slowly, peering out his windows and searching for some sign that he was in the right place. Wooden houses slumped side by side, some with tarps thrown over half-sunken roofs. Paved roads turned suddenly to unpaved, muddy slush that nearly spun out his car. Cows wandered through the streets.

He would stand out, in his Moscow wool trench coat and cashmere scarf. Sergey tugged his hat down low over his forehead. A shitty disguise, but it was all he had.

Eventually, he found the mechanic's shop, a plywood-and-rusted-steel claptrap just off the muddy main drive. A cow mooed at him when he drove in and stormed away when he parked too close.

The mechanic, the owner of the shop, didn't want to talk to him until he passed over a bottle of vodka. Suddenly, he had loads to say. The man he was looking for, the man in his proffered picture, yeah, he worked there. Had come to town a few weeks ago, looking for work. Hitchhiked in. He worked long hours and never complained, and he made shit pay. The man was proud of how he stiffed his employees.

Had his employee fucked up Sergey's car? Should he sack him? He'd be glad to, show that pretty-faced newcomer who was the boss.

No, no. Sergey rushed to reassure him that his car was in perfect order, thanks to the man in the picture. He'd helped him when his tire had blown and he just wanted to thank him. Could he see to it that the vodka was given to him?

Of course. The mechanic beamed, showing his rotten five teeth.

Also, did the mechanic happen to know where his employee lived?

HE STOMPED THROUGH THE snow and trees, cursing Sasha with every breath. Sasha had to bury himself in the woods and in the snow. Wasn't he sick of snow? He had to disappear in one of the most inaccessible parts of the country. He had to be difficult, always.

And then, he stumbled into the clearing.

Ahead, a tiny wooden cabin squatted between the trees in front of a small clearing. A fire pit and a spit, unused, lay covered in snow next to a slushy parking area marred with tire tracks.

Sasha wasn't home.

He headed for the cabin anyway.

It was old, ancient even, without a door lock. Who would be traipsing through the woods outside of Shipunovskaya, anyway? Not much risk of a robbery there. And, from the looks of it, any potential robbers would go right on by. The only thing valuable about the cabin was the wood it was made of.

He shouldered open the creaking door and ducked into the cramped, one-room shack.

No power, no running water. No kitchen. No doors signaling a toilet. Sasha had a wooden table, hand-carved by Cossacks from the rough look of it, a sagging, broken couch, and a thin mattress on the floor in the corner. A fire lay banked in a stone fireplace opposite the couch. Beside the hearth was a stack of newspapers.

The cabin was bone-crunchingly cold, and he went to the fireplace, grabbing a poker and balling up newspaper to rekindle the flame. He reached for another sheet—

A picture had been cut out, an empty square in the newsprint, beneath a headline he recognized. A headline about him, from a week prior, opening the Duma, the parliament, for the first time after the coup.

Sasha cut out my picture.

His hand hovered over the newspaper, not touching, not moving, as he struggled to process the fact. *Sasha cut out my picture.* Why? What would Sasha want with his picture? He was the one who had left. He was the one who *always* left.

Sergey tipped his head back, sighing—

He froze, his jaw dropping as he spotted the wall beyond the fireplace, hidden from view by the bulky river rock mantel.

Hundreds of photos and headlines were tacked to the wall. Photos of him, headlines of him, from the day he'd returned to Moscow until just days before. Everything he'd done. Opening the Duma. Addressing the nation. Rebuilding the Kremlin. Visiting towns and cities devastated by Moroshkin and the coup. Working with his legal team on charges for the traitors, and a path forward for the nation. Commending the FSB and the federal police for their staunch support of his government throughout the coup.

Everything he'd done, every moment, Sasha had cut out and kept and had tacked to his wall. Headlines that shouted his deeds. Pictures of him, like a parade, or a shrine.

Why? Why would Sasha track his every move? Cut out his every picture? The stack of newspapers by the fireplace had been cut apart, every item of him taken from the pages and put on the wall.

Sasha was the one who had left. Why would he want to know anything about Sergey, when he was the one who had walked out?

An engine rumbled, drawing closer. Tires slid on snow. Brakes squealed.

Sergey jumped up, running his palms down his coat, nervous energy propelling him. He shifted his weight back and forth across his heels. He didn't know what to do with his shaking hands.

A truck door slammed outside. Boots crunched through the snow, up the wooden steps of the cabin.

Sergey shoved his hands in his pockets. He took a breath, trying to harden his heart.

Sasha shouldered open the door of the cabin, took two steps in, and stopped in his tracks. Snow slid off his boots and puddled on the roughhewn floor.

He stared at Sergey, his inscrutable expression hard and unreadable. If he was shocked to see Sergey standing in his cabin in the middle of the bitter Russian north, he didn't show it. He carried a small paper bag in one hand and a paper cup of coffee in the other. Three newspapers were stuffed under his arm.

Seeing Sasha again was like taking a cannon blast to his chest. Sergey blinked, and then nodded to the newspapers. "More pictures for your collection?" He breathed in sharply after he spoke, trying to contain his wince.

Sasha dropped the newspapers, his coffee, and the paper bag on the table and turned, striding out of the cabin.

Fuck. Sergey raced after him, down the uneven wood steps, and out to Sasha's mangled truck. It looked like a salvage yard reject. Sasha hauled open the tailgate and dragged out a bundle of firewood.

He ignored Sergey completely.

"Sasha... Look at me."

Nothing. Sasha strode by him, back to the cabin.

Sergey followed him all the way back inside. He watched Sasha drop the wood, cut the ties with a knife, and place three logs into the hearth. While Sasha fanned the coals, sparking a roaring fire, Sergey emptied the bag Sasha had dropped on the table and unfurled the newspapers.

Him, again, on the front page.

A glass bottle of pills rolled across the newspaper, the prescription label handwritten in scratchy, old script. He reached for the bottle, frowning at the antiquity of it. They were Soviet-era medications.

Sasha snatched it away from him, throwing the bottle onto his mattress. As Sasha moved, he coughed, a wracking, heaving cough that rattled his bones. He didn't turn around. Didn't face Sergey again.

"You left for this? A shack in the woods? Working as a mechanic for a man who cheats you every day?" Sergey kept his voice soft. His thoughts wouldn't add up. Had Sasha truly not wanted him? Had everything they shared all just been in his head? Was this Sasha's escape? Did he bury himself in the woods, as far off the grid as he could get, because it was the only way he thought he could be free of Sergey?

Had he made a huge mistake tracking Sasha down?

"I left for *that*." Sasha nodded to his wall of Sergey, his pictures and the headlines that screamed Sergey's accolades, his achievements, his work rebuilding Russia. "Everything you have done..." He broke off, a rib-cracking cough shaking his body again.

"What is wrong with you? Are you sick?" He stepped closer, or tried to. Sasha held out his arm, palm forward, holding him back.

"You may remember I have no spleen," Sasha choked out, spitting a wad of phlegm to the rough cabin floor. He'd lost his spleen after the attack at Andreapol, when his fellow pilots had beat him so badly Dr. Voronov had to remove it before he bled to death internally. "I am always sick. The medicines I get are useless." He glared at his mattress and the pill bottle he'd thrown there.

"Sasha, we have medicine in Moscow. Dr. Voronov can treat you—"

"I am not in Moscow."

Sergey came up short, like he'd been slapped. "You could be," he finally said, softly.

"*Nyet.*" Sasha threw out one hand, pointing to his wall. "I told you, Russia needs you. You are the best hope for our country. Our future. You cannot risk ruining that. Too many lives are at stake."

Growling, Sergey turned away. "You would make the Politburo proud, Sasha. Everything for the might of the state. The state must always be right."

"Stop being selfish, Sergey—"

"I am a *man!*" Sergey exploded. "Not a robot like you are! I *feel!* I *desire!* I *love!*" He swallowed hard.

Silence filled the cabin, until Sasha finally spoke. "I feel, Sergey," he grunted. "I love."

"You love to *leave*."

Sasha's eyes slipped closed. "I told you I would not apologize for doing what was right. For what needs to be done. One day, you will see that I am doing this, all of this, for you."

"*Nyet*, do not say these things," Sergey snorted, disgust crawling through him. "Do not tell me breaking my heart was for my own good, Sasha. Do not lie to me. You have done that enough. You left because you do not want me or want what we could have had, or else you would have fought for it."

"Sergey, that is not true—"

"I should not have come." He turned to go.

"How did you find me?" Sasha followed him to the door, his voice suddenly different, softer, almost pleading. Almost desperate. "Why *did* you come?"

Sergey stopped on the second step. He stared at the forest, the snow-covered pine boughs and the frozen ground. It seemed, for a moment, like Siberia all over again. His aching heart, missing Sasha like a piece of his soul was missing. Snow that fell and tried to match his frozen hope. "I started looking for you the night you disappeared. I searched everywhere. Morgues. Hospitals. Traffic accidents." He saw Sasha look down, stare at the wooden deck. "I finally found something. A picture from Lubyanka Prison. You flew back with the prison transports, not with Anton and Aleksey like you said you would. You hid from me."

Sasha said nothing.

"I searched for reports of newcomers in rural areas. If you were going to run, you would want to disappear. I started outside of Moscow and searched in bigger circles, following the highways. Where would you go if you had to hitchhike? Eventually, a police report from Velsk gave me a clue."

Cursing, Sasha shook his head. "Punks there figured I was military. They thought I was Moroshkin's forces." He finally looked up, into Sergey's gaze. Pure misery hung in his eyes. "You are so popular," he breathed. "Even punks in Velsk want to prove they love you."

Sergey ignored him. "From Velsk, I tracked you here, and I called as if I were FSB. People were happy to tell me all about the man who had arrived a few days after you disappeared. He worked as a mechanic, and he lived outside of town. Your descriptions matched."

"Ilya helped you?" Sasha scuffed his boot against a warped board.

"No. I found you myself." Every night, when he couldn't sleep, when he just wanted to scream, or cry, fall apart and beg for answers. When he needed to know why Sasha had left when they'd finally seemed to be on the same page.

What had he discovered, though? His heart, if possible, hurt more than it had before. The pit inside him opened deeper, yawned blacker. He trudged down the last steps.

"Why did you come?" Sasha followed him until they were both standing in the snow.

He fumbled in his jacket, pulling out a long, crisp envelope. He'd dreamed of this going differently. "Sasha Andreyev, you are invited to the Heroes' Ball in Moscow, honoring the fighters who took back our country from the traitor Moroshkin and his followers. You will be named a Hero of Russia and awarded the Hero's Gold Star medal." He kept going, even as Sasha stumbled back and fell to his ass, landing in a pile of snow. His face went white, as white as the wasteland surrounding them. "Everything you need is in there. The reception begins at four in the afternoon." He hesitated. "In three days."

Sasha stared at the envelope but didn't take it. Sergey finally dropped it in the snow. He headed out, storming through the drifts as he followed the track back to the muddy road where he'd left his car.

And then, he turned around. His jacket flared around him as he stormed back, straight for Sasha, still sitting on his ass in the snow. "The only thing that would be different in those damn headlines, if you had stayed," he growled, shaking with fury, "is that you would be helping me make things even better. I believe in you, Sasha. I believe in your heart. I love you, all of you. I wanted you by my side for what you could bring to this country. But you think love is fickle because *you* are fickle, Sasha. You have no faith in me or in the world. Or in us, and what we could be."

Finally, Sasha looked up, blinking before he glared. "I lost my spleen to faith," he snapped. Standing, he ignored the envelope in the snow and stormed back into his cabin, leaving Sergey all alone.

74

Washington DC

SCOTT WOKE THEM BEFORE dawn, knocking on the door to his study and bringing in two steaming cups of coffee. "Finally." He grinned. "Real coffee." He smiled at Jack and Ethan's bedhead, their hair sticking straight up from beneath the blanket that covered their naked bodies. Scott winked and then left them to get dressed.

They were on the road fifteen minutes later, driving down to Andrews Air Force Base. Jack stared out of the window for the whole drive, his eyes tracing Washington's skyline, the lights of the capital reflecting off the Potomac, scattered stars sparkling behind the monuments. The pale glow of the predawn light, just starting to streak gold and pale pink over the horizon.

Scott badged his way into the base and drove them to the flight line. A small executive jet was already prepped, the engines warm and idling as they waited to taxi to the runway. Air Force officers made themselves scarce, looking away when Scott pulled up.

"All right, HOTUS and POTUS," he said, spinning in his seat. "Have a good trip to Texas."

Ethan groaned as Jack laughed.

"I had to." Scott winked at Ethan. "Levi would never let me live it down if I didn't get it in."

Jack tried to smile, but it wavered, and then fell. He looked down, exhaling shakily. How could he ever thank Scott the way he deserved? From the first moment until the last, Scott had been their steadfast friend, a bulwark against the world. How many times had Scott saved their lives? Stood up for them? Helped them when no one else would? How many drives had Scott done for each of them? From the big gestures to the tiny. How many times had he turned from the front seat with a friendly smile, just doing what he could to help? "Scott… I can't ever say thank you enough—"

"No, stop." Scott waved him off. "You've got nothing to thank me for, Mr. President."

"Yes, I do. Scott—"

"Tell you what." Scott grinned. "You can thank me by making this guy happy." He reached out and grabbed Ethan, shaking his shoulder. "Treat him right. He deserves an awesome husband. *You.*"

Ethan flushed and knocked Scott's hand away as Jack finally smiled. "He deserves everything," he breathed, looking at Ethan. "Far better than me. But I'll do my best." *How can I treat Ethan the way he deserves if I am in prison?*

His thoughts turned dark again, grinding over anxieties that chewed on his every waking thought. Panic was never far; he felt like he was drowning, being swept out to sea by crashing waves, and his legs were getting tired of treading water. How much longer could he keep his head above the surface? He could barely breathe anymore.

Ethan kissed his hair and took his hand. "Let's go."

Scott watched from the SUV as they boarded the jet, and then drove off as the pilot started their taxi out to the runway. "We'll be in Texas in four hours," the pilot said curtly over the intercom as he turned off the lights. Jack's lips thinned, and he closed his eyes.

When they took off, Jack's knuckles went white as the engines screamed and they roared into the sky. The pilot twisted the jet around to fly over Andrews and then skirted the no-fly zone above Washington.

Jack pressed his forehead to the window, gazing over the capital as dawn washed her in golden light.

"It's not supposed to end like this," he whispered. "Sneaking out of DC. Staring down the barrel of a life in prison."

Ethan's hand snaked through his, holding tight.

"Presidents Harding, Pierce, Tyler, Nixon… and Spiers-Reichenbach." He squeezed his eyes closed, and his lips trembled again. "Presidents who left office in disgrace. The most reviled in history."

"Jack…" Ethan slid into the seat beside Jack and pulled him close, turning him away from the window. Jack folded into his arms. "You're not reviled. You're not a disgrace."

He wanted to believe Ethan, he did. But Madigan's words, spat at him on the ice at the top of the world, played on a near-constant loop in the back of his mind. A joke president no one believed in. An afterthought who became a disgrace, a national regret. Hadn't Senator Allen affirmed as much? Everything he was, everything that had held him up as a man, was falling away, a house of cards that tumbled into a black abyss in the center of his soul.

"Have I ever told you about the days before you moved into the White House? The transition before your inauguration?"

Jack shook his head.

"Everyone in DC was excited. There was a buzz in the air. A lot of times, no one cares about the incoming guy. It's either boring—another stuffed shirt—or someone you dread. But you were someone everybody was excited about. You built bridges. Worked across party lines. Had a reputation for getting things done. Being honest and ethical. Having integrity. We all looked forward to you."

It should have helped, but Ethan's words just made him want to disappear. If that were true, then he'd shredded people's hopes in a blisteringly short eighteen months. In political timetables, that was the speed of a rocket plowing into the earth. How fast he'd tanked. Where had it all gone wrong?

Ethan kissed his temple, nuzzled his cheek. "You shouldn't have come for me," he breathed, whispering into Jack's ear. "This is all because you came after me in Russia. Jack…"

Jack sat up and turned to face Ethan. He held Ethan's face in both of his hands. "No. No, I'll never regret that. Never regret coming back to you and putting us back together. No matter what happens." He smiled, finally. "I will always choose you first. You are my everything. Always."

Maybe he was compromised. He'd put Ethan before everything, before his presidency, before Madigan, before the end of the world. But he could live with that. Living without Ethan, on the other hand…

Ethan's hand rose, cradling Jack's face in return as he pressed their foreheads together and smiled back. Their wedding rings glinted in a ray of sunlight falling through the windows, scattering prisms around the cabin, rainbow diamonds that danced over their tearstained faces.

75

Texas

IT WAS ETHAN'S TURN to be wracked with anxiety as they pulled up the gravel drive leading to Jack's parents' house.

Jack's parents lived on a small ranch outside of Austin, just enough land to grow hay on and need a tractor. But still close enough to the city to have decent cell reception, Jack had said with a smile.

A car had been left for them at the Austin Executive Airport, and they'd driven an hour into the country together, holding hands. Jack had started telling story after story of his parents, about growing up an only child, being a rascal who got into too much trouble.

Ethan tried to remember to breathe as the trees blurred together, and the golden Texas hills rolled on and on.

Eventually, they'd turned off the highway and wound through the backroads, and then turned up a narrow gravel drive.

A man and a woman were already sitting on the porch. As they turned in, both sprang to their feet. Moments later, they charged down the porch and ran across the drive, shouting. "Jack! Jack! My God! Jack!"

Jack parked and tumbled from the car, racing to his mom and dad. His mom, short and plump with thick gray hair, threw open her arms as Jack neared, and she wrapped him up, holding on to him and rocking back and forth like he was still ten years old. Sobs wracked her, wordless shouts as she clung to her son. Jack's dad grabbed them both and pulled them close, a three-way hug as he kissed the top of Jack's head.

Jesus. Ethan's hands shook as he climbed out of the car. Would they blame him for everything that had gone wrong? For Jack's downfall? History would put a pin through Ethan's face, marking him as the turning point in Jack's presidency.

He lingered behind Jack and his parents, fidgeting.

Jack's dad saw him first. Smiling, he reached for Ethan and held out his hand. "Ethan."

"Hello, sir." He shook Jack's dad's hand.

Jack's dad pulled him in, wrapping him up in a hug. "Thank you for bringing our son home," he breathed in Ethan's ear, his voice shaking. "Thank you for loving him."

EVENTUALLY, THEY MADE THEIR way inside. Andrew and Mary, Jack's parents, hustled them into the kitchen, where Mary had food waiting. A TV droned in the background, turned to TNN. Speculation raged on Jack's future, on the committee's deliberations. Unnamed sources from the Capitol went back and forth in the comments, first declaring Jack was on the way to prison, and then bitterly arguing the opposite.

Andrew turned the TV off as soon as they walked in. Ethan spotted pictures of him and Jack hanging everywhere—framed and on the walls, propped up on the mantel, stuck to the refrigerator. The signs of a proud family.

"When President Wall called, we thought the worst," Mary said, her voice wobbling. "We couldn't prepare for what she told us. You were alive… but we had to pretend you were dead." Andrew held her hand on top of the table as tears rolled down Mary's cheeks. "No, let's talk about something else." Mary wiped her face and tried to smile.

They spent the afternoon talking, getting to know each other as if there wasn't the risk of life in prison hanging over Jack's head. Andrew and Mary wanted to know all about their life in the White House. About Sergey, Jack's best friend, and Ethan's time in the Secret Service. What being the very first First Gentleman was like. Ethan's life before Jack.

No one brought up Madigan's name, or the strike in the Arctic, or Jack's flight to Russia. No one asked about Ethan's bruises, either, but Jack caught Andrew and Mary staring at them with wide, terrified eyes.

Eventually, though, Mary did ask about their wedding. "I wish I had been there," she said, her hand resting on top of Jack's.

"It was fast. Cramped. We were at war a few hours later. But Captain Anderson was great. For speaking off the cuff, he spoke beautifully." Jack smiled and reached for Ethan. "It was ours, and that made it perfect."

Mary beamed as Ethan flushed, gazing into Jack's eyes. Andrew smiled too, clapping Jack on the shoulder before he stood. "So, Ethan," he said. "Are you an outdoorsy guy?"

"Yes, sir. I grew up on a farm. I helped my dad out around the place."

Andrew brightened. "Oh yeah? What kind of farm did you guys have?"

"He didn't own it, sir. He was a farmhand. We lived on the land, and he worked for the owners. It was dairy and beef."

Andrew looked contrite, but pushed through quickly. "Well, if you'd like, I can show you around this place. We've got just under a hundred acres. Some good spots for deer hunting. A few wild boars that I'm trying to get rid of."

"I'd love to see it." Ethan rose and followed Andrew, but stopped and dropped a kiss to Jack's lips first. Jack snaked his hand around Ethan's neck and pulled him closer, deepening their kiss with a grin. On the way out of the back door, Ethan flashed a smile back to him.

Mary smiled at Jack and squeezed his hand on top of the table. "He's wonderful, Jack. He really is. He takes good care of you?"

Jack smiled. "He treats me too well, Mom. He's the love of my life. I'm so happy with him."

Mary's smile wavered and then fell. She licked her lips. "Jack, honey… there's something I need to show you." She sniffed as she rose, walking slowly to the kitchen counter. An envelope lay there, yellowed on the edges from age. She looked down at it and closed her eyes, exhaling carefully.

"What is it, Mom?"

Wordlessly, she passed it to Jack. She wouldn't look him in the eyes.

It was a letter from Leslie addressed to his parents. The postmark was sixteen years old.

His breath caught. Sixteen years to the month of her death, exactly.

"Mom…"

"Just read it, honey. I never knew why she sent it here, but… maybe after everything that happened, you do. I never showed this to you because I thought it would hurt you too much. I just can't keep this anymore." Her voice faded away, and she turned to the sink, grasping the white tile as she stared at the faucet.

He slid the worn paper from the envelope.

Dear Jack,

I hope this gets to you. I'm sending it to your parents. I'll tell you why when I see you again.

You need to know how much I love you, Jack. I love your goofiness, your terrible cooking. How you always want to do what's right, even in a crazy, complicated world. You keep me honest, Jack. Keep me stable.

Which is why I've decided to leave the Army. After this tour, I'm going to resign my commission. I don't know what I'll do. But I do know that whatever it is, I want my future to be with you.

All my love,
Leslie

He checked the date, scratched into the top of the paper in her slanted cursive.

She'd written the letter two days before her death.

Madigan's voice, again, crashed into his brain. *She was on the verge of joining my team. I recruited her myself.*

She'd said no. And Madigan had killed her for it.

Leslie… How did we get trapped in this madman's world? His eyes closed as he folded the letter and set it on the table.

She didn't deserve what Madigan had done to her. No one in the world deserved what he had done. How many lives had he torn apart? He and Leslie were just two people, just two out of thousands and thousands of lives he'd shredded.

But, for the first time, conviction settled in his blood, in his bones. Since he'd snapped Madigan's neck, the world had seemed broken, twisted at the same angle as Madigan's wrecked body, everything just off-center as if he were watching the world in a carnival fun house. He'd delivered a cold justice, the justice of revenge, of a raging, furious man. And he'd doubted himself every day since.

Leslie's smile, and then Ethan's, played in the darkness behind his eyelids. *I got him, Leslie. I got the bastard who killed you.*

It seemed, for a moment, that Leslie smiled back, nodding like she heard him. The image of her turned to Ethan, beaming and radiant. She laid her hand on Ethan's shoulder and smiled at Jack before walking away, fading into the darkness.

Quiet sobbing made him open his eyes. Mary squatted on the kitchen floor, holding on to the sink with one hand and covering her eyes with the other as she tried to stifle her bawling. "Jack, I'm so sorry," she gasped. "I should have told you. I shouldn't have kept it from you. But Madigan, and everything he's done to you, and to our family—" Her hand rose, covering her mouth.

"Mom, Mom, Mom." He sank down beside her, pulling his mom into his arms. Her gray hair tickled his chin as he held her. "It's all right. This answers a question I needed to know."

"This is all connected, right? She was leaving because—"

"She was a *good* person, Mom. She wanted to do what was right. And she paid the price for it."

"God, I'm so sorry to give it to you now. When you're happy with Ethan. I don't want to mess up what you and Ethan have—"

"You aren't. Leslie is gone, and nothing will ever change that. Yes, I loved her, but that love belongs in the past. Even if she did come back—and she wasn't a clone when she did—" He tried to smile, but Mary just groaned and closed her eyes. "Even if she did walk in the door right now, by some miracle, my heart would still belong to Ethan. I told you: he's the love of my life. For the rest of my life."

Mary nodded, breathing slowly as her tears subsided. She rested her head against the cabinets, wiping away her tears and thin black lines of mascara running down her cheeks. "God, I'm a mess. I wanted to look good for your husband."

"You look great, Mom. You always do."

She snorted, wiping at her eyes. For a moment, she seemed to gather herself, pull herself together.

And then, the sobs started again. "Jack, what if—"

He stopped her, pulling her into a hug. "No, Mom, don't. Don't say it. Don't ask. Not now. Just, please. Don't."

She nodded and then tried to pull herself together again. Her sobs turned to sniffles, and then deep breaths. Finally, she spoke. "I, uh. I didn't know what to get you two… you know, for supplies. Do you use condoms?"

"Mom."

"I bought a couple different kinds of lube and a few boxes of condoms, just in case. They're up in your room."

"*Mom!*"

"What? I'm trying to help." She smiled helplessly, shrugging. "You're my son. I just want you to be happy, no matter what."

ANDREW AND ETHAN SPENT the whole afternoon together, running around the ranch and working on Andrew's old truck. Ethan, sling-free, was elbows-deep in an oily engine when Jack found him again. A smear of oil had transferred from his arm to his forehead, and Jack wanted to lick it off.

"Dad, Mom asked for you inside." Andrew disappeared through the back porch door as Jack sauntered toward Ethan. Ethan wiped his hands and grinned, watching Jack's prowl.

He pushed Ethan against the truck's bumper and trailed his hands down Ethan's sweaty t-shirt. "Hey sexy," he purred. "I think there's a problem with my engine."

"Oh yeah?" Ethan wrapped his arms around Jack's waist and squeezed his ass.

"It's all revved up, and I need your help getting somewhere to go."

Ethan laughed. "You are shameless. Absolutely shameless."

"Mom wants us to get ready for dinner. I'm supposed to tell you to go take a shower." Jack winked.

"And, by 'tell me', you mean you're going to watch, right? Verify this shower takes place?"

Jack felt Ethan's cock harden against him, an answering hardness to his own. "Watch? I'm going to join in."

They slipped upstairs, dashing past the kitchen, trying to hide their erections as Mary and Andrew hovered over the stove. Jack ripped his pullover off on the stairs and started in on his jeans as Ethan pulled his t-shirt over his head. Ethan pushed him against his bedroom door, kissing him deeply, pressing his body against Jack's, owning him.

Jack moaned. "God, I want you. Take me, Ethan. Make me yours."

"You are mine. And I'm yours." Ethan steered them into Jack's bedroom, sparing half a glance for the old football posters and high school textbooks still on his bookshelf.

In the bathroom, Ethan dropped to his knees and sucked Jack deep as the water warmed.

Another day, Jack might have jumped into Ethan's arms, asked him to hold him up as he wrapped his legs around Ethan's waist and bounced on his cock. But Ethan's ribs were still bruised, and though he'd completed his bone-growth treatments and taken off the sling and the bandages around his chest, he was still sore. Instead of jumping him, he guided Ethan into the shower and pressed him against the wall under the spray, kissing him breathless as he slid their bodies together.

Hard cocks slicked together, then thighs and wet bodies. Ethan's hands trailed down Jack's sides, and Jack's hands over Ethan's chest. Ethan spun him around, backing Jack into the wall, and kissed his way down Jack's chest, all the way to his cock. He swallowed Jack again as his hands rose on Jack's thighs, soapy fingers sliding over his ass.

Jack spread his legs and moaned, his fingers running through Ethan's hair, pulling away when Ethan's blowjob became too much and his balls rose, tightening. "Not yet," he breathed. "Want you to fuck me."

Ethan's eyes blazed. He backed into the spray, panting as he washed, soaping up and rinsing in record time, while Jack leaned against the tiles and slowly stroked his spit-slick cock.

They stumbled from the shower and ditched the towels, heading, soaking wet, straight for Jack's bed. Ethan wrapped his arms around Jack from behind, sucking his neck, his collarbone, kissing down the curve of his shoulder. Jack moaned and grabbed at him, rubbing his ass against Ethan's crotch, over his hard cock, rocking into him.

Growling, Ethan spun Jack, tipping him backward onto the bed before climbing on top of him. Jack fumbled for the bedside table, grabbing one of the three brand new bottles of lube his mom had bought. Cellophane tore and flew through the air. He pumped lube into Ethan's palm, and then arched back, almost shouting as Ethan pressed deep into him, sliding his lubed fingers inside Jack's hole.

"Love you so much," Ethan breathed into Jack's ear. Water dripped from his nose, from the ends of his hair. He lined up his slicked cock at Jack's entrance. "Fuck, I love you."

Ethan pushed inside slowly, and Jack's body opened beneath him, welcoming his lover, his husband. His thighs spread wide. Ethan's forehead pressed against his shoulder, his breath scorching over Jack's neck as Ethan grabbed his hips with both hands.

He loved this, loved every moment of this. Ethan, buried inside him, their bodies so close it felt like the barrier between them collapsed. Like if they pushed just a little bit harder, their souls would merge, become one. He shared his breath with Ethan, rocking against him, rolling into his thrusts, their bodies surging together. Ethan's lips mapped his skin, the contours of his neck, the pounding of his pulse. His hands slid up Ethan's spine, his nails digging into the flexing muscles along Ethan's back. He squeezed his ass and tried to pull Ethan closer. Sweat prickled along his skin, along Ethan's skin, making their bodies slide.

Ethan grabbed his legs and kissed Jack's ankles before laying them over his broad shoulders. Both hands gripped Jack's ass as he drove deep, sliding all the way into his body.

Panting, Jack stroked Ethan where he could, reaching for his chest, his arms, his thighs. He had to touch him, caress him. Hold him and never let go.

And then Ethan surged forward, bending Jack in half as he kissed him, plunging his cock into Jack.

Jack wailed against Ethan's lips, against his kiss, his spine bowing as pure pleasure shot through his body. Ethan kissed him again, driving his cock in and out of Jack's hole. He kept his eyes open, staring into Jack's as they made love, kissing with each deep thrust.

Ethan's cock sank deep inside Jack, into the center of his soul. Into the center of his heart, and deeper.

He never wanted this to end. In Ethan's arms, his soul burned, lit on fire, and escaped his body, sliding over his skin until Ethan breathed him in, took him inside of his own body, and their hearts beat as one. He was never more open, never more vulnerable, than he was in Ethan's arms, and he loved it. Craved it. Needed it. Needed Ethan's love.

How could he ever live without this?

His orgasm almost took him by surprise, a slow burn that turned to a sparkler, igniting in his veins. Jack's cock was rock-hard, painfully hard; any harder, and it might burst. He thrashed, bucking beneath Ethan's hold, his come pulled from the center of his being, so scorching hot he could feel every inch of it leaving his balls and traveling through him until it burst free, wave after wave painting his chest and Ethan's. He screamed against Ethan's kiss again, pressing their cheeks, their foreheads together as his fingers dug into Ethan's straining, flexing muscles.

Ethan gasped, breathed his name, and moaned, sliding his cock as deep as it could go. He stared down at Jack, his eyes seeming to paint every moment of Jack's bliss into his memory. "Jack," he whispered, kissing Jack's eyelids, his cheekbones. His ankles, next to Ethan's face, and then back to his lips. "I love you."

MARY AND ANDREW DIDN'T say a word when they finally came down for dinner—late—but Andrew couldn't smother his grin. And, Ethan couldn't stop the burn flaring over his cheeks and down his neck, the flush he knew was darkening his skin.

Jack headed for the kitchen table but came up short when he saw it was empty. "Mom? Where are we eating?"

"Outside, honey. Go on out. I'll be there in a second."

He took Ethan's hand and steered him for the back door, for the large porch that overlooked a grassy field and two oak trees. Jack had told him about climbing those oak trees when he was a kid and lying in the hammock strung between them, staring up at the clouds and the stars and making up wild stories about distant lands and adventures he'd have one day.

They stepped onto the porch and froze.

Candles sat in clusters around the porch, casting a golden glow. Lanterns made from mason jars swayed from the overhang. Bunches of tulips and daisies were stuffed in short vases and tied with ribbon, scattered around the porch and between the candles. Soft music played from the stereo, something romantic and gentle. Red rose buds floated in a bowl on a long picnic table, draped in a white tablecloth with crimson petals scattered over the top. Hung between two posts, a sign read *Just Married*.

Andrew and Mary came out behind them, clapping. "Surprise! We wanted to celebrate your wedding. Have a little home reception for you both." She winked. "I always knew you were going to be late to your own wedding, Jack."

Jack seemed caught between laughing and crying and settled for wrapping his mom up in a hug. Andrew joined in, and then pulled Ethan in for the group hug, too.

They ate first, diving into barbecue and homemade coleslaw, mashed potatoes and grilled corn on the cob. Mary brought out a cake, complete with two grooms perched on a heart of icing. Jack laughed, but he pulled Ethan in and posed for a picture, the two of them beaming over the homemade cake.

Andrew gave them each a knife with a wink and a smile and said, "Have at it."

Ethan fed Jack a slice of cake carefully, turning crimson when Jack started lasciviously sucking the frosting off his fingers. Andrew laughed and looked away as Mary swatted Jack with her napkin, leaning over the table and telling him to behave. Jack dissolved into giggles, and then pulled himself together to feed his own slice to Ethan.

Of course, Jack got goofy with his slice. He missed Ethan's mouth a few times, smearing frosting on his lips, his chin, and part of his cheek. Mary and Andrew laughed, and then rolled their eyes good-naturedly when Jack insisted on cleaning the mess he made himself. A dozen kisses later, and Ethan was as red as the rose petals. Jack looked very pleased with himself.

Andrew rose and changed the music, putting on a soft love song. "I believe it's time for your first dance."

Ethan pulled Jack to his feet and held him close, swaying across the porch as the music played on. He caught the lyrics on the second refrain: a love song sung between men, a man singing to the man he loved. It was a simple thing for Andrew and Mary to do, but it carried a deep message. He smiled at Andrew over Jack's shoulder.

The song ended, and another one came on, an older love song, a crooning ballad about love finally coming at last. Mary and Andrew rose. Mary went to Ethan, and Andrew held out his hand for Jack. "Parents' dance."

Jack laughed as he and his dad tried to negotiate arms and feet. Andrew let Jack lead, and he stumbled, staring at his feet as they both giggled. Ethan swept Mary around the deck, both of them laughing at Jack and Andrew. Halfway through, Mary clapped her hands and switched places with Andrew, taking Jack into her arms.

"You can lead," Ethan said, smiling as Andrew approached him.

"I never learned the other way." Andrew shrugged. "Guess I won't fit in back in DC. Jack can dance with anyone. I remember the news played that clip of him and the Russian president for a week straight."

Ethan laughed, and then followed Andrew's lead into a spin. "He threw everyone for a loop with that one. It was Sergey's idea, though. He loves being unpredictable."

Andrew shook his head. "I still have a hard time believing that one of my son's closest friends is the president of Russia."

"He was his best man, in fact."

Andrew spun him again as Jack dipped Mary. She smacked his shoulder and demanded to be put back while Jack giggled himself silly.

"Thank you for this." Ethan swallowed as Andrew's hand landed on his hip. "Thank you."

Andrew grinned, a lopsided quirk of the lips that seemed like an echo of Jack's easy, effortless smile. "Thank *you*," he said, "for loving him. For making him happy again. We hoped, for years, that he would find love after..." Andrew shrugged. "And, for what it's worth... I've never seen him this happy, ever."

The song ended before Ethan could respond, and they broke apart, laughing when Jack kept spinning Mary around and around, ignoring her protests.

Eventually, Ethan stole Jack back, and they danced together in the candlelight, beneath the stars and the swaying branches of the oak tree, until Mary and Andrew turned in and the music player died. And then they danced in silence, staring into each other's eyes as time seemed to fall away, and each kiss lasted for a hundred years or more.

76

Moscow

"Mr. PRESIDENT, HE HAS ARRIVED."

Sergey's stomach flip-flopped as the usher whispered in his ear. *Sasha.* He'd come. He'd actually come.

His fingers trembled, and he almost dropped the champagne flute he held. Ilya gave him a sharp look, trying to cover for Sergey's sudden gobsmacked expression by talking loudly with the Federation Council members.

"Excuse me," he demurred, bowing out. He caught Ilya's stare and hoped the helpless look in his eyes conveyed enough.

Ilya gave him a small, tight smile.

He wound his way through the hotel ballroom, standing on his toes to peer over the heads of everyone, trying to catch a glimpse of Sasha. Where had he gone? He hadn't turned around and left already, had he?

"Mr. President."

Sergey froze. He spun, slowly.

Sasha stood behind him, both hands clasped behind his back. He wore the tux Sergey had left on his hotel bed, the tux he'd had made at the Kremlin for him, what seemed like years ago. It fit him like a dream, like carnal temptation, like every desire Sergey had ever had wrapped into one.

Hopefully Sasha had availed himself of the IV antibiotics he'd left as well.

He tried to smile as his eyes traced Sasha's body, from his head to his toes and back. "You look perfect," he breathed. He should be used to this ache in his chest by now, this Sasha-shaped hole in his life.

Except now Sasha was standing in front of him, close enough to touch, to hold, to pull close and beg him to not leave again. That ache in his chest could be cured.

But, no. Sasha had left. He had to remember that. Sasha had walked away. He'd chosen to leave.

And then had created a wall devoted to Sergey in his bedraggled cabin.

There were some things he would never understand, as long as he lived.

Sasha's eyes slid away, darting over the crowd, seeming to count the people in the room, trace an escape route through the masses, catalog his exits as if he were planning a military operation.

Sergey swallowed. Damn it, Sasha hated these things. He hated big public gatherings, giant events. He'd be miserable tonight.

Why had he come?

"You look good as well," Sasha said softly, his deep voice rumbling. His eyes flicked back to Sergey, down his body, and then away again. He cleared his throat, a flush rising on his cheekbones.

Sergey blinked. "Have you… found your seat yet?" A dozen tables were scattered around the edges of the ballroom in front of a podium where he'd deliver his remarks later and pass out the Gold Star medals. He'd have to lay the medal around Sasha's neck and *not* kiss him in front of all of Russia.

"No."

"Let me show you." He gestured for Sasha to go first, and then guided him across the ballroom. The Kremlin was still in disarray, and they'd moved the reception to the Moscow Ritz-Carlton. All the heroes, and Sergey, were staying there tonight.

Sasha's table was at the very front, where the heroes earning the highest honors, the Hero of Russia award, were seated. Anton, Aleksey, Vasily, Ilya, and Sasha. And Sergey, as president.

He'd put Sasha on the opposite side of the table from him, but someone had moved his place setting. It was right beside Sergey's. He coughed. "Sorry, this was supposed to be over there." He switched Sasha and Vasily, quickly.

Sasha said nothing. He stared over the crowd, his jaw clenched.

"I will see you during dinner." Nodding, Sergey strode away, cursing with every footstep. Damn him and his foolish heart. Damn him for falling for Sasha. Damn him for still, even now, hoping for a miracle.

WHEN DINNER BEGAN, SASHA sat right beside Sergey, his nametag back where it had been before.

He wanted to crawl out of his skin, and his fork trembled when he held it, steak balanced precariously on the end. He barely ate, his eyes sliding sideways every other second, watching Sasha's stiff back, his strong arms encased in his dark tux. The way he sliced his food, speared his steak. The clench of his jaw as he chewed. The wine glass he left untouched.

Sergey downed his glass of wine faster than he should have and asked for another. Ilya sent him a sharp look across the table, blowing cigarette smoke harshly in-between glaring at Sasha.

And then, it was time to speak.

He'd practiced his speech for a week, extolling the sacrifices and heroism of the men and women he was honoring that night. He told a story about each, something that allowed their acts to shine. When he got to Sasha's, his voice caught, cracking as he described Sasha's one-way overflight of Madigan's position and the intelligence that had formed the backbone of the plan to save their nation, and the world.

The crowd rose in a standing ovation when he finished speaking.

Sasha looked like he wanted to disappear, crawl under the table and quietly die.

The medal ceremony was stilted, but he shook each hero's hand, thanked them profusely, and draped the Gold Star medal around their neck. When Sasha stood before him, he averted his gaze, staring at Sasha's shoulder instead of his eyes. "*Zvezda moya*," he breathed, gripping Sasha's arms. "Now the world knows what I always have: you are a true hero."

He heard Sasha's quiet exhale, saw his eyes slide closed.

And then, he moved on, past Sasha, grasping Anton's hand and smiling wide, presenting him his medal. And then Aleksey, and on and on, until he could pretend he had forgotten all about Sasha Andreyev.

LATER, HE'D BLAME THE WINE.

Sergey didn't drink wine to excess. A glass with dinner, maybe one after. He preferred whiskey when given the choice. Something to restart the heart, a firebrand to the soul. Wine was too insidious. It sneaked up on him. He was past the point of good sense before he saw the first warning sign.

Waiters had brought out the dessert, trays of *ptichye moloko* cake cut into delicate star-shaped slices. Whipped marshmallow quivered on top of a thin slice of spiced cake and beneath a coating of drizzled chocolate. More wine flowed, and Sergey found his glass refilled.

Dancing had started, a mix of Russian pop hits belting from a DJ and a live band dipping into classical Russian anthems. He watched everyone spin on the dance floor and took turns dancing with beautiful Russian women, flirting gently with each of them. They left lip-gloss kisses on his cheeks and batted their eyelashes at him, but when the dances ended, he bowed politely and escorted each lady back to her friends.

The night thrummed, humming through him, filling him with wild energy. Anything could happen on a night like this. Potential hung in the air, so close he could snatch it.

He went back to his table. Two men hadn't danced once all evening: Ilya, who never danced, and Sasha, who would rather be anywhere else, with anyone else, by the look on his face. Sour disgust, and sullen dejection, turned his beautiful features ugly as he played with his napkin. His *ptichye moloko* cake sat uneaten, the delicate marshmallow melting and sliding sideways on the plate.

Ilya arched his eyebrows and lit a fresh cigarette as he approached. Sergey pulled Ilya's cigarette from his lips with shaking hands and took a deep drag, blowing it out slowly.

His gaze fixed on Sasha, slumped in his seat. His Gold Star Hero's medal lay on the table, carefully folded and set off to the side of his coffee.

He collapsed into the seat beside Sasha. His legs bounced, nervous, frantic energy racing through him. Hope buoyed him, made him light, as light as the marshmallow cake. Sasha had come to the ball. That had to mean something. Maybe, maybe there was hope. Maybe.

He leaned forward, balancing his elbows on his knees as he flicked ash on his empty dessert plate. "What if," he said carefully, "I were to ask you to dance with me? Hmm? What would you say?"

If Sasha looked dour before, he looked downright miserable after Sergey spoke. He rolled his napkin around his fist, grimacing as frustrated rage played over his face. He sat forward, hunching over his lap. "Why do you do this, Sergey?" he growled. "Why do you keep pushing? You know we—" His voice cut out, and he shook his head, looking down.

Hope crashed and burned. Sergey's heart crumpled, paper crunched in a closed fist, or ash flicked away, useless and unneeded. He'd never learn, it seemed. He had an open wound named Sasha, and he loved to pick at it, pluck the scab off and keep it bleeding.

Sergey nodded, mostly to himself, and took another drag of Ilya's cigarette. He stubbed it out in Sasha's untouched marshmallow cake and then stood. Silently, he buttoned his jacket and walked away. Every step ached and felt like failure. If he only tried harder, if he only tried to reach inside Sasha, where maybe there still was an ounce of affection—

No. He'd done all he could do. He had to move on.

ILYA STARED AT SASHA across the table, burning holes through him as the smoke from Sergey's cigarette ash continued to curl over the table. "You are a fool, Sasha." He pulled out another cigarette and stood, shrugging into his white smoking jacket. His medal gleamed, proudly displayed over his heart. A Hero of Russia.

Sasha glared at Ilya, his former boss, and Sergey's closest friend. "Russia needs him. You know that."

"What about what he needs, hmm?" Ilya grasped the back of his chair and leaned over the table, growling at Sasha. "What about his happiness? Maybe you are okay with being a Soviet-era drone, but the rest of us have moved on. We live in the twenty-first century, yes?" Ilya shook his head, snorting. "You should not have come. You gave him false hope, and when you leave, I will have to pick up the pieces." He slammed his chair against the table. "Again."

Ilya stormed away, crossing the room and shedding his wild anger as he sauntered up to a group of politicians, Federal Councilmen who worked closely with the FSB. Arms thrown wide, he greeted them warmly and then passed out cigars to all the men.

"Tati..."

Sasha whipped around, glaring.

Anton stood behind him.

He looked away. "Do not call me that."

"I thought you were going to try and fix things with Sergey."

He said nothing. He stared at Sergey's cigarette, stuffed into the melted marshmallow cake. Soon, the whole dessert would fall apart, slide into its component pieces across the plate. "Tatiana stuck to her convictions," he said slowly. "She knew what was right. She did her duty."

"And she was miserable her whole life." Anton slid out a chair and sat down, facing Sasha. "It is a cautionary tale, Sasha, not a prescription. Not something to look up to."

Ilya was right. He shouldn't have come. Sasha looked down, glaring at the floor. How fast could he get out of there? His flight wasn't until the morning. Could he hitchhike that night? "Misery is a small price to pay for a better world."

"Is that what you think this is?" Anton's frown twisted until he stared at Sasha with a mixture of pity and frustration. "You think no one will accept it—"

"You have no idea what I have been through!" Sasha's blood boiled, surging through him as his gaze snapped to Anton. "I *know* it will not be accepted! I *know* how bad it gets!" He'd been beaten for who he was. He'd almost died. Had almost been killed because he'd been born loving men. There was no world, no place for him. Certainly no place for him and Sergey, and their ill-fated love. Had stars ever been crossed in a worse way? It was the worst thing in the world for Sergey to love him back.

Sergey thought the world would open before him, that people would always love him, would always accept him. He was too much of an optimist, sometimes disgustingly so. A Western trait. How had he come to see the world so brightly?

"Do you not understand? We already accepted it."

Silence. Sasha stopped breathing.

Anton kept going. "You think we did not know about how you felt? *Everyone* knew. We all called you Tati."

"Shut up..." Sasha hunched forward again, clasping his hands together. "Do not say another word!"

"We *all* knew, Sasha. Everyone in the insurgency. How are you kidding yourself that we did not, with how obvious your feelings were?"

"Shut *up!*"

"You and he were our favorite gossip, Sasha. All those nights we spent fighting, on patrol, on guard duty. We always would say, 'when would they finally get together'? When would you crack and finally kiss him? When would he realize what was right in front of him? We had money on it—"

He stormed away, heading for the balcony doors. The room spun, the walls bleeding gold and crystal as braying laughter and revelry mixed with the tinkle of glass and the blaring music. He needed air. Space. Needed to get away. Maybe he'd jump, fling himself from the balcony. He'd have space then.

Anton followed him outside. "Sasha!"

"What?" He whirled, throwing his hands wide, and faced Anton. "What do you want from me? Why are you saying these things? Why do you want to—" His lips clamped shut. He couldn't say another word. He'd fly apart if one more word passed through his lips. He'd fall to pieces, lying on the ground with his soul shattered like glass.

Anton shook his head. "I want you to see what we already see. That it is okay, Sasha. What you feel. What he feels. It is okay." He shrugged. "Maybe not for everyone. Maybe do not have a gigantic wedding. Just a small one." He tried to grin.

Sasha stared at him.

"I am your friend, Sasha." Anton stepped forward, grabbing his arms. "I would not lie to you. I tell you these things so that you can choose different from Tatiana. Yes?" He shook Sasha gently. "You have people who support you. Whatever happened before… you are not there anymore. You have friends now." Anton tried to catch Sasha's gaze, but Sasha stared out over the balcony, over Moscow, and said nothing.

Sighing, Anton left him, disappearing back into the ballroom.

There was no way. No way at all. He *loved* Sergey, loved him so deeply. But loving Sergey would put Sergey in danger, deadly danger. He still felt his comrades' fists at times, heard their snarls and insults in his nightmares.

The only way for Russia to, eventually, be truly safe and for others like himself to love freely would be for Sergey to lead her.

The only way to keep Sergey safe would be to be far away.

True love, sometimes, meant walking away.

Sasha stayed on the balcony until the chill penetrated his bones, and he was certain the shaking in his hands was from the cold and nothing else.

POUNDING ON HIS HOTEL room door woke him far too early. Cursing, he stumbled out of bed, grumbling as he threw open the door.

Ilya glared at him. "Get downstairs. Breakfast in the ballroom."

He frowned. "That was not on the schedule."

"Is just for you." Ilya turned on his heel and walked away.

Groaning, Sasha thunked his head against the heavy hotel door and closed his eyes. Breakfast just for him. What were the odds that Sergey would be there as well?

On his way back to his hotel room the night before, he'd passed Sergey's suite, right as Ilya was leaving. Sergey had leaned in the doorframe, his shirt unbuttoned down his chest, cuffs undone, jacket long gone. He'd looked, in the dim light of the suite's low lamps, perfect. Absolutely perfect, like how Sasha remembered him in his dreams. Ilya must have said something funny. A smile had warmed Sergey's face, and he was chuckling, rich and deep.

And then he'd seen Sasha, and his expression had melted, falling so fast it almost startled Sasha. But, no, he shouldn't have been surprised. He wasn't privileged to Sergey's happiness anymore. He wouldn't see his smile ever again.

He pulled on his pants and a dark sweater, brushed his teeth, ran his hands through his bed head, and headed down to the ballroom. Maybe this was the final goodbye. He steeled himself, closing his eyes before pushing open the door.

When he entered, two men rose from a table near the front of the ballroom. Sergey… and another man. They'd clearly been talking, sharing a breakfast tray and a pot of dark coffee. They sat close together… side by side.

His skin prickled as his shoulders tightened, watching Sergey laugh with this strange man. American, by his accent. Tall, broad-shouldered. Blond hair, cut neatly. He wore a suit, even though Sergey had dressed down in jeans, a button-down, and a pullover.

Sergey gave Sasha a tight smile, waving him over to join them. His grin didn't meet his eyes; instead, sadness poured from his gaze.

Sasha's lungs seized. When had *this* happened? When had Sergey moved on? Who was this American? Someone from the embassy? Someone Jack had set Sergey up with?

He wasn't ready for this, to see Sergey with another man. His hands clenched, making tight fists that shook as he crossed the ballroom.

"Sasha Andreyev, Hero of Russia," Sergey said carefully, nodding to him. "Meet Colonel James Sharp, United States Air Force, and an officer at NASA."

Colonel Sharp held out his hand as Sasha stumbled over nothing, tripping as Sergey's words slammed into his brain. "Whoa there! Colonel James Sharp, pleased to meet you. I am the lead recruiter for all prospective NASA astronauts."

Sasha took his hand, pumping twice, and then sat in the chair Colonel Sharp pulled out for him. Sergey faded away, sitting at a table with his laptop just close enough to eavesdrop.

"So, Sasha. Can I call you Sasha?"

He nodded, glancing at Sergey.

"I hear you're interested in becoming an astronaut."

He'd told one person that. *Exactly* one person. Only Sergey knew about his dreams, dreams that had vanished after his attack. His eyes boggled, and he blinked, his gaze bouncing from Colonel Sharp to Sergey and back again. "I… am not qualified," he grunted. "My spleen was removed. Following an… incident."

"Well, the wonderful thing about modern medicine is that we can fix things like that nowadays." Colonel Sharp grinned and stuck out his leg. "I lost my left leg from the knee down in Afghanistan on a bad chopper landing. But that didn't stop me from applying to NASA. They have a medical program for people who apply who aren't in perfect physical shape. NASA will get you the rest of the way, if you're accepted. We can grow a bio-identical spleen from your stem cells. Pop it right back in you." He smiled wide.

Sasha stared, his eyes sliding sideways to Sergey again.

"Your application package is amazing, I have to say. Recommendation letters from three world leaders, a stunning military and civil service record, a Hero of Russia medal." Colonel Sharp winked.

"Three world leaders?"

"Yep. President Puchkov, President Spiers-Reichenbach, and President Wall."

"May I see that?" He reached for the file Colonel Sharp had flipped open. A complete application to NASA in his name lay there, stuffed full with recommendation letters and accolades.

He stared at Sergey, willing him to turn his way. Sergey kept typing away at his laptop, ignoring them completely.

"So, let's talk about your future at NASA, Sasha. Because based on your application, I think you'd be an amazing fit."

They talked for hours, Colonel Sharp first explaining about NASA and the astronaut training program, and where Sasha could go in the international program. A pilot first, and then, after several missions, he could rise to mission commander. Or he could serve tours on the International Space Station as a pilot and a crewmember. Sasha finally spoke about his dreams, about how he wanted to fly into space. How he'd dreamed of space shuttles since he was a little boy.

As they spoke, his heart unclenched, like a fist that had closed around it was loosening. He'd thought this was gone. Flushed away, never to be had. He'd buried it, buried his hopes in the same place he buried his love for Sergey. He couldn't have either.

Colonel Sharp sat across the table from him and told him he *could* be an astronaut.

"Training lasts for two years. As a pilot, we'll train you in the T-38 in Florida, in addition to your standard astronaut training in Houston. That will prepare you to pilot the spacecraft. You'll progress with a class through a specific set of modules, one new course every eight weeks. You have six weeks of instruction and then two weeks of leave. We changed our courses around to try and better support our international candidates. Give them time to head back home." Colonel Sharp smiled again, flashing his wide, bright grin. "Astronauts spend enough time away from their loved ones. No sense prolonging that in training."

His heart twinged. "When would training begin?"

"Our next class starts up in two months. I need to take your file back to Houston and get it rubber-stamped by the higher-ups. But I can tell you this: if you want in, I'd be glad to have you."

He shook his head. "How are you here? Why are you talking to me?"

Colonel Sharp gestured to Sergey, who was packing up his laptop and trying not to look at Sasha. "Your president requested that we send a representative. He said he had someone he wanted to strongly recommend to the NASA space program. Said you'd be a good fit. And he was right." Colonel Sharp stood. "I'll be in touch, Sasha. We look forward to seeing you in Houston soon."

And then, he strode out of the ballroom, all-American swagger and wide hips, smiling like he had all the secrets in the world. He constantly smiled, never seemed to stop. Sasha watched him go, his mind whirling a thousand different directions.

"So." Sergey spoke from the nearby table, leaning against it and crossing his arms. "You will be an astronaut?"

"You turned in an application for me?"

Sergey nodded, pursing his lips. "It is your dream. It is what you want."

His hands shook again, anger building as the fist around his heart closed again. Why would Sergey be kind to him after everything he'd done? "Why are you doing this?" he snapped. "Why would you put this application in for me? Why would you send me to NASA?" His thoughts spun, trying to connect the dots. Sergey wasn't cruel enough to set him up for failure. "You want to send me away. That is it, yes?"

"Sasha—"

"I was already far away, Sergey. I can go farther if you want me to—"

"I do not want you to go anywhere! I want you to come home! Back to Moscow!" Sergey turned away, his hands on his hips as his shoulders slumped. "I applied for you," he finally said, "because I want you to be happy, Sasha." He faced Sasha again, looking him in the eyes. "I thought, once, that I would be a part of that. That *I* could make you happy. But…" He shrugged and shoved his hands in his pants pockets.

Sasha scrubbed his face with his hands. Too much, it was too much. Sergey, Anton, and now NASA. Too many people, too many things pulling him in different directions.

What he wanted, he couldn't have. What he needed to do made his heart scream with anguish. And what he deserved was nothing. He certainly didn't deserve Sergey's kindness, or his attempt to make Sasha happy by fulfilling his lifelong dream. He didn't deserve any of that.

"Living in that shack is not for you. Please." Sergey stepped forward, slowly approaching, until he stood before Sasha. He reached out, his hands gently wrapping around Sasha's arms. "Go. Get away from this place. Chase your dreams, Sasha. Become an astronaut. And then, someday, come back to Russia and help us rebuild our space program."

Sasha's jaw dropped. His head spun again, the world tilting wildly as dizziness threatened to knock him on his ass.

"Just, please, Sasha. When you are in America." Sergey's lips thinned, and he looked down before he spoke. "Find someone. Find someone who can make you happy."

Panic clawed at Sasha's soul and tore at his spine. Tried to shred apart his mind. His heart squeezed, no longer in a fist, but in a vise. He could feel it straining, almost about to burst. His whole chest ached. "You are telling me to leave… and to find someone else?"

Sergey closed his eyes and nodded.

Breathing felt like being stabbed in the back, a knife sliding between his ribs. It was one thing to leave, to walk away, but entirely another to have Sergey tell him to go. And tell him to move on, to put an end to their love. He clung to their memories, relived the moments he'd spent at Sergey's side every night, lying alone on his thin mattress. He'd close his eyes and pretend to be anywhere else, just back with Sergey. Watching over him in the forest and at the bunker, so close he could reach out and brush his fingers over Sergey's eyelashes. Holding him on the sand on Simushir Island. Kissing him, tasting him, beneath the Arctic ice, huddling together on *Honolulu*.

Like a classic Russian romance, he'd played the part of the tragic lover perfectly. Clinging to their love, deluding himself into thinking that as long as he still yearned, as long as he still ached for Sergey, their love would remain alive. Kept sacred in the empty spaces, the pull between their souls.

But Sergey wasn't a Russian hero from the days of old, and he wasn't going to cling to an illusion of love and make empty, rotten temples in his soul to what-could-have-beens. He was a man of the now, of the future, and he would leave Sasha behind, spinning onward as Sasha kept turning over his memories, over and over again.

A groan slipped past his lips. How could he keep Sergey safe when he was the one thing that could destroy Sergey's future? Wasn't loving someone about making the hard choices? All he wanted was to protect Sergey. The vise around his heart squeezed again. His heart bled, agony slipping down the inside of his ribs. "I will never be able to find someone in America."

"Sasha—"

"I will not be able to. Only one man has ever captured my heart. Only one man has ever made me love him."

Sergey tried to pull away, but Sasha grabbed him, kept Sergey from turning. "You must know, Sergey, you must. You are the only man I have ever loved. The only man I ever will love."

Sergey wrenched free, shoving Sasha back. "Then *why?*" he shouted, exploding. "Why have you done this? Why did you rip us apart? Why did you leave? *Again?*"

"I want what is best for you! Only what is best for you! The hatred, the rumors… they will poison your presidency. I *have* to keep you safe! If you were attacked like I was… I could not live with that!"

"*You* are best for me." Sergey reached for him, putting one hand on the side of his face. "You made me feel alive. And I am not afraid, Sasha. I am not afraid of the world. You are worth everything, every risk. This love… it is bigger than any fear I might feel. There is nothing that could come between us, if you only let us have a chance."

He closed his eyes, leaning into Sergey's touch. He ached, he yearned, to close the distance between them, mold his body to Sergey's. Press him back against the nearest table. Undress him slowly and spread him out, worship his body. He'd never taken his time with a lover before, but he wanted to with Sergey. His mind swirled, a raging tornado, thoughts spinning too fast to grab on to. Need, fear, desire, and panic. What was the right choice? A life with Sergey, looking over their shoulders, or a life alone, with only his misery to keep him company?

"If we try," he breathed, speaking slowly. "If we try… could you keep it quiet?"

"I am not looking to lead a parade. Twenty years I waited for my anti-corruption purge. Do you think I am a man of fast impulse? No, I just want you in my life. I want to *love* you." He tried to smile, but it came out like a grimace. "I was not planning on engagement announcements for at least a year. Maybe two." He swallowed hard, his joke falling flat.

Sasha watched his Adam's apple rise and fall.

"Maybe we could start to go public in two years. After your training." Sergey's voice turned wistful. "So much could change in two years. What you fear… the world may be different then. Maybe *we* will have changed it." Sergey cupped his other cheek, cradling his face. He spoke in a whisper. "Are you telling me you want to try this? Us?"

Sasha's breath bounced off Sergey's face. What he wanted, he couldn't, shouldn't have. He shouldn't give in.

"We are stronger together," Sergey breathed. "I am stronger with you *because* I love you. You are stronger when you love me, yes?"

He nodded. He couldn't speak.

"Then let us be *strong*." Sergey inched closer until their bodies were almost touching. "You will need that to be an astronaut."

Sasha frowned and almost pulled away. "You still want me to go?"

Sergey's chin rose, defiant. "I want you to have everything you ever wanted, Sasha."

"If I say that is only two things: being an astronaut and being with you?"

Sergey's eyes fluttered closed for a moment, and he slid forward the last inch, pressing his body against Sasha's.

It felt like a bomb had gone off behind him, the force, the power, the thrum that shot through him. He grabbed Sergey's hips, struggling to keep his feet.

"You have both in your hands. You can have everything you want, Sasha. You deserve it. But... you must be careful. This heart is fragile and already bruised. I cannot take it if you leave again."

"But NASA—

"Would you come home every six weeks? Come back to me? Maybe let me visit you if I cannot stand being away from you for another night?"

Sasha nodded, breathing in shakily. Coming home... to Sergey. This was all a dream. It had to be. "I always came back," he whispered, leaning in. Sergey's lips were so close, so close he could feel their warmth.

"You never had to leave. You never had to run." Sergey dropped the first kiss to Sasha's lips, a dry, chaste slide that only fanned Sasha's desire, turning his soul white-hot. Sergey pressed their cheeks together, their noses. "Sasha.... *please.*"

What he wanted was right in front of him. The man he loved was in his arms. Anton's words swirled in his brain, crashing against Sergey's pleas and promises, his hope for their future. His own desire was a physical pull, a tug on his soul that he'd felt from the first moment he'd met Sergey. He stood on the edge of a black hole, poised on Sergey's own event horizon. If he tipped forward, fell headfirst into this love, what would happen? The best... or the worst?

He closed the last millimeters, capturing Sergey's lips in a slow, deep kiss. His tongue teased open Sergey's mouth, and then dipped within, tasting his love. Sergey responded, surging into Sasha, wrapping his arms around Sasha's shoulders as he pressed tight against him, and his hands slid into Sasha's hair.

Sasha's hands trailed over Sergey's body—down his chest, around his back, across his shoulders. Sergey was a lure, a siren's song, a sweet addiction with no cure. Together they were a rocket, blasting into orbit and riding an eternal flame.

Maybe the world wasn't ready for their love yet. The world was still crazy, still mad and upside-down. But they could carve a piece of it away for themselves. Find their own home, where men like Anton and Aleksey and Ilya lived, and where they could truly love each other. Until then, until they found that place, they'd keep their love safe in the shelter of their hearts.

"Come home?" Sergey whispered against Sasha's lips.

Slowly, Sasha nodded.

77

Texas

Sunday morning, Mary made far, far too much food. They ate together on the back porch, stuffing their faces until their bellies groaned. Jack complained that he was going to get fat, but Mary kept sliding more French toast on his plate.

Both of their shirts hung looser, and Ethan could feel Jack's ribs when he put his hands on Jack's back. Their strike mission and everything that had happened had taken so much from them, and since coming back, Jack hadn't eaten much. He moved his sausage to Jack's plate.

Andrew spent the day working on his old truck. Ethan helped for a while, passing tools back and forth and chatting about the upcoming football season.

When Jack and Mary went for a walk down to the creek that passed through the back of the property, Andrew finally asked Ethan about Madigan, about the Arctic, and about the hearings. A small TV hanging on the wall in the garage was set to TNN. It was muted, but the crawl on the bottom screamed Jack's name over and over. Eventually, Andrew fell quiet, and he started setting his tools down harder, banging around the truck's engine as a deep scowl furrowed his face.

Ethan found Jack walking back with his mother, holding her hand as she rested her head on his shoulder. He watched them come up the grassy hillside, sunshine scattering gold in Jack's hair. Mary's khaki shorts clung to her wide hips, flared over her knees. She wore a blue shirt with an American flag and a country barn stitched across the chest, a Norman Rockwell warmth in the homespun crafting. Jack's jeans hung loose on his hips, and his white T-shirt flapped in the light breeze. Ethan's Secret Service sweatshirt dangled from his free hand.

Jack looked up, saw Ethan, and beamed. His smile went straight to Ethan's soul, to the center of his heart. A buzz rolled through him, a heady, summer thrum, honey-warm. Jack's smiles made his heart beat, made his soul catch fire. He smiled back, matching Jack's wide, glowing expression, his gaze overflowing with love.

They lay together in the hammock through the afternoon, Ethan holding Jack close, pressed against his chest. Sometimes they talked, reminiscing about the first time they met, their early friendship. How nervous they both were in the beginning, desperate for their relationship to work, and scared it would all fall apart. They laughed over their foibles and gaffes. Relived their best moments.

Ethan never brought up the future. Neither did Jack. Would they even have a tomorrow?

Mary and Andrew huddled together inside the house. Andrew watched TNN, hunched on the couch, his hands fisted over his mouth. Behind him, Mary ironed, working through what seemed like every plaid shirt Andrew owned.

The sun dipped in the sky, rays of light sparkling through the wavering branches of the oak and falling across their faces. Ethan cupped Jack's cheek and stared into his eyes. Everything, everything in his life, came down to this moment, to the man in his arms. He'd never known how deeply he could love, how all-consuming that love could be. How loving Jack could rewrite his entire life. How happy he could be, just holding Jack, and gazing into his soul.

Jack tried to be brave, holding Ethan's hand and smiling. But fear hung in his fractured blue eyes. His breaths came fast, almost strangled puffs against Ethan's skin. "I'm scared," he whispered. "I don't want to be apart from you."

"You will never be apart from me." He stroked Jack's cheek, dragged his thumb across his flushed skin.

Jack's phone rang.

Ethan grabbed him, holding tight, as if he could stop time if he just held Jack close. Everything he'd kept buried burst, a volcano erupting inside of him, and he gasped, pressing his lips to Jack's forehead. It was too soon, too soon. He didn't want to face this, not now, not ever. It wasn't fair. Jack had saved him, saved everyone, but the cost was too high.

Hadn't that been the problem from day one? Jack was always being ripped apart for his heart and his choices made out of love. Love for the country, love for the world. For his friends.

And his love for Ethan.

Ethan kissed his hair, blinking back his tears.

Jack's hand shook as he pulled out his phone. His other hand clenched down on Ethan's, their knuckles going white. He swiped to answer. "Hello?"

"*Jack. It's Elizabeth. Senator Allen just called. The committee finalized their recommendations.*"

They held their breaths, staring into each other's eyes. *I love you so fucking much.* Ethan tried to speak through his gaze, tried to pour his love into Jack. He could never explain how much he loved Jack, put into words how deep his love went, but maybe if Jack could feel what he felt, feel the force that seized him when he thought of Jack, like a tornado lived in his soul.

A single tear slipped down Jack's cheek. He mouthed to Ethan, *I love you.*

Elizabeth took a deep, steadying breath. *"They are not recommending charges against you for violating the Logan Act. They agreed that you and I were working together and that I endorsed your activities in Russia."*

Jack exhaled hard, and Ethan's eyes slipped closed. Their hands squeezed.

"They spent most of their time on the Espionage Act charges. There's a damning statement they're going to release, saying that it is a felony to mishandle classified information, including exposing foreign nationals to Top Secret information or installations, in either an intentional or negligent manner. That you are, by the black-and-white letter of the law, guilty."

Ethan curled around Jack, burying his face in Jack's hair, gasping as a bomb burst in his chest. *Guilty.* The word hit him like a shotgun blast, shattering his bones and atomizing his soul.

Jack went pale, the blood draining from his face. "Oh God..."

"However," Elizabeth said, speaking fast. *"They're* not *recommending charges be brought, and the Department of Justice has confirmed they'll abide by the recommendations of the committee."*

The world lurched, a hard jerk to the right. Had he heard that correctly? Or was that just his imagination?

Jack sputtered, searching for words. "What— No charges— You said guilty—"

Elizabeth cleared her throat, her voice changing, obviously reading from a statement. *"'It is the opinion of the committee that prosecution of these charges would not be in the nation's best interest. While the exposure of Top Secret information to foreign nationals was clearly intentional, it was not malicious in nature, and served the goal of American national security. That does not excuse the dangerous, dreadful errors in judgment shown by President Spiers-Reichenbach. However, it does provide context and clear mitigating circumstances that led to these decisions. This additional context leads us to conclude that we believe a prosecution would not, ultimately, be successful. Successful prosecutions for violations of the Espionage Act have historically centered on the malicious, willful release of classified or Top Secret information to harmful foreign nationals. The foreign nationals working with President Spiers-Reichenbach were not named allies, but were operating in a cooperative and non-hostile manner at that time.'"*

Ethan stared at Jack, his jaw hanging open. "What does this mean?" he grunted when Jack stayed silent.

"It means the Attorney General is not *going to press charges. It means you're free, Jack,"* she said carefully. *"The committee does think you're guilty, but the DOJ won't prosecute. The case won't hold up. It's too complex. Your reasons for what you did were made in a fluid environment. The law is rigid, written for an inflexible world. What you went through, the choices you had to make... they can't be quantified on paper, charted out in black and white and weighed for public review."* She sighed, long and loud. *"There will be people*

around the country who will be furious at this. At you. There's going to be backlash..."

Elizabeth kept talking, but her voice faded away, a low warble as the truth landed in the center of Ethan's heart. Jack was *free*.

Jack beamed, smiling as tears rolled down his cheeks. He dropped the phone on Ethan's chest and cradled his face, pressing kiss after kiss to his lips, around his wide smile.

They could deal with backlash. They could deal with anything. Together.

"*Jack, Senator Allen is still on the line. I need to get back to him. I'll call you later. We'll discuss next steps. I know Pete wants to give you a call, ask about a statement.*"

"Later, Elizabeth. I need to let this sink in."

They heard the smile in her voice. "*I know. It's a relief for us all, Jack. We've been biting our nails all weekend. The whole team is here. I'm going to announce it to them after this call.*"

"We'll wait for it to leak to TNN."

She laughed. "*Senator Allen says they're going to release soon, too. It will all be over in a few hours.*"

Jack breathed out. "Thank you. Thank Stephen for me. Whatever he did... it helped."

"*Politics. You never know who your friends and enemies are, do you?*"

"You always know who your true friends are." Jack smiled, his gaze fixed to Ethan. "I'll talk to you soon, Elizabeth."

78

Washington DC

Elizabeth TRANSFERRED BACK TO Senator Allen. "He's been told."

"*I'm sure he's relieved.*"

"We all are, Senator." Elizabeth leaned forward, flicking through a manila folder. A Top Secret cover sheet lay nearby. "Now, let's discuss the findings from your Senate Select Committee investigation."

"*It's all there. We started with the president's testimony, and then went through Reichenbach's and Agent Collard's as well. Investigators pulled data from Madigan's freighter, and his house of cloning horrors shipwrecked off Saudi Arabia, and from the sunken Veduschiy in the Arctic.*"

"And the committee is confident in these findings?"

"*Greater than ninety percent confidence. Madigan created five clones. Leslie Spiers, Noah Williams, and three more, still unaccounted for.*"

Elizabeth sighed, closing her eyes as the words swam on the pages before her.

Senator Allen spoke again. "*Are you going to share this with President Spiers-Reichenbach?*"

"I think he's earned a reprieve, don't you? Let him sleep at night. This is our problem now."

"*We have Americans still being held in Lubyanka Prison, with the other Madigan trash. We're working on extradition orders for them. Since they were actively serving military officers who fled with Madigan, it's a delicate maneuvering between three court systems. It could take time.*"

She shrugged. "I won't weep if any of Madigan's men are inconvenienced in Lubyanka Prison. It might take quite a while to extradite them."

He grunted. "*And General Moroshkin is still at large.*"

"I'm not worried about him. He left Nunavut a broken man. He was the one who let the dog in the back door in Russia. I wouldn't be surprised if we find his bones off St. Petersburg in the Gulf of Finland one day."

"*We can hope.*" Allen sighed. "*Our teams in the Arctic recovered the bodies of the SEAL team as well. They're coming home under honors. I'd like to be at the base with you when they land.*"

"Absolutely. I'm reaching out to their families. Senator, what about Madigan's network? His supporters in the United States? General Bell's testimony says he's convinced there are more of his followers still out there."

"*We think this was his last stand. His infrastructure was crumbling. Reichenbach and his team dogged his every move. He was penned in in Somalia until Sergeant Wright, working for Madigan, killed his teammate and put Lieutenant Cooper's team out of commission. These were the acts of a man scraping his forces together for a final battle.*"

"But did we get them all?"

Senator Allen was quiet. "*I can't answer that. And neither can our intelligence community.*"

She shook her head. "What about the rest of the world? The threat forecast for the future looks pretty bleak."

"*We took big hits with this one. Madigan, Moroshkin, and his Russian forces on our back door. The Chinese turned their navy around, but we still had two of the world's biggest armies heading for us at the same time. One hundred and ninety-six countries saw that. They watched Madigan give us bloody noses, again and again. We're still bleeding. Russia's broken. Europe took a step back from us. We're going to have a hard time for a while.*"

Elizabeth chewed on her bottom lip, staring at the committee's final recommendation. "One of the committee's assessments and recommendations is the creation of an off-the-books black team. Under presidential oversight, and reporting back to the president and your Senate Select Committee. A team that could act, decisively and quickly, when needed. Politically, diplomatically... clandestinely."

"*We need this kind of team. We can finance it through our black asset program. Who knows what we'll be coming at us now? More internal threats? Who can we definitively trust right now? This team needs be people we can rely on, one hundred percent.*" Allen sighed, and leather creaked over the phone like he was leaning back in his own chair. "*We're going to face outside attacks. People are going to want to take a swing at us right now. We need to be able to stop them. Ideally, before they get a chance to strike.*"

"I agree, Senator. And I have a few ideas."

79

Texas

J ACK ROLLED INTO ETHAN, his hands running over Ethan's face, his neck. Ethan held Jack, beaming.

They heard a loud whoop rise in the house, Andrew's hearty cheer, Mary's gasp, and then sobbing. TNN played in the background, the news alert falling from the screen door on the back porch.

"We're free. Ethan, we're free." Jack laughed, joy pulsing through him. He was free, and he was in Ethan's arms.

Their future unfolded before them, open and wide, full of opportunity. Of choice.

"Now what?" Jack cradled Ethan's face, looping one leg through Ethan's thighs and scooting as close as he could on the hammock. They swayed, rocked by the late-afternoon breeze. "We can do anything."

"First—" Ethan smiled, covering Jack's hand with his own. "We're going on our honeymoon." He kissed Jack, slowly. Pulling back, he pressed their foreheads together, his half-lidded eyes warm as they held Jack's gaze. "After that, we can do anything. Anything we want."

"What Elizabeth said the other night..." Jack's brows furrowed, his thoughts starting to string together, possibilities he hadn't considered at the time, had refused to think about, bubbling up to the surface.

Ethan kissed him again, smiling. "Anything, Jack. It's your life."

"It's *our* life. Together."

Smiling, Ethan laced their hands together, brought Jack's fingers to his lips, and kissed Jack's wedding ring. "And I'm with you all the way."

The End

Author's Notes

Thank you for reading my book. If you enjoyed it, would you consider leaving a review at your favorite retailer?

A novel and a series of this length and magnitude would not be possible without the assistance of so many, many people. I have so many individuals to thank, not the least of whom are my editors throughout the series—Raevyn, Barb, Jay, Christina, and Rita. And, always, my husband, who read every draft, listened to every idea, helped with the research, and was the world's best cheerleader to me. Thank you.

Research for this series was extensive. White House procedures and locations are as accurate as practicable and possible. Locations throughout this series are all accurate. Sakhalin Island, Simushir Island, Wrangel Island—all of these tiny islands exist in the world.

Kilaqqi belongs to the Evenk tribe of Eastern Siberia. My research into the Evenki people led me to the Russian Museum of Ethnography and numerous Doctors of Anthropology in the field of Siberian Anthropology. I even listened to a few online video lectures about the Evenki language, enough to get the basics. "Kilaqqi", in fact, means "rocky hills" (多石坡) in Evenki. This was one of the most fun aspects of my research.

Arctic navigation is accurate. This represents one of the most hair-pulling aspects of research. For days, I hovered over Arctic oceanographic charts, plotting courses and bearings, mapping out underwater passes, and exploring the soaring ice sails and plunging ice keels, all from the confines of my office. It was rigorous research, but I was very proud of the final result. *Honolulu's* scenes are some of my favorites.

The Russian Arctic, and in particular the Kara Sea, was a Soviet nuclear dumping ground. In addition to K-27, scuttled illegally in shallow waters in the Kara Sea in the 1980s, official figures show that the Soviet military dumped a huge quantity of nuclear waste in the Kara Sea: 17,000 containers of radioactive, nuclear waste; 19 vessels with their reactors intact; 14 nuclear reactors, five of which contain hazardous spent fuel. Some radioactive liquid waste was poured directly into the sea. The Bellona Organization (www.bellona.org) based in Oslo, Norway, works to combat pollution in the Arctic and years of Soviet damage to the environment. They run research expeditions to the Kara Sea often to explore the radioactive dangers of the dumping ground. Complicating matters recently, however, the Russian government has been drilling for oil extensively in the Kara Sea, sometimes right on top of nuclear waste. The waste has not been adequately mapped, and some reactors are still missing. "Mapping for sunken radiological hazards in the Arctic devils Russian authorities" – an article by Bellona.

Anton references lines from the novel, Евгéний Онéгин/Eugene Onegin, written by Alexander Pushkin and first published in Russia as a novel in verse in serial form from 1825-1832. The entire novel is composed of three hundred eighty nine lines of iambic pentameter, and is a seminal classic of Russian literature.

King Faisal al-Saud is a fictionalized representation of the current push in the Saudi Royal Family to modernize. The Saudi Royal Family has attempted, in recent years, to push for modernization, and has begun to strike down at the incredible and toxic influence of the strict Wahhabism taught throughout the Kingdom. Political watchers of the Saudi Royal Family predict that future leaders, including the Crown Prince, will move toward drastic modernization, including greater rights and freedoms for women, and improved liberties for the Saudi citizenry.

King Faisal and Uncle Abdul's study of the Quran reflects the religious beliefs of Progressive Muslims, a branch of Islam that embraces evaluating the Quran in a historical context, and treating the sacred text like a living, breathing document, as well as evaluating all sacred texts for deeper inclusive meanings. They promote inclusiveness, equal rights, and above all else, love. I am deeply indebted to organizations in this space, both for helping me with my research, and for their incredible work promoting equality and inclusiveness: Muslims for Progressive Values (www.mpvusa.org); *Al-Fatiha* and Faisal Alam; SalaamCanada (www.salaamcanada.info); The Inner Circle (www.theinnercircle.org.za) and Imam Muhsin Hendricks; The Muslim Alliance for Sexual and Gender Diversity (www.muslimalliance.org); LGBT Muslim Retreat, an annual retreat for LGBT+ Muslims from around the world. For many attendees, the retreat is the first time they have met another LGBT+ Muslim (www.lgbtmuslimretreat.com). This list in non-inclusive, but represents some of the amazing work being done by Progressive Muslims.

The cloning process and accelerated cell growth I based Leslie Spiers's resurrection off of is rooted in the science of induced pluripotent stem cells, pioneered by Dr. Yamanaka. Dr. Yamanaka was awarded the Nobel prize for this work in 2012. IPS cells can be made from donated cells and DNA from the host (in this case, fictional Leslie Spiers), and then directed to grow as needed. Examples of current research has centered on growing retinal cells out of skin stem cells for patients with macular degeneration.

Glossary

US Based Terminology

CIA – Central Intelligence Agency

DARPA – "Defense Advanced Research Project Agency"; Department of Defense research & development agency

Espionage Act – The Espionage Act made it a crime to: gather, transmit, or lose defense information, gather or deliver defense information to aid a foreign government, photographing defense installations, and disclosure of classified information, to include '…knowingly and willfully communicating to an unauthorized person any classified information to any foreign government, faction, party, military, or representative…'

"H Street" – Secret Service Headquarters in Washington DC

MAMs – "Military Age Males" – any male-identified roughly from age 15 through 65

National Security Staff – The staff who works 24/7, 365 days a year in the Situation Room, supporting the president of the United States and the National Security Advisor/intelligence communities.

QRT – "Quick Reaction Team"; a rapid response tactical unit deployed in emergency or developing situations

SOCOM – Special Operations Command

Twenty-Fifth Amendment – The 25th Amendment to the United States Constitution established procedures for filling in vacancies for both the president and the vice-president. It also allows for the involuntary removal of the president by a majority consensus of the "principal officers of executive departments". It also allows the president to resign his office voluntarily.

USS Honolulu – a fictional Los Angeles class (SSN) fast-attack submarine

Waterboarding – an interrogation technique simulating the experience of drowning, where a person is restrained face up while large quantities of water are poured over the face and into the breathing passages.

White House Bunker/PEOC – The Presidential Emergency Operations Center, located in the White House Bunker beneath the footprint of the White House. Its exact location is classified.

Arabic Translations/Terminology

Alhamdulillah – Praise be to Allah
Allah u Akbar – Glory to Allah/Allah is great
'Am - uncle
Ana Bahibak – I love you
Bismillah – In the name of Allah
Barakah Allah – with Allah's blessing
Du'a – individual prayers to Allah
Faisal – "one who has strength"
Habibi – My love
Hafeed – grandson
Ibn akh - nephew
In shaa Allah – Allah willing/If Allah wishes
Imam – Islamic leadership position; leader of a congregation/mosque/Muslim community
Maa shaa Allah – Allah has willed/Allah willing
Mahr – the gift given by a groom to his prospective bride to begin wedding proceedings
Nahn eayila – We are family
Nikaha/Nikha – Islamic marriage/ceremony
Shaytan/s – devil/s
Shahada – statement of faith that all Muslims must proclaim every day as part of their daily prayers. To convert to Islam, all one has to do is speak the Shahada aloud in front of a witness.
Subhanallah - Glory to Allah; for praise
Thawb – long, white gown worn by men in Saudi Arabia and parts of the Middle East
Wallah/Yallah – for emphasis, for frustration, for exclamation
Wahhabism – strict conservative Muslim sect opposed to all practices not explicitly sanctioned in the Quran. Wahhabism believes that the Quran is not a living document, but must that society must change to conform to the exact specifications of the Quran

Russian Translations/Terminology

Govno - Shit
Krasivyy - Beautiful
Lyubov moya - My love
Nam pizdets – We're fucked
Pozdravleniya - Congratulations
Spetsnaz – Russian Special Forces
Udachi – Good Luck
Uronit' vintovku – Don't move
Ya lyublyu tyeba – I love you
Yobaniy nasos – An exclamation of amazement. Literally, "fucked pump." "Fucking amazing" would be a colloquial translation
Zvezda moya – My star

About the Author

Tal Bauer is an award-winning and best-selling author of LGBT romantic thrillers, bringing together a career in law enforcement and international humanitarian aid to create dynamic characters, intriguing plots, and exotic locations. He is happily married and lives with his husband and their Basset Hound in Texas. Tal is a member of the Romance Writers of America and the Mystery Writers of America.

Other Books By Tal Bauer

Please visit your favorite ebook retailer to discover my other books

The Executive Office Series
Enemies of the State
Interlude
Enemy of My Enemy
Enemy Within

Hush

Connect With Tal Bauer

Visit my website: www.talbauerwrites.com
Email me: tal@talbauerwrites.com
Friend me on Facebook: https://www.facebook.com/talbauerauthor
Follow me on Twitter: @TalBauerWrites

Printed in Great Britain
by Amazon